The Father Tom Mysteries:

By

J. R. Mathis and Susan Mathis

Mercy and Justice Mysteries, 2021

First Printing, November 2021

Contact: mercyandjusticemysteries@gmail.com

Cover Photo: Depositphotos

Cover: Annie on Fiverr

Editing: Anna Palmer Darkes

Also by J. R. Mathis and Susan Mathis

The Haunted Heritage

The Father Tom Mysteries, Book 10

First Printing, September, 2021

Contact: mercyandjusticemysteries@gmail.com

Cover Photo: Depositphotos

Cover: Millie Godwin

Editor: Anna Palmer Darkes

One

There is nothing like a trip through the western Maryland mountains in the early fall to restore the spirits. Today, the first Saturday in October, is the perfect day for it. The fall colors are nearing their peak, with a clear blue sky and crisp air that's just about perfect for a drive through the area.

Particularly if one is alone with one's much loved soon-to-be-wife.

Even if she does want to shop.

Helen has insisted on going to the outlet mall in Hagerstown at least once a month since we got engaged, saying again and again that she needs just "one or two" more outfits for our honeymoon cruise. At this point, I don't see how any ship could possibly stay afloat with all the luggage she appears to plan on taking with us.

But I admit, it's not a bad way to spend a day. We're away from the trials and tribulations of our respective vocations. For Helen, that means there are no criminals to interrogate, no crime scenes to tromp through. For me, it means no emergency phone calls to the hospital, no confessions to hear. She doesn't wear her sidearm, and I don't wear my collar.

But since neither of us is ever really off duty, she does carry her backup weapon, carefully tucked in her mysterious thigh holster, and I carry my stole and a bottle of holy oil in case someone needs anointing of the sick.

Or last rites.

Fortunately, in our approximately half-dozen trips, Helen has not once had to chase down a perp through the food court, and I have not had to give the last rites of the church to an elderly person struck down by the kiddie train that runs by with alarming speed and regularity.

Our trips typically follow the same pattern. We leave right after 8 a.m. Mass, swinging by The Muffin Man for coffee—and, of course, muffins—to enjoy on the long drive. Once we get to the mall, I drop Helen off at one of the plus-sized women's clothing stores and then park the car. I go inside and take a seat near the fitting rooms, where I spend the next hour or so oohing and ahhing over everything she tries on.

Since I love and appreciate Helen's wonderful curves, this is the highlight of the day for me.

Unfortunately, my enjoyment is limited, because when she's done with the regular clothes, she shoos me out into the mall "to get us something to drink." She and I both know that this is unspoken code for "OK, Tom, I'm going to shop for lingerie now, so you need to go."

Neither of us speaks of it because, well, it's unspoken.

I wander around for a while, staying close enough for Helen to find me but far enough away so that I can't see what she's buying. After a while, she comes out.

Then I carry the bags to the car, laden down like a pack mule, usually with at least three store bags and one dress bag.

Inevitably, Helen catches me trying to sneak a peek. "You might as well give up, Tom," she usually says with a giggle. "I always have the clerk put the unmentionables at the bottom of the bag underneath everything else."

"I know," I usually sigh, "but you can't blame me for trying."

"Tsk, tsk, Father Greer," she says, shaking her head. "What would people think if they saw a priest trying to catch a glimpse of a woman's underwear?"

"Why do you think I never wear my collar?" I say.

After this exchange, we go to a late lunch at one of three restaurants we particularly like. Since we always go on the last Saturday of the month, when Father Wayne comes out to celebrate the 4:30 p.m Mass, we drive back to Myerton. There we usually end our day together with a long, luxurious kiss when I drop Helen and her purchases off at her apartment.

We have just reached the point in the day when I have been shooed out of the store and am wandering up the wide hall in search of a comfortable bench when I see a blue-haired young woman in a wheelchair being wheeled toward me by a flustered-looking young man.

Of course, I think. *Nate and Gladys had the same idea for a relaxing drive up into the mountains.*

It's actually a relief to see them together—and by together, I mean somewhere other than my office or Mass. In the couple of weeks since the revelations about Nate's activities leading up to the murder of Ashley Becket, when he hired her as a prostitute in a frankly idiotic plan to lose his virginity, the three of us have met together to discuss their relationship. Nate is intent—almost desperately so—to show Gladys how sorry he is and is willing to do anything it takes to earn her forgiveness. Gladys—well, let's just say she's been a little mercurial, alternating between merciful and forgiving one moment and angry and accusatory the next.

So, the fact they're together in a mall in Hagerstown the first weekend of October, apparently not arguing with each other, is a good sign.

Since no one wants to run into their priest—even one who is out of uniform—when they're on a date, I try to make myself scarce. Unfortunately, before I can escape I hear Nate say loudly, "There's Father Tom. We should ask him what he thinks."

My heart sinks even as I paste on my best pastoral smile. The reason that I assume people don't want to run into their priests is that I, said priest, don't want to run into them. All I wanted was a nice, quiet, drama-free day with Helen. We haven't had too many of those lately.

Oh, well, it's too late. At the very least, chances are this encounter will be interesting.

"Hi, you two," I say pleasantly, when they reach me just past the Boardwalk Fries. "What brings you here today?"

"Shopping, because of Nate's irresponsible behavior," Gladys scowls without hesitating. Even with an IQ on the high end of genius, she often lacks the gift of discretion.

"This situation is not just my fault," Nate snaps, at least for the moment refusing to be cowed. "You could have believed in me. 'Stand By Your Man,' you know?"

"Are you really trying to win me over by using song lyrics from a bad 1970s country song?"

"No, but I am saying—"

"Hey, guys," I say, trying to head this same argument that I've already heard off at the pass, "Why don't you just tell me what you're shopping for?"

"Halloween costumes," they say in unison.

I just stare at them. "Halloween costumes," I say. "That's what you're arguing about today?"

"Uh-huh," Gladys says firmly, "and it's all his fault."

"It is not my fault," Nate says. At her glare, he shrugs. "OK, it is my fault. But you didn't have to cancel the plans we had already made."

"Why would I have her waste her time when I didn't know if you'd even be out of jail by the time we needed them!" Gladys shouts, causing several people to stop and stare.

"Gladys," I say quietly, "please tell me why you two are almost coming to blows over Halloween costumes."

She takes a deep breath. "Because Nate and I were a couple, we needed to have matching Halloween costumes. We talked about what we were going to be since June, and we settled on The Little Mermaid and Flounder. I had already lined up someone to construct a rock around my chair and to custom make our costumes—I'd be the Little Mermaid, of course, and Nate would be Flounder."

"OK, those both sound nice," I say. "So, what's the problem?"

Gladys grits her teeth and says, "Nate had to go and get arrested for murdering a hooker. I just assumed I'd be alone again and cancelled the costumes. But now, we're back together, since he didn't actually kill her, so now we have to find new costumes. OFF THE RACK!"

She's pretty agitated by now and getting loud as more people begin to stare and Nate turns eight shades of red. I try to calm her down by saying, "Well, I'm sure it shouldn't be too hard to find something. What about Raggedy Ann and Andy?"

"Dad, really?" Gladys snorts.

"Yeah, Father," Nate says, rolling his eyes. "We're not kids."

"OK," I say, wracking my brain for something even moderately helpful. "What about something from the classics, like Anthony and Cleopatra?"

"I like the sound of that," Nate says, grinning at Gladys in a way that I'm pretty sure is not appropriate for my eyes.

"No," Gladys says sharply. "I'm not going to dress up like some Egyptian Queen in that scanty sort of harem outfit"

"Gladys, that is hardly what I was imagining," I insist, blushing.

"I want to do something from Star Wars," Gladys says, shooting Nate a look, "like Princess Leia and an Ewok, but he won't do it."

"An Ewok," I say, grinning, "Hey, that's a great idea. You'd be so cute as an—"

"No," Nate says with a dismissive wave. "It's too undignified for someone who now has his own business. I'm still trying to recover from that issue with the murder accusation."

I refrain from pointing out that two people in their mid-twenties standing in the Hagerstown outlet mall arguing about Halloween costumes is hardly dignified in the first place.

"Anyway," Nate continues, "I think implying there's a relationship between Princess Leah and an Ewok is bordering on bestiality, which I know is against the Commandments."

"Hah!" Gladys says loudly. "You're one to talk about something being against the Commandments."

"For the millionth time, Gladys, I didn't actually commit fornication!" Nate yells.

When I visualized what my life as a priest would be like, and even when I visualized my life as a parish priest, I never foresaw that it would include standing in a mall in Hagerstown, Maryland, talking about bestiality as it relates to Princess Leia and an Ewok, with two people, one of whom just yelled the word "fornication."

But then, as my professors always said, you never know.

"OK, Nate," I say, desperate to bring this increasingly uncomfortable conversation to an end, "you don't want to be an Ewok. What if you were Han Solo? He was her boyfriend."

Nate grins. "Hey, I like that!"

I feel a flush of triumph and I think I have a winner. Then Gladys says caustically, "He's not tall enough to be Han Solo."

I look at her like she's lost her ever-loving mind, because that's the only thing that can explain her behavior.

Then, I take a closer look at Gladys. She doesn't appear angry. She doesn't even appear hurt. She looks . . . disappointed.

This is not about the costumes. This is about something else.

"Hey, Nate," I say, keeping my eyes on Gladys, who is looking at her clasped hands. "Can you go in that store and tell Helen to meet us down at the ice cream shop? I know she'd like to spend a few minutes with y'all. Gladys and I will go ahead and head that way. You stay here and help carry Helen's packages."

I take Gladys's chair and we head towards the Baskin Robbins. On our way, I say, "OK, Gladys. You and I both know this isn't about Halloween costumes."

"It is," she says quietly. "It's just about the costumes. I know it sounds stupid to you, Dad—"

I push her over to a wrought-iron table right outside the ice cream parlor and sit down. "Gladys, I may not understand it, but I don't think it's stupid. I don't think it's about the costumes, though. So, what is it?"

She looks up at me, a tear trickling down her face. "OK. It's not the costumes themselves. Not really. It's . . . it's what they mean. Or, what they meant."

I sit quietly, knowing she'll tell me in her own time without prompting from me.

"Halloween was always my favorite holiday as a kid, even more than Christmas," she says. "Not because of the ghoulish stuff, but because I got to dress up, become someone else. Especially after I lost my ability to walk, I could be anybody. I put on a Wonder Woman costume, and I was Wonder Woman for a few hours. Everyone else saw the chair, but in my mind I could run, and jump, and fight the bad guys. Everything I couldn't do in real life."

"I can see that," I say, "but it still doesn't explain—"

"I was by myself, Dad," she whispers. "I didn't have a brother or sister to dress up with. And when I was a teenager, I didn't have a . . ."

"A boyfriend," I say quietly. And with that, things become clear.

"Right," she says with a pained smile. "I was homeschooled, I didn't get to know guys my own age, and even if I did, you know how insecure teenage boys are. They were never going to go for the genius in the wheelchair."

"And in college," I say, "you didn't have a boyfriend, either."

She laughs bitterly. "I loved Richard, or I thought I did, but he wasn't exactly the kind of man who would dress up in a costume. Then of course, the guys and girls I had sex with, well, they weren't really interested in a relationship that had any real meaning to it. Honestly, by that time, I wasn't, either." She takes a deep breath. "But I've told you that."

I stay quiet, and she clears her throat. "By the time I came to Myerton and took the job at the police department, I'd given up on relationships of any kind. I decided I was just never going to have a real boyfriend. As far as imagining dressing up for Halloween with the man I loved—well, I'd given up on that years ago."

She pauses for a moment. Quietly, I say, "And then you met Nate."

She looks at me, a smile lighting up her face. "I know everyone else thinks he's goofy, but Dad! He was like a dream come true! I mean, not only was he interested in me as more than an easy lay, he liked *me*. He loved *me*. He liked costumes, and dressing up, and Halloween, and cosplay, and everything I liked. He was different."

Gladys' smile disappears. "Except he really wasn't. He really isn't. And that's why I'm so upset. Because he's not what I thought he was."

"Gladys," I say, "you know he still loves you, in spite of what he did."

"But what I still cannot get my mind around, Dad, is that he did it in the first place. He says he loves me, but I'm still having a hard time believing that."

"Let me ask you a question," I say, folding my arms. "Did you expect Nate to never disappoint you?"

"I never expected him to hire a hooker," Gladys says.

"Frankly, I didn't expect that, either," I say. "And it was wrong. It was sinful. It hurt you. And it's something that he's confessed to you and asked forgiveness. He's been to confession and received absolution."

"I know all that," Gladys says, nodding her head. "But it's like I don't know who he is anymore."

"He's still Nate," I say.

"But he's not who I thought he was," Gladys whispers.

I consider my next words carefully, for my own sake as well as hers. "You worked with Helen on her investigation into Joan's murder, right?"

She nods. "Yes."

"I don't know if you're aware of this, but one of the most difficult things for me about that was not having to relive her murder," I say. "It was discovering that the woman I loved—still love, really—was not who I thought she was."

Gladys looks at me. "Oh," she says quietly. "I never really knew for sure if you knew. Mom never told me."

"No reason she shouldn't have," I say with a shrug. "But yeah. I didn't know about her struggles with mental illness. I didn't know about her multiple hospitalizations as a teenager. And I certainly didn't know about her first marriage."

"How did you feel when you found all that out?"

"Hurt," I say with a tight smile. "Angry. Confused. I was that way for a while. You know I left town and went to a monastery as their chaplain for a few months after Helen solved the case. One of the things I came to grips with during that time was what I learned about Joan. I finally realized that she didn't hide who she was from me to hurt me. She didn't mean to deceive me. She did it because she was afraid if I knew the truth, I wouldn't love her anymore."

"But that's ridiculous!" Gladys declares. "She was sick! You wouldn't have stopped loving her!"

"Of course not. I still loved her, even after I learned the truth. I was disappointed, true. But it wasn't the first time Joan disappointed me. And I disappointed her plenty of times. And Gladys, Nate will disappoint you again. It's inevitable. Not because he's a particularly bad or evil person. But because he's human. He's a flawed and sinful human being, as we all are."

She says nothing, so I press forward. "And you will disappoint him, too. I'm sure you have."

"Me!" she says indignantly. "How?"

"He said it. You didn't stand by him, not the way he thought you should. Now we can argue whether or not he's right, but that's how he feels."

"But he—"

I hold up my hand. "You heard him tell you that when he first met you, he assumed you were a virgin because you seemed so sweet and innocent. Gladys, do you think he wasn't disappointed when you told him otherwise? You don't think he struggled with anger and sadness over that?"

"I don't know," Gladys says quietly.

"Did he ever berate you about it? Did he bring up your past over and over again?"

She shakes her head. "No."

I take a deep breath. "The point is, Gladys, you can wallow in your disappointment over finding out that Nate isn't who you thought he was. You can continue to be angry with him over something that he's already sought your forgiveness for. You can give him hell for hiring Ashley Becket in the first place for the rest of his life. But if that's what you want to do, then end things with Nate right now so you can find a man who will never disappoint you, and so he can find a woman who won't disappoint him. And when you do, I want to meet him."

Gladys looks at her hands. "But I don't want anyone else," she whispers. "I want him."

I sigh. "Then Gladys, you need to decide if you can accept him as he is. Flawed. Sinful. And very likely to hurt and disappoint you in the future."

She doesn't say anything and I don't say anything. I leave her at the table and order ice cream cones for Helen and me—butter pecan for her, chocolate caramel swirl for me. By the time I get back to the table, Nate and Helen are there. The young man looks as weighed down with packages as I have been on occasion.

"Hi," I say, handing Helen her cone and giving her a kiss. "Mission accomplished?"

"For today, anyway," she says. "Oh, butter pecan. My favorite."

"I know, that's why I got it for you."

While we're talking, I'm aware that Gladys and Nate are sitting next to each other quietly. I wonder if I'm going to have to continue counseling them when Gladys says, "You know, Nate, I've thought about it, and I think that you'll make a wonderful Han Solo. Let's go back and get those costumes we saw when we first got here this morning."

"Really?" Nate says, a smile breaking out on his face. "Are you sure?"

Gladys looks him in the eye and says, "Yes, Nate. For the first time in weeks, I'm sure."

Nate clearly looks confused by this, but I give Gladys a smile. "Well, you two have fun. Helen and I are going to wander the mall eating our ice cream cones like teenagers."

"We are?" she asks. I give her a look, and she says brightly, "Oh, we are. How fun will that be?"

We tell Gladys and Nate goodbye as Nate says, "Don't forget I'll be by tomorrow afternoon to talk to you about the Myer Mansion."

I have been dreading this but know that it's an important part of promoting the Haunted Mansion, so I say, "Yes, Nate, 5:00 p.m, right?"

"Yes. See you then," Nate says. "Oh, and at Mass."

My work finished, Helen and I walk off to stroll happily through the mall, licking ice cream cones like two little children out of school for the first day of the summer. When we get some distance from them she asks, "What was that about?"

"Nothing you need to be concerned with. File it under pastoral counseling and don't give it another thought."

Much to my surprise, she grins at me and says, "Thankfully." Then, having finished her ice cream cone, she slips her arm through mine and we head back towards the car, carrying the latest additions to her honeymoon wardrobe.

Two

One of things that I have been both looking forward to and dreading since the beginning of the new school year is meeting with this year's group of First Communicants. These kids, generally going into second grade, will spend the coming school year preparing to receive First Holy Communion in the spring.

Normally, I would not meet with them until sometime during Lent. Their initial instruction would come from Saint Clare's Director of Religious Education, and I'd only come in to talk to each child individually near the designated time.

But we hardly have a normal situation this year. I have not yet hired a Director of Religious Education to replace the crazy woman who shot Helen a few months ago. I've managed to resist Anna's best efforts to get me to advertise in the Archdioceses of Baltimore and Washington for a new DRE, since I'm reluctant to take any chances hiring another person who turns out to be a lunatic. There's always the possibility we'd wind up with an actual serial killer instead of simply the daughter of one.

I have put in a request, through the Archdiocese, to the Nashville Dominicans for a qualified sister to serve as the DRE. But it's one of hundreds of similar requests from this order of teaching nuns—one of the most rapidly growing religious communities in the country, with young women eager to serve God and His people—and the likelihood of receiving one in my lifetime is small. But I'm hopeful.

So, because of my determination—or stubbornness, depending on who you ask—I am taking on the responsibility of leading the children, and their parents, through the first steps. That is why, at 9:15 a.m., I'm seated on a child-size chair in the first grade classroom, surrounded by about a dozen inquisitive looking youngsters and their obviously nervous parents.

Technically, not all the parents are nervous. Alan Trent, who was just made chair of the Department of Philosophy and Theology at Myer College, and is arguably better qualified than I am to teach this class, is here with his youngest, Betty. She is the ninth—and last—Trent child to prepare to receive her first sacraments at Saint Clare's

Louise Harrell is there with Martin Maycord's two older nieces, Lucy and Sophie—the latter, at eight, being the oldest child in the group. I'm gratified to see them here. Since their father was imprisoned for various crimes ranging from drug trafficking to being an accessory to murder, they've made remarkable progress, thanks to both the stability provided by their uncle and the counseling provided by their therapist—and Martin's girlfriend—Mae Trent. The girls are still shy, but Louise more than makes up for their awkwardness with her warm, encouraging smile and helpful comments.

Miriam Conway, on the other hand, looks like she's about to throw up. Now, that may or may not be related to her very obvious pregnancy. She is in her seventh month and due in late-December. Both she and Dan are hoping for a girl to, as Dan says, "help civilize the three hooligans"—his affectionate term for his twin boys, Max and JP, and their brother Andrew.

Sitting next to Miriam is their daughter, Catherine, who is not quite seven. If it were any child other than her, I'd wonder if she were ready for her first sacraments. But it seems appropriate that Saint Clare's little seer should be spiritually precocious. Of course, wondering what her daughter might say is probably contributing to Miriam's nausea.

I know the other parents and children less well, but all are regular attendees at Mass and have been in religious education before, so I don't foresee any problems.

My optimism will be the death of me.

I'm about to start when Helen slips in the back and takes a seat by Miriam. She gives the mother of her godchild-to-be a hug and blows a kiss to Catherine. She catches my eye and gives me a smile and a wink.

"OK, boys and girls," I say with what I hope is a friendly smile. "In church, we always begin everything with a prayer. So, let's start by saying the Lord's Prayer."

After making the sign of the cross—and noticing my first job will be to teach a few of the children the proper way to make the sign of the cross—I begin the prayer by saying "Our Father." From there, the children all join in, some more than others, including one little boy with a very short hair cut who seems to think that God will hear him better if he yells.

"Very good, very good," I say, encouraged that most of them at least seemed familiar with a prayer we say at every single Mass. "OK, so, who here knows who I am?"

Several hands go up, and I call on a little blond girl who says, "You're Father Tom."

"That's right," I say.

I think, *This is going to be easier than I thought*. "And what is your name?"

"Emily," she says pleasantly. "Father Tom, I have a question."

"OK, sure" I say, happy to meet such an enthusiastic student.

"Why don't you have heat in your house?" she says with perfect seriousness.

"What?" I ask, obviously caught off guard.

"My Daddy says that you're a priest and if you're cold at night, you should get a blanket, not a wife."

There are a few stifled chuckles from the adults—including Helen, bless her heart—and I see Emily's mother lunging for the child from the back row. I wave her back to her seat with what I hope is an understanding smile.

I then turn my attention back to Emily and say, "Oh, Emily, thank you for asking. I do have heat in my house but I haven't had to use it in a while because it's been summer time. But now the fall is coming and it's time to start talking about Sacraments. Who knows what a sacrament is?"

The boy with the short hair, whose name tag reads "Daniel," waves his hand.

"Yes, Daniel," I say.

Standing up, he belts out, "They are the divine helps which God gives us to enable us to believe the truths of faith, live according to God's moral code, and grow in the gift of divine life."

"That's very good, Daniel," I say, as his mother beams with pride. "So a sacrament is something that God has given us to help us be closer to him. There are Seven Sacraments. The first is one that you've all had, right after you were born. Does anyone know what that was?"

A little boy named "Pio" raises his hand, and when I call on him says confidently, "Circumcision."

"No," I say as the parents in the room try desperately not to laugh. "This involves water and usually a baby wears a white outfit for it."

At this the entire class erupts with "baptism" and I smile on them beatifically as I say, "Right. Baptism is the first sacrament you receive and the second is called reconciliation. Now, does anyone know what reconciliation is?"

A little girl named Alice raises her hand and says, "It's when a husband leaves the whore he's been shacking up with and moves back in with his wife."

There are a few audible gasps, and I wonder if the sun has gone behind a cloud or if I am about to pass out, when a deep voice from the back corner of the room commands, "Alice Elisabeth McDermott, you need to shut your mouth!"

Wanting to defend little Alice, who looks about to cry, I say, "That's sort of right. It is when two people who have not been getting along say they're sorry and become friends again. With the sacrament of reconciliation, we admit that we've done some things that are wrong and have kept us away from God so that we can be close to him again. We do this in Confession. Who knows what Confession is?"

Catherine Conway throws her hand up confidently. "Yes, Catherine," I say, noticing too late the look of horror on Miriam's face.

I soon understand why.

"Father Tom," Catherine says authoritatively, "a confession is when a perp admits he is guilty, but sometimes you have to beat it out of him."

Helen almost bursts out laughing. Miriam looks like she wants the floor to open up and swallow her. Around Catherine, little boys and girls are expressing horror.

"No, no, Catherine," I say quickly, trying to maintain a smiling countenance, "that's not—"

"But Father Tom," she continues with surprising dignity, "you will not have to beat a confession out of me. Mommy has made me keep a list of all the things I've done wrong ever since I could spell 'hit' and 'bit'."

"That's good, Catherine," I say weakly as Miriam struggles to remain upright in her chair.

"Father Tom!" Daniel yells, "Are you going to beat us?"

"No, of course not," I say hastily. "Catherine—"

"No, Father Tom's not going to beat us," Emily says. "He's nice."

"Thank you, Emily," I say, thinking things have turned a corner.

"He'll get Miss Helen to do it," she goes on. "She's a cop."

From the back of the room, I hear Helen begin to laugh uncontrollably. She stands up and exits swiftly.

"Daddy will do it for you," Catherine says, "if Miss Helen can't. I've heard Mommy and Daddy say—."

"OK," I say with as much dignity as I can muster, "We're out of time. Miss Helen has some treats for you in the other room. I need a minute or two to talk with your mommies and daddies and then we'll come in there, too."

As soon as the last child has cleared the door, I look at these desperate parents and say calmly, "I assure you that I treat all comments that come to my ears with the utmost charity and encourage all of you to do likewise. Please check your email Tuesday morning for a set of printable worksheets that the children can complete at home in the coming week. I will go over the material with them during next week's session. Obviously, the Socratic method is for the birds. Class dismissed."

***

After the First Communicants class debacle, the rest of the morning goes smoothly. The 10:30 a.m. Mass is its usual mixture of reverence and chaos, with the proceedings highlighted by my first triple baptism—two boys and a girl from three different families, the continuation of the parish's baby boom prompted by a particularly snowy January and February.

After Mass, Helen and I eat a delicious lunch of pork that has been slowly braising in cola all morning. Helen brought her brussels sprouts cooked with bacon and brown sugar, as well as rolls and cheesecake, courtesy of The Muffin Man.

"So tell me, Tom," Helen says with a smirk, "is there a Vatican-approved paddle for beating confessions out of children, or would you like my old nightstick?"

I roll my eyes. "Well, according to Emily, I'm too nice to beat anyone, so you're going to do it."

Helen laughs as I add, "Though Catherine did say Dan could do it if you couldn't."

"I think I need to have a little talk with him," Helen says as tears roll down her cheeks, "about his interrogation techniques."

"Eh, he probably uses them on the twins," I shrug.

After this bit of banter, Helen says, "Nate and Gladys looked good. I mean, I didn't see her scowl at him once. Has she finally forgiven him?"

"I sure hope so," I sigh. "After yesterday, I think things will improve."

"By the way, what was all that about?"

"You're not going to believe this," I say. "They were in a battle royal over Halloween costumes, of all the ridiculous things."

For some reason, Helen's smile disappears. "You think Halloween costumes are ridiculous?"

"Well, not for kids. But they're full grown adults. I mean, I know they do all the cosplay stuff with Age of Artemis at comic book conventions, but dressing up for Halloween at their age?"

Helen's frowning now. "So, tell me, Tom," she says. "If I said we wouldn't be having that argument because I'd decided a couple of months ago what we're wearing—"

"You're not serious, Helen!" I exclaim.

"Of course I am, Tom," Helen says. "You know the last night of the Acutis Society's haunted house—what are they calling it again?"

"Fairy Tales and Frights," I say, "to emphasize that there is family-friendly stuff earlier in the evening."

"Well, the last night is on Halloween," she continues. "And they're having a party afterwards. And someone in this room promised Mae Trent that we'd be chaperones."

"Yes, chaperone," I say. "Not dress up."

"But Tom," Helen says with a smile. "You know how much I love to dress up for Halloween."

"I thought you'd outgrown that in 20 years."

"Honestly, I haven't in a long time—about 20 years," she says. "I'm really looking forward to this, darling. And the costumes I picked out are perfect." She lowers her voice. "And, Father Tom, I can guarantee you're going to like my costume in particular."

Her sultry tone sends a thrill through me, and I'm suddenly aware that I need to turn the heat down in the Rectory.

Rallying my last remaining shreds of dignity, I whine, "But you know how much I hate Halloween."

Helen rolls her eyes. "Yes, Tom. I remember. And I remember *why* you hate Halloween. But shouldn't you be over that by now?"

"Listen, being awakened every day in October year after year by Nola Greer wearing a hideous witch mask is not something you get over easily."

"That was forty years ago!"

"And the scars are still there."

Helen leans forward and pouts. "Oh, come on, darling, won't you do it for me?"

"I guess so, but only if you insist."

"Anyway, Tom, it'll be good for you."

"That's what you always say."

Three

Helen leaves just before 5 p.m, and Nate arrives at the Rectory. He volunteered to write an article about the Myer Mansion, the parish's plans for the estate, and the haunted house to stir up interest and frankly, sell tickets. This is a fundraiser, after all.

We sit down in my office and he pulls out a digital recorder. "Do you mind if I record you, Father?" he asks with enthusiasm.

This gives me an uncomfortable sense of déjà vu. For a moment, I'm taken back to when Nate and I first met and he was working on a documentary about my late wife Joan's murder. It was his work that ultimately led Helen to reopen the case and catch her killer.

I manage to brush those thoughts away. "Not at all, Nate," I say with a smile. "I'd like you to quote me accurately."

"Oh, don't worry about that," he says. "I'll make sure to write exactly what you tell me."

Nate pulls out a notebook from the messenger bag dropped on the floor by his chair. Flipping it open, he says, "I have some questions, Father Tom, about the mansion."

"Well, I'm happy to talk about the mansion and our plans for the Myer estate. This project is very close to my heart, and I'm just so happy that the Acutis Society is hosting Fairy Tales and Frights for the families of Myerton. I know that the Saint Francis Education Center it's raising funds for will be a real benefit, not just to the parish, but to the town as a whole."

"I understand from Gladys that you've done some research into the history of the house?"

I nod. "Yes, some, though I can hardly claim to be an expert on its history. The house was built before the Civil War and was added onto over the years. Interestingly enough, it was the first structure in town wired for electricity—that was done by Thomas Edison himself."

Nate's writing something down—probably noting what I just said as a good quote to include in the story—when he looks up at me and says, without preamble, "So, Father Greer, have you ever heard anything about the Myer Estate being haunted?"

The question catches me off guard, and all I can manage is, "Excuse me?"

"Yes," he says, seriously. "It's one of the oldest houses in Myerton, and there have been some stories over the years about strange noises being heard, lights being seen from the outside, and other unexplained phenomena."

"OK," I say, still trying to figure out how to respond. I clear my throat and say, "Well, the house has seen its share of tragedy over the years—"

"I'm talking about Victoria Myer," Nate says.

I take a deep breath. "Victoria Myer," I repeat. "She was a daughter of Winthrop Myer, the founder of the town and the one who built the Myer Mansion. I remember there being something in the family history about a wounded Confederate soldier who fell in love with her while it was being used as a hospital after the Battle of Antietam. He died in her arms or something like that?"

"Well, yes and no," Nate replies. "The story is that the soldier went looking for her in the dark one night. She couldn't sleep and saw him. For some reason, she had a knife—why, no one knows, apparently. Victoria thought he was an intruder, met him in the dark on the staircase, and stabbed him. Seeing what she had done, she held him while he died and then killed herself with the same knife. Ever since, Victoria Myer's been walking the halls of the house, still carrying a knife."

"Well, that certainly is an interesting story, Nate," I admit, "but I'm not sure what kind of light I can shed on it."

"So when you were in the Myer Mansion," Nate says, "you didn't see anything strange?"

"Look, Nate, I saw a family tragedy unfold in that house, one that was all too human and had no, shall we say, supernatural involvement," I say, getting just a little irritated with him.

"Just tell me about your own experience at the mansion."

"Well, to be fair, it was pretty unique. I highly doubt anybody else would go through what I did."

"Still, it will give readers a sense of what the mansion is like today."

I hesitate. It seems like forever since the events involving the Myer family, the Watsons, and Father Leonard. Horrible, tragic events that included the deaths of four people. Events that triggered my crisis of faith and downward spiral that ended in a cabin during a Florida thunderstorm, with Helen stopping me from throwing my priesthood away. They are events I don't like to think about, much less discuss.

Against my better judgement, I say, "OK. Not long after I returned to Myerton, I went there to talk to Win Myer, who left the estate to the church. The house was dark when I got there, but I knew Win was home because his car was in the driveway. I tried the door and it was unlocked so I went in. I could see a light off in the distance. It was coming from under Win's office door so I went that way but when I opened the door, no one was inside. I started to leave but someone grabbed me from behind and I blacked out.

"I woke up hours later in a shed behind the house. I didn't know who put me there. I was not locked in, so I got out and went back to the house. I won't say anymore than this: what I discovered there was tragic, Nate, and we will not exploit it. Do you understand? It was the final chapter in a long, tragic story that no one needs to rehash."

"Understood, Father. But would you care to comment about the ghost story as it relates to the mansion?"

"No, I would not like to comment. The Bible says 'let the dead bury the dead' and I think that's a good idea here."

Nate nods. "OK, Father, that's fine. What is the Catholic Church's official position on the existence of ghosts?"

"I do not believe the Church has a position one way or another," I say. "I have not studied the question. The Catechism, in line with Sacred Scripture, does prohibit necromancy—the attempt to communicate with the dead."

"So," Nate says, "no séances."

"Definitely not," I say.

"Oh," he says, sounding disappointed. "But of course the Church teaches there is an afterlife?"

"Of course, Nate," I sigh. "The Church teaches that the soul lives on after the body dies."

"So there could be ghosts?"

"I suppose, but it's much more likely that Victoria Myer's soul is in Purgatory than walking the halls of the Myer Mansion."

"Do you believe in ghosts, Father?"

I smile. "Nate, I believe what the Church believes. I won't comment further. I pray for the souls in Purgatory, as all Catholics should. Other than that, I have more interest in the living than the dead."

Four

"He asked you about what?" Helen exclaims over coffee at The Perfect Cup the next morning.

"The ghost of Victoria Myer," I say. "He basically asked me if I'd ever seen her when I was there."

Helen sits back and folds her arms. "You didn't, did you?"

I shake my head. "Did you?"

"Sorry, I was too busy dealing with the dead body in the study and the very live murderer in the living room," Helen says. "Honestly, where did he get that?"

"Oh, it's an old family legend, actually," I say. "I ran across it in my own research on the house. You know me, still the archivist at heart."

"So there really *is* a ghost?"

I look around to make sure no one is listening, then lean forward. "Can you keep a secret?" I whisper.

Helen's eyes light up as she leans forward. "What?" she whispers back.

I look furtively to the side, then whisper, "No," before breaking into a laugh.

Helen plops back in her chair, scowling, and says, "You, Father Greer, can be a real Balaam's donkey, you know that?"

I nod. "But, you love me anyway."

She sighs and smiles. "Yes, I just have a weakness for you."

"And on that note," I say, standing up, "I need to get back to the Rectory."

"And I need to get to the station," she says. I kiss her on the forehead, and she says, "I love you."

"I love you. I'll stop by this afternoon."

Her eyes sparkle as she says, "I'll be counting the hours."

***

I am just beginning my research for this week's homily—I've learned never to put my preparation off until later in the week—when the front doorbell rings. Anna answers it and there's muffled chatter approaching my office door just before a light knock.

"Yes?" I call.

I'm both surprised and pleased when Martin Maycord sticks his head around the door into my office.

"Martin," I say, "come in and have a seat. What's going on?"

"Hi, Tom, are you busy?" Martin says as he comes in. "I don't want to interrupt you, but I was on my way home from work and I thought I'd stop in for a few minutes and take a chance that you might be available."

"If you can take time to stop by and visit with me after you've pulled an all-night shift at the hospital, I can certainly make time for you."

Martin sits down. "Well, I have two things to talk to you about. One wonderful, the other terrible. Which do you want first?"

Trying to be more optimistic about life, I say, "Why don't you tell me the wonderful thing first."

Though I'm pretty sure I know what it is.

The usually serious doctor breaks into a grin, looking happier than I've ever seen him before. "Tom," he says, lapsing into the Southern accent that betrays his Georgia roots, "I'm going to ask Mae to marry me."

"That is wonderful news, Martin," I say, reaching across the desk to shake his hand. "I'm sure you'll both be very happy."

"So you really do believe it's wonderful news?" he asks, surprisingly sheepishly. "I mean, we've only been dating for three months, and I know that she's a good bit younger than I am. But Tom, I've never met anybody like her in my life. I've talked to her parents—at her insistence, I might add—and they are ready to give us their blessing. Both my parents are dead, so it's not an issue with me. Not to mention the fact that, well, I'm much older and I have lived out on my own for quite a while now."

"To answer your question, Martin, yes, I do think it's wonderful," I say with a smile. "You're right about the age difference, and about the fact that you haven't known each other that long. But just remember, you two have to go through six months of premarital counseling before the wedding. By the time you make it through, I feel confident that it will confirm what I already believe seeing the two of you together—you two will make a great match. From what you've told me, you don't have any major conflicts."

"No, we don't, no major ones," he chuckles. "One of my pet peeves with her is that she's too thrifty. She acts like she has to squeeze every penny until it screams and I'm just not accustomed to that."

"And what bugs her about you?" I ask with a grin.

"She feels like I worry too much about making other people happy. Especially her. She insists that she's content most of the time with her life the way it is, and that I drive her a little crazy by always asking if there's something I can do to make it better."

"Martin," I say, shaking my head, "I've got to say, if you're leveling with me and those really are your pet peeves with each other, I don't think you have much to worry about. But we will go through all that later. Now, you're giving her your mother's ring, right?"

"Yes, but I'm having it re-designed for Mae. My father got my mother's ring when he was in graduate school, and it has a beautiful but small diamond. I'm going to have another, larger, diamond added beside it and then a matching diamond on the other side. She'll have my mom's ring, but it will be more in keeping with what I plan to provide for her, if that doesn't seem boastful."

"Not at all, Martin. Lord knows you're a generous person, and there's nobody who deserves generosity more than Mae. So, have you decided when you're going to pop the question?"

"Yes, this Friday night," he says. "I've got it all arranged. I've chartered a boat from Annapolis, we'll dine on board, then at just the right moment, fireworks will go off and I'll drop to my knee and ask her to become my wife."

Frankly, I'm surprised Martin's going for something so sedate.

"Besides," he says, "it has to be this weekend. After that, it's going to be full steam ahead getting the haunted house ready. I don't think she and I are going to have a single moment to ourselves until after Halloween."

"Well, they've already done a lot of work setting it up," I say. "I was there Thursday and it already looked like a cross between The Twilight Zone and Clash of the Titans. They really are going all out. So, Martin, has Mae roped you into helping?"

Martin rolls his eyes and sighs. "Of course."

I grin. "You're a character, aren't you?"

"Now don't give me a hard time, Tom," he says, pointing at me. "You know love can make a man do crazy things."

On that, he's absolutely right. "So, what are you?"

"Well," he says, "Mae is Little Red Riding Hood. And . . . I'm The Big Bad Wolf."

I burst out laughing. "Tom," he says with a scowl, "not really a good idea to laugh at your doctor a few days before your physical."

"I am sorry," I say, regaining control. "But, The Big Bad Wolf? Like, you'll be dressed as a wolf?"

"Right down to the head," Martin says. "Costume's as hot as hell, but all I have to do is chase Little Red Riding Hood playfully for the children early in the evening, but be scarier and more aggressive later on. It's for a good cause, so I don't really mind."

He pauses. "Unfortunately, I also have something unpleasant I'd like to make you aware of."

"What's that?" I ask, an ominous feeling creeping into my bones.

Martin takes a deep breath. "I've seen one of your parishioners in the ER several times since I've been here. Every time, it's been some sort of injury that is consistent with domestic abuse."

"Oh, My Dear Lord," I say, raising my eyes to the ceiling. "How bad?"

"A black eye, a couple of bruised ribs, a shoulder sprain consistent with someone yanking her arm backwards. No broken bones—yet."

"And you're sure she's being abused?"

"Tom, I've seen enough battered women in Baltimore to know the signs," he says. "In my professional opinion, the injuries came from physical abuse by her husband."

"Have you tried talking to her, or having Mae talk to her?"

He nods. "I haven't involved Mae yet, but I have tried again and again to talk to her about filing charges against her husband or at least getting away from him. But every single time, she refuses, insisting that she's just clumsy, that she fell—you know, the same old story. She came in again last night. She claimed she fell, but there was bruising on her arm like she had been grabbed tight before she was pushed. I tried to talk to her but she just pushed me away, insisting that her husband was a good man and it was her fault for making him mad."

"So, she basically admitted her husband did that to her," I say. "What can I do?"

"Well, since she won't go to the police," he says, "you're about the only one who stands a chance of doing anything. Tom, this has got to stop before someone gets killed. You know I can't tell you her name or any more details—she's not a minor, otherwise I could report it. But please be on the lookout for anyone that you see in church or around town who looks like they might have been beaten. I am hoping that if you reach out to her, she might listen to you. Otherwise, I don't know where this is going to end, but it won't be anywhere good."

I consider what Martin's just told me. One of the things they teach us in seminary is that domestic violence will be one of the most difficult issues we will have to deal with in our work as priests. I admit that, since being at St. Clare's, I have not come across this particular problem in the confessional. I guess I just wanted to believe that it would not happen in our happy small-town parish.

Obviously, I was wrong.

"Martin," I say, "I really appreciate the heads-up. I know this pushes the boundaries of doctor/patient privilege, but rest assured it will not go any further."

"Including Helen," he says, "although I'll be calling her myself if there's a next time."

"Including Helen," I say. "But let's pray that there isn't."

"Of course," Martin says. "But I've seen this too many times, Tom. Barring a miracle, there will be a next time."

Five

Since Martin can't tell me the name of the woman in my parish who's being abused, there's little I can do right now.

But I know someone who might have an idea who she is.

"Anna," I say, standing at the door of her office. "Busy?"

"Always," she says with a smile, looking up from her laptop. "Does this have something to do with Martin's visit? Now don't look at me that way, I didn't hear anything."

"Oh, I know that," I say, trying to figure out how I can get the information I need without connecting it to Martin and thus betraying his confidence.

"So he told you he's going to ask Mae to marry him?" she says.

I look at her incredulously. "I thought you said—"

"And I didn't," Anna said. "I had lunch with Doris Trent a couple of days ago and she said Martin had invited her and Alan out to dinner, just the three of them. Took them to a really fancy place in Baltimore. He told them he loved Mae, wanted to ask her to marry him, and basically asked for their blessing. Well, Doris is just thrilled about it. I mean, he's Catholic, he's a doctor, and apparently he's quite comfortable."

"Comfortable doesn't begin to describe it," I say. "Martin's quite wealthy. You say Doris is thrilled. Did she say how Alan feels about it?"

Anna hesitates, then says, "Well, he gave his blessing, but I think he still has some questions about Martin. But he's not about to stand in the way of his little girl being happy, so he's keeping his concerns close."

I sigh. "Well, I can't say I'm surprised. Martin's made such a remarkable turn in such a short period of time. If I were a father, I might be concerned."

Anna sits back and folds her arms. "Tom, do you have concerns?"

I consider her question for a moment before answering. "Concerns? No, not really. I know Martin and Mae love each other—that's evident any time you see them together. Martin's devoted to her, and Mae seems equally devoted to him. I don't have a problem with the age gap between them from a morality standpoint or anything like that."

"Then what is it, Tom?"

"Well, honestly, they come from two completely different backgrounds. They have very different life experiences. And frankly, Martin is not as firmly grounded yet in his faith as Mae is. I think that may raise issues they haven't even thought about yet. But," I smile, "it's nothing that we can't work through in the next six months."

"Exactly. Now, is there anything else?"

"Yes," I say, remembering something, "Last week I saw a piece on the news about how domestic violence often goes up near the holidays. I was thinking about asking Helen for a brochure or something that I could put in the church bulletin but then, I wonder, do you think it's even an issue in the parish? I mean, you know more women than I do."

Anna looks to one side for a moment, like she's trying to decide what to say. Finally, she turns to me and says, "I'm afraid it is a problem, Tom, at least for Bridget Davis."

I take a deep breath. "Oh," I say.

"Yeah," Anna says, nodding her head.

Shaking my head, I say, "That's not an easy situation, is it?"

"No," Anna replies. "It's too bad you didn't know the Davises a few years ago. She and Rusty would never miss a Mass, their boy Terry was a sweet kid—still is, though I think he's ten or eleven by now. All their kids were sweet."

"So what happened?"

Anna says, "I don't really know the details. Rusty lost his job—some accident, I think—and he hasn't been able to find another. Bridget teaches at Myerton Elementary, but he just stays home. From the state of the house, it doesn't look like he does much of anything except drink, from what I hear."

My heart goes out to Rusty—a little bit—as Anna tells me what she knows. He sounds like so many people I knew back home as a kid. The dad would lose his job for some reason and, at least for a time, he couldn't find another one. First, depression would set in, then the drinking to try to alleviate the depression—a foolish choice, since alcohol is a depressant—which would lead to more depression. Eventually, the dad would either find another job or, as happened far too often, he'd be declared disabled and start receiving a monthly check from the government. Between that and the wife's wages, the family would manage to keep afloat somehow.

Many times—not often, but often enough—the dad would begin taking his anger and frustration out on his wife and kids. Usually with screaming, but sometimes with his fists. More than once, one of the kids in my classes would show up at school wearing long sleeves or a sweater to hide the bruises. On a couple of occasions, the guidance counselor would show up to our class, asking someone to come down to their office.

We were old enough to know what that meant. Child Protective Services. Foster Care.

Inwardly, I shudder at what Bridget and her children may be going through.

"Do I have anything this afternoon?" I ask Anna.

"It's supposed to be your day off," she answers. "And, except for your daily lunch with Helen, your calendar is clear."

I nod and stand. "Can you send the Davises' address to my phone? I know they live on the same street as the Conways, but I can't remember the number."

"What are you going to do, Tom?" Anna asks with a worried look.

"What I'm supposed to do," I say. "I'm going to check on a hurting member of my flock."

"Look, Tom," Anna says. "That's very admirable, but Rusty Davis has a temper. Just be careful."

I smile. "Do you think he'd take a swing at a priest?"

When Anna doesn't answer, doubt begins to creep into my mind.

***

Turns out, I don't need the address.

The Davis house sticks out like a sore thumb among the lovingly maintained houses on the street, just five houses down from where I pass Catherine Conway and her brothers playing in the yard while Miriam keeps a careful eye on them. After Catherine's fall from the large tree in their yard, neither she nor Dan let the kids play outside unsupervised. The tree is ablaze in fall color, but the carefully mown brownish-green lawn shows only a few stray red and gold leaves. The flower beds near the house show recent mulching, and there are fall annuals planted. Their garden statue of Mary sports a crown of white chrysanthemums, and a statue of Saint Francis that doubles as a bird feeder has a couple of small diners nibbling on the seed filling the bowl in his concrete hands. In all, the Conways' home exudes love and happiness.

In contrast, the Davises' home reeks of sadness and desperation. The lawn is overgrown, looking like it hasn't been mowed in weeks. The flower beds are in desperate need of weeding, with a few hearty survivors poking weak blooms through the mess. A child's wagon, more rust now than metal, sits in the middle of the driveway. The house is in desperate need of power washing, and there's the unmistakable sign of water damage from where the gutters—no doubt filled with leaves and other refuse—overflowed.

Parking my car in the cracked driveway—it needed resealing against the elements long ago—I sit for a moment and say a quiet prayer. I'm not sure what if anything I hope to accomplish. It's like I told Anna. I'm reaching out. If Rusty accepts what I have to offer, wonderful. If not, I can at least say I tried.

And as I've learned, trying is about all I can do for some people.

Unbidden, the image of a dead Richard Davenport flashes in my head. Except for myself, Helen, Anna, Nate, and Gladys, he had no mourners at his funeral. I must remember to add his name to the list of people for the All Souls Day Mass.

I walk to the door and press the doorbell. Hearing nothing, I knock.

And wait.

"Maybe no one's home," I mumble, and I knock again.

"OK, OK, keep your pants on!" says a groggy and slightly slurred voice from inside. I step back as the door swings open.

"We don't want—Oh!" Rusty Davis is obviously surprised to see me standing on his front porch. From his messy blond hair and glazed eyes, I must have gotten him out of bed. He looks like he hasn't shaved in days, the tank top undershirt he's wearing is soiled, and his baggy gray sweats are stained as well.

In addition, he reeks of a combination of body odor and alcohol.

"Father . . . sorry, I can't remember your name," Rusty says. I can smell the alcohol on his breath.

It's ten in the morning.

"Father Tom," I say with a smile, extending my hand. He looks at it warily, but doesn't take it.

"Oh, yeah," he mumbles, running a hand through his mop of hair. "That's right. Sorry."

"I'm sorry if I woke you," I say, trying to maintain a lilt in my voice.

"I have a condition," he says defensively.

"I'm very sorry to hear that," I say, trying to sound sympathetic. With my thumb I point to the driveway. "When I didn't see a car in the driveway, I—"

"Bridget's at work," he growls. "She takes the car. Leaves me here."

"I understand she works at Myerton Elementary?"

"Yeah, yeah. Just *loves* it there." His voice drips with bitterness and sarcasm. "She'd probably live there if she could. Damn school."

"Well," I say, groping for what to say, "It's good that she has a job—"

"She has a job," he spits, "and I don't. Is that what you're trying to say?"

"No, no, not at all," I say quickly, seeing my visit is careening out of control fast. "I just meant it's good that she has a job that she loves."

"Huh!" he grunts. "She should be here taking care of me. Woman should care more for her husband."

"Oh, I think—"

"Good morning." I turn to see a letter carrier coming up the driveway, a stack of mail in her hands.

"Great," Rusty mutters. "More bad news."

"Morning, Father. Rusty, here ya go," she says cheerfully, handing the stack to him.

"Thanks for nothing," he spits as she hurries off. Looking through the envelopes, he says, "Damn bloodsuckers. Greedy bastards. It isn't right, Father, it just isn't!"

One of my less admirable skills is the ability to read upside down. Even from where I stand, I can see "collection agency" on some of the envelopes.

"You know, Rusty," I say carefully, "if the parish can ever be of any help to your family. I know times are tough for a lot of people."

He stares at me, his face growing red with anger. I take a step back. "We're not charity cases, Father!" he yells. "What, you don't have enough damn illegal aliens to take care of, huh?"

"Rusty," I say, trying to maintain my own temper, "I was just—"

"Leave us alone, Father," he growls, "and get off my property!"

With that, he slams the door in my face.

Turning away, I look up to the clear early fall sky. "Well, Lord," I say quietly. "I tried."

Six

On Tuesday, Helen is able to join me for my hospital visits. We've talked often about what her role in the parish should be, given the demands of being Chief of Police, even in a town the size of Myerton. The two of us agree that her primary role in the parish, as my wife, will be supporting me in my different ministries. So, she joins me in greeting parishioners after Sunday Mass. When she can, like today, she joins me at the hospital. There are nursing home and shut-in visits on Wednesdays, and she's come along a couple of times.

Helen can be very patient and gentle when dealing with someone who is suffering or in pain, empathy drawn from her own experience. It's a trait that I appreciate, but it can make for a very long afternoon when we have multiple people to see.

At the same time, however, she is not particularly patient with those who just want to criticize the nursing staff and complain about the hospital. Helen remains grateful to the hospital staff for saving her life, and is thus intolerant of those who would speak ill of it.

Worst of all are the few only slightly ill patients who want to grill her about the details of some investigation they've heard about. She is pretty good at deflecting prying questions, but last week, she finally looked at one kid—in traction because he was speeding and wrecked his father's car—after he badgered her for details about her being shot, and asked, "Can you keep a secret?"

He got all excited and said, "Sure."

Helen grinned broadly and said, "So can I," and walked out.

Today, there are only a few parishioners to visit, so we have time to go down to the ER and see the nurses. We know them by name, having been there several times in the last few months, and they always joke about being glad to see us under our own power or, in my case, not covered in someone else's blood.

"Not very busy today," I say as I look around the almost empty waiting room.

"Oh, it will pick up," Sally says. "Flu season is just around the corner. Not to mention Halloween."

"That's our busy time, too," Helen comments.

"Yeah. There's just something about this season that really brings out the crazies." Sally looks at me. "I just hope I don't see you in here again."

I laugh. "I'll try really hard, but you know me. I can't make any promises."

Sally looks at Helen. "Can't you keep him out of trouble?"

Helen sighs and shakes her head. "No. Why do you think I'm marrying him?"

Another nurse, hearing her, mutters, "I'd think that was obvious. One fine looking man right there."

***

"How about an early dinner?" I say as we leave the hospital.

"Sounds good, then I'll need to go home to get ready for tonight," she says.

"Tonight?" I ask. "What's tonight?"

Helen looks at me quizzically. "Oh, Tom, you know what tonight is."

I rush through all the important dates in our lives together—both recent and past—in my mind and come up empty. "No. Should I?"

"I'm teaching that self-defense course to the Ladies of Charity tonight. And you're supposed to act as my attacker. Remember now?"

"Oh, dear Lord," I say, rolling my eyes. "You mean you're actually doing that?"

"Of course I am, Tom," she says, a hint of exasperation in her voice. "And you volunteered to help me."

"I don't remember volunteering," I say. "My memory is that Anna looked at me and said, 'You'll help her, won't you, Tom?'"

"And you said you'd be glad to."

"I was being sarcastic. I thought you and Anna were just making that up to drive me crazier than I already am."

"Now, Tom, really!"

"No," I plead. "Please, Helen. Don't make me do this."

She's about to respond to my admittedly childish request when instead she smiles and gets a twinkle in her eye. "OK, darling. Of course you don't have to if you really don't want to."

I sigh. "Thank you."

"I mean, it's really not fair," she says, looking out the window. "After all, I am professionally trained and in reasonably good shape. This is definitely my turf."

"What do you mean," I say, my ego getting the best of my good sense, "'it's really not fair' and all that? I'm in good shape."

"Of course you are, Tom," she says somewhat condescendingly. "I'll call Nate and see if he'll be willing to help me out. Gladys is planning on coming anyway. Besides, he is younger, so I won't have to be as careful when I struggle free from his grip."

"Wait," I say, suddenly paying attention. "What do you mean, 'struggle free from his grip?'"

"Well, there are several moves aimed at getting away from someone holding you close around the chest or waist."

"Oh, really?" I say, becoming intrigued.

"And also, Nate will probably be easier to throw to the ground and sit on."

Now I'm very intrigued. Clearing my throat, I say, "Helen, you know, you're right. I should support you in this. I'm sorry for being such a poor sport. I'll be glad to help you with your class."

"Oh, darling, would you?" she says with a smile of triumph. "That would be lovely."

Yes, I know she played me like a violin. And I let her.

Am I proud of that? Eh, life is a series of compromises.

And honestly, I'm up for any excuse to hold Helen.

***

It's only when Helen asks me if I have an athletic cup that I question my decision to give into my, for lack of a better word, temptations.

"Why?" I ask.

"For your protection," she says matter-of-factly.

"You're not planning on—"

"Oh, of course I'm not planning on hitting you there," she laughs. "But that is the most vulnerable area on a man, and I will be demonstrating some strikes to disable an attacker."

"But darling," I say nervously, "I mean, I was injured there not that long ago."

"I promise I'll pull my punches. But, accidents can happen."

Fortunately, I'm able to find the one I purchased for my ill-conceived plan to play softball in seminary, and promptly at 7 p.m., I am in the church basement wearing sweatpants, a t-shirt, and said cup. I'm standing in the middle of a circle of seated Ladies of Charity and Gladys next to Helen.

"Now ladies," Helen says to the attentive women, "there's nothing special about these moves. Anyone, regardless of how old or how young, can use them to fight back against someone trying to hurt them. In fact, I helped another officer teach some of these to elementary schoolers when I was in D.C. And let me tell you, a nine-year-old can be as ferocious against an attacker as any of you.

"Tom has offered to assist me, probably because he wants to know how dangerous I really am before we get married."

This gets a laugh, especially when I add, "Oh, I know already. I'm just a brave sort of guy."

Then, we begin. And I again question the wisdom of my decision.

Helen proceeds to demonstrate something she calls a "Hammer Strike," which involves her trying to punch my eyes out with her car keys while screaming "Stop" and "No" in my face. She knows very well that I hate anything that threatens my eyes and I very nearly turn and run from the room.

Moments later, when she moves on to the "Groin Kick," I wish I had. She doesn't actually make contact, but the threat itself is terrifying.

She goes on to nearly strike me in the throat several times, using everything from the palm of her hand to her elbow.

Everyone seems pretty tired at this point and so we break for refreshments. Helen is caught up in something to do with new curtains for a home for unwed mothers the Ladies of Charity is helping to redecorate, so I take my drink and cookies and find a seat on the edge of the cacophony.

I am just beginning to relax when Margaret Benson toddles over. Margaret is in her early 80s and completely convinced that the nation is in danger of being taken over at any moment by any one of several groups. I plaster a smile on my face and stand as she approaches, taking my arm and digging her claws into it.

"Father," she says, her voice crackling with age, "I just want you to know how much I appreciate Helen doing this for us. You know, the time may come when women like me have to fight to the death to avoid being killed, or worse."

"Yes, ma'am, that's true." I say, wondering exactly what "worse" she has to worry about at her age. "You never know."

"Why, just today I saw where there are secret agents going around to nursing homes and stealing patients' phones and signing them up as organ donors without their permission. Then, the first time someone sneezes, it's curtains for them and their kidneys are on their way to China."

"Yes, ma'am. That is terrible," I say, wondering why someone in China would want an 80-something-year-old American kidney but not wanting to ask.

I am desperately trying to think of a way to change the subject when Helen claps her hands and says, "OK, everyone, let's gather back around."

Once everyone has reassembled, Helen looks at me and says, "OK, Tom, I want you to grab me from behind."

At first, I don't think I heard her right. "Excuse me?"

"You heard me," she says, turning her back to me. "Grab me from behind."

"OK, ah, how exactly?"

Looking over her shoulder, she smiles. "Just use your imagination."

Normally, grabbing my voluptuous bride-to-be from behind would be a dream come true. But the presence of 28 pairs of unblinking eyes takes some of the joy out of it.

I walk up behind her and wrap my arms around her waist. I'm just beginning to relish the feel of her when she suddenly drops down, spins, and simulates a dangerously close strike with her palm to my groin. Needless to say, this elicits a few giggles, with Gloria MacMillan shouting from the back row, "Drop him to his knees, Helen!"

Helen demonstrates a similar move when I trap her arms and then when I grab her around the neck. By this time, I have had enough and so I am incredibly thankful to hear her say, "That will be all tonight, ladies. Thank you for your kind attention." She turns the meeting back over to Anna and I slip out the back door to hide in the Rectory until everyone goes home.

***

Anna and Helen turn up about 30 minutes later, just as I am finishing a beer.

"But you really like that blue one with the big flowers?" Anna is asking Helen as they come in.

"Yes, Anna, I do," Helen says, "but I really don't see why you're asking me. It's not like I know anymore about this kind of stuff than anyone else does. I probably know less."

"Yes, but these are young women and we need a young woman's perspective."

"But Anna, I'm hardly a young woman. Most of these unwed mothers are in their teens. You should ask someone like Mae Trent or Gladys."

Anna sits down as Helen plops on the couch next to me. "Well, Mae is too busy being wooed by her handsome and wealthy doctor, and Gladys—well, is Gladys. Lord knows I love that girl, but her tastes are . . . unique."

"Still talking about the home for unwed mothers?" I say. "That's been going on for a couple of months, hasn't it?"

"Tom, these things can't be rushed," Anna says. "The home they have is adequate and in good repair, but it just doesn't look homey and comforting. You know what some of these girls have been through. We, with the Knights supplying the labor, are going to paint and do new curtains and everything. And, thanks to Helen's input, we have the entire color scheme."

"I just hope everyone else likes it," Helen says. "Again, I'm hardly a decorating expert. You've seen my apartment."

Looking at me, Anna says, "Changing the subject, how was your visit to the Davises?"

I sigh as Helen looks at me. "You went to the Davises?" she asks.

"Yes," I nod. "And to answer your question, Anna, not great."

"Let me guess," Helen says. "Rusty was there alone. He looked like he'd just woken up, and he smelled and sounded like he was about halfway through a six-pack."

"So you know him," I say.

"That's a terrible situation," Helen says, shaking her head. "We've been called out to that house on several occasions responding to 911 calls about fights. Same old thing—we get there, and the husband says everything is fine, they were just having an argument, the wife backs him up, says there's no problem."

"Did any of your officers ever see evidence Bridget Davis was abused?"

Helen takes a deep breath. "Not that anyone could see, but one time when Nina Hallstead responded with Potter to a call, she pulled Bridget aside and basically told her she knew he was hitting her, that she didn't have to put up with it, and to just say the word and they'd arrest him."

"How did she know?" Anna says.

Helen pauses before saying, "I don't want to betray a confidence. Let's just say there's a reason Nina learned how to fight."

We sit quietly with this for a few minutes. Helen finally stands up and says, "I'm getting a beer. Want another, darling?"

"No, I'm good. You, Anna?"

"Oh, no," she says, "In fact, I'm going up to bed. You two be good."

"We have for almost five months," I say.

Anna goes upstairs, and Helen returns with her beer. Snuggling down on the couch next to me, she says, "I liked your arms around me tonight."

"I liked having my arms around you," I say, "until you tried multiple times to hit me in the groin."

She chuckles. "All in the interest of education." She takes a swig of beer and snuggles closer. "Twelve more weeks," she whispers.

"Not that much time."

"I know," she says. "You know what I'm looking forward to the most about being married to you?"

I grin and say, "Well, I have some idea."

"OK, there is that. But it's just the fact that at the end of the evening, I don't have to leave to go back to my lonely little apartment."

I kiss the top of her head. "I feel the same way," I whisper. "Very much so."

She looks up at me, her eyes glistening. "Do you know how much I love you, Tom Greer?"

"As much as I love you, Helen Parr."

"Will you kiss me?"

"Gladly."

Seven

I arrive at Martin's office at the hospital just before 10 a.m. on Thursday. He meets me at the door and says, "Good morning, Father. I reserved an exam room for us down the hall."

As we walk along, Martin tries to make small talk but I find it hard to follow the conversation. Finally, he says, "Tom, are you really that nervous about this?"

I croak out, "I guess I am," expecting some sort of sympathetic response.

Instead, he claps me on the back and laughs. "Good. Now you know how I felt before my first confession with you."

This does make me laugh, as well as put things in perspective. After all, I am not going to learn anything today that could endanger my immortal soul.

He shows me the room and a nurse comes in to do my vitals. She frowns at my blood pressure and then takes it again in my other arm. She makes some notes on a tablet, throws a gown on the exam table, and leaves. I strip down to my underwear, putting on the hospital gown and sitting on the exam table trying to retain some of my dignity.

Martin comes in about five minutes later. "So," he says as he looks in my ears and eyes, "I think I have a possible donor on the hook for the Education Center."

"That's wonderful," I say, in addition to "ahh."

"Yeah," says as he puts his stethoscope against my chest. "Take a deep breath, please. Have you heard of the Fielding Corporation?"

I shake my head, still breathing deeply.

"I'm not surprised. They make pediatric medical equipment using natural and recycled materials. Anyway, they're still a new company and I went to med-school with their founder. I gave him a call, told him about what you want to do, and he admitted it's intriguing. He's especially interested in developing the land as an outdoor learning area."

"That sounds amazing," I say, finding myself surprisingly relaxed. "What do you need from me?"

"Just relax, Tom—Oh, not much," Martin says. "He's in Ohio so I told him to pick a day and we'll fly up to meet him. OK, that's fine. Bring Helen if you like. Mae'll probably come since they haven't met yet and the helicopter seats four."

This freezes me in my tracks as I ask, "Wait—what?"

"Oh, sorry. Yeah, I figured I'd fly us up myself. I need some hours to keep my license and we can leave early so we can enjoy the fall foliage. Greg assures me there's plenty of room to land on his property. We'll meet with Greg and his wife over lunch and then fly back. I want to land before dark, not because I can't land on instruments but because I'm just a bit out of practice."

I'm thoroughly intrigued by now and ask, "When did you learn to fly a helicopter?"

"Oh, well, when I was training to go to Afghanistan, they made all the field surgeons take ground school so that we could take over in case the pilot was injured. When I got back to the states, I decided to complete my certification."

"And you own a helicopter?"

"Yes and no," he says casually. "I lease it to the hospital for a dollar a month to use as a stat-flight. But I still own it, so when I want to borrow for a few hours, they arrange back-up from a big hospital in Baltimore. Normally, a hospital this small would not have a stat-flight at all, so even with having to depend on help from Baltimore for a few hours a month, it's a win-win."

I want to find out more, but Martin shocks me by saying, "OK, we're all done. Get dressed and meet me back in my office."

I am amazed to find that I was so caught up in his story that I was paying no attention at all to what he was doing. When I get back to his office, I tell him this and he just smiles, saying, "Someone once said that priests and doctors have similar vocations in that they should comfort the troubled and trouble the comfortable. You were obviously troubled, so I hope my random chatter comforted you."

He looks at the tablet in front of him, takes a deep breath, and says positively, "Frankly, Tom, I'm pleasantly surprised at how healthy you are. Your labs look good—cholesterol's a little high, but overall, not too bad. Everything else is normal."

I smile. "Well, I'm glad something about me is."

"To be honest, Tom," Martin continues, "the only thing that's really bothering me is your blood pressure. With your family history, we can't afford to let it get out of hand."

I take a deep breath, trying not to panic, as he says, "I've been looking at your records, and it seems that it has been on a slow but steady rise since you came to Myerton. Prior to that, there does not appear to have been any problem. Now, part of it could be your age but I'm wondering if there is anything else in play. What did you do before coming here?"

"I was the archivist for the Archdiocese of Baltimore."

"Uh-huh. And before that?"

"I was in seminary, after spending time in formation with the brothers of Our Lady of the Mount."

He contemplates this before he continues, "Sounds pretty quiet, not very stressful. Would that be a fair assessment?"

"Oh yeah, especially compared to now."

He smiles at this as if he's gotten the answer he is looking for. "Look Tom, I'm going to show you the honesty and grace that you have always shown me. I can put you on blood pressure medication, but I hate to do that if your only real problem is managing stress. Now, I don't see anything here about medication for your panic attacks. Do you take anything for that?"

"No. I've had a few sessions with a therapist and she taught me some coping techniques."

"Such as?"

"Mainly focusing on my breathing and my surroundings, being aware that I am not trapped in that basement again, that Helen is safe, that kind of thing."

"And that works for you?"

"Yeah, pretty well."

"OK, good. Then hopefully this will, too. Tom, before I prescribe blood pressure medication, I want you to make a concerted effort to find a way to cope with your stress, and I'm not just talking about the stuff that's bugging you, but the stuff that you don't even know is bothering you, like what your Mom might say at the wedding."

I eye him oddly and he says, "Helen gave me a call before you came over. You know I can't tell her anything without your permission, but she can tell me whatever she likes."

He pauses and then continues, "We are two very blessed men, Tom, to have found love again after our early losses. We owe it to God to make the most of these blessings. So just like you laid it all on the line with me about valuing Mae enough to wait for her, I'm telling you that you need to value Helen enough to find something to do that helps you relax. Any ideas?"

"Well, I pray," I say. "That's comforting."

"I'm sure it is," Martin says, "but I have to wonder how relaxing it is, especially when you are responsible for bringing the needs of hundreds of people to God's attention each day. No, I was thinking maybe something more physical. What about cycling? This is a wonderful time of year for it. Getting out in the country for even just half an hour each day could do you a world of good."

I hesitate. I mean, I have a bike. A very nice one, in fact, that Helen picked up for me at a police auction.

Suddenly, I'm visualizing Helen and myself biking into the country on a crisp autumn day, a delicious picnic lunch strapped to the back of my bike. We spread a blanket under a tree, have some wine.

It could be even more fun after we're married.

Martin sees my smile and says positively, "Well, I think we may be on to something. So, I am prescribing one hour of bike riding every day."

"Wait," I say, coming out of my reverie, "Every day?"

"Yes, weather permitting." He pauses, then adds, "Tom, you did me an amazing favor when you confronted me, gently as you did, about the state of my soul. I am trying to do the same for you about the state of your body. Please, take my advice as seriously as I took yours and we'll both be better off."

I have no other response to this so I say, "OK. And thank you. I know how hard it is to tell people something they don't want to hear."

"Then you also know that it's not as hard when you really care about the person and want what's best for them."

"I appreciate that Martin," I say with a smile. "So, tell me, how are preparations for popping the question going?"

"Everything is in readiness," he says. "I'll admit, I'm getting a little nervous about it. I mean, what if she says no?"

"I seriously doubt she will, Martin," I laugh. "She's about as good at hiding her feelings as you are. Do you think she suspects something?"

"She's a very smart woman, so I'd be surprised if she didn't. She even asked me if I had something special in mind. I had to think quickly about an answer."

"What did you say?"

"I honestly can't remember, I was so befuddled."

At that, we both laugh as we stand up. Martin puts out his hand. "Tom, let's get back together in about a month. I'll check your blood pressure again—by the way, it might be a good idea to get a home monitor so you can keep track yourself—and see if my prescription is doing its job. Helen asked me particularly to make sure you were in good shape for the honeymoon."

"Oh, really?" I say, blushing. "Well, if that's what she wants, I better do what you say."

***

The day is so nice after Noon Mass and lunch that I decide to go ahead and take Martin's advice and take a bike ride. Helen texted me earlier and said she couldn't make lunch, because she had a conference call with other Chiefs of Police in the area. So I pull the bike out of the garage and dust off the cycling helmet that Helen bought me.

I'm wearing my clericals, but the sun is bright enough that I'm sure cars can see me. Being a college town, Myerton has an excellent system of designated bike lanes and bike paths. Drivers are used to students sharing the road with them, and I cannot remember the last time there was a serious accident involving a cyclist and a car.

I'm determined not to be the first of the year.

I decide to take a relatively easy ride out to the Myer Estate. It's mostly flat, and a good portion of the route is a bike path through the wooded areas backing up to the college.

I ride past the gorge where I often parked when Helen was in the hospital. Sitting in my car, I'd play loud heavy metal music and scream. I haven't done that in a long time.

It only takes me about thirty minutes or so to bike out to the estate. By the time I get there, I'm sweating, breathing heavily, and my underused calf muscles are protesting loudly. I'm thankful I brought a bottle of water with me, and I quickly gulp down most of it.

"It's for Helen," I gasp to myself. "I'm doing this for her. Lord knows I wouldn't do it otherwise."

The estate is in much better shape than it was last year this time, as the church has spent a lot of money to clean up the grounds and powerwash and paint the interior. But even in the middle of the day, the sight of the mansion sends a shiver down my spine when I remember all that happened there.

Nate's business van is in the drive, along with a motorcycle I don't recognize. I'm confused, because I wasn't aware that any members of the Acutis Society drove a motorcycle.

I walk up the steps to the front door and turn the knob. Finding the door unlocked, I push it open and step into the foyer.

Inside it's clean and freshly painted; the only cobwebs on the large chandelier are the artificial ones put there to prepare for the haunted house. It doesn't even open for a couple of weeks, but there's already been a lot of work done to turn the antebellum house into—well, I'm still not exactly sure what.

I wander through the rooms, transformed by lumber, paint, paper mache, and chicken wire into various scenes. One room is a forest scene, giving way to a vine-covered area that looks like it's out of Sleeping Beauty. Another room is a Greek palace, or maybe Atlantis, probably out of Age of Artemis. There are a few other rooms still in progress, so it's hard to tell what they're meant to be.

"Nate!" I holler, not having found the young man as I did my walk-through. "Nate!"

My heart stops for a moment when I hear muffled voices and shuffling coming from upstairs.

"It's just Nate and someone else," I say to myself. "There's no ghost."

"Father Tom!" Nate calls from the top of the stairs. Standing next to him is another young man, wearing black leather motorcycle gear, sporting a bushy head of hair and an only slightly less bushy beard.

"Hello, Nate," I say as he scurries down the stairs. He seems out of breath and nervous for some reason. The guy behind him is much more relaxed, walking down the stairs at a more leisurely pace.

"What are you doing here?" Nate asks. There's a smirk on his friend's face as he comes beside him.

"I was riding my bike," I say—

"When did you start riding a bike?"

"Since about thirty minutes ago," I say. "Dr. Maycord said I needed more exercise. Anyway, I thought I'd stop and take a look at everything. I have to say, you all have done a great job."

"Uh-huh," Nate says distractedly. "Well, I don't want to keep you, Father."

"You're not, Nate," I say. Looking at the other young man. "I don't think we've met."

"Naw, we haven't Father," he says. "But you're that priest who's getting married, right?"

"Right."

"Cool," he says, nodding his head.

"Father Tom," Nate says, "This is Larry. He's a friend of mine. We met playing Age of Artemis."

"Oh, are you here to help with the haunted house?"

"In a manner of speaking, I guess," Larry says, again still smirking.

"Yeah, yeah," Nate says quickly, licking his lips. "So, yeah, we were just—yeah, we were just getting something ready for the house. Yeah."

Why Nate's so nervous is a mystery, so I ask, "Is everything all right, Nate?"

"Huh? Yeah, fine. Everything is fine. Listen, I'd love to keep talking, but we've got a lot of work to do."

I get the strong feeling Nate's trying to get rid of me. Like he's up to something he doesn't want me to know about.

Like he's hiding something.

"Nate," I say.

"Hey, Nate," Larry says, "I have to leave in a little while, so are we going to do this thing or not?"

"Yeah, yeah," Nate nods. "Excuse me, Father."

Together, they turn and go back up the stairs.

I take a deep breath. "So what are you up to now, Nate?"

Eight

Friday afternoon, I stop by Helen's office with lunch and find her door closed. This is unusual, as she usually keeps it open so that she can, as she says, "Keep an eye and ear on what's going on, and let everyone know that she's doing so."

Not wanting to interrupt her if she's in a meeting, I go back to the front desk. I ask the new officer, Brandon Hicks, who I had only met the day before, "Excuse me, is Chief Parr in with someone?"

He looks at his computer screen and says, just as formally, "No, sir, Father Greer, not according to the log."

"Could you buzz her please and let her know I'm here?"

"Certainly, sir." He calls back and I hear Helen answer, "I don't want to be disturbed right now."

"But ma'am," he says, "Father Greer is here." I am a little taken aback to hear her sigh and say reluctantly, "OK, send him back."

I go back to her office and knock on the door. As soon as I hear, "Come in," I know something is wrong.

I open the door to find her sitting behind her desk, teary-eyed. "Close the door," she says gruffly.

"Honey?" I say as the door closes behind me and I go to her, wrapping my arms around her as she sits. "What's wrong? Has something happened to someone?"

I know only too well that that is the unspoken fear that we all carry around. I've known it now for just a few months, but Helen has known it for years. It's with Dan and Miriam when they tuck their kids in, and with the younger officers when they go out on dates. It's with Nick and Nina Hallstead when they kiss each other good-bye at the start of her shift. I wonder if Officer Hicks has met it yet—probably not, for they can't teach it at the police academy. It's something that you first meet when the phone rings and someone you know is in the hospital with a gunshot wound from a warrant service gone bad or internal injuries from a beating or, in our case, a gunshot to the shoulder and massive blood loss.

She looks up at me, and I'm amazed and gratified by the fact that she's not even trying to hide her fears from me.

"Not yet," she whispers. "But someone could be, and I've got to get ready."

"What do you mean?"

"I mean that one of the things they recommended at that Chief's meeting I went to in August is that I have an outline of a eulogy ready in case I lose someone under my command."

She picks up a couple of sheets of paper covered in her illegible scrawl. "So, Tom, I'm sitting here imagining what I can say to Miriam or Christopher or Cheryl or Nick or any of the other spouses to somehow make them think that sacrificing the life of the person that they love most in the world is worth it to catch bad guys. And I've got nothing." She crumples up the pages and tosses them in her trash can.

I say nothing but instead gently pull her to her feet and lead her over to the couch where she has spent more than one night lying awake so that the people of Myerton can sleep safely. We sit down and I pull her head onto my shoulder.

"Honey," I say gently, "I'm going to do that thing that you tease me about and tell you something I learned in seminary. You have nothing because there is nothing. No, don't get me wrong; for Christians, the hope of heaven can be a comfort and it will be, ultimately. But in those first days and weeks, especially when death has come suddenly, there is nothing you can say or do that will make things better. We both know that from bitter experience."

"Then why am I bothering with this?"

"Because there are others, friends and family who are close, but not the closest, who you can help. And by helping them, you indirectly help those hurting the most."

She sighs. "I guess I can see that. But I think about something happening to Dan—you know how much he means to me, how much I love Miriam and the kids. I imagine myself trying to explain to Miriam what happened, or tell Catherine her . . . her daddy won't be tucking her in at night anymore. And it's more than I can stand."

I nod. "You're right. That's a horrible thought to process. But another thing you can do for your people—that you already do with the Conways—is to be a part of their lives. Really get to know them and treat them like your own family. That way, you help them build up the strength they'll need if the worst ever does happen."

"So what about the eulogy?"

"Go ahead and write it now, but write what you think you'd want to hear, what you'd want to know. Then put it away and work on it again later. And, by the way, this is also an area where you can tap your police chaplain for help."

I smile at this and she smiles back before wiping her eyes and asking, "Thanks, darling. I do feel better."

"Do you feel up to eating?"

She grins. "When have you ever known me to not feel like eating?"

***

We enjoy dinner that night at the Rectory—meatloaf and mashed potatoes, with Helen providing salad and dessert courtesy of The Muffin Man. She does not bring up what we discussed earlier in the day, but instead fills me in on a mentorship program for new officers, in which more seasoned veterans are assigned to keep an eye on them.

"But isn't that what they do anyway?" I ask. "I mean, I remember seeing something like that on *Adam 12*."

"It is similar, in that they do have a training officer when they first join the department. This is for after they've finished training. I want them to have someone that they can go to with questions or even complaints about me, someone that they can talk with about their personal life if need be. The truth is that while I am perfectly comfortable being a woman in this role, I know that my perspective is different than a man and the guys need men to talk to, just as the women need women."

"That's a very thoughtful thing to think of," I say.

"Thank you," she says. "Now, what are we watching tonight?"

"Well, I knew you had a bad day so I thought that you might want something special, even though it's not Christmas,"

Her eyes brighten as she grins, "Are you serious? You said that we could only watch it at Christmas."

"I know, and I still consider it essential holiday season watching. But you had such a bad day, so yes, I've got *Die Hard II* to all queued up."

I always say stuff like this to her so that she will think that I'm making some kind of sacrifice. Truth be told, the *Die Hard* movies are some of my favorites of all time.

That is why I am particularly aggravated when, just as Bruce Willis is saying "Yippee ki yay," and dropping the lighter into that wonderful stream of aviation fuel, my phone rings. Knowing that a priest is never off duty, I check to see who it is and say to Helen, "It's Anna," just as the plane explodes in a spectacular ball of fire.

Ironically, the ball of fire on the screen is nothing compared to the one on the phone.

"Anna, what is it?" I ask, trying to make myself heard over her shouting. "What? . . . Tomorrow's paper? . . . Huh? . . . OK, fine. We'll be here."

"What was that about?" Helen asks.

"Apparently she and Bill stopped by the Food & Gas Mart just now and they had copies of tomorrow's *Myerton Gazette* on sale, so she got one. It seems that Nate's article on the Myer Estate is on the front page, below the fold."

"Isn't that a good thing? I mean, since it is for publicity?"

"I would think so but for some reason, Anna does not."

I don't have to speculate much longer because Anna sweeps in at that very moment and tosses the paper in question on the coffee table in front of me.

"Remind me again why we didn't just let the boy rot in jail?" Anna screeches. "Just look at what that idiot wrote!"

Bending forward to pick it up, I see the headline.

MYER MANSION HAUNTED? MANY THINK SO.

"Oh, no," I groan, as I begin to read.

More than 100 years ago, the Myer Mansion in Meyerton, Maryland, was used as a hospital for hundreds of sick and wounded soldiers from America's Civil War. According to one story passed down across the decades, one of those soldiers was a young Confederate, far from home. While recovering in the family's home, he fell in love with Victoria Myer, the pretty young daughter of the house.

The article contains a picture, captioned "Victoria Myer", of a beautiful young woman with black curls, a stereotypical southern belle.

"She shared his feelings, and they agreed to run away together. But tragedy ensued when, the night before they were to elope, the young soldier wandered through the dark house looking for her. Thinking she heard a prowler, she emerged from her bedroom carrying a lantern and a knife. Seeing a dark form on the staircase, she stabbed the man whom she loved. Discovering her horrible mistake, she took her own life with the same knife, their blood mingling together on the steps. To this day, some insist that the tortured soul of Victoria Myer still walks the halls of the Myer Mansion—open weekends beginning October 22 to those who want to experience its terror themselves."

"Well, that is the most ridiculous thing I've ever heard," Anna huffs.

"The story is part of the family history," I say. "And the ghost legend's been repeated through the years."

"I know. I grew up here, remember. But that's a story we told around the bonfire, just so we'd get scared and the boys would put their arms around us."

"Really?" I say with a grin. "Anyone we know, Anna?"

Bill looks at her, and she blushes. "Oh, just keep reading."

I look a little ahead and whisper, "Oh, boy."

"When asked about the house's history of violence, Anna Luckgold admitted, 'There is certainly something different about the Myer Estate. When I was a teenager, we heard from our parents that it was haunted, especially the staircase. We were warned never to try to go upstairs unless you were a member of the family. Otherwise, you might not make it down alive.'"

"Anna," I ask, incredulously, "Did you really say that?"

"Yes," she admits. "I also told the idiot we soon figured out that our parents told us that story to keep us from trying to slip upstairs and make out during parties. The boy genius there chose to leave that out. And if you ask me if it was with anyone in particular, Thomas Jude Greer, I'll call Archbishop Knowland and tell him I caught you and Helen *in flagrante delicto*!"

I hold up my hand. "I wasn't going to say anything!"

"Hmm," Anna says. "Now, read the rest. It doesn't get any better. You'll especially like the next part, Helen."

I read silently until I get to the next big quote.

"Chief of Police Helen Parr agrees with Mrs. Luckgold's appraisal. 'The place can be really spooky at night . . . We get calls here at least once or twice a month from people who see strange lights in the windows. Oftentimes, our officers hear the sound of running footsteps as they pull up and find signs that there has been something . . . going on in the house, even though no one's there.'"

I look at Helen quizzically as she declares, "What he didn't say is that the place is spooky, which is why it attracts mischievous teeenagers. He also didn't mention that there is no one there ANYMORE, but we inevitably find their syringes and beer bottles. He also fails to mention that was last year, after Win Myer's murder and the house was abandoned for a while. We haven't had a call out there since the parish started maintaining the property."

"What got into him?" I say, shaking my head.

"Oh, do keep reading, Tom," Anna says. "The best is yet to come."

I glance down the page. "Oh, frankincense and myrrh," I exclaim.

"Tom!" Anna says. "No—wait, what?"

"Never mind," I say. "Just listen to this."

"Perhaps the most harrowing story told to this reporter came from Father Tom Greer, pastor of St. Clare's Catholic Church, which owns the property now. He tells of one of his early encounters with the haunted house. Father Greer recalls, 'I remember there was something about a wounded Confederate soldier who fell in love with the daughter of the house while it was being used as a field hospital and he died in her arms.'

"He then admits to experiencing his own harrowing encounter at the mansion, saying, 'Not long after I returned to Myerton, I went out there . . . The house was dark when I got there . . . I tried the door and it was unlocked so I went in. I could see a light off in the distance . . . I started to leave but someone grabbed me from behind and I blacked out. I woke up hours later in a shed behind the house. I didn't know who put me there . . . I got out and went back to the house. I won't say anymore than this: what I discovered there was tragic . . . It was the final chapter in a long, tragic story.'"

But one has to wonder, is it really the final chapter? Those who want to find out can visit the mansion—"

"The rest looks like just a summary of the Fairy Tales and Frights, the days and hours of operation, ticket prices, and it's a fundraiser for the parish," I say, tossing the newspaper on the coffee table. "Not a single mention of the education center."

We all sit quietly for a long time. Finally, Bill says, "Perhaps the Gazette can print a retraction?"

"It won't come out until next week," I say. "Besides, nothing he wrote in there was blatantly false. We all said the things he wrote that we said."

"But it's completely out of context," Helen exclaims.

"It is certainly that," I say.

"Tom, you're being very calm," Anna says.

"Oh, then I'm doing a great job of acting," I say through gritted teeth, "because I want to strangle that idiot right now. I mean, he's made us a laughingstock! The Myer Mansion, haunted. Yeah, parents are going to want to line up to send their kids to an education center that's haunted!"

"Now, Tom, no one is going to believe it," Helen says, trying to calm me down. "Besides, it's the Myerton paper. And almost everyone in town knows the story of the house, knows Nate, knows us. They'll see he's exaggerating."

Just then, my phone rings. Pulling it out, I growl. "Well, speak of the devil," I say, answering, "Nate, I was just going to call you. About this article you wrote. I—"

"Oh, you've read it already," Nate says, excitedly. I can hear Gladys squealing in the background. "Isn't it great?"

"Now, I wouldn't—"

"I can't believe it! It's such a break for me, for my journalism career!"

"What are you blabbering about, Nate?" I say, thoroughly confused.

"The article. The Baltimore paper picked it up, and it's going in their Saturday edition."

I can feel my blood pressure begin to rise as I stammer, "The—the—"

"Yeah," he says. "But that's not all. The wire service thought it was such a great story for Halloween they're making it available to all their papers! That's hundreds of papers across the country!"

I collapse on the couch. I hear Helen say, "Darling? What is it?"

"Nate," I rasp. "No, Nate, please—"

"Within days, the Myer Mansion's going to be the best known haunted house in the country!"

Nine

"I don't understand why you're so upset, Dad!"

Gladys and Nate are in the Rectory living room at 10 a.m. the next morning. Helen's there, mostly to make sure I don't try to kill Nate with my bare hands. Anna's sitting in a chair with her arms crossed, scowling at the young man.

"Gladys!" I say, pointing at Nate. "The article he wrote will make Saint Clare's the laughingstock of the entire country!"

"I don't see how, Father Tom," Nate says. "There's nothing in the article that casts the parish or you in a bad light."

"You put words in my mouth!"

"No, sir," Nate says firmly. "I recorded every interview. Everything I wrote is a direct quote."

"You took what we said out of context, Nate," Helen says. "You left off important details that changed the entire meaning."

"Oh, can't you just arrest him, Helen?" Anna says with irritation.

"Huh?" Nate says, his eyes getting big.

"You can't arrest my Bae, Mom!" Gladys says. "He has freedom of the press!"

"I'm not going to arrest anyone, Anna, Gladys—Nate, close your mouth. You look simple when you do that," Helen says.

"Nate," I say, trying to be calm, "I want you to print a retraction. I want you to rewrite the article, using exactly what we said, and have the Gazette print that and send it to the Baltimore paper."

"But . . . but . . ." Nate stammers, looking crestfallen. "But what about my journalism career?"

"You don't have a journalism career, Nate!" I explode. "You're not a reporter! You wrote a piece of lurid fiction and passed it off as a factual news story! You clean up blood for a living! For God's sake, Nathaniel! When the hell are you going to GROW UP!"

The only sound in the room is my breathing. My pulse is pounding in my ears, which feel like they're on fire. I don't need a blood pressure cuff to know my little outburst just sent it sky high.

Everyone is staring at me. Anna and Helen both look surprised. Gladys looks shocked. Nate—Nate looks crushed. But beyond crushed, betrayed.

He stares at me, tears beginning to flow down his cheeks. "Father Tom?" he says weakly.

I close my eyes, shame replacing my anger. "Oh, son," I whisper, shaking my head. "I'm—I'm so sorry I said those things. This article just has me so upset and worried, but that was no excuse for exploding at you like that. Can you ever forgive me?"

He takes a deep breath. "Father Tom," he says quietly. "My dad used to yell at me like that. Say something similar. But he never, ever said he was sorry. He never ever asked for my forgiveness."

Nate stands up and comes over to me. He puts his hands on my shoulders. "I know I drive you crazy sometimes," he says. "But you've always been there for me. Even when everyone else abandoned me. When people believed I killed Ashley, you said I didn't. You helped me see how I wronged Gladys. You brought me back to the Church. You're helping me become a man who'll be a good husband and a father. Of course, I forgive you."

Then, he hugs me.

I don't quite know what to do at first. So, I hug him back.

I hear a couple of sniffles, then Gladys cries out, "Oh, that was so beautiful, Bae!"

Nate finally stops hugging me, and nods. "You're right, Father." Looking around the room, he says, "You're all right. I twisted what you said to make the article more interesting. Because I really believe the house is haunted, and I want everyone else to believe it too."

I sigh. "Nate, the house isn't haunted."

"We'll just have to agree to disagree—you know, 'more things in heaven and earth, Horatio'—but what I did was wrong and unethical. So I'm going to call the Gazette right now and ask them to get to work on a retraction, and I'm going to write another story—this time, Father, about the education center. That's the one I should have written in the first place."

I smile and clap him on the back. "Thank you, Nate," I say. "That's very mature of you."

Just then, the theme from *Camelot* starts playing. Gladys rummages through her bag and finds her phone.

"Hi, Mae," she says with a smile. "What's—wait, what? Can you repeat that? Hold on." To the rest of us, she says, "Mae checked out ticket sales. Both weekends are sold out, and we're getting flooded with requests to be put on a waiting list!" To Mae, she says, "So how many?" Her eyes get huge. Amazed, she says, "Mae says at least 2,000 people."

I collapse on the couch. "How many tickets did you allocate?"

"Across both weekends, Dad? Two thousand at ten dollars a ticket."

"That's $20,000 dollars," Anna says. "And if you get another 2,000 printed for those people who want them, that's another $20,000—Tom, that's $40,000 dollars!"

"We'll need to add another night to each weekend to accommodate everyone," Gladys says, still on the phone with Mae, "but we can do that."

"We'll need to change some schedules," Helen says, "But we can provide crowd and traffic control for an extra night.

I'm still stunned by this turn of events. I look at Nate, who's looking at me questioningly.

"Nate," I say, "I still want that retraction. But maybe it can wait until after Halloween."

He grins. "Sounds good to me."

"Wait, what did you just say, Mae?" Gladys says, her grin disappearing. "He did. Last night. Oh." She gets quiet, then says. "No, it's wonderful. Congratulations. Yeah, I'll see you tomorrow." She ends the call and stares at her phone for a moment.

"What is it, Gladys?" Helen says.

With a forced smile, Gladys says, "Mae. Martin Maycord asked her to marry him last night."

Anna claps her hands and says, "Oh, that's wonderful."

Helen looks at me and says, "Did you know about this?"

I nod. "I was sworn to secrecy, but yeah, Martin told me Monday he was going to do it last night. He had this whole elaborate plan to pop the question. I guess she said yes."

"Oh, that's just fantastic," Helen says with a grin. "Gladys, how did Mae sound?"

Gladys doesn't answer right away. Finally she says, "Happy. Ecstatic." But her voice is flat.

"Bae, are you feeling OK?" Nate asks.

"Huh? No, actually I'm feeling kinda weak all of a sudden."

"Here," he says, standing up. "I'll take you home."

"No, Nate," she says, turning her chair around. "I'll drive myself. I'll talk to you later. Good-bye, everyone."

"Gladys," Nate says, "can I do anything for you?"

She stops her chair. "No," she says bitterly, "you've already done enough."

Gladys leaves, slamming the door behind her, leaving Nate looking hurt and confused.

Before I can talk to Nate, my cell phone rings. "Oh, I've not been looking forward to this call," I say, shaking my head.

"The Archbishop?" Helen asks.

"Oh, yeah."

"Give me your phone, Tom," Anna says, walking to me with her hand out. "I'll talk to him."

"No, Anna. It's my job."

"Well, in this case, son, let me handle him," she says with a wink.

I nod and hand her the phone.

"Hello, Your Eminence" Anna says. "No, I'm sorry, he can't right now. I offered to speak to you." She begins to walk from the living room towards the kitchen, the Archbishop loud enough for me to catch some of what he's saying.

"Don't worry," she whispers to me. "It will be fine." Talking into the phone again, she says, "I understand, Your Eminence, but if you will just allow me to . . . Now . . . Now . . . Will you just be quiet and listen for a minute, Walter Joseph Knowland! . . . Thank you. . . Now, here's what happened . . . "

Anna continues talking as she walks into the kitchen and slams the door. Nate's sitting on the couch, looking forlorn again.

"I . . . I don't understand?" he says quietly. "What did I do this time?"

"I'm sure nothing, Nate," Helen says, trying to reassure him.

"It happens when I'm not expecting it," he says. "Things will be fine, then all of a sudden, she'll just lash out." Looking at me, he adds, "If I didn't love her so much, if I didn't want us to have a life together so much, I'd . . ." Nate shakes his head. "But, I'm not going to do that."

I say, "Nate—"

But he interrupts me, saying, "Father, I'm going to leave now. I think I'll go out to the Mansion, check on a few things. Larry's supposed to come by later. I'll see you tomorrow."

Helen and I watch Nate as he trudges out of the room. When the door closes, Helen says, "I thought you said things were going better?"

"They were."

"So, what was that all about?"

"I don't—wait," I say as a thought occurs to me. "Oh, I bet that's it."

"What?"

I turn to Helen. "This isn't about Nate," I say, "at least not directly. It's about Mae."

Helen looks at me questioningly, then smiles. "Oh, of course. Mae's engagement."

I nod. "Gladys wants to marry Nate, has for a while. She was certain Nate was about to pop the question when the whole mess with Ashley Becket started. That set things back a lot."

"Not to mention the fact that Gladys and Nate have been dating longer than Martin and Mae have—not by much, but enough," Helen points out. "She's upset it's Mae getting engaged and not her."

"She's upset and jealous and angry at Nate."

"So, Father Greer, what are you going to do?"

I look at Helen. "You know, right now, nothing. I've talked to Gladys until I'm blue in the face. She's going to have to decide what she wants. Then, I'll talk to her. Maybe then she'll actually be ready to listen."

Ten

"Oooo, would you look at that!"

"It's so gorgeous!"

"You say it was his mother's ring? How romantic!"

"Were you surprised? Did he get down on one knee?"

I'm standing with Helen after Mass on Sunday, greeting parishioners as they file out. But today, we're taking second place to the newly engaged Mae Trent.

"Good morning, Father Tom, Helen," Miriam says as she scurries—or rather, waddles—past us on her way to the crowd of young women of all ages jockeying to see The Ring and hear The Story.

"Father Tom, Helen," Dan says, looking at the sight. Catherine is clutching his hand, while Max, JP, and Andrew are—well, nowhere to be seen. But since Dan doesn't appear concerned, I choose to believe all is well and they're at the playground or something.

"Hi, Miss Helen," Catherine says, "Hi, Father Tom."

"Hello, Dan, Catherine," I say. Helen squats down and says to Catherine, "How about a hug, sweetheart?"

Catherine throws her arms round Helen's neck. "Daddy, can I go to the playground?"

"Sure, just be careful. And keep an eye on your brothers," Dan says.

Catherine says, "I will," and scurries off.

Turning to us, Dan says, "So, have you seen the happy couple?"

"I haven't been able to get close to Mae since she got here," Helen says. "I'm dying to see that ring."

"If it's what Martin described to me, it's an impressive one," I say.

"I saved for months to buy Miriam's ring," Dan says. "A single diamond. I told her it's because she's a one-of-a-kind."

"I got Helen's ring for our first engagement," I say. "I wanted a stone that matched her eyes."

Helen grins with pride as she shows Dan the ring. "Hmm, nice," he says. "So, Father Tom, you kept that after you two broke up?"

I open my mouth to answer, when Helen interjects. "No, I kept it. After throwing it at the door when he left, of course."

"Why did you keep it?"

She looks at me and smiles. "I thought he'd come to his senses and come back to me."

"I did," I say. "It only took twenty years and a papal dispensation."

Dan shakes his head. "I still have a hard time believing it."

I laugh. "You're never going to get used to us being married, are you?"

He shakes his head. "No, I can't believe you left her in the first place. If I had been around, I'd have kicked your ass."

"Aw, Dan," Helen says, "that's sweet."

"I would have deserved it, too," I say.

He looks at me and with all seriousness says, "Don't think I won't do it, Tom, if you ever hurt her."

"Daddy! Daddy!" Catherine comes up and flings herself at her father, clutching his leg. "Daniel called me Spooky Catherine again!"

Dan sighs and rolls his eyes even as I feel the anger beginning to radiate off Helen. "Who is this . . . little fella?"

Dan says, "Daniel Wright. He's just a little snot. Started calling Catherine that a few months ago."

"Yeah," I say quietly. "Apparently, it caught on."

Helen squats down and looks Catherine in the eyes. "Sweetie, I'm so sorry someone called you that. But I'm sure your Daddy told you that some people are just mean, and eventually, he and I wind up arresting them and throwing them in jail. He'll be punished."

"Oh, I'm sure he feels punished now," Catherine says matter-of-factly. "When they heard him say that, Max and JP jumped on him and started beating the fire out of him."

"What!" Dan exclaims. "Why didn't—oh, Catherine—excuse me Father, Helen." The ex-Marine grabs his little girl's hand and hurries off.

Helen growls, "I don't know why he's in such a hurry to break it up. Sounds like the little . . . spawn of Satan—"

"Helen!" I say quickly. "Daniel Wright is not the spawn of Satan. For crying out loud, he's the son of a parishioner! You can't say things like that!"

"Well, it's a lot better than what I would have said a month ago."

"You know, I rue the day Vivian gave you that book. It's just—I mean, I appreciate you trying to stop cursing. But honestly, some of the things you say instead are just weird!"

"Well, Father Greer," she says, jutting her chin up proudly, "I guess I'll just have to be weird, then. I am not going to be known as the foul-mouthed priest's wife!"

"Father Tom, Helen." We turn to see a positively beaming Martin Maycord and starry-eyed Mae Trent come up.

"Well," I say, extending my hand, "I guess congratulations are in order."

Martin shakes my hand, and I bend down to give Mae, who's somewhat smaller than Helen, a hug. Helen gives both Martin and Mae a hug.

"Oh, I'm just so happy for both of you," Helen says with a grin. "Let me see that ring."

Mae extends her left hand. The ring is impressive, just as Martin described it to me. A large diamond set between two smaller ones, it sparkles in the sunlight.

"Isn't it just the most beautiful thing you've ever seen?" Mae says breathlessly. "I just about passed out when I saw it. I mean, I thought Mama's ring was beautiful. But this—I just never imagined I'd have something so beautiful."

Martin kisses the top of her head. "You deserve the best, my darling," he says. "And this is only the beginning."

She playfully slaps at him. "Oh, Marty, you're going to spoil me!"

He looks at us and smiles. "She doesn't quite get that that's exactly my plan."

We all laugh as Mae blushes. "So," Helen says, "how did he ask you? Did you have any idea?"

"Well," she says with a shy smile. "I kind of suspected he had something up his sleeve when he flew us all the way to Annapolis."

Helen looks at Martin. "You flew?"

"He has his own helicopter," I say to her. "More on that later."

She nods as Mae continues. "So we landed, and he had a car and chauffeur waiting. We drove into Annapolis and right up to the pier. There was the most beautiful yacht waiting. He told me we were dining on the boat, and that he had hired the chef at one of my favorite restaurants in Baltimore to cook for us. Oh, it was just lovely! Out on the Chesapeake as the sun was going down behind us. We ate—the food was just fantastic, so many courses, I almost couldn't eat dessert. We talked and laughed. Then, I hear music, and on the upper deck is a string quartet. We danced as the moon rose over us and the stars came out. Finally, we got to this little point somewhere. All of a sudden, fireworks lit the sky, and Martin dropped to one knee and asked me to marry him!"

"Wow," I say. "That's really something. I asked Helen in front of the altar."

"And it was just perfect," Helen says to me, slipping her arm through mine.

Martin looks at his watch. "Oh, darling! We're going to be late for lunch. I don't want to keep everyone waiting."

"It's fine, Marty," Mae says. "You go to the car. I need to talk to Father Tom and Helen for a moment."

He gives her a kiss and whispers, "I'll count the minutes." He tells Helen and me good-bye and hurries off.

Mae sighs. "He's so good to me," she says. "I just hope . . ."

"What, Mae?" I ask.

She turns to us. "Oh, nothing. I wanted to ask, is Gladys OK?"

Remembering her abrupt departure from the Rectory the previous morning, I say carefully, "As far as we know. She was at Mass this morning."

"I saw her," she nods. "I'd been trying to call her, but she won't answer. She hasn't returned any of my texts. I was hoping to catch her after Mass, but I guess she went out another way. And I really want to talk to her. I mean, she's become one of my best friends. I want to share this with her."

I open my mouth to say something when Helen says, "Oh, I'm sure everything's fine. She's been very busy lately. When I see her, I'll tell her you want to talk to her."

"Oh, thank you so much, Mrs. Parr."

Helen smiles. "Mae, you're engaged to be married. You're a grown woman. Please call me Helen."

Mae says, "OK, Mrs.—I mean, Helen. And thanks."

She hurries off down the steps as we watch her leave.

"Well, sounds like we were right," I say. "Poor Mae."

"Poor Mae?" Helen says. "Poor Gladys. I can just imagine how she's feeling."

I sigh. "Well, like I said, if she wants to talk, she can talk. But I don't know what else I can do about her and Nate."

"Oh, Tom," Helen sighs. "You're such a man."

"What?"

She shakes her head. "Nothing, darling. Come on, let's get you out of this. I'm getting peckish."

We walk into the church. It's empty, except for one lone figure in a wheelchair, parked in front of the tabernacle. Her head's down, and her quiet sobs echo through the space.

"Gladys," I say and start to walk to her.

"Wait, Tom," Helen says quietly as she grabs my arm. "Let me talk to her. I've got a good idea how she's feeling."

I nod. "I'll see you in the Rectory."

***

I've changed out of my clericals into a pair of sweatpants and a t-shirt, checked on the food a couple of times, and checked out a little of that afternoon's NASCAR race by the time Helen arrives, with Gladys in tow. Both look like they've been crying.

"Hey," I say, standing to give Gladys a hug. "You all right, sweetie?"

She sniffs and wipes a stray tear with her lace handkerchief. "I am now, Dad. Thanks to Mom."

I look at Helen. "Looks like I wasn't needed for this."

"There are some things, Tom, that only another woman would understand."

"Well, why don't I get us some food and you can try to explain it to me."

A few moments later, we're at the dining room table, digging into my beef stew and munching on homemade biscuits.

"You're going to have to teach me how to make these for Nate," Gladys says.

"Good luck," Helen says. "I've tried to get him to. But it's a secret Greer family recipe."

"Which I will be glad to share with you as soon as you're a Greer," I say with a smirk. "I can't have you learning the secret to great biscuits and then deciding to marry another priest."

"There is absolutely no other priest I have my eye on—well, except maybe the Archbishop. He's such a sweetie."

"I think you'll have to wrestle Anna for him, darling."

"What?" Gladys exclaims.

"I'll tell you some other time," Helen whispers.

We chat about this and that, finish our stew, then retire to the living room for coffee and pound cake—not mine, but Nick Hallstead's a better baker, anyway.

"So," I say, "who wants to tell me what's wrong?"

"Was wrong, Dad," Gladys sighs. "I'm better."

"What I don't understand is, why were you mad at Nate?"

"I wasn't—not directly," she says. "It wasn't about him—not exactly."

I look at Gladys. "It was Mae, wasn't it?" I say quietly.

She nods. "She had been telling me for a couple of weeks that she was certain Martin was getting close to proposing. I'd tried to ignore it, thinking that either it wouldn't happen, or wouldn't happen so fast. They'd only been seeing each other for a couple of months, and I just thought Mae was dreaming. Getting ahead of herself."

Gladys takes a deep breath. "When she told me Martin had proposed—that she was engaged, with a ring and everything—it just hit me all at once."

Helen says quietly, "It wasn't you."

"No," Gladys says, "it wasn't me. I thought I'd be engaged to Nate by now. That I'd be the one calling Mae so excited. That I'd be the one showing off my ring after Mass. But after everything that's happened . . . it's like, I'm starting over again, and Mae's hurrying along ahead of me. I—I felt—"

"Left behind," Helen says.

"Yeah, exactly."

I sit back. "You know, Gladys," I say slowly, "we've talked in our sessions about the work you and Nate have to do to get back to where you were before Nate did what he did. Nate has to do a lot of work to earn your trust, not to mention doing some growing up."

"Yeah, Dad," she says. "You made that clear yesterday."

I grimace. "OK, I didn't say it very well, but he does. But doing work like that takes time, Gladys."

She swallows. "I know. That's one reason I asked Mom if I could join you both for lunch today. I wanted to tell you, I've definitely made up my mind. Nathaniel Eduardo Jorge Rodriguez, warts and all, is the only man I want. He's my soulmate, the one I want to marry, and have kids with, and grow old together with. And I'm willing to wait, and do the hard work with him, for however long it takes. When we do become engaged, I want our foundation to be as solid as possible. As solid as Martin and Mae's."

I smile. "I am so happy to hear you say that, Gladys. And it will take hard work. And it will take time. But I really believe that you two will get there."

Just then, the Rectory doorbell rings. "I wonder who that is?" I say.

"I'll get it," Helen says.

When she leaves, Gladys says, "I am so glad Mom talked to me."

"I am too. But I'm curious what she said?"

She hesitates, then says, "Well, she said she felt the same way I did for a while after you left and some of her friends wound up getting engaged."

My heart breaks when I hear this, and I'm about to say something when Helen says, "Look who's here."

I turn and see Mae standing in the hallway.

"Mae," I say. "This is a surprise."

"I hope you don't mind me just showing up," Mae says. "But I had a feeling Gladys would be here. Hi, Glad."

"Hi," Gladys says quietly.

Mae steps forward and clears her throat. "I've been trying to call you since yesterday."

She nods. "I'm sorry, Mae," she says. "I haven't been a good friend to you. I am happy for you and Martin, you know that, don't you?"

"I know," Mae says, coming up to her and squatting down by Gladys. "And I'm the one who's sorry. I'm the one who hasn't been a good friend."

"No, Mae—"

"No, now listen. I was so excited over everything, and I wanted so much to share it with my best friend, that I didn't even stop to think how you'd feel. You've been talking about marrying Nate almost since we became friends. And here I go, becoming engaged to a man much older than me, who I've known just three months! I mean, it's crazy when you think about it!"

"No," Gladys says, "It's not crazy! You've found your soulmate in Martin, just like I've found mine in Nate. He and I just have to take more time to grow into the couple you and Martin are now. You fell in love with Martin the first time you saw him, you told me. I thought Nate was an idiot for a long time before we started dating, and it took me a while to fall in love with him."

She reaches out for Mae, and the two young women hug. "I love you so much," Gladys whispers. "You were the first person other than Father Tom and Helen that I told about my past. The love and compassion you showed—I probably wouldn't be where I am now if it weren't for you."

"Oh, Glad," Mae says. "I love you, too. I've never met anyone like you. You've taught me so much, I can't even tell you."

They separate and Mae says, "So? We good?"

Gladys nods and grins. "We're good."

"Great!" Mae says. "Because I've got a big ask for you. You know, Martin's already talking about this huge extravagant affair, and I don't know anything about fashion or decorating or anything. I'm going to ask Katie to be my maid of honor—she's my sister, after all—but I'm really going to need your help. I was hoping you'd be my wedding planner?"

Gladys emits an ear-piercing squeal that I'm sure disturbs every dog in town. Clapping her hands, she says, "Yes! I'd love that! Oh, Mae, between Martin's money and my ideas, you're going to have an incredible wedding!"

With one last hug, Mae stands up and says to Gladys, "Come on. Let's go to Sprockets. We can discuss ideas, and I can show off Marty's engagement present."

"What did Martin get you as an engagement present?" I ask.

Mae sighs. "I told him he didn't have to, but he insisted on buying me a new car."

"He bought you a car?" Helen asks, incredulously.

"Uh-huh," Mae says. "I tried to tell him that I didn't need a car. That the one I had only had 100,000 miles on it and still drove fine. But Marty insisted that I needed a better car. Fortunately, I was able to convince him that I didn't need the Porsche, so he settled for the four-door Audi I liked."

I can't believe my ears. "You—you turned down a Porsche?"

"It was between the Porsche, the Jaguar, and the Audi," she says with a shrug. "The Audi was the only thing I thought was sensible."

"You turned down a Porsche and a Jaguar?" I say, absolutely incredulous.

"Come on, Tom," Helen says. "It's a beautiful day. I'll run home and get my bike. How about a nice ride in the country?"

I nod, even as I wonder about the youth of today.

Eleven

My initial concerns over Nate's . . . creative, shall we say, article about the Myer Mansion proved unfounded.

Mostly.

Over the next couple of days, I received about half a dozen calls from various people calling themselves "paranormal investigators," wanting to come to Myerton and try to get what they call scientific evidence of spectral activity in the Mansion. I turned them down, of course, not so much because I think such things are bunk—which I do—but because I didn't want the plans for the Fairy Tales and Frights house disrupted.

Requests for tickets continued to pour in, causing the Acutis society to add Thursdays to the schedule. Even then, they had to stop selling tickets when they topped a total of 5,000.

That's $50,000 dollars for the St. Francis Center. Even Archbishop Knowland was impressed—of course, it could have been due to the fact that it was Anna, instead of me, who told him.

Wednesday morning, I arrive at the Myer Mansion—this time, in my car. I'm meeting Martin and Miriam, as the chairs of the Fundraising Committee and the Education Committee respectively, to look over everything.

Martin arrives not long after I do, driving the Porsche convertible that is such an occasion of envy for me. He has the top down and actually wears sunglasses and driving gloves.

I guess surgeons really have to take care of their hands.

"Hello, Tom," Martin says. "Fine day, isn't it?"

"It's beautiful," I say, looking at the car.

He gets out of the car and comes around to stand by me. "You've, ah, ever driven a Porsche?"

"Oh, nooo," I laugh. "Only in my dreams."

"I won't lie to you, Tom. It's a really great car. Technically, I don't own it," he says. "My LLC leases it."

"You have an LLC?"

He nods. "Just makes accounting easier at tax time."

Curiosity finally gets the best of me. "Martin, can I ask you a question?"

"Sure."

"How—how can you afford your house, this car, a helicopter? I mean, how much does Myerton General pay you?"

He sighs and smiles slightly. "Actually, Tom, they really don't pay me a whole lot. About half what I earned in Baltimore."

"Then how—"

"Oh, I have other sources of income," he says. "I have several patents on medical devices I've invented. That's what I really love to do—I mean, I love surgery, and I'm very good at it, but I do love working on a new device to solve a surgical problem, or invent a new process or procedure. I have a small lab in the basement of my house. I'm usually down there in the evenings tinkering on something."

"Mae told me one time about a foundation you have?"

"Yes, I have the foundation," Martin says. "And the rehab centers in New England. And a couple of other charities. Honestly, Tom, I give away more than I keep for myself—though, now that I have a family, I may have to rethink that."

"Well, you've been very generous with the parish," I say. "Not to mention all your help with this."

"Really, it's my pleasure. Say, wasn't Miriam Conway supposed to meet us? I have a surgery just after lunch."

"She said—oh, here's her van now."

The Conway family van comes to an abrupt stop. Miriam climbs out, waddles around to the other side, and opens the door to reveal Catherine, Max, JP, and Andrew, all buckled in.

"Sorry I'm late," she yells over her shoulder. "Mom woke up with a fever and couldn't watch the kids. I promise they'll be no trouble."

"I doubt that," I mutter. Martin shoots me a look. "Oh," I whisper. "Catherine's great. Those boys are little hellions at times."

"Oh, my!" Martin says, his eyes big.

"Hey," I laugh. "Just think of it as a glimpse into your future."

Martin looks at me, but he's not laughing. "Uh, yeah," he says. "Yeah."

Before I can say anything else, Miriam is with us. "Shall we go in?"

We walk into the house, Miriam repeating to her kids not to run off, not to touch anything, and under no circumstances to go outside. Nate, Dominic, Dominic's girlfriend Therese Shepherd, and Nate's friend Larry are all working on painting something.

The sight of wet paint prompts Max and JP to run forward. Before they can touch it, Nate says, "Whoa! Whoa! Don't touch it! The paint is wet." He looks up and sees us.

"Oh, hi!" he says, putting down his paintbrush and wiping his hands on his paint-covered jeans. "I forgot you were coming by." He looks down at Catherine. "Hi, Catherine!" he says with a grin.

"Hi, Mr. Nate," Catherine says with a smile.

He squats down. "Have you come to see what we're making?"

"I'm here," she says, "because Mimi couldn't watch us today and Mommy said she had to bring us hooligans with her."

"Hahaha, oh, Catherine," Miriam says nervously.

"Well, I think there's lots of things here you'll like," Nate says. "You just look around all you want to."

"Hey, Nate!" Larry calls. "Some help over here!"

"Yeah, be right there, man," Nate answers. "Sorry, I've gotta get back to work. I hope you like everything."

Nate goes back to work, and I say, "Well, shall—"

"I've gotta go potty!" screams Andrew.

"I told you to go before we left," Miriam says wearily.

"I did," the boy says. "I've gotta go 'gain."

She smiles apologetically at Martin and me. "Sorry, we're really trying to get him trained before the baby comes. Bathroom?"

"Uh, I don't know," I say. "Dominic, where's the bathroom?"

Dominic comes over to us. "Just follow me, Mrs. Conway," he says. "The one this way is fully functional."

As Miriam, Andrew and Dominic scurry off, I hear Martin mutter, "Potty training. Didn't think about that."

"What?" I ask.

"Huh? Oh, nothing." Looking around, he says, "They've done an impressive amount of work. I see some state-of-the-art lighting equipment. Did the church pay for all this?"

"Oh, no. Gladys did."

"Gladys Finklestein? How much does the city pay her?" he asks with a laugh.

"She's actually independently wealthy—not as wealthy as you, I don't think. An inheritance from her parents and grandparents."

Martin nods and continues to look around. "There's the forest I'll be chasing Mae through."

A blood-curdling scream from the paper mache forest causes both of us to jump. Suddenly, JP bursts through one of the trees, covering himself in brown paper and chicken wire, as Max chases him with a wooden sword he found somewhere.

"Good God!" Martin exclaims.

"Boys, stop!" I yell as I grab JP and put my hand up to stop Max.

"We were just playing, Father," JP says.

"Yeah," Max pants, "he's the dragon and I'm the knight about to kill him."

"What in the world?" Miriam says as she waddles back with Andrew. Looking at her sons, then the damage they caused, she puts her hands on her hips and says, "Look at what you did! All this hard work."

"Mrs. Conway," Dominic says calmly. "Please don't worry about it. It's easily fixed."

"You two, sit on that step!" Miriam orders, pointing to the bottom of the staircase. "Andrew, sit!"

"What if I have to go potty!" he yells.

"You don't!" Taking a deep breath, Miriam says, "Father, Martin, shall we look around?"

***

We spend the next half hour looking at the Acutis Society's impressive work. They've obviously spent hundreds of man hours on this project, and the quality of workmanship is evident.

"Dominic," I say as we finish looping through the rooms, "You all have done an amazing job."

"Yes, Dominic," Martin says. "Amazing."

"The kids are going to love this," Miriam says.

"Thank you, but really, I'm just a laborer," he says. "Nate and Gladys, and Larry, they did the design work. They drew up the plans and figured out where everything would go."

"Is there going to be anything upstairs?"

"No, just downstairs," Dominic says. "Tim Cooper advised that, while the upstairs is structurally sound, it was not advisable to have a lot of people walking around up there."

"Well, he's the architect," Martin says. "He'd know best."

I happen to glance at the staircase, then do a double-take.

"Uh, Miriam, didn't you tell the boys to sit there?" I ask, pointing to the step bereft of children.

She gasps, then stomps her foot. "BOYS!" she bellows, her voice echoing through the house. "Oh, I'm so going to turn them over to Dan when he gets home," she says through gritted teeth. "Catherine!" she calls. When her daughter doesn't answer, she stomps her foot again. "Where is that girl now?"

"I'll look for them upstairs," I say. "You two look for them down here."

I run up the stairs. I don't hear Max or JP, but I run right into Andrew.

"Andrew," I say, "What are you doing up here?"

"I had to go potty," he says, pointing at a door just down the hallway, "but it was locked. I really had to go."

An odor tells me, yes, he really had to go.

"Oh, Andrew!"

"I'm sorry," he says, beginning to cry. "You're not going to beat me, are you, Father Tom?"

"Oh, of course not, Andrew," I say with a forced smile. "You go downstairs and I—I'll just take care of your little accident."

He goes down, and I walk the short distance to the locked door, the odor getting stronger as I get closer.

Stopping at the door, I look down and mutter, "Oh, crap."

Because really, what else am I going to say?

Now, I don't have a weak stomach. But never having been a dad, and being too young when Sonya was born, I never changed a dirty diaper and therefore never had to deal with . . . this situation. So I feel sort of out of my element. I begin to look around for a room that might have a towel or something, even a plastic bag to pick it up with. But all of the rooms are empty.

As I'm walking to the last upstairs room, I hear Catherine say, "Why are you so sad?"

I stop outside the door, which is slightly ajar. No one answers Catherine, but she says, "Oh, that is bad. I'm sorry. Yes, I'll be sure to tell him. He's a good priest. He'll do it."

Pushing the door open, I say, "Catherine?"

She doesn't turn around, but instead says, "Uh-huh, this is Father Tom." She pauses, then looks over her shoulder at me. "She says you look nice."

Taking a step inside the room, I ask, "Who are you talking to, Catherine?"

"The lady who lives here."

A cold chill goes up my spine. "Where is she?"

Catherine says, "Oh, you can't see her, can you, Father Tom?"

"No, no, I can't."

"That's OK. She's gone now anyway. Besides, she told me what to tell you."

I look into her earnest eyes, eyes that have a seriousness and a wisdom beyond her years. I have no reason to believe Catherine is making up what she's telling me, and every reason to believe she's telling the truth.

But frankly I'm nervous to go any further.

"She mentioned me?"

"Not by name. She said she needed a priest to pray for her and to say Masses for her."

Now the hairs on my arms are standing on end. "Catherine, what did she look like?"

"She was younger than Mommy," Catherine says, "maybe even younger than Miss Mae. She had curly black hair and was wearing a white dress, like in an old movie."

A thought occurs to me. "Come with me, Catherine," I say. We go out the bedroom door—and run right into Nate.

From the grin on his face, he heard us.

"Nate," I say slowly.

"What did you see, Catherine?" he asks excitedly.

Catherine steps behind me as I say, "Leave it alone, Nate."

"But I heard her say something about a lady," Nate says. "Did you see something Catherine? Did you?"

I open my mouth to speak when Catherine pops out from behind me and says, "I was playing with Charlotte."

I look down at her and am about to ask what she's talking about when Nate squeals with excitement. "Charlotte? She said her name was Charlotte? Not Victoria?"

"No. Her name's Charlotte."

"Nate," I say firmly. "You need to go downstairs right—"

"Did she have anyone with her?" Nate asks. "Another lady, maybe?"

"No, Charlotte doesn't have any brothers or sisters."

Suddenly, I think I see what she's doing.

Why, the little con-artist.

I try to suppress a smile as Nate looks more and more confused. "No brothers or sisters?"

"Uh-uh," Catherine says, shaking her head. "She lives in a cabin in the woods with her Mommy and Daddy, and she wanted to see the big house, too, so she came with me today. She's my friend."

Crestfallen, Nate asks, "Catherine, is she your imaginary friend?"

"Well, that's what Mommy calls her, especially when I say she broke something."

His shoulders sag. "Oh. I thought—"

"Catherine, you go downstairs. I need to talk to Mr. Nate for a moment."

"OK, Father Tom," Catherine says. "Come on, Charlotte, let's look around downstairs."

As the little girl walks down the steps, Nate looks at her crestfallen. "I really thought she—" he mutters.

Crossing my arms, I cock an eyebrow and say, "What did you think, Nate?"

Looking at me, he says, "Well, you know—I mean, she has the gift, right?"

"You listen to me, Nate," I say firmly. "Whatever gift Catherine may or may not have is none of your business. And it certainly should not be used by you to feed your ghost obsession."

"I—I'm sorry," he stammers, his Adam's apple bobbing as he swallows. "I just thought—"

"Well, Catherine told you what was going on," I say, "and you should just take her word for it. Got it?"

"Yes, Father."

We walk downstairs quietly, When we're on the first floor again, Nate returns to the work area. Catherine is standing by the door to the study.

"Come with me, Catherine," I say. Leading the little girl into the room, I walk to the fireplace. Over the fireplace still hangs an old family portrait.

I point to one of the girls. "Is this her?" I ask Catherine.

Catherine nods. "Yes. Can you help her, Father Tom?"

I don't answer. I just stare at the young woman in the painting.

It's Victoria Myer

Twelve

"So, what, Tom? You think the ghost of Victoria Myer really is walking the halls of the Mansion?"

Helen asks the question with a look I've seen her use in response to a suspect's shaky alibi.

I don't blame her. I'm still shaken by what Catherine said to me, even after a nice relaxing meal and a couple of beers.

"No, I didn't say that," I say, shaking my head. "I just told you that after what Catherine told me—"

"You really believe she's telling the truth?"

"Helen," I say, looking at her seriously. "After everything we've experienced personally with her, you're going to question if she's lying or not?"

Helen takes a swig of beer and considers this for a moment. "No," she says. "Catherine's been right on everything. I agree with you that she has some kind of gift. It's just hard for me to get my mind around."

"It is for me, too," I admit. "A message from beyond the grave, asking for prayers? I'm not quite sure what to make of it."

"But Tom," Helen says, pointing to me, "you do admit you've seen Joan, that she's delivered messages to you. She said God wanted you to become a priest."

I nod my head. It's true. Seeing Joan appear in the Grotto at Our Lady of the Mount is what led me into the priesthood. Then, she appeared to me when I was unconscious after my severe beating in Bellamy.

So, why am I having such a hard time with this?

"It just seems so fantastic," I say, answering my own question. "And, frankly, I feel a little bit guilty for giving Nate such a hard time."

"But Tom, what Nate wrote about—it's hardly the same thing."

"I know, I know. But still—I mean, it doesn't look like he was necessarily wrong."

"Are you going to tell him that?"

I look at Helen. "Are you kidding? That'll just get him all revved up again. He'll start talking about getting one of those paranormal investigator shows to come out and try to catch Victoria on tape or something stupid like that."

"Victoria?"

"Helen, I looked her up in the old parish records. She was baptized Victoria Marie Myer, March 24, 1844. She was confirmed in 1858. There's no record of a funeral Mass, probably because she committed suicide, but she is buried in a grave in Myerton Cemetary, with the date of death October 23, 1862. Which fits with the story of her falling in love with a Confederate soldier wounded at the Battle of Antietam and convalescing at the mansion when it was a hospital. The bottom line is, she's my concern just as much as any living person in the parish is."

"OK," Helen smiles, "so what are you going to do, Mulder?"

I laugh. "Well, Scully, I'm not sure. This is not something they teach us in seminary."

"Really? I'm shocked!"

Ignoring her sarcasm, I continue, "I really should contact an expert. I need to talk to Father Wayne."

"Father Wayne?" Helen says with surprise. "Why do you need to do that?"

I hesitate for a moment. "Well, I can tell you, but you need to keep this to yourself."

"OK," Helen says warily.

Taking a deep breath. "In addition to being a tough but incredible spiritual director and the Archbishop's right-hand man, Father Francis Marion Wayne is the Archdiocesan exorcist."

***

"I was wondering when we'd be meeting about your little haunted house."

Father Francis Marion Wayne, a man transferred out of the Marine Corps as a chaplain because he was too tough on his men, actually looks amused as he hands me a cup of coffee Wednesday morning in his office in Baltimore.

"I didn't really expect to, Father," I say as I take a sip and feel the liquid burn on its way down my throat, warming me from the inside out. "I just thought the story of the ghost of Victoria Myer was a legend, a story made up to frighten little children and fascinate adults."

"I take it you don't believe in ghosts," he says as he looks at me.

"No," I say, shaking my head. "Frankly, I thought ghosts, and ghouls, and things like that were just superstitious nonsense."

"I find that surprising, considering your own encounters with the souls of the dearly departed."

"You know," I say with a smile, "Helen pointed the same thing out to me."

He pats his hand on the desk. "She's a great woman, that one!"

"Oh, I totally agree," I say nodding my head. "I didn't have a good answer for her. I guess I'm just a natural sceptic. My encounters with Joan . . . well, I thought those were just unique events. That it wasn't the same as the soul of a dead person roaming the halls of an antebellum mansion."

"Skepticism is always a good thing for a priest," Father Wayne says. "At some point, you'll have a parishioner claim to see the image of the Blessed Mother in a toasted English muffin, or possibly have someone claim to be receiving messages from Saint Michael, or Saint Joseph, or even Our Lord himself. The Church always begins with skepticism about the miraculous or the supernatural. So, in and of itself, your skepticism is not a bad thing."

He pauses to study me for a moment. "So what's changed?"

I take a deep breath and begin to tell the story of Catherine Conway. I recount the accident that put her in a coma, and her awaking with the knowledge that Helen and I would marry. I tell the stories Dan told me, about Catherine telling Miriam that Andrew was sick when she had no way of knowing that and mentioning to her dad about the Myer Mansion being turned into a school before the plans were announced to the parish. I recount the almost unbelievable story of her stepping out in front of Leslie Williams' bicycle, causing an accident that bent the sight on the disassembled rifle in her backpack just enough to throw her aim off. I finish with the latest, her telling me about a lady asking her to have a priest pray and say masses for her, then identifying the lady as Victoria Myer.

Father Wayne listens quietly, nodding his head at points, but not asking questions. When I finish, he leans back in his chair and stares at the ceiling for what seems like forever.

Finally, he says, "This Catherine Conway, how old is she?"

"She'll be seven in February."

"And what you've told me about her, all this can be verified by her parents?"

"Yes, and Helen. Except for the most recent thing, about Victoria Myer."

"And you have no reason to believe she could be making the story up, based on what she's heard?"

I consider the question for a moment. "Well, I believe Catherine is as capable of lying to get out of trouble as any other child her age. But I don't think she'd make up a story like this. And I seriously doubt her parents would have even discussed that newspaper article."

Father Wayne nods. "Well, my only question for you is why is this the first I'm hearing of Catherine? I mean, a six-year-old visionary doesn't happen every day."

I shrug. "I just didn't think—I mean, she's just a child."

"She's a child with an extraordinary gift, it would appear. As her priest, you need to take great care with her. If knowledge of this gets out, it could open her up to ridicule or worse."

"Some kids already call her 'Spooky Catherine,'" I say. "It happened at the church playground after Mass on Sunday. Her younger brothers beat up the boy who called her that."

Father Wayne grins and punches his hand with his fist. "That's the spirit! Good for them! Frankly, I'd never have thought that Dandy Dan Conway would produce kids with such fire in them!"

"Dandy Dan?" I ask, confused.

"My nickname for him," he says. "In Iraq, he was known for being quite the ladies' man. Dandy Dan was, shall we say, cleaner than what his comrades called him."

I nod. "So, what should I do?"

"Well, Father Tom, I'd think it'd be obvious," Father Wayne says. "Catherine told you what the woman said."

"To pray for her and say Masses for her soul." I sigh at the thought.

"What's the problem?"

"Well," I say, "I mean, you know?"

He stares at me like a bulldog about to pounce on a raw steak. "No, Father, I don't know. Why don't you tell me?"

I take a deep breath and say in a rush, "I'm just afraid that if I start saying masses for the soul of Victoria Myer that people will think it's—well, odd. That I'm odd for doing it. That I believe there's a ghost running around the Myer Mansion."

Father Wayne looks at me, bursts out laughing. "Odd?" he says through his laughter. "You—you're afraid of people thinking you're odd? I'm sorry, son, that ship sailed long ago!"

I sit up straight, feeling insulted. "What do you mean?"

"Father Tom," he says, clearing his throat. "You're a later-life vocation. You fell in love with a woman in your parish and received a dispensation to marry. The woman in question is in law enforcement. And in the last year or so you've been involved in several murder investigations—one where you were the prime suspect—and you've been beaten, shot at, and stabbed. Compared to all that, praying for the soul of the dead is small potatoes."

"But Victoria Myer's been dead almost 150 years. Why now? And why me?"

"Did she come from a Catholic family?"

"Yes, they were very devout. They helped rebuild Saint Clare's after a fire in the 1850s."

"What about in recent years?"

I take a deep breath. "I would say later generations were less devout."

He shrugs. "There's your answer, Father. All this time, she's had no one to pray for her soul. We don't understand the mechanics of these things, and won't this side of heaven, but I agree with a lot of theologians—including Aquinas—that God sometimes allows the souls of the dearly departed to appear to the living, even to wander among them for a time, seeking the prayers of someone to help them leave purgatory. Maybe for Victoria Myer, the mansion is purgatory. We just don't know."

I sigh and nod. "OK. Thank you, Father Wayne. Now I know what to do."

"You knew what to do," he says firmly. "You just needed a kick in the ass to do it. Now, I have a meeting with His Eminence. Tell that lovely bride of yours I look forward to our next meeting. Let her know I've been practicing."

I'm confused. "Practicing, sir?"

"Shooting," he says. "She's an excellent shot. Really puts me to shame. So I've been putting time in at the pistol range."

I nod. Of course Helen and Father Wayne would shoot together.

"I'll be sure to tell her, sir," I say, shaking his hand. "She'll love the challenge."

***

I'm just outside Baltimore on I-70 when my phone rings. To my surprise, it's Dan Conway.

"Hi, Dan," I say.

"Tom," he says, sounding serious. "Are you still in Baltimore?"

"I just left," I reply. "What's wrong?"

I hear him take a deep breath. "You need to meet Helen at the Myerton General ER."

I clutch my phone as my stomach tightens. "Dan," I whisper. "Is—is she—"

"She's fine. But Terry Davis is not. His dad beat the shit out of him." I hear Dan's voice crack as he adds, "Tom, he's only 10 years old and they say he may not make it."

I punch the accelerator and send the needle on the speedometer sailing past 90.

Thirteen

I get to Myerton General in record time, pulling into the clergy parking space just about ninety minutes after getting Dan's call. I'd asked him to meet me with my sick kit, and I see his car parked next to Helen's.

Rushing through the ER's doors, I go immediately to the nurse's station. Betsy Rawls is on duty tonight, and on seeing me, she says, "Father Tom, they're all up in surgical waiting."

"Thank you," I say. "Any word on Terry Davis?"

She takes a deep breath. "No," she says quietly. "He's in surgery with Dr. Maycord. Internal injuries, broken bones. Dr. Maycord asked for Dr. Sims, the orthopedist on call, to assist." She swallows. "He also contacted a plastic surgeon to . . . to . . . " She can't say anything else, but turns away and busies herself with a stack of papers.

I take the elevator to the all-too familiar floor and walk down the all-too familiar hallway to the all-too familiar waiting area. There, in a secluded corner, I find Bridget Davis. Sitting with her is Mae Trent, holding her hand and talking to her softly. Dan and Helen are standing some distance off in deep discussion.

I walk over to them. When Helen sees me, she takes a deep breath and says, "Tom, this is bad."

"Betsy told me Terry's in surgery," I say. "Martin's asked for a plastic surgeon?"

"Probably to fix the damage that bastard did to the boy's face," Dan said. "Hallstead broke down in tears when she saw him, so you know how bad it is."

"What happened?"

"We got a call just after 11 a.m., saying there was another fight at the Davises," Helen says.

"I happened to be at home when I heard the call on my radio," Dan continues. "I ran down there to see what was going on. As I got there, Rusty was burning rubber out of the driveway. Bridget was standing on the porch, hysterical." He swallows and shakes his head. "What that man did to that boy—he'd better pray I'm not the one who catches him."

"How did it start?"

"We're still trying to piece that together," Helen says. She looks over at Bridget. "Apparently, Rusty started on Bridget, and Terry decided to defend his mother. Brave kid. I hope her staying with that son of Sodom was worth the loss of her boy."

"He's in God's hands now, Helen," I say. "And God's using Martin's hands. He'll pull him through."

She looks at me with a grim look on her face, but doesn't say anything. "I'm going to check to see if we've found Davis yet."

"He's not in custody?"

"No," Helen says. "Like Dan says, he drove off, too cowardly to face arrest, I guess. He left his cell phone, but he's made some cash withdrawals west of here, so he seems to be heading that way."

"Anything I can do?"

"Just do what you usually do," she says. "Pray. Talk to Bridget Davis. Try to get her to see sense this time."

I nod and walk over to where Bridget and Mae are. Mae looks up at me, but Bridget doesn't seem to know I'm there.

"Father Tom," Mae says, standing up.

"Mae," I say. "Hello, Bridget."

Bridget glances at me and nods slightly.

"Bridget," Mae says, "I'm going to check and see if there's any word on how Terry's doing."

She walks off, and I sit down next to Bridget. "Bridget," I say quietly, "I am so sorry that this has happened."

She nods. "Dr. Maycord said he had internal injuries but he wouldn't know how bad until he got him in surgery. Oh, Father," she says, falling into my arms, "I called the police on Rusty. I called them on my own husband. I didn't want to but Terry was unconscious. I had to do something. I couldn't stop him. He just kept kicking him, no matter how I tried to pull him away."

"You did the right thing, Bridget. You had to get him away from you and your children. Now, where are the younger kids?"

"They're at the Nacombs. They live next door and Sara rushed over then she saw the ambulance and took the little ones home with her. Oh, Father, what must they think of us?"

"First, it doesn't matter what they or anyone else thinks. But second, in my experience, no family is free of bad situations, even those in the Church. But Bridget, do you feel like telling me what happened?"

She takes a deep breath. "Terry woke up with a cough and a runny nose. I didn't want to send him to school, but I also knew Rusty couldn't watch him. I called in. For some reason, when Rusty woke up, he got angry that I was there. I told him about Terry being sick, and he started screaming at me that I was saying he wasn't fit to take care of his own son. I tried to calm him down, but once he . . . Rusty knocked me down. I tried to stay down, but he was yelling at me to get up, and he kicked me. I yelled, and Terry must have heard me. I don't know what he was thinking, but all of a sudden, Terry jumped on his back and tried to knock him down. But Terry, he's only ten, he's still a little boy, and Rusty just threw him off. I thought he would keep after me, but he turned on Terry and started punching him and kicking him. I tried to pull him off but I couldn't, so I grabbed the collar of his shirt and pulled with all my might. He tried to sling me off but I wouldn't let go so he finally turned around and grabbed for me. I ran then, hoping he'd come after me and leave Terry alone. I got into the yard before he caught me. There was a couple walking their dog so I started screaming for them to call 911. The woman did and the man came running up to help me. When Rusty saw him, he let go of me and started saying that there was no need to call anyone, that it was just a family argument. But I kept screaming that my son was hurt and the man stood between Rusty and me and told me to go inside and check on Terry. The man must have turned away or something, because the next thing I know Rusty's pulling out of the driveway in our car."

Exhausted from sobbing and recounting the terrible story, she just leans against me. I quietly pray for her, for Terry, and for Rusty.

After a few minutes, Bridget says quietly, "Rusty was a good man, a loving husband and father, a hardworking provider, until the accident."

"What accident?" I ask, gently.

She sighs and continues, "Two years ago, Rusty was working a job in Baltimore. He was a structural engineer with Delmarva Enterprises. They build high rises in all the big cities locally. Rusty was the one who would go out, inspect the work, and sign off on it. Anyway, I went to pick him up at a site because his truck was in the shop. He wanted to drive home, but I didn't want to get out and switch because we were stopped in traffic, so I was driving. We were on our way home on the Baltimore Beltway when some guy a few cars up lost control of his car. He spun out and the next car hit him. Then another and then I hit the third car. I was not speeding and the police insisted there was nothing I could have done, but Rusty hit his head on the window. It was a bad concussion and he developed epilepsy. Medication can control the seizures to a certain extent but they took his driver's license, so he can't drive.

"The company tried to keep him on at first, told him they'd give him a desk job, but he couldn't stand being cooped up inside all day and so he quit. That's when he started drinking too much. I'd come home and he'd be drunk. At first, I could just stay out of his way and he'd pass out and sleep it off. But then, his benefits ran out and money got really tight. My parents could help us some but not much. I knew his parents had plenty and so I asked them for help.

"They were glad to do it and really nice but that seemed to push Rusty over some kind of ledge. The next time he got drunk, he started yelling at me that it was all my fault, that if he'd been driving, none of this would have happened and he wouldn't have to go begging to his dad. I tried to reason with him but he just got madder and madder. That was the first time he hit me. The next day, he saw the bruise on my cheek and asked me what happened. He didn't even remember and when I told him, he accused me of making it up. He grabbed me and tried to wipe the bruise off, saying I had made myself up to look that way. When he couldn't get it to come off, he changed his story, said he hoped I'd learned my lesson about arguing with him. I promised I had and everything was OK for a week or two.

"Then it all happened again, and then again. I didn't end up in the hospital until he sprained my wrist. That was about six months ago. After that, I knew Dr. Maycord was suspicious, so I'd try to hide in the kids' rooms when he'd get home from a night out drinking. The thing was, he was never that drunk when he'd get home, I guess the bars would kick him out before he started trouble there, but he'd always pick up a couple of six packs on the way home and start in on those as soon as he got in."

She starts sobbing again and I think of all the things I could say, might say, should say. But in the end, all I can see in front of me is a woman broken by a life that she never could have even imagined, much less chosen.

Finally, I say, "Bridget, you need to understand that none of this is your fault. You have done nothing wrong. You have consistently tried to do the best you could for your family and if you have made mistakes along the way, they are just that, mistakes. Now you have a chance to reach out for help, and I promise you there are people all around you who want to help you get back the family life you had before or, if that is not possible, make a new life for yourself and your children. Would you be willing to let us, your Church family, help you with that?"

Bridget nods her head, slowly, as if trying to wrap her mind around what I have said. Just then, Mae returns to the waiting room. I catch her eye and point to a corner. She nods and I walk over to meet her.

"She says she wants help," I say quietly to Mae, "and I will be glad to do anything I can, but this is your department, so just let us know where we fit in."

"Thank you, Father. I have some news on Terry and, if she's willing, I'd like to have you with us when I tell her."

I follow Mae back to Bridget. She sits down and says, "I have some news on Terry. Is it OK if Father Greer stays while I share it with you?"

Bridget nods, so Mae continues, "Doctor Maycord is still in surgery with him, but he says that he will definitely be all right in time. But he will have to stay in the hospital for a while. He's going to require more surgeries, especially to repair the damage done to his face. But Terry is going to be OK. Do you understand what I'm saying, Mrs. Davis?"

Bridget nods her head, tears filling her eyes as she collapses on Mae's shoulder and begins to hug her. Mae holds and pats her until Bridget pulls back.

Then, Mae draws herself up and says firmly, "Mrs. Davis, Terry is a minor, and therefore, I have contacted Child Protective Services. They will be coming here to interview you sometime today and will speak to Terry before he leaves the hospital. They will need to determine if the other children can be safe in your custody, or if they need to be placed in foster care."

Bridget begins to cry again as Mae continues, "I assure you that everyone involved in this situation wants very much for you to keep your family intact. To that end, are you prepared to get a restraining order against your husband and to commit yourself to keeping him away from your home and your family?"

Surprisingly, Bridget pauses at this and looks at me, saying, "But he's my husband. They are his children. How can I do such a thing, Father?"

"Bridget," I say, sitting down across from her, "Rusty is in a very bad place right now, and you need to protect him by keeping him from doing something he will regret the rest of his life. You say that he has been a good husband, a good father in the past. Then you need to keep him away from you and his family until, God willing, he can be that again. Otherwise you are just placing him in the near occasion of sin. You don't want to do that, I know, and in this case, there are laws in place to keep you from doing that, if you are willing to obey them. The only question is, are you willing?"

She looks at me firmly now, her eyes determined, and says, "Yes. I will do that." Then, turning to Mae, she says, "Get me whatever paperwork you need me to sign."

Fourteen

It was another two hours before Martin came out and told Bridget that Terry had made it through. The boy would spend the rest of his life without a spleen, and Martin couldn't say what his kidney function would be. He was concerned with some swelling on the brain, but after consulting with a neurosurgeon they decided to watch and wait. He was in a medically-induced coma to help him heal. The plastic surgeon Martin had flown from Baltimore—a personal friend of his—said it would take a couple of surgeries, but she'd be able to repair the damage to Terry's face.

Helen made finding Rusty Davis her department's top priority. She sent BOLOs out all over the state, eventually including West Virginia, western Pennsylvania, and southern Ohio. The Friday after Rusty's disappearance, state police in Ohio found the car abandoned in a truck stop. After that, the trail went cold.

The first time anyone heard from Rusty was Monday, when Bridget, who'd been sitting by her son's bedside since he got out of surgery, received a text. He said he was sorry, and he knew he'd have to spend time working on himself before he could be a good husband and father again. He told her he was in Minnesota with cousins and would be in touch. Bridget told him about the restraining order. But since there was a warrant out for his arrest, the likelihood of him showing up was small, anyway.

Miriam got the Meal Train up and running, organizing the other moms to provide meals to the Davis family so Bridget could spend as much time at the hospital with Terry as possible. Families took turns watching the younger children, and there was a steady stream of women from the church sitting with Bridget in the hospital, or offering to give her a break so she could go home and get a shower and change of clothes.

I'm pleased with the way the parish rallied around Bridget and her family. This is the way it should be. This is the way it was when Helen was shot. We could not have gotten through that crisis without our parish family. I know the Davises will be stronger with the same support.

Tuesday, I'm sitting at my desk working on my homily when my text messaging buzzes.

"Thank you, Lord," I say with a grin.

It's from Helen. Just four words. "He's awake. He's fine."

***

Not long after receiving Helen's text, Anna walks into my office with a cup of coffee.

"That's such good news about Terry Davis," she says.

Taking a sip of the much needed restorative, I nod. "A real answer to prayer. Bridget was so concerned about brain damage, but at least right now there doesn't seem to be any."

"That's so good to hear." Anna pauses, then says, "Tom, about Deacon Roderick."

I sit up and put my coffee cup down. "Is there a problem?"

"Oh, no, of course not," Anna says. "He's making the transition to the parish well. I've heard no complaints."

"I'm still glad you made the suggestion to the Archbishop. He's really proven helpful, not just at the altar, but with the visits. Apparently, he managed to charm Gloria MacMillan."

"He must be some kind of magician if he can pull off that trick. No, but we haven't really had the chance to get to know him. I haven't even met his wife."

"I know he's taking an apartment here in Myerton," I say, "beginning very soon. But his wife's staying in Baltimore."

"Taking care of a sick mother, from what I understand. But still, you should get to know him on a more personal level."

"What do you suggest?"

She smiles and her eyes light up. "A dinner party."

I sit back and consider this. "A dinner party. Hmm. Not a bad idea. We can invite Clark and Vivian—it's been forever since we've done anything with them."

"And you and Helen don't need to worry about a thing," she says. "I'll do all the cooking."

I grin as I reach for my phone. "Sounds great! I know he's going to be here this weekend. We can do it Saturday after the 4:30 p.m. Mass."

"Wait, what about Fairy Tales and Frights?"

I shake my head. "I don't have anything to do with that after Thursday, until the Halloween Party after the house closes on the 31st."

She nods and leaves as I dial Deacon Roderick's number.

"Hello, Father Tom," he says. "How are you today?"

"Fine, just fine, Deacon Roderick," I say.

"Father Tom," he says. "We've been working together for a couple of months now. Please call me Derek."

"Then you must call me Tom," I say. "The reason I called is, you're going to be here Saturday, aren't you?"

"Yes, I'm going to be at the Vigil Mass then both Masses on Sunday."

"Very good. I know this is somewhat last minute, but I was wondering if you and your wife could join us for dinner Saturday evening?"

When he doesn't answer right away, I think I've lost the connection. "Derek? Are you—"

"Yes, yes, I'm here," he says quickly. "Saturday evening, you say? The both of us?"

"Yes. We haven't met your wife yet. I thought we could get better acquainted. She and Helen can get to know each other. I also thought I'd invite Reverend Applegate and his wife, I think I've mentioned them to you."

"Well, I'll have to check with Linda—she cares for her elderly mother, you know."

"I understand," I say. "So, if she can't—"

"Oh, I'm sure something can be arranged," he says. "Just plan on the two of us, and if something comes up, well, it will just be me."

"That sounds fine. We're nothing if not adaptable around here."

He sighs. "Thank you for your understanding, Father Tom. I look forward to getting to know you and Helen better. From what I already know, she's a remarkable woman."

I can't help but to smile. "That, she is."

As soon as I'm off the phone with Derek Roderick, I text Helen:

Are you off Saturday night?

A moment later, she replies:

Yes, I'm leaving Dan in charge.

I smile and type:

OK, Deacon Roderick and his wife are coming for dinner after the 4:30 Mass.

There is no response for a number of minutes, but then my phone rings. "Hi, Darling," I say, innocently.

"Tom?" Helen says, without preamble, "I swear I thought we were engaged and getting married in 10 weeks. But now, I know that I've obviously been hallucinating all this time and that we are just friends. So I will be busy Saturday night cancelling the plans I have made in preparation for becoming your wife and therefore I will not be able to accept your—I guess it was an invitation?—to dinner."

Sensing that I have made a mistake, I ask, "Helen, have I done something wrong?"

"That depends," she says patiently. "If we're just friends, not at all. If we are to be married soon, then you should never, repeat, NEVER, make social plans without me."

"OK, I understand. But it was Anna's idea. She said she'd cook and I figured I'd invite Clark and Vivian, too. So you could just sit back and not worry about anything."

"First, I would prefer if WE invited Clark and Vivian. Second, don't you think it's time that we begin to transition to acting in as many ways as morally possible like a married couple? I mean, the transition to living together is going to be a shock no matter what we do, so I'd at least like to get in some practice at doing a few things together."

"So what do you want to do?" I ask, realizing that's what I should have done in the first place.

"I like the idea of having a dinner party but want time to think things through. We can discuss this over lunch. But Tom, this is something I want us to do. You remember how much

I liked entertaining when we were together. And frankly, I haven't had much—well, any—opportunity to do it since John died."

"I understand, and I'm sorry," I say. "I should have thought of that. I'll tell Anna that you're going to be in charge."

"Now, don't tell her that way," she says. "Just tell her that I want the practice of hosting. Tell her we want her and Bill to be there as our guests."

"All right. I'll see you in a couple of hours. Love you."

"I love you too, Tom," Helen says. "But next time, just remember to ask me stuff first?"

We hang up and I go to Anna's office. I'm nervous about the conversation, because I have a sense she's not going to be too happy about being replaced—though that was going to happen anyway in a couple of months.

"Anna," I say, "I just got off the phone with Helen."

"Oh, good. Can she be here Saturday night?"

I hesitate. "About that, Anna. Um, Helen—well, she pointed out to me that she's going to be my wife soon and, well, she wanted us to host the dinner party. With her doing everything."

Anna's smile fades, and I see a hint of disappointment in her eyes. "Oh," she says quietly. Then, she squares her shoulders and says, "Of course she does. I'm sorry, Tom. I should have thought about that. I'm just so used to . . . but she's right. Let her know I'll be glad to help if she needs it."

"Anna, we want you and Bill to be there as our guests," I say. "But I'll let Helen know."

"And Bill and I will be glad to attend," she says, standing up. "If you'll excuse me, I need to—I'm sure there's something in the kitchen I need to do."

She hurries out of the office. I hear a sniffle, and feel my own heart breaking for her.

* * *

Two hours later, over chicken salad sandwiches at her desk, Helen springs the details on me.

"We'll invite everyone, including Anna and Bill—you told her, right?" she asks.

I nod. "Yes. She said they'd love to be there."

Helen sits back. "How did she take it?" she asks quietly.

"Honestly," I sigh, "I think she was a little disappointed. But she also said she understood. And she told me to tell you she'll be glad to help."

She smiles. "I'll be sure to do that. Now, I'll make dinner and have everything ready when Mass is over."

Her face lights up with excitement. Helen used to love having people over for parties, though back then I did most of the cooking.

I turn my attention back to what she is saying as she continues, "We'll start with hors d'oeuvres around six and then have dinner about seven. That way, we'll be done before it gets too late, since everyone has to be up early the next day."

"Wait," I ask, my heart leaping. "You said hors d'oeuvres. Does that mean Nibbles?"

"If you insist," she says, laughing at my excitement.

Years ago, before she learned to cook well, Helen mastered one recipe and tweaked it to make it her own. She took an old Southern standby that I first made for her called sausage balls and changed it up, keeping the biscuit mix base but trading out the sausage for finely chopped bacon and the cheddar cheese for Swiss. The result is one of my favorite snacks of all time, one I never tried to make after we split up and one that she has been promising to make for me ever since we got engaged.

"Oh, joy!" I say, jumping from my seat and coming around the desk to kiss her. I growl slyly in her ear, "You know what those things do to me."

"Keep this up and I'll serve canned cheese on saltine crackers," she giggles back before wrapping her arms around my neck and pulling me close for a kiss.

Of course, we hadn't shut her door completely, and so the next thing we hear is Dan Conway's voice saying, "Nope, I'm never going to get used to this."

"Oh, Dan," Helen says, letting me go but refusing to be embarrassed. "Tom is just excited because I promised to give him Nibbles Saturday night."

I turn red and am about to explain when Dan puts his hand up and declares, "Please, no more. I'm barely coping as it is. Let me just believe that it's some sort of snack."

"But it is!" I gasp, as Helen giggles beside me.

"Uh-huh," Dan says, "I'm sure it is. But now, Helen, please just give me that Davis file and I'll get out of here."

"Any news on that?" I ask, anxious to change the subject.

"Not really. She insists that she's only heard from him through the occasional text and that he claims he's staying somewhere in Minnesota. Apparently, he has some distant cousins there that he's mentioned through the years. Problem is, she doesn't know anything about them, not even where they live."

"Well, I guess all that really matters is that he leaves her and the kids alone," I say.

"I'd still like to nail that son of Sodom's hide to the wall, but yeah, it looks like that's going to have to be enough."

Dan and I both look at her funny, still taken aback by her increasingly odd attempts to avoid cursing. Dan admits, "I'm afraid so," before leaving us to continue talking about Nibbles and all the good things that follow them.

"Listen," I finally say, "just tell me what you need me to do."

"Nothing, really," she says cheerfully. "Just be available Saturday in case I have a last minute crisis, which I'll try to avoid."

Fifteen

"So, is everyone clear?"

The members of the Acutis Society, along with other members of the parish they've roped in, are seated in the basement on Wednesday evening. Gladys has just finished going over the final instructions for Fairy Tales and Frights, giving a speech that reminds me of George C. Scott's in the opening scenes of *Patton*.

Martin—or, I should say, The Big Bad Wolf—is of course seated next to Mae—or Little Red Riding Hood. I've not had much of a chance to talk to either of them about their engagement since they announced it. I assume everything continues to go well for Saint Clare's latest betrothed.

But looking at them, I get the feeling that all is *not* well. Martin looks distracted, and Mae looks slightly upset.

"Father Tom," Gladys says, "you're going to be there for the ribbon cutting, right?"

"Tomorrow night, 6 p.m.," I nod. "I'll bring my own scissors."

"You'll be there early enough to pray with us, right?"

"Oh, of course."

"And you'll go through the house with the first group?"

At that, I hesitate. No one said anything about me going through the house. I don't like haunted houses. I don't like being scared.

"I'm sure the kids will like it," Gladys continues.

I breathe a sigh of relief when I realize she means going through the family-friendly version earlier in the evening. If it's for little kids, I think I can handle that.

"I'm looking forward to it," I say.

Seated next to me, Helen whispers, "Coward."

"There is nothing you can say or do that will get me to go in the scarier version."

"Maybe not this year," she mutters.

Suddenly, the basement feels much warmer.

"OK, remember," Gladys is saying. "Everyone be at the Myer Mansion at 4 p.m. for one last run-through. Thanks!"

The crowd begins to disperse. Turning to Helen, I say, "So, are you off?"

She sighs. "Yes, I am."

"Well, don't sound so disappointed," I say with a smile.

"It's not that," she says. "This Davis situation still bothers me. I wish I could have got my hands on that son of Sodom."

"You know," I say, "your profanity substitutes are getting weirder and weirder."

"Look, I'm trying, da-arn it," she huffs.

"Is he in Minnesota?"

"That's what Bridget says. She hasn't heard from him in a couple of days."

"Well, he's not in town. His family's safe. That's the important thing."

Helen nods. "So, what did you make me for dinner?"

"Chicken enchiladas, Vivian Applegate's recipe."

"Ooooh, those are good—oh, here comes Martin."

I turn just as Martin walks up and says, "Hi, guys."

"Martin," Helen says, "How's Terry?"

"He's a strong kid," he says. "He's recovering very well. Had the first reconstructive surgery yesterday. Mae's been meeting with him daily."

"He's probably going to need a lot of counseling," I say.

"Speaking of which, Father," he says, "do you have some time now? I've got something I need to talk to you about. It's kind of urgent."

"Sure, let's go to the Rectory." Turning to Helen, I say, "can you—"

"I'll go talk to Mae," she says. "I haven't talked to her in a while."

Martin and I walk from the basement of the church to the Rectory. The usually loquacious surgeon is strangely quiet, confirming my suspicions that something is wrong.

Once in my office, Martin says, "Father, there's something I need to talk to you about."

"Considering you're calling me Father instead of Tom," I say, "am I right that this is something serious?"

"No. Yes. I—I don't really know. That's why I'm here."

I sit back. "OK. Why don't you tell me what's up?"

He takes a deep breath. "Now that Mae and I are engaged, we are obviously getting serious about wedding plans. I want us to have a long honeymoon—I'm thinking about a month, preferably in Italy and perhaps several other European countries."

"Sounds lovely," I say, wondering where this is going.

"When I first hired her at the hospital, it was so Mae could save money to go visit Rome, so I am just thrilled to be the one to take her there."

"So, what's the problem?" I ask, by now completely in the dark.

"Well, I mentioned to her that I wanted to buy her a new wardrobe for our new life together. She's always dressed well, but I know that she's rarely had anything new in her life. I thought that would be fun for her, you know, to pick out exactly what she wanted and just charge it to me."

"But she didn't like that idea?"

"Oh, no," he says, shaking his head. "She was excited about the clothes."

I'm really trying to figure out what exactly has Martin in a state, but am failing miserably. "Martin, I'm sorry, but—"

"She said she wasn't sure it made much sense since she hoped to be in maternity clothes by our first anniversary!" Martin exclaims.

"Uh-huh," I say, just now beginning to see the problem. "And this caught you off guard?"

"You better believe it did. I mean, I know what the Church teaches about artificial contraception, and I have personally seen enough cases of damage caused by hormonal drugs to be concerned. But I don't really have a problem with barrier methods myself. I hope that does not offend you, but I just don't."

"It doesn't offend me, Martin. The question is, does it offend God?"

"Honestly, Tom, I don't know that I'll ever have to face that issue. Mae is adamant that we do nothing to even try to space out having kids, not even to try to avoid getting pregnant for a few months so we can, you know, have some time to get to know each other without having to worry. I even told her I'd be open to Natural Family Planning, though it's far from my first choice. I mean, I've read the literature and know that it can be very effective, but only if those using it are very disciplined. Frankly, I don't want that, not for our first year together."

"What did Mae say about NFP?"

"Oh, she talked about how she believed it should only be used by couples who were suffering some sort of hardship that made it a really bad idea to have another child, and that would certainly not be an issue with us."

"Would it be an issue, Martin?"

"Not technically," he admits. "Money certainly isn't an issue. And we have more than enough room. But, I mean, Father, doesn't it make more sense to get our marriage off on the right foot before we bring a child into the mix? Not to mention, we'll already have the girls to deal with. I mean, isn't that enough?"

I sit back and look at my friend. "Martin, you and I can debate this issue all day long. But you're talking to the wrong person. Now, you've seen the syllabus for our pre-Cana meetings. You know we're going to discuss this, and I'm going to present you with the Church's teaching."

"Yes, I realize that," he says.

"But I'll tell you what I've told others in different contexts. I'm not the sex police. I am not going to be watching Mae's waistline at Mass each week trying to determine if you're being open to life. I'm not going to search your house for condoms or anything like that. All I can do is tell you what the Church teaches."

"But Tom," he says, now reverting back to a more familiar address, "you and I both know that most Catholic families in the country use some form of artificial contraception."

"Yes, and every time they do, they're violating Church teaching. It doesn't make it right. But that's between them and their priest, should they even bring it up in confession, which I seriously doubt they do. Look, ultimately this is something you and Mae will have to work through, together."

"But Tom, if we do nothing, and she's as fertile as her mother is, we could have like, I don't know, a dozen kids. In addition to the girls. That's getting into reality show territory."

"Martin, what exactly were you hoping I would say?"

"I don't know," he says, shrugging. "I guess I hoped there was some sort of loophole that I didn't know about."

I laugh. "Sorry to let you down, my friend. But look, part of being married is listening to the other person, and really trying to hear what they're saying. I suggest you and Mae keep talking about this, and we'll discuss it more in the weeks to come. In the meanwhile, I'll keep you in my prayers, asking God to give you clarity and understanding."

"That sounds like something I say when I've done all I can and I still don't know if the patient will make it."

"I don't think that's the case here, Martin," I say with a smile. "You and Mae are just beginning your life together. It's way too early to consider the patient terminal."

Sixteen

"OK, everyone," Gladys hollers as she claps her hands. "Let's gather around for prayer!"

It's Thursday night, the first night of the Acutis Society's Fairy Tales and Frights. Helen and I are here, first for me to pray with the Society's members, then walk through the mansion with the first group of little boys and girls.

"You can do what you want, Tom," Helen said to me at lunch, "but I'm going back later in the evening to go through the scary version."

"I'll drive you," I said, "then we can grab a snack from Sprockets."

"Don't you think it's time you worked through this fear you have haunted houses?"

"They never said anything at seminary about that being a qualification for a parish priest."

Helen had rolled her eyes at that one.

In front of me are the members of the Society, dressed up in their costumes. Mae's in a particularly fetching Red Riding Hood costume, looking the picture of youthful innocence. Martin's standing in his Big Bad Wolf costume, sans head, of course. Dominic and Therese Shepherd are dressed as a knight and Sleeping Beauty, respectively. Someone's in a dragon costume, and Nate's in a rather authentic looking suit of armor. There are various other costumes from different fairy tales and, considering the Hellenic look, the MMOG Age of Artemis.

"The Lord be With You!" I intone.

"And with your spirit," comes the response.

"Let us pray." The assembly bows their heads, and I continue, "Almighty God and Heavenly Father, we who are gathered here ask you to bless the efforts of these young men and women. May they entertain the people of this town, even as they raise money to further your Kingdom. We ask this through Jesus Christ, your only Son, our Lord, who lives and reigns with you and the Holy Spirit, God, forever and ever."

And all God's people say, "Amen."

"Thank you, everyone," I say, "for all your hard work. The Saint Francis Educational Center is a project very close to my heart. And thanks to you, we're going to have an additional $50,000 dollars towards making that dream a reality."

Helen and I step away as Gladys begins to bark out the final instructions. "She's a real taskmaster, isn't she?" I say.

"I taught her everything she knows about leadership," Helen says.

"Aren't you afraid she'll try to take your job?"

She laughs. "I said I taught her everything she knows, not everything I know."

We're laughing at this when Little Red Riding Hood walks up.

"Father Tom," she says, shyly. "I'm sorry to interrupt you and Mrs. Parr—"

"Mae," Helen says with mock firmness, "I must insist you call me Helen."

"Sorry, Helen," Mae says with a smile. "I'm still not used to being treated by people like a grown-up instead of a kid."

"You haven't been a kid for a while, Mae," I say. "Can I do something for you?"

"Um, actually, yes, if you have a few moments, can we talk. Privately?"

Helen smiles and says, "I'm going to check with Hallstead and Potter, make sure they've got their marching orders."

As she walks off, I say, "Don't you need to get in place or something?"

"We have a few minutes, and I doubt this will take long."

"OK," I say, warily.

She takes a deep breath. "Father Tom, you know how much I love Marty."

"I suspect I do, yes."

"And I am so looking forward to becoming his wife."

"I'm sure."

"But—but—Father Tom, you just have to talk some sense into him!"

I have a feeling I know what she's talking about, but I ask, "Mae, what do I need to talk some sense into him about, exactly?"

"About children. Birth control. Being open to life. That sort of thing."

"Mae," I say slowly, "does Martin not want children?"

"Oh, no," Mae says, shaking her head. "It's not that exactly. But we were talking the other day about the honeymoon—oh, it just sounds wonderful! He wants us to spend a month in Europe. Visit Rome—I've always wanted to see the Vatican. He even talked about using some connections he has to get a private audience with His Holiness to bless our marriage."

"That sounds like some honeymoon," I say, trying to keep the envy I feel from creeping into my voice.

"He wants me to buy a whole new wardrobe from these high-end places in Baltimore—even said we could fly up to New York. I told him it didn't make much sense to buy too much, since I was probably going to be in maternity clothes by our first anniversary."

"Oh?" I say, trying to keep my face neutral. I cannot betray that Martin already spoke to me about this. "What did he say?"

"Well, for a moment he didn't say anything. Then, he started talking about how he wanted to have children, but not right away, and we should put it off until we'd been married at least a year so we could really get to know each other. I told him I didn't see how we could do that since I wasn't going to be using contraception."

"Which is completely in line with what the Church teaches," I nod. "What did he say to that?"

She sighs. "He said he completely agreed about hormonal birth control. He'd read the studies, and he knew from seeing patients how harmful it could be. But he asked if my objection extended to condoms, and I said it certainly did."

Having just agreed with her that she's no longer a child, I'm still shocked and slightly embarrassed that the innocent-looking Mae said the word 'condoms' to me. It's not like I haven't heard the word before—and indeed, there was a time in my sordid past that I bought them for myself—but it's still jarring.

"Then," she continues, "he said he'd been reading up on Natural Family Planning and knew it was highly effective, but it also required discipline. He wasn't sure he wanted us to worry about our first year at least. I told him that NFP was only for people who had a compelling reason to limit or space their children, and that certainly wasn't the case with us.

"Well, it kind of went downhill from there. It wasn't an argument, exactly—or maybe it was, we just didn't yell at each other. Anyway, we had to leave it unresolved because we had to go to the meeting at Saint Clare's about this fundraiser."

She looks at me with earnest eyes, as if she expects me to understand instinctively what she wants me to tell her fiance. I know very well what she wants me to say, because it's the mirror of what Martin wanted me to say to Mae.

"Mae," I say with a smile, "if you're expecting me to tell Martin that you're right and he's wrong, I hate to disappoint you."

"What?" she says with obvious surprise. "But Church teaching—"

"Is very clear on artificial contraception, yes. When we talk in our pre-Cana classes—and you've seen the syllabus, so you already know this—we're going to talk about how you're expected to be open to life and other aspects of Catholic sexual ethics. But ultimately, all I can do is tell you what the Church teaches. What that looks like for you and Martin is something for you two to figure out between yourselves."

"But Father Tom," Mae says, "Martin's wrong!"

"Is he, Mae? About contraception, yes, if that's his opinion. But you know, you could be wrong about NFP, too?"

From the look on her face, Mae's not someone used to being told she might be wrong. "How?"

"Mae, NFP is a practice that people—not just Catholics—have used for years to avoid getting pregnant without using artificial means. You are correct that a ff couple using it should have a serious reason for limiting or spacing their children. You've read Saint Pope Paul VI in *Humane Vitae,* I'm sure. He wrote, 'responsible parenthood is exercised by those who prudently and generously decide to have more children, *and* by those who, for serious reasons and with due respect to moral precepts, decide not to have additional children for either a certain or an indefinite period of time.' But he didn't say what constitutes a 'serious reason'. That, the Holy Father left up to the prudential judgement of each couple."

Mae's quiet, so I say, "Ultimately, this is something you and Martin are going to need to decide for yourselves. I'll be glad to give advice, and be clear where the Church is clear, but that's all I can or will do."

She sighs, and says, "I understand. Thanks, Father."

Just then, Gladys' bullhorn-amplified voice booms, "OK, everyone! Get inside and to your places!"

Mae shakes her head. "Whoever gave her that da-arn bullhorn," she mutters as she walks back to the house.

"Yeah," I say to myself. "They've got a lot more to work on than a lot of people would think."

"Hey!" I look up and see Helen walking towards me. "Ready to get—well, slightly startled?"

Smiling, I say, "Sure. Lead on."

As we walk to the small crowd of children and parents gathering in front of the mansion, Helen asks, "Is everything OK? I mean, with Mae and Martin?"

"Helen, you know—"

"I know you can't say specifically. But in general, is there a problem?"

I stop and look at her. "If there's one thing I've learned in the last few months," I say, "it's that every couple, no matter how much in love they are, has problems."

She nods. "Do you think they can work it out?"

"If they both want to," I say quietly. "If they both want to."

***

"Thanks everyone, for coming," a grinning Gladys, dressed as a medieval princess, says through her bullhorn. There are about twenty children and parents, including Miriam with Catherine, Max, and JP. Louise Harrell is there with Martin's three nieces—Sophie, Lucy, and Therese. Most of the others I recognize are from the parish, but there are a couple of Helen's officers with their children.

"We're really excited about being able to present this, Saint Clare Catholic Church's first—but hopefully not last—Fairy Tales and Frights. If you don't already know, all the money raised is going to help fund the renovations of this wonderful historic house necessary to turn it into the Saint Francis Education Center."

There's some enthusiastic applause from the crowd as Gladys says, "I'd like to ask Father Greer of Saint Clare's, and the person behind the Education Center, to come and cut the ribbon."

I walk up to the wide red satin ribbon stretched across the entrance, and Gladys hands me a pair of large cutting shears. "Thank you, Gladys," I say. Turning to the crowd, I say, "I want to thank you all for coming tonight. The Acutis Society of Saint Clare's has worked and planned for months for this night, and I want to thank them all for their hard work. I've seen some of it, and I can assure you that you are all in for a treat."

Placing the ribbon between the open shears, I say, "I declare Fairy Tales and Frights now open!" The cut's a clean one, and the ribbon separates into two parts that flutter to the ground. I open the doors, and step aside as Gladys rolls through, the small crowd of excited children and their parents following.

"You did that very well," Helen says.

"I got a gold star for paper cutting in kindergarten," I quip. Offering her my arm, I say, "Well, darling, shall we?"

She smiles and slips her arm through mine, leaning her head on my shoulder as we walk through the door.

I've seen it in progress, but I'm still amazed by the transformation. Helen whispers, "Wow! I'm not sure what I was expecting, but this is amazing!"

"They did a great job, that's for sure," I whisper.

"What's the theme for the family tours?"

"I think Gladys told me it's 'A Scary Walk Through Wonderland.'"

Just at that moment, a life-sized Gingerbread Man pops out from behind a tree and says to the children, "Hello, boys and girls!" In response, the children laugh and giggle, some saying hello. He walks along with us for a few moments, talking to the children.

Suddenly, a young man dressed as a small child pops out from behind a rock and screams, "Cookie! I'm hungry!" and begins to run at the Gingerbread Man.

The Gingerbread Man jumps, screams, "Oh, No! I need to get out of here!" and runs away as the greedy child yells "I want the Cookie!" This scene causes the children to laugh.

We walk further through the enchanted forest when we're greeted by Mae, dressed as Little Red Riding Hood, complete with a wicker picnic basket.

"Why, hello," she says with a big smile. "What are you doing in my forest?"

One of Mae's sister's says, "We're here to see the forest, Little Red Riding Hood."

"What do you have in the basket?" Therese, Martin's youngest niece, asks.

"Oh," Mae says with exaggerated sadness, "my grandmother is sick, so I'm taking her some soup. My mother told me to be careful, because The Big Bad Wolf lives here. Have any of you seen him?"

"No!" the children all say in unison, some shaking their heads.

"Oh, good!" Mae says with a smile. "Then we should—"

Just then a loud "Roar!" comes from behind us. We turn around to see The Big Bad Wolf trotting towards us..

"Eeek!" Mae screams. "The Big Bad Wolf!"

The children scream and part like the Red Sea. The Wolf runs between them, passing right by me. I catch a whiff of antiseptic as he does, telling me Martin is really underneath all that fur.

"I'm going to get you, Little Red Riding Hood!" he growls. "And when I catch you, I'm going to eat you!"

"Oh! Oh dear! I must run for my life! Good-bye, boys and girls!" Little Red Riding Hood says, before running through the forest and up the staircase, the Wolf hot on her heels.

"Art imitating life?" Helen whispers.

"More than likely." I whisper.

Gladys continues to lead us through the Enchanted Forest. We encounter the Wicked Witch of the West coming after Dorothy and Toto. The children yell at Snow White not to do it as an ugly old woman tries to get her to eat an apple. On a bed covered in vines lies a sleeping girl—Therese Shepherd, dressed as Sleeping Beauty.

Gladys says, "Now, poor Sleeping Beauty is under a curse. The only way the curse can be lifted is by a kiss from a handsome Prince."

On cue, Dominic hacks his way with his sword through the paper mache vines and branches to reach Sleeping Beauty. He stops, and bends over the young lady in such a way that no one can tell if he's kissing her or not. Still, there are the requisite "Eww, gross!" comments from some of the children. Therese opens her eyes, sits up, and throws her arms around Dominic to thank him for lifting the curse.

"And the curse is broken!" Gladys says, and begins clapping. The children clap and cheer as Therese and Dominc continue to hug.

"Do you think you should stop them?" Helen says.

I shrug. "This is Dominic, after all. I'm not concerned."

We're walking past a rather impressive-looking cave when all of a sudden, a huge dragon rushes out. There's no fire, of course, but an impressive amount of smoke coming from the dragon's nostrils.

"Oh, no!" Gladys squeals. "We woke the dragon! He hates being awakened!"

"I can understand that," Helen mutters.

"Who will save me!" Gladys yells.

"I will, my lady!" Leaping from behind one of the "rocks" is Nate in a very authentic-looking set of chain-mail and metal helmet. He runs at the dragon with his sword, driving the ferocious beast back into the cave to the cheers of the children and Gladys.

"My hero!" Gladys says breathlessly as Nate very gallantly bows and kisses her hand.

"Your most devoted servant, my lady," he says. Standing up, he turns to the children and says, "And with the dragon vanquished, that ends our little trip through Wonderland. Did you have fun, kids?"

The children jump up and down and scream, "Yay!" Their parents, Helen, and I all applaud vigorously.

"If you follow Sir Nate," Gladys says, "we have some little treats and refreshments for you. Thanks for coming!" She grins and waves at the kids as they follow Nate past her.

When everyone has gone and Helen and I are alone with her, Gladys breathes a huge sigh of relief. "So? What did you all think?"

"Fabulous, sweetie!" Helen says.

"Truly, truly wonderful, Gladys," I say, giving her a hug. "You all did a fantastic job. This is going to be a huge success."

"I hope so, Dad," Gladys says with a grin. "I know how important it is for you." She looks at the time. "OK, we have another tour starting in three minutes, so we have to reset everything." Wheeling off, she yells, "Great job, everyone! Now, let's get set to do it all over again!"

Helen and I laugh. "Like mother, like daughter," I say.

"I have taught her well. Now, Father Greer, how about some treats?"

"Right this way," I say, walking through the door that Nate took the children. The children are eating cookies and drinking punch, while their parents talk to each other.

We walk up to Miriam, who smiles and says, "Father Tom, this is just incredible!"

"The Acutis Society did a great job," I say.

"You look tired, Miriam," Helen says. "Do you need to sit down?"

"Oh, Helen! I'm fine," she says. "This is—"

"Hey, Spooky Catherine, did you see the ghost!"

The entire room falls silent. I look in the direction of the familiar voice. Daniel Wright, the loud boy from my first communion class, is grinning mockingly at Catherine. Max and JP are standing by her, clearly wanting to defend their big sister.

"That little—" Helen says, and takes a step forward.

"You're not kidding, Helen," Miriam says, also rushing to her daughter.

Helen wants to follow, but I gently grab her arm and say, "Helen."

She stops and looks at me. "Miriam can handle this, can't she?" she says.

I nod, looking at the pain in my beautiful bride's eyes. It's one of those rare occasions that I'm aware just how much not being able to have children hurts Helen. She loves little Catherine as much as she could her own daughter, and the desire to protect her is strong.

But it's not her role.

"I said," Daniel says, "did you see any ghosts, Spooky?"

By this time, Miriam is by Catherine, and the boy's mom has him by the arm. "Daniel, you apologize to Catherine right this minute."

"It's all right, Mrs. Wright," Catherine says to the mom. Looking at Daniel, she says, "I did see a ghost. And she had something she wants me to be sure to tell you."

"Oh really? What's that?"

Taking a step forward, she gets right in his face and says, "She said for me to tell you that you are a real poopyhead."

Miriam gasps, but Helen bursts out laughing.

"That's my girl," she says under her breath.

Miriam grabs Catherine and drags her back to us. "Catherine Elizabeth Conway, where did you hear that?"

"From Daddy," Catherine says matter of factly. "Only he didn't say poopyhead."

Helen takes Catherine by the hand and says, "Come on, sweetie. Let me get you some more punch."

As the two walk off together hand-in-hand, Miriam says, "She's going to be the death of me."

"Me, too," I say with a smile.

"Catherine?"

"No," I say, shaking my head. "The other one."

Seventeen

"Anna!" Helen calls from the dining room early Saturday afternoon. "Can you come here for a moment?"

I'm reviewing some emails sent by people, thanking Saint Clare's for "wonderful," "amazing," and "thoroughly entertaining" Fairy Tales and Frights at the Myer Mansion. A few express disappointment that the ghost of Victoria Myer did not make an appearance, but I choose to believe they're being tongue in cheek.

But after my conversation with Father Wayne in the wake of Catherine's—what, vision? I'm still not sure what to call her gift—of Victoria Myer, I'm a little offended by their flippant attitude.

"Yes, Helen?" Anna says as she comes out of her office and walks past mine. Curious about what's going on, I leave my emails to go investigate.

Anna enters the dining room, where Helen is standing in front of the Rectory's china cabinet. People may be surprised that the Rectory even has china, much less a china cabinet. But there are occasions when the Rector is expected to entertain. Priests who've served in my position have had other priests, archbishops, and parishioners for dinner over the years. I expect Helen and I will give quite a few dinner parties, considering she likes entertaining and we both like cooking.

"I never realized," Helen says to Anna, "that the Rectory has so much nice china. Where did it all come from?"

"Oh, various sources," Anna says. "That amber depression glass has always belonged to the church. My mother used to recall how, when she was a girl, that's all they used for potluck dinners and other events."

"You're kidding?" Helen says, incredulous.

"No, I'm not. I still remember when they put it out on tables and let people take what they wanted because they wanted to get rid of it. Apparently, Father Avery, who was the rector at the time, insisted that 12 place settings be kept at the rectory, since at that time he was eating off melamine from the fifties."

"And this?" Helen asks, holding up a piece of delicate white china with what the back label certifies is 24 carat gold trim.

"Father Avery's successor, Father Cleveland, left that behind when he moved on in the early 1980s. He was going into a retirement home and assured us he had no one else in his family who wanted it. Apparently, he brought it home to his mother from Japan when he was stationed there as a young man. That was a common practice during the post-war years. I have to say, it's a little garish for my taste, but very valuable now that gold is so high."

"But this," Helen says, picking up another plate, "this is so understated and tasteful. I love it."

"Thank you, dear. That's mine. I just unpacked it a few weeks ago. It stayed stashed away long enough. You and Tom will be able to make good use of it."

I admire the obviously high end plates with their creamy glaze and narrow platinum bands around each edge. "I've seen these before," I say softly, "but not here."

"That's true," Anna agrees matter of factly, "I used them the first time Joan brought you home for dinner, and then for most holidays. I . . . I haven't had them out in a while."

"Fifteen years?" I ask.

"Yes," she says with only a slight tremor in her voice. "But now they're back in circulation, being used to bless others, as beautiful things should be."

"Then we'll use them Saturday night," Helen declares pleasantly.

"No, don't," Anna insists. "This is your night. Use the depression glass. It's such a good look for fall. And a great conversation starter." Then, briskly, "Now, let me show you where the table linen is. Oh, and you'll want to use the silver."

"The Rectory has silver?"

"Oh, yes. Donated by the Myer Family in the 1870s to show their appreciation for Father O'Riley's work during the typhoid outbreak of 1871."

"Thank you, Anna," Helen says.

Anna takes Helen's hands and says, "My dear, I should have shown you these a long time ago. It's your responsibility now."

I turn away and walk back to my office, smiling because at least for this moment, all's right with my little corner of the world.

***

After the Vigil Mass, I'm greeting the departing parishioners when Deacon Derek walks up with a woman in her sixties, very attractive for her age, with blond hair and blue eyes.

"You must be Mrs. Roderick,," I say with a smile, offering her my hand.

"Oh, Father, please call me Linda," she says, giving me a hug. "I'm just so happy to meet you, finally. Derek has told me so much about you."

I want to say the same thing, but the fact of the matter is I know very little about her.

"I was telling Linda," Derek says, "that Helen is cooking tonight."

"Yes, she is, and you're both in for a real treat. She's making some of her specialties and my favorites."

"So, your fiance is Chief of Police and an excellent cook?" Linda says. "I can hardly wait to meet her."

"Well, let's not wait any longer," I say.

After returning to the Sacristy to change out of our vestments, we walk over to the Rectory. When we walk in, we're greeted by a feast for the senses. On the coffee table is a heaping platter of Nibbles, along with a tray of cut vegetables arranged around a bowl of white dip and a plate of crackers with a large cheese ball next to it. There is music playing softly in the background, obviously coming from the small but powerful set of speakers that Helen borrowed from Gladys. From the kitchens wafts a delicious smell that I recognize as Helen's lasagna. I also catch a whiff of the fresh rolls she made yesterday and let rise in the refrigerator overnight.

"How lovely!" Linda exclaims.

"Tom?" Helen calls from the kitchen.

"Yes, darling," I say. "Linda and Derek are here with me."

Helen walks in the living room, and she takes my breath away.

My beloved bride-to-be is clad in a soft grey skirt and deep purple sweater that compliments her curves without unduly emphasizing them. I want very much to take her in my arms and whisper in her ear how much it means to me to come home to all this, but that will have to wait until later.

"Helen," I say, "this is Linda Roderick."

"Linda," Helen says with a smile, "it's so nice to finally meet you."

"I am just so happy to finally meet you, Helen," she says. "Derek's told me so many stories about you and Tom and your—unusual activities together?" Turning to me, she says, "Derek says you're the real Father Brown."

I laugh. "I don't know about that. Helen's the master detective in the family."

"Though I admit," she says, slipping her arm through mine and giving me a light peck on the cheek, "he can be useful on occasion."

"Well, I want to hear all about you two," Linda says. "Derek is a terrible source of information."

"We're really boring," I say.

"Just an ordinary couple," Helen adds.

"Sorry, you two," Anna says, materializing in the hallway with Bill. "There is nothing boring or ordinary about you."

Derek introduces Anna and Bill to Linda while I answer the door. It's Clark and Vivian, and I introduce them to Derek and Linda.

Helen claps her hands and says, "Dinner's going to be another thirty minutes, but we have some hors d'oeuvres and Tom is going to pour some wine. Just sit, talk, enjoy some Nibbles, and have a good time!"

Everyone begins to follow Helen's instructions, and Helen signals to me to join her in the kitchen.

"Helen," I say softly once we're alone, "you look beautiful tonight. Everything looks just great."

She pats my cheek. "Thank you, darling. Hearing that means a lot. Now," she says, taking a bottle of wine from the counter and handing it to me, "please pour our guests this. We'll have a white with the salad, and a chianti with the lasagna."

"Yes, ma'am," I say with a grin.

I take the bottle back into the living room in time to hear Viv say, "So you're going to be in Myerton full time?"

Derek nods. "Yes, to help out Father Tom for the next couple of months. After they get back from their honeymoon, then I'll probably go back to just coming for the weekend—assuming the Archbishop doesn't reassign me."

"And Linda, you're staying in Baltimore?"

"Yes," Linda says. "My mother needs a lot of care, and we just can't afford someone full time. I'll come out on the weekends, when I can."

Bill says, "Won't you find the separation hard?"

Linda shakes her head. "Actually not. Derek had so many naval deployments, as a Navy wife I got used to not having him around. It will actually be a break."

We all laugh as Clark says, "I was in the Army for several years. When I was stationed in Korea, Viv and I were apart for a year. I think it was harder on me than on her."

"Well, I did have two rambunctious boys to keep me busy," Vivian says, "not to mention my work for President Wright."

"Well, I really appreciate your sacrifice, Linda," I say. "Derek has been so helpful to me, not just after I was stabbed, but ever since."

"Thank you, Father," he says with a smile. "It's been a pleasure to serve."

"Is Tom taking care of you?" Helen asks when she walks in and takes a seat next to me.

"He's a great host," Clark says. "You're training him well."

"Hardly the first time I've done this with Helen," I say. "It's just been a while."

"Oh?" Linda says.

Vivian says, "Oh, you haven't heard the story of these two? Helen, you have got to tell her. Linda, it's just remarkable."

So, egged on by Vivian, Helen begins to tell our story, beginning with our college engagement and ending with the night I asked her to marry me. I fill in with my comments and perspective. She, of course, leaves out some of the more intimate details of our journey.

"So, God really did bring you two back together?" Linda says in amazement.

Taking Helen's hand, I say, "And I praise Him every day for it."

There's a silence in the room, only broken when Helen says, "Well, I think dinner is just about ready. Let me go check and put the finishing touches on everything."

She leaves the room, and Clark turns to me. "Tom, I haven't had the chance to tell you how amazed I was by Fairy Tales and Frights. I went with the youth department to the 9 p.m. tour last night. Just incredible!"

"The Acutis Society worked very hard on it," I say. "I'm very proud of them."

"And scary! My word," Vivian says. "I screamed the entire way through, and I'm not at all familiar with—what's the name of that game some of it was based on?"

"Age of Artemis," Anna says. "It's kind of a mash-up of different myths, mainly Greek."

"Do you play, Anna?" Clark asks with a laugh.

"Oh, no," Anna says. "When Gladys had her computers set up here when we were trying to clear Tom's name, I watched her play some and she explained it."

"What do you mean, clear his name?" Linda asks.

I open my mouth to speak, but Anna says, "Oh, the former State Attorney tried to frame Tom for murdering a young woman years ago. He was completely innocent, of course. Man was motivated by jealousy."

Looking at me, Linda says, "You lead a very unusual life for a parish priest."

"You could say that, yes," I say, drinking the last of my wine.

"OK, everyone," Helen calls from the dining room. "Come to the table. Just leave your glasses."

The table is as stunning as the living room. The amber-colored depression glass dishes against a rust-colored table cloth scream autumn. Plated at each place is a caesar salad—I made a small contribution to that by making my special caesar dressing—with a glass of white wine and a glass of ice water.

"Everyone, please sit," Helen says. She takes her place at the other end of the table, and I take my place at the head. Looking at her, bathed in the candlelight from the centerpiece, I'm once again filled with contentment.

At this moment, everything is perfect.

***

By the time everyone leaves around 10 o'clock, Helen and I are both exhausted but thrilled with how well the evening went. Anna steps outside to say goodbye to Bill and then heads to the stairs saying, "Tom, if you're still up when the dishwasher finishes, please go ahead and empty it and put on a second load. Just leave everything stacked on the counter; I'll put it away tomorrow since I know where everything goes."

I want to retort, "So do I," but before I can, she pauses and walks across the room. Hugging Helen closely, she kisses her on the cheek and says, with gentle tears of affection in her eyes, "My dear, you did a wonderful job tonight. Things could not have gone any better. Get some rest this evening and dream sweet dreams of all the dinners and parties you'll be giving here in the future." She then turns quickly and heads up the stairs, sniffling softly as she goes.

"That was sweet," I say as Helen and I collapse on the couch, "and, I might add, correct."

I kiss her the way I've been wanting to all evening. "It was a wonderful party. One of the best this old place has ever seen, especially since I've been here."

We hear Anna's door shut and automatically prop our feet on the coffee table. "So," I say, placing my arm around Helen, "What did you think of Linda?"

"Oh, she's lovely," Helen says. "They're obviously very devoted to each other, if not in such a romantic way as newlyweds would be."

"As we will be in just a few months," I murmur into her soft, dark hair, in which tonight the smell of vanilla has been overpowered by garlic.

"Yes," she says contentedly, snuggling a little closer. "Anyway, Linda wants to continue to care for her mother as long as she can. I admire her for that."

"Me, too. And hey, if it works for them, it works for me."

After a few minutes, just resting on the couch and basking in each other's presence, Helen's phone starts playing the theme from *Camelot*.

"What's Gladys doing calling you at this hour?" I say. I check the time. 11:00 p.m. The Haunted Mansion closed an hour ago.

Helen gets up and scurries to the kitchen where her tote bag is. "Hi Gladys, what's—wait, just calm down," I hear her say. She says nothing else, but rushes from the kitchen to the gun safe.

I jump to my feet as she punches her code in. My blood runs cold when she asks, "Are you sure he's dead?" I begin to pray, not just for the soul of whoever is dead, but that, selfishly, that it's not any of a long list of people who I know are there right now.

She reaches in the safe and pulls out, not her Smith and Wesson, but her smaller backup. "I understand. I'm on my way. Keep everyone there until I get there, and call Dan." She hangs up, and I reluctantly but automatically turn my back as she straps on her thigh holster.

Looking at me, she says, "We've gotta go now."

"What's going on?" I ask as we head out the door."

Helen takes a deep breath. "They found a dead body at the mansion."

Eighteen

"Oh, dear Lord! Who is it?" I ask after the initial shock wears off.

We get in Helen's car and pull out of the driveway. "His name is Larry Daniels."

"Wait, Larry Daniels?"

"Do you know him?"

"I only met him once," I say. "He's a friend of Nate, apparently."

"I don't know about that. He's not a member of the parish but he is an avid Age of Artemis player. He's been playing online with the group for a while now and wanted to help with Fairy Tales and Frights. Gladys ran a background check on him and he came up clean, so they let him. Now he's dead."

"Why didn't she call come over your radio?"

"Gladys didn't want to let anyone know it had happened at the Myer Mansion," Helen explains. "She doesn't want the bad publicity."

"Well, I can't argue with that," I say. "First Nate's stupid article, now a murder. Oh, boy!"

"Maybe the house is cursed, you ever think of that?"

"I'm really beginning to wonder," I mutter.

"Anyway," Helen says, "Martin was there to pick up Mae and he confirmed the guy was dead. Everyone else was gone except Gladys, Nate, Martin, and Mae. Oh, and Dominic. Apparently, he immediately used some duct tape and yellow crepe paper to rope off the area as a crime scene."

"You're kidding?"

"Nope, you know Dominic. I'm only a little surprised that he didn't have crime scene tape in that big backpack he carries around."

We drive along for a while, then I say, "Helen, you are the Chief of Police. But aren't you playing a bit fast and loose with procedure?"

"Yes and no," she sighs. "Gladys has contacted the police. We are on our way. I'll get the crime scene techs out and contact the State ME. We'll process the scene and file all the correct reports and, of course, open an investigation. We just won't tell anybody exactly where the body was found."

"You can't hide a murder from the press."

"No, but if asked, I'll just say it occurred at an undisclosed location on the north side of town. I'll also update Angela on what's going on just to make sure I don't miss anything."

"You know how things are, Helen," I say. "It won't take long before the whole town knows it occurred at the Myer Mansion."

"We only have to try to keep it under wraps for another week," she says, "unless you want people to demand their money back?"

"No, no. I'm sure you know what you're doing. Now, what do you want me to do when we get there?"

"Just what you normally do, please. Keep people calm. Deal with any emotional fallout. Nate found him, so I don't know how that's going to go down, especially since he was a friend."

There's one other question I don't want to ask, but I need to. "Helen, will they be able to open Fairy Tales and Frights? I really hate to see all their hard work go for nothing."

"It's not open tomorrow, is it?"

"No, the only Sunday they're open is Halloween. It doesn't open again until Thursday."

She smiles. "That won't be a problem, Tom."

"Thanks for that, and for not judging me too harshly for asking."

She looks at me with an expression that I rarely see, and only when she is speaking to me as a cop and not just the woman I love. "Tom," she says firmly, "my job is hard enough without letting it shape how everyone around me sees reality. The sad truth is that people die everyday, many of them tragically. Life has to go on for the rest of us, and in this case, it has to go on for a bunch of twenty-somethings who have poured their hearts and minds into putting this amazing project together for the community. The harsh truth is that, just because one person is dead, they don't have to be."

I ponder this for a minute and then ask, "Do you think that is part of what Jesus meant when he said 'let the dead bury the dead?'"

"I don't know," she says. "That's your department, not mine. I mean, Burying the Dead is a corporal act of mercy, but that could be, at least in part, so that the dead are indeed buried, laid to rest for good, so that we, the living, can go on with our lives."

I would love to continue this discussion, but by this time, we are turning into the mansion driveway. We pull up to the front entrance and find Gladys outside waiting for us, flanked by Nate, Mae, and Dominic.

When we get out, they come up to Helen. "Thanks for coming, Mom," Gladys says.

Helen gives her a hug. "We came as soon as we could, sweetie," she says quietly. She then hugs each person in turn, asking if they're OK.

"As fine as we can be, Helen, Father," Mae says, rubbing her arms like she's cold.

"Where's Martin?" I ask.

"He is in with the . . . with Larry," Dominic says, solemnly.

"Gladys told me you roped off the crime scene," Helen says. "I appreciate the initiative."

He takes a deep breath. "It was Gladys' idea," Dominic says. "I just had stuff in my backpack."

Helen nods and turns her attention to Gladys. "I need you to contact the techs and get them out here. Also, call the ME's office and have them send someone out. Dan will be here in a couple of minutes, but I want Hallstead and Thompson back out here. They were handling security and crowd control tonight, right?"

Gladys nods. "OK," Helen says. "Tom, you want to come with me?"

I bite my tongue before I answer, "of course." We walk into the foyer and immediately see Martin sitting on the floor. On the first landing of the staircase, which is roped off with yellow crepe paper and duct tape, is a large gray lump.

Martin stands when we come in and says, "I didn't want to contaminate the crime scene, but I also knew someone needed to keep an eye on things so I figured I'd stay here, since I am obviously more accustomed to the sight and smell of death than the others out there."

Helen nods and thanks him before going over to the staircase. Martin and I follow her up the steps to the landing.

There, laying in a puddle of his own blood, is The Big Bad Wolf with the head of Larry Daniels. The wolf mask is laying by the body.

Helen squats down on one side while Martin squats down on the other. Scrutinizing the body, she says, "Martin, what's your take on this?"

"I'm not a forensic pathologist," he says, "but I'd say he hasn't been dead long—an hour at the outside."

Helen stands up and digs through her bag for her small flashlight. She shines the beam on the body—the lights are on, but this, she tells me, gives her a better ability to see details. "This body was moved."

"Yes," Martin says. "I did roll him over and take the mask off in hopes of reviving him, but he was already gone."

"Care to guess the cause of death?"

Martin shakes his head. "I don't need to guess. He was stabbed—from the cut in the costume there, I'd say a knife. Can't tell you what kind, that will be up to your experts. Given the stab wound and the amount of blood, I'm going to guess that the knife pierced the lung and the guy bled to death in under a minute or two. Again, I'm just guessing. I backed off as soon as I determined he was gone. You'll know more when you get the costume off of him. As for fingerprints, I'm assuming you still have mine on file." He says this with a wry smile as he continues, "Besides rolling him over and taking off that mask, I don't think I touched the body itself, but I might have."

"Thanks, Martin. The more I know starting out, the better off we'll be."

Helen shines the flashlight up the steps, revealing blood splatter and smears on each one. "He wasn't stabbed here," she mutters, and walks up the steps. When she gets to the upper landing, she calls, "Hey, can you two come up here?"

I start up the steps. Martin says, "Do you think she meant me, too?"

I look at him and shrug. "She said 'you two.' Just don't let it go to your head," I say with a grin.

He starts up on the other side of the stairs. "I prefer that the bodies I work on wake up after I'm done with them, thank you very much."

Helen's standing, shining her lights on the blood-stained carpet. "Here," she says. "This is where he was stabbed. But what was Larry doing up here in the first place? This wasn't part of the haunted house."

"Maybe he was going to change out of his costume?"

"The changing areas for the cast are in the back of the house on the first floor," Martin says. "The only people who come up here are Little Red Riding Hood and The Big Bad Wolf when the latter is chasing the former."

"Maybe he was lured up here?" I say.

"That actually is the most likely explanation," Helen says. She shines the light on the carpeted floor.

"Wait," she says finally. Squatting down, she points at something on the floor. "I think that's a boot print in blood."

"It's kind of faint," I say.

"If the killer stepped in the blood stain here," Martin says, "he wouldn't have tracked much blood."

She shines her light on the floor and walks up the hallway, then back down. She stops at the locked door that Andrew mistook for a bathroom. Squatting down, she says, "There's a brown stain here."

"I can explain that," I say. "Andrew Conway had a little accident."

"Eww," Helen says, wrinkling her nose. "OK, I think we can definitively say this doesn't have anything to do with the crime."

"Did you see any other footprints?"

She shakes her head. "I'll have the techs look with their equipment, but other than that print, I didn't see any. Martin, no one saw anyone strange leave the house?"

"Not out the front door, which is where everyone was," he says. "The murderer could have gone out the back. There are several back exits."

"Or, the murderer could still be here," I say. "It's a big house."

Helen nods as we hear Dan call from downstairs, "Hello!"

"We're up here, Dan," she says. "Stay there, we're coming down."

A moment later the three of us join Dan, Officers Hallstead and Thompson, and both of Myerton Police's crime scene techs. Helen fills them in briefly on the scene and what she found.

"Dan, before we begin working the crime scene," she says to them, "I want this house searched from basement to attic. If the murderer is still here, I'd rather we found him before he either manages to sneak out or hurts someone else. You're going to need more officers. Get who you need. I'll authorize overtime for anyone you have to get out of bed."

"Right, Chief," he says.

"Once the scene is cleared, Edward, Tina, I want you both to concentrate on the upstairs hallway. If the murderer did get out after murdering that poor kid, I want to know how. Dan, I'm going to talk to everyone outside. Tom, you can go do what you need to do now."

I nod, and she, Dan, Martin, and the techs leave. Thompson tells Hallstead, "I'll stay with Father and the body."

She nods. "I'll start the search."

Hallstead moves off in the direction of the study, and Thompson accompanies me to Larry. Once there, I squat down by his lifeless body and place my purple stole over my shoulders. Taking out a small vial of holy oil, I say the prayers that I've memorized by this time.

After making the sign of the cross over him, I stand up and say to Thompson, "I'll leave you to your post." But as I walk away, Thompson says, "Can I ask you a question, Father?"

"Of course, Thompson."

He hesitates. "You know, I'm not a Catholic. I'm not really much of anything, I guess, though my Mama took me to church every Sunday when I was a kid, so I believe in God and all that. But I just wanted to ask you. Do you—do you think Victoria Myer did this?"

I'm unable to hide my shock. "Really, Officer Thompson? Are you asking me if a ghost killed this boy?"

"Well, I mean, he was stabbed, on the staircase, just like that soldier was."

"Thompson," I say, shaking my head. "I will not be telling Chief Parr about this conversation, because I'm pretty sure she wouldn't think too much of an officer who actually asked if a ghost was responsible for this. But to answer your question, no, Victoria Myer was not responsible for this. The last life she took in this house, tragically, was her own."

Without another word, I walk down the stairs and out the front door.

***

Outside, Helen and Dan are having a conversation off to the side. Mae is leading Gladys, Martin, Dominic, and Nate, in prayer, obviously taking the lead in helping them process what's happened. I join them and then, after the Amen, say calmly, "I know this has been an awful experience for you, especially you, Nate. I also know that Mae is better qualified than I am professionally to help you work through this, but I am still around if you need me."

They murmur their thanks. Helen walks up and announces, "OK, guys, I want to assure all of you that I will do my best to keep things quiet so that you can reopen on Thursday. Does anyone here know anything about Larry's family situation?"

"He lives with his parents in Hagerstown," Nate says quietly, the first words he's said since Helen and I arrive. "I don't have their number. But it's probably in Larry's cell phone."

Helen nods and says, "OK. Dan's going to take statements from each of you. But can anyone tell me the last time you saw Larry alive?"

They all look at each other until Dominic says, "I saw him about an hour ago. We had closed and most everyone had gone home. He came out in costume and was teasing Mae, chasing her and stuff. Then he said he thought he'd left his phone in the house and he went inside to get it. When he didn't come out after a few minutes, I went looking for him. I mean, he seems like a nice guy and all but we've got some expensive gear in there and I didn't want him making off with anything. That's when I found him."

"Did you hear anything? Footsteps? Someone running?"

Dominic shakes his head.

"Did anyone hear Larry scream, or fall down the stairs?"

Gladys says, "Mom, the walls are pretty thick and the door is solid oak. We were out in the driveway, away from the house."

"There wasn't a sound," Nate says, a distant look in his eyes.

"Other than you guys, are you aware of anyone else here at that time?"

Again, they all look around at each other before shaking their heads.

"OK," Helen says, "I'm going to leave you with Dan now. As much as possible, we need to keep this quiet, for several reasons. One, the less the murderer knows that we know, the better. Also, if we are able to open the mansion back up, it will be best that as few people as possible know about the murder. I'll do all I can to keep the exact location out of the papers but you guys need to keep quiet if you want this to work." She glares at Nate specifically, and he bobs his head up and down like the dog my mother used to have in the back window of her car.

As Helen and I are walking off, Nate comes running up behind me, saying, "Father Tom, I really need to talk to you about something."

"Nate," I say, holding up my hand, "Unless it's an emergency, you need to talk to Dan first. Why don't you stop by the Rectory tomorrow after Mass? Bring Gladys and stay for lunch. Anna is cooking and she always makes plenty. Are you free then?"

"Uh-huh. But I need to talk to you privately, so can we go off by ourselves after lunch?"

"Sure," I say, "we can meet in my office."

As Nate turns around to return to the group, I find myself suddenly concerned about what he needs to talk about. I begin to pray for wisdom as Helen and I drive back to the Rectory.

Nineteen

My concern over what Nate wants to talk to me about nags at me through Mass and lunch. He seems cheerful enough, and everything seems fine between him and Gladys. I begin to hope it may be something more positive, like he wants to discuss popping the question.

I'm not entirely sanguine about that. In my opinion, they still have a lot of work to do on their relationship before they get engaged.

Anyway, I try to focus on keeping an open mind as we retire to my office after lunch, leaving Helen and Gladys to talk wedding details. Even at this late hour, Gladys is still trying to persuade Helen to wear some kind of vintage 1950s wedding dress she has her heart set on. As I close the door, I hear Helen say, "Gladys, for the last time, I'm not going to stand in front of a church full of family, friends, and dignitaries looking like a white chrysanthemum!"

Not wanting to prolong the agony for either of us, I ask as casually as I can, "So what's on your mind, Nate?"

"Well, um," he says, clearing his throat, "it's just this. You know, Father Tom, since everything happened with Ashley Beckett, I have been working very hard to be a better person. I am also taking my faith more seriously and that has helped."

I nod, with what I hope is a warm and understanding smile. "Yes, I know that. I've been very impressed with what I've seen."

"Thank you," he says, wringing his hands. "But Father, I'm afraid I've stumbled, and the magnitude of me causing more harm to the people around me is just overwhelming."

"I see, Nate," I say, trying to keep my face neutral. This is exactly what I was afraid of—he wanted to talk to me about another sexual transgression. "Would you be comfortable telling me who your stumbling has hurt?"

"I guess it doesn't matter since he's dead, but it is—was, I don't know which is right—Larry Daniels."

"Larry Daniels?" I say calmly, even as I'm struggling inwardly to maintain my composure.

"I want you to know, Father Tom," Nate says earnestly, "that I would never have started anything if I'd known where it was going to lead. I was just curious, you know, about life on the other side and one thing led to another and now Larry's dead."

"Nate," I say, weighing my words carefully, "are you saying that you killed Larry?"

"Oh, no, Father! Absolutely not! I really liked the guy. I thought we were on our way to a long-term friendship, and Gladys liked him, too, so that was cool."

"Wait," I say, my head—or is it the room?—beginning to spin. "Gladys knew about your—your—friendship with Larry?"

"Yeah, and as I say, she liked him. But of course she didn't know about everything we were doing. I mean, I was afraid if I told her she wouldn't approve."

I feel a cold sweat breaking out on my brow as I say, "I can see that. But why are you telling me now?"

"Because I'm afraid that I introduced him to the woman who killed him."

I lean forward, my brow furrowed. "So you think you know who did it?"

"Yes, Father."

"Have you told Helen?"

"No, Father, I'm afraid to. I feel like she's just beginning to respect me again, and I don't want her to know what Larry and I were doing."

"And what exactly were you doing?" I ask, dreading the answer to my questions.

Nate sits back in his chair and takes a deep breath. "As I said, it started out all innocent. We started talking one day and found out that we had a lot in common, including curiosity about how it was on the other side, you know?"

I just nod my head, dumbfounded by what I'm hearing.

"We started looking at some websites," he says, "and sending information back and forth about what we learned. Then one night we got together and ended up spending most of the night discussing what we'd been reading about. One thing led to another, and now he's dead."

"But where does the girl come in?"

"We learned about her together, though I was more into her than he was. Still, he was game for including her when I wanted to."

"Oh dear Lord," I say, losing my temper. "You mean to tell me you got involved in all this, got mixed up with someone who may have killed someone, after you promised Gladys you'd behave yourself?"

"I really didn't think she'd mind. I mean, we've discussed this kind of thing some but she's just never been into it."

"Aaagh!" I say, almost jumping across the desk. Then, composing myself, I say, "Nate, we obviously have a lot to talk about but the first thing you need to do is to tell Helen about this girl. I'll go get her and stay in here with you to make sure you tell her the whole story, and to keep her from harming you physically. After that, we have to talk to Gladys."

"OK," he says, shaking his head forlornly, "but she's going to be mad."

Fortunately, by this time I'm halfway out the door so I'm not able to simply throttle him then and there. Instead, I say pleasantly, "Oh, Helen, can you step in here for a minute, please?"

Helen comes in and sits down, hands in lap, obviously hoping for some good news, when Nate blurts out, "Helen, I think I know who killed Larry Daniels. I wasn't going to tell you but when I told Father Tom about her, he insisted you needed to know."

Helen is alert now as she says, "Who, Nate?"

He takes a deep breath and exclaims, "The ghost of Victoria Myer!"

"What?" Helen and I both say as we jump in our seats.

"Yeah, and it's my fault. Like I told Father Tom, I was curious and then I started reading more about ghosts and hauntings and the paranormal, and then I got Larry involved. He obviously went looking for her and she killed him, right there on the staircase where she stabbed her lover all those years ago."

Helen fixes me with a glare and says, "And Tom wanted you to share this with me, why?"

"Because he said it was vital that you know. I didn't want to because I didn't think you'd believe me or even that it would make any difference, but he insisted that it did."

Desperate to regain control of this situation, I say firmly, "Helen, that is not what happened. I thought he was having some kind of affair with Larry. At some point they got another person—the girl in question—involved in their . . . activities, and she killed Larry."

Now they both stare at me as Nate says with tremendous hurt in his voice, "Father Tom, that is a terrible thing to say, not only about me, but also about Larry. I mean, I don't know about him, but I've never been interested in men. Oh, people used to say I must be gay since I didn't have a girlfriend, but I never thought you'd be the kind of person to jump to that conclusion."

"I didn't, I haven't," I stammered, looking desperately at Helen—who, bless her heart, is obviously enjoying my discomfort. "I thought that was what you were trying to tell me. You know, curiosity about life 'on the other side' and stuff."

"The other side of death," Nate says, obviously still hurt. "I'm sorry, Father, but I am disappointed that you jumped to such a conclusion."

"Nate," Helen says, "I think you need to cut Father Tom some slack here. I mean, I'm not sure anyone would assume you were talking about a ghost."

Nate looks at me. "Look, son," I say, "I am sincerely sorry I jumped to the wrong conclusion about you and Larry. I can only hope you forgive me."

He smiles. "Oh, Father. Of course. I think I understand the confusion. I should have been clearer."

"Thank you. Now," I say, folding my hands and glancing at Helen, "why do you think Victoria Myer killed Larry?"

Helen shoots me a disapproving look, but I shake my head slightly. After having misjudged him so badly, he deserves a chance to tell his story.

"I met Larry like everyone else," Nate says, "playing Age of Artemis. You know—or maybe you don't—that you have your avatar—your character name—but you can talk in real time to the other people you're playing. You can also send closed chat messages to single players. Well, Larry joined one of the Acutis Society's group sessions a couple of months ago, out of the blue. He got along well, seemed like a nice guy and everything. So, he'd join us whenever the Society would play. After a while, he and I would play. We'd talk about different things, you know, guy stuff."

"What kind of guy stuff," I ask, a frown creasing my forehead.

"Oh, nothing like that, Father!" Nate says. "I mean, he did know about Ashley and everything from the papers. He did ask me all about that. But mostly just gaming and stuff. He never mentioned a girlfriend, Father, but I don't think he was gay."

"Now, Nate—" I say.

"OK," Helen interjects, "so you got to know Larry personally. When did you meet him?"

"Well—um, is this private? I mean, you're not going to tell Gladys anything."

"What did you do, Nate?" I sigh.

"Well, he asked me if I'd ever gambled, and I said I had once—you know, that story I did for my vlog when I had one, that is—and I wasn't any good. He told me he could teach me a few things. So, we met at the big casino just outside Hagerstown." He looks down at his hands. "It didn't really go well."

"How did Larry do?" Helen asks.

"Larry? Oh, great! He won a bunch. Even showed me how to place wagers on horses. Said if I was ever game, he'd introduce me to his bookie."

"He mentioned a bookie?" Helen says, alert now.

"Uh-huh. Didn't mention his name or anything."

"So where does Victoria Myer come in?" I ask.

"Well, I told him about the research I was doing, and the story about the ghost. Turns out he was big into all that stuff. I have to tell you, Father, I know I made a big mistake getting in as far as I did. But by the time you told me, it was already too late."

"What do you mean, too late?" I ask.

"You told me the Church was against seances. Well, you see, um—Larry and I tried to make contact. A couple of times. Including one time after I knew better."

"Nate!" I say sharply. "You shouldn't have done that!"

"I know, I know, that's why I wanted to come here and talk to you! To make my confession."

"What you did was very, very dangerous, Nate," I say. "Necromancy and other occult practices can really endanger your soul, leaving you open to demonic influence."

"Oh, Tom," Helen says. "That's—that's just nonsense."

"You want to tell Father Wayne that?" I snap.

Helen's eyes flash with anger, but she doesn't say anything.

"Nate," I say slowly. "How did you try to contact Victoria Myer?"

"Well, other than asking Catherine Conway if she could sense anything, you mean?"

"What the Hades fire, Nate! You did what!" Helen exclaims.

"Oh, don't worry, Helen. Father Tom already yelled at me about that. But yeah, we tried once before I wrote the article—I mean, that was a complete bust. No cold chills, unearthly moans, knocking or anything like that. The second time was the day you came over to the Mansion, Father."

"That's what you were doing upstairs," I say. "I thought you looked guilty about something."

"We were in the middle of trying again. Larry had brought an old Ouiji board from his grandmother's."

"Oh, good grief," Helen whispers, rolling her eyes.

"I thought Larry was pulling a prank or something," Nate says. "But now—now, I think we made her mad."

A chill goes down my spine. "What happened, Nate?"

Nate swallows, beads of sweat appearing on his forehead. "Well . . .well, we were at it for about 30 minutes when that little triangle piece started moving across the board. Larry asked, 'Is someone here?' The piece pointed to 'yes'. Then, I asked, 'Who are you?'" He pauses for a minute. "The piece started moving. It pointed to the letter V, then the letter M."

Helen and I stare at Nate. "Anything else?" Helen asks.

"No," he says, shaking his head. "That's when we heard Father Tom. I knew he wouldn't approve, so we hid everything and acted like we were doing something related to getting everything ready." He looks at me. "Larry swore to me that he didn't do anything. I mean, I didn't know him very well, you know, but he was freaked out. After that, he didn't want to have anything else to do with trying to contact Victoria Myer. But I . . . I couldn't leave well enough alone. And then I heard Catherine and you talking, and I thought—well, I know now she was just playing a game.

I sit quietly, looking at Nate, trying to figure out what to say next. "You did something very foolish, Nate," I say quietly. "But I can say, and I'm sure Helen will back me up, that Larry wasn't killed by the angry ghost of Victoria Myer."

"What about a demon?" Nate asks. "I mean, could we have—"

"Nate," Helen says, the exasperation evident in her tone, "unless it was a ghost or demon who wears size thirteen hiking boots, I can definitely say we're looking for a killer very much of this world."

Nate looks at her, then me. He lets out a big sigh of relief. "Oh, thank God! I was just certain I'd done something else to get a good person killed. Father Tom, I promise you, I'm done with all that stuff. No more ghost hunting for me."

"I'm glad to hear that, Nate. Now, why don't you go to the living room. I'm sure Gladys is wondering what we've been talking about the whole time. And I strongly suggest you tell her."

Nate nods his head. "Well, I guess you're right. I was only dabbling in the supernatural. It wasn't like I was seeing another prostitute."

He stands up and walks out of my office, leaving Helen and I alone.

"Tom," Helen says firmly, "I apologize for what I said, but please don't snap at me like that again in front of other people."

I hold up my hand. "I'm sorry. I was on edge. It won't happen again."

Helen softens. "Oh, it probably will," she says with a slight smile. "I know how provocative I can be sometimes." She pauses and looks at her hands. "Tom, um, there is something strange about this case. I didn't want to mention it in front of Nate because I didn't want to get him all riled up."

"What is it?"

"We did find size thirteen hiking boot prints," she says. "Hallstead tracked them down the hall, but the hall was a dead end. We searched the whole mansion and came up empty. Tom, I have no idea how the killer got in and got out that night."

***

I'm lying in bed, trying to wrap my mind around the events of the last twenty-four hours. Helen assures me that they'll be done with the crime scene no later than Monday afternoon, and Nate said, even though there was a lot of blood on the staircase, he'd have no problem cleaning it or the upstairs landing. The news of the murder was reported on the *Myerton Gazette's* website, but there was no mention of the Myer Mansion, Fairy Tales and Frights, or even Larry's name. If the full truth can just wait until after Halloween—

"Darth Vader's March" alerts me that my mother is calling. Helen has scolded me on more than one occasion for having this as my ringtone for her, but I insist that it is important that I know it is her calling so I can psyche myself up to answer.

Having done so as much as humanly possible, I answer. "Hi, Mom," I say, with as much cheerful sincerity as I can muster.

"Hi, Tommy," she replies, more cheerful than usual.

A little hope creeps into my voice as I ask, "How are you?"

"Oh, I'm actually doing pretty well. I've been feeling better lately and getting some stuff done around the house."

"That's wonderful, Mom!" I say, thinking, *This is actually going well.* "What have you been doing?"

"Well, Tommy, that's the reason I called. I wanted to let you know that I've moved a bunch of your old stuff out of your room and into the garage."

"OK," I reply tentatively, my optimism beginning to fade. "Why?"

"Well, you see, Tommy, I need the room for a young woman who's been staying with me and helping me out around the house."

I say nothing to this, and she continues, "Her name is Tonya and she's Trevor's sister. You remember Trevor, don't you?"

Trevor? Trevor? "Vaguely, Mom," is the best I can do.

Mom sighs, her disappointment in me clear when she says, "Oh, Tommy. I would have thought as a priest, not to mention one who's about to become a husband, that you'd be a better listener. Well, maybe you listen to everyone except your mother—after all, I'm only the one who carried you through the hottest Florida summer on record when the air conditioner went out."

"I know, Mom," I say, staring at the ceiling. "I just have a lot on my mind. Now, who is Trevor again?"

"He's the sweet young man who brought me home from the hospital a few weeks ago. Well, he has been such a godsend, taking me to the grocery store and cooking for me and helping me go through a bunch of Sonya's old things."

"Uh-huh," I say, not liking where this is going.

"Well, he said he didn't like the idea of me living alone. So he suggested that Tonya come and stay with me and help me out around the house."

"How thoughtful of him," I mutter.

"Wasn't it though? Oh, Tommy, Trevor is just so wonderful like that. You could learn a lot from him."

"Sure, Mom. Sure," I say, silently wishing I'd get a call and have to rush out to the hospital to give last rites to a bus accident.

"Anyway, it turns out she's a nurse but isn't working right now because there's a nursing glut and she wants someone who's just getting their start to have a chance. Isn't that sweet?"

A nursing glut? In Florida? When has that ever happened? "So," I say, "she's going to move into my room?"

"Uh-huh. She and Trevor have been working night and day up there, making it into a cozy little nest for her. He really is the most devoted brother. I mean they get along better than any two siblings I've ever seen. I just wish you could have loved Sonya the way he does her. He's been in and out visiting with her so much that I finally gave him a key."

All of this sounds alarm bells in my mind. Carefully, I say. "Mom, do you think it's a good idea to take in strangers like this?"

"But they're not strangers, Tommy," she whines in that nasally tone of hers that sets my teeth on edge. "Not really, anyway. You remember my friend from high school, Shirley Chessworth? Her father owned the drug store?"

I don't remember her but, OK.

"We were talking last night and it turns out that she is Trevor and Tonya's great-aunt."

"Mom," I say, afraid I'm being drawn into The Twilight Zone again—and not the one with Rod Serling, "how did you find this out? How did Shirley Chessworth come up anyway?"

"We were going through my Bellamy Senior High School Yearbook—they were really interested in it, you see—and I saw a picture of Shirley and Trevor said to Tonya, 'Hey, isn't that Great-Aunt Shirley?' and Tonya said 'You know, I think it is.' I asked them if they knew if their great-aunt's father owned the drug store and wouldn't you know it, he did!"

"Amazing, Mom."

"Isn't it? Anyway, I wanted to try to get in touch with her, you know, for old times sake, but it turns out she's dead. In fact, all her family is gone, except Trevor and Tonya."

"Oh, that's a shame, Mom. What happened?"

No, I don't know why I ask what happened. It's just there is always a point in a phone call with Mom that I just give in to the insanity.

"It is a tragic story," Mom says, gleefully mournful, "but one I've always been warned about. Their family was having a big reunion down around Winter Park. Well, poor Shirley—she never was real bright, really as dumb as a post—she made potato salad that morning and not only did she not chill it first, but she made her own mayonnaise with raw eggs. Then she just piled that whole big bowl in her car and went to church. Well, you know they were some kind of Pentecostal. I swear, I don't know how those women stay so big with all the jumping around they do in church every Sunday. Do you know, Tommy?"

"Why would I know, Mom?"

"Oh, I just thought they taught you about other denominations in seminary. Anyway, that potato salad with those raw eggs sat out in her car until she got to that reunion and a bunch of them ate it and the next day, the old ones were shouting with their maker. Fortunately, Trevor and Tonya weren't there but Trevor did say that they probably would have been OK anyway since he doesn't like potato salad. Isn't that funny, Tommy? Just like you."

"Hilarious, Mom," I say, taking a moment to offer up my current suffering for the Pentecostal souls in Purgatory who will never again be able to enjoy the taste of fresh potato salad.

Unless, of course, there is potato salad in heaven.

Which I highly doubt.

Twenty

As I've said on more than one occasion, Monday is a priest's traditional day off. And after the weekend I had, no one would fault me for hopping in my car—or hopping on my bicycle, just in case Martin Maycord is watching—and riding out into the mountains to enjoy some peace, quiet, and fall foliage.

But there are things more important than my own comfort. Hurting members of my flock hurt just as much on a Monday as any other day. While Deacon Derek can—and regularly does—handle sick calls and hospital visits, there's one person I need to check on myself.

Which is why I'm at Myerton General this morning around 10 a.m., sitting with Bridget Davis while her son Terry undergoes another surgery to repair the damage done to his face by his father.

After I give her communion, she says quietly, "Everyone has been so nice since it happened. I think each member of the Ladies of Charity has been by to stay with Terry while I ran home to take care of his brother and sister."

"Are you still staying with him?"

She nods. "I'm scared to leave his side, Father. I know what the doctors say, that he's recovering well and he should be able to go home in another week, but I'm just so afraid that something will happen if I'm not here."

I take her hand to comfort her. "Bridget, this wasn't your fault."

She begins to cry. "Everyone keeps saying that," she wails. "But if I had just been strong enough to leave a long time ago, Terry wouldn't be in this hospital." She shakes her head. "But I wasn't. I wasn't strong enough. And Terry will never forgive me."

"Yes, he will," I say, putting my arm around her as she cries softly. "You're his mother, and sons have an infinite capacity to forgive their mothers."

OK, definitely a case of do as I say, not as I do.

"Can I tell you something, Father?"

"Of course."

She sits up and sniffles. Looking away from me, she says, "About a month ago, I decided I'd had enough. Enough of the drinking. Enough of him blaming me for the accident. Enough of him hitting me. So, late one night, he was passed out drunk. I had been sneaking clothes and other things out of the house, putting them in the trunk of the car—he never drove, it wasn't a problem. So I told the kids to get dressed and carry their shoes. We snuck out of the house and I got them in the car. I was all set to leave, drive to my parents in Virginia."

Quietly, I ask, "Why didn't you? You know, the Church teaches that separation, even a civil divorce, is appropriate in abuse situations."

"I knew that," she says, "I'd found one of those websites, 'Canon Law for Dummies,' or something like that, done by someone who's an actual canon lawyer for the Archdiocese of Miami. Someone else had asked the question, and the lawyer told her that. No, I didn't leave because of my pride. My foolish, foolish pride."

She digs through her purse, probably for a tissue, so I produce the handkerchief Anna insists I always keep with me for occasions like this.

"I imagined myself having to walk up to my parents' door," she whispers, "and tell them I'd left Rusty. That my marriage was over. And, I'd have to tell them the reason. And I knew what they'd say. You see, Father, my parents—especially my mother—never liked Rusty. They didn't want me to marry him. I did it just to rebel against them, to assert my independence. Well, twelve years later, I was running back home with my tail between my legs. And that, I couldn't stand."

"So you stayed," I say.

She nods. "If I had known what was going to happen, Father . . ." She doesn't finish, but instead begins to cry again.

I knew what she was going to say. I've heard it hundreds of times in the confessional. "If I had known" x, y, or z was going to happen, "I wouldn't have done it," or "I would have done things differently."

"I just don't understand, Father," she suddenly says through gritted teeth. "We were a happy family. Rusty was a good husband, a good father. He never raised his voice, much less his fist, to me or the children. Why did God let all this happen to us? What sin did we commit? Is he punishing us?"

The eternal question, another one I've heard a thousand times as a priest. It's a question I asked myself a lot about a year ago, during my crisis of faith that almost led me to break my vows and leave a priesthood I no longer cared about.

It took a lot of prayer, even after Helen helped me turn things around, for me to come up with an answer.

"Bridget, the fact of the matter is, yes, God allowed this to happen. But not because He's mean, or He's punishing you for a sin you've committed. Really, the very fact that bad things happen is a consequence of living in a fallen world. But, God allows these trials for reasons we may never know, at least here on Earth. Or looking back later, we'll see that what happened to us resulted in some good things. Now, I'm not saying this to minimize your pain, or Terry's pain, or your anger at God."

"I'm not angry at God," she says emphatically.

"But if you are, that's OK, too. I've been angry with God, not all that long ago in fact."

"I'm not angry," she says with less conviction. "I just feel . . . abandoned."

"But even in this, he hasn't abandoned you," I say with a smile. "He's here with you. He's with Terry. He's here when someone comes to visit you, or brings a meal to the house, or watches your kids. See, all the people in the parish who love and care about you and your family are being used by Him to show you His love, to show you His presence. So when you feel like God's left you, call one of us. Call me. Call Anna. Call Miriam."

She takes a deep breath. "Thank you, Father. It's hard for me to admit, but I don't know how I'm going to do this alone."

"The good news is," I say, placing a comforting hand on her shoulder, "you don't have to."

We sit quietly for a moment when I hear an unfamiliar cell phone chime. I know it's not mine, but Bridget digs her phone out of her purse.

"Oh," she says. "It's Rusty."

"What does he say?"

She shakes her head as she reads. "Oh, same old thing. Says he's sorry. Says he knows he needs to stay away. Says he knows he made a huge mistake. Says he's going to make everything right before he comes home."

Without responding, she puts the phone back in her purse.

"Do you know where he is?"

"Not exactly," she says. "He says he's staying with cousins in Minnesota. He didn't say where and frankly, I didn't ask. I told him about the restraining order, said Mae Trent helped me with that, and that I was getting the kids the help they needed. I also told him there was a warrant out for his arrest."

"What did he say to that?"

"Nothing at first. A few days later, he said he would fix everything so we could be a family again."

"Well," I say, "I hope he's serious."

She takes a deep breath. "I hope he is, too. I still love him. God help me, I still love him."

***

After the Noon Mass, I decide to go to the police station to take Helen to lunch. She's in her office talking to Dan and as I walk in, I hear him say, "So that's what his parents said. They're obviously devastated, but they said that he'd borrowed money from them on several occasions, each time insisting that 'he'd be in big trouble' if he didn't pay up. I have his laptop and Gladys is dumping it now, along with his phone."

"Anything so far?" Helen asks, as she motions for me to take a seat on the couch.

"Actually, yes. One number that he's gotten a lot of calls from recently popped for a bookie in Baltimore, Grisham Clay."

"That must be the bookie Nate mentioned to us, Helen," I say.

Dan looks at me and says, "Yeah, Helen told me about your conversation with Nate. I swear, that guy can get some crazy ideas sometimes. Really wonder what Gladys sees in him."

Turning back to Helen, he continues, "I have contacted Mr. Clay and invited him to come in for a chat. He says that he will be glad to and that he has nothing to hide. He also says his lawyer will be with him."

"He must be doing pretty well if he has an attorney on retainer and is able to pay him his going rate to drive out here from Baltimore," Helen comments.

"He seems to be a pretty big fish in the pond, though I haven't found any organized crime connections yet."

"What about connections with violence?"

"So far, nothing significant. It seems that a few of his clients have been known to show up at hospitals in the Greater Baltimore area with mysteriously broken bones. But they always insist that they fell down a flight of stairs."

Turning back to me, Dan asks pleasantly, "Speaking of which, Father, how is your case coming?"

This catches me off guard and I reply, "My case? What case? Dan, I have not interfered with anything in . . . well, weeks."

"Calm down, Tom," Dan says with a grin. "I am talking about the situation with the Davises. Helen told me you are keeping up with Bridget, as you should as her priest. But since her husband also assaulted the hell out of their son and has a warrant out on his ass, I thought you might be trying to get her to help us locate him."

"I wish I could. Lord knows I've tried, but she insists she doesn't know where he is and doesn't want to, as long as he stays away from where they are. Just that he's somewhere in Minnesota. She got a text from him while I was with her at the hospital this morning. He insists that he won't bother them, that he promises to fix everything so they can be a family again. So that's hopeful."

"Hopeful for an eventual return to family life, yes," Helen reminds me, "But not until after he's done some serious jail time for what he did to that boy."

"Obviously," I agree. "But if there were some way that he could be sent to a rehab facility instead of prison, wouldn't that be better for the family?"

"No," Helen says with surprising ferocity. "Tom, I worked with juvenile victims in D.C. for a year. It was hands down the worst year of my career, but I learned something. Men who get drunk and hurt children, even teenagers, do not quit. I'm sure there are cases out there of one or two men who did, just like I'm sure there were saints who could levitate. But I cannot base my decisions about humanity on the likelihood of either."

"OK," I say, "I bow to your judgment, at least on this." I smile at Dan and ask, "How am I doing?"

"Not bad, Father. I think you're on your way to making a good husband, although you need to learn to bow to her judgment on everything if you want any sort of happiness and peace in life."

We both laugh while Helen scowls and mutters, "I'm glad to see you are both learning the great truth of the universe—that women are always right."

"Yes, dear," I say.

"Yes, Chief," Dan says.

"Now, back to work," she says, pointing at her detective. "When is Clay getting here?"

"This afternoon about 3 p.m, so you two have time to ride to Sprockets and get some snacks to enjoy while you sit behind the glass and watch me interview him."

"Dan," I say, "I was not planning on—"

"Letting me know you were there? Look, Tom, I know how little the church pays you and it's a cheap date. Enjoy."

"Shall we?" I say to Helen.

Standing up and hefting her tote bag over her shoulder, she says, "OK, Dan, you're in charge. Make sure Gladys doesn't try to stage a coup while I'm gone."

A short time later, we're in Helen's car on our way to Sprockets. "Hey," I say, "Why is Dan in such a good mood all of a sudden?"

"He hasn't said exactly," Helen chuckles, "but based on past experience, I suspect that Miriam has hit the third trimester mark. Apparently, based on some veiled references he made to me one time, she feels really good and especially affectionate during this time."

"Oh, I see," I say.

"Yeah. So I always allow more leeway for coming in late, and he remains in a very good mood."

"Hmm. I'd say I wish Miriam were pregnant more often but that seems nearly impossible."

***

Promptly at 3 p.m, Helen and I are sitting behind the glass in the viewing room, waiting to watch Dan interrogate Grisham Clay.

There are a number of things that strike me as odd from the very moment Clay enters the room. For one thing, he doesn't look like a bookie. Now, I know that you cannot trust a book—or in this case, a bookie—by its cover, but I expected someone who was either overly gregarious or ominously taciturn. Clay is neither. Nor is he dressed in the cheap suit, probably some variety of plaid, that I would associate with a bookie. Instead, he appears to be about my age, with slightly graying hair, obviously well cut and maintained. His suit is not extremely high end, but neither is it cheap. He has a friendly face that reveals no sort of discomfort with his surroundings, and I get the feeling that he is pretty comfortable wherever he finds himself.

I would not be the least bit surprised to see him at Mass on a Sunday or a Knights of Columbus fish fry on Friday night. I don't think he would stand out at either.

When Dan comes in, Clay stands and shakes his hand, introducing him cordially to his lawyer. The three men sit down and Dan begins, "Thanks for agreeing to see me, Mr. Clay, and for traveling here from Baltimore."

"Not a problem at all, Detective," Clay says with a pleasant, almost disarming smile. "I have family in the area, and I'll be joining them for dinner later."

"I'm glad we did not inconvenience you, then." Dan pauses before getting down to business. "Mr. Clay, the reason I've asked you here today is to try to learn anything I can about Larry Daniels, who died Saturday night under some rather mysterious circumstances."

"Yes, I was saddened to hear that when you called, both for personal and professional reasons."

Clay's lawyer shoots him a warning look as Dan asks, "So you knew Larry in both capacities?"

"I did, indeed. He has been a client of mine since right after he turned 18. He was a good kid who was still learning his limits, but that is the case with most young men his age, don't you think, Detective?"

"Perhaps, but most young men his age do not become involved in illegal gambling."

"Who said anything about anything illegal?" Clay asks as his lawyer gives him a warning tap on the arm. "I only deal with legal adults who want to wager money within the legal confines set down by the State of Maryland. And as far as the other part of your comment, that is actually incorrect. Most young men do place bets at some point in their lives, though you are right when you say that, typically, those bets are in no way illegal."

Dan obviously decides to avoid challenging the legality of Clay's business dealings in general in order to focus his attention on the bookie's involvement with Larry. "OK, so you admit that Larry placed bets with you. How was his luck?"

Clay shrugs and says, "More or less like everyone else's. You win a few and you lose a few."

"It is my understanding that Larry has been losing more than a few in recent weeks."

"Well, Detective, as I said earlier, he needed to learn his limits."

"And you were teaching him those limits?" Dan asks evenly.

Before Clay can answer, his attorney speaks up and says, "Don't answer that, Gris." Then turning to Dan, he says firmly, "My client is a well-respected businessman in Baltimore and I do not like what you are implying."

"I am not implying anything," Dan says pleasantly. "I would assume a mature businessman like Mr. Clay would have policies pertaining to dealing with young losers like Larry."

"I would never refer to any of my clients as losers, Detective," Clay says sanctimoniously.

"But he has lost money to you, right? And was in pretty deep debt to you? At least, that's what he told his parents."

The lawyer speaks up again, insisting, "My client does not have to disclose personal information about his clients and their financial situations. That would be privileged information."

"OK, then," Dan says, leaning his arms on the table. "Let me ask you a hypothetical question. I understand that this has nothing to do with reality, but just suppose someone was in significant debt to you, how would you handle it?"

The lawyer starts to object but Clay waves him off saying, "In complete honesty, Detective, that would depend on a number of factors. But for the sake of this hypothetical situation, let's just say that it was a young man who was into me for less than $1,000. If he did not pay up, the first thing that would happen is that he would not be allowed to bet anymore. I would attempt to contact him by phone, email, and text. If none of that worked, I would send an associate to talk to him at his home. Talk, Detective, not rough up or harm in any way. If that failed to produce results, I would send the same associate to his place of business to talk to him. In almost every case, this would be the final step because, honestly, nothing is more upsetting to a gambler than having his family or co-workers find out what he's up to. But in the rare cases where I still have gotten no results, I would pass the word to every bookie in the tri-state area that he was a deadbeat, and he would not be able to place another bet in this area for the rest of his life."

"So, you are telling me you would not hurt someone who stiffed you?"

"Not a young guy, and not for less than $1,000, which, by the way, is what Larry owed me."

He pauses for a minute and then continues, "Look, Detective. I'm a businessman. A kid like Larry is good for a million dollars or more across a lifetime, but only if he stays alive. His friends are good for that much, too, but not if they hear my name bandied about at his funeral so, to answer the question you are dying to ask, I did not kill that kid and I know nothing about who did."

"I assume you have an alibi."

"Indeed I do. I was at the Ravens game. They lost big, I won big, but I had seats in the skybox and Mr. Lawson here will provide you with the names and phone numbers of everyone who was waiting on me that night. I'm a big tipper. It makes me memorable."

Lawson hands Dan a sheet of paper and announces, "I believe we are done, here, Detective. My contact info is at the top of that page. Please let me know if we can be of any further assistance."

They leave and Dan comes into the observation room, shaking his head. "So, what do you think, Helen?"

"I have to say, Dan, he didn't look guilty to me. What about you?"

"Me neither. If this alibi checks out, and I'm sure it will, then I think we need to start looking elsewhere."

"Yeah," I say quietly, looking at the now empty room. "Elsewhere."

Twenty-One

That night, Helen and I make dinner at the Rectory.

Since we both like to cook, it's an activity that we can do together that has nothing to do with crime or criminals. Cooking together is fun, something we enjoy doing, and relaxes both of us.

"You're adding too many onions," I say at one point.

"You always say that," she retorts.

"You always add too many onions."

I'm chopping vegetables for our chicken stir-fry when she peers over my shoulder and says, "You're not cutting them the same size."

"You always say that when we stir-fry," I pout.

"Well, if you don't want me to say that, then try cutting the vegetables the same size next time."

"I'm sorry you find my knife skills lacking," I say, "but I was the best chopper in my home economics class in high school."

She looks at me. "How did I miss this? You took home ec?"

"Uh-huh," I say. "Junior year. My coq au vin won a ribbon. Also, I was the only guy in class, so—" I waggle my eyebrows.

She hits me with a towel.

Jealous.

Once the preparation of the meal is out of the way, we have the same discussion we always have.

"Shall I set the table?" she asks.

"Oh, not tonight," I say, with a pained expression on my face. "Let's just eat on the couch. It's so much more comfortable, and Anna's not here so we can prop our feet up on the coffee table."

"All right," Helen says with a sigh. "But once we're married, we're eating at the table every night like civilized people."

"Absolutely," I say, without really meaning it and suspecting Helen doesn't, either.

So an hour later, we're sitting on the couch eating and talking. By mutual agreement, the TV stays off until Jeopardy.

"You mean you really don't think there's anything to the gambling angle?" I ask Helen.

"No. Clay's alibi checks out, and he confirms that Larry owed him about $800. We can't find any evidence that Larry placed bets with any other bookies who may not have Clay's long-term business strategy."

I shake my head. "So where do you go now?"

Helen shrugs. "We'll start over, look at Larry again, see if we can find anyone in his life who may have had a motive. The thing is, from everything I've heard, except for his gambling problem, Larry was a pretty normal, salt of the earth kind of guy. Everyone we talk to speaks highly of him. No one can think of anyone who would want to harm him."

She shoves a forkful of rice in her mouth, then says, "What makes it even more difficult to figure out who might have killed him, of course, is that he wasn't even supposed to be where he was."

I look at Helen with surprise. "What do you mean?"

"I mean, Larry was a last minute replacement for Martin," Helen says. "He had an emergency at the hospital, so they needed a wolf. Larry was the only one who could fit in the costume."

I stare at the blank TV screen. "I hadn't thought of that. But that's right. Martin was supposed to play The Big Bad Wolf. I mean, he should have been wearing the wolf costume that night. Not Larry."

I sit back, aware that Helen is staring at me. "What?" she finally asks

I blink and look at her. "What, what?"

"You've got something, don't you?"

I shrug. "Maybe. Follow me here for a minute. So we've been assuming whoever stabbed the man in the wolf costume was going after Larry, right?"

"Right," Helen says.

"But for that to be true," I say, warming quickly to my train of thought, "the killer would have to know that Larry was in the costume. And according to Gladys, he was a last-minute replacement."

Helen nods, a smile appearing on her face. "For Martin Maycord."

"Exactly," I say. "So what if the killer stabbed The Big Bad Wolf thinking they were killing Martin?"

Helen takes a deep breath. "If that's true, Tom," she says gravely, "then Martin is still in danger." She takes out the phone. "This is Chief Parr," she says. "I want an unmarked car in front of the Maycord residence. I also want an officer covering the entrance to the hospital."

Hanging up, she calls another number. "Hi, Joe, it's Helen," she says. "Listen, is Dr. Maycord working tonight? . . . OK, can you give your people a heads up to keep an eye out for any suspicious looking people, particularly anyone asking to see Dr. Maycord? . . . Thanks."

"You really think Martin is in that much danger?" I ask.

"It's just a precaution right now, in case you're right," she says. "Which, by the way, I think you are."

I sigh and shake my head. "I wish I weren't."

"Now all we need to do is figure out who would want to kill Martin. I mean, he has had longer to accumulate enemies than Larry had. The poor kid was only 21."

"Well," I say, finishing off the rest of my stir-fry, "the obvious suspect would be someone who lost a relative that they think Martin should've been able to save."

"That's one possibility, but Tom, Martin owns several rehab facilities and where there's rehab, there's drugs, and where there's drugs, there's organized crime."

"Do you think it could have anything to do with Bethany's death, or with his brother-in-law?" I ask.

"I don't think so," Helen says, shaking her head. "The Feds rolled-up the operation his brother-in-law was a part of. I guess it could have something to do with that, but stabbing a man wearing a wolf costume in a haunted house is not quite their style."

She stretches. "Anyway, I'll talk to Dan in the morning, probably have a talk with Martin, see what he has to say about possible enemies."

"Speaking of Dan," I say with a grin. "I can hardly wait to see what Miriam has him dress up as this year. He was hilarious last year as that tree with all the kids running around him dressed as little forest animals."

"Oh," Helen says casually, "he'll be a farmer this year."

"How do you know?"

"Because Miriam only makes new costumes when she's not pregnant. When she's pregnant, and showing, everyone in the family, except Dan, goes as a pumpkin. Dan dresses as a farmer and, voila!"

"That is really wonderful," I say, smiling. "They really are an incredible family."

"They are," Helen says, wistfully. "Tom, when we marry, will you consider us a family, even though we'll never have kids?"

"Of course," I say, wrapping my arms around her. "Families begin on the day of the wedding, not the first baptism."

"Thank you for that," she says, placing her palm gently on my chest and letting her pinky slide between the buttons of my shirt.

I am suddenly aware that Anna is not here, and am about to say that I'll get dessert when she purrs, "Tom, I love the idea of us being a family. But there are certain aspects of that that we don't *have* to wait on, you know?"

Damn, I think, *I should have seen this coming*. I've been aware that my own, shall we say, physical desire for Helen has slowly increased as the wedding gets closer.

It would only make sense that Helen would have the same feelings.

I know I should stand up, move away, go get pie or a cold drink, but I figure my self-control can tolerate a few more seconds of her heavenly touch. I clear my throat and say, "Well, I suppose that is true. But it obviously depends, Helen, on what you mean by 'certain aspects.'"

She's lightly purring in my ear now, and I am sure that I need to get off this couch and maybe take a lap or two or seven around the block.

But she pours cold water on all my urges by saying, "I was just thinking about our Halloween costumes."

"What?" I asy, jumping back so quickly that a button pops off my shirt. "What the hell, Helen? You were serious about that?"

"Of course I was," she says. "Did you think I was kidding?"

"Part of me was, yes. I mean, you know I hate dressing up."

"No, I know you used to," she says defiantly, dropping to the floor to look for the button. "I hoped that you had moved past that, especially after what you just said about the Conways."

"Helen," I say, now on my knees also looking for the button, "they have children."

"And we never will. Does that mean that we can't have fun on Halloween?"

I know that never being a mother haunts her, that it is a wound that never heals, but I also know that she's pretty ruthless when she wants to win an argument. I am trying to look her in the eye when she begins to laugh and then says seriously, "Give me that shirt. I have a sewing kit in my tote bag and I'll sew that button back on before Anna gets the idea I was trying to tear your clothes off while she was gone."

I look at her, horrified, and say, "No, Helen, I don't have anything on under this."

She rolls her eyes. "Tom, I have seen you with your shirt off before and while I do find you very attractive, I promise that the brief sight of your unnaturally pale chest will not drive me into uncontrollable passion."

"When have you seen me without a shirt?" I ask, ignoring the remark about my chest.

"Uh, let's see. In Bellamy when you were in the hospital. In Myerton after Martin sewed you up. In the pool at the July 4th Picnic. Last week when you were pretending to work out at the police department gym."

"That last was only for a moment, until I could change into a clean shirt. And what do you mean, pretend?"

"My point is that I could have had the button back on the shirt and the shirt back on you if you weren't arguing."

I stand and head upstairs. "Where are you going?" Helen asks.

"To change shirts. I'll throw this one down to you."

I can hear her eyes roll again as she follows me to the base of the stairs. I decide to take this opportunity to use the bathroom before taking my shirt off and throwing it downstairs to her, calling as I do, "I hope you can fix this before Anna gets home. I wouldn't want her to think we were up to anything."

I am buttoning up a badly wrinkled but still moderately clean shirt as I come down the stairs. There, on the landing, are a wide-eyed Gladys and an obviously very embarrassed Mae Trent.

I feel myself turning fifty shades of red as I say awkwardly, "Helen is sewing a button back on my shirt. I went upstairs, by myself, to change so she could have the shirt."

"Well, obviously," Gladys says.

I am completely caught off guard by this. My surprise must register on my face because Gladys adds, "What, do you think we don't have enough faith in you and Mom not to jump to the worst possible conclusion?"

"Er, no," I stammer, finishing buttoning the shirt, "no, of course not. But what are you doing here? I didn't hear the doorbell?"

"It was unlocked so I let myself in," Gladys says.

"I told her we should have knocked," Mae says, "since you and Helen were—on a date?"

"And I told her," Gladys says, "that the only action you two were probably up to was a wild game of Risk. By the way, Dad, have you won yet?"

"No," calls Helen from the living room. "I'm the Queen of the World!"

I shake my head and say to Gladys, "Listen, sweetie, I'm always glad to see you—you too, Mae—but again, why are you here?"

Gladys looks serious as she rolls past me and into the living room, "Mom, we need to talk to you. Something important has come up."

"Now, Gladys," Mae says as she walks after her, "I really think—"

"Mae, trust me!" Gladys says. "We have to tell Mom about this."

Helen bites off the thread and hands me the shirt, the button firmly in place. Folding her hands, she asks, "OK. I'm listening."

Mae sits on the end of the couch, Gladys staying by her. "Mom, Dad," she says, taking a deep breath, "Mae was just reminding me that Martin was supposed to be in that costume the night that Larry was killed."

We nod our heads and Helen says, "Yes, Tom and I were just thinking about that ourselves. I've got hospital security keeping an eye out, and there are unmarked cars in front of the hospital and his house, just in case."

"Oh," Mae says quietly, shaking her head, "I don't think that's necessary."

Helen continues, "I'm going to talk to Martin about it more tomorrow, to try to get a feel for who might want to harm him."

Gladys looks at Mae. "Tell her what you told me," she says quietly.

Mae looks down as she says sorrowfully, "Helen, I think I might know."

We look at her as she continues, "A few months ago, before I even met Martin, I dated a guy named Dale Riddle. We only went out a few times, but he was very possessive and I told him pretty quickly that I wasn't interested in continuing our relationship. I thought everything was fine. I mean, he is one of those guys who says he's going to win you back, but you know a lot of guys say that, so I didn't pay a whole lot of attention. Anyway, after I broke it off, I didn't hear from him."

"Did that change?" Helen asks.

Mae nods, biting her lip. "Last week, after Martin and I got engaged, Dale started texting me. At first it wasn't too bad, he just said things like I was making a mistake and he thought that I'd be happier with him. He said Martin was too old for me and that kind of stuff but, again, I just more or less ignored him. But in the past few days he's gotten a lot more aggressive in his messages."

"What do you mean by that?" Helen asks.

Mae takes her phone out of her pocket and reluctantly hands it to Helen. "I guess it would be better if you just read them for yourself," the young woman says quietly.

Helen looks at the screen and I take the opportunity of sitting close enough to her to look over her shoulder to see:

Mae, you know I'm the only guy for you. I know that doctor fella makes a lot of money but there's more to life than just money. I can't believe you're such a golddigger. I already tried once to stop this. Next time I'll get it right.

"What do you think he means by that, Mae?" Helen asks.

Mae is nearly in tears now and shaking her head as she says, "I don't know. I'd like to be able to say that Dale is not a violent guy, but he kind of is. I mean, he was always trying to get me to go hunting, and I don't have a problem with anyone who hunts, but it's just not something I'm interested in."

"What else can you tell us about him?"

"Well, he never wanted to do things with my family. He always said that they thought they were better than everyone else, which I always told him was far from the case, but he insisted that they looked down upon him and his family because they didn't have much money." May laughs at this as she says, "I kept telling him, 'Listen, most of my clothes in my entire life have either been hand-me-downs from my cousins or bought from the thrift store.' But he just insisted that people look down on his family. He took me to meet them like on our second date, and I'm sure they're nice and all, but all they seemed to want to talk about was how everyone else had it better than they did and how the government was out to get them and stuff like that. As I say, I don't want to judge anyone but it just made me uncomfortable."

"And you say he's been pretty unhappy that you were dating Martin?"

"Oh, yeah, he insists that I'm only interested in Martin because Martin has lots of money, which, I mean I guess he does. I don't really know. It's not something we've ever really talked about."

I furrow my brow at this. They haven't talked about money? Between this and the issue of children, maybe things aren't as good as I thought they were.

I may have my job cut out for me—and they're both in for a rude awakening when they begin to look at what life together will really look like.

"But Helen," Mae says earnestly, "you've got to believe me. I want to marry Martin because he's wonderful and good and kind and generous, and loves not just me but my family. I wouldn't care if he didn't have a penny to his name and we were looking at living in a one-room shack."

Helen smiles and pats her gently as she says, "I have no doubt about that, Mae. It sounds like Dale is the one with the problem, not you. So, based on this text, do you think he may have been the one who stabbed Larry, thinking he was Martin?"

"Oh, no, I don't think that at all," she says, shaking her head. "I would never think that about anyone. Gladys is the one who said that she thought we had to tell you about this. I didn't want to."

She looks at Gladys pleadingly as Gladys takes her hand firmly and says, "Mae, you've been blessed to have been around really good people for most of your life. And I know that you've had a lot of training in all the bad that is out there. But I've seen it firsthand. And I can tell you that anyone, especially a man—no offense, Dad—who wants something from you can make you believe whatever he wants you to."

Mae takes a deep breath. "Gladys, sometimes you seem so jaded, but I know you have a good reason to be. I guess you could be right about Dale."

She turns to Helen. "So to answer your question, I just don't know. I certainly would never have thought he was someone who could kill a human being, or I wouldn't have been dating him. But I suppose—I mean I guess he would know how to do it if that's what he wanted to do."

"What do you mean by that, Mae?" I ask.

She sighs again and says softly, "Well, you know I told you he's a hunter, and I have cousins who hunt and fish. They like to talk about what they've killed, like all hunters and fishermen do. But looking back, Dale always got kind of this creepy gleam in his eye when he talked about killing a deer. I mean, he would go into a lot of gory detail, like he wanted to either shock or impress me, I never knew which. He would talk about cutting its throat and all the blood and stuff."

She laughs wryly at this. "I guess that's one thing I like about Martin. He's more interested in saving lives than taking them. Oh, he's told me about his wilderness survival weekends and the things that he would kill and eat but it's not like he did it just for fun or that he wanted to impress me—though he did, at least a little bit. But it was more about overcoming the elements than anything else."

She looks down her hands and says, "I guess I'm not making a lot of sense. The bottom line is, I suppose Dale could have killed Larry if he'd wanted to. I just find it hard to believe that he would want to, not a human being"

"OK, Mae," Helen says gently, "You've done everything you need to do. Dan and I will take it from here. But we will need his address and phone number. Can you text that to me?"

"Sure," Mae says, taking her phone back from Helen. "What will happen now? I mean, you won't just run out and arrest him, will you?"

"Of course not," Helen says cheerfully. "Chances are he's not even guilty. However, we need to talk to him, to see if he has an alibi for where he was the night of the murder."

Mae and Gladys both frown at this. Mae's expression looks forlorn but Gladys' defiant.

"I can tell you right now, Mom," Gladys says firmly, "that he doesn't have an alibi. In fact, Nate saw him prowling around the house after we closed. He claimed he was just looking around, that he'd never been inside such a fancy place before. Dominic came up about then and Dale looked at him and said something like, 'I guess your sister's looking forward to living in a big house like this, looking down on the rest of us like the bitch she is.' Dominic lunged at him, but Nate grabbed him and told Dale to get out."

"And no one thought to tell me this, why?" Helen asks impatiently.

"Because we saw him leave the property. Nate followed him to his car and saw him peel off. Anyway, he'd never met Larry so we saw no connection."

"But obviously, he could have doubled back," I say. "There are plenty of back roads in that area. If he'd come back, no one would have seen him. He could even have left his car somewhere and walked through the woods to the back of the house."

Helen shoots me a look but keeps smiling as she turns back to Mae and says softly, "Honey, I'm so sorry. I have to admit it does not look good for Dale. But so far everything we have is circumstantial. Now you need to go home and get a good night's sleep. I know from personal experience that being friends with a genius who only needs four hours of sleep a night can be exhausting." She smiles at Gladys as she says this and then stands, walking with the girls to the door. They go on down the path to the driveway but Helen pauses as they make their way out and says, "Tom, I need to go home, too. I'll talk to you tomorrow."

Standing on tiptoes, she kisses me tenderly on the cheek and nuzzles my ear for just a brief moment before whispering, "I love you, darling. Please pray. This may be about to get messy."

"I love you, too," I say, adding, "And I will."

Then, I complete our parting ritual by making the sign of the cross on her forehead and saying, "May God bless your going out and your coming in, may He keep you and those in your charge protected so that mercy and justice may be done throughout the land."

Twenty-Two

I am looking over the sick list when Helen calls, "Hey," she says, "What time are you going to the hospital?"

"About 3 p.m. Why?"

"Is there anyway we can leave right after Mass and I can go with you? Dan's car's in the shop, so he took mine up to Baltimore to pick up some evidence in that hit-and-run last month. Martin just called and says he's working the ER so he can't come to the station. I asked if it would be OK for me to come there and he said, 'Sure,' so I was hoping to catch a ride with you?"

"Of course," I say. "Any opportunity to spend time with you."

"Oh, Tom," she says sweetly, "you flatter me. Especially when you and I both know that the real reason is because you want to sit in on the interview."

"Helen," I say with mock sadness, "you cut me to the core!"

"Am I wrong?"

"Of course not, but you could at least pretend."

She laughs and says. "I'll just walk over for the Noon Mass and we can go from there."

"I'll count the hours until we meet again," I say dramatically.

"Oh, good grief," she mutters before hanging up.

I've no sooner returned to my list when Anna walks in waving a copy of this coming Sunday's parish bulletin. "Tom? What is this?" she says, placing it on my desk and pointing at a particular item.

I peer at what she's pointing at. "Well," I say, "it looks to me like that's the Mass intention for this Sunday, October 31."

"I know what it is," Anna says, "but why does it say Victoria Myer?"

I lean back in my chair and look up at her. "Because that's who I'm saying the Mass for."

"But why?"

"Why not?"

Anna opens her mouth to say something, then thinks better of it. Finally, she shakes her head. "You know, you're right. Why not say a Mass for her soul? Poor girl."

"Exactly," I say. "It probably won't register with most people. And if it does, I'll just explain."

Anna sits down and crosses her arms. "And what will you tell people if they ask you why you're saying a Mass for a ghost?"

"I'll say I'm not saying a Mass for a ghost. I'm saying a Mass for a holy soul in Purgatory, who died a tragic death, purportedly by her own hand, and is in need of our prayers."

"You're not afraid of what people might think?" Anna asks.

"No," I say, shaking my head. "I'm a priest. I'm saying a Mass for a departed soul. End of story."

She nods and says, "OK, then." Anna stands up and begins to walk out, but she stops. Turning around, she says, "You've come a long way, you know that?"

I frown. "What do you mean?"

"Just this," she says with a smile. "When you came here the first time, I knew this was the last place you wanted to be. When you came back at the Archbishop's request, you accepted the assignment after Father Leonard's arrest out of a sense of duty. But your heart wasn't in it."

I swallow. "I'm not proud of that," I say quietly.

"You were suffering. We all saw it. We just didn't know what to do about it. Then, whatever happened in Bellamy, whatever happened between you and Helen, when you came back, I knew you were going to be all right," she whispers. "And I knew it was because of her. That's what I told Walter when he asked for my opinion—that you could become a fine priest if given the chance. If given the opportunity to have a wife. To have Helen."

I kiss the top of her head. "We are so grateful to you, Anna," I whisper. "For everything."

Anna nods and straightens her shoulders. She lifts her chin and says, "Well, you have a Mass to prepare for, then hospital visits."

"Yes," I say. "Helen's going with me."

"Oh? On your visits?"

I hesitate before saying, "Well, not exactly."

***

We get to Martin's office at about 1:30 p.m. Knowing that he could be called away at any moment, Helen gets right to the subject.

"Martin, have you ever met a guy named Dale Riddle?"

His eyes narrow and his voice takes on a growl as he says, "Once. Why?"

Not answering Martin's question, Helen asks, "When?"

Martin leans back in his chair and says evenly, "The day after Mae and I announced our engagement."

"I see. How did you meet him?"

"He showed up at the house that Sunday evening. I was getting out of the car when he stopped me and introduced himself as 'someone with some special information about Mae Trent.' I told him to get lost, but he said if I wouldn't listen to him, he'd find someone that would, so I let him in the house. Aunt Louise and the girls were still at Mae's, talking about wedding plans. I had only come home early because I wanted to grab a nap before a night shift."

"So you let him in. What happened?" Helen asks.

"Helen," Martin says, "will you tell me what this is all about?"

"Martin," I say. "Just answer her questions. I'm sure Helen will tell you after she's done."

Martin looks at me, then nods. "All right," he says slowly. Turning his attention back to Helen, he says, "I did not invite him to sit down but instead gave him five minutes to say what he had to say."

"What did he say?"

Anger flashes in his eyes as he says with a clenched jaw, "He said Mae was a promiscuous gold-digger who had slept with every boy that she had ever met and that she was only 'playing the good girl' to get me to marry her so she could have my money."

Helen and I both exhale at the same time as she asks, "Then what happened?"

"Actually," Martin says with a slight smile, "I feel like I handled things extremely well. I only applied enough pressure to his esophagus to make him think he couldn't breathe instead of actually choking him, which was my first impulse. While I had his undivided attention, I told him he had three options. The first was that he could show me evidence to support what he was saying, in which case I would destroy it but not him. The second was, he could admit he was lying, in which case I would allow him to walk out of my house on his own power. The third was to stand by his story, without evidence, in which case he'd be carried from my house on a stretcher—alive, but in a world of hurt. He chose the second option. I then let him go, telling him that should he try to accuse me of any wrongdoing, I would certainly insist that Mae sue him for defamation of character and that I would spend every cent of my substantial income to make sure that he never had a penny to call his own again."

"And then?" I can't resist asking.

Helen is so caught up in the story that she doesn't even shoot me a look as Martin shrugs and says, "He left."

I feel let down as he takes a deep breath and then asks, "So, I've answered your questions, Helen. *Now* will you tell me why you are asking about that piece of shit?"

Helen says, "We know that you were supposed to be The Big Bad Wolf that night, and that Larry didn't get called in until that last minute."

"That's right. I got called in to deal with a particularly nasty farm accident."

"So," she says, "we are trying to determine if whoever killed Larry was actually after you."

"I see," he says, appearing thoughtful. "But how'd you learn about Dale in the first place?"

Helen and I look at each other and she says, "Gladys Finkelstein brought him to our attention."

Martin looks at both of us, then nods. "Oh, I see," he says. He seems to accept what Helen said, but his eyes remain sharp, like he doesn't believe he's getting the whole story. I remember some doctor character on TV once insisting that all patients lie, and I wonder if Martin's experience has taught him to spot questionable truths.

Taking my chances, I look at Helen and say quietly, "Helen, if you're finished, I need to talk to Martin alone for a minute."

She seems to understand what's going on and says, "Sure. I'll meet you in the car."

After she leaves, I look at Martin evenly and ask, "Did you tell Mae about this incident?"

"Of course not," Martin scoffs. "There was no reason to upset her, and I certainly did not want her to think that I believed that psychopath."

I take a deep breath and say, "Martin, there are actually a number of very good reasons why you should have told Mae. One is that this guy might tell his nasty tales around town. Another is that he might try to approach Mae herself, and she needs to be prepared for that. But the biggest reason is that you two are supposed to be building a life together and that involves sharing with each other, facing problems like this together. That is why God created marriage. If you plan to handle all the problems in the future on your own, then why do you want a wife?"

He seems to ponder this for a minute and then asks, not belligerently but in the tone of someone looking for information, "Do you and Helen share all your problems with each other?"

"No," I answer honestly. "The nature of our professions means that there are many problems that we have to bear alone. And, I have to admit, I kept things from Helen when we were first engaged because I felt I was protecting her. Likewise, she kept things from me for the same reason. But it was a mistake, and we are both working on doing better."

Martin looks thoughtful, then says, "Openness, frankness. Those weren't a high priority in my house. My parents kept a lot of secrets from each other. Some, I found out only recently."

"I suspect that it will be easier for Mae to be open with you than it will be for you to be honest with her, primarily because she is part of a large, caring family and you are more accustomed to living on your own. But Martin," I insist, looking him in the eye, "believe me when I say that you need to start now."

"All right," he says. "I'll take your word for it. I'll tell her tonight."

"Sounds good," I say. "Now, I'll let you get back to work."

"Thanks for this, Tom," he says, shaking my hand. "I know I have a lot of work to do to become the man Mae deserves, and I really am trying but, damn, the habits of a lifetime, you know?"

"Oh, yeah, buddy. I know better than you can imagine."

***

I get back to the car and say to Helen, "I need to call Mae when I get back to the Rectory."

"Don't bother," she says, "I already did."

I look at her, surprised, and she says, "Hey, I know I'm not a priest but I am someone who has dealt with trust issues—in fact still am dealing with—so I know what I'm talking about when I told her she needed to tell Martin about the texts."

"Do we have plans tonight?" I ask, driving back toward the police department.

"Not really. I figured I'd pick up something for dinner. Why?"

"Oh, nothing, really. I just think we need to be prepared for me to get a phone call from two love birds who are about to have their first big fight."

"I'll try to get off early," Helen says with a laugh.

Twenty-Three

Helen's at the Noon Mass on Wednesday and comes back to the sacristy while I'm hanging up my robes.

"Any news about Dale?" I ask.

"Yes and no," she replies guardedly.

"What does that mean?"

"Simply that I have news but not from him personally," she sighs. "He is not answering his phone. When I had Gladys ping it, it showed him at his parents' home. However, when I called them and asked to speak to him, they admitted that his phone was there but insisted he left early this morning without saying where he was going. I am thinking about going by there this afternoon to try to talk to them."

"Mind if I tag along?" I ask, pulling my suit coat on.

"I was going to ask if you could go with me, you know, to sort of smooth the way, get them to talk to me. I get the distinct impression that they don't trust the police. I have seen them at a few church functions, though, so I don't think they'd have a problem with you."

I shake my head as I say, "Helen, I've told you before. I will not use my position as a priest to help you gather evidence."

"Unless, you always add, it's a matter of life and death," she says gravely. "And Tom, this very well could be."

"In what way?"

"Well, if he was after Martin and failed, he might come after him again. I mean, I have someone watching his house and the hospital, but we can't keep that up forever. Besides, if Dale is the person we're looking for, and he's determined enough, I could have a hundred officers protecting Martin and Dale could still get him. No, I need to get to Dale so I can talk to him, and arrest him if necessary."

"OK," I say, reluctantly. "I'll go with you, and I'll encourage his parents to talk to you because it could either clear his name or keep other people from getting hurt. But I will not try to elicit information from them myself, or frame anything in terms of sin and morality. Is that good enough?"

"Yes," she says, kissing me lightly on the cheek, "Now, let's go before you change your mind."

***

The Riddles live on the edge of town is a smallish-sized farmhouse behind a tall wood fence. We pull up to the gate and I get out to open it, even as Helen calls them to let them know that we're coming in. Because of this warning, both the Riddle adults meet us outside on the front porch.

"Father," Mr. Riddle says without preamble, "you're welcome to come on in, but the Chief there is not."

This takes me aback and I am trying to think of what to say when he continues, "We know our rights in this family and we know that she cannot come in our home without a warrant."

Before I can say anything, Helen pipes up with a pleasant smile and says, "You're absolutely right, Mr. Riddle, and it does my heart good to hear you say that. Far too many people these days are ignorant of the law and it leads to nothing but trouble." Then she looks at me casually and says, "I do have a couple of questions for you, but if you'd like to talk to Father Tom here first, I'll be glad to wait in the car."

This obviously catches him off-guard and, after a short hesitation, Mr. Riddle says reluctantly, "No, I don't guess we have anything to talk to the Father about."

Mrs. Riddle pops up now and says softly, with the voice of someone rarely allowed to speak, "Jacob, it's nice weather today. Wonder if we could just sit out here on the porch?"

Mr. Riddle looks around briefly and shrugs, saying, "If you don't mind sitting on this old run-down porch, I reckon you're welcome."

"Thank you, Mr. Riddle, Mrs. Riddle," Helen says, smiling. "And I think your porch is lovely. It reminds me of my grandmother's house back in Nebraska."

"Oh?" Mrs. Riddle asks now, obviously excited to have someone new to talk to, "Is that where you're from?"

"Yes, ma'am," Helen says graciously. "I grew up on a farm. We lived on it and worked on it with my mother's parents.

I look at Helen with surprise. I knew she was from Nebraska, but I really didn't know much else about her life there. I had no idea she was a farm girl.

My bride-to-be is still chock-full of surprises.

"Well, isn't that nice," Mrs. Riddle begins. She looks like she'd like to say more, but a look from her husband silences her.

Mr. Riddle glares at Helen., "So you have some questions for us, Chief Parr?"

"Yes, sir. Just a few. I'm sure you've heard about the young man who was killed the other night." They both nod slowly as she continues, "I am trying to talk to everyone that was at Fairy Tales and Frights near the end of the evening, just to see if they saw anyone or anything that might help us find the killer."

"What's that got to do with us?" Mr. Riddle scowls. "We're just barely getting by. Don't any of us have the money for something fancy like going to a haunted house, especially one in a big fancy house owned by a rich man who killed himself."

He pauses before turning to me and going on. "Really, Father, I'm disappointed that the parish is even hanging on to that house. Ought to sell it to use the money to help needy folks, not to give fancy parties for people that got more money than sense."

"The young people of the parish are putting on Fairy Tales and Frights to raise money for an education center for the children of the community," I say, trying to conceal the irritation in my voice.

"Rich people's children," he snorts. "I bet folks like us can't afford it. I mean, I guess it's better than lettin' the government teach our children all their left-wing socialist ways. But it ain't gonna do us any good."

I'm about to continue to argue when Helen steps in. "Well, obviously Mr. Riddle, the center has already brought a certain level of tragedy, since Larry Daniels was killed there. Honestly, I doubt anyone in your family knew him. He was not from around here. But I know Dale was there that night, and so I am hoping he might have seen something that could help us find Larry's killer."

"Finding murderers ain't our business," he says, shaking his head.

"Certainly not," Helen agrees, continuing her charm offensive. "But I know from your reputation, Mr. Riddle, that you love this nation and our Constitution. I know that you would agree with me that the guarantee of a right to 'Life, Liberty and the Pursuit of Happiness' must be protected. All I am asking for is your help to bring to justice the person who took away this young man's right to life."

I am beginning to consider letting Helen write my homilies when Mr. Riddle says slowly, "What do you want to know?"

"Nothing from you or your wife, sir. But we would like to talk to Dale. Can you help me get in touch with him?"

"No, ma'am, I can't. As I told you on the phone, he's gone up into the woods somewhere, to think, he said, and get away from bad memories. I guess you heard about how that Trent girl broke his heart?"

Helen says gently with just the hint of a smile, "Nothing is as fickle as young love, Mr. Riddle. I bet you broke a few hearts yourself back in the day?"

He shakes his head firmly. "No, ma'am. Not like this. That little girl just didn't think Dale was good enough for her and her snooty family. Just 'cause we didn't have the money to send him to a fancy college, and 'cause he misses church once in a while to go huntin' on the only day off he has each week. She tried to say that they just weren't a good mix. But boy, she sure found she was a good mix with that fancy doctor quick enough. Yes, sir. She wasted no time getting her claws into him."

I want to intervene to defend Mae. But I know the rules, so I let Helen continue. "You aren't worried about him being alone without any way to get in touch with you? I mean, especially since he's so upset and all?"

"Shoot, that boy don't need us," Mr. Riddle grins, showing a good number of discolored and broken teeth. "He'll hunt and fish for his supper and sleep under the stars. It'll do him good."

"It gets dark early," Helen says.

"It's just past a full moon. He has one of those big flashlights. Besides, he can see really good in the dark. Eyes like a cat."

"My daddy hunted, deer mainly. What about Dale?"

"Deer, rabbit, anything you can eat."

"You know, I'll never forget one time Daddy hit a deer on the way home from picking me up at school. He jumped out and cut that deer's throat so fast that we were able to use the meat."

My stomach lurches as Mr. Riddle says, "Yep, Dale could do something like that."

"You gotta have a sharp knife, though," Helen says. "Daddy sharpened his every Sunday afternoon. Dale use a grinder or a whet stone?"

"Whet stone, so he can take it with him when he goes off by himself."

"Can he really keep it sharp with just a whet stone?"

"Lady, he keeps that knife sharp enough to shave with. He knows I won't tolerate him walking 'round here looking like some kind of homeless, so he'll trim off his whiskers before he comes home."

"He got a blade long enough for that?"

"Eight inches."

Helen nods. "Well, I reckon that'll do it. I still got Daddy's knife. I don't know for how much longer, though, because years of sharpening have made it pretty narrow."

"That's why I told Dale, 'Boy, if you gonna pay good money for a knife, get one with a wide blade.' His started out two inches but I bet he's already sharpened an eighth or more off."

"I bet," Helen says, standing. I join her and she says pleasantly, "Thanks for taking time to talk to me. Please tell Dale that after talking to y'all, I don't need anything else from him. I hope y'all have a blessed day." We shake hands all around and return to Helen's car.

She pulls out of the driveway and heads back to Myerton. "Want a snack?"

"Sprockets?"

"It's on the way," she says. Picking up her phone, she presses speed dial. "Judge Hastings, please."

I look at her. "Why are you—"

"Shush," she says quickly. "Judge Hastings? Chief Parr. . . Fine, your Honor, how are you? . . . Oh, I am glad to hear that. Your Honor, I'm calling because I need a warrant . . . Arrest . . . Murder . . . . Dale Riddle."

"What?" I mouth quietly. She holds up a finger. "Yes, I'll have the affidavit on your desk this afternoon. I just wanted to let you know it was coming. Thank you, your Honor."

She hangs up and I ask, "So, are you going to tell me?"

Helen takes a deep breath. "According to the preliminary autopsy report, Larry Daniels was stabbed with a knife that was about 2 inches wide and eight inches long. There were fibers in the wound, mostly from the wolf costume. But there were a couple of hairs from a white-tail deer."

I whistle. "So it looks like Dale's your guy."

Helen nods. "Yeah. Too bad we can't find him. But he can't stay out in the woods forever. We'll keep an eye on the Riddles' farm. When he comes home, we'll be ready."

We drive along in silence for a while, then I say, "How did I miss that you were a farm girl?"

She shrugs. "Frankly, it's not something I really wanted known when I was in college. I came to Maryland because I wanted to get away from the farm. I wanted to be more sophisticated, I guess."

"Did you hate it? Home? I mean, that's why I left Bellamy."

She smiles and shakes her head. "No," she says quietly. "I loved it. I really loved the farm. But by the time I graduated high school, I'd already lost my grandmother and my mom and my dad. My aunt and uncle took over the farm. I just wanted to get away from the memories."

I look at her. "Do you miss it?"

"I miss the farm from when I was a little girl," she says with a smile, "when Mom and Dad were alive, and Grandma, so it's not that I miss the place. I miss the time."

I nod. "I understand that. I don't miss Bellamy—oh, heck, no—but when we were back there, I remembered all the times I had with my Dad, and what my Mom was like before he died, and even the fun Sonya and I had playing when we were younger. That, I miss."

We lapse into silence as we ponder our memories of childhoods past. Finally, I ask, "That story you told the Riddles, about your Dad cutting the throat of that deer he hit. Was that—"

She nods. "One hundred percent true. Best venison I've ever had came from that deer."

"And you still have your Dad's knife?"

She turns her head slightly and, with a wicked smile, she says, "I never told you I only carry *one* knife, darling."

***

After our pit stop at Sprockets, we drive past the Myer Estate.

"No wonder people think it's haunted," I mutter. "That place is spooky at night, especially tonight with the moon out and the sky clear."

Something catches my eye. A flash of light in an upstairs window.

"Helen," I say, looking over my shoulder as she speeds past. "I saw something in an upstairs window. A light."

"Oh, Tom," Helen says.

"No, I'm serious. We need to go back and check. I think someone is in there."

"Who? Victoria Myer?"

"Would you just turn around?" I say, a bit louder than I mean.

"OK, OK," Helen says with exasperation. "You're getting surlier the closer we get to the wedding."

She makes a u-turn, and a couple of minutes later, we're going up the driveway to the front of the Myer Mansion.

I see the light again. "There," I say, pointing through her front window.

"I see it," Helen says. "Probably a prowler coming to check the place out because of that stupid story Nate wrote. Or, it could be someone after the equipment. Either way, I'd better check it out."

She reaches under her skirt and pulls out her back up, then into the glove compartment for her flashlight. Picking up her radio, she says, "This is Chief Parr. Investigating a possible prowler at the Myer Mansion. Requesting backup."

There's a crackle of static, but the familiar voice of Mike Thompson responds, "Unit 4 en route. ETA, five minutes."

"Approach without—repeat, without—lights and sirens, Thompson," Helen says. "We don't want to scare him off."

"Roger, Chief. Out," Thompson says.

"OK," she says as she opens her door. "You stay here."

"Oh, no," I say, shaking my head. "I'm going with you."

"Fine," she spits. "Just stay back, OK?"

Helen gets out and heads for the door. I follow well behind her, per her instructions. She opens the door and walks in, gun out and raised under the flashlight. I stand by the door out of the way as she swings her light slowly around the room and then proceeds toward the stairs. She shines that flashlight upstairs and continues up, the stairs creaking as she goes. I remain at the bottom of the staircase, well aware that no one will benefit from me getting in her way.

At the top of the stairs, she suddenly swings the light to her left and shouts, "Police! Freeze!"

At that moment, I hear a high-pitched blood-curdling scream. A slightly familiar voice shouts again and again, "Don't shoot. Please don't shoot me. I work here."

"Face down on the floor and lace your fingers behind your head."

It sounds as if the perp is complying and I hear her cuffs come out as the voice on the ground cries, "Helen! It's me. Nate."

I get to the top of the stairs as she grabs him by his arms and sits him up, shining the flashlight in his face.

"What the frankincense and myrrh, Nate?" she yells as I reach around and turn on the light.

He's talking too fast for me to understand but I am able to make out "ghost," "haunted," and "evidence." She uncuffs him and he stands up as she turns away from us and holsters her weapon. Then she looks at him with barely contained rage and commands, "Slow down, Nate, and say that again."

Nate's breathing so heavily, his words come out stattaco. "I was—checking out—for tomorrow—the   upstairs—on   the   left—there's—evidence—something—spectral activity—maybe."

Rightly fed up with this gibberish, Helen finally says, "Nate, why don't you show this to me instead of trying to tell me."

He nods. "OK. It's this bedroom here," he says, pointing to the door at the end of the hallway that Andrew Conway mistook for a bathroom.

"But this door's been locked from the inside," I say. "How did you get in?"

"I was up here looking over things and I noticed this door was slightly open," Nate whispers. "That's when I found the evidence. This is where she is, Father! Victoria Myer!"

"Dammit, Nate!" I exclaim. "Helen already told you Larry wasn't killed by a—a ghost! Besides, Victoria Myer wouldn't hurt anybody!"

I must be tired or something, because I didn't mean to say what I just said. Helen jerks her head around to look at me. Nate looks startled. "Father?" he whispers, a smile forming on his face. "Do—do you—"

I take a deep breath and say quietly, "Nate, now, I'm going to tell you this—"

"Tom?" Helen says, her voice edged with a warning.

"—but you must not tell anybody—"

"What the hell are you doing?" Helen growls through gritted teeth.

"—but when I was here recently—" I take a deep breath, "Victoria Myer spoke to me."

Helen breathes a sigh of relief as Nate squeals, "Really? She—she appeared to you?"

"No," I say. "She didn't take a form. And it wasn't an external voice I heard. But I did feel a presence, and a voice in my head said she was Victoria Myer."

"Oh," Nate says, looking a little disappointed. "But she's definitely here."

"Yes," I say, nodding my head. "And she's suffering."

"Why?"

"Because she has had no one to pray for her soul, Nate," I say, placing my hand on his shoulder. "I've done my own research. Some theologians—including Saint Thomas Aquinas—believe that ghosts are actually souls in Purgatory. They 'haunt' a place because they're hoping to run across a loved one who can pray for them. But Victoria Myer, in all these years, has found no one."

Nate actually looks downcast. "So, she's not like I described in my article."

I shake my head. "No. Probably, that's how the story got handed down—complete with the knife—because it was creepier than the truth. Also, that's how many people see ghosts."

"That's so sad," he says.

"It is, Nate."

He looks at me, and says, "Well, she has someone to pray for her now."

I nod my head. "That's a good idea."

"Ahem."

We look up and see Helen standing in the doorway. I've been so wrapped up in my conversation with Nate that I totally missed her actually going in the room.

"Well, Nate," she says, "it may not be the ghost of Victoria Myer. But someone's definitely been staying here."

"Chief!" Officer Mike Thompson calls from downstairs.

"Thompson," Helen yells. "Get the techs down here. I want this room torn apart."

"Did you find something?" I ask.

"Oh, yeah," she says with a smile. "Come. I'll show you."

I walk behind her into a small bedroom. The bed does indeed appear to have been slept in, recently. There's no dust on the sheets but there are hairs and some traces of dirt, as if the person staying there isn't particularly fastidious. There are also various empty snack bags in a box in the corner.

"Someone's been living here," I say. "A homeless person, maybe?"

"It would have to be recent," Nate says. "We never found any sign that someone was living here. Besides, the doors to the outside are all locked."

"Whoever it is must have found a way in," I say.

"Well, whoever's been living here is likely the one who killed Larry Daniels," Helen says. She motions us over to a small closet.

"Look at this," she says, picking up a pair of hiking boots. "This is the same tread pattern as the prints made on the carpet."

I peer at a hole in the leather upper. "What's that? A cut of some kind?"

"Looks more like a burn to me," Nate says. We both look at him. "Well, it does."

"Maybe some kind of acid," Helen mutters.

I look past Helen into the closet. "You've seen this," I say, pointing at a leather belt hanging from a nail.

"Uh-huh," Helen says. "I haven't touched it, but it looks like the right length. And the crime lab will have to confirm it. But I just bet that's the knife that killed Larry Daniels."

Twenty-Four

"Thanks for coming down, Mae."

We're in Helen's office Thursday afternoon. Gladys is with Mae, offering moral support, no doubt. I'm seated on the couch—my traditional location when Helen is talking with someone.

"Glad to do it, Helen," Mae says, "though I'm still not sure what help I can be."

Gladys takes her hand. "The Chief just wants to show you some photographs and see if you can identify them."

"Photographs of what?"

Helen opens a folder on her desk and takes out something and hands it to Mae. "Do you recognize this knife?"

Mae looks at the picture of the knife we found in the bedroom in the Myer Mansion. She turns the photograph around, looking at it from different angles. "I'm not sure," she says slowly. "It's a hunting knife—it looks a little familiar. It looks like one that Dale has, I think."

"You've seen his knife?"

"Oh, yes," Mae says. "We went for a day hike and he took it with him. Showed me how sharp he keeps it. He said it cuts through a deer's throat like a hot knife through butter." She says this last with a visible shudder. "It was not long after that that I broke things off with him."

"But you're not sure it's Dale Riddle's knife?" Helen says, taking the picture from her.

Mae shakes her head. "I don't know whether I should be sorry or not," she says. "I still have a hard time thinking Dale would want to hurt a person, much less kill them."

Gladys says, "We've talked about this, Mae. You don't know what people are capable of. You may think you do. But you don't. Trust me, I know."

"But I know Dale," Mae insists. "We practically grew up together. I mean, we weren't close—his family is, you know, the kind to keep to themselves—but I've known him a long time."

"And I thought I knew Nate," Gladys says sorrowfully, dropping her head.

"Glad," Mae says, putting her hand on her shoulder, "I thought you put that behind you?"

Gladys takes a deep breath. "I put it behind me every day," she says softly. "But it still hurts. I love him, and it still hurts."

We're quiet for a few minutes when Gladys straightens up and looks at Helen. "Sorry, Chief," she says firmly. "You had something else for her to look at?"

Helen nods. "Do these look familiar?" she says, handing Mae another photograph.

Mae looks at it for only a moment when she says, "These are Dale's boots."

"Are you absolutely sure?" Helen asks.

"Yes, ma'am, I am," Mae says. "I recognize that hole in the upper. I don't know how he got it, but he said if his dad ever found out, he'd catch hell for it. When we were in the woods, he'd cover the hole with duct tape. He kept saying he needed to buy a new pair, but he didn't have the money."

At Helen's slight look of triumph, Mae says quietly, "Have I just connected Dale to Larry's murder?"

"You've done what I asked you to do," Helen says gently. "No more, no less."

Mae hugs herself tightly. "Oh, my God! Oh, my God!" she says quietly. "He did kill Larry! He . . . he wanted to kill Marty! All . . . all because of me!"

I'm off the couch and over to Mae before Helen and Gladys can say anything. I kneel down beside her and say firmly, "Mae Trent, you need to get that out of your head right now! If Dale did kill Larry—if he wanted to kill Martin—he didn't do it because of you. The only person responsible is Dale."

"But I broke up with him," she whispers. "If I hadn't—"

"You've spoken to Bridget Davis," I say. "When she tells you it's all her fault, that she shouldn't have made Rusty angry, what do you tell her?"

"I tell her she's not responsible for another person's actions," Mae says. "That whatever she may have done, it did not give Rusty the right to hit her or her children."

I nod. "That's right in her case. And, Mae, it's right in your case. You went out with a guy you figured out you weren't compatible with. Then, you found one with whom you were. Happens all the time. There's nothing wrong with that. Whatever possibly drove Dale to murder, it wasn't anything you said or did."

Mae sighs. "I still can't believe it."

"That, sweetie," Helen says with a smile, "is because you're a good person. Me, I just look at the evidence. And you've given me enough to arrest Dale for the murder of Larry Daniels."

***

"You look pensive," I say.

We're in Helen's car outside the Riddles' property, Officer Nina Hallstead in a marked Myerton Police patrol car parked behind us. Helen had told me she wanted back-up when she made the arrest, "just in case."

"I wish you hadn't come with me," she says, looking at the front gate.

"Sick of me already?" I say with a grin, trying to lighten the mood.

I realize I failed when Helen says, "This could go sideways really quickly, Tom. The Riddles are a disgruntled family who believe the world is out to get them, and they have a distinct distrust of the government. They also have a good number of registered firearms in that house and probably more that are unregistered and of dubious legality."

"Then why didn't you contact the State Police?" I say, now alarmed. "They could have sent their SWAT team to do this."

She shakes her head. "That would have provoked a showdown, possibly a barricade situation, and people would have been hurt. Frankly, I'd like Martin to go a few weeks without having to fix up a member of law enforcement."

"But Helen," I say, "you or Hallstead could be hurt."

She looks at me and smiles. "We're both wearing vests," she says to reassure me, "and we'll leave at the first sign of trouble. But Tom, no matter what happens, you stay in this car. Got it?"

I want to protest, say I want to be with her, argue that things might go smoother if I'm where they can see me. But I know she's right.

"Got it," I say firmly.

"OK. Well, this is it," Helen says, a tone of regret in her voice.

"Are you even sure Dale's here?"

She nods. "I asked Mae to text him, ask how he was. He responded right away. It wasn't a nice response, but Gladys was able to ping his phone. It's still here. Which means he's here."

Helen lapses back into silence. "There's something else, isn't there?" I ask.

She sighs. "I have to admit, Tom, I really didn't want it to be Dale. I mean, I know he's a creep and has been pushing Mae much too hard. But when you see the way he was raised, it just seems like he's more of a mixed-up kid than a murderer."

"I know," I say sadly, "but really, honey, don't most murderers start out as mixed-up something? I mean, well-adjusted individuals don't typically kill people. We've seen that, haven't we?"

She sighs, "You make a good point. But that does not make this any easier." She lapses into thought, then says, "Also, Tom, something about this doesn't sit right with me. The evidence we found is circumstantial at best."

"But the crime lab said the knife's definitely the one that killed Larry," I said. "The blade's consistent with the stab wound, the blood stains they found match Larry, there are only one set of fingerprints on the handle, and the knife had fibers consistent with the wolf costume. Not to mention the fact that Mae identified the boots you found as Dale's"

"All that is true," she says, still pensive.

"So?"

Helen turns to me. "So Dale's an outdoorsman. Why would he hide in the mansion after killing Larry? Why didn't he hide in the mountains somewhere?"

I shrug. "OK, I see your point about that. But the knife—"

"And that's another thing," Helen says. "The knife still had blood on it."

"Yeah?"

"Tom, remember that story about my daddy slitting the deer's throat?"

"I don't think I'll ever forget that, frankly."

"The first thing he did when we got home, after hanging the deer in the shed to dress it, was clean his knife. He always told me to be sure to clean my knife after using it. A hunter always cleans his knife. Why didn't Dale?"

"Maybe he was in a hurry?" I say. "Maybe he panicked?"

"Maybe," Helen says. "But if you're going to stab someone in the dark, chances are you don't panic easily."

"So are you saying he didn't do it?"

"No, I'm saying things aren't making sense to me."

I take a deep breath. "Well, until you bring him in and talk to him, you won't know."

She nods. "Right. So, let's do this." She gets on her radio. "Ready, Hallstead?"

Hallstead radios back, "Ready when you are, Chief."

Helen starts her car and pulls back onto the road. Pulling up to the gate, I get out to open it. Back in the car, we drive slowly up to the house, with Hallstead right behind us.

"Nina, pull off," Helen says on the radio, tension beginning to creep into her voice. "Remember what we discussed."

"Right," Hallstead responds. After a pause, she says, "Be careful, Chief."

"That's my plan," Helen says with a wry smile.

She stops her car about ten feet from the house. I turn around and see that Hallstead has pulled onto the grass off the driveway and has opened her door.

"OK," Helen says. "Remember Tom, no matter what happens. Stay here."

She turns to get out when I pull her around, giving her a kiss we usually don't allow ourselves. Pulling back, I whisper, "Come back to me. Please."

She smiles and strokes my cheek. "I always do," she whispers. Then, squaring her shoulders, she gets out of the car and starts walking to the house.

It's then I notice something that startles me.

She left her gun.

"What are you doing, Helen?" I whisper to myself. I hold onto the fact that she knows what she's doing, but hope she has her backup.

I know from hearing the stories that the most dangerous moment of any arrest is when you knock on the door, so I am holding my breath and praying as Helen steps up on the Riddles' porch. She crosses the shallow space forcefully and knocks firmly.

"Mr. Riddle," she calls loudly, "it's Chief Parr. Open up, please!"

She then steps back, giving herself some maneuvering room. As instructed, I remain in the car, my eyes fixed on the front door, my fingers on my Rosary beads.

Mr. Riddle opens the door and growls, "Lady, I didn't give you permission to step on my property!"

"Unfortunately, Mr. Riddle," Helen says, pulling a sheet of paper out of the inner pocket of her coat, "I don't need any. I have a warrant for Dale's arrest for the murder of Larry Daniels. Please ask Dale to come out here."

Mr. Riddle looks Helen up and down. "Or what? You gonna shoot your way into my house?"

She opens her coat. "I'm unarmed," she says.

"I know you cops. You got a backup?"

Helen says, "Mr. Riddle, I usually carry a backup. But I know you're too much of a gentleman to ask me to show you where I keep it. So you're just going to have to take my word that I don't have that, either. Now, would you please ask your son to come out?"

"I ain't gonna do it," he yells. "My boy didn't do anything wrong and I ain't gonna turn him over to no government agency just so he can take the fall for some rich doctor."

"You are going to turn him over, Mr. Riddle," Helen responds, "or I am going to arrest you for obstruction of justice."

She takes a step forward and crosses her arms. "Now, I know you're considering your next move, and I want to provide you with all the information you need to make it. I know that you have a number of weapons in your home, some of them registered, some of them not. Therefore, I want you to know that behind me and to my left is officer Nina Hallstead. She has a rifle trained on you, one of police issue but extremely similar to the one she used when she won an Olympic gold medal for shooting."

I turn around again. Sure enough, Nina's crouched down behind the door of her patrol car, a rifle trained on the porch.

"So," Helen continues, "If you or any member of your family display a weapon in such a way as to make Officer Halstead think that I am in any danger, she will use the rifle to protect me."

Mr. Riddle says nothing, but instead stares past Helen at Hallstead, his eyes narrowing.

"I'm going to tell you one more time, Mr. Riddle," Helen says. "Call Dale out here now. If Officer Hallstead and I have to go in to get him, I'll have to secure the scene. That means I will have to locate and confiscate every weapon in this house and report any that are illegal to the Bureau of Alcohol, Tobacco, Firearms, and Explosives. Then you'll be in real trouble. You don't want that, do you, Mr. Riddle?"

He scowls at Helen, then calls over his shoulder into the house, "Dale! Get out here!"

It seems like forever, but finally a young man in his early twenties plods out the front door. He's somewhat clean-shaven, but his lip is curled into a sneer. With a tone to match his look of defiance, he snarls, "I didn't do nothin' wrong, lady."

Helen takes her cuffs out and says, "Dale Riddle, I'm arresting you for the murder of Larry Daniels. Please turn around and put your hands behind your back."

He starts to comply, when suddenly he rushes past her and leaps off the porch. He begins to run across the yard towards the woods, separated only by a wood fence.

"Stop!" Helen hollers. "Hallstead!"

"I've got him," Hallstead yells as she dashes past Helen's car at a full sprint, her long legs propelling her headlong across the space between her and the boy who, while younger, is no match for the former MMA fighter. She gets to him and makes a flying tackle, landing on top of Dale.

Helen and Mr. Riddle come off the porch and run over to the officer and her prisoner, who's still struggling under her.

"Be still before I break your damn arm!" Hallstead yells at Dale. For emphasis, she grabs one of his arms and yanks it forcefully behind his back. The young man howls like a wounded animal.

"Dammit, bitch," he cries.

"It's not broken, you big baby," she says as she cuffs him. Hallstead gets off of him and jerks him to his feet. "What do you want me to do with him, Chief?"

Helen brushes some stray hairs from her face. "Read him his rights and take him to the station. Book him for murder. Add resisting arrest and assaulting a police officer."

"I didn't assault nobody!" Dale yells.

"You pushed me out of your way," Helen says firmly. "That's assault."

"Come on, you," Hallstead growls as she pulls Dale by the arm towards her car.

Turning to Mr. Riddle, Helen says, "You better get him a lawyer. He's in a lot of trouble."

"Can't afford no fancy lawyer," he says. "Don't need one anyway. He can speak for himself. Taught him all the law he needs to defend himself."

"Mr. Riddle," she insists, "that's not a good idea. Dale's facing some pretty serious charges."

Just then, other cars pull up, including the crime scene van, no doubt waiting somewhere for Hallstead's call.

Pointing at the vehicles, Mr. Riddle asks, "What are they doing here?"

Smiling, Helen says, "Oh, didn't I mention that? If you read the warrant carefully, it also authorizes me to search your house for evidence. And since I'm not exactly sure what I'm looking for, I'm ordering my men to remove any weapons—gun, knives, you know—as well as electronic devices or anything that looks suspicious."

Mr. Riddle stands with his mouth open. Finally, he stammers, "Now—now wait just a damn minute—"

Still smiling, Helen says, "Have a nice day, sir."

Twenty-Five

About an hour later, Helen and I are sitting in Gladys' office, looking at the large center screen at a shot of Dale Riddle sitting alone in the interrogation room.

"Why aren't you doing the interview?" I ask.

Helen shrugs. "Simple. It's Dan's case. And we're shaking things up a bit. I'm trying to learn that I don't have to do everything."

Something occurs to me when she says this. "Wait, shouldn't Dan have gone out and made the arrest?"

"Technically, yes," Helen says. "But this needed a little finesse. Dan's a great guy and a fine detective, but he has all the finesse of the Incredible Hulk."

I nod. "Yeah, I see your point."

"Quiet, you two," Gladys says. She has a headset on, and I'm trying to figure out what she's listening to.

"Hear anything?" Helen asks.

She shakes her head. "He's just tapping his foot."

"He's nervous," I say. "That's natural."

"What do the sensors say?" Helen asks.

"What sensors?"

"Oh," Gladys says with a grin. "Mom let me wire the suspect's chair with sensors. I can monitor heart rate, respiration, that sort of thing."

I frown. "You mean like a lie detector?"

"Sort of," Helen says. "It's not admissible in court, but it does help us figure out if a suspect is telling the truth or not. It's just another tool in our bag of tricks."

"Ah," I say. "So that's why we're here instead of in the viewing room."

"Exactly," Helen says.

On screen, Dan enters the room. "Showtime," Gladys says, pressing a few buttons.

"Pay attention to his reactions, Gladys," Helen says.

"Right, Chief."

"Hello, Dale," Dan says. "Do you know who I am?"

Dale nods. "I've seen you at church. You're the cop with all the kids."

"Detective Conway," Dan says, nodding. "I understand from Officer Hallstead you waived your right to a lawyer?"

"Yeah, I told that dyke that I didn't need a lawyer."

"Ooooh," Gladys says. "Nina's not going to like that."

"And she's not going to hear about it, understand?" Helen says firmly.

"I don't like you referring to one of my colleagues like that," Dan says. "And I doubt she or her husband would appreciate it."

Dale looks chastened. Swallowing, he says, "Yes, sir."

"That made him nervous," Gladys says. "Heartbeat and respiration spiked."

"Hmm," Helen says. "Typical bully."

"I didn't kill nobody!" Dale yells suddenly. "I didn't know that guy!"

"We'll get to that in a few minutes," Dan says. "Let's start by talking about Mae Trent."

He snorts. "Yeah. What about her?"

"It's my understanding you two dated for a while."

Dale shrugs. "Yeah, so what? We went out some. I go out with lots of girls."

"So she wasn't anyone special, is that what you're saying?"

Dale doesn't say anything for a long time. "No," he finally says quietly. "No one special."

"He's lying, Mom," Gladys says.

"Press him on that, Dan," Helen says into a microphone.

"Are you sure? Because Mae gave us some text messages that would say otherwise."

Dale looks at Dan, then slumps in his chair. "OK. Yeah, Mae was special to me. But to her, I was nothing."

"What makes you say that?"

"Oh, lots of things," Dale says. "When we first started going out, I thought she was a nice girl, you know? But she soon showed her true colors."

"I still don't get what you're saying."

"She showed me she was a stuck-up bitch. She looked down on me and my whole family because we don't have the money that her family does. Living in that big fancy house on a hill, just so they can lord it over everyone."

The Trents live in a restored Victorian-era home in an older part of town. It's large and sprawling, perfect for their big family. But it's hardly fancy, and it's not on a hill.

Besides, the Trents are among the humblest people I've ever met.

"Did she tell you that?" Dan asks.

"Not in so many words," Dale says. "But I could tell by her attitude. First time I brought her home for dinner, she had this look on her face the entire time, like where I lived wasn't good enough. My mom made perfectly good venison, and Mae barely touched it."

"Mae told me about that," Gladys says indignantly. "Mr. Riddle had talked in detail about how he killed the deer. It made her lose her appetite."

"I tried to interest her in things I like," Dale says, "like hunting. But she was too delicate for that, whining that she couldn't shoot a defenseless animal."

"Well," Dan says, "I don't see much point in it myself."

"I guess not. You'd rather kill defenseless women."

In a flash, Dan bolts from his chair, knocking it over, and lunges at Dale.

"Stand down, Detective!" Helen commands.

But Dan doesn't. On the screen, I see his shoulders heaving as he leans across the table, his hands curled into fists.

I grab the microphone and say calmly, "Dan, it's Tom. It's OK. Just calm down. He's not worth it. You and I both know that."

At first, Dan doesn't seem to have heard me. Finally after what seems like an eternity, he stands up, his arms hanging loosely down his sides. Dale's grinning up at him in triumph.

"Let's take a break," Dan says, his voice a low rumble. As he exits the interview room, Helen says to me, "Go." I dash out of Gladys' office and down the hallway.

Dan's standing outside the door to the room, bent over with his hands on his knees. I walk up to him and place my hand on his back.

"You OK?" I ask quietly.

"I was going to kill him, Tom," he rasps. "Smarmy little asshole."

"Do you want Helen to take over? She'll do it, you know, no questions asked."

Dan stands up and looks at me. Shaking his head, he says, "No, Tom. I'm fine now. Thanks for pulling me back."

I clap him on the back. "Anytime, buddy. You know that. Tell you what. Stop by the Rectory later tonight. It's been a while since we've had beer and cigars on the back patio."

He smiles. "Sounds like a plan, Father."

"But remember, you can't do that if Helen has had to lock you up." I say this with a grin that he returns.

I leave Dan and go back to Gladys' office. Helen looks up when I come in. "How is he?"

"He says he's fine now," I say.

"Good," Helen says. Then, keying the mic again, she says, "OK, Dan. Go on to asking about Martin. We've got the fingerprints back from the knife. They're a match to his, and there are no other prints. But I want you to ease into it."

I see a slight, almost imperceptible nod, as Dan says, "OK, so you and Mae broke up."

"Ah, she dumped me, just so we're clear," Dale says, almost proudly.

"OK, she dumped you. How long ago was that?"

"Four months ago, back in July."

"Huh," Dan says. "It wasn't too long after that, I think, that Mae started dating Dr. Martin Maycord. Am I right?"

On screen, we see Dale shift in his seat. "OK, that got a reaction," Gladys says, looking at the lines and numbers on a screen.

"She couldn't get rid of me fast enough before she started on that rich doctor," Dale says bitterly. "I mean, he's way older than she is. That's when I realized what a real gold-digging bitch she was."

"So you think Mae dumped you for Dr. Maycord?"

"That's what happened!"

"Did she tell you that?"

"Of course not. Too deceitful to tell me the truth. When I texted her after I found out, she swore to me her breaking up with me had nothing to do with her seeing Maycord. But my Daddy didn't raise no fool, Detective! I know how the world works."

"So you weren't happy about them dating." Dan leans forward, resting his arms on the table. "How did you feel when you heard about their engagement?"

"Well, that just confirmed it, didn't it? I mean, they only knew each other, what, three months? Mae and I practically grew up together—maybe we weren't in the same circles or anything like that, but we've known each other."

"So you don't believe Mae loves Dr. Maycord?"

"Are you kidding?" he laughs. "He's old! Drives around in a fancy sports car, lives in a mansion. He can give Mae everything her greedy little heart desires."

"So, did you decide to pay Dr. Maycord a visit to warn him?"

Dale freezes at that. "How did you hear about that?" he says nervously.

"Oh, Dr. Maycord told Chief Parr all about your little visit. Telling him Mae was a promiscuous gold-digger who was only after his money. That was what you said to him, right?"

"Dan's got him cornered, Mom," Gladys says, continuing to look at her screen.

"Look," he stammers. "He—he attacked me. That's assault, right? I mean, I was just trying to get him to break up with Mae so I could get her back. That's all. I didn't mean any of it. Hell, Mae turned me down flat a number of times."

"Good for her," Dan says evenly. "So, was it after that that you decided to kill Dr. Maycord?"

"What? No!" Dale protests.

"Oh, so you decided before you talked to him?"

"No! I—the—what does this have to do with that guy who was killed?"

"Well, Dale," Dan says. "It's like this. Larry Daniels was playing The Big Bad Wolf last Saturday night. But he wasn't supposed to be. No, you see, Mae had persuaded Dr. Maycord to do that for Fairy Tales and Frights—I guess she liked the idea of being chased by him, I don't know—but Dr. Maycord had an emergency at the hospital. So Larry was a last minute substitution." Leaning across the table, he adds in a low, rumbling voice, "So you see, Dale, our theory is that Larry wasn't the intended victim. Dr. Maycord was."

The blood runs from Dale's face. He swallows and says, "Now—now look, Detective—"

"Didn't Nate Rodriguez find you skulking about inside the mansion after it was closed?"

"I was just looking around," Dale says.

"You weren't looking for Dr. Maycord?"

"I didn't want to get anywhere near him!" Dale cries. "He had me by the throat! I thought he was going to kill me! He—He scared the crap out of me!"

"So why were you at the Myer Mansion!" Dan asks loudly.

"It's like I told that guy and Mae's holier-than-thou brother, I'd never been inside such a nice place and I just wanted to look around."

"So after they kicked your sorry ass out," Dan growls, "where did you go?"

"Where did I go?" Dale asks. "I—I just went back to my cabin."

"Your cabin?"

"Yeah," he says. "I have a little cabin in the mountains just outside town. It ain't much, really, it's more of a lean-to, but I built it myself. I go there when I want to hunt, or just be alone to think."

"Did anyone see you there that night?"

"No," Dale says. "Like I say, I go there when I want to be alone."

"So, you have no alibi," Dan says.

"I guess not," Dale says. "But I didn't kill anybody!"

"The evidence says otherwise."

"Huh! What evidence?"

"Here it comes," Helen mutters as Dan opens a folder in front of him and takes out a photograph. "Do these look familiar?" he says to Dale.

Dale looks at the photograph and licks his lips. "They're hiking boots," he says.

"We showed this photo to Mae Trent," Dan says. "She identified these as your boots."

"She would say that," he mutters.

"Are you saying she lied?"

Dale sighs. "No. They're mine. But I don't have them anymore."

"Well, no. We have them in evidence."

"No, I mean I haven't seen them for days."

"Gladys?" Helen asks.

"It's hard to say, Mom," Gladys says, looking at the screen. "He's so nervous right now, he could be lying, or he could be telling the truth."

"Do you mind explaining that?" Dan asks, sitting back with his arms crossed.

Dale flops back in the chair and says, "Look, here's what happened. A couple of weeks ago, I was at my cabin when some stranger wandered up. He looked out of place, you know. He wasn't dressed for hiking or even being in the woods. He had, like, athletic shoes on, jeans, a sweatshirt and a light jacket. Told me he was homeless and had been camping in the woods about five miles away with a friend of his. Said they got in some kind of fight and the guy threatened to kill him, so he ran off with only the clothes on his back."

Dan nods his head. "He give you a name?"

"I didn't ask him."

"What did he look like?"

Dale thinks a minute. "Just like a guy—ordinary, nothing special. I mean, he had blood on him, but he'd said he's been in a fight. His knuckles looked roughed up, you know, like when you punch someone a lot."

"OK. So what does this guy have to do with those boots?"

"Well, they were an old pair of boots—I'd just bought a new pair, the one's I'm wearing, see, and let me tell you, Daddy gave me hell about buying brand new boots when he saw them—and he didn't have any, so I gave them to him. We happened to be about the same size. Also gave him an old army jacket I'd picked up at a thrift store a few months back. It wouldn't do for winter, but it'd keep him from getting too cold at night. Anyway, like I say, seemed like a nice enough fella. I'd made venison chili, so I invited him to eat. After we ate, we talked for a while then bedded down."

Dale pauses and shakes his head. "Learned a hard lesson that night. Don't trust nobody."

"Why is that?"

"Because," he says angrily, "when I woke up, the guy was gone with a bunch of my stuff. A sleeping bag, another coat, my—" Dale stops talking suddenly and looks away from Dale.

"There's a spike, Mom!" Gladys says. "He's scared about something."

Dan asks, "What else did he take, Dale?"

Dale shakes his head. "Nothin'. Just that."

From the folder, Dan takes another photograph and places it in front of Dale. "Is this your knife?"

Dale glances at it, then looks away.

"According to your Dad, you have a hunting knife just like this."

Dale still says nothing.

"Is. This. Your. Knife?" Dan asks firmly.

Dale looks at Dan and nods. "Yeah," he says quietly, licking his lips. "Yeah, that's my knife. That guy—the one I was talking about—I couldn't find it after he left. I didn't want to say he stole it because, well, my Dad gave that knife to me and I knew he'd be really upset."

"Well, you'll be glad to know we found it," Dan says matter-of-factly, "just exactly where you left it."

"What the hell are you talking about!" Dale shouts. "I told you it was stolen!"

"Yeah, by some guy who didn't give you a name who you gave your old boots to—which, by the way, we found *with* the knife!"

Dale looks frantic now. "Listen, Detective I—I don't know what's going on here."

"Our crime lab boys tell us that knife is the murder weapon," Dan continues, ignoring Dale's comment. "And guess what, Dale? There is only one set of fingerprints on it. Yours."

The young man almost collapses inward at the force of Dan's last word. "So, Dale," the detective says calmly, "you want to tell me what happened?"

Dale's mouth moves, but no words come out. "Let me help you," Dan says, folding his hands and leaning on the table, "You resented Dr. Maycord having what you couldn't. So, first, you decided to try and get him to call off the engagement by telling him a bunch of crap about Mae Trent. When that didn't work, you decided to kill him. You knew about Fairy Tales and Frights, and somehow found out that Dr. Maycord was going to play The Big Bad Wolf to Mae's Little Red Riding Hood. And I bet the thought of that rich doctor running around chasing your ex-girlfriend just about drove you nuts. Am I right?"

Dale's still quiet. "So, you at some point snuck into the Mansion and decided to hide out in one of the upstairs bedrooms. We found your food and know you slept there, so it had to be for several days. The night of the murder, you got careless, though, and Nate found you wandering around inside after the house had closed. You made up that story on the fly. After they kicked you out, you doubled back and re-entered the house. You figured you didn't have much time left before you were discovered, so you knew you needed to act quickly.

"I bet you just couldn't believe your luck when you saw The Big Bad Wolf come into the house. You were upstairs on the landing. What did you do? Call him upstairs by name? Or did you pretend to be a ghost, make a noise just to lure him into your trap?"

Dale's still staring at Dan when the detective says, "Anyway, it doesn't matter. You stabbed the wolf, thinking it was Dr. Maycord, and saw him tumble down the stairs. Then, you went back into your hiding place like the sniveling little coward you are."

Dale slumps back in the chair, just staring at the detective. Finally, he says, "But none of that happened. I didn't do it."

Dan stands up and says, "I suggest you take the public defender when one's appointed for you. You're going to need one."

Dan's about to leave when Dale starts to laugh. "Wait! I know what all this is! It's a set-up! Yeah. My daddy told me all about the government's tricks to get good, law-abiding citizens behind bars, especially if they challenge the rich and powerful. You, that lady Chief, her priest-lover, Mae, that doctor—you're all trying to frame me. I bet that rich doctor's paid you and that Chief a lot of money to do this, hasn't he?"

Dan looks back at Dale. At first, I'm afraid he's going to lunge at the young man again. But instead, he looks sorrowful and shakes his head.

"Son," he says gently. "No one's out to get you. You're not that important."

Twenty-Six

Being smarter than his father, Dale Riddle accepted the public defender when offered. At the arraignment Friday morning, the young man pleaded not guilty to all charges. In spite of State Attorney Angela Jenkins' argument for no bail, the judge set bail at $500,000.

Not long after the hearing, a Dale Riddle Defense Fund popped up on the Internet, appealing for all "true, God-fearing Americans" to donate to "save an innocent young man from being ground under the jackboots of Big Government and their wealthy benefactors."

Looking at the site in Helen's office that afternoon, I say, "Do you own a pair of jackboots?"

"No, just regular thigh-high leather ones," she says without missing a beat.

"Ah, really?"

"Of course not, Tom," she says. "I couldn't get to my thigh holster if I did."

I have to admit to being a little disappointed.

"So, are you satisfied that you have your man?"

She shrugs her shoulders. "All the evidence points to him."

I look at Helen. "That's not a yes, you know?"

Helen nods. "I know," she says, then returns to her work.

***

Saturday morning, I visit the Davises at their home. Terry was released from the hospital a couple of days before, and he's outside with his brothers and sisters when I arrive.

I look at the children playing in the overgrown, leaf and stick-filled yard. They look happy, probably because their brother's finally home. But the area where they are playing is just not suitable for young children. I must talk to Bill about having the Knights of Columbus do some work around the house, since there's no telling when or if Rusty will come back to his family.

"Hi, Father Tom," Terry says, walking up to me. He's still recovering, so he moves slowly. The bruises on his face are fading, but the plastic surgeon did a good job fixing the damage Rusty did.

"Hi, Terry," I say. "Playing with your brothers and sister?"

"Yeah," he says with a smile. "They've missed me, you know? I'm their big brother."

"I take it you're happy to be home?"

The boy's smile fades a little. "Yeah, I guess. It's different without Daddy. I asked Mommy where he is. She said he's living somewhere else for a while. She says he still loves us, and he's really sorry for what he did to me. I know he didn't mean to do it, Father. I mean, he's been so sad lately. And when he drinks, he's not himself."

I nod, wondering at the almost infinite capacity of children to forgive.

"Mommy says when he gets his life together and stops drinking and gets a job, it will be like it was before," Terry says, beaming again. "Then we'll be a family again. We used to play catch when he got home from work. It's been a long time since I've had anyone to play catch with."

"Twerry," his little sister calls, "you're holding up the game!"

"Be right there, Tina," he calls. "Sorry, Father. I've gotta get back to them. I'm the man of the family now, you know. At least until Daddy comes back."

He runs off, and I blink back a tear and swallow the lump in my throat.

The man of the family. At ten years old.

What a heavy burden he's going to carry.

"Father." I look over to see Bridget walking from the house to me. "I didn't know you were here until I saw you through the window."

"I was talking to Terry," I say. "He seems like he's doing well."

"He is," Bridget says with a grin. "According to the doctors, he'll be back to 100 percent in just a couple of months. They think he may have lost some of his hearing in one ear because of the . . . anyway, they're waiting to see if he'll recover it or if it's permanent."

"He misses his father," I comment.

Her grin fades. "Yes," she says, sadly. "Mae Trent's talked to him about that. She says it's normal for children to miss their abusers."

I nod. "Well, Mae would know. She's the expert. Have you heard anymore from Rusty?"

"A couple of texts, nothing more," Bridget says. "I hope he's OK. It's getting cold up in Minnesota already. He left his snow boots and heavy coat here when he left. Of course, he was in a hurry, trying to keep from being arrested."

Her statement jiggles something in my mind. "What was he wearing when he left?"

"What? Oh, I don't remember. I think a sweatshirt. His windbreaker's gone from the front coat rack, so I guess he grabbed that on the way out. It was a little chilly that day."

"Yes," I mutter. "I remember that."

She shakes her head. "I don't know why I care so much, after all he's done. He left me a long time before he took off, Father, truth be told. I've been doing things myself for a long time. I always thought, if I worked hard enough to keep the family together and the household going, he'd see it and appreciate it. It would inspire him, somehow, to get help, you know, with his drinking and his anger. But I guess I was being a fool."

"You were being hopeful," I say, reassuringly.

"Perhaps." She squares her shoulders and lifts her chin. "But hope's dead. At least for now. So, I just need to put my head down and make the best life I can for the kids."

"Just remember, the parish is always ready to help," I say.

She smiles. "Thank you, Father. Really, I appreciate everything the parish has done through all this. But I can't be dependent on the church forever. I have to stand on my own two feet sometime."

"Oh, Bridget, you don't—"

One of the children screams, "Mama, Ricky hit me!"

"I'll be right there, Tina!" Turning to me, Bridget says, "I have to go, Father. I'm planning on taking the kids to the Fairy Tales and Frights tonight. Will you be there?"

"No, no," I say. "I'll be there tomorrow night. I'm chaperoning the afterparty."

"Are you and Mrs. Parr going to be in costume?"

I roll my eyes. "Yes. She insisted. Wouldn't tell me what she decided on, but I said I'd do it."

She laughs, even as her eyes look sad. "You're going to make a good husband, Father."

"I certainly hope so," I say. "I certainly hope so."

***

Unfortunately, Helen has to work Sunday, so she's not at Mass that morning. She promises, however, that she'll be at the Mansion "with bells on," as she put it.

"I haven't heard you this excited since our engagement," I tell her on the phone after Mass.

"I'm just so looking forward to dressing in our costumes," she says.

I roll my eyes. "Well, my darling, that makes one of us."

"Oh, Tom," she says with a pouting tone, "are you going to be grumpy all night because of this?"

I sigh. "No. Of course not. Unless, of course, I'm supposed to be Grumpy from Snow White."

She laughs. "I assure you, it's not that."

"And you still won't tell me?"

"OK, I'll give you a hint. Everyone who sees it will say it suits you perfectly."

After I hang up, I go back to the Rectory, eat the lunch Anna prepared before going over to Bill's for the afternoon, and then decide that if I'm going to be up all hours, what I really need is a nap. So I go up to my bedroom, change into some comfortable sweats and a t-shirt—I only wear my pajamas at night—and lie down.

I must have fallen asleep right away, because the next thing I know it's 5 p.m. I yawn and stretch, feeling refreshed but also needing another shower to loosen my aging joints. After my shower, I feel less like an old man and more like a—well, not a young man, certainly, but not old in any event.

Not having any idea what Helen wants me to wear, I put the gray sweats and t-shirt back on. When I pick up my phone, there's a cryptic text from Helen:

I stopped by but I guess you were asleep upstairs. I left a package for tonight on the kitchen table. I'll be there around seven.

Slipping on my slippers—my feet get cold, and the floors of the Rectory downstairs aren't carpeted—I go to the kitchen and find a large, green hat box.

Intrigued, I lift off the lid and find, nestled in tissue paper, an authentic saturno—the traditional black, wide-brimmed, wool felt hat worn by priests for generations.

Including a rather famous fictional priest created by G.K. Chesterton.

I smile. "Father Brown," I say. "Of course. But what is Helen wearing?"

Looking again in the box, I find a pair of round wire-rimmed glasses with plain glass and a note in Helen's tortured handwriting. Fortunately, I'm able to decipher what it says:

Dear Father Brown: Please wear this tonight, along with your collar, cassock and umbrella. Love, Bunty.

I peer at the note, my eyebrows raised. "Bunty?" I say. "Who the hell is Bunty?"

A quick internet search on my phone for Bunty brings up nothing at first, so I add "Father Brown" to the search engine. I hit paydirt, and learn that "Bunty" is a character in the new *Father Brown* TV series from the BBC. I've not seen the series, primarily because it has little relationship to the original stories by Chesterton that I love. It's set in the 1950s, not the 1920s, and includes new characters.

Including, apparently, this "Bunty" person.

"Great," I growl. "Helen's dressing as some non-canonical character. Probably the housekeeper."

I scroll down further and find a picture of Bunty.

My heart skips a beat when I finally get a look at her.

She's definitely not the housekeeper.

"Wow," I say as I stare at the picture. "If Helen really is planning on dressing up as her tonight, I'll wear anything she wants me to."

Looking at the time, I see it's already 6:15 p.m. I grab the box and go upstairs to change. I haven't worn my cassock in a long time, and the first thing I notice is that it's a little tighter than I remember.

"Must have shrunk the last time I had it cleaned," I mutter.

Still, I manage to get it on and notice only a tiny bit of stress on the buttons. I get my collar on—again, the neck is tighter than I remember—put the glasses on, and settle my new hat on my head.

"Not bad," I say with a smile as I look at myself in the mirror.

"Father Brown?" Helen calls from downstairs.

"Coming, darling," I say. I get to the top of the stairs and am about to say, "OK, I'll concede, you—" when I am dumbstruck by an altogether enchanting sight.

Helen is indeed dressed as this Bunty character, in a classic, bright-red 1950s dress with a fitted top that accentuates her curves to perfection and a full skirt that falls a few inches below her knee. She has obviously done something to her hair because it is bigger and more brazen than I have ever seen it. She's also wearing bright red lipstick and dainty white gloves.

I confess to being immediately concerned that we are alone in the Rectory and come downstairs quickly to meet her.

"You look incredible," I say, leaning in for a kiss.

I am startled when she pushes me away, saying firmly, "Tom, if I kiss you with this red lipstick, the whole world will know. You'll have to mind your manners."

I try not to look crushed as she says, "I'm going to have to go back to the office tonight for a few hours to keep an eye on our prisoner, so we need to take separate cars. I just wanted to make sure you're wearing your costume before I go on out."

"Well, I am," I say, "though I don't know why."

"Because you love me and I love costumes. But, if you're that unhappy, you don't have to wear it."

"Really?" I say hopefully.

"Of course not. I'll just run home, wash this makeup off my face and change into a pair of jeans and a sweatshirt. Then I'll meet you there."

"Oh, no, you don't," I say, pulling her into my arms. Helen giggles as I say, "You know, I think I'm beginning to like wearing costumes." I then try again to kiss her, but she ducks so I have to be satisfied with kissing her chastely on her forehead. With that she's out the door and I go back to the kitchen for a cup of coffee and a few more minutes of peace before I face the throng at Fairy Tales and Frights.

It's about 7:30 by the time I decide I have to leave. I go out to start my car, only to have the engine refuse to crank.

I try turning the ignition again, pumping the accelerator this time. Still, nothing.

Now, I love cars, but I really know nothing about repairing them. Since nothing at all happens, I assume it's the battery. I pull out my phone and realize I don't have time to call roadside assistance for a jump. Besides, there's always the chance the battery's no longer holding a charge.

The fact of the matter is, I really need a new—or at least, newer—car. It's been a faithful machine, but it's pushing 200,000 miles, and while I keep it in good repair, it's been acting increasingly temperamental.

I sigh and get out of my car. I run through my options. Most of the people I could get a ride with—Nate, Gladys, Martin—are already at the Myer Mansion. I hate to trouble anyone else on Halloween night, since kids are probably beginning to Trick-or-Treat.

As I contemplate my predicament, my eye falls on the garage.

Inside the garage is my bicycle.

Pulling up the door, I stare at the two-wheeled vehicle that I'm still not really enthusiastic about. There's still some light, and the bike has a really good headlight and tail light. Taking the paths through campus, I can avoid roads.

Then, I remember how I'm dressed.

"You couldn't have planned this better, Helen, could you?" I mutter. "Oh, well, in for a penny, in for a pound."

So I pull out the bike, leave my umbrella since I don't know how to ride the bicycle with it, hike up my cassock so it's clear of the chain, and start pedaling towards the Myer Mansion.

Twenty-Seven

I manage to get to the Myer Mansion without incident—thought riding across campus does elicit quite a few looks. Of course, the students were dressed in a myriad of costumes ranging from the sublime to the ridiculous to the scandalous, so I didn't really stand out.

Because he's such a well-known character, when I get to the Mansion I am greeted several times as "Father Brown." The cast of Fairy Tales and Frights applauds and laughs, Gladys in particular commenting, "Wow, Mom told me what she'd decided on. I had no idea she'd go all out."

"The saturno is authentic," I say. "The cassock came out of my closet."

"Looks like you're going to pop a button, Dad," she says.

"It shrank," I say.

"Uh-huh," she says with a grin.

"So, did you and Nate settle on a costume for the afterparty?"

"Oh, yeah," Gladys says. "It's perfect for us."

"I can hardly wait."

Helen arrives about an hour later. Now, I created a small stir when I rode up on my bicycle. But when Helen—ah, Bunty—strides to the house from her car, the swaying of her hips causing her skirt to swish back and forth, she's greeted with a storm of applause, whistles, and cat-calls.

Helen beams as she gets to me. "Father Brown," she says with a curtsy.

"Ah, Bunty," I say, taking her gloved hand and planting a kiss.

"Mom!" Gladys says. "That turned out fabulous! I still can't believe you made that!"

Helen's shaking her head quickly when I look at her. "You made this?"

She sighs and smiles, swaying back and forth. "OK. You discovered my little secret. Yes, I found a vintage pattern to a dress that looked like one the character wore on the show and made it myself. I had to make some alterations, of course. But I'm pleased with how it turned out."

"Where did you learn to sew like this?"

"You're not the only one who took Home Ec in high school. At Saint Monica's School for Girls, I was hopeless at cooking but I excelled at sewing."

"So," I say slowly, "can you, like, mend altar linens and things like that?"

She steps forward and says menacingly, "Yes, I can. And don't you dare breathe a word to Anna."

"Why not?"

"Because I'm not coming home from our honeymoon to find the dining table piled high with altar cloths, purificators, and the like that should have been disposed of years ago for me to mend. Got it?"

"Of course," I say with a smile. Putting a finger to my lips, I say, "Your secret is safe with me."

She smiles. "Good. Shall we, Father?"

"Absolutely, Miss Bunty."

***

Fairy Tales and Frights closes up at 10 p.m., and by 10:30 p.m. the afterparty is in full swing. The young people have a warm bonfire built, and the music is blaring from Gladys' van, the Mystery Machine. Most people have stayed in their costumes from the house, but some have changed. Mae is still in her Little Red Riding Hood costume, but Martin's no longer The Big Bad Wolf. Instead, he's dressed as—well, as Martin Maycord.

"Where are Gladys and Nate?" I say. Helen and I are sitting at a distance, close enough to keep an eye on everything but far enough away not to cramp their style.

"I guess they're changing into their costumes," Helen says. "By the way, what did they finally agree on?"

I shrug. "Last I heard, it was Han Solo and Princess Leia."

Helen is looking past me towards the front door of the house when she begins to laugh. "OK, that's definitely not Princess Lea and Han Solo."

"What?" I turn around to see what she's looking at. "Oh, you have GOT to be kidding me!"

Coming toward us is a tall President John F. Kennedy and First Lady Jackie Kennedy in a wheelchair. Thanks to a black wig, she at least doesn't have blue hair.

She is, however, wearing a very familiar looking pink suit.

"What do you think?" Gladys asks. "Isn't it perfect?"

I look at Nate. "So. Not Han Solo, huh?"

He shrugs. "This makes her happy," he says.

"Good man," I say with a nod.

"It's just . . . Gladys, I have no words," Helen says.

"Thanks, Mom," Gladys grins. To Nate, she says, "Come on, Bae. Let's join the others."

The President and the First Lady go off toward the group dancing around the bonfire.

"Helen," I say. "Gladys is dressed like Jackie Kennedy at Love Field."

"Yes," she says, "yes, she is."

I watch them join the others at the fire. Gladys begins to move her wheelchair in time to the music, Nate dances with her—if the flapping of his arms and moving of his legs can be called dancing.

I can't help smiling. "That's a sight I like to see. That's how they are meant to be."

"I think you're right, Tom," Helen says. "Those two belong together."

"So, how much longer do we have to stay?" I ask Helen, trying not to sound like I'm whining.

"Oh, honestly, Tom," Helen says, her ruby red lips stretched into a smile. "It's not even 11 o'clock and it is a beautiful, starlit evening. We could even go closer to the bonfire if you want to and dance. The music sounds pretty fun."

"Helen, when I dance, it is an excuse to hold you close. I am not going to go over there and jump around with a bunch of teenagers. No, I'm going to sit here and pull out my phone and check the results of this afternoon's race."

"Spoilsport."

Before I can come up with a smart retort, Martin sort of limps over, looking completely wrung out. He collapses in one of the Adirondack chairs we have set up.

"You OK?" I ask with a grin.

He looks at me and smirks. "Oh, yeah. I'm in great shape, for a 36-year-old man trying to convince his child bride-to-be that he is still young and cool."

"I'm sure you're both those things," Helen says reassuringly.

He shakes his head. "I don't understand it. I regularly stand for five or six hours during a surgery, but this is killing me."

"It's the stress," I say, causing both of them to look at me like I've lost my mind. "Seriously, I know that surgery is stressful, but it's also something you're familiar with, a situation you're in charge of. Out here, you're still trying to impress Mae, at least in part by pretending to be something you're not.'"

Martin almost looks hurt at this and asks, "Are you calling me out, Father?"

"Of course not. We all do it. I mean, when Helen got me that bicycle, I acted like it was the best thing she'd ever given me, even though until you told me I needed more exercise, I had absolutely no intention of ever riding it."

We all laugh at this, then Martin says, "I've been meaning to stop by the Rectory to talk to you, Tom."

I glance at Helen, who says, "I think I'll go hang out with the young people for a little bit."

"Oh, Helen, you can stay," he says. "We're all friends here. You know part of it, anyway."

"What's up?"

He takes a deep breath. "Well, after we talked about my encounter with Dale Riddle, Mae and I had a . . . well, it was a fight. Oh, was it a fight. We didn't yell or scream or throw things.

But things were really tense. Pointed even. I discovered a few things about Mae. For one thing, she really does know her own mind. Second, she doesn't back down when she thinks she's right. Third—and this surprised me for some reason—she's also ready to admit when she's wrong. Fourth, and finally, she's the most forgiving person I've ever met."

"So," I say, "things are OK between you?"

He looks at his hands. "Better than OK, Tom," he says. "Once we resolved the whole Dale thing, we sat down and talked about the other elephant in the room."

"Children," I say, prompting Helen's eyes to get big.

"Yeah," he sighs. "This time, we really listened to each other. I told her my concerns—that I wanted the time for us to grow together as a couple before we had children, since we haven't dated that long and, well, the age difference. She told me how important a big family was to her, because that's what she grew up with. I told her I understood that, but I didn't, and it was going to take time for me to adjust. She said she understood that, and she also realized we'd already have children in our home. So after a while, we agreed to a compromise."

"Which is?" Helen asks, eliciting a look from me for a change.

"Well," Martin says, blushing a little. "We're going to practice NFP faithfully for the first six months we're married. After that, well, we'll just see what happens. We may decide to keep using NFP, or we'll leave it in God's hands."

I smile. "That sounds like a perfect compromise to me."

Martin sighs. "Well, we'll see."

In spite of this good news, I do feel compelled to say one thing. "Martin, it's good that you and Mae are talking about these things now. But I hope you realize that it would have been better to talk before you actually got engaged."

Martin sighs. "Yes. That's another thing we agreed on. We realized that there were a lot of things we should have talked about. I know we talked, I just guess it wasn't about the important stuff. So we covered a few things we didn't really talk about before."

"Like?" I ask.

He takes a deep breath. "Well, my net worth, for one. I'm not sure she's quite recovered from the shock."

We're laughing at this when Helen gets a text message. She looks at it and ends her three-day not-cursing streak.

"What?" I ask, knowing full well that she may or may not be able to tell me in front of Martin.

"Dale Riddle made bail," she says with a disgusted look on her face.

"You're kidding me," I reply. "I thought his parents insisted they didn't have two nickels to rub together."

"Well, it turns out that the Riddle's fundraising website raised enough to cover the ten percent they needed to put down. Mr. Riddle picked Dale up a couple of hours ago."

"Why are you just hearing this now?"

"Dan stopped by the department to check on him and found out."

"What'll happen now?" Martin asks, obviously agitated.

"I don't know yet, Martin, but you have got to listen to me," Helen says firmly. "I am here tonight and I will put an officer on your home to watch you, but you cannot, I repeat, cannot do anything yourself. I hate to bring this up, but you are on probation and subject to ending up in jail. The only reason that you got away with that little stunt last Sunday was because Dale didn't pursue it and I for one believe that you made the whole thing up just to try to impress me."

Martin looks at her and begins to smile as I say, "And with that thought ringing in my ears, I'm going to go get a beer. Want one, Helen?"

"No, can't."

"Why not?"

"Because I'm armed and I have instituted a department-wide policy that no one can drink alcohol while carrying a weapon."

"Why'd you do that?"

"Because my favorite instructor at the academy used to say, 'If you have a gun in one hand, you sure as hell better not have a drink in the other.'"

"You know, Helen," Martin says, "one beer is not going to affect a woman of your size, especially if you drink it slowly."

"Perhaps," she says. "And thank you for recognizing the advantage my size gives me in holding my liquor. But I have to practice what I preach, or at least that's what Tom keeps telling me."

I am blushing now and stand to go get the drinks. "What about you, Martin?"

He shakes his head. "I'd better not. Technically, I'm on call tonight."

"So, Helen, you want a diet cola, I know. Martin, what—"

Suddenly, a blood-curdling scream cuts through the night air.

We look in the direction of the bonfire and see shadowy figures wrestling on the ground while a figure wearing a cape continues to scream.

Martin leaps to his feet. "That's Mae," he whispers.

Twenty-Eight

The three of us rush to where the bonfire is still sending sparks into the night. Martin gets there first and goes straight to Mae. She's still standing, looking down at her stomach.

In the firelight, I see the blood staining her white blouse.

"You bastard!" I hear someone scream nearby. I turn in time to see Helen pull Dominic Trent off of a figure on the ground. It's hard to tell, but it looks like someone wearing a Grim Reaper costume.

Helen lets Dominic go, and the young man turns toward Mae and Martin, just as the trauma surgeon says loudly but without panic, "Dominic, get my bag." He tosses the keys to his car to Dominic as he says this. Dominic catches them in mid-flight and dashes towards Martin's Porsche. I pull out my phone to call 911 and am giving the operator our location as I turn and see Martin gently lowering Mae to the ground.

"He stabbed me, Marty," Mae's saying over and over again, her eyes wide with shock. "He just walked up to me and stabbed me!"

One look at the blood gushing from her abdomen onto the ground is all I need. "Get an ambulance out here, now," I bark into the phone. "We have a woman bleeding to death. She's been stabbed at least once." I then toss the phone to Helen, who gives more commands.

Kneeling down by Martin, I ask, "What can I do?"

"I need something to hold pressure on this," Martin says calmly as he looks at the wound. I instinctively gather up the skirt of my cassock and press it toward his hands. Dominic is back by now, carrying a large black backpack with a Red Cross on it.

"Dominic, open the main zipper. Tom, take over here." Using my crumpled cassock, I push down as hard as I can on the wound, even as Mae begins to cry from the pain that's setting in. Martin is digging in his bag, saying calmly to Mae, "I know it hurts, honey, but I'm about to give you something to make you feel better." He draws up a syringe of clear liquid and injects it into her arm, never even breaking his stride.

"Now," he says with a false cheer, "Dominic is going to hold your hand and talk to you while I check out how well you're doing."

Martin is in full-blown surgeon mode now and says, "Dominic, hold her hands down so I can get a look at this." By the time the words are out of his mouth, Dominic has her hands and is holding her.

Martin is tearing open a pouch and ordering me, "Move your hands." When I do, he begins packing the hole in Mae's lower abdomen with what looks like ice cube-shaped bundles of gauze.

As soon as he's done, he says to Mae, "You're doing great, honey." She's calmer now and Martin continues, "Don't worry, I've got you."

She smiles as the drug hits her system with its full force and then, as she's drifting off, I hear her sigh, "I love you, Marty. I want to be your wife."

"You will be, honey, you will be" Martin says, even as he barks, "Where's that damn ambulance?"

"It should be here any moment," Helen assures him before asking, "What can I do?"

"Send someone to get her family. I want them to be at the hospital when we get there. I," and here his voice falters, "I may need to ask them something." Helen is on her phone with dispatch before he can finish his thought and soon Hallstead is on her way to the Trents.

By the time the ambulance arrives two minutes later, Martin has started an IV and has removed the packed gauze. There is still blood oozing from the wound at a pretty steady rate and I hear him say, "Shit," before shoving his right hand into the wound and saying, "Where are you, you little bastard?"

He continues probing the wound with his fingers, saying, "Come on, you're here somewhere." Then, seeming to find what he's looking for, his professional mask slips for a moment.

"No," he whispers. "Please, dear God. Not that."

"What is it?" I ask.

He looks at me and shakes his head, but doesn't answer. He keeps his hand in place, even as the ambulance backs into where we are. The EMTs seem startled to see this, but before they can say anything, Martin barks, "I am Dr. Martin Maycord. Get this girl on a gurney and get us the hell to the hospital!"

As they are loading her I hear him say, "Get the hospital ER on the line and tell them I am coming in hot with a stab wound to the abdomen, likely a nicked uterine artery. We are going straight to the OR. Have a team standing by at E4. Get Reynolds in there and have her set up for an arterial repair and a possible hysterectomy. I want Franks to assist. If Geralds is home in bed, wake him up, I want him as my anesthetist. Then give them our ETA."

He then turns to me and says, "Come on, Tom, you're going with us." This catches me off guard but he speaks with such authority that I follow him into the ambulance.

As soon as the doors close he looks at Mae and says, "You need to anoint her, Tom." He says nothing else but the look on his face says everything. It is only then that I realize I'm wearing that stupid Father Brown costume. Digging under everything to my pants pocket I get out my purple stole and begin the Rite of Anointing of the Sick. I know how little time we have, so I speak clearly and with as few words as possible.

I am just finishing up when we pull into the ambulance bay. Martin is out before the doors are open and yells, "Get her into surgery, now!" even as he sprints off ahead of them.

***

Thanks to Helen's driving skill and knowledge of all the back roads that are too rough to transport a patient over, she's at the hospital by the time I get out of the ambulance.

I wrap my arms around her as she says, "How's Mae?"

"I don't know," I say, shaking my head. "Martin looked—I don't know."

"She's in good hands," Helen says. "We both know that."

I nod. "Was it Dale? What's he saying?"

Helen hesitates before saying, "Not now, Tom. Later."

I open my mouth to protest, but something in her eyes warns me not to. "Let's go," I say.

We go in the side doors, Helen flashing her badge at the security guard who tries to stop us. Martin is already out of sight. We barely get through the doors when her radio goes off.

"I have the Trents," Hallstead says in her steady, authoritative voice.

"We're at the Emergency waiting room," Helen says. "Get them here ASAP. Lights and sirens. And Nina . . . you need to step on it."

After a pause, Hallstead says, "10-4, Chief."

Minutes later, the Hallstead ushers the obviously shaken Trents through the doors of the ER.

"Good job, Officer Hallstead," Helen says. "Get back to the scene."

Helen hugs both the Trents, saying, "I'm so sorry this happened." Still in shock, the Trents say nothing. We escort them straight to the elevators. Going up to the fourth floor, we're soon in the surgical waiting room, a room I know too well.

"I'll go see if I can find a nurse," Helen says. She leaves and I take the Trents by the hands and try to reassure them, saying, "Martin has been with her the whole time, so she has been in great hands."

"But what happened, Father?" Doris Trent moans.

"The officer only told us Mae had been in an accident and was being rushed into surgery," Alan Trent says. "Please, tell us what happened to our daughter."

Before I can answer, Martin runs through the doors and comes straight to where we are. He quickly hugs Alan and Doris and says, "Let's go in here." He leads us to a small meeting room—the same room he talked to me in after Helen's surgery.

The Trents collapse into a couple of chairs as Martin squats down beside them. "I only have a moment before I have to scrub in," he says quietly. "I don't know how much you know yet, and I don't have time to tell you everything. But this is what you need to know. Mae was stabbed in the abdomen. The knife nicked her uterine artery. The normal procedure in cases like this is to do a hysterectomy, but you know how much she wants—how much we both want children." He pauses then says, "Now, I believe I can repair the artery and save her uterus. However, that is a much riskier procedure. She's already lost a great deal of blood, and she'll lose more if I do this. I may not be able to do the repair, so to save her life, I'd have to perform the hysterectomy anyway. But I would like your permission to try."

Alan stares at Martin like he can't decide whether to punch him or hug him as Doris bursts into tears. Martin continues, "Alan, I know you haven't known me long. You may still have your doubts about me as a suitable husband for your daughter, and you may be right. But please, do not doubt my skills as a surgeon. I can do this."

Still staring at Martin, Alan gives a brief nod. Martin says nothing but sprints out of the room.

"Let's go back to the waiting room," I say quietly. "This is going to take a while."

We're met by a nurse with paperwork for the Trents. I know what the next 24 hours are going to be like, so I take advantage of their distraction to slip into the men's room to wash up.

This turns out to be a bad decision. As the water washes the blood off my hands and I see it swirling down the drain, I'm taken once more back to the night that Helen was shot.

Is this the same restroom I was in? No, I remember, Thompson took me back to get a shower. There was more blood that time, but it smelled the same. I see my cassock for the first time, crumpled and stiff with Mae's dried blood. I snatch it off, afraid somehow that if I keep it on, I will be taken back to that basement, transported against my will to that cold floor, or worse, to that warm parking lot where I held Joan. Not caring that Anna will complain, I toss the garment into the trash.

"Just hang on," I whisper. "Someone will be here soon. I promise. Don't leave me. I love you."

I don't know who I'm talking to, Joan or Helen, but I know who Martin's thinking of now. I offer up the sense of panic, of helplessness, to be united with the very blood of Christ on the cross, for Martin's benefit and more so for Mae.

"Oh, God in heaven," I pray fervently, "Make Martin's hands steady and wise."

I take a few more deep breaths, splash some cold water on my face, and emerge from the restroom looking nothing like a priest of this century or the last but just some guy in a t-shirt and sweatpants.

I find the Trents in the waiting room with Helen. Gladys and Nate arrive a few minutes later with a few of the Trents in tow.

"Martin's Aunt Louise is with the younger ones at their house," Gladys explains with tears welling up in her eyes. "Dad, is—is Mae—"

"She's in surgery," I say. "She's lost a lot of blood, but Martin's with her."

Gladys nods and wipes her eyes. "I can't lose someone else," she whispers. "I just can't." She clutches at Nate, who wraps his arms around her as she cries.

Dominic comes in a few minutes later with Therese Shepherd, his girlfriend. His jaw is firm, his face set. Stoically, he walks over to his parents and gives them a hug.

Therese says to Helen and me, "Domie's spoken to his older brother Vincent. He's on his way from Pennsylvania. He'll be here in a couple of hours."

"I'll send Thompson to meet him at the state line," Helen says, "give him a police escort in." She goes off to call the station.

In groups of two and three, the other members of the Acutis society arrive over the course of the next half hour. They're all young, and most of them are afraid. A person they care about, and who is in many ways their leader, lays critically wounded on an operating room table.

I motion for all of them to gather around me in another part of the waiting room, away from the Trents. "I know this is a very, very distressing and scary time for you," I say, "and you're probably worried and wondering what you can do. Right now, the most important thing you can do is to pray for Mae, and for Dr. Maycord, and all the others working to save our friend's life."

They sit down in chairs. I hear and see Rosaries being pulled out, and am gratified when I hear Nate say, "In the name of the Father, and the Son, and the Holy Spirit," to begin the prayers.

"Father Tom?" I turn to see one of the surgical nurses I remember from Helen's time here. She motions for me to come to her and we walk to a quiet corner.

"Dr. Maycord asked me to talk to you," she says quietly. "There's a problem."

"Is she—"

"No, she's still alive, but she's lost a lot of blood. She has a very rare blood type, B negative, and the hospital blood bank is out of that type and the other types she can receive. He was hoping you may be able to get people from your church to come donate?"

"Does she have enough time for me to do that?"

She opens her mouth, then shakes her head. "No. We need that blood now."

I look over my shoulder at the praying group of young people and say, "Come with me." We walk over to the group and I say quietly, "I am sorry to interrupt your prayers. Mae is in desperate need of blood. Now, I don't know if you know your blood types or not, but she specifically needs B negative. Is anyone B negative?"

With tears in her eyes, Gladys looks up and says, "I am. She can have as much as she needs."

I smile. "Anyone else?"

The group looks back and forth, some people shrugging their shoulders. "Just follow this nurse to the blood bank. Even if you can't help Mae, you can help someone else."

The Acutis society members, joined by Dominic, follow the nurse out of the waiting room. Helen comes back and says, "Tom, I need to get back to the station. I've got to sort out this mess."

"You still didn't answer my question about Dale. Why did he stab Mae?"

Helen looks at me, and in her eyes, I can see she's still hesitant to tell me anything. Finally, she says quietly, "All I can tell you, Tom—and please keep this to yourself for right now—is that chances are, we'll never know the answer."

I open my mouth to ask another question, but before I can the elevator doors open and she gets on. The doors close, and I turn away to go back to my hurting flock.

***

We spend the next several hours hoping, waiting, and praying. One by one, the members of the Acutis society return from giving blood, the bandage in the bend of their arm mute testimony to the small sacrifice each gave so Mae—or some other person in need—could have a chance at life. As they come, each stops by to ask if there's any word.

"Not yet," I say quietly. "You still need to pray."

Gladys comes back and wheels herself over to the Trents. "Mr. and Mrs. Trent," she says. "I'm Gladys Finklestein. I don't believe we've met formally, but I'm a friend of Mae. I consider her my best friend in the parish—really, my best friend anywhere. I've been through a lot of stuff in my life, and I've been working to become a better person—a better Catholic. I—I just want to tell you that Mae, more than any other person except the Father here, has been the greatest influence on me. I told her some secrets about myself—things I've become ashamed of—and her kindness and compassion gave me so much courage about facing them. I—I love her. I'm an only child, my parents are dead, so I don't have any siblings. I just want you to know that I consider Mae the sister I've never had."

By this time, Gladys is sobbing. I have to admit some tears are flowing down my cheeks, too. In the midst of her own grief, Doris reaches out to Gladys and wraps her arms around her.

"Mae's mentioned you, Gladys," she whispers, "how she's come to consider you her best friend. She calls you 'my quirky genius of a friend.' She talks about how smart you are, and your blue hair, and your love of vintage clothing. And she's mentioned how big a heart you have. Thank you for what you just said. It means the world for me to hear that about my daughter."

After a moment, Gladys slowly pulls away from her and nods. Turning around, she goes over to join the other members of the Acutis Society.

The time passes slowly, as it always does at times like this. Finally, Martin comes out, looking exhausted but smiling.

"Doris, Alan," he says, his southern accent more pronounced than usual because he's so tired, "let's go over here to talk."

Doris grips my hand, a wordless request to accompany them. Martin shows us to the same side room where we sat—has it only been hours? It seems like days—before.

Once he closes the door and we're seated, he collapses in a chair himself.

With a weary grin, Martin says, "She will be fine. She lost a lot of blood and it will take her some time to recover, but she should be fine. We'll keep her in the hospital for a few days to rest, and so we can stay ahead of any infection, but she should be home by her birthday."

Doris sits up in her chair. Raising her chin, she asks, "And children?"

"Ma'am," Martin says, "she can have a whole housefull if she wants to."

Doris begins to cry softly as Alan puts his left arm around her and sticks his right hand out. As Martin shakes it, he says firmly, "Do you think you can handle that, son?"

Martin's grin widens. "Sir," he croaks, his voice heavy with emotion, "if God gives them to us, we'll raise them."

Twenty-Nine

After hours that seem like days of waiting, the Trents are finally allowed to go back and see Mae briefly. Knowing how traumatic this will be for them, and how short a time they'll be allowed to stay, I decide to wait for them to come back out. The sorrow and worry that had hung like a cloud over everyone has lifted, and instead of quiet prayers of sadness, laughter and happy chatter fill the waiting room.

Gladys and Nate come over, still dressed as Jack and Jackie, though she's taken off her black wig, pillbox hat, and gloves.

"You look tired, Father," Nate says.

"I am," I say with a weary smile. "What time is it anyway?"

"Almost 6 a.m.," Gladys observes.

"That's what I thought," I say as I yawn and stretch. "I don't think I'll ever get used to these all-night vigils."

"We've had quite a few of them recently."

I nod. "Well, here's hoping the rest of the year will be a quiet one." I rub my eyes then say, "I'm going to wait for the Trents to come out, then go back to the Rectory and get a couple of hours of sleep. I've got the Noon Mass plus a 7 p.m. Mass tonight."

"Why two Masses?" Nate asks. "It's Monday."

"November 1," I say. "All Saints Day. It's a holy day of obligation, remember?"

"We'll be at one of the Masses, Dad," Gladys says.

"Um, isn't All Soul's Day tomorrow?" Nate asks.

"Yes, it is; now that's not an obligation, you know."

Nate nods. "Oh, I know, I know," he says quietly.

Just then, the Trents return. Dominic, Vincent, and the older Trent children rush to them.

"How is she?" Dominic asks, Therese holding his hand.

Alan smiles, tears of relief flowing down his cheeks and onto his beard. "She's awake and talking," he says. "She's going to be fine."

Everyone breaks out into cheers. "Wonderful news," I say, shaking Alan's hand and hugging Doris. "Gather around, everyone, and I'll lead us in prayer."

The entire crowd of young people surround the Trent family, bowing their heads and joining hands with each other. I begin a heartfelt prayer of thanksgiving for Mae's survival and for the medical team that saved her.

"Amen," we all say in unison at the end. I turn to the Trents and say, "I'm so glad. I need to go, but I'll make sure an announcement is sent to the entire parish about Mae. I'll come visit her tomorrow. If you need anything, please call me."

Doris hugs me. "Thank you, Father Tom, for everything. You're such a blessing to the parish. I want you to know that our family prays for you, and for Helen, and your upcoming marriage every day."

"Thank you," I say. "I need all the prayers I can get."

I go to the elevator and press the down button. The doors open and I'm about to step on when I see Helen in the car.

"Hi," I say, surprised to see her. "I was just—"

"We need to talk, Tom," she says in full cop mode. "The Trents are still here, right?"

"Yeah, they're over there. What's this all about?"

Instead of answering, she walks to the nurses station. "Is Dr. Maycord still in the hospital?"

The nurse checks her computer. "The system says he's still here. Would you like me to page him to come here?"

"No," Helen says. "I need to meet him in his office."

The nurse looks a little surprised at this, but she nods. Not long after she sends a page for Martin over the hospital PA system, he calls.

"He'll be there as soon as he can," she says, "I'm to call someone from security to let you in."

"Thank you," Helen says. To me, she says, "Get the Trents, please, and meet me there."

She begins to walk off, but I reach out to her and touch her shoulder. "Helen? What is all of this about?"

She looks at me with pain in her eyes. "Answers," she whispers.

***

We're all seated around Martin's large desk, his obviously high end ergonomic chair awaiting its exhausted owner. Finally, he comes in and walks immediately to the Trents.

"She's all tucked in," Martin says. "She was only awake for a few minutes after you left, and she won't wake again for at least eight or ten hours. You need to go home and try to get some sleep. You'll want to be fresh when you see her later today."

"And what about you, son?" Alan, always the dad, asks the man not at all young enough to be his son.

Martin smiles wearily at this and says, "Please don't worry about me, sir. One of the perks of my position is that an orderly will come in and make that couch into a very comfortable bed as soon as I ask him to. I'll stay here and go home after y'all get back to stay with her. I can check on the girls then."

I am touched by the fatherly ways Martin has so obviously slipped into as Helen says, "Martin, I know you're exhausted, but I need to talk to you and the Trents briefly about the man who tried to kill Mae."

"Oh, yes. I had forgotten about him in all our own sorrow. Have you spoken to Dale's parents yet? They must be absolutely heartbroken." Doris says.

Helen takes a deep breath and says quietly, "I have spoken to Dale's parents, and to Dale himself, to tell him that he is no longer a murder suspect."

No one says anything as Helen takes another deep breath, obviously giving everyone a chance to process this information. "Alan, Doris, Martin. Dale Riddle did not try to kill Mae tonight. He almost certainly did not kill Larry Daniels. Rusty Davis was the man in the Grim Reaper costume." She pauses and adds, "I should tell you also, that Mr. Davis was pronounced dead at the scene. When Dominic tackled him after his attack on Mae, Mr. Davis landed on the knife. It will take an autopsy to say for sure what happened, but from what she could tell at the scene, the ME believes the knife severed an artery. He bled out within seconds."

Again we all sit in silence until Doris says, "I don't understand, Helen. Why would Bridget Davis' husband want to harm Mae? I mean, everyone thought he was far away from here."

"Besides," Alan says, "Mae never mentioned knowing him."

"Alan, since their paths crossed within the confines of her work at the hospital, I'm sure she never did mention him. Martin knows what I am talking about and I am sure he is even now piecing together why Mr. Davis acted as he did."

I glance at Martin. From the look in his eyes, he's already figured it out, or at least some of it.

"We still have a lot of work to do to piece everything together," Helen says. "I don't have a lot of answers right now. So I am asking for your patience and forbearance. Please, for the next few days, just focus your attention on helping Mae get better. The man who attacked her is dead and will never hurt anyone again, of that you can be sure. I will get the rest of the information to you as soon as I can."

"Of course, Helen," Doris says, "You do your job and we'll do ours."

"And I'll do mine," Martin interjects, seeming to just get his head above the fog of exhaustion that's enveloping him, "And right now that requires me to kick you out of my office and send you home to get some rest so I can, too." He stands, smiles and hugs the Trents and Helen, and shakes my hand firmly, saying, "Thank you for everything, Tom. We wouldn't have made it through without you."

***

Helen leaves to return to her apartment, grab a quick shower, and change into something more befitting a chief of police than her Bunty costume—which she's still wearing. The only remaining part of my Father Brown costume is my saturno, looking out of place sitting on my head while I'm wearing sweats and a t-shirt.

Though I am tired, I made a commitment after Helen's hospitalization to always make time to stop by the chapel for a few minutes to thank God for her recovery, to pray for those in crisis, and to check to see if there was anyone who needed comfort. I slip into the back of the beautiful, dimly lit room.

This place is truly a marvel for, while many modern facilities have up-to-date, religiously neutral decor, this chapel was moved, piece by piece, from the previous hospital and is still 100 percent Catholic. The designers placed the non-sectarian facility front and center on the first floor of the new hospital, but the Myer family paid to move this one to its out-of-the way space on the fifth floor. Still, I love how dim and sacred it is.

It's quiet this morning. I go forward, light a candle for Mae, and kneel briefly, offering prayers for her and her family, present and future. I am only there a few minutes before I stand and turn to go. It's then that I notice a disheveled head bent over a pew. I don't recognize the person until I start to pass by and he speaks, asking, "You got a minute, Father?"

"Of course," I reply, as I sit down by an obviously physically, mentally, and emotionally exhausted Martin Maycord. "I thought you were going to get some sleep?"

"So did I," he says. "But I felt drawn here. You know, I only found this place a month ago? It's the hospital's best-kept secret."

I say nothing as he sighs. "That was the worst thing I have ever been through in my life, Tom, and it makes no sense. I have been a rotten, reprobate bastard much of my adult life and nothing happened to me or anyone I cared about. Do you know how many good guys I saw die in Afghanistan? But did anything happen to me? Nope. One guy I knew said a Hail Mary, out loud, in front of everyone, everytime we took off. His plane went down in a fireball. Another guy, completing his ROTC obligation before entering seminary and who read his Bible every night, got his head blown off not six feet from where I was standing. But me, who cussed and drank and fooled around with anything in a skirt—including, truth be told, a few local girls I paid for the privilege—slept every night safe and sound.

"Then, I come back to God, start trying to be a better person, to be the man Mae deserves, and look what happens. Tom, she almost died. I'll never tell her or her parents this, at least not anytime soon, but her heart stopped twice—once because there was just not enough blood for it to pump, and once because it was just under so much pressure. I got her back both times, saved her ability to have our children, and she's going to be fine. But I have to wonder, where was God when this was happening?"

I want to say nothing. I want to tell him to go and get some rest, to take a shower and then he'll feel better, more clear-headed and ready to talk, but his eyes are burning into mine, demanding an explanation. So I give him what little I have.

"God was in that operating room with you," I say, putting my hand on his shoulder, "guiding your hands, restarting her heart. Just like He was there when you met Mae on the steps of Saint Clare's, just like He was there to welcome home the two men you saw killed and the others who slipped from this life to the next loving Him. He was there beside you, allowing you to make good and bad choices, loving you while slowly and inextricably bringing you to this moment in time. He will be there when your first child is born and when the last gets married. And no matter how hard we try to ignore it, someday He will be with Mae or you, when one finally loses the battle against sin that inevitably takes them from this earth.

"Martin, I can't explain to you why things happen the way they do, anymore than you can explain to me the intricacies of the surgery that just saved Mae's life and her chance for motherhood. But you know surgery, and that's enough. God knows his plan, too, and that has to be enough, because otherwise, what do any of us really have?"

He nods, and I think I've managed to comfort him, at least a little. I stand up and look down at the exhausted doctor and say, "Now, having said that, listen to your priest. Go back to your office and get some rest. After that and a shower, things will look a little better."

Wordlessly, he stands and together we walk out of the chapel, turning in tandem to genuflect before the flickering flame that reminds us that, no matter what burdens we bring in or take out, Jesus is still right here, the Light in an often very dark world.

Thirty

Nate and Gladys drop me off at the Rectory—my dead car is still in the driveway, and my bicycle is at the Myer Mansion—a little before 8 a.m. I'm immediately peppered with questions from Anna about what happened and if Mae is all right. I answer as briefly as I can and ask her to send a note around the parish email chain giving everyone an update before trudging upstairs, setting my phone alarm for 11 a.m., and throwing myself on the bed.

I must have fallen asleep right away, because my alarm wakes me with a jolt. Feeling surprisingly refreshed, I shower and get dressed and walk downstairs to the kitchen. Anna has made a fresh pot of coffee, and I pour a cup and take it into the living room for a few moments of peace before I walk over to the church to prepare for Mass.

"I thought I heard you," Anna says, walking into the room and sitting down. "Did you manage to get any sleep?"

I nod. "Yeah, I think I'll make it through the rest of the day."

She shakes her head. "I still can't believe it. Of all the people in the world, Mae Trent is the last person I'd think of someone wanting to kill. Who hated her that much?"

I hesitate a moment before saying, "Helen's probably made the notification, but keep this to yourself for now. Rusty Davis is the one who tried to kill Mae and probably killed Larry Daniels thinking he was killing Martin."

Anna's shocked. "But—Rusty wasn't even in Myerton! He told Bridget he was in Minnesota. And he was hiding in town all this time?"

"That's what it looks like," I say.

"What did he have to say for himself when Helen arrested him?"

I shake my head. "He couldn't say anything. He's dead. Killed by the same knife he stabbed Mae with."

Anna sighs and closes her eyes. "Oh, Tom. Does Bridget know?"

"Probably by now," I say. I put my now empty cup on the coffee table and stand up. "I better get over to the Church. I've got a lot of work to do."

***

Much to my surprise, Dominic is vested and has already set up the altar. He looks tired. But more than tired, burdened.

"Dominic," I say. "You don't have to do this. I can manage."

He takes a deep breath. "No, Father. Mae would want me here."

I'm also surprised to see Helen slip in as I start Mass. No longer dressed as Bunty, she's wearing her usual professional suit, a blue blazer with matching blue skirt. Even from where I am, it's clear she got little if any sleep.

After Mass is over, I find her waiting in the church.

"Hi," I say, giving her a hug.

"Hi," she says quietly.

"You OK?"

She pulls away from me and shakes her head. "Not really."

"What's wrong?"

She closes her eyes and takes a deep breath. "Tom, Mae's in the hospital because of me."

"Oh, now, Helen, that's ridiculous!"

"Is it?" she asks, tears beginning to show in her eyes. "I knew there was something that didn't fit with Dale Riddle being the killer. My gut told me there was more going on, and I didn't listen to it. I didn't bother to have Dan follow up on Dale's story about the homeless guy—who was most likely Rusty Daniels. I thought everything was set, so I let my guard down. I should have had a couple of officers there."

I put my arms back around her and pull her to my chest. "You've got to stop this, Helen. You and I both know it doesn't lead anywhere good. The fact of the matter is, Dale made perfect sense as a suspect. Everyone thought Rusty was out of town. You had no way of knowing he was in town. Helen, you can't know what you don't know."

I can feel her smile against my chest. "Did they teach you that in seminary?"

"Maybe," I say with a grin.

She takes a deep breath. "I need to get a statement from Mae. Will you go with me?"

"Of course. I need to go check on her anyway. Then I need to check on Bridget."

"We've done the notification," Helen says. "I'll go with you in case she has any questions."

"I'm almost certain she will. I know I do."

***

We arrive at the hospital to find Mae is out of the ICU and ensconced in Myerton General's only VIP room, complete with a wall of windows, a small kitchen, and a comfortable seating area near the patient's bed. There is no nurse in the room at the moment but she has no lack of medical care, as the chief of trauma surgery is sitting by her bedside monitoring her condition assiduously. She is still pale from the blood loss, a condition that I am familiar with from Helen's incident of a few months ago.

Helen crosses the room to her and, carefully maneuvering around the tubes, gives her a gentle hug. I do my usual friendly in-hospital gesture of patting the patient's foot before shaking Martin's hand.

"Good to see you both," Martin says. He waves us to the couch and pulls out his phone to send a text message. A few minutes later, an orderly arrives with drinks and snacks. I have never been in this part of the hospital before and am quite impressed.

Mae eyes our snacks hungrily and says, "That's beginning to look good."

Martin takes her hand and says, "Nothing so crunchy for you, my dear; in fact, nothing at all before tonight. But then I have a bowl of egg drop soup being delivered from China Palace."

She smiles at this and squeezes his hand, saying playfully, "But you hate that place. And anyway, I thought you told me you are not my doctor, but only my fiancé?"

"I'm not," he assures her, looking into her eyes and smiling, "because if I were your doctor, you'd be eating green jello with everyone else. However, Dr. Drake assures me that you should be able to handle that vile soup."

Helen takes advantage of this to say, "Mae, if you feel up to it, I'd like to get your statement about what happened."

"Helen," Martin says firmly, "I'd really rather you wait until Mae's more rested. I don't want her getting upset or tiring herself out."

Before Helen can reply, Mae surprises us by saying just as firmly, "She asked me, Martin, not you, and I am fine telling her what I remember." Then, looking at Helen she adds, "Which I'm afraid isn't much."

"I completely understand," Helen says. "Why don't you just start where you first noticed the Grim Reaper" She activates her phone's recorder and asks, "Is it OK if I record this? I'll have someone at the station transcribe it and then bring it by tomorrow for you to read over and sign."

"That will be fine," Mae says. Taking a deep breath, she begins, "We were all just sort of hanging out. Some people were dancing and I had been, but had stopped to catch my breath. Jill and Heather were there and they were asking me about where Martin was and teasing me about him being an older man and I had just said—" She pauses and blushes a little. "I probably shouldn't say. Oh, well, it's not that big a thing. I told them an older man knows how to treat a woman like a lady."

She grins at Martin, who blushes slightly before saying, "Or at least is capable of learning."

Mae takes his hand and continues, "Someone said, 'Let's make s'mores' and Heather and Jill went over toward the bonfire. I don't like marshmallows so I was about to go find Martin when this guy came up to me. He was wearing a Grim Reaper costume and had his hood up and his face covered with this sort of thin fabric so I didn't know who he was. I figured he was just someone's boyfriend or something. Anyway, he said, 'Mae Trent?', like he wanted to meet me, and I said

'Yes.' Then he said, 'I have an engagement present for you and the doctor.' I was about to thank him when he pulled out the knife. It had a bow around it and in the instant that I saw it, I thought, 'Oh, that's good. We'll need a good knife.'

"But then, before I could say or do anything, he stabbed me, hard, in my stomach. The first thing I felt was the hilt hit me and I thought it was one of those trick Halloween knives. But then he pulled it out and I saw the blood and I think I started screaming."

The three of us nod our heads slightly, for that is indeed what we heard. "I wanted to run," she says, "to get away but I couldn't seem to move. I saw that he was raising his arm and I knew he was going to stab me again. I started to duck and put my arms up but the next thing I knew, Domie had knocked him to the ground. Martin got there right after that and I just remember him telling me that I was going to be all right and thinking, 'He's a good doctor. He would know.' After that, I don't remember anything else until I woke up here." She waves her arm around the room.

Helen turns off the recorder and says gently, taking Mae's other hand, "That's everything we need." Then, with a playful smile, "I'll now turn the floor over to my esteemed fiancé who has much more important work to do here than I."

Both Martin and Mae visibly relax as I prepare to give Mae another anointing, this time with communion. I use the short form, which still allows places for Helen and Martin to make responses and then gently place the Holy Eucharist on her outstretched tongue.

"Thank you, Father Tom," Mae says weakly. She's clearly exhausted, so I say, "Helen and I will leave you now to get some rest. I'll try to stop by tomorrow."

I carefully pat her, and Helen and I turn to go. Mae says, "Marty told me it was Rusty Davis?"

Helen and I turn. "Yes," Helen says.

"Marty told me he's dead?"

Helen nods. "Yes. When Dominic tackled him, Rusty fell on his own knife."

Mae nods. "How's Bridget?"

"We're going over there to see her." I say.

"When you do," Mae says, "can you give her a message? Tell her I'll be praying for her and her family, and as soon as I get out of here, I'll get her and the kids any help they need."

I smile, impressed but not at all surprised.

***

"You know, Tom," Helen says as we walk to the car, "this is the second time in as many weeks that we have come to this hospital together, both in our professional capacities. Do you think all those reporters who have questioned how we would be able to both live out our callings as a married couple would be surprised?"

"Probably, but they really shouldn't be. There are more similarities in what we do than meets the eye?"

"Oh?" she says. "Pray explain, Father Greer."

I take on the challenge vigorously, for I have been thinking about this a lot since we became engaged. "Follow my train of thought. We are both in charge of encouraging people to follow laws that we ourselves did not make. The laws are in fact very similar, not as similar as they once were, but in most cases, the Ten Commandments still provide the inspiration for many of the laws on the books.

"I instruct more than you do, but even you have programs that reach out to remind people to obey speed limits, not to steal, etcetera. You do more enforcing than I do, but only after a moral failing has led to a legal one, for it is rare that someone breaks a law without also breaking a commandment.

"And finally, we both often meet people when someone has broken a law or has hurt them in some deep and lasting way. As a detective and even more so as the Chief of Police, you don't typically get called out to the so- called 'victimless crimes.' You get called by someone who has been hurt, either emotionally or physically, by someone else. So do I. You offer the hope of justice in this world, I of mercy in the next. Whether they know it or not, most of the time when someone needs you to help them, they also need me."

She seems to ponder this as we reach the car and drive off. Then she says, "But there are contrasts, too, Tom, ones that we need to take into account in our desire 'to act justly and to love mercy and to walk humbly with God.'"

"What are those?" I ask.

"Mae has all the resources in the world: a large, loving family, a wealthy fiancé, youth, beauty, education, everything she can possibly need to survive and thrive. Bridget Davis has precious little, maybe even less now, for while she could once keep her husband's misdeeds private, the whole world knows of them now, as do her children. How are we, as a church and a community, going to reach out to her, to show her family mercy and justice?"

"That is a very good question, one I'm glad you asked," I say thoughtfully. "We definitely need to come up with a plan to support her and the children in the months ahead. Give me a couple of days and I'll think of something, unless there's something that I need to do right now."

Helen shakes her head. "No, right now, Anna has the Ladies of Charity living up to their name. They'll take care of everything between now and the funeral. We just need to make sure that the support keeps up, even after the flowers are dead and the casseroles have been eaten."

"Well, that will be one of the things I'll ask her when we see her."

***

I'm pleased to find several cars in front of the Davis house, including Anna's, when Helen and I arrive.

When we knock at the door, it's Anna who greets us. Letting us in, she says quietly, "The children are next door. Poor darlings, I don't think they really know what's happened. Except for Terry. He's in his room."

"I wanted to speak to Bridget for a moment," I say quietly.

Anna nods and looks at Helen. "I know you'll need to talk to her, but can it wait until tomorrow?"

"Of course," Helen says. "I'm here as her priest's fiancé, not Chief of Police."

Anna nods and leads us to a back room that looks like a den or a family room. Bridget is seated at the window, staring out at the backyard.

"Bridget, dear," Anna says quietly. "Father Tom and Mrs. Parr are here to see you. Do you feel up to talking to them for a few minutes?"

She nods slightly. "Yes," Bridget says quietly and turns around to face us.

Anna leaves us, and Helen and I sit on the couch near her. "Bridget," I say quietly, "I just want to tell you I'm so sorry about Rusty. Is there anything you need from me right now?"

She shakes her head. "No. I've told Anna I just want a quiet graveside service. No funeral Mass. He hadn't been to Church in months, so I don't think he'd care."

"That's fine," I say. "What about funeral expenses?"

"Anna said Bill Brandt and the Knights will pay for a space at the cemetery. He'll be cremated." Turning to Helen, she asks, "When will you be done with the body?"

"He's at the state medical examiner's office in Baltimore," Helen replies. "I'll check tomorrow, but I'd say they'll release the body Wednesday."

Bridget takes a deep breath. "Wednesday. Good. Then we'll have the funeral on Friday. Get it over with. Is that all right, Father?"

"I'll make sure my schedule's clear."

"Thank you." She lapses back into silence and turns to look out the window. "I had no idea he was in town," she says. "I thought he was in Minnesota. You have to believe me that I would have told you if I knew."

"I believe you," Helen says. "We had no indication he was in Myerton, either."

"Oh, that poor boy! And Mae!" she wails, collapsing into sobs. "Mae tried to help me and the kids, and Rusty did this to her! She must hate me! Her parents must hate me!"

I go from the couch to her chair, squatting by it and saying, "No, not at all. In fact, Mae told me to tell you that she's praying for you and your family, and that she'll be glad to help you in any way she can after she's healed."

Bridget looks at me, tears still flowing down her cheeks. "She—she said that?"

I nod, and the new widow collapses into my arms, sobbing. I put my arms around her to comfort her. Helen soon joins me, the arms of justice and mercy holding her as she cries.

We stay like that for a long time before she calms down. Finally, all cried out, Bridget says, "Thank you for coming, both of you. But I'd like to be alone now."

We assure her of our continued prayers and tell her to contact me if she needs anything. We leave the room, only to run into Anna outside the door. She's holding a white envelope.

"This just came in the mail," she says, handing it to Helen. "I figure you'd want to look at it before Bridget does."

Helen takes one look at it and takes a deep breath. "Well, maybe we'll have some answers after all."

The envelope is addressed to Bridget, with a Myerton postmark showing it was mailed Saturday, October 30.

Thirty-One

Tuesday being All Souls Day, I get to the Church early. For the past month in the narthex, people have had the opportunity to write the names of their dearly departed in a book of remembrance. It's a common practice for the names collected to be placed on the altar. I want to get the book in place before Mass starts.

But not before making some additions of my own.

I'm gratified to see the book about half-full. Scanning it, I see some familiar names and handwriting. I put Joan's name in when I set the book out, along with my dad and my sister Sonya. I also wrote in the name of Father Leonard McCoy. Right below, Helen wrote John's name along with those of her parents and grandparents.

Flipping through, I see other additions. In Gladys' flowing handwriting, I see her parents and grandparents. I'm startled to see she included Chad Hudson and Richard Davenport.

"You have come a long way, my darling daughter," I whisper.

I take the pen by the book and open to the last partially filled-out page. I'm about to write a name when I see someone's already included it.

"God bless you, Nate," I say. He wrote the name Victoria Myer.

Underneath, I write Rusty Davis and Larry Daniels.

One a murderer, the other his victim.

Both souls in need of prayer.

***

That night, Helen and I have just finished dinner and go, as we do as often as possible, into the church to say Evening Prayer. The door is unlocked, as it always is until I lock up at night, and we slip into the dimly lit place where, everyday, God comes once again to his people on earth.

I see someone in a pew, praying. Since I often mention that anyone here at this time is more than welcome to join us, I am not surprised to hear Dominic Trent making the responses along with Helen. Given all that we have been through, the words that begin Evening Prayer are especially poignant: "Oh God, come to my assistance, O Lord, make haste to help me."

The Church, knowing that this is prayed at the end of a long day by people who are weary, keeps this form short and Helen and I stand back up and head for the door less than a quarter hour later. We are careful not to disturb Dominic but he stands as we do, so I turn to meet him. He is obviously distraught and as soon as I see him, I say, "Would you like to come over to the Rectory for a chat?"

I can tell he wants to but he hesitates, saying, "I don't want to intrude."

"Dominic," I say firmly, "You are never an intrusion. No one who needs me ever is or ever will be. Now come on."

Still, he hesitates. Then, Helen takes him firmly by the arm and propels him toward the Rectory, not exactly in a perp walk but reminiscent of one, saying, "I have a pumpkin bread that I just took out of the oven before we walked over and a pot of hot apple cider simmering in the slow cooker." She gently squeezes his hands, saying as she does so, "You're freezing. I've touched corpses that were warmer. Father Tom will stir up the fire, and I'll leave you two men to talk."

We're walking in the door now and Dominic says, "No, Mrs. Parr. I kinda need you to stay. I mean, I know you mentioned to my parents that you needed to get a statement from me."

"I did," Helen says calmly, "but it will wait if you need to talk to Father Tom."

"No, ma'am. I really think I need to talk to both of you. I mean, I may need to confess to one or both of you but I don't know, so I need you to tell me."

We look at each other over Dominic's bowed head and I say, "Dominic, my father always insisted that everything looks better over a plate of something sweet. Let's get you something to eat and drink and then we'll talk."

He seems to accept this, so we all go inside. I lead Dominic to the seat closest to the fire, thankful that I had just banked it before going over to the church instead of putting it out entirely. It takes only a little effort to get it started again and Dominic is instinctively warming his hands when Helen returns with a tray of mugs of hot cider and thick slices of still-warm pumpkin bread.

We eat for a few minutes in silence before I say, "OK, Dominic, what's on your mind?" I ask the question as if I don't already know, as if I hadn't been praying for the hell this fine young man has no doubt been going through, as if I hadn't anticipated this meeting since Halloween night.

"Father Tom, Chief Parr," Dominic says, without preamble, "I killed a man and I wasn't sorry."

Helen looks at me and I nod for her to go first, since the first half of his question deals with the facts of the case, not his moral culpability. "Dominic," she says calmly, speaking to him with a level of respect that she always uses when dealing with those struggling to do the right thing. "You are incorrect. I have questioned everyone there that night, and will take your statement, too, but Mr. Davis fell on his own knife, a knife you never touched, held in a hand you never touched. In fact, from everything I have been able to glean from the witnesses, you could not have even seen the knife from the angle you approached him. Did you see the knife, Dominic?"

"No, ma'am, I didn't. I knew he had something and that he was trying to hurt Mae, but I didn't get past that before he was down."

"Exactly. He went down. He fell and in the process, the knife—which he was raising to stab Mae a second time—entered his own body. Based on eyewitness testimony, which the coroner's report backs up, when he began to fall, he lowered the arm holding the knife, instinctively trying to break his fall. This caused the knife to catch him in the throat, severing his carotid artery. He was most likely dead before you even got to your feet."

"But I pushed him."

"Why?" I ask. He stares at me like I am crazy as I ask again, "Why did you push him, Dominic?"

"Because I was afraid he was going to hurt Mae."

"Going to hurt?" Helen asks.

"Yeah, I didn't know he'd already stabbed her until I heard Martin talking about the blood. I wasn't looking in that direction. I heard her scream, saw him with something in his hand, and tackled him to stop him."

"So you didn't even know he'd done anything to Mae." I say, smiling. Again Dominic looks at me with confusion and I add, "Dominic, this is wonderful. You could not have had even the slightest intention to take some sort of revenge on him. You were defending your sister, a person made in the image of God, from harm. In doing so, you did not use what I believe are your considerable martial arts skills to try to hurt him. You simply prevented him from hurting her."

"That may be, Father, but when I saw what he'd done to her, and I later found out he'd died, I wasn't sorry. At that moment, I was glad that he was dead. I was furious about what he'd done to Mae, especially when we were at the hospital and we didn't know if she was going to make it or not. It wasn't until after Martin came out and told us that she was going to be OK, that she could still have kids and all, that I thought, 'OK, now I'm sorry he died.'"

"So let me get this straight, Dominic. During a time of heightened stress and fear, you entertained some very nasty thoughts, but as soon as the situation returned to normal, you regretted your initial feelings."

"Yes, Father, that's pretty much it."

"Dominic," I say with a smile, "the most that I can say spiritually is that you're guilty of venial sins committed under extremely difficult circumstances. Mention this to me the next time you come to confession and then try to put it behind you. As far as your legal position, Helen?"

"Dominic," Helen says brightly, "I still need a formal statement, so please stop by the police station sometime tomorrow and tell Detective Conway what you told me tonight. He will ask you to write it down and then sign it. Then, as Father Tom has already said, you need to try to put this incident behind you."

"I just wish I could," he says, forlornly.

"You've got to give it time, son. It will take a while and you will always remember this, but eventually you will come to see what happened in its proper context," I say.

"Speaking of time," Helen says, standing, "it's time for me to go. I have an early day tomorrow."

I stand to walk her out and Dominic also stands but says quietly, "Father Tom, may I stay a few more minutes? I need to tell you something else, in private."

"Of course," I say, and Helen gives Dominic a hug before saying, "I'll see myself out." I look at her hand and see her tap her engagement ring with her thumb, our signal for all the things we'd like to say and do if we were alone. I do the same, touching the place where she will place my wedding band in less than two months, and she goes out the door.

Dominic and I sit back down and he says, "Father, I wanted you to know that I've made up my mind. I am breaking off my relationship with Therese and entering seminary as soon as I graduate. It's the only way I can make atonement for taking another human life."

I say nothing for a moment, taking care to choose my words carefully before I say, "I am so sorry, Dominic. That will not be possible."

He looks at me aghast, saying with horror, "Is it because of Mr. Davis? Because you just said that I didn't really kill him."

I shake my head and say, "Oh no. I'm sure there are priests out there who have killed, perhaps in the military, perhaps while on a police force, perhaps by participating in an abortion. St. Paul himself was much more complicit in the death of St. Stephen than you were in Davis'. No, it's because you will need a letter of recommendation from your parish priest and I will not be writing one, at least not anytime soon."

Again, he looks at me dumbfounded and says, "Father, I don't understand. In fact, I am completely confused."

"You are indeed, Dominic, about a lot of things. You need to take the time to straighten out all that you've been through before you can be in any proper state of mind to even begin to discern a calling. If you'll take my advice, you'll keep dating Therese, each of you conducting yourselves in ways that you intend to please God. You'll also keep in touch with me, and let me help you when you need it. Talk to your parents. And when some time has passed, if you still want to go to seminary, then we'll talk about that letter."

He sits quietly for a long moment before saying, "I see what you're saying, Father, but I'd still like to do something, maybe not to make up for what I did but at least to, I don't know, help bring some good into the world?"

This idea pleases me because it opens a door to another idea that has been playing on the edge of my mind since Helen and I returned from visiting Bridget Davis. "Dominic," I say, clapping him on the back, "I think I have just the thing for you."

Thirty-Two

I ring the doorbell at the Trents' sprawling Victorian home on Thursday morning.

While we wait for someone to open the door, I say to Helen, "Are you ready for this?"

She takes a deep breath. "It's all part of the job, Tom. I promised them answers. Fortunately, I now have some to give them."

The door is opened, not by one of the Trents, but by Martin Maycord. "Hello, Tom, Helen," he says, stepping aside to let us in.

"Thanks for making time for this in your schedule," Helen says.

"Well, I'm not just here for this," he says with a smile.

"Marty! I need my laptop!" calls Mae from the direction of the living room.

Rolling his eyes, he looks at Helen and says, "You'll be happy to know that you're no longer the most stubborn patient of my career. Come on, she's in here."

We walk in to find the Trents' living room transformed into a hospital room, complete with a bed that reminds me of the one Helen had for the first few weeks after she got out of the hospital. Except, in addition to the bed, there are beeping monitors and IV stands at the ready.

At our amazed looks, Mae explains, "Marty told my doctor he'd keep an eye on me once I got home. What he didn't tell him was—" she waves her arm around the room.

"If you were my patient," Martin says, "you'd still be in the hospital for a couple more days."

"But I'm not your patient," she smiles sweetly up to him.

"It's a good thing, too, because if you were, I couldn't do this," Martin says, right before leaning down and kissing her.

"Ahem."

We turn and see Alan and Doris Trent have entered the room. Much to my surprise, Alan looks amused at the doctor's obvious embarrassment.

I guess there's nothing to thaw a dad's heart towards his daughter's fiancé like him saving her life.

"Is the guest room OK, Martin?" Doris asks.

"Guest room?" I say, cocking an eyebrow.

"Oh," Mae says, "Mom and Dad are letting Marty stay for a week, you know, so he can keep an eye on me."

"Letting?" Alan mutters. "More like insisting."

"Everything is perfectly above board, Father," Martin says.

"Damn right it's above board," Alan mutters. "I'm sleeping on the couch in here."

"Oh, Daddy," Mae says, rolling her eyes. "I'm a twenty-four-year-old woman!"

"Now Mae," Martin says, "I completely understand your father's feelings. I don't mind at all."

"You know," Alan says, smiling a little. "I'm liking you more and more each day."

"Well, since everyone is here," Helen says, "let's sit down. I don't want to tire Mae out, but I think she should hear what I have to say. It won't take too long."

The Trents take a seat together on the love seat, Alan putting his arm around his wife. Martin sits in a chair next to Mae, holding her hand. Dominic comes in and asks, "May I sit in as well?"

"Of course," Helen says, and he throws his lanky frame into an armchair.

"Alan, Doris, Martin," Helen says. "When I told you that Rusty Davis was the person who tried to kill Mae and did kill Larry Daniels, I told you I had very few answers as to why. Over the last few days, Dan Conway, the other officers under my command, and I have been working long hours trying to piece together what happened. But it wasn't until yesterday that we were able to put everything together. Some of what I have to tell you is still speculation, but Dan and I are confident that we know why Rusty Davis did what he did."

She sits back on the couch and begins, "It all started Wednesday, a week before Fairy Tales and Frights opened. That day, Rusty assaulted and severely beat his ten-year-old son, Terry. Rusty fled in the family car before we could arrest him. The car was found abandoned in a truck stop just across the Ohio-Maryland border. We were unable to track him because he left his cell phone at his house. But between his home and the truck stop, he stopped at three different ATMs and withdrew a total of $900." She pauses and says, "Bridget only discovered this the next day. It was practically all the money they had left. Fortunately, the bank canceled Rusty's debit card."

"So not only did he beat his son, he left his family to starve?" Alan says, appalled.

"Yes. Were it not for the generosity of the parish, the Davises would have been in a terrible bind until Bridget's next paycheck," I say.

"What he did next is unclear," Helen continues. "We do know that he texted Bridget on a couple of occasions, each time from a different cell phone number. We believe he purchased a couple of pre-paid phones to use. It was in these texts that Rusty mentioned going to Minnesota to get himself straightened out. Now, it turns out that he does have cousins living in a small town in the western part of the state. We contacted them, and they said he had asked about staying with them for a while, but they never heard anything else from him.

"In a couple of her messages, Bridget told him about the restraining order and the role that Mae played in getting that. She also mentioned that Mae was counseling their kids to, as she put it, 'undo the damage' Rusty's behavior had done. I should also say, we had an active warrant and a 'be on the lookout' out for him, so he had every incentive to stay far away from Myerton."

"But he didn't," Martin says.

"No, he didn't," Helen says. She pauses for a moment, then says, "On Monday, Bridget Davis received a letter mailed to her the previous Saturday from Myerton." She pulls a folder from her tote bag, opens it, and pulls out a couple of sheets of paper, "This is a copy of that letter. In it, Rusty explains why he did what he did next. According to his own words, Bridget's text set something off inside of him. He developed a hatred of Mae, seeing her as someone who was trying to take his family away from him and turn his children against him. He wrote, 'I decided to hurt that bitch the way she hurt me, by taking someone she loved from her.'"

"But how did he even know about me and Marty?" Mae asks.

"The engagement was public knowledge by then," Helen says. "He must have heard about it. Or maybe Bridget said something in one of her texts that clued him in that your relationship with Martin was more than just professional."

"So instead of playing it safe," Doris says, "he came back to Myerton for revenge?"

"That's what his letter indicates," Helen says. "From the truck stop, it appears that he hitched a ride back in the direction of Myerton with a trucker. He may have walked or hitchhiked some of the way, but when he got closer to Myerton, he started walking through the woods. Only one problem—he wasn't dressed properly for hiking in the Maryland mountains in mid-October, since he was still wearing the clothes he left home in."

"That's when he came across Dale Riddle," I say.

"Dale!" Mae exclaims.

"By one of the biggest coincidences I've ever run across in my career in law enforcement," Helen says, shaking her head, "Rusty came across Dale at his camp site. They had never met before, and neither had any idea how much they shared."

"A hatred of Martin and Mae," Dominic pipes up.

"It was a very unfortunate encounter for Dale," Helen says, "because Rusty stole his old hiking boots and, most importantly, his hunting knife. Those two pieces of evidence pointed conclusively to Dale—or so we thought.

"Anyway, eventually Rusty made his way back into Myerton, probably walking through the woods or at night through the streets, making sure to stay clear of any police cars that might drive by. After a day or two, he reached his goal—the Myer Mansion."

"Why there?" Alan asks.

"I can explain that," Martin says. "All the publicity for Fairy Tales and Frights mentioned Mae as one of the organizers and listed me as a patron. But it didn't say anything about me being The Big Bad Wolf?"

"No, it didn't," Helen says. "That's something Rusty learned while he was in the house."

"What?" Mae and Dominic exclaim.

"One night when everyone was gone, Rusty snuck into the mansion. In his letter to Bridget, he mentioned that he knew the house very well, because his father had done some work on it when he was a little boy. He learned all the little nooks and crannies, including a room locked from the inside that had a secret way in and out. It took consulting with Tim Cooper, who found some old plans for the home in the family archives at Myer College, to confirm that the room Rusty hid in had a small staircase leading to the kitchen. It had been covered over in a remodel, but Rusty remembered it was there. No one noticed it, because no one ever went into the old kitchen."

"That's right," Mae says. "No one ever went in and out of that part of the house."

"He was concealed from everyone, and was able to see everything going on. Probably him walking upstairs is what fed Nate's ghost obsession. According to his letter, one day he saw Red Riding Hood being chased up the stairs by The Big Bad Wolf. He heard the wolf growl, 'I'm going to get you, Mae Trent.' So he figured out who you were, Mae." Helen pauses and clears her throat. "He only knew you were the wolf, Martin when he saw, and I'll use his own words here, 'the guy take off the wolf head, pull Red Riding Hood into his arms, and lay a kiss on her that almost set the house on fire.'"

Martin and Mae turn beet red as both Alan and Dominic glare at the doctor.

I guess there's only so much credit saving someone's life can earn a person.

"So with that knowledge, he put his plan into action. The first Saturday night of the house, Rusty lured the wolf upstairs and stabbed him. He fled back to his hiding place before he found out he'd killed the wrong person. In his letter, he does express regret for killing Larry, but also says his anger just grew. He decided the only thing he could do was to kill Mae." Helen pauses. "And you know the rest."

Everyone is quiet after Helen finishes. We're all trying to absorb what she's revealed over the last half hour. One man's desire for revenge cost a young person his life, almost cost another hers, but in the end cost him his own life.

Sad. So very, very sad.

The doorbell rings. Doris begins to get up, but I hold my hand up. "I'll see who it is," I say quietly.

Going to the door, I open it and am surprised to find Bridget Davis standing on the porch.

She looks surprised to see me. "Father Tom! I—I didn't expect to see you here."

"Hello, Bridget," I say with a smile.

She swallows and licks her lips nervously. "Ah, I went to the hospital—I wanted to see how Mae was, and maybe—well, they told me she'd been released and was at home, so I decided—I have this plant, see," she says, holding up a spider plant, "and the last time I was in her office, I saw she didn't have a plant, and I thought she should have one, because most offices have plants, so—"

"Would you like to come in and give it to her yourself?" I ask gently.

"Oh—oh, no," she says, shaking her head. "I—I—I just couldn't. If you could give this to her—"

I reach out and gently take her arm, pulling her inside the Trents' house. "I think she'd like to see you," I say, as I lead her to the living room. People have already turned to see who the visitor is.

"Mae, you have a visitor," I say cheerfully, gently shoving Bridget towards Mae's bed.

Bridget walks up to Mae, who's looking at her visitor with a smile on her face.

"Hello, Bridget," Mae says brightly.

"Mae," Bridget says. "I—I—ahem—I brought you this plant. For your office." She thrusts the plant toward her.

"How lovely," Mae says. "Thank you so much. How thoughtful."

"I'll just take that," Martin says, carefully removing the potted offering from her hands.

"How are you feeling?" Bridget asks.

"Much better, thanks. How are the kids?"

"They—they're OK," she whispers. "They still don't understand."

"It will take time," Mae says gently.

Bridget nods, then says, "Mae, I am so sorry Rusty did this to you! You were only trying to help me and my kids, and—-and—oh, can you ever forgive me?"

Mae takes Bridget's hand. "There is nothing for me to forgive. You didn't do this. You're not responsible for this. So, don't give it another thought. You need to focus on your children now. And when I'm out of this bed and back to work—"

"—which won't be for a while yet," Martin says sternly.

Mae shoots him a look. "As I was saying, once I'm back at work, I'll meet with them to help them process everything. Until then, one of my colleagues from Hagerstown can come in and meet with them."

Bridget nods, then breaks down into sobs. I take a step to her, but Doris stands up and goes to her, taking the hurting woman into her arms.

"There, there, my dear," Doris says quietly, patting her back. "We're all here for you. It will be OK. Maybe not right away, but someday. You'll see."

Thirty-Three

Saturday morning dawns bright and clear, one of those fall days that always makes me glad to be alive. So glad in this case that I am actually excited to head out for my morning bike ride. Normally, I ride out into the country, but today I decide to take a spin through some of the more populated parts of our small town, wanting to have a look at some work being done on one of the local homes.

I leave the rectory and pedal north past The Muffin Man bakery. Nina Hallstead is coming out with a large box of donuts that I remember Helen always orders for the station on the first Saturday of each month. Not noticing me, Nick, her husband, follows her out and grabs her around the waist, swinging her around for a kiss that reminds me that my wedding day cannot come soon enough. I speed up and make a point of looking the other way, just in case they do notice me and feel embarrassed.

A few blocks past the bakery, I enter the historic part of town and ride past the Trents. The girls seem to be having some sort of tea party on the lawn joined by Martin's nieces, who I guess will soon be their nieces, too. This is obviously far from their minds as the fuss over mismatched cups and saucers, teddy bears, a doll or two, and a large beach umbrella that refuses to stay put. On the porch, Mae is propped comfortably in a wicker chaise, supervising the girls while Martin supervises her. She waves as I pass but Martin is too busy tucking a blanket around her to notice me.

I turn onto another residential street and pass Amy and Tim Cooper's house, where a new blue banner proudly proclaims, "It's a Boy." I offer a brief Prayer of Thanksgiving for a new life safely arrived and make a mental note alert Miriam to get a Food Train started for them. In fact, I am passing the Conways' now and am tempted to stop, but I see that the family is busy. Little Andrew runs out of the house naked, with Miriam waddling to catch up with him. Fortunately, Dan's in the driveway with the rest of the kids, washing the car, a task that I need to tackle myself before the weather gets any colder. Laughing at the little streaker, he quickly catches him up in his arms, laughing more as he returns him to his mother, who is unsuccessfully stifling a laugh herself.

A few blocks later, I come upon the project I want to take a look at. I slow my speed but do not stop as I pass by the Davises' home, where more than a dozen members of the Acutis Society are hard at work. One of the older boys is on a ladder, cleaning out the gutter, while several others work on the opposite side, power washing the house. Gladys is sitting with Bridget and one of the girls, pulling weeds in the flower beds and planting some cold-hardy mums.

But the sight that warms my heart the most is that of Dominic, diligently raking leaves into a pile with the help of the two Davis brothers, the oldest still moving slowly but obviously recovering. He sees me and raises his hand in a wave just as Therese throws a handful of leaves into his carefully combed hair. He immediately grabs his own handful of leaves and goes after her, as she tries to hide behind Gladys and Terry Davis tries to help Dominic corner her.

Content that at least on this day, at this moment, my beloved flock is dwelling in green pastures, I turn my bike toward the police station, where my own "still waters" is hard at work.

The Fatal Fall

The Father Tom Mysteries, Book 11

By

J. R. Mathis and Susan Mathis

First Printing, October, 2021
    Contact: mercyandjusticemysteries@gmail.com

Cover Photo: Depositphotos
    Cover: Millie Godwin
    Editor: Anna Palmer Darkes

Also by J. R. Mathis and Susan Mathis

Prologue

November 1928

I look at myself in the mirror, wearing a light blue dress with the beading I love so much. I think this one will have to do. All the others I've tried are simply too tight.

We're getting out just in time, because it's getting impossible to hide my secret anymore. My husband is never around, so I'm not worried about him noticing. But my friends have already commented that I've gained weight the last few months. I've laughed and told them it's because of our new cook. But I think a couple of them suspect the truth.

I hope none of them mention it to my husband.

I look at the time. He's already waiting for me.

No luggage, he said. We can't arouse suspicion. We'll buy everything we need when we get to wherever we're going.

A new life together, away from here. Away from my husband, his wife.

I know it's a grave sin. I know I'm going to hell. I know it makes no sense.

But I look down at my ever-expanding stomach, and know I have no choice.

I put on my green coat—it's chilly outside, plus I need it to hide my shame—and walk to my dressing table. Opening the jewelry box, I grab a few things and stuff them in my pockets. I'm still wearing the locket my husband gave me as an engagement present.

I look at my wedding band. It symbolizes the vow I'm breaking. But my love said to keep it on, since it would support the lies we're going to tell.

Turning, I grab my green cloche hat and set it on my head. Looking at myself in the mirror, I take a deep breath.

"You can do this," I whisper. "It's not that much longer."

I turn around and march out of my bedroom without looking back.

One

"Tom," Helen says to me over lunch on the first Sunday of November, "what are we going to do for our first Thanksgiving together?"

This question catches me off guard. "Well, I hadn't thought much about that," I say. "I mean, I guess I thought that we'd just do what we did last year and help with the community dinner. Don't you remember?"

Helen blushes at my question and takes a sip of sweet tea. "Ahem, yes, I remember."

I'm a little curious about her reaction. "You were there with a few other officers from the police department, right?"

The redness in her face deepens, and she takes a sudden interest in the remains of the shepherd's pie on her plate. "Yeah," she says without looking at me.

I stare at her, not comprehending why she's acting this way. "What is it?" I ask. "Why are you blushing like that?. Did something happen that I don't know about?"

She takes a deep breath. "Tom," her gaze still fascinated by the gravy on her plate, "last Thanksgiving was not my finest hour. Not by a long shot."

"Really? I don't remember anything embarrassing happening to you."

She finally looks up at me. "Tom," she says with a slight smile, "I have a confession to make."

"Shall we go into the Church, or is this not that kind of confession?" I say with a grin.

Helen takes my hand and casts her eyes downward. "I really don't know. Maybe, maybe not."

"OK?" I say slowly.

She pauses for a minute, as if deciding whether she's going to admit something to me, and finally says, "Tom, I know that my actions that day were good, but my motivation was far from it."

I stare at her until she continues. "I came up with the idea of the department participating so that I could spend the day with you. It was a very difficult time for me, and I didn't want to be alone. I also didn't want to have to fend off offers from sympathetic people who were only asking me because I was a widow or otherwise just pitiful. I will not say that my feelings for you at that moment had reached a level of potential sin, but I was certainly on my way, and I should have stopped then."

I really don't know how to respond. Obviously, I can say that everything worked out for the best since I have been dispensed to marry.

But it could have turned out very badly.

We both know it almost did.

"Helen," I say, squeezing her hand, "one thing I've learned in my decade in the priesthood is that God does a great job taking the things we get wrong and making them right. Our situation is one of my favorite examples."

She smiles. "Of course you're right about that. But still, we were taking a terrible chance, or at least I was. I would not recommend it to anyone else."

"I agree, and I would not recommend what we have done to anyone else. We are very fortunate in how our story has turned out, but then again we also made some hard choices in the beginning."

We both sit and contemplate this for a moment or two before Helen says, "You know how much I love the holidays, Tom. And I want this to be special for us."

I have some information that I need to share with her that she is not going to find amusing. Trying to ease my way into the topic, I ask, "Helen, how important is it to you that we cook a whole turkey for ourselves?"

"Just for us?" she asks, incredulously, "Not that important. I mean, I don't particularly care for endless leftovers. Why do you ask?"

Instead of answering her question, I ask, "So, suppose we got a tray of pre-cooked sliced turkey and then you made whatever side dishes you wanted to go with it? It could be just us, or we could invite Gladys and Nate and Anna and Bill."

"I'm liking this idea better and better, Tom, but I suspect there's something you're not telling me."

"Only this," I say, taking a deep breath, "We'll have to eat in the evening because St. Clare's is hosting the Community Dinner this year."

Helen is only briefly crestfallen before admitting, "I remember that, now. Look, Tom, we'll have plenty of other Thanksgivings together. We can just—"

"We can just offer to do the heavy lifting the day before and in the early morning. Then we can excuse ourselves as soon as we finish serving. In fact, you don't have to be there at all."

"Oh, yes, I do. Not just as your future wife, but as the Chief of Police. No, I can't ask my people to volunteer for something that I'm not doing myself."

"And that, my darling, is one of the things I admire about you. But," I add, "you can still certainly leave early, and I can get to the Rectory as soon as I can."

"It'll be a long day but I can do a lot of the prep work in the days leading up to Thanksgiving."

I sit up as something occurs to me. "Wait a minute. I just remembered. Will you have to work Thanksgiving? I mean, I know that Dan has a lot of family that comes to town."

"Miriam has a lot of family," Helen corrects me, "including several sisters who blame Dan for the size of their family and are often after him to 'get snipped.'"

"You're kidding?"

"Not at all. Now, beyond issues related to Church teaching, he finds the idea both frightening and appalling, as he ends up telling me at some point every Thanksgiving weekend. So the upshot is that he works on Thanksgiving, taking a long lunch break when everyone's eating and inclined to have their mouths too full to say much. Then, I work on the day after so that Dan can stay home and redeem himself in the eyes of his in-laws by watching the kids while Miriam shops the Black Friday sales."

"OK, so are we set then?"

"Sounds good to me. I'll start looking online for recipes."

"Please," I insist, raising my hand to make my point, "just don't read them to me. My mother used to do that and it drove me crazy."

"Speaking of your mother, shouldn't we invite her for Thanksgiving?" Helen asks. "I mean, she is alone now."

"No!" I cry, putting my hands over my face. "Please, no, not that."

"Tom," Helen begins, obviously warming up to lecture me about being nicer to my mother, the way adult orphans love to do.

I decide to stop her by saying, "Helen, do you really want my Mom here watching every forkful of food you place in your mouth and commenting on it on Thanksgiving?"

She pauses at this, obviously remembering that my mother is more than a little obsessed with Helen's weight. Finally, she smiles kindly and says with obviously false generosity, "Well, I suppose it would be a bit much to ask her to fly up here twice in less than a month."

"It would," I agree.

"We'll send her a nice flower arrangement instead."

"She'll like that."

I look at her plate. "Do you want any more?"

She shakes her head. "I couldn't eat another bite. That was delicious."

"Why, thank you, my dear," I say, inclining my head. "I'll clear."

Helen stretches and asks, "So, what time's the race this afternoon?"

"Not until later," I say, placing the plates in the sink. "Last one of the season."

"Oh, dear, are you going to be OK?" she asks with mock seriousness.

"Well," I say, bending over her, "fortunately, this off-season I'll have plenty to keep me occupied."

"Oh? New hobby?" she grins.

"No," I whisper as I lean in to kiss her. "A new job I'm very much looking forward to."

***

"Are you sure Mae's expecting you?" Helen asks.

"She asked me to come by after Mass and bring her communion," I say as I ring the doorbell at the Trents' sprawling Victorian home. "Apparently, Martin's insisting that she wait two weeks before coming back to Mass."

Helen rolls her eyes and shakes her head. "He hovers over that girl more than you did me."

"The only reason I didn't was because you didn't want me to."

"Oh, I wanted you to," she smiles. "I just didn't want you to treat me like I was frail."

I roll my eyes. "You are never going to let me forget that, are you?"

"I don't plan to."

The door opens to reveal not one of Mae's parents, but Vincent, her oldest brother.

"Father, Mrs. Parr," he says with a smile, extending his hand to me. "Please come in."

Helen and I enter the warm and inviting foyer. "It's good to see you again, Vincent," I say. "I'm surprised you're still here. I thought you'd have to go back to school."

"I'm actually just down here for the weekend," he says. "I'm leaving in an hour to drive back."

"I know your parents are happy to see you," Helen says. "As is Mae."

Vincent laughs. "Frankly, Mae only has eyes for Martin. I'm not even sure she's aware I've been home this weekend."

We walk toward the Trent's living room. The pocket doors are closed, and there's a gaggle of little Trents and Martin's young nieces gathered outside with their ears pressed against the wood.

"Hey," Vincent says, causing the children to jump and turn to us. "What do you think you're doing?"

The youngest Trent child present, Kateri, says, "Listening."

"Hush, Kat," Martin's niece Sophie says.

"Eavesdropping, huh? That's not very nice."

"We were just trying to hear what Mae and Martin are arguing about," Isabella Trent says.

I cock my head to one side. "Why do you think they are arguing?"

"Because we heard Mae yell at Uncle Martin," Lucy, Sophie's sister, says.

"Why in the world did she yell at Martin?" Helen asks.

"I think she was afraid he'd break her doll," Kateri says.

The three of us look at each other. "What, Kat?" Vincent asks.

"Uh-huh," she says, nodding her head with her eyes as big as saucers. "Martin said she needed to take it easy, and Mae yelled that she wasn't some frail china doll that needed to be surrounded in bubble wrap."

Helen and I look at each other. "Ahhhh," we say in unison. "Are they still yelling?" I ask.

"No, they've been quiet since then," Sophie says.

"OK, go outside and play," Vincent says. "It's chilly so don't forget your coats."

The girls grumble as they walk away from the door. Vincent knocks. "Go away, girls!" Mae yells.

"Mae, it's Vince. Father Tom and Mrs. Parr are here."

There are indistinct whispers coming from the room and sounds of movement. Finally after a moment, Mae says, "Let them in, please."

Vincent slides open the doors and Helen and I walk into the living room, changed into a hospital room for Mae's recovery from being stabbed. Mae's sitting up in bed wearing a sweatshirt from the prestigious Catholic university she attended, while Martin is seated in a comfortable-looking armchair.

What's striking is the distance between them, and the fact that neither looks particularly happy.

"Father Tom, Helen," Mae says, smiling. "So good to see you."

"You're looking even better than you were a couple of days ago when we were here," I say. "Apparently, Martin's taking good care of you."

Her smile slowly disappears. "Oh, yes, Marty's been just wonderful, making sure I don't exert myself in the slightest," she says sarcastically.

"Now, Mae," Martin says, "that's not—"

"I'm surprised he'll even let me feed myself," she continues. "I half expect him to thrust a bottle of formula into my mouth!"

"Really, Monica June!" Martin says. "You're acting like a child!"

Mae sits up, her eyes ablaze in a way I never expected from her. "A child! Marty, did you just call me a child!"

Martin looks sheepish. "Now, Mae, darling, I didn't—"

"If I'm acting like a child, Dr. Martin Joseph Maycord," Mae shouts, "It's only because you're treating me like one!"

"Oh, don't be silly," Martin says.

"Silly! Silly! Don't you call me—"

"OK, you two, that's enough," I say. They lapse into silence and look at me.

"Now," I continue, "Helen and I came here to visit, to see how Mae was doing, and so I could give her communion. Breaking up an argument wasn't part of our plans for the afternoon."

"We weren't arguing, Father Tom," Mae says.

"No, we were just having a discussion," Martin says. "I was trying to get Mae to be reasonable about her recovery."

"And I was trying to get Marty to understand that I didn't see the need to lay around the house all day like I was still in the hospital," May says, "when I feel fine."

"And I was explaining to her that her injury was serious, it has been less than a week since Rusty Davis stabbed her, and she really should still be in the hospital."

"And I—"

I hold my hand up. "We get the picture," I say with a slight smile. "This sounds familiar, doesn't it, Helen?"

"I do have a distinct feeling of deja vu, Tom," Helen says with a smile.

"Now, look you two," Martin says, "Mae's situation—"

"Is not nearly as serious as Helen's was," Mae says.

"True," Helen says. "I was in the hospital a lot longer. But Mae, the only reason Martin discharged me was because I made Tom promise he'd change my bandages and the like. And even with that, I still made his life difficult because I didn't want to accept that I still wasn't a hundred percent."

"Thank you, Helen," Martin says. "See Mae—"

"Not so fast, Martin," I say. "I made Helen's recovery more difficult than it should have been because I was so worried about something happening to her that I wouldn't let her do even simple things."

"Well, you tried," Helen says.

"I rarely succeeded, admittedly. But we finally realized that we were both wrong and we were both right."

"Is that some kind of weird logic they teach you in seminary?" Martin asks.

"No, it's just common sense. I recognized that I needed to let Helen do what she could for herself."

"And I," Helen says to Mae, "realized I needed to let Tom help me."

"Mae, it doesn't mean that Martin thinks you're frail or a child or anything like that," I say. "And Martin, I'm sure Mae doesn't want to get up and start training for a marathon. You need to let her do some things, and Mae, you need to let him take care of you."

Mae and Martin look at each other. "Another compromise, huh?" Martin says.

"We do seem to be making a lot of them lately," Mae says with a smile.

"Sorry, darling," Martin says as he approaches Mae's bed.

"I'm sorry, too," Mae says. With a smile, she adds, "I actually don't mind you taking care of me."

"It's something I love to do, Mae, and always will."

Taking a deep breath, I say, "Well, now that that's settled, why don't I do what I came here for."

Two

"I have the boxes you requested, Father Greer."

I look up from my laptop at the student assistant, who's just wheeled a cart carrying four six-inch by twelve-inch gray archival boxes to my table in the Myer College Archives and Manuscripts Reading Room. She's a young, bespeckled coed wearing a burnt orange sweater and a skirt that catches her just below the knee.

She bears no resemblance to another young coed I met in the same area fifteen years ago, but she still makes me uncomfortable.

"Thank you, Gwen," I say quietly. I peer at the labels. "So these are Father O'Connor's papers from when he was Rector at Saint Clare's? Doesn't seem like very much."

"This is just his personal correspondence," she replies. "Also his diary, which is fairly detailed. The parish records are at the Archdiocesan Archives."

I smile slightly. "Yes, I know."

"He was at Saint Clare's during the Depression? That was a hard time for this area."

I look at her. "I'm doing my senior honors thesis on that period," she explains.

"Ah, I see. Well, he was here at the beginning. He was assigned in 1927, but died in his sleep in 1933. Which is interesting in and of itself, considering he was only forty."

Gwen's eyes get big. "Really? You—you don't think—I mean, is that why you're—"

Changing the subject, I say, "So, you're majoring in history? That was my major as an undergrad."

"Was that before you became a priest?"

I look at her and smile. "Oh, yes," I say. "A while before I became a priest. I didn't even think about becoming a priest then. It wasn't until—"

She gasps and puts her hand to her mouth. "Oh! Of course! I remember now. I'm so sorry, Father."

I put my hand up. "It's fine. I'm surprised you even know the story."

"Are you kidding?" she squeals. "I mean, you and the Chief of Police are a big deal among my friends, and most of us aren't even Catholic. It's just such an incredible story. So romantic." Gwen pauses, looking like she wants to ask me something.

I raise my eyebrows. "You have a question, Gwen?"

She blushes even as she says, "Well—er—ah—we were talking—my friends and I—and one of the other girls—well, she said she saw it in an interview, and Mrs. Parr said that—well, that is to say, she said—"

"Yes," I say simply, knowing what she's trying to ask.

I know, because it is THE BIG QUESTION Helen and I get in every interview we've done since the Pope granted me a dispensation to marry and our engagement was announced to the world.

Gwen's mouth falls open. "Really? You mean, you two have never—"

"That's right," I nod.

"I mean, I know you *can't*—what I mean is, you can, but you're not supposed to. Right?"

"Yes, they're very strict about that," I say.

"Gwen!" I turn in the direction of the sharp voice and see Linda Danes, the head archivist—my old job—glaring at her young student.

"Yes, Ms. Danes?" Gwen says quickly.

"Please leave the patrons alone," she says. "This is not the place for you to add to your no-doubt ample supply of gossip."

The young lady swallows, nods, and scurries off. To Danes, I say, "She wasn't bothering me, Linda."

"I just thought you'd like me to run off another—do you call them fans?" she says with a smile.

"I call them fans," I chuckle. "Helen, well, has another word for them."

"When am I going to meet this woman, Tom? You need to bring her sometime."

I sit back and shake my head. "Alas, Helen does not have my love of dusty stacks and the smell of old paper."

"That's unfortunate, considering you share her love of solving crimes," she replies.

I wave away the comment. "I don't love it, in spite of any evidence to the contrary."

"You could fool me," Linda says. "If the papers are right, you're the real Father Brown."

"They exaggerate—though Helen did buy me a saturno for Halloween. No, I just find myself involved. I don't go looking for it. Sometimes, it seems that a crime finds me."

"You need to be more careful, then," Linda laughs. "I'll leave you to do your research."

She walks away from my table and I open the box with my white-gloved hands. Removing a folder, I lay it on the table and carefully open it, revealing exquisite handwriting in blue ink on aged, lined paper.

"You did have excellent penmanship, Father," I whisper with admiration. I begin to read the first letter and start transcribing the contents.

Now, you may wonder what I'm doing in the Myer College archives, reading the 100-year-old correspondence of my predecessor. Frankly, I decided I needed a hobby to help relieve stress. After Dr. Martin Maycord told me that I needed to lower my blood pressure, I began riding my bicycle regularly. I've come to not entirely hate it—especially when I'm riding with Helen—but along the way, I realized I needed something to relax my mind as well.

And what's more relaxing to a former archivist than a couple of hours immersed in the records of the past?

Minutes later, I'm reading a letter from Father O'Connor's sister—his actual sister as well as a Sister with the Daughters of Charity in Emmitsburg—when someone taps me on the shoulder.

I jump and turn to find Nate Rodriguez grinning down at me.

"Hi, Father Tom," he says. "What are you doing here?"

"Morning, Nate," I respond. "Just doing some research."

He peers at the box on my table, and the letters in front of me. "Oh, Father O'Connor, huh?"

"Yes. You recognize it?"

"Oh, yes," he says. "I looked at the same boxes researching Victoria Myer for the article I did for the *Gazette*."

I try not to grimace. That article he wrote, saying the Myer Mansion was haunted by the ghost of Victoria Myer, was at best a mixed blessing to the parish. It sent ticket sales to the Acutis Society's Fairy Tales and Frights through the roof. It also put us on the map of every "paranormal investigator" in the country.

It also made me much more aware of my responsibilities to pray for all the members of my parish, even those who died over 150 years ago.

"I spent some time reading Winthrop Myer's letters as well. There's actually a copy of a letter Myer wrote about Victoria's death in one of his letterbooks," Nate says. "So, what are you researching?"

"Frankly, Nate, your article—for all the problems I had with it—got me interested in the history of the town in general and the parish in particular So, I decided to do some research into Father Liam O'Connor. I learned about him in seminary. He was well known in Maryland for his work against the Ku Klux Klan in the 1920s."

"Interesting," he nods. "Are you going to write a book?"

I smile. "Oh, I don't know. It's just a way of relaxing, taking my mind off things for a few hours. What are you doing here?"

"Just researching another article for the *Gazette*," he grins.

"Oh?"

"Yeah. There was so much attention for my article about the Mansion, they wanted me to do an article each month about something related to the history of the area."

"That's great, Nate," I say. "And you're still cleaning up crime scenes?"

"Oh, yeah. I mean, this is fun and what I really like to do, but that pays the bills. Besides, I still owe Gladys for the money she loaned me to start the business."

"I haven't seen you two in a few days. How are things?"

He smiles. "Really good, Father. Best they have been in a while. We're still working through some things, but at least we're talking instead of yelling." He pauses. "A few days ago, Gladys asked me if I was disappointed in her after she told me about her past."

I don't say anything, letting Nate tell me what happened in his own time.

"I didn't answer for a long time," he says quietly. "I wasn't sure I wanted to tell her the truth. Then I admitted that I was."

"Did you tell her why?" I ask.

He nods. "That I'd built this vision of her in my mind, and in one fell swoop, she knocked it down. She wasn't the sweet, innocent girl I thought she was—I'd known she wasn't, you know, after she told me about Richard Davenport, but I still—I don't know—I thought that was an anomaly, I guess. So yeah, I was disappointed. But I realized I still loved her and, even though I did something wrong and stupid for the dumbest of reasons, that never changed. And it wasn't going to."

I stand up and clap him on the shoulder. "That took a lot of courage, Nate. I'm proud of you."

He swallows and manages to say, "Thank you, Father. That means a lot."

"Nate," Gwen says behind him. She has another cart, but with only one box on it this time.

"Oh, great! Thanks, Gwen," he says. "Sorry, Father, I've got a job this afternoon, but I want to look at this first."

"Totally understand," I say. Looking at the time on the clock in the reading room, I add, "I don't have much time before I need to meet Helen for lunch. By the way, what's the article about?"

Nate grins, his eyes flashing with his usual exuberance. "No ghosts this time, Father. Buried treasure."

I blink. "Excuse me?"

"OK, maybe not buried treasure. I'm doing an article on the embezzlement of $150,000 from the Bank of Myerton in 1928."

"I don't think I've ever heard of that?"

"Oh, it was a huge scandal back then. The vice president of the bank took off with a Western Maryland and Ohio Railroad payroll and neither he nor the money was ever seen again. There have been all sorts of rumors over the years about what happened to the money. Well, I think I've figured it out."

"Oh? So, where's the money?"

Nate grins again. "You'll just have to find out with the rest of the town."

He grabs his cart and goes to a table on the opposite side of the room. I return to the nun's letter, trying to focus on the contents.

But I can't help feeling disquieted about Nate's latest project.

***

I'm walking down the hallway at the police station toward Helen's office when I pass a conference room. Glancing inside, I stop at the site of my bride-to-be, the Chief of Police, talking to a group of children and their moms.

I recognize most of the group as Saint Clare's homeschooling co-op. Miriam Conway, one of the leaders, is there, along with her daughter Catherine. Other moms and children from the parish are listening in rapt attention to Helen speak.

"So," she's saying with a smile, "when we need to track a bad guy through the woods, or see if a car or van has drugs in it, we call on Sergeant Cupcake here for help."

I walk in and smile at the sight of the proud German shepherd standing next to Helen. She has her hand firmly on the leash, more to emphasize her control than to prevent Cupcake from hurting the children.

Unless given a command to attack, Cupcake is as sweet and gentle a dog as I've ever seen.

A hand shoots up. Helen smiles at the questioner. "Yes, David?"

Daniel Wright, child of the parish—and a nemesis of Catherine, truth be told—asks in his usual loud way, "Is she trained to kill?"

That produces startled gasps from some of the children. But before Helen can answer, Catherine steps forward to Cupcake and drops to her knees, wrapping her arms around the dog. In response, the dog whines and licks her face."

"I know, I know," Catherine says. "That's just Daniel. He's a poopyhead."

Miriam says, "Catherine, what?—"

The girl looks up at her mom with her wide brown eyes. "Daniel hurt her feelings. She doesn't like it when people think she's a bad dog, just because she works for the police."

Helen says quickly, "That's right, Catherine. Cupcake is highly trained and only attacks on command—not to kill, just to stop a bad person. Now, that's the end of our tour, who—"

Daniel laughs and says, "What, Spooky? You can talk to animals, now?"

Catherine stands up and turns to face her tormenter. But before she can say anything, Cupcake growls menacingly at Daniel.

"Aahh!" the boy screams. Cupcake growls a little louder and stands up, taking a step forward.

"Down, Cupcake! Obey!" Helen commands, pulling at the leash.

"I thought you said she wasn't dangerous, Chief!" Daniel's mom Lilith says, grabbing up her now-scared son.

"She's not," Helen says, still pulling on the leash.

"Don't let her eat me!" Daniel says. "I'm sorry, Catherine! Tell her I'm sorry!"

Calmly, Catherine turns around and says to Cupcake, "He's sorry. You can stop now."

Immediately, the shepherd stops growling and sits. Catherine pats her on the head. "Good girl," she whispers.

"Um—I—I'm sorry about that," Helen stammers. "Ahem, now, we have some treats for all of you right over there. I'll just take the Sergeant back to her partner."

Quickly, Helen walks from the room, leading Cupcake. I realize that no one has made a move to the table ladened with punch and cookies.

Instead, all eyes are on Catherine. And Miriam.

I decide an intervention is in order, so I clear my throat and say, "The Lord be With You!"

Automatically, the moms and children respond, "And with your spirit!"

"Bless us, oh Lord, and these Thy gifts, which we are about to receive, from thy bounty, through Christ our Lord, Amen."

"Now," I say with a smile, "with those tempting treats properly blessed, eat up!"

Deciding that cookies are more interesting than what just happened, the children clamor to the table. Catherine walks with the group, but I notice no one is speaking to her.

"Miriam, you need to do something about her!" I turn to see Lilith talking to Miriam, who visibly stiffens at this.

"What do you mean, Lilith?" she asks with her chin up.

"What do I mean? Look, I thought all this talk about 'Spooky Catherine' and her seeing visions and angels and everything like that was just something the kids made up. I heard the rumors about her predicting that Father Tom and Helen Parr were going to get married, and dismissed them as foolish. But after what I saw today—I'm sorry, there's something wrong with her. Even dangerous."

I open my mouth to step in, but Miriam says, "Lilith, there is nothing wrong with Catherine, and certainly nothing dangerous. She sees things the rest of us can't. Other than that, she's just a normal little girl."

"You really think—"

"And before you start showing concern for my daughter, perhaps you should talk to Daniel about how bad bullying is. Because that's what he is. A bully."

Lilith stiffens and walks away, grabs Daniel out of the line for the treats, and begins to lead him away from the table.

"Miriam, I'm sorry," she says across the room, "but we won't be at co-op anymore."

"Have a nice day," Miriam grins and waves.

As soon as the angry mom clears the doorway, Miriam's shoulders sag and she sinks into a seat. The other moms are busy with their children, so I walk over to her and sit down next to her.

"Are you OK?" I ask, placing my hand gently on her shoulder.

She looks at me and sighs. "Yes. No. I don't know," she says. Looking over at Catherine, who is eating cookies and laughing with a couple of other girls, she adds, "I wish she had never fallen out of that tree and hit her head. It jarred something, Father. The doctor's say her scans are perfectly normal, but ever since then—she's been like this."

I nod my head. Catherine's gift is as undeniable as it is inexplicable.

"Dan and I are at a loss," she continues. "It was one thing when we could keep it private. But now, it's like the entire parish knows. And today's not going to help." Turning to me, she asks, "Any advice?"

I take a deep breath. "Miriam, I pray for your family every day, and for Catherine in particular. But beyond that, this is a little above my pay grade. I do think one thing that might help is if you start teaching Catherine to be more discreet in what she says and who she says it to. You, Dan, me as her priest—that's fine, but she needs to keep anything she sees or hears private otherwise."

Miriam nods. "I just don't want her to be shunned by the other children."

Just then, there is a burst of girlish laughter. We turn to see a group gathered around Catherine, and they're all chattering animatedly about something.

Pointing to the scene. "I don't think you need to worry too much about that, Miriam. From what I've observed, children have an easier time accepting one of their own who is different than many adults do."

Three

"I *should* have let Cupcake eat that little—"

"Now, Helen," I say as I throw the dice and move my car three spaces—fortunately landing on a property I own, "you couldn't do that and you know it."

"I know," she sighs. "The paperwork for something like that is a nightmare."

I shake my head. "Well, Lilith gave Miriam an earful about Catherine."

"Oh, for heaven's sake!" Helen says as she shakes the dice. "She's just a child!"

"I know, I know, but she's an unusual child, and people are afraid of things they don't understand."

Helen pauses and looks at me. "It's only going to get worse, isn't it?" she asks quietly.

"I don't know about that," I shake my head. "Catherine may grow out of it, or her gift may get stronger. I did advise Miriam to teach her to be a little more discreet."

"Well, that should help. I mean, people have short memories. Unless she starts levitating or gets the stigmata."

I laugh. "Well, let's hope that it doesn't go that far. Though Father Wayne is interested in meeting Dandy Dan's daughter."

Helen looks at me with a grin. "Dandy Dan?"

"Dan wasn't always the upstanding man we see now. Are you going to throw those dice or not?"

Helen wrinkles her nose at me, throws the dice, and starts moving her piece. As she moves more spaces, she slows down and her eyes get bigger. Finally, she lands on the last blue square on the board.

I grin in triumph. "Park Place. I own it."

"I don't believe it," she says. "I just don't believe it." She looks up from the board. "I'm bankrupt."

I jump up, my arms stretched over my head in triumph. "Yes! Yes! Finally! I won! I won! After sixty-two games, I finally beat you!"

"Congratulations," she says with a frown.

"Oh, what's the matter, Chief Parr," I say mockingly. "Can't take losing?"

She crosses her arms and fixes me with a glare. "You know I hate losing. And aren't you supposed to be humble or something? You know, gracious in victory?"

"Probably," I say with a grin, "but not tonight!"

Helen sighs and shrugs. "Oh well. You got lucky. I'm still ahead of you 61 to 1."

I lean over so I'm inches from your face. "Well," I whisper, "we have the rest of our lives together for me to get number two."

She grins. "Never."

We kiss, then I whisper, "I'll be on the couch waiting for my beer."

Helen scowls but, being an honorable woman, begins the loser's task of putting the game away. I sit on the couch, basking in the glow of my triumph.

Do I really think it will ever happen again? Not really. But for tonight, I'm enjoying the sweet taste of victory.

A few minutes later, Helen joins me on the couch with two beers. Handing me one, she says, "So how was your day?"

"Good, good," I say, taking a drink. "Sorry I had to skip out on lunch, but I had a call from Bridget Davis."

Helen looks at me over her beer. "Is everything all right?"

"Yeah," I sigh. "She's still trying to recover. I went over there and listened. Terry's really taking his father's death hard. He doesn't understand why everyone's so mad at him."

"I don't know how you explain to a ten-year-old that his father died after trying to kill someone. I'm just amazed, after the beating Rusty gave him, that he's so upset."

"Children are more forgiving than adults sometimes," I say.

We both sit quietly, then Helen says, "So, how's the great project going?"

"It's not really a project—I'm not sure if I'm going to do anything or not—but Father O'Connor's papers are really interesting. I barely scratched the surface, but Nate said—"

"You ran into Nate at the college library?"

I nod. "Yes. Apparently the *Myerton Gazette*'s given him a monthly assignment to write on some aspect of the area's history."

"Oh, what the frankincense and myrrh," Helen says, rolling her eyes. "That can't be good."

I hear the door open as I say, "He promises no more paranormal stuff. Nate said he's working on an article about some bank robbery in town in 1928."

"What was that, Tom?" Anna says, coming into the living room. "Hello, you two."

"Hi, how was dinner with Bill?" I ask.

"Fine, fine. What were you saying about Nate and a bank robbery?"

"Yeah, I was just telling Helen that Nate's writing another article for the Gazette. Something about the First National Bank of Myerton being robbed in 1928 of $150,000, or something?"

Helen chokes on her beer. "What? That's a lot of money."

"It really was back then," I say, "I'm not sure what it would be worth now, but maybe a million or more?"

While Helen and I are talking, Anna lowers herself into an armchair. She's gone white, and she has a far-off expression.

"After all these years," she whispers. "I thought it was over."

"What's wrong, Anna," Helen asks. "You look like you've seen a ghost?"

"Maybe I have," she says quietly. She shakes her head. "I'm just glad he's not alive to see it."

"Who, Anna?"

Anna looks at me. "My grandfather. The First National Bank of Myerton was his."

***

Helen hands Anna a cup of tea. "I put a little brandy in it," she says. "It looks like you can use it."

"Thank you, dear," she says. Taking a sip, she closes her eyes and says, "Ahh, yes, just what the doctor ordered. Sorry about that. It was just a shock to hear that after all these years."

"Anna," I say, "Joan never told me your family owned a bank."

"That's because I never told her," she replies. "We certainly didn't by the time she was born. It was a dark family secret that by the time she came along, most people in town had forgotten about."

"But your grandfather," Helen says, "he owned a bank in the 1920s?"

"Not just a bank, Helen," Anna says. "The First National Bank of Myerton was the only bank in town for years. Everyone did their banking there, including the Myer family. Between their personal fortune and their business accounts, the Myers were the bank's biggest depositors."

"Did your grandfather start the bank?" I ask.

"Oh, no," Anna said, shaking his head. "His grandfather founded the bank just after the Civil War. My grandfather—his name was Ashton Stewart, by the way, but everyone called him Ash—took over the bank after his father died in the flu epidemic of 1918."

"He must have been young," I say.

"He was twenty-two," Anna nods. "Fresh home from the war and thrust into a position he thought he wouldn't be in for another twenty years. Young, inexperienced. Probably why he made the mistakes he made, including trusting the wrong person."

"Nate told me the vice-president of the bank stole the money?" I say.

Anna nods. "Kent Stirling," she says, her voice tinged with bitterness. "He was Grandpa Ash's best friend. They served in France together. Somehow, both managed to survive combat in the Meuse-Argonne, but then they were only at the front lines for a couple of months before Germany surrendered. They came back, Grandpa took over the First National, and he hired Kent as his Vice-President."

"So his best friend embezzled from the bank?" Helen says with rapt attention.

"Mm-hmm, and Grandpa Ash never forgave him."

"Anna, obviously you weren't alive when it happened," I say. "How did you learn about it?"

"Family stories around the dinner table, especially at Thanksgiving," Anna sighs. "My father was only two when everything happened in 1928, and he and my mother had me in 1952. Grandma was gone by then—I never met her, and she was never spoken of in the house. Grandpa came to live with us, and he was always telling the story about how Stirling's betrayal ruined the family."

She pauses. "For decades, the Stewarts were one of the major families in Myerton and the surrounding area. We were wealthy, socially prominent, lived in one of the big houses in what is now the historic district where the Trents live. Now, we were no Myers, but the families did rub shoulders. Grandpa Ash and Winthrop Myer III grew up together until Myer's father shipped him off to prep school near D.C. The families were friendly. That's one reason I was invited to parties at the Myer Mansion with . . . well, other prominent families when I was a teenager."

"But wasn't it a Myer company payroll that Stirling stole? Nate told me the Myers stopped doing business with the bank," I say.

"Yes, they stopped using Grandpa Ash's bank for their businesses, but they still kept their personal accounts there. According to Dad, Winthrop Myer made it clear to Grandpa that he didn't hold him responsible; it was a business decision made by his Board of Directors. Grandpa . . . well, he never had a kind word to say about the Myer family until the day he died."

"I'm still not clear what happened?" Helen says. "How was the bank robbed?"

Anna shakes her head. "Even after almost a century, I'm not sure anyone really knows. Piecing the story together from what Grandpa said, the Western Maryland and Ohio Railroad paid their employees on the fifth of every month. A payroll shipment, all in cash, of course, would arrive on the fourth from Baltimore and would be locked in the safe. The next day, the head of payroll for the railroad would come to the bank with an armed guard, get the money, and take it away for distribution down the line." She takes a deep breath. "It was a large sum of money to handle at one time, so Grandpa put the man he trusted the most in the world in charge."

"Kent Stirling," I say.

"Kent Stirling," Anna nods. "On November 2, 1928, the payroll shipment arrived—"

"Wait," I say, holding up my hand, "I thought it arrived on the 4th."

"That was a Sunday that year," she says. "It arrived late afternoon on the previous Friday. Stirling accepted the shipment, signed a receipt, and locked it in the vault. Grandpa swore he saw Stirling lock the money in the vault. Right at 5 p.m., he and Stirling left the bank. That was the last Grandpa—or anyone—saw of Kent Stirling.

"Monday morning, according to Grandpa, he got a phone call from an irate customer wanting to know why the bank wasn't open. Apparently, Stirling always arrived at the bank, made sure the teller stations were set up for the day's business, let in the staff, and opened the bank promptly at 9 a.m. Well, Grandpa called Stirling's house. His wife answered and said Stirling hadn't been home all weekend, telling her he was going fishing in the mountains for a weekend and would be back Sunday night."

"But he hadn't come home." Helen says.

"No, he hadn't. Harriet Stirling—that was the wife's name, Harriet—even called the police to report him missing. Grandpa hurried down to the bank to see what was going on. Once there, he found a few customers, his tellers and clerks, and the men from the railroad waiting.

"He unlocked the door and Grandpa went straight to the vault. Not only did he have to turn over the payroll money, he had to get the teller drawers set up—something he'd come to rely on Stirling to do. But as soon as he got the vault opened, he realized he had trusted the wrong man."

We're all quiet for a few moments, then Helen says, "Did they ever find Stirling or the money?"

"No on both counts," Anna sighs. "The police looked for Stirling, but it was like he fell off the face of the earth. The robbery was big news, not just in Myerton, but in Baltimore, too. Soon, the entire state knew that my Grandpa's bank had lost a fortune to an embezzler. The publicity was awful. People in town began to take their money out, saying that a mattress was safer than the bank. The bank never recovered from losing the Myer businesses as clients. But somehow Grandpa managed to keep the bank open—he sold the big house they lived in and moved into the more modest one that I grew up knowing—and for a while, things looked like they were going to be OK. And they probably would have been, but then the Depression hit and, well, that was that."

"What happened to your Grandpa and his family? Were they left destitute?"

"Fortunately, no," Anna says. "Grandpa had never invested in the stock market, so he didn't lose everything when it crashed. And he didn't keep all his money in his own bank. The family was never wealthy again, but we were comfortable enough. Of course, that only fueled the rumors."

"What rumors?" I ask.

"When it first happened, no one believed Grandpa had anything to do with Stirling's embezzlement. But after the bank failed, and people who still did business with him lost their life savings, the rumors started that he and Stirling were in cahoots, that the reason the money was never found is because he and Grandpa split it, with Stirling fleeing the country with his half and Grandpa hiding his away somewhere in the area."

"You're kidding!" I say. "What, like he buried it in the woods?"

"The woods, under the floorboards of his house, in his mattress, used it to buy artwork—the list was huge. That really made Grandpa bitter. Not only did he lose his best friend and his business, he lost his reputation."

Anna wipes a tear away. "I don't have many memories of Grandpa—he died in 1962, when I was ten—but what I do remember is a bitter old man who would not let go of something that happened long before I was born. And now, Nate's going to stir everything up again."

"I don't think it will be as bad as that," Helen says. "Myerton's a lot bigger than it was back then. Most people have probably never heard of the story."

"Helen, you grew up in a small town," Anna says. "Tom, you did too. You know that people have long memories, and those stories are passed down from one generation to the next. No. There are enough families with roots deep in Myerton's past who will remember. And they'll talk. And—" she swallows "—and my Grandpa's name is going to be dragged through the mud again because someone let that idiot near a keyboard again."

"Anna, if you're concerned about what Nate's going to write," I say, "maybe you should let him interview you? You know, tell your family's side of the story?"

"I agree with Tom," Helen says. "You should talk to Nate."

Anna brings her fist down hard on the arm of the chair. "Absolutely not," she declares. "I want nothing to do with that article. The last thing in the world I am going to do is to be interviewed by Nathaniel Eduardo Jorge Rodriguez."

She stands up and walks to the door of the living room. "I'm going to bed. Helen, it's about time for you to go."

"Anna, don't you think—" I start to say.

She wheels on me and, shaking a bony finger at me, shouts, "Thomas Jude Greer, you will not mention that article again, or you can find another secretary! Good night!"

She walks out of the room and stomps her way up the stairs, leaving Helen and me open-mouthed in astonishment.

Four

I've spent the last couple of days dodging Anna. Each morning, I checked the *Gazette* website to see if Nate's article appeared. Fortunately, it hasn't. I'm hoping he's given up on the idea.

No, I don't know why I would think that, either. Nate with an idea is like a dog with a bone. I just hope whatever he writes doesn't set off my mother-in-law and church secretary.

In any event, by the time Thursday rolls around, I am relieved to be able to spend the morning out of the Rectory. Not only do I have hospital visits, but it's also the day of my follow-up appointment with Martin. After he warned me about my blood pressure, I took his advice seriously, riding my bike almost everywhere I could for a total of an hour a day just like he recommended.

I'm optimistic he'll have good news after he checks me out.

I'm still optimistic after the nurse checks my vitals and doesn't grimace this time at my numbers.

Then, Martin comes into the exam room, and I see the look on his face.

"Tom," he says, shaking my hand, "how are you doing?"

"I was doing OK until you came in," I say nervously. "You have the same look I get when I need to give someone I'm giving spiritual counsel a firm talk."

Martin nods. "Well, that's why I'm here, Tom, unfortunately."

I take a deep breath. "OK."

He takes a look at his tablet. "Now, I'll retake it in a little bit, but your blood pressure is still a bit higher than is good for you. In fact, it's a few points higher than it was last month."

I slump and shake my head. "How can that be? I've been riding my bike like you told me—you've seen me around town. I've even taken up a hobby that I find relaxing. You said if I reduced my stress, my pressure would go down. I don't know how I can reduce my stress anymore. Does this mean medication?"

"Not yet," Martin says. "There's still some things you can do with diet. The good news is your weight is down a few pounds, so that will help some. Watch your salt intake, limit caffeine and alcohol. Those three changes should help."

I sigh as I try to imagine my life without coffee. "So, when you say, no caffeine—"

"No more than two cups of coffee a day and no cola drinks. You don't need the sugar."

"I prefer lemonade anyway," I say. "But two cups of coffee a day?"

"What's your normal intake?"

I think for a moment. "Maybe five or six?"

"Tom, for a man with your blood pressure, that's way too much. Look, you can try this, or I can put you on blood pressure medication right now."

"Well, why don't we do that, then? I mean, I'm probably going to have to go on it anyway. I mean, it's genetic, right?"

Martin sighs. "There is a genetic component, yes. And since your Dad had high blood pressure, that's a contributing factor to your problem. But medication is not inevitable, not if you continue to get exercise, control your stress, and watch what you eat."

I don't say anything for a moment, then say, "OK, you're the expert."

He smiles. "That's the spirit, Tom. Now, let me finish the exam and send you on your way. As much as I enjoy seeing your smiling face, we both have other people to take care of."

As he looks in my ears, I ask, "Speaking of patients, how's your fiancée?"

He chuckles. "She's still complaining about being cooped up in the house. I've stopped hovering, and she's beginning to do some light activities. I think we may even be at Mass on Sunday."

"She'd like that," I say.

"I know, which is why I'm considering it. As long as she takes it easy, she should be fine."

He finishes the exam and retakes my blood pressure. He smiles when he sees the readings. "Much better," Martin says. "Must have been nerves. But that doesn't change my advice."

I begin to get dressed. "Do you want to see me again before Helen and I go on our honeymoon?"

He strokes his chin. "Hmm, no, I don't think so. Have you bought a blood pressure cuff yet?"

When I shake my head, he says, "Tell you what. Buy one. Check your pressure in the morning and text me the numbers. I'll keep track, and if I think things are getting out of hand, I'll bring you in. How does that sound?"

"Like a very sound plan, Martin," I say with a smile.

"Good. Now get out of here. You have souls to save, and I have bodies to put back together."

***

After my hospital visits and Noon Mass, I settle into my office to put the finishing touches on my homily for the coming Sunday. Anna seems to have gotten over being upset over the entire issue of the article and is acting a lot more pleasant.

I'm in the middle of rewriting my conclusion—they always give me trouble—when the Rectory doorbell rings. A moment later, Anna knocks on my office door.

Peeking inside, she says, "Tom, Steve Austin from the Hoot-n-Holler is here to see you."

I lean back in my chair. "Really? Did he say what he wanted?"

"No, he just asked if you had a few minutes."

"Sure, send him in."

Anna steps back and Steve walks into my office. Instead of what he usually wears when tending bar—a tight t-shirt and jeans—today he's wearing trousers, a button-up shirt, and a light blue blazer.

"Thanks, Anna," he says when he comes in. "I haven't seen you at my place in a while."

"Oh, well," she chuckles. "After the last Ladies of Charity social night there, we've been laying low."

I'm startled by the conversation. "Anna? The Ladies of Charity goes to the Hoot-n-Holler?"

"Why not?" Anna says. "It has plenty of room, the food is not bad, and Steve always gives us a good deal on the drinks. Besides, you go there."

I open my mouth to say something when Steve grins and says, "Oh, he's just upset because he can only stop by when no one else is there."

"Ah," Anna says. "Quite sensible. You don't want a priest cramping everyone's style."

"Cramping—now wait a minute—" I protest.

Anna just laughs at me and leaves Steve and me alone in my office.

"She keeps you in line pretty well, it looks like," he says.

"That, she does," I say, offering Steve a seat.

"I won't take up too much of your time," he says. "I just wanted to talk about the Community Thanksgiving Dinner. I understand Saint Clare's is hosting this year?"

"Yes, it's our turn," I say.

Steve looks at his hands, then says, "Look, I'd like to help out this year. I mean, I don't have any family—none that will have me, anyway, because, well, you know, they still haven't accepted that I'm gay, which is fine most of the time. But it does make for a lonely holiday season."

"I am sorry about that, Steve," I say.

He shrugs. "Like I say, it usually doesn't bother me. I'm not bitter or anything. I still love them, and I look forward to the day when they can love me again."

The big ex-Army Ranger clears his throat. "I've known about the dinner ever since I bought the Hoot-n-Holler, but I haven't approached anyone about helping out. I mean, I wasn't sure the churches in town would accept anything from a gay man. Then, I met you and got to know you, and you've always treated me great, so I thought this year, well, I'd take the step."

"And I'm glad you have, Steve," I say with a smile. "We can always use the help. Did you have something in mind?"

"Well, I can donate a couple of kegs of beer—I don't know if anyone would object to the alcohol. If you think that would be a problem, I can donate a soda machine. I can also help on the day of the dinner. I usually close the bar and spend the day alone."

"Frankly, I think the soda machine might be the better idea. We don't want to scandalize the Baptists, you know."

Steve laughs at this. "Oh, I know. I was raised Baptist. Know all about them. Two things are always kept in the closet in a Baptist home, and one of them is alcohol."

I don't know what to say to this, so I just say, "I'll let everyone know about the donation and your willingness to help. I'll send you more details as the date approaches."

"Sounds good," Steve says.

Just then, Anna knocks on the door again. "Tom, sorry, but Bridget Davis is here. She's stopping by for a list you have?"

"Oh, right," I say. "Just show her in. "Steve, I'm sorry—"

He waves his hand. "I have a few more stops to make before I leave town. I'll let you get back to your work."

As Steve stands up, Bridget comes into the office. "Father Tom, I'm—Oh! I didn't know I was interrupting."

"We were just finishing up. Steve Austin, Bridget Davis."

"Davis, Davis," Steve says. "Have we met?"

"No, Mr. Austin," Bridget says coolly. "But my husband was a frequent customer of yours."

There's a flash of recognition in Steve's face. "Rusty Davis was your husband."

Bridget nods. "Yes," she says quietly.

Steve lowers his head and slowly shakes it. "Ma'am, I—I am just so sorry about everything that's happened to your family. Yeah, Rusty came in a lot. I'd cut him off after a few drinks and send him home." He pauses. "If I had any idea what he was doing to you and your kids after he got home, I'd have kicked his ass myself. He was nothing but a bully, and I've had to face a lot of bullies in my time."

Bridget appears surprised. "Well, Mr. Austin. Um, that's—that's very kind of you to say. And really, none of what Rusty did was your fault. He'd always pick up more beer on the way home."

"Still, had I known, Mrs. Davis . . . "

She smiles and says, "Thank you, Mr. Austin."

There's a strange silence between them for a moment. Then Bridget seems to shake herself out of a fog. "Oh! Yes, Father. I came here for that list of handymen?"

"I have it right here," I say. To Steve, I explain, "Bridget has quite a lot of work that needs to be done on her house. The church has a list of parishioners, licensed contractors, who do that sort of work." I don't say at a discount since I don't want to embarrass Bridget, but Steve seems to pick up on what I mean.

"What kind of work do you need done?" Steve asks her.

"Well, a little bit of everything," she says. "Some outlets don't work, and the faucet in the kitchen needs to be replaced, for starters. Before he—well, Rusty used to take care of everything. But it's been a long time."

Clearing his throat, Steve says, "Mrs. Davis, I'm not a professional, but I'm pretty good with my hands. I handled most of the work fixing up the Hoot-n-Holler after I bought the place. I could do the work for you, and you wouldn't have to pay me anything."

"Well, that's very kind of you, Mr. Austin, but you have your own business—"

"My business is only really busy at night," he grins. "My days are more or less my own." He hesitates, then adds, "Let me do this for you, Mrs. Davis. I didn't help you before, let me help you now."

Bridget's eyes light up and she smiles—the first real smile I've seen in a long time. "Well, you're just a Good Samaritan, aren't you?"

"Maybe in more ways than one," Steve says.

"All right, Mr. Austin," she says. "Thank you. Um, I know you're a busy man, but can you come by the house so I can show you what needs to be done?"

"Saturday's my day off," Steve says.

"It is?" I ask. "I thought you worked Saturdays?"

He shoots me a glance. "I just started taking Saturdays off." To Bridget he says, "I'll stop by, see what needs to be done, then get what I need to make the repairs. How does that sound?"

"It sounds like you're an answer to prayer, Mr. Austin!"

He laughs. "Mrs. Davis, I have never had anyone call me that. And it's Steve," he says, extending his hand.

"Bridget," she says, taking his hand. "Thank you, again."

"It's the least I can do," he says quietly.

I look at the two of them and wonder what I'm seeing. "OK, well, this seems to have worked out great for everyone."

Bridget looks at me and says. "Yes. Thank you, Father. Steve, I'll see you Saturday morning?"

"See you then," Steve says.

Bridget leaves, and Steve watches her go. "That's very nice of you to offer to do that," I say.

"Huh?" he says. Then turning back to me. "Oh. Yes. Well, she seems like she needs help. Anyway, Father Tom, I'll let you get back to work."

He leaves, and I sit in my chair. Shaking my head, I mutter, "What was that? I mean, it looked like—nah! Tom, don't be ridiculous."

Dismissing the impossible thought from my mind, I return to my homily.

Five

"Tom, can you go ahead and uncork the wine?"

I've just set the plate of Nibbles—a Helen specialty and my all-time favorite hors d'oeuvre—on the coffee table. "Sure. Which one?"

"The chianti we're having with dinner," she answers from the kitchen. She's putting the finishing touches on the meal, featuring her chicken parmesan using homemade marinara sauce—a secret recipe she refuses to divulge.

Which is only fair. I have yet to give her Grandmama's biscuit recipe.

I walk into the kitchen and ask, "Where is it?"

She points to the bottle, fat-bottomed and covered in the traditional straw basket. "Time?" she asks.

I check. "They'll be here anytime now. You know, it's only Clark and Vivian. They've had dinner with us before."

"I know," Helen says as she shakes the bottle of vinaigrette dressing for the salad. "They have high expectations now."

"They're not judging you, you know. They're our friends."

"I know they're our friends," she says as she lifts a pot lid to check something. "That's why I don't want to disappoint them."

"Frankly, I'm surprised you wanted to have them over. I mean, we're not going to have too many Friday nights all to ourselves coming up."

"Vivian and I need to discuss some wedding details, I know you and Clark need to talk about Thanksgiving, and this dinner party is a great way to take my mind off of everything."

Before I can ask what she means, the doorbell rings. "Ah, that's them," I say as I walk to the door.

"Take them into the living room," she calls. "Offer them a drink and some Nibbles."

"Sorry," I say with a grin. "Already ate them all!"

"You didn't, Thomas Jude—"

"Of course not, darling, just pulling your chain."

"Hrumph!"

I open the door to Clark and Vivian Applegate, our friends and fellow clerical couple. Clark's the pastor of Myerton Methodist Church, my closest friend among the ministers in the area, and my best man. Vivian, his wife, has become a friend and confidant to Helen over the last few months. In fact, Vivian is overseeing the wedding.

"Hey, come on in, you two," I say.

"Tom, so good to see you," Clark says, extending his hand.

Vivian hugs me. "I'm just thrilled you asked us over. I'm dying to try some more of Helen's cooking."

"And I want more of those little—what are they called?" Clark asks, looking to the living room with anticipation.

"Nibbles," I laugh. "They're a favorite of mine."

"Man, I've thought about them ever since you had us over the last time," Clark says, helping Vivian off with her coat and hanging it up before doing the same with his own overcoat. "It's really chilly out tonight!"

"Well, the fire's warm," I say. "Come on, sit down."

"You two go ahead," Vivian says. "I'm going to slip into the kitchen and see if Helen needs any help."

Clark and I go into the living room and sit down, he in one of the armchairs, I in the recliner—we're leaving the couch for Helen and Vivian.

"So, have you recovered from all the Halloween excitement?" Clark asks.

I roll my eyes. "Yes, finally. If it weren't such a success, I'd say no more haunted houses as long as I'm Rector here."

"You raised a lot of money for the education center?"

I nod. "Over $50,000. Mainly from ticket sales, but we also had people give separate donations. Most of those were from non-parishioners, which surprised me."

"There's a lot of enthusiasm in town for what you're doing, Tom," Clark says. "Including at my church. Now, that may be because everyone knows we're friends, but I really think people recognize the merit of the center. So, how close are you to opening?"

"Oh, we're still a long way off. But we're going to be able to start renovations this month with the money we already have. I still need to decide about a director for the center, and I still need a Director of Religious Education for the church. Money's still the major thing, but Martin Maycord's been a godsend in that area. I don't know where this project would be without his fundraising prowess."

"I've met Dr. Maycord, briefly," Clark says. "Seems like a nice guy."

"He is, he is," I nod. "Great surgeon too."

"Vivian mentioned he's engaged to Mae Trent?"

"Yes, that happened a few weeks ago. It was in the *Gazette*."

"I know Mae from her job as a social worker at the hospital. A very caring and compassionate young woman. But isn't there quite an age-gap between her and Dr. Maycord?"

I laugh. "Yes, twelve years. But it's also a real life, love-at-first-sight romance."

Clark rolls his eyes. "Oh, I know all about those. Vivian reads them. Is almost addicted to them. She's just finished one, *Blooming Love*, or something like that.

"It's *Blooms of Love*, Clark," Vivian says as she and Helen walk in.

"Oh, that's Erin Wright's latest," Helen says. "Is it good?"

Vivian sighs. "Only if you like a handsome cowboy falling in love with a voluptuous florist."

"Maybe I'll take it on the honeymoon," Helen says, smiling slyly at me.

"Do you think you're going to have time for reading?" I ask, my eyebrows raised.

"Well, we have to rest sometime, you know?"

"Hey, you two," Clark says, shifting in his chair, "this conversation's getting a little too racy for me."

"Oh, Clark," Vivian laughs. "You're such an old fuddy-duddy!"

"I am not," Clark retorts.

"You are, too," Vivian says.

"So, what were you two talking about?" I ask Helen as I pop a Nibble in my mouth.

"The wedding, what else?" Helen says. "Just going over some stress points with Viv."

"And by stress points, you mean Mom?"

"Her name did come up, yes," Vivian says. "And I promise to keep an eye on her."

I breathe a sigh of relief. "Good. You never know what she's going to say or do."

Clark grabs a handful of Nibbles off the plate and starts popping them in his mouth. "Well, I'm sure it will be OK. She's your mother. She's not going to do anything to embarrass you on the day of your wedding. Did she at your last wedding?"

I grimace. "No. But then, she wasn't there. I didn't invite her."

Vivian looks surprised. "You didn't invite your own mother—"

"Trust me, Viv," Helen says quietly. "I've met Nola Greer. It was for the best."

We're all quiet for a moment, then Clark asks, "So, are all of the other wedding plans in place?"

"Just about," Helen says. "I have my dress. Gladys is still trying to decide what she's going to wear. The Archdiocese is handling the press and the catering. The Myer Mansion is being transformed from a sinister enchanted forest into a reception hall."

"Doesn't it have that huge ballroom?"

"Uh-huh," Helen says. "That's where the main reception's going to be, but some of the other rooms downstairs are going to handle any overflow."

"Do you have any family coming, Helen?"

At that, Helen looks a little sad. "I don't have much family, Clark," she says. "My aunt and uncle are still alive but they're not able to make it. I have cousins scattered around, but I'm not really close to them. I'm an only child, so I have no siblings."

She clears her throat and squares her shoulders. "I've come to think of Saint Clare's as my family," she says with a smile. Looking at me, she adds, "And I'm so glad to be marrying into it."

"Helen," Clark says, "that's one of the most beautiful things I've ever heard."

"I mean it," Helen says. "I've known that ever since Archbishop Knowland told us about the possibility. I'm not just marrying Tom. His parish family is my family. He's their shepherd, and I'm blessed to be one of his lambs."

"My most beloved one," I say quietly.

We exchange a glance across the room, forgetting for a moment that there is anyone else around. I'm struck by how beautiful she is tonight, the flames from the fireplace dancing in her eyes, the light reflecting off of her black hair. She's wearing a burgundy sweater, paired with a forest-green skirt. It's so tempting just to cross the short space between us, take her up in my arms, and—

"All units, report of a disturbance at 6155 Lily Lane, the Lancelot Apartments," a staticky voice I recognize as one of the county's 911 operators says. "A woman banging on the door of Apartment 13B."

"Did—did she just say the Lancelot Apartments?" I ask Helen.

"Uh-huh," Helen says with a frown. "Apartment 13B. Oh, crap!"

"What is it?" Vivian says.

"Probably nothing," I sigh. "That's just Nate Rodriguez's apartment."

"Do you need to go, Helen?" Clark asks. "Because Vivian and I—"

I see Helen start to say something, then close her mouth. She puts a smile on her face and says, "No. An officer can handle it, and I've got a good crew."

Just then, Helen's radio says, "Car 14 en route. ETA is three minutes."

"That was Nina Hallstead," I say.

Helen stands up. "See? All handled. Hallstead is one of my best officers."

"Wait—did you say Nina Hallstead?" Vivian asks.

"Yes, have you met her?"

"No, but our boys loved a woman MMA fighter named Nina Hallstead. Had a poster of her in their room and everything."

"That's her," I say. "She went into law enforcement after she retired."

"Well, well, imagine that!" Vivian says, shaking her head.

"And with that crisis in the capable hands of Officer Hallstead," Helen declares, "let's go to the dining room."

***

Helen just sits down after bringing out the main course when "Eye of the Tiger" starts playing from the kitchen.

"Oh, I am so sorry," she says, standing up. "Let me just take care of that really quickly and I'll be right back."

She hurries from the room. Clark turns to me and says, "Do you think it's anything serious?"

"Hmm, it's hard to tell," I say. "If she comes back to the table and sits down, it's nothing. If she goes to the gun safe, there's a problem."

I take a sip of water and say, "So, Clark, I had a volunteer from the community for the Thanksgiving dinner."

"Oh, wonderful!" Clark grins. "The Ministerial Committee's been wanting more participation from the non-church community. Who is it?"

"Steve Austin from the Hoot-n-Holler," I say. "He's going to donate a soda machine and help serve. He first offered a couple of kegs of beer, but I thought our Baptist brethren may not approve."

"Some of my own congregation wouldn't approve of that," Clark says with a chuckle. "You were right to turn that down. I'm glad Steve's participating. He's a good guy. From what I understand, the Hoot-n-Holler used to be a real dive. It's become more respectable."

"Apparently so, if Anna's right."

"Oh, yeah," Vivian says. "Anna's invited me to more than one Ladies of Charity social night. Boy, you Catholics can really tie one on!"

"Anna?" I say with a laugh. "I don't think I've ever seen her tipsy, much less drunk."

"Let me tell you, Tom, it's a sight," she says. Before Vivian can say anything else, Helen rushes back into the dining room. "Tom," she says quickly, "everyone, I'm so sorry, but there is a situation that I need to take care of. I'm afraid I need to leave."

Clark and Vivian both say what a shame it is and how they understand completely. I stand up and say, "Darling, I thought Dan was covering things this evening?"

"He was—he is," Helen says. "But I need to take care of this."

"But can't you just call—"

"No, Tom," Helen says sharply. "I'm the Police Chief. It's my responsibility. Now I'm sorry, but I need to go."

With that, she flies out of the dining room past me, closing the door to the Rectory with a resounding bang. I'm left with Clark and Vivian, confused, embarrassed, and a little angry.

I turn to our guests, who are both looking a little embarrassed themselves. Sitting down, I say, "Sorry about that, Clark, Viv. I—I didn't handle that well."

"It's fine, Tom," Clark says.

"Yes, Tom," Vivian agrees with a nod. "These things happen."

"Usually if there's a call," I say with a slight smile, "I can go with her. I mean, we talked about the possibility of plans having to be changed or interrupted because of our jobs. I just didn't think it would happen before we were married."

"But Tom," Clark says, "you really can't expect to go with Helen every time she gets a call, can you? I mean, not anymore?"

I shrug. "Maybe not. Still, I owe you both an apology for my behavior. And I owe her one too."

"Well," Vivian says brightly. "You don't need to apologize to us. Helen will forgive you. But right now, let's eat this delicious meal she left for us."

"Good idea, Viv," Clark says with enthusiasm.

I smile at our friends—our patient, understanding friends—and say, "Well, I happen to know dessert's a tiramisu from The Muffin Man."

Vivian claps her hands. "Wonderful!"

For the next fifteen minutes or so, we return to our food and our conversation. Still, my mind is on Helen.

What was so important that she had to handle it herself?

Why didn't she mention what it was?

I stop mid-chew and turn to look over my shoulder. From where I'm sitting, I can see the gun safe.

She never went anywhere near it. Which means she left without her gun.

Inwardly, I breathe a sigh of relief. Whatever it is, it isn't something she thought was dangerous.

There's that, anyway.

I've just started talking to Clark and Vivian about the developing plans for an outdoor learning area as part of the education center when there's a frantic pounding on the Rectory door. It so startles me, I jump in my chair.

"What in the world—" I say, standing up quickly and knocking my chair over. The pounding increases, now joined by cries of "Father Tom! I need your help!"

I yank open the door, and a frantic Nate Rodriguez rushes in.

"Oh, my God! Oh, my God!" he blabbers. By this time, Clark and Vivian are standing in the doorway to the dining room to see what's going on.

"Nate! Nate!" I yell above the stream of unintelligible words coming from his mouth. "For goodness sake, what's wrong?"

"Father Tom! You have to hide me! I claim sanctuary! That's still a thing, right?"

Whatever's going on, it can't be good. "Nate, just calm down—"

"Calm down! Calm down!" he screeches. "She attacked me! I was walking along minding my own business, and she ran at me, screaming and beating on me! I ran away, but you have to hide me! She's going to kill me!"

"What did you do to Gladys this time, Nate?" I ask, rolling my eyes.

"Oh, it wasn't Gladys! It was Anna!"

"Anna?" I say. "Anna who?"

"What do you mean, 'Anna who!'" he screams. "Anna Luckgold, the parish secretary!"

I'm too stunned to speak, but I overhear Vivian say, "You know, honey, our church is boring compared to Tom's."

Six

"What are you talking about?" I say incredulously. "Anna attacked you? Why did she attack you?"

"I don't know, Father Tom," Nate says frantically. "I swear, if I did, I'd tell you."

He paces back and forth, running his fingers through his hair. "I've been trying to think while running here from my apartment."

The mention of his apartment causes something to click in my mind. "Wait a minute, Nate," I say. "This happened at your apartment."

"No," he says, shaking his head quickly. "On the sidewalk in front of my apartment. I was coming home from Gladys', and I'd just parked my car. I saw a police car, and Officer Hallstead talking to Anna. I wasn't sure what was going on—I thought maybe Anna had been mugged, though why she was in my neighborhood at night, I have no idea—so I hurried up to where they were. I called her name, she turned—and that's when it happened!"

Now it all makes sense. Anna was the disturbance at Nate's apartment, the one that Nina Hallstead answered.

And it was probably the issue Helen had to take care of.

"Nate," I say to the somewhat calmer young man, "I don't know what's going on or why Anna would attack you. But you can't hide from her here."

"But—but—you can't throw me out into the cold! I asked for sanctuary!"

"But Anna lives here, Nate!"

He stops and looks at me for a moment. "Oh. I forgot that. Maybe I'll hide at Gladys' for a while."

"You're not going to hide anywhere," I say, taking him firmly by the arm. "What you are going to do is sit in the living room and wait until Anna gets back—"

"What! NO—!"

"—so we can get to the bottom of this."

He looks at me with the sad eyes of a dog. "You will protect me, won't you?"

I take a deep breath. "Yes, Nate. I'll protect you."

He nods and collapses on the couch. I return to Clark and Vivian and say, "Well, this has been an interesting evening."

Clark claps me on the back. "Buddy, it seems like you have your hands full. Vivian and I'll be going."

"What?" Vivian says. "I want to stay and see what happens."

"Come along, Viv," Clark says, taking his wife gently by the elbow. "I'm sure Anna will tell you all about it."

They say their good-byes, and I slip into the kitchen to call Helen.

"Hi, honey," she says when she answers. "Listen, I'm sorry about that—"

"No, I am," I say. "We've discussed how something like this was bound to happen, given our careers."

"Well, I've got everything straightened out, so I'll be back in a few minutes."

"Uh-huh," I say. "So is Anna coming with you?"

"No, I called Bill to—" Helen stops. "Ahem. Tom, how did you find out Anna was involved?"

"Well, when Nate showed up here yammering that Anna had attacked him, it didn't take me long to figure it out."

Helen sighs. "I was hoping to not get you involved. I know how much you care about her."

"Well, the idiot savant of Myerton got me involved," I reply. "Can you tell me what happened? Why is Anna so mad at Nate?"

"Frankly, it's that article he's been working on. Apparently, it's appearing in tomorrow's print edition of the *Gazette*."

"OK," I say slowly. "We know she wasn't happy he was doing the article. But why did she attack him over it?"

"Because, Tom," Helen says, "in the article, Nate accuses Anna's grandfather of murder."

***

"But I didn't!" Nate declares.

"Yes, you did, Nate," Helen says. "I've seen the article."

Not long after our conversation, Helen arrives back at the Rectory. Nate has calmed down—well, as calm as he ever gets. I am still completely in the dark about what he wrote that set Anna off.

"What did you write, Nate?" I say, wondering again why anyone thought him writing another article for the *Gazette* was a good idea.

"Only the truth, Father, I swear," he says, holding one hand on his heart and raising the other like he's being sworn in to give testimony at a trial.

"That's what you said last time."

"But I didn't do what I did last time," Nate says firmly. "I stuck to the facts I uncovered in my research. I quoted everyone I interviewed exactly. I've got the notes and the recordings to prove it. And I didn't say anything about Anna's grandfather!"

Helen and I look at each other. "Helen, did the article mention Ashton Stewart?"

"Yes, he's mentioned throughout the article."

"Of course he is," Nate says, "he was the president of the bank when it was robbed. He's the one who allegedly murdered the vice president."

"What?" I exclaim.

"We'll get to that in a minute, Tom," Helen says, holding up her hand. "Nate, do you know what Anna's maiden name is?"

When he shakes his head, Helen looks at me. "That's it. He didn't know."

"Know what?" Nate asks.

I shake my head. "Anna should have told him."

"Told me what?"

"It still wouldn't have changed what he wrote." Helen says.

"What wouldn't have?" Nate says, getting more confused by the second.

"Maybe, but then he'd have gotten both sides of the story."

"Excuse me!" Nate says loudly, causing both Helen and I to look at him. "Can you please tell me what Anna should have told me?"

I take a deep breath. "Nate, Ashton Stewart is—was—Anna's grandfather."

The young man's eyes get huge and his mouth falls open. "Wha—What?"

"That's right, Nate," Helen says. "Before she became Anna Luckgold, she was Anna Stewart."

Nate collapses back in the chair and covers his face with his hands. "Oh, no! Oh, no!" he wails. "No wonder she hates me."

"Now, Nate, Anna doesn't hate you," I say, patting him on the back. "She's actually quite fond of you when you're not doing something to upset her."

"I didn't know, I swear," Nate says, beginning to rock back and forth. "If I had, I would have interviewed her. I would have given her family's side of the story, instead of just Roland's."

"Roland?" I ask. "Who is Roland?"

"Roland Crescent," Nate says. "He's the grandson of Kent Stirling, the vice president of the bank alleged to have stolen the money."

"Nate, I haven't had a chance to read the article, so why don't you just give me the high points," I ask, settling in for a long story.

Nate sits up and leans forward. "Well, you know the basic story, I think, if Anna told you about her grandfather."

"She told us the other day. She said the whole affair was a dark family secret, that her grandfather remained bitter about it for the rest of his life."

"Well, he had a good reason," Nate says. "From my research, Ashton Stewart and Kent Stirling fought together in Europe during World War I."

Helen says, "Anna mentioned the Meuse-Argonne, I think."

"That's right. Well, I came across a record of a commendation given to a Sergeant Kent Stirling for bravery, specifically saving the life of his unit's Lieutenant, Ashton Stewart."

"So that's why Stewart hired Stirling as vice-president when he took over the bank."

"That's the only reason I could find. Stirling was originally from Georgia, according to his service records. I found his family in the 1910 census. He was the oldest of ten children. His father listed his occupation as tenant farmer."

"So, no banking experience at all?"

"The service records indicate he dropped out of school after the sixth grade."

"Why would Ashton Stewart hire him as vice president of a bank, a position he wasn't qualified for?" Helen says.

"Gratitude for saving his life, more than likely," I say.

"Probably," Nate nods. "Anyway, they both came back from overseas. Stirling returned to Georgia, I think—I couldn't find anything on him between 1918 and 1920—and Stewart came back to Myerton. Then his father died in the influenza epidemic of 1918, and Ashton Stewart inherited the bank. I found a news article in a 1919 issue of the *Gazette* talking about his taking over. It called him 'the Boy Wonder of Western Maryland,' and 'Myerton's Mellon'—I, ah, had to look that one up. Anyway, he took over the bank, and by 1920, Stirling was named vice president."

"Anna mentioned they were close, that Stewart gave Stirling some major responsibilities," I say.

"The records of the bank bear that out," Nate says. "Lots of documents were signed by Stirling. It appears that Stewart gave Stirling oversight of investing some of the bank's assets. I asked a forensic accounting friend of Gladys' to take a look at some of the bank's records. According to him, by early 1928, the bank was actually operating at a loss."

"At a loss?"

"Uh-huh. The bank was almost insolvent, partly due to Stirling's investments."

"But Anna never mentioned any of this," Helen says. "She said the bank only went under because of the Depression."

"As best as Gladys' friend could figure," Nate says, "Stewart used his own assets to keep the bank afloat. He sold off thousands of acres of land and invested the cash back in the bank. By late summer of 1928, the bank was in good financial shape again."

"And Stirling was still vice-president?"

"Yes. He remained in that position until the embezzlement was discovered."

"Sounds like Stewart was loyal to a fault," I say.

"Wellll, there may have been another reason," Nate says. "In 1922, not long after Stirling moved to Myerton, he married Harriet Stewart, Ashton Stewart's younger sister."

I whistle at this news. "Anna never mentioned that."

"I suspect there are a lot of things Anna didn't mention to us," Helen comments.

"She may not have known because of what happened later," Nate says.

"What do you mean?"

Nate takes a deep breath. "Well, the basic details of the theft of the railroad payroll are pretty well known. But the authorities were never able to figure out a couple of things. First, what happened to the money. And two, what happened to Stirling. One of the things I wanted to do was answer both questions."

He pauses for dramatic effect, sitting with a slight smile on his face. He's clearly enjoying having us in the palm of his hands for once. Nate sits quietly like that for several minutes.

Finally, Helen barks, "Well? Did you?"

Nate jumps and his smile slowly turns to a frown. "No, not definitely. There were lots of rumors printed in the *Gazette* about Stirling—the favorite one being that he took off to South America with the money. It was when I was trying to track down Stirling that I ran into Roland Crescent."

"And he's the one who accused Ashton Stewart of murder. How did you run into him? Who is he, even?" I ask.

"I came across him while doing research on the internet, looking for traces of Stirling. He's in his early sixties, and he claims that Kent Stirling was his paternal grandfather."

"Wait—claims?" Helen asks.

"Uh-huh," Nate nods. "I found a posting from him on a genealogy message board, asking for more information about Kent and Harriett Stirling. He said he'd been doing research for years, and wanted to talk to other Stirling family researchers. Well, I contacted him, and he consented to an interview."

Nate clears his throat. "Looking back, I should have known something was wrong. He lives in Baltimore in this run-down townhouse, not in the worst part of the city but the neighborhood's clearly seen better days. Roland answered the door wearing a bathrobe and slippers, looking like he'd just rolled out of bed. His apartment—well, you know those cable shows about the hoarders? Yeah, it looked just like that.

"So, anyway, we sat down and he started this rambling story that really didn't make too much sense at times. I recorded the whole thing—you can listen for yourself."

"What did he tell you?" I ask.

"He claimed his father was the son of Kent and Harriet Stirling, born in 1923. His dad was five years old at the time the money was stolen. According to Roland, his father told the story of how Ashton Stewart came to their house in a fury, screaming at Harriet and demanding to know where Kent Stirling was. She claimed she didn't know—the story she told the police, that was printed in the paper, was that he'd gone fishing for the weekend. His father told Roland that that sent Stewart into a rage, that he grabbed and shook Harriet, saying she was lying, saying if she knew how he'd betrayed both of them, she wouldn't be protecting him, that if she didn't tell him the truth, she'd be dead to him and the rest of the family. Stewart's last declaration was 'I'm going to find that bastard, and when I do, I'll kill him with my bare hands.'"

"And that's what you wrote in the paper," Helen says.

"I only reported what he said, Helen," Nate replies. "It was a common rumor that Stewart had killed Stirling for robbing his bank and buried the body somewhere on the outskirts of town. The *Gazette* even printed supposed eyewitness accounts of seeing Stirling going into the woods after the robbery, followed by Stewart."

"So Nate, you really didn't say Anna's grandfather killed anyone," I sigh.

"Not in so many words, Tom," Helen says. "But by printing the rumors, he gave them credence."

I shrug. "Sorry, I'm on Nate's side on this. I think Anna overreacted." I pause a moment and contemplate my hands. "There's something else here, though. Anna really didn't want to talk to Nate for some reason."

"Maybe she was afraid of the rumors coming to light," Helen says. "She's a very proud woman, you know. Maybe she didn't want the embarrassment. The whole story is pretty sordid, after all."

"You haven't heard the worst part," Nate blurts. "I didn't even write this in the article."

Stunned that Nate actually showed some discretion, I ask, "What's the worst part?"

"So, after Ashton Stewart's confrontation with his sister, she had some kind of mental collapse. Roland didn't have any details, but I was able to find a record of her being committed to the State Hospital in Sykesville. According to the hospital, she died there in 1940."

"That's awful," Helen gasps. "What about her child?"

"According to Roland, his father was placed in an orphanage and eventually adopted by a family on the Eastern Shore, the Crescents. He went on to have a pretty good life, apparently, became a pharmacist, married, and had three children. But, tragically, he killed himself in 1964. Apparently, he had a mountain of debts, so his death left the family destitute. Roland blames Ashton Stewart for his father's death."

"That makes no sense, though," I say. "If anyone is to blame, it is Kent Stirling."

"But Ashton signed the commitment paper on Harriet," Nate says. "And when Roland came across the speculation in the papers at the time about Ashton Stewart's role in Stirling's disappearance, well, he decided Ashton Stewart killed his biological grandfather."

"But he has no proof, Nate, and you printed what he said for the whole world to see."

We turn to see Anna in the entrance to the living room. Bill's standing next to her, a comforting arm over her shoulder. From her bloodshot eyes, it's clear she's been crying.

"Anna," Nate says as he stands up. "I am so sorry. If I had any idea Ashton Stewart was your grandfather, I would never have put that in the article."

"How long have you been standing there, Anna?" I ask quietly.

She takes a step towards Nate—who, to his credit, doesn't scurry away to hide behind the chair—and says, "Oh, not very long. Just long enough to hear about what my grandfather did to his sister—my grandaunt, I guess, I never knew I had one. And I suppose that Roland is my second cousin or something like that."

"Yeah, something like that," I say.

She nods and looks at Nate. "Son," she says with genuine sorrow in her voice, "I'm—I'm sorry for attacking you like I did. I don't know what came over me. I saw my grandfather's name and murder and just went crazy, I guess."

Nate smiles and approaches Anna. "It's OK," he says. "I understand now why you were so upset. If I had known—"

"And the reason you didn't was because I didn't follow Tom and Helen's advice to talk to you," she says, shaking her head. "That whole thing destroyed my family—it even affected me growing up—and I didn't want to dig it all up again. But, I guess things can't stay buried forever."

With that, Anna hugs Nate. "I do care about you, even if you do act like an idiot sometimes"

Hugging Anna, Nate chuckles. "I love you, too, Anna. And I'll still interview you."

Breaking the hug, she nods. "I'll think about that, Nate. But I'm not making any promises."

Looking at the rest of us, she says, "Helen, Bill, it's late. You two need to go home so Tom and I can get some sleep. It's been a long evening, and I'm exhausted."

Helen and I stand as Nate says, "Yeah, I need to go too. Mr. Brandt, can you give me a ride home? I'm kinda tired after that run."

He laughs and says, "I'd be glad to, young man. And it's Bill. Hey, I've been meaning to talk to you about joining the Knights of Columbus."

Anna tells Bill goodnight, while Helen hangs back so we can exchange our goodnights in private. Nate tells Helen and me goodnight, and gives Anna another hug. Bill puts a fatherly arm around Nate and begins to tell him all the virtues of the Knights.

But as they leave, one last question occurs to me. "Hey, Nate? The money. You told me in the library that you figured out where it was?"

He turns and breaks into a grin. "Oh, yeah! That was actually the most exciting discovery I made. It's still here in Myerton."

"What do you mean, still here?"

"The college manuscript collection has one box of Harriet Stirling's papers, including a diary I didn't have the chance to look at. In there is a note, apparently sent to her by Kent Stirling the day he disappeared with the money. It's really weird, some of the things he said, but he tells her that what he stole from his best friend was buried in the gorge on the edge of town."

"The gorge on the edge of town?" I say.

"Yeah. I checked a 1928 map of the area, and the only gorge he could be talking about is the one that borders Myer College. That's where the stolen money is!"

Seven

The sounds of pans clattering and dishes clinking awakens me around 6 a.m. on Saturday. I need to get up anyway, since I'm saying 8 a.m. Mass, and I'd like to have time for a little something before.

I shower and dress before going downstairs, thinking about the big day ahead of me—one I'm looking forward to with a mixture of fear and excitement. Excitement over where Helen and I will be going, fear over how we're getting there.

My life is just one adventure after another, you know?

In the kitchen, I find Anna sitting at the table, nursing a cup of coffee, a copy of the weekly print edition of the *Myerton Gazette* spread in front of her.

"Good morning," I say as I walk to the counter to pour myself a cup of coffee—reminding myself that I'm only allowed one.

"Morning, Tom," she says, her eyes still on the paper. "Your breakfast is on the table."

I look at the table. "Where?"

"The bowl, at your place. Oatmeal. It's good for your blood pressure."

I roll my eyes. Helen must have talked to her. But because I know she means well, I don't complain. I just sit and look at the bowl of—well, it's the consistency of wallpaper paste, but looks like something else.

I plunge the spoon into the mixture and am surprised it tastes better than it looks. "Hey," I say around the oatmeal, "this isn't bad."

"Maple and brown sugar make all the difference," she says with a smile. "I'll add blueberries and strawberries next."

I spread my arms dramatically and declare, "I feel myself getting healthier already."

She rolls her eyes and shakes her head. She closes the paper and says, "It's actually a very good article. Well written. Nate sure did put a lot of research into it. I just wonder when he had the time, with the Fairy Tales and Frights just last month?"

I shake my head. "I don't think he sleeps that much. Like Gladys, he can get by on little sleep. Edison didn't get that much sleep. Geniuses usually don't."

"We're talking about Nate, not Gladys."

I shrug. "According to Gladys, Nate's I.Q. is only a few points below hers."

"I demand evidence before I'll believe that." She hands me the paper. "Do you want to read it?"

"No thanks," I say. "Nate summarized it for me."

I suddenly notice she's bleary-eyed. "You don't look like you got much sleep, Anna."

She yawns. "I actually didn't. This whole thing about my grandfather—not the robbery or that absurd accusation. No, he committed his own sister to a mental hospital and put his nephew in an orphanage. I mean, what kind of man does that?"

"Maybe a man who thinks he doesn't have any options?" I say. "Maybe a man was so overcome with grief, he wasn't thinking clearly?"

Anna shakes her head. "No. If that were the case, he wouldn't have let his sister die alone in an asylum. And as far as options, he had a wife. They only had one child, my father. They could have easily raised another."

I chew on my oatmeal—it's beginning to grow on me, by the way—and think for a moment. "You never knew your grandmother, right?"

"No, not on my father's side," Anna sighs. "It was like she never existed. She wasn't spoken of. I don't even think I ever saw a picture of her."

"Didn't you think that was strange?"

"Frankly, yes, but the one time I asked about her, I was told by my father in no uncertain terms that I was never to bring up the subject again. So I didn't." She lapses into silence. "My family was under a cloud the entire time I was growing up," she says quietly. "We didn't talk about things. My dad—he was a good man, but he'd taken on my grandfather's bitterness over the loss of the bank and all the hatreds he carried. It almost made the atmosphere around the house toxic. My mom tried to compensate for it, but there was only so much she could do. It was only in high school that any light really came into my life—and that was for so short a time."

I bite my tongue to keep from asking what—or who—that light was.

But I'm pretty sure I already know.

"Well, aren't you curious now about what happened to your grandmother?" I ask carefully.

Anna looks at me, peering at me the way she does when trying to see through my feeble attempts at being mysterious. "Does Nate know something about my grandmother?"

"No," I say slowly. "At least, not that he said. But you pointed out he did a lot of research for that article. There's more than he put in, remember?"

Anna sits back and crosses her arms, staring off to the side. Finally, she takes a deep breath and says, "I don't know if I want to know the truth, Tom. I've lived just fine without it for almost seventy years. Maybe I should be content with that."

***

"Y'all comfortable back there!"

I barely hear Martin over the sound of the rotors of his helicopter, but I manage to say, "Fine. Just fine."

Certainly, getting a donation for the Saint Francis Educational Center is worth any sacrifice on my part. And according to Martin, his friend in Ohio is prepared to make a sizable one. We're flying to his estate right now to discuss the details.

I'm just not convinced any amount of money is worth risking my life.

It's a cliche, I know, but it's not so much that I'm scared of flying as that I'm scared of crashing. And while Martin has assured us his helicopter is as safe as any airplane, the craft we're in seems awfully fragile to me.

Helen taps me on the shoulder. I lean over and she whispers, "That's my shooting hand you're squeezing."

With great force of will, I let go, Helen shaking and rubbing her hand to get the circulation back.

"I'm just about back to where I was before I got shot," Helen grumbles. "And now I think you fractured my trigger finger."

"I didn't squeeze it that hard," I whisper-shout. "As you often point out, my grip isn't as strong as yours."

"And how do you know how strong her grip is, hmm, Tom?" Martin says over the headset.

I blush, Helen laughs, and Mae slaps her fiancé on the shoulder. "Marty, that's terrible," she says sweetly.

He turns to her and says, "I guess you need to work harder to reform me."

"I'm looking forward to it," she replies with a smile.

He leans over and kisses her as I scream, "Eyes on the—ah, clouds! Eyes on the sky! You could run into something!"

"Tom, don't worry," Martin laughs. "We're perfectly safe. Mae will tell you."

"Father Tom, Marty's right," she says looking back at me. "I was terrified the first time he took me up. But after a while, you just get so enraptured by all the beauty of God's creation you can see from up here."

"I'm quite content with taking in God's creation on the ground, thank you very much," I say. "And Mae, when we're among friends or I'm not wearing my clericals, please just call me Tom."

"All right, Tom," Mae says. "I'll try, but my Mama always taught me to be respectful to priests. It's gonna take some getting used to."

"Tom," Helen says, slipping her arm through mine and leaning her head on my shoulder, "you really should take a look out the window. The fall colors are gorgeous! You can see so far!"

"You've been in a helicopter before, Helen?" Martin asks.

"Only in an official capacity," she says. "Never for fun."

I question just how much fun flying in an oversized closet is, but I've added to my reputation as a coward enough today.

"Martin," I ask. "Are you sure I shouldn't have worn my clericals?"

"Definitely, Tom," Martin says. "My friend isn't anti-religion, but he's not religious himself. He believes in God, sort of, but doesn't take him too seriously."

"You mean like you used to?" Mae asks.

Martin hesitates before saying, "Not quite. I just think the less attention drawn to the fact that the education center is going to have a Catholic foundation, the better."

He can't see my frown as I say, "Martin, he does know it's sponsored by Saint Clare's, right?"

"Oh, of course," he says. "But, I, ah, may have emphasized the community part over the parish part."

I clear my throat and say, "I see."

"Besides, Tom, he's interested in the outdoor learning area. There's nothing explicitly Catholic about that, now is it?"

I look at Helen, whose brow is furrowed with concern. "No, I suppose not."

With that, I lapse into silence for the rest of the trip, looking out the window at the splendor of God's creation, and wondering what the hell I'm getting into.

Eight

By the time we land in the field behind a house that makes Martin's look like a shack, I've just about gotten used to Martin's pride and joy.

I figure I might as well, since it's the only way of getting back to Myerton.

"Well, that was as smooth a flight as I've ever had," Martin says with a grin. "Remember our flight to Atlanta, Mae?"

She laughs and says, "I think I said all twenty mysteries of the Rosary on that one."

I snap my head around to look at Helen, who looks like she's just had a massage instead of experiencing two hours of terror. "Why don't we just rent a car and drive back home?" I whisper.

"It will take all night, and you have Mass at 8 a.m. tomorrow. Martin got us here safe, he'll get us home safe. If we don't fly back with him, you'll insult him. And after all he's done for us, Tom," Helen answers.

As usual, her common sense is unassailable. "All right," I sigh. "But if you see me drinking more than usual, don't stop me."

"Dutch courage. Really, Tom?"

"Hey, it got me through my first homily in seminary," I grin.

She starts at that. "You were drunk when you—"

"Not really drunk. Just relaxed."

Very, very relaxed. Too relaxed as it turns out. As soon as I finished, I passed out.

But our homiletics professor gave me an A on the assignment, so he overlooked that. Fortunately.

We're piling out of Martin's copter—I'm strongly tempted to kiss the ground—when he says, "Oh, good, here comes Greg."

I look up to see two golf carts headed towards us. One of them is driven by a well-built, brown-haired man with a confident air about him, the other by a young man who looks to be in his late teens.

"Martin," the older man calls with a grin.

"Greg," Martin says, shaking the other man's hand as he gets out of the golf cart. The younger man, who bears a resemblance to Greg, parks and gets out to stand beside him.

"Larry," Martin says, shaking the younger man's hand. "You look good. Princeton's treating you well."

"Thank you, Dr. Maycord," Larry says. I notice him looking at Mae with a smile. "Hello," he says.

"Hello," Mae says pleasantly.

"You must be the woman who finally captured this guy's heart," Greg says. "It's a pleasure to finally meet you, Mae. The last few months, every call and email's been 'Mae this', and 'Mae that'." He looks her up and down. "Yes," he says quietly, a smile spreading across his face, "I can definitely see why."

"You are too kind," Mae says, as she slips her arm through Martin's.

Greg nods and turns to me. "And you must be the reason we're all here today."

"Greg Fielding," Martin says, clapping me on the back. "May I introduce Father Tom Greer."

"Father Greer," Greg says pleasantly. "Martin's told me a lot about your efforts. I'm hoping we can come to a mutually beneficial arrangement."

I'm thrown off for a second by the phrase "mutually beneficial arrangement," but accept his offered hand and say, "It's a pleasure to meet you. I'm excited to share our plans with you. And please, call me Tom."

"Well, Tom, it is," Greg says. "And you must be Helen," he says, extending his hand to her.

"Nice to meet you, Greg," Helen says brightly, turning on all the charm in her ample arsenal.

Greg looks at us both and says, "I saw something months ago on the news about you two, but didn't pay too much attention. Not being Catholic, I don't understand all the archaic rules or really care what the Pope does. But when Martin said he knew you, and what a great couple you were, I admit I got excited to meet you myself. I mean, it's not often that I have two revolutionaries under my roof."

"Dad," Larry says, "we had that group from South America not that long ago."

"Oh, I know, I know, but Tom and Helen here," Greg says, waving at us, "are rocking the foundation of one of the few patriarchal institutions left on Earth. It's exciting."

I'm trying to get my mind around what he just said, when Helen says, "Oh, you flatter us, Greg. We're just two people who were fortunate enough to be allowed to marry. We're hardly revolutionaries."

"Yeah, Dad," Larry says. "I mean, Ms. Parr is a cop. She's the oppressor."

I feel Helen stiffen and I'm about to say something, when Martin says quickly, "Well, let's not let politics ruin our lunch. It's been ages since I've seen Betsy."

Clapping him on the back, Greg says, "Quite right, old buddy. You and Mae hop on behind me. Larry, you take Tom and Helen."

"Sure, Dad," Larry says, looking at Helen with barely disguised distaste.

I glance over at Martin, who catches my eye. He smiles apologetically. Mae looks upset.

I don't even need to look at Helen. I can hear her teeth grinding.

This is going to be one long lunch.

Nine

"We're vegetarians," Greg's wife Betsy says as she sits down. "I do hope that's all right with everyone?"

Everyone nods and mumbles polite assurances. "I was actually vegetarian for two years," I insist.

"Oh really?" Betsy asks.

"Yes, I lived with a monastic order that did not eat meat."

"Oh," Betsy says, obviously uncomfortable.

Helen, on the other hand, is a real carnivore. I suppose it's her Nebraska roots. But I also know she's a good guest and will eat whatever is put in front of her.

Trying to make pleasant conversation, I say, "I have read that a plant-based diet is better for you. Martin advised me I need to eat more veggies."

"Yes, well," Greg says, "when we decided to run the corporation as a zero-carbon footprint enterprise, we realized we were part of the problem in our personal life."

"So we switched to a plant-based diet," Betsy says, "all organic, of course. I never realized until I read an article how bad for the environment raising animals for food was."

Helen stabs her fork a little too hard, causing her plate to clatter.

"So, Betsy," Mae says, "you seem really concerned about the environment."

"Oh, I am. I think it's incumbent on all of us to do what we can. It's the only planet we have, after all. It's the main reason Greg and I were so committed to having only one child."

"Mom, I thought it was because when you saw me, you'd achieved perfection," Larry says with a wry grin. He winks at Mae, causing her to frown.

"Of course, dear," Betsy laughs. "But really, Mae, certainly you agree as a young career woman that having a small family is just better all around?"

I look at Mae, who's looking at Martin. Martin looks a little pale, frankly. I don't think this is the lunch he was expecting. So far, I'm not impressed by his wealthy friends.

Mae opens her mouth to speak, when Helen says, "Well, I'm an only child, and I know growing up on my family's cattle ranch in Nebraska, my parents would have loved to have more children." She turns to Mae and says, "How many are there in your family, remind me?"

"Ten," Mae says matter-of-factly. "I'm the oldest."

"Ten!" Betsy says, genuinely shocked. "That's—that's amazing in this day and age."

"It's more common than you think, Betsy," I say.

Greg looks at Martin. "So, have you two decided to have a large family?"

Martin's looking at Mae as he takes her hand and says, "I took a huge risk a couple of weeks ago to make sure we could."

There's an uneasy silence at this, so I try to steer the conversation to the real purpose of our visit. "Greg, Martin tells me you're particularly interested in our plans for an outdoor learning facility associated with the center."

"Yes, very much so," Greg says. "Martin shared with me the plans for the house and the property, as well as the center's mission statement. I think it's all very exciting, what you have planned, but I do have some questions."

"Well, I'll try to answer them."

He folds his hands under his chin and looks right at me. "I'm concerned about the center's commitment to diversity and inclusion."

"I see," I say, ignoring the fact that what he framed as a question was a statement. "Well, all of our documentation makes it very clear that everyone from the community is welcome to use the center, regardless of race, color, sex, or national origin."

"If you're Catholic."

"No, not at all," I say, shaking my head. "Anyone of any creed—or no creed at all—can participate in any of the center's programs. We've already been approached by several of the churches wanting to use the space for different activities."

"I guess that's what I'm trying to get at," Greg says. "You don't say anything about sexual orientation or gender identity. Now, I know the Catholic Church formally discriminates against the LGBTQ+ community—"

"Excuse me, but that is not accurate at all," I say firmly. "The Church discriminates against no one."

"You say homosexuals are going to hell," Larry says.

"The Church," I say slowly, "doesn't say who is going to hell. We do not claim that knowledge. If you mean the Church teaches that homesexuality is a sin, that's also not correct. The Church is very clear that same-sex attraction is not in and of itself a sin. Homosexual acts are sinful, as is adultery and fornication—because they take place outside of marriage."

"So, what, you tell them they have to deny the way God made them?" Betsy says.

"The origin of same-sex attraction is an open question and, frankly, above my pay grade. But I will tell you this. I went to seminary with men who are priests today, who identify as gay, and are leading very happy lives—as celibate men. Just like every straight priest does. Just like I have, and will continue to do, until Helen and I are married."

"Wait—you two aren't having sex now?" Larry cackles. "Oh, that's rich!"

"What do you mean?" Mae says, her look reminding me that she's Dominic's sister.

Martin covers her hand with his. "Greg," he says with a tone that doesn't match the pleasant smile on his face, "what's all this about? I mean, when we talked about the center, you didn't mention any of these things. Besides, it's for children. None of these issues will come up, I'm sure."

Addressing me instead of his friend, Greg asks, "OK, so what if a same-sex couple wants to enroll their child in, say, a music program?"

"We would allow the child to enroll," I say, "just the same as the child of an unwed mother, an African-American family, a Latino family, a Muslim family, an atheist family—would you like me to go on?"

"Well, what if a biologically male child shows up to a program wearing a dress because they identify as female?" Betsy asked.

"I think it unlikely, but if it happened, they'd be allowed to participate as long as they were not disruptive."

"Would you call the child by their preferred pronoun or name? Say, a Richey who wanted to be called Rose?"

"Look," I say, getting exasperated, "I'm sure I know several transgender people. For all I know, there may be some in my parish. But unless they tell me they were once male or female, I'm going to call them by what they look like. And, let me say, common decency and civility would demand that I call them anything they prefer."

"Greg, Betsy," Helen interjects, "you seem to be focused on this one aspect of the education center's mission. But you haven't explained why?"

"It's very simple, Helen," Greg says with a tone of condescension. "Ours is a socially-conscious company committed to a more diverse and inclusive world. It's in our mission statement, published on our website for everyone to see. We also, through our company foundation, donate to numerous organizations dedicated to making a better world. Pro-environmental groups, organizations to promote women's health, and several LGBTQ+ rights organizations."

"I think I'm beginning to see," I say slowly. "You want to make sure that you don't contribute to a cause that may not reflect those values as you define them."

"I want to make sure that we always act in ways that are consistent with our enlightened values," Greg says.

"As do I. But then, I suspect that the Catholic Church's views are not enlightened, in your opinion," I say with a smile.

"Not just my opinion, Tom. There are a lot of people—including some in your Church—who agree with me."

"That doesn't make them right."

"Well, how do you know the Church is right? Blind obedience?"

"Oh, Dad," Larry says with a sneer. "Of course it is, since everything they believe is just a set of myths to maintain their dominance over the ignorant."

At this, Mae leaps out of her chair. "Ignorant! I'll have you know, my father and mother both have Ph.D.s, and I have a Masters degree, and we hold to the teachings of the Church!"

"Even the highly educated can be unenlightened," Betsy says to Mae. "Look at yourself. You've bought into the patriarchal domination of an organization that teaches that a woman is no better than breeding stock."

"Greg," Martin says, by this time obviously incensed, "if you really believe all this, then why are we here? Did you just arrange this to insult my friends and my fiancée?"

"Oh, now, Martin," Greg says, "of course not. And I apologize if you found our statements insulting. I invited you here so we could engage in a dialogue and try to come to some mutually beneficial understanding."

"That's the second time you've said that," I point out. "What do you mean?"

"Tom," Greg says with a smile that is meant to be ingratiating but comes across as insincere, "just this. If you would be willing to make certain small changes to the center, my company's foundation is prepared to make a very sizable donation for the creation of an outdoor learning experience."

"And what small changes do you have in mind?"

"Well, let's just say a more secular presentation of the purpose of the education center."

I lean forward over the now cold vegetables on my plate. "And by 'more secular presentation,' what exactly do you mean?"

"Dropping Saint Francis from the name in favor of something more generic," Greg says. "Explicitly including reference to sexual orientation and gender identity in the center's documents. Allowing for a diversity of viewpoints to be presented."

"Completely disassociate from the Catholic Church," Helen, who has been fairly quiet to this point, says firmly.

Greg blinks and says, "Oh, Helen, nothing that—"

"Greg, I've been sitting here quietly listening to you and your . . . charming wife and son. It's what I'm trained to do as a detective, to listen, to try to separate out the truth from fiction. Over time, I've become very good at spotting a con artist when I see one." Pointing at our host, "You had no intention of making a donation to the center in the first place, did you?"

"Now, really, Helen—-"

"The entire purpose was—what, to make us look foolish? Only a complete sociopath would go to this much effort, and you don't strike me as a sociopath—though I'm withholding judgment on your son, who's spent this entire meal undressing Mae with his eyes."

"What!" Martin growls.

"How dare you!" Betsy says. "Larry would never objectify a woman like that!"

Helen laughs derisively. "Oh, come on. He doesn't believe a word you and your husband have spoken. He just mouths the same platitudes, probably so you'll keep sending his no doubt substantial allowance."

For his part, Larry slumps down in his seat and refuses to meet his parents' eyes.

"No," Helen says, shaking her head. "You might as well tell Martin—your old friend—the truth."

Martin looks at Greg. "Well?" he barks.

Greg sighs. "Listen, old pal. When you first told me about the center, I was excited. But when you sent me the information and I saw how religious and reactionary it was, well, I didn't want to have anything to do with it. But since I knew what you were like—"

"What do you mean, 'what I was like'?"

"Oh, come on, Martin!" Greg laughs. "You know what I mean! You never darkened the doors of a church in med school. Hell, you were more likely to be sleeping off the night before—usually in someone else's bed." Peering at Mae, he says, "Has he ever told you his nickname? We called him 'Do 'em and Dump 'em Maycord.' And now here he is, prancing around like he's all holy, hanging out with priests, and engaged to some Vatican calendar girl."

Martin starts around the table, fury in his eyes, obviously intent on doing some serious bodily harm to his old friend.

"Marty, don't," Mae cries.

"Martin," I say calmly. "Don't do something you'll regret."

Martin stops just as he gets to Greg's chair. He looks down at his friend and says with barely-contained anger, "You always were a prick, you know that, Fielding." He marches back to his chair and says to Betsy, "Thank you for a most . . . enlightening lunch. But we will be going now."

"Oh, Martin, not yet," Helen says with a smile, still looking at Greg. "We came here for a donation, remember? Greg still hasn't written the check."

I look at my darling bride-to-be like she's lost her ever-loving mind. Martin and Mae both look confused. Greg, after the initial shock, bursts out laughing.

"Oh, that's funny, Ms. Parr," he cackles. "If—if you think I'm going to give your lover's little project a dime of my money, you're—"

"We were good enough to hear your conditions, Mr. Fielding," Helen says calmly. "All I ask is that you listen as I tell you ours."

He's still laughing as he says, "Oh, I am all ears."

Helen clears her throat. "My darling fiancé is a good man—one of the best I've ever known. He's kind, thoughtful, and compassionate. But he's not perfect."

I'm not sure I'm liking where this is going.

"He has a number of flaws."

No, definitely not liking where this is going.

"One of his biggest flaws—and really, one that makes him so endearing—is he's too trusting. He's not naturally suspicious of others."

OK, I have to admit she is right about that.

"I, on the other hand, tend to be too suspicious. Probably I've grown cynical because of the job, I don't know. But when I learned about your interest in the Saint Francis Education Center, I did a little digging."

"A little abuse of police power, huh?" Larry says, obviously rallying from Helen's earlier smackdown.

"Oh, hardly," she says, still smiling. "Just some basic internet searching, checking out your company's website. I paid particular attention to the list of donations your foundation's made over the years. An impressive list. But what was striking to me was the absence of a single religious organization. Not one.

"So I got to thinking. Why would a corporate foundation that had never donated to a religious cause all of a sudden be interested in a little project in a small town in Maryland?"

"He was a friend, Helen," Martin says, emphasizing the 'was.'"

"Yes. Which told me he probably had no interest, but was doing it for a friend. When I learned about this lunch, I decided to dig a little deeper. You see, one of my close friends is an investigative reporter—you won't have heard of him, but he's quite good."

I look at her with surprise. Is she talking about Nate?

"His girlfriend is a computer genius. She's like the daughter I've never had, so we're very close."

I cover my mouth with my hand. She's talking about Gladys.

"I shared my concerns with them—that something just didn't seem right to me. So they did some deeper digging and found some interesting information. About you, Mr. Fielding."

"About Greg?" Besty says with a laugh. "He's an upstanding member of the community, a highly respected philanthropist, and well-regarded as a medical innovator."

"Yes, now. But five years ago, he was a Pediatric Surgeon at a top hospital in Cincinnati. Isn't that right, Mr. Fielding?"

Greg's no longer smiling. Instead, he's frowning, his eyes showing fear.

Helen's spooking him.

"Yes, that's right," he says. "What of it?"

"You resigned rather suddenly, isn't that right?"

"Greg had a vision," Betsy says. "A vision that became the Fielding Corporation. A totally green approach to the medical device industry."

"That's the official story," Helen says. "But my friends found a paper trail of some rather nasty accusations of a, shall we say, sexual nature?"

Betsy's mouth falls open. She looks at her husband and whispers, "What is she talking about?"

"Nothing," Greg says quickly. "Lies and slander."

"Hmm, probably why you settled the accusations and agreed to resign your position as part of the settlement agreement. Now, my friends don't have any details—nasty things, those non-disclosure agreements—but they have found a couple of people who were not part of the complaints who are willing to talk about their experiences."

Greg's lost all of his self-confidence and is as white as a sheet. "What do you think you are doing?" he hisses. "Is this some kind of sick joke?"

"Do I look like I'm joking?" Helen says firmly. "I have sat here while you vilified the man—not to mention the Church—I love, embarrassed the man who saved my life, and belittled a young woman who has more character in her little finger than that son of yours has in his whole body. Now, this is what is going to happen next. Martin is going to write down a number and hand it to you. That is the amount of the check you will hand Tom before we leave."

"And if I refuse?"

Helen pulls her phone out of her purse—no tote bag today, it would have made the helicopter over-weight—and says, "Then I make one call and the story of your personal misdeeds is page one in every paper in the country by tomorrow morning. Your company stock will tank, and all those enlightened organizations you've funded will be returning your money and vilifying you in press conference after press conference."

Greg stares at Helen. "You know, the Governor of Maryland is a friend of mine."

"So? The Archbishop of Baltimore is a friend of mine," Helen says. "And he doesn't face re-election next year. In this day and age, the governor is not going to defend someone accused of this behavior. And if you do talk to him and he has me removed as Chief, it won't help you. The story will get out. I'll be out of a job—true, priests don't make a lot of money, but we'll get by—but your name will still be mud. Your company, worthless." She turns to Betsy. "I doubt you'll be giving any more speeches about empowering women." To Larry, she says, "You might want to start looking for a job, because your allowance will probably be cut."

Helen sits back and crosses her arms, cocking her head to one side and looking at Greg the same way I've seen her countless times at a suspect. "Ball's in your court, Greg?"

After a moment, the defeated man clears his throat. "Martin," he says quietly, "do you have a number for me?"

Martin removes a card and a pen from his pocket and writes something on it. I lean over trying to see, but he turns his back so I can't.

When he's done, he tosses the card to Greg. It lands in front of him, the side with the writing down. He picks it up, takes one look, and his mouth drops open. "You can't be serious, Martin?"

"Oh, I most certainly am," he replies.

Greg stares daggers at Martin, then stands up. "I'll go write the check," he mutters.

"I'll make sure the donation is listed as from an anonymous donor," I say, smiling. "I'm not sure I want our center to be associated with the values you represent."

He grunts, and stalks out of the room, leaving his son and one clearly angry wife.

There's an uneasy silence in the room, broken only when Mae says, "Well, Betsy, I want to thank you for a most educational lunch. I learned so much here."

She turns to Helen and winks.

***

I almost pass out when Greg Fielding hands me a check for $5 million.

I'm so stunned I don't even mind that I'm once again in Martin's helicopter, flying away from one of the strangest luncheons I've ever attended.

"I can't tell y'all how sorry I am," Martin says sorrowfully.

"Marty, Tom still got the donation for a center," Mae says.

"But what they said about you—how they treated everyone. I should have known better. Greg was always a prick in medical school. Still don't know why I've remained friends with him all these years."

"Mae's right, Martin," I say. "It doesn't matter. We've got the donation. This is enough to really get work on the center rolling. With this, we'll have no problem opening next fall."

"That's wonderful, Tom," Helen says, kissing me on the cheek.

"You don't have a moral or ethical problem with how we got it, Tom?" Martin asks.

"No, why should I?"

"Well, Tom," Mae says, "Helen did basically blackmail Greg back there."

"Oh, that," I say with a dismissive wave. "Helen didn't have anything she said she did. She was bluffing."

"What?" Martin and Mae say at the same time.

"Tom," Helen says with surprise, "how did you know?"

"My darling, I have watched you interview numerous suspects over the past few months. I can tell when you're bluffing to get someone to crack."

"Huh," Helen says, shaking her head. "Maybe I need to change my tactics."

"Is Tom right, Helen?" Mae asks.

"Pretty much," Helen nods. "It's true I did some research into him online. When I ran across his rather sudden departure, I did ask Nate to do some digging, but he ran into a stone wall." Shrugging, she says, "I had a gut feeling it had something to do with sexual harassment. As soon as I met the man, and saw how he was looking at you, Mae—"

"What?" Martin yells. "You said Larry—"

"A little bit of misdirection, so to speak," Helen says. "Anyway, I knew I was right. It was just a question of waiting until the right time."

Martin laughs. "As someone who's been on the receiving end of one of your interrogations, I should have seen what you were doing. Well done."

"Say Marty," Mae says, "when we get back, can we grab a bite? I'm starving after that rabbit food!"

"I know a great steakhouse in Pittsburgh. Let me call—"

Just then Helen's phone rings.

"Who is it?" I ask.

Looking, she says, "It's Dan. He wouldn't call unless it was important." Answering, she says, "Hi, Dan, What's—what's that—wait, can you say that again?—And they're doing what?—Oh, crap!—He is?—OK, pull every officer in and have them report there to get this thing under control. I'll be there in—" To Martin, she asks, "How long to Myerton?"

"At this speed, about 90 minutes."

"Can you go faster?"

"What's wrong, Helen?" I ask.

"Yeah, I can have you there in an hour," Martin says.

"Dan," she says into the phone, "we'll land at the hospital in about an hour. I'll be there as quickly as I can. In the meantime, just try to keep things from getting more out of hand."

She tosses the phone back in her purse. "Well, Nate Rodriguez strikes again!"

"What's wrong, Helen?" Mae asks

"Oh, nothing," Helen says sarcastically. "It just appears that the entire student population of Myer College and half of the town's swarming the wooded area on the edge of campus looking for Nate's buried treasure!"

Ten

At Helen's request, Martin flies over Myer College so she can get a bird's-eye view of the situation.

Frankly, it's chaos. What looks like hundreds of people are swarming all over the area, with most of them concentrating on the gorge where Nate claims Kent Stirling buried the money he stole from the bank in 1928. Designated as a protected area several years ago by the college, the gorge is about 200 feet deep, consisting of a sheer rock face of about 50 feet and a slope of another 150 feet of rocky terrain ending at a small creek. The rest of the area is wooded, though at this time of year, the branches are bare.

"They look like ants down there," I say. "Greedy little ants."

"All of this because of Nate's article?" Mae says.

"Has anyone thought of hiding his laptop?" Martin asks. "It just seems like when he writes an article, something like this happens."

"It's not Nate's fault, really," I say. "People are just greedy."

"Well, right now, they're trespassing," Helen says. "Thanks, Martin, you can head to the hospital."

"I can set down in that area over there," Martin says, indicating the open plaza between the Arts and Sciences building and the Fine Arts department.

"Are you sure there's enough room?" I ask.

"Plenty. I'm pretty sure," he says, flashing a smile over his shoulder. "Hold on."

Martin sets us down dead center between the two buildings. Helen and I unbuckle to get out, but I'm surprised when Martin cuts the helicopter's engines.

"What are you doing, Marty?" Mae asks, a little confused.

"Hanging around to have a look," Martin says. "You haven't seen those two in action yet, have you?"

"Well, no, but—"

"Ah, you're in for a treat. Besides," he turns to Helen, "there's always a chance someone will do something stupid and get hurt."

"Fine, just stay out of the way," she says to them. Turning to me, she adds, "You, too, Tom."

"I always do," I say.

Rolling her eyes, she steps out of the helicopter and marches quickly towards the general area. As she does, Officer Nina Hallstead comes up to her and hands her a radio.

"What's the situation?" Helen asks,

"There are about a hundred people or so in the gorge and surrounding woods," Hallstead says. "Most of them have shovels, some of them have metal detectors. They've been peaceful up to this point, but I'll tell you, the president of the college is furious."

"Where's Conway?"

"He's down in the gorge with Potter and Thompson, along with about ten other officers and a dozen campus security monitoring the situation, waiting for orders."

"Go join them," Helen says. "Tell Dan I want him to begin to move people out of the area. Use as little force as possible. I really don't want to have to arrest a bunch of young people tonight."

"Roger, Chief." Hallstead runs off.

We're getting closer to a small group of people. I recognize Nate and Gladys, who's unmistakable in her bright teal wheelchair. A man I know is the president of Myer College is screaming at Nate, while another man I don't recognize seems to be trying to calm him.

When the president sees Helen, he marches to her and yells, "Chief Parr! It's about time you showed up!"

"I was out of town on a personal engagement, President Connor," she says calmly. "I returned as soon as I learned of the situation."

"I've explained to President Connor that the police will assist campus security in any way necessary to remove the students," the other man says. He looks to be thirty-something going on twelve, with a nervous air that matches his high-pitched, reedy voice. His suit is stylish, but between the real-wood frames and the high-end tennis shoes, he looks like he's trying a little too hard.

"Excuse me, who are you?" Helen asks with a tone that's more profane than her spoken words.

"Oh, we haven't met yet," the man says with a nervous smile. He clears his throat and extends his hand. "I'm Lexington Luther, the new Deputy Mayor. Mayor Chillings appointed me last week."

Helen shakes Luther's hand, her grip causing the shorter man—yes, he's shorter than she is, believe it or not—to wince.

"Nice to meet you, Mr. Luther," Helen says in a tone that indicates it really isn't.

"Oh, please, call me Lex, everyone does." Turning to me, he says, "You must be Father Greer."

I take the offered hand and shake it with less force than Helen did. "So, your name is Lex Luther?"

"Yes, we're German. Distantly related to Martin Luther. But I assure you, Father, I have no sectarian biases."

I nod. "Glad to hear it."

"Listen, while you are standing here," President Connor says frantically, "those students are trampling over a protected area. I mean, college biologists tell me that it's one of a handful of places in this area that has a population of the Northeastern Cattail."

"The Northeastern Cattail," Helen repeats. "And that is?"

"Well, it's—it's a very endangered species of plant, from what they tell me," Connor says.

"And Mayor Chillings is committed to the environment," Deputy Mayor Luther says, "as her extensive overhaul of the town's recycling program demonstrates."

That extensive overhaul consisted of replacing the yellow recycling bins every house and business has with blue ones.

"I am sure that Chief Parr understands her responsibilities to protect the Northeastern Cattail, don't you, Chief?" Luther says.

She takes a deep breath. "President Connor, my concerns are for the safety of the students and other persons down in that gorge. Frankly, I couldn't care less if some coed with a metal detector stomps on a plant."

"It's not just a plant!" Connor declares. "It's a rare Northeastern Cattail!"

"Certainly. Sorry. I should have said, I couldn't care less if some coed with a metal detector stomps on a rare Northeastern Cattail."

Helen walks towards the edge of the gorge, where Nate and Gladys are watching the chaos. Mae and Martin had hurried ahead to join them. I follow Helen, while behind me are an irate college president and a rookie deputy mayor who've both had their first taste of Helen Parr.

I'm really going to enjoy this.

Catching up to her, I ask, "You OK?"

"Of course. That president's not like Davenport. I mean, he was a degenerate Balaam's donkey, but at least he didn't act like—well, like that."

"I see what you mean. What do you think of the new Deputy Mayor?"

"I think he's going to be trouble, Tom. I just don't know how yet. Hi, Gladys, Nate."

"Hi, Chief," Gladys says.

"Helen, Father Tom," Nate says, transfixed on the scene unfolding below. "Maybe I should stop writing and stick to cleaning crime scenes? It never seems to end well."

"Oh, Nate," I say. "It's not your fault that those students are overcome by greed."

"They look like fire ants after you kick their mound over," Martin says. At our looks, he says, "I grew up in Georgia, remember?"

"Well, it's not like they have a map or anything," Gladys says. "All Nate wrote was what Stirling told his wife—it's buried in the gorge. I've spent hours analysing that note, thinking maybe it's some code, and have come up empty."

Helen thumbs the radio. "Dan, where are you?"

At the bottom of the gorge near the creek, a bulky figure starts waving his arm over his head. "Right here," Dan's voice comes over the radio. "Can you see me?"

"Do you have enough manpower to clear the area?"

"Yes."

"Hold on." She looks at the rapidly retreating daylight. To President Connor, she says, "We don't have a lot of daylight left. If it's going to be done safely, we need to start moving those people out of there now."

"Well, what are you waiting for?" he snaps.

Helen clenches her jaw. "Sir, since that is campus property, I need your permission before we proceed."

"Yes, yes," he says, waving his hands. "But be careful. Remember, it's one of the—"

"—few populations of the Northeastern Cattail," Helen sighs. "I don't think I'll ever forget the Northeastern Cattail." Into her radio, she says, "OK, Dan."

"Right." Down below, Dan cups his hands together and his voice echoes off the walls of the canyon. Just as he finishes commanding the students to stop what they're doing, there's a blood-curdling scream.

"What's that!" the President yells.

The entire area is shocked into silence. Peering over the edge, I see what looks like a dirty soccer ball rolling down the slope and stopping at Dan's feet.

Looking down, Dan says, his voice picked up by the radio, "Well, damn. A skull."

Nearby, I hear Mae whisper, "You're right, Marty. This is fun!"

"Wha—What did he just say?" Connor wheezes.

"Dan," Helen says into her radio, "can you repeat that, please?"

"Chief, we've got a human skull here," Dan says. "It rolled down the incline from where two—no, three knuckleheads were digging. Hey, you three, stay right where you are! Drop those shovels!"

"Oh, no! Oh, no!" Connor says frantically. "They must have disturbed an ancient native burial site! Oh, this is bad! Very, very, bad!"

Helen glares at the president. "Dan," she says slowly, "how old does the skull look?"

"There's no tissue left, if that's what you're asking. I'm no expert, but I'd say it's been in the ground for a while."

The president grabs Helen's radio. "Now be careful with that! That's a very valuable archeological find!"

"President Connor, if that's who this is," Dan says, "considering this skull has four gold fillings, I highly doubt it's more than a hundred years old, if that!"

Grabbing her radio back, Helen says to Dan, "OK. We need to talk to those students who found the body."

"They're not going anywhere, Chief."

"Good." She looks at Gladys. "Call the state crime lab and the ME's office. We need a forensic anthropology team here right now. Call the state highway department. I want this whole area lit up."

Helen walks to the edge. "Listen, everyone!" she hollers. "This is now a crime scene. Everyone needs to leave now. Except for the three who found the skull. Stay where you are."

She turns to the President, who is now as white as a sheet. "Crime scene! Crime scene! What do you mean, a crime scene!"

Luther says, "I'm sure what the Chief meant to say was—"

"Mr. Deputy Mayor, I'm quite capable of speaking for myself," Helen says firmly. "President Connor, I've got skeletal remains down there. Now, since this isn't a cemetery, and that skull is obviously not some dead Native American chief, it should definitely not be there. Of course, I'm just guessing here, but from my experience as a detective, the fact that there's a skeleton where none should be tells me that someone put it there, on purpose, to conceal a crime. That means this is now officially a crime scene."

Around us, students are emerging from the gorge quietly, no doubt stunned by the turn of events, and dispersing across campus. Helen looks at them, then turns back to the small cluster of people around her. "I need anyone not associated with what is now a criminal investigation to leave. That means you," she points to the president, "and you," she points to the Deputy Mayor.

"Oh, Chief Parr," the Deputy Mayor says, "I think I really should stay and observe so I can give the Mayor a full report."

Smiling her sweetest and most terrifying smile, Helen says, "I'll have a full report on your desk first thing Monday morning. By that time, I might actually have something to report."

Deputy Mayor Luther gulps, then nods. "That will be fine. Have a good evening, Chief." As he walks away, he pulls out his phone, no doubt to call the Mayor.

President Connor says, "I trust you will keep me apprised of the investigation?"

"Now, why would I do that?" Helen says. "I will be sure to give you a copy of my final report, but that's all you're entitled to."

"Listen, Chief!" He snaps. "I am the president of this college! This is college property! I expect—"

"Oh, now, Jeffrey, just calm yourself down, ya hear?" Martin says in his best southern drawl as he claps the president on the back. "You're getting yourself worked up over nothing. Now, why don't you just go on home and pour yourself a nice stiff drink."

"Martin, I—"

"Just do as I say, hmm? Or I may find myself too busy to teach that course on trauma nursing that you asked me to do. Free of charge," Martin says with a grin.

Connor looks at Martin, then at Helen. "Have a good evening, Chief," he mutters before walking off.

My admiration for Martin Maycord grows by the day. I turn to Helen and say, "I guess I should leave you to it. I can walk to the Rectory from here."

"Thanks, Tom," she says with a smile. "I doubt I'll be at Mass tomorrow. It's going to be a long night."

I kiss her on the forehead. "I'll see you when I see you. Just be careful, OK?"

"I better get that chopper back to the hospital," Martin says. "Tom, Helen, It's been an interesting day, to say the least."

"Who do you think it is, Helen?" Mae asks solemnly.

"Oh, Mae, it's way too early," Helen answers, looking down at the three hapless students who uncovered the remains. "Frankly, unless there's something with the remains to identify them, we may never know."

"I already know who it is!" Nate says suddenly. "Roland was right! That's the body of Kent Stirling! Ashton Stewart killed him and buried the body before taking off with the money stolen from his bank."

"Now you stop that right now, Nate," I say firmly. "There is no evidence that that body has anything to do with the bank robbery! It could be totally unrelated!"

"But it was buried in the same place where Kent Stirling said in the last note he wrote to his wife that he buried the money! It's so obvious."

"No, it's not, Nate!" I say. "Helen, tell him!"

Instead, Helen says to Nate, "Can you give me all your research into the bank robbery? Everything, including your interviews?"

"What are you doing, Helen?" I ask.

"Sure," Nate says. "Can I get an exclusive?"

"Yes, but when I say so."

"Helen, you can't seriously believe—"

"Tom, a word," Helen says quietly. We walk away from the others.

"Listen," Helen says softly. "Before you ask me, yes, I believe those remains have something to do with the 1928 robbery. Now, I don't know who that is down there. The problem is, Nate thinks he does."

"He thinks it's Kent Stirling," I say.

"Right. And knowing Nate the way we do, his first impulse is to write a story saying that, and accusing Anna's grandfather of murder. Right?"

A light bulb goes off. "But now he can't," I say with a smile, "because you just offered him an exclusive."

"Precisely. Besides, Nate's a good researcher. I may need him before this is over."

"So, you really are going to investigate this as a murder?"

"Tom, there is no statute of limitations on murder, you know that," Helen says. "It's my duty to conduct as thorough an investigation as I can."

I shake my head. "The chances of solving a crime after this much time—I mean, it's been almost a hundred years."

She takes a deep breath. "All the witnesses are dead, plus we have the barest of forensic evidence. It's an almost impossible task."

I study her closely. "You're looking forward to this, aren't you?"

Helen grins and her eyes flash. "Oh, yeah!"

Eleven

"Tom!"

I'm jarred out of a sound sleep by the sound of Anna yelling my name and pounding on my bedroom door. Instantly awake, my heart pounding, I leap out of bed and dash to the door.

Yanking it open, I say, "Anna! What's wrong! Are you OK!"

Anna's a combination of distraught and furious. She's holding her tablet computer and shaking it at me. "No, I am not OK! What is that fiancée of yours doing?"

"Whoa, whoa," I say, rubbing the sleep from my eyes. "Just calm down—"

"Don't you tell me to calm down, Thomas Jude Greer! I want to know what Helen thinks she's doing!"

She thrusts the tablet at me. It takes a second for my eyes to focus on the screen. When they finally do, I grab it out of her hands.

"Dammit!" I spit.

It's the Sunday morning digital edition of the *Myerton Gazette*. The headline reads:

HAS KENT STIRLING FINALLY BEEN FOUND?

"Nate," I say through gritted teeth, "you promised Helen—"

"Oh, it's not Nate," Anna says. "Look at the byline. I don't even know who that is."

I sigh when I see the name. "I do. Elisia Drakes. She's the reporter who published the article right after Ashley Becket's murder, identifying her as working for Freshy Fresh."

Anna frowns. "I remember now. Helen hadn't even told the Beckets yet."

"No, she hadn't. Drakes got the information from Rick Richardson, her then-boyfriend. I've met her once. It seems that lurid sensationalism is her stock-in-trade."

Handing the tablet back to Anna, I say, "I need to take a shower and get dressed. After I do that, we'll look at this. OK?"

Anna nods, then walks away. I close the door and lean against it. I whisper, "Helen is not going to be happy about this."

***

"Darn reporters," Helen grumbles over lunch.

"I knew you wouldn't be happy when you saw it," I say.

Chewing a forkful of chicken crepes, she says, "It almost cost me my 42-day non-cursing streak. Dan's got a sign in the break room."

"You're kidding?"

"Go see for yourself. Apparently, my officers have a pool among themselves for when I'll crack. You pick a date and throw a dollar into the pot."

Looking at her with bemusement, I ask, "So what date did you pick?"

"December 26," she says with a twinkle in her eyes that causes me to blush.

"Ahem, well," I say, avoiding her gaze, "I hope you win."

"Oh, I'm pretty sure I will."

We're still giggling when the phone on Helen's desk rings. "Yes?" she says when she answers. "Wait, who?" Helen lays her head on her desk. "Sure, why not, send him back."

Hanging up, she says, "Well, this day just got better."

"Who's here?" I ask, finishing the last of my food.

"Deputy Mayor Luther. He's been calling me, demanding an update. I stopped answering his calls an hour ago. Evidently, that was the wrong thing to do."

A moment later, there's a knock on her door.

"Come in," Helen calls.

Luther walks in, dressed more casually than yesterday in khaki trousers, a green polo shirt, and a brown tweed blazer.

"Good afternoon, Deputy Mayor," Helen says pleasantly. "Tom brought me lunch. Would you care to join us? I believe he brought plenty."

"No, thank you," he sniffs, looking at the small casserole dish, the fresh green beans with bacon, and the fluffy rice spread between Helen and me. "I'm vegan."

Of course he is.

"Too bad. I'm very fortunate to be marrying a good cook. You don't know what you're missing," she says.

"Perhaps, but I didn't come here on a Sunday afternoon for this. I came by for an update."

"Lex—can I call you Lex, saying Deputy Mayor all the time is such a mouthful—the update is the same one I gave you when you called at 8 a.m. And 9 a.m. And 10 a.m. Which is the last update I gave you because I stopped answering your calls at that point."

"The Mayor wants to be kept apprised of this investigation," Lex says. "She wants to know what's going on."

"Then tell her what I already told you," Helen says calmly. "The Office of the State Medical Examiner in Baltimore has the remains. Their top forensic anthropologist is going to examine them and try to come up with an age on the bones, as well as a cause of death. The crime scene team, with assistance from the state crime lab and some of Myer's archaeology students, are sifting every bit of soil for evidence. So far, they've come across some buttons and a wrist watch. We're hoping to get lucky and find something we can use to I.D. the person."

"Lucky?" he says with surprise. "That's what you're relying on? Luck?"

Helen takes a deep breath. "Sometimes that's all a cop has."

"This is the twenty-first century, Chief Parr!" he says indignantly. "You have all the modern scientific resources available to you through both state and federal sources. Not to mention this department's substantial budget."

"Deputy Mayor Luther," Helen says, "I know what century it is. I assure you I am using all the resources available to me to identify those remains. But we're talking about a crime that happened almost a hundred years ago, probably. Unless there's a crime lab out there that has a time machine, we may never know who those students dug up! And frankly, I'm not sure why the Mayor cares so much about something that happened before anyone in this room was even born!"

Lex clears his throat and tugs at his collar. "It is not your job to question the Mayor's priorities," he says with a nasally tone that reminds me a little too much of my Mom. "Your job—"

"I know my job," Helen says. "Now, if you will excuse me, I have not eaten since late yesterday afternoon, and my lunch is getting cold. I assure you, when I find out something I believe you need to pass on to the Mayor, I will call you."

"The Mayor may want to hold a press conference at some point," he says. "You will be there."

"Of course. Have a nice day, Lex," Helen says, returning to her food.

Without another word, Lex stalks out of the office.

"I told you he was going to be trouble," Helen says to me, stabbing her fork into a green bean.

"Well, he's young," I say. "He's new. Probably throwing his weight around a little."

"Huh. Well, he's going to have to learn not to interfere with my investigation."

"I don't think he was interfering—"

Leaning across her desk and glaring at me, she says, "Are you defending that little . . . Deputy Mayor?"

"No, Helen," I say patiently. "I'm just trying to get you to see things from another perspective. One perhaps not as confrontational?"

"I didn't think I was being confrontational?"

"You weren't," I say. "But you didn't tell him you've already learned some things, did you?"

The look of surprise on Helen's face causes me to grin. "How do you know that?"

"You just told me," I say, my grin getting wider.

Helen's at a rare loss for words, then she begins to laugh. "You're learning all my tricks, Tom!"

"Not all of them," I say. "I've just gotten very good at reading you. So, what have you found out? Is it something you can tell me, or something you can't?"

She sits up in her chair and contemplates her hands for a moment. Finally, she says quietly, "Tom, I could tell you, but right now, I want a tight lid kept on what we've found."

"And that includes me," I say, matter-of-factly. "That's fine. We've talked about this, so it's OK—"

"But I want to tell you why, Tom." Helen takes a deep breath. "The few clues we've found so far don't fit what we think we know about the 1928 robbery."

"I'm not sure I follow."

"And I can't say anymore without giving something away. But I'm telling you, Tom, if the anthropologist's report says what I think it's going to say, some people are going to be very upset."

***

Since Helen is tied up with a case, and the weather is clear, if a little crisp, I decide when I get back to the Rectory to take a bike ride through town. Myerton on a Sunday afternoon in the fall is relatively quiet, with shoppers strolling up and down Main Street, and the Myer College students either sleeping off the events of last night or studying for another week of classes. With the leaves well past their peak, people no longer flood the area to enjoy the fall color. There are a couple of farms outside of town that feature pumpkin patches, hayrides, and other fall fun, but mostly it's families from the area, or perhaps Frostburg, who travel out to enjoy them.

Riding past the Conway house, I'm surprised to see an addition to the usual brood of four. I stop and wave to Miriam, who's sitting on the porch swing trying to look relaxed as she keeps an eye on her very active children.

Catherine runs out to meet me. "Hi, Father Tom!" she says brightly.

"Hello, Catherine," I say with a smile. On her heels is Terry Davis, Bridget Davis' oldest son.

"Hello, Terry," I say. "You two look like you're having fun."

"I wasn't," Terry says with a smile. "But I am now, thanks to Catherine."

"Oh, and what did Catherine do?"

"Ever since Daddy died trying to hurt Miss Mae, I've just known he was in Hell with the devil, because that's where bad people go when they die," he says. "I know everything my Daddy did was wrong, but it made me really sad to think I was never going to see him again, because I want to be a good boy and be with Jesus when I die."

"Did you tell Catherine this when you came over to play?"

"No, I didn't say anything about it. But Catherine told me that I didn't need to be sad, that Daddy wasn't in Hell, that right before he died, he told Jesus he was sorry for all the bad things he had done, and he was happy right now because where he was, he could see heaven and knew he'd be there some day."

I nod. "Did you say this to Terry, Catherine?"

She looks up at me with those soulful brown eyes of hers and nods.

"Is Catherine right, Father Tom? Will I see my Daddy in heaven someday?"

I look down at this ten-year-old who's suffered more than many people three times his age and place my hand on his shoulder. "Jesus' love for us is so big," I say with a smile, "we can't understand everything about it. I'd say it's very likely that what Catherine says is true for your Daddy, as it is for any bad person who is sorry for what they've done right before they died.

"But," I add, "you don't need to worry about that right now. It's a beautiful day, and you two should go back to running around."

With that, Catherine and Terry run off to continue whatever game they were playing. I look at Catherine, wondering again about the burden such a gift is to one so young, and also how I can possibly have the wisdom as her priest to guide her as she gets older.

I walk to the porch, where Miriam is reading a book. I recognize the title as a romance novel Helen's read.

"I see she's got you reading them, too," I say with a smile.

Miriam looks up from her book. "Just a little harmless diversion, Father. I mean, every woman can use a little romance now and again."

She offers me a chair, and I take it gladly after biking so far. "Dan isn't the romantic type?"

At my question, her cheeks get red and she smiles shyly. "Oh, no. Dan's quite . . . wonderful in that area." She clears her throat and says. "I saw you talking to Catherine and Terry."

"Yes," I say. "Are the other kids inside?"

"No, they're at Bridget's house," Miriam says. "Terry was getting a little underfoot, so she asked if he could come over to play with Catherine."

"After all he's been through, it's good to see Terry playing like other kids."

Miriam nods. "He looked so sad when he came today. I'm proud of Catherine for helping him."

I look at her. "Did she tell you how she helped him?"

"Oh, yes. She told me. Actually, she asked me if she could tell Terry what she'd seen in her dream. We'd had a long talk the other day about how God gave her a special gift, that He wanted her to use it to help people, but she should tell Dan or me about anything she saw or heard." Miriam chuckles. "I'm not sure she realizes that not everyone can see what she sees." Looking at me, she asks, "Did I do the right thing, Father? I mean, this gift she has—God does mean her to use it, right?"

"Oh, Miriam," I say with a smile. "I'm trying to figure all this out, just like you and Dan are. But I think in this case, you did the right thing."

We watch Catherine and Terry play a rather enthusiastic game of tag for a while. "Father," Miriam finally says, "did you know that Steve Austin from the Hoot-n-Holler is spending a lot of time at Bridget's?"

I furrow my brow. "Now, Miriam," I say gently, "I thought you'd learned your lesson about rumors and gossip."

"Oh, Father, I'm only telling you what I've seen myself," Miriam protests. "In fact, the reason Terry is here today is because Steve's over there working on something and Bridget thought Terry was getting in the way. But this is like the third or fourth time this week."

"I do know that Steve was kind enough to offer to do some repairs Bridget needed done," I say. "I don't think there's anything more than that."

"Oh, Father Tom, I think you misunderstand me," Miriam says. "I'm not saying anything, well, inappropriate is going on. Steve's a great guy and I like him—he was really good about Dan when he had his problems after shooting Leslie Williams—but Bridget's been through a lot. These last few years, she hasn't really known a man's kindness. And Steve—I mean, he's a good-looking man."

"He's also gay, Miriam," I say.

"I know that, and you know that. But does Bridget know that? I happened to be over there the other day, and Steve was doing some yard work. He'd taken off his sweatshirt and was in a t-shirt and jeans. And Bridget was looking at him like a starving woman at a banquet."

I think I'm beginning to understand. "You don't want to see Bridget hurt."

"Exactly. Now, I could talk to her, tell her about Steve. But she might not believe me."

"No, and it's not your place anyway." I take a deep breath. "If anyone is going to tell Bridget, Steve's going to have to be the one to do it."

Twelve

"Would you like the same boxes as last week, Father Tom?"

I look at Gwen across the reference desk. "Um, no, I'd like something else. I believe the collection has some papers from Harriet Stirling?"

"Oh!" Gwen says with surprise. "Harriet Stirling? Wasn't she the wife of the man whose body—or what's left of it anyway—they found Saturday afternoon?"

"Gwen," I say firmly, "those remains have not been identified."

"But that story in the *Gazette*—"

"—was premature. In any event, I'd like to see her papers, please."

"Of course, Father. I know right where they are. I've served them a few times to Nate Rodriguez over the last few weeks."

As she goes to retrieve the box, I wonder what I think I'm doing. What do I hope to find, looking in the letters and diary of a woman broken by life, abandoned by her family, condemned to spend the rest of her life locked up as a mad woman? What connection can they possibly have on those old bones now lying on an examining table in Baltimore?

Well, if it is the body of Kent Stirling, maybe his wife's papers can shed some light on what happened to him. How did he wind up buried on the edge of Myer College? What drove him to betray the friend who'd placed so much confidence in him?

And if it isn't Kent Stirling whose skull landed at Dan's feet? Well, maybe something in the box will point to the person's identity.

"Here you go, Father," Gwen says as she places one gray archival box on the desk and hands me a slip to sign.

"Thanks," I say. I take the box and a pair of white cotton gloves to my table, where my laptop is already open and waiting for me. I carefully place the box down and take my seat. I open the lid and examine the contents.

I'm disappointed there's not more. Three folders and one volume, obviously the diary Nate mentioned. I pull one of the folders out. The first one is full of handwritten notes in blue ink on lined paper, all signed "K"—Kent, I assume. From feelings expressed in a few of them, they're love notes to Harriet from her suitor, written before their marriage, presumably. Each is full of such things as "my heart yearns for you" and "I count the minutes until I can see you again" and "my life has no meaning apart from you."

On the surface, heartfelt. But are they? By all accounts, the same man who wrote these stole from her brother and abandoned her and their son only a few years later.

The second folder looks like more official correspondence, consisting of letters and bills from local businesses. Interestingly enough, they all date from the remaining months before the theft in November. Some are polite reminders of accounts that are past due. Others are less polite, with one saying "final demand" and threatening suit.

What's really odd is they're all addressed to Harriet, not to Kent Stirling. Taking out my phone, I use the calculator to add up the amounts owed.

I'm so astonished, I add the numbers again to make sure I didn't make a mistake. But I come up with the same figure.

Harriet Stirling owed different businesses in Myerton, Baltimore, and Washington D.C. $2,000 dollars in 1928. I check an inflation calculator online, and today, that would equal over $30,000.

I have no idea what Kent Stirling earned as Vice-President of the First National Bank of Myerton, but from all the past due notices, it appears they were living beyond their means.

Or rather, Harriet was spending beyond their means. The bills and notices are all from clothiers, furriers, jewelers, and high-end boutiques.

Was this Stirling's motive? If so, stealing $150,000 dollars to pay $2,000 dollars in debts is excessive, to say the least.

I shake my head and close the folder. Placing it back in the box, I take out the third folder. This is social correspondence—invitations to teas, garden parties, luncheons, that sort of thing. There are a couple of invitations from the Myers to engagements at the Myer Mansion. None of this is surprising. Obviously, as the sister of the bank president and the wife of the bank vice president, she'd be invited to such things.

Sighing, I sit back and rub my eyes. Glancing at the clock, I see it's already 11:30 a.m. I'm not saying daily Mass on Mondays until Advent begins, but I am joining Helen for lunch at The Bistro at noon.

I'm about to put the folder back in the box when I realize I haven't seen the letter Nate talked about in his article. I look again in the folder and, not seeing it, check the first folder. I find it there.

From the way Nate described it, I thought it was only a couple of lines. But it's actually a full page, written on paper bearing the letterhead of the First National Bank of Myerton. He used a pencil instead of a pen, and some of the words are smudged. But I can make out what it says.

Placing it on the table, I begin to type:

Dearest Harriet:

By now you know everything. I am so sorry. I've hurt you and your brother in unspeakable ways. There is no excuse for what I've done. I just couldn't take it anymore. I guess I wasn't strong enough. I needed out. I wanted out. I wanted a reason to laugh again. But now, it's all gone. The light is broken, and all is darkness. The precious thing I stole from your brother is buried in the gorge on the edge of town.

Good-bye.

K.

My phone vibrates, and a text message notification pops up. When I see the message, I quickly gather my things.

It's from Helen. It reads simply:

Come to the station now.

***

"I got your message," I say as I close the door to Helen's office. "What's wrong?"

She takes a deep breath. "Remember I told you we've already found something, but I didn't want to tell you what it is?"

I nod. She leans forward and rests her forehead on her hands. "So, I need to tell you now, because the search uncovered something where the remains were found. And I'm going to need your help."

"My help? Why do you need my help?"

From the folder in front of her, she removes a photograph and slides it across to me. It's a gold locket.

"This was found near the body?" I ask. "Are you telling me the remains are those of a woman?"

Helen nods. "I just got off the phone with the ME's office. The skeleton is definitely female, probably in her late twenties when she was buried." Taking a deep breath, she adds, "They also found fragments of bone consistent with an unborn child, about five months."

"Dear Lord," I say. "So this poor woman was pregnant when she was killed—and I assume she was killed?"

"That's still unclear. The examination found several fractures and broken bones, including a blow to the head. The anthropologist says the injuries are consistent with a fall."

"So, she was pushed. Or jumped. If she was an unwed mother, in the late 1920s—"

"No, Tom," Helen says. "The remains also had a wedding band. So we're looking at a married woman in her late twenties, who was pregnant at the time of her death."

I look at the photograph of the locket again. "I'm still not sure why I'm here?"

"The locket has an inscription on the back," she says, sliding another photograph to me. It's a close-up, showing just two words on its glittering surface.

My jaw drops open. "Helen, you can't be serious?"

The locket says, *From Ash to Theia.*

"I had Gladys look in the county marriage records," Helen says. "Ashton Stewart married Theia Bradshaw in February 1925."

"Helen, do you know what you're saying?"

"I do, Tom. That's why you're here. I need you to come with me and help me tell Anna that the remains are those of her grandmother."

Thirteen

"She's not at the Rectory," I say, pocketing my phone. "I think she told me she had some shopping to do."

Helen sighs. "It's just as well. I'm starving."

We're sitting at a table in The Bistro, looking at a couple of menus. We agreed when we left her office that it'd be better if we told Anna about her grandmother on a full stomach.

Besides, today is a perfect day for tomato bisque and grilled cheese.

"Have you decided—oh, Father Tom!" I look up from my menu and see Gwen from the library standing there, her pen poised above an order pad.

"Gwen? I didn't know you worked here?" I say.

"Yeah, well, I just started this week," she says. "You know, Myer's kinda on the pricey side and the job at the library doesn't quite cover my living expenses. I got tired of Cup-of-Noodles for dinner every night."

I look at Helen. "We remember those days, don't we?"

"It's been a while, but yeah, I ate many cups while studying," she says. "Since Father Tom's not going to introduce us, I'm Helen."

"Oh, I know who you are, Chief Parr," Gwen says brightly. "I'm Gwen Tolson."

"Gwen works in the manuscript section at the library," I say. "I just saw her this morning."

"What are you studying at Myer, Gwen?" Helen asks.

"History, but my minor's in criminal justice."

"Looking at law schools?"

She hesitates. "I was. That's what my parents want me to do. But I've really become interested in criminal justice. I was actually thinking of law enforcement."

Helen grins. "Well, we can always use more bright young women in the field. You know, it's not an easy career, especially these days."

"Yeah, that's why I haven't told my parents what I'm thinking about. Listen, I don't want to be presumptuous—I mean, I know how busy you are, with being Chief and preparing for a wedding—but I was wondering—"

"Of course, just give me a call. I'll show you around the station and we can chat."

Gwen's eyes light up and she bubbles, "Oh! Oh, that would be wonderful. Just great! Thank you!"

She turns and takes a couple of steps away from the table, then comes back. "Almost forgot to take your order."

We tell Gwen our orders and she trots away from the table. "Look at you," I say to Helen. "Changing young women's lives."

"She seems like a bright, intelligent young lady," Helen says. "And if I can answer some questions she has, it's time well spent."

"Well, I guess not everyone can become an archivist," I shrug.

"Oh, Tom, the world has enough curmudgeons, don't you think?"

I try kicking her under the table playfully, but miss and hit the table leg with my shin instead. "Ow!" I grimace, reaching under to rub the sore spot.

"That's what you get for being naughty," she says with a grin.

Rolling my eyes, I sit back and cross my arms. "So, how are we going to tell her?"

"That's your job," Helen says.

"Oh, I see," I say, nodding my head. "You want me to do your dirty work."

"Don't put it that way, Tom. You have a lot more history with Anna than I do. You were married to her daughter. She loves you."

"She loves you, too," I protest. "I mean, she's as responsible for us being able to marry as anyone except the Archbishop."

"I know Anna's quite fond of me," she says. "But deep down, she still sees me as the woman who tried to take you away from the priesthood—and by extension, her. If I'm the one who tells her that the grandmother no one would ever speak of has been buried in that gorge for almost a century, that may bubble to the surface. She's going to be upset no matter who tells her. I'm just hoping she'll be less upset with you than with me."

"So what are you going to do?"

"I'll answer any questions she has, fill in details, you know, that sort of thing."

"I still don't understand—"

"Tom, do you want me to spell it out?" she whispers. "We're getting married in six weeks. We've survived pre-marital counseling with the Archbishop. Somehow, we've managed to behave ourselves. I don't want anything to mess things up now."

"What, do you think Anna would get so angry she'd call the Archbishop and, what, tell him not to allow us to get married?"

"I don't know, but I don't want to give her any reason to do just that!"

"You're being ridiculous, not to mention paranoid."

"Maybe, but do you want to take that chance?"

I sigh and wave my hands in surrender. "All right, all right. I'll break the news to her. But you'll have to give the details, since I don't know anything."

She lets out a deep sigh. "Thank you."

Just then I hear a familiar voice say, "Now, my Pashto isn't great, but somehow I managed to talk my way out of it without getting killed."

A woman's voice asks, "And you weren't scared?"

After a pause, the man says quietly, "Sometimes, you've just got to decide you're not going to be scared. It's the only way to survive."

"Who is that?" Helen whispers.

"Well, if I didn't know better, I'd say that was Steve,"

"Steve? You mean, Steve Austin? The owner of the Hoot-n-Holler?"

"Yeah, that one."

"But—he sounds like he's with a woman."

"He is," I say. "And it sounds like Bridget Davis."

"Bridget Davis? What is he doing with her?"

"Well, since they're together at a restaurant around lunchtime, I'd say—"

"Oh, don't be Balaam's Donkey about it. You know what I mean."

"He's been doing some work for her—home repairs, yardwork, that sort of thing. Maybe she took him to lunch to thank him?"

Just then, Bridget erupts in laughter at something Steve said that I couldn't hear. "Steve, you are such a bad, bad boy, you know that?"

"I'm not that bad, Bridge," Steve says.

"Maybe not, but I've never met anyone like you, Steve."

"Yeah, that I can believe."

Helen and I stare at each other across the table. "What's going on?" she whispers.

I shake my head. "I don't know. But maybe I should have a talk with Steve about a few things."

Gwen brings our orders and sets them in front of us. "Enjoy your meal," she says brightly.

Between having to face Anna and what's going on at the other table, the chances of that are slim.

***

Helen and I are sitting in the living room of the Rectory when Anna gets back.

"Bill, I hear what you're saying," Anna says, "but I'm telling you, we need to make a good impression on the community this year. The last time we hosted was a near disaster."

"Hey," I call.

Anna and Bill appear in the doorway to the living room. "Oh, hi, Tom. Helen, what are you doing here this time of day on a Monday?"

Helen looks at me. "We need to talk to you, Anna. It's important."

"Oh," Bill says. "Well, from your tone, it doesn't sound like good news."

"I'm afraid it isn't."

"Anna," Bill says, taking the two bags she has from her, "I'll put these in the kitchen then slip out the back way, so you three can have some privacy."

"No, Bill," I say, "you can stay. I think it would be for the best. Helen?"

"I agree," Helen says. "Anna, I'm so sorry."

Anna's jaw stiffens and she raises her chin. Unbidden, she sits on the couch, perched on the edge with her hands folded. Bill sits beside her and puts his arm around her.

"I think I already know," Anna says matter-of-factly. "It has to do with that body you found buried near the college."

Helen looks at me. To Anna, I simply nod. "Yes, it does."

"I see." She begins to wring her hands together. "So, that reporter was right. It is Kent Stirling. And, it looks like someone killed him. And you're here to tell me you think it was my grandfather. Well, I don't know what possible evidence you could have of that, but it's not true. My grandfather did not kill Stirling, though he probably felt he had a right to after what that man did to him!"

Anna's beginning to get worked up so I jump in carefully. "That's one reason we're here. You see, they've found evidence that indicates it's not Kent Stirling."

Visible relief washes over Anna. Her shoulders relax. "Oh?" she whispers. "Oh, what a relief! I've been so afraid, since no one knows what happened to him—I take it you didn't find the money?"

I haven't thought to ask Helen this question, and I'm kind of surprised that Anna has. I look at Helen, who says, "We've found no trace near the body, but a team is still looking. We're going to bring in a ground-penetrating radar from Baltimore to help in the search."

"You won't find it," Anna says firmly. "It's just like Grandpa said, Stirling left the country, probably died in South America somewhere, maybe Cuba."

"As Helen said," I say, trying to steer things back to why we're here, "it's not Kent Stirling." Taking a deep breath, I add, "It turns out it's not a man at all."

"What are you saying, Father Tom?" Bill asks. "It's a woman those kids found?"

"Yes."

"So it has nothing to do with the robbery," Anna says. "Was she killed?"

"The ME says there are signs of a fall from about 100 feet, likely the edge of the little cliff there," Helen offers.

"How awful," Anna says, shaking her head. "But what does that have to do with me?"

"Anna, in searching the spot where the body was buried," I say, "they found buttons and some jewelry. Including this."

I hand her the photograph of the gold locket. "How beautiful," Bill says. "My mother had something similar. I remember she wore it until the day she died. It had been her grandmother's."

At the mention of his grandmother, Anna looks up from the photograph. She looks at Helen, then at me. "That's why you're here, isn't it?" she whispers.

"There's an inscription," I say in answer, handing the other photograph.

Anna squints to read, "From Ash to Theia."

"Gladys looked in the marriage records," I say. "Your grandfather married Theia Bradshaw in February 1925."

Anna stares at the photograph. "That body—the one you found—found murdered—are you saying it's my grandmother?"

I look at Helen. That's the kind of question she should answer.

"Anna," she says quietly, "after so long, it's difficult to make a positive ID. Since we really know nothing about her, what she looked like, how tall she was, all we have to rely on is that locket. So, it's possible that it could be someone else who just happened to have your grandmother's locket—say, a housekeeper who stole it."

"The skull had some gold fillings, I remember reading in the *Gazette*," Anna says. "Is that right?"

Helen nods. "Yes."

"Not likely that a housekeeper in Myerton in the 1920s would have gold fillings, would you agree?"

"I would."

She leans forward. "Helen, my dear," she says with a smile. "I know how good a detective you are. I trust your instincts. So I have two questions for you. First, do you think that's my grandmother?"

"Yes," Helen says firmly, "I do."

Anna nods. "OK. Do you think my grandfather killed her?"

I look at Helen, who looks at me. To Anna, she says, "I don't know who killed her, or even if she was killed. She could have committed suicide, or it could have been a tragic accident and she fell while she was taking a walk or something."

"Helen, you don't believe that," Anna says.

Taking a deep breath, Helen says, "No. Someone killed her, and then carefully hid the body."

"Why do you say that, Helen?" Bill asks.

"It's simple, really. They found the remains four feet down, carefully laid out, then covered over. If it was suicide or an accidental fall, she'd have been closer to the surface. Because of predators, the skeleton would not have been intact. She might not have been found at all."

Anna nods. "Perfectly logical."

"But having said that," Helen says, "even if she is your grandmother, and she was murdered, we have no indication who did it."

Anna stands up and walks to the mantle. Playing with the brick-a-brack, she says, "My grandfather would make the likeliest suspect, though, wouldn't he? Most people are murdered by those closest to them, am I right?"

"Yes," Helen says, "statistically, that's true, but—"

"And it would explain a lot," Anna continues, "namely, why he never spoke about her, why she was never allowed to be mentioned in front of him. He killed her for some reason and buried her body, then erased her from his life."

Turning around and crossing her arms. "So what's the other thing you haven't told me?"

Helen and I both start at this. Rolling her eyes, she says, "Oh, come on. I've become very good at telling when both of you are hiding something. I mean, that's how I knew how you felt about each other before you did."

Bill looks at her. "You did?"

"Not important right now," Anna says, waving at Bill. "So, what is it?"

I open my mouth but Anna puts her hand up. "I'm not sure why Helen asked you to break the news to me, Tom, but I want to hear from her. She is, after all, the Police Chief."

I glance at Helen, who swallows before saying, "I won't go into exactly how we know, but your grandmother was about five months pregnant when she died."

Anna closes her eyes and nods. "I see," she whispers. She walks back and sits on the couch again, laying her head on Bill's shoulder. Bill puts his arm around her, and Anna closes her eyes. I think I see a tear fall from her eyes.

We all sit quietly for a while—I don't know exactly how long—when Anna finally sits up. With a look of determination, she says, "OK, Helen, so what's next?"

"I'm not sure what you mean?" Helen says.

"The investigation. Now that you know who was murdered, what do you do next?"

"Well—if this were a normal crime, I'd start interviewing suspects, looking for who had a motive to kill her."

"But everyone is dead," Anna says. "So what are you going to do?"

"Anna, are you asking Helen how she's going to investigate your grandmother's death?" I ask.

"You have to know," Helen adds, "that after so much time, I can't do any of the things I'd normally do. It's very unlikely we'll ever know exactly what happened."

"So you're saying you're not going to do anything," Anna says firmly.

"Anna, what do you want from me?" Helen asks, a hint of exasperation in her voice.

"I want you to do your job!" she yells. "I want you to find out who did this to my grandmother!"

"Anna," Bill says, touching her arm.

"I know what I'm asking is difficult," she says, tears beginning to flow down her cheeks. "And you may never find her killer. But I need to know something. I need to know what happened to my grandmother."

She swallows and looks at her hands. "She was a forbidden subject in my house," she says quietly. "I so much wanted to know what she was like. I'd often lay awake at night and imagine what she looked like. I always wonder if I looked like her, if I was like her."

She looks at Helen. "I know I may be asking you to do the impossible," she pleads, "but can you try? Please, for me?"

Helen has tears in her own eyes. I feel the emotion behind the request. But I also know that Anna is asking her to do something she just can't do.

"Anna," I say quietly, "I know how important this is for you, but Helen—"

"Of course, Anna," Helen says. "I'll give it my best shot."

I'm speechless for a second, then say, "But, Helen, you just said—"

"I know what I said, Tom," Helen says quickly. "Anna, I may not be able to find out who killed her, but I'll try really hard to give you some answers."

"That's all I ask, dear," Anna says with a smile.

"Now," Helen says. "I need any information you have about Theia Stewart."

"That's the problem, Helen. I don't really know anything. I didn't even know her name until you told me."

"Do you have any of your grandfather's papers?" I say, giving in to the inevitable. "Letters, a diary perhaps. Photographs."

"A photograph of her would be terrific," Helen says. "We might be able to get a more positive ID with that one."

"There is an old trunk up in the attic of my house," Anna says. "It was in Dad's house when he died. It's locked. I'm not even sure it's my grandfather's."

"It's a place to start," Helen says. "We don't know when she was killed, but I can't believe she disappeared and no one took any notice of it. Maybe there's some mention of her going missing in the *Gazette*."

"I can look into that," I say.

"I think that's a job we can ask Nate to do," Helen says. "He's good at that. Do you think there may be some records at the college library that might help us?"

I ponder the question for a moment. "There might be," I say. "I can check the next time I'm there. My schedule's pretty packed this week, but I can get over there on Thursday."

"There's something you'll need to do first, Tom," Anna says.

"What's that?"

"I need you to go up in my attic and get down that trunk."

Fourteen

Now, my love for Anna Luckgold knows no bounds. She's been more of a Mom to me over the years than my own Mom. Certainly, conversations with her are a lot less painful. She's supported Helen and me every step of the way, probably even in ways I'll never know. She's also not afraid to tell me when I'm wrong or just acting like an ass. There have been several occasions since I came to Saint Clare's when I've needed that. So, I have a very hard time saying no to her.

Which is why I'm standing in her dusty, smelly, stuffy, and cobwebby—is that a real word?—attic on Tuesday afternoon in search of an old trunk.

Once again, I'm struck by how different Anna is from my own Mom. I know I shouldn't compare them, but it's hard not to when the differences are so starke. Right now, I'm comparing Anna's very orderly way of storing, with boxes and plastic containers neatly stacked and labeled, with my Mom's, which can best be described as 'it's here somewhere.' Nothing's labeled, at least not clearly. The boxes are often torn open, spilling their contents on the floor. And there's little separation between trash and treasure. I remember one time looking through a box for something of my Dad's and coming across an empty cereal box with an expiration date of 1968. I have no idea why she kept it, but when I asked her, she insisted she had a very good reason, but just couldn't remember what it was.

Even though it's orderly, it is still far from clean. It's also surprisingly warm, considering how chilly it is outside. Somewhere in my mind I remember that heat rises, and since the heat is on to keep pipes from freezing at night, my guess is that all the heat's decided to reside in the attic.

The first thing I do is take off my jacket and shed my Catholic University of America sweatshirt, leaving me clad in a white t-shirt and gray sweatpants. I look around, but don't see the trunk. Anna said it was rather large, and I'd probably need some help to get it down.

Which is the excuse I gave to Steve when I called him.

OK, I have an ulterior motive for getting Steve over here. After what Miriam told me, and what Helen and I observed at The Bistro, I feel compelled to talk to him about Bridget.

I know, I know. I'm not the sex police. And I don't think for a moment anything like that's going on. But I'm concerned about Bridget. I just don't want her to get hurt.

Heaven knows, she's been hurt enough by a man.

I start moving boxes, hoping to uncover the trunk fairly quickly. All that happens is that I start sweating. Soon, my t-shirt is sticking to my skin and sweat is pouring down my face. Trying to get comfortable, I peel off my t-shirt. My chest hair is wet and matted, and I use the t-shirt in a feeble attempt to wipe my face.

"Tom!"

"Up here, Helen," I yell down. "Hey, could you get me a glass of water? It's as hot as seven fires up here!"

"It's the middle of fall," she yells. "It got below freezing last night."

"What can I tell you, it wasn't in Anna's attic! Can you just bring me water!"

There's a pause before Helen growls, "Certainly, your majesty!"

I sigh. "I'm sorry. This is just a lot harder than I thought it would be."

I move some other boxes and am about to pick up another when I hear Helen walking up the steps. "I don't see what the—oh, my!"

I turn around. Helen's standing just inside the attic, a glass of water in her hand, her eyes as big as saucers.

"Tom," she gasps. "What—why—you're—I—I mean—"

"Are you all right, Helen?" I say, taking a step towards her.

"Uh-huh," she says, still staring at me. "You're right," she whispers. "It is hot up here."

"I told you it was," I said.

She begins to walk towards me with the water. "I guess so," she says. "Here's your water."

"Thanks." I take it and drink it so fast, some of the water misses my mouth and dribbles down my chin. When that happens, I think I hear Helen . . . whimper.

"Ah, I needed that," I say. "Thanks."

"Sure, sure," she says, then she takes her coat off. "It really is hot up here, isn't it, Tom?"

There's a tone in her voice and a look in her eyes that tells me maybe I should give us some space.

"Um, Helen," I say with a grin. "Are, ah, are you sure you're all right?"

She nods, her eyes locked with mine. "I just stopped by to see how it was going."

"Fine."

"Have you found it yet?"

"No."

She nods. "I should go."

"Uh-huh."

Instead of moving away, she steps closer. "But I don't want to," she whispers.

"And," I say, beginning to lose myself in her azure blue eyes, "I don't want you to either. But you really need to, Helen. Go."

She takes one step back, then turns on her heels and walks across the attic to the stairs, then down. It's only a moment before I hear Anna's front door slam.

I close my eyes and breathe a deep sigh of relief.

"Too close," I whisper. "Much too close."

I thank God I had the presence of mind to tell her to leave, to get away from me as quickly as she could. Another few minutes—

"Hello?" someone—this time, a man—calls from downstairs.

"Up here Steve," I answer, quickly standing up and pulling myself together. I grab my t-shirt and pull it on just as he enters the attic.

"Tom," he says with a bemused smile.

"Thanks, Steve, for coming," I say, shaking his hand.

"Well, when you called saying you needed some help getting something heavy out of Anna's attic, I have to say I was intrigued."

"Oh?" I shrug. "It's just a trunk, for a case Helen's working on."

"Yeah, about Helen, is she OK?"

"She's fine, why?"

Steve shakes his head. "Because when I pulled into the driveway, Helen ran out the front door to her car and burned some serious rubber pulling away."

"Oh," I say quickly. "Yeah. She was late for a meeting."

"Must have been an important one."

"Well, you know," I say as nonchalantly as I can. "She's Chief of Police. Important meetings all the time. As I say, I really appreciate the help. From what Anna told me, there's no way I could get it down myself."

"And you decided to call me for help, huh?" Steve asks, a slight smile on his face.

"Yeah," I say. "And I really appreciate you taking the time."

He shrugs. "Well, if you can't get a member of your parish to help you, I figure the gay, agnostic bartender can come to your rescue."

I laugh nervously. "Exactly." I look around and add, "I still haven't found it, but Anna tells me it's here somewhere. Can you start moving the boxes on that side, and I'll keep working over here?"

"I'll be glad to, Tom," Steve says, crossing his arms, "if you'll tell me the real reason you called me."

I look at him and try to bluff. "I don't—"

"Tom, you are a fine man—one of the finest I've ever met, and I've known some fine men—but you are a terrible liar. Which, considering you're a priest, is a good thing. So what is it?"

I take a deep breath. "You're right, Steve," I say. "Maybe we should sit down."

I find a couple of old folding chairs and hand one to Steve. We sit across from each other, and he says, "If you wanted to talk about something, you could have just come to the bar."

"No, I need to talk to you in private," I say.

Steve grins. "What is it, Tom? Are you coming out or something?"

"Sorry to disappoint you, Steve," I chuckle, "but no."

"Darn," he says, snapping his fingers. "And you'd be such a good addition to the local community. So if it isn't that, Tom, what's so important that you couldn't talk to me at the bar?"

I pause for a second. "Steve," I say slowly, "it's about Bridget Davis."

"What about her? Is she OK? Is something wrong? I just spoke to her last night and she seemed fine. It's nothing to do with one of the kids, is it?" Steve asks, a look of concern on his face.

"No, no, it's nothing like that, Steve," I say. Seeing the other man relax, I decide to dive in. "You've been seeing a lot of Bridget, haven't you?"

Steve looks at me. "I don't know what you mean by 'a lot,'" he says slowly. "I mean, I've been over there a lot. The house needs some work. It's clear Rusty didn't lift a finger to do anything for a long time. She has kids, Tom. They need a good place to live."

"I know, I know," I say quickly, "and I'm glad you're able to help her."

"Are you, Tom? Because I'm getting the feeling that you don't approve."

"Oh, don't misunderstand me, Steve. It's nothing like that. But I'm just . . . concerned, I guess?"

"About what?" Steve asks, getting noticeably irritated.

"About your relationship with Bridget," I blurt out.

"My—my relationship with Bridget?" Steve says. "We've become friends. Turns out we have some things in common. I enjoy her company. I think her kids are great, especially after everything they've gone through."

"Helen and I were at The Bistro the other day and saw you two having lunch."

"Gays have lunch, you know?"

"But usually not with recently widowed women who were married to an abusive man who didn't show her the least bit of positive attention for a long time."

There's silence in the attic as Steve and I just stare at each other in some kind of standoff. Just as I'm about to say something else, Steve says, "She knows, Tom."

"She knows you're gay," I say.

"Uh-huh. Turns out Rusty came home one night, sore as hell that I cut him off before he was ready, and referred to me as 'that damn faggot.' The first day I was working for Bridget, she asked me about that. Honestly, I was expecting her to tell me to leave—I've had that happen before, especially in a family with boys. You know, the real perverts give us a bad name. But I'd decided a long time ago not to lie about who I was, so I told her yeah, it was true. Do you know what she said?"

I shake my head. "She sighed with relief, saying she was glad she didn't have to worry about me. She'd had enough of men and was glad I was someone she could trust," Steve says with a laugh. "I tell you, Tom, it's been a long time since anyone said that to me."

"She probably feels safe with you."

He looks at his hands. "Probably knows I'm not going to come on to her, or attack her, or hit her or belittle her. I mean, it's really sad in a way. Bridget is an attractive woman. She's only in her early thirties. But Rusty just did such a number on her—not just with his fists but with the crap that came out of his mouth—I'm not surprised she's soured on men."

"Sounds like she's shared a lot with you," I say. "I've had trouble getting her to open up. She told me about the beatings and said he blamed her for the accident."

"Oh, it went beyond that," Steve says. "Bastard blamed her for everything rotten that had ever happened to him. Said if she were a better wife—more of a woman—he wouldn't hit her. When he was really drunk, he'd start talking about all the women he'd had before her, and how she didn't hold a candle to any of them."

"That's terrible," I say, shaking my head. "I'm glad she feels she can trust you."

"Well," he says, taking a deep breath, "my dad belittled me every chance he got. Called me sissy, queer, faggot, not a real man."

"Was this after you came out?"

"Oh, no," he laughs. "That was before I even knew what gay was. I was 11 or 12, and I guess I just wasn't masculine enough for him."

Considering what Steve looks like now—taller than me, with a powerful build no doubt honed during his years as an Army Ranger—I find that comical.

"He only beat the crap out of me when I was seventeen and told him I was in love with a guy. Of course, that's before he threw me out, with my mother screaming that she'd have no Sodomites living under her roof." Steve shakes his head. "Mama was the real Bible-thumper in the family. Knew scripture backwards and forwards. Daddy was a deacon in our church, but the only verse of scripture he knew by heart was 'spare the rod and spoil the child.'"

"Did you share any of this with Bridget?"

"Oh, yeah," Steve says. "I told her a lot of things. Some of it I've never told anybody—well, except you just now. I have a hard time trusting people. Bridget's the first person I've found in a long time who I can be myself with."

"Well," I say, shaking my head, "I feel foolish now. Sorry I even asked the question."

"You know, Father, it's OK," Steve says, holding up his hand. "Bridget's a member of your church. One of the things I like about you is how much you love your people."

"They're my family, Steve," I say.

"Family," Steve says. "Must be nice to have one." He looks at his hands and says, "I probably shouldn't tell you this, but Bridget's been getting crap from hers ever since Rusty died."

I furrow my brow. "How so?"

"Basically, his family blames her for everything, saying if she'd been a better wife, he wouldn't have done what he did—like treating the SOB better would have kept him from murdering that kid and stabbing that poor Trent girl. Her family—now, they are a real piece of work—have basically taken the attitude that she deserves what she got for marrying Rusty against their wishes."

"She'd told me her family didn't want her to marry him," I say, shaking my head. "I can't believe they're being so cruel."

"Father, you should know that family can treat you worse than total strangers."

I take a deep breath. "Oh, yes," I say quietly. "I know something about that."

We sit quietly for a minute, then Steve stands up. "Well, we're not going to find that trunk just sitting here. You wanted me to look on this side?"

Standing up, I say, "Yeah, if you don't mind helping after I basically tricked you."

Steve laughs. "We're good, Father. You're the kind of guy it's hard to stay mad at. I mean, you have such cute dimples."

"I take that as a compliment," I laugh.

"Hey, don't let it go to your head," Steve says with a grin. "You really are not my type."

We both laugh, and then get back to moving boxes looking for that elusive trunk. After about thirty minutes, we're both hot, sweaty, and dirty, with Steve and I both now working without our t-shirts.

"Anna must spend a fortune on heat," Steve gasps.

"I need to have a talk with her," I say. "A Florida summer's cooler than this attic."

"Listen, I like Anna, but was she sure it was up here?"

I move one more box. "Not entirely. But she doesn't store stuff in the basement. She's had a couple of floods."

"OK," Steve says, lifting another box off a stack and putting it on the floor. He's about to move another when he says, "I think I found it."

"Thank the Lord," I say, exhausted. "I don't think I could move another box."

Steve moves a few more boxes out of the way to reveal an old green footlocker. Like everything else, it's covered in dust and cobwebs. The metal fasteners are pitted and tarnished. But other than that, it's in good shape.

It's also locked.

"Don't suppose Anna said anything about having the key?" Steve says, looking at the trunk with his hands on his hips.

"Not a thing," I sigh. "I'd hate to carry that thing down, just to open it and find out it's not what we're looking for."

"I think it's the only footlocker up here, but I agree about not lugging it down those steps." Steve opens a small leather case on his belt and pulls out one of those multitool things—you know, the one that has a whole bunch of different knives and screwdrivers. Squatting on the floor, he says, "So, let's get you open."

After working the lock for a couple of minutes, I hear a click.

"Got it," Steve says. He unfastens the clips and lifts the lid.

"Well, Steve, I think we found what we're looking for," I mutter. Squatting beside him, I pick up a framed wedding picture near the top. I turn it over.

Written on the back is, *Ash and me on our wedding day.*

Fifteen

Steve and I manage to wrestle the trunk down the staircase and out to the trunk of my car. After thanking him, Steve says, "Listen, I'm more than happy to help anytime I can, Father. But I don't want you to worry about me and Bridget. We're just friends."

"I hope you understand, Steve," I say, "that I never thought you'd do something deliberately. You're a good man, and I know you'd never hurt her like that. I just wanted to make sure she didn't hurt herself, you know?"

Steve laughs. "I know. And I tell you what—if she ever throws herself at me, you'll be the first to know."

"Well," I say, "I doubt that will happen. But thanks."

He drives off, and I head back to the Rectory for a much-needed shower and change of clothes. I need to take the trunk to the station so Helen can see it, but I don't want to offend anyone because of my rank odor.

I also need time to think about what to say to Helen after our close encounter.

Arriving at the Rectory in about fifteen minutes, I see a red scooter parked behind Anna's car. Knowing no one off the top of my head who rides a red scooter, I assume it's a parishioner who has come to see me on an urgent matter.

It's only when I get out of the car that I hear Anna yelling.

"I told you, Ms. Drakes, that I have nothing to say to you or any other member of the press."

"Don't you want your family's side of the story told?" a younger woman says.

"We don't even know if I'm even related to that body they found," Anna yells. "And even if it is—"

"According to my sources, they're about to officially identify the body as that of Theia Stewart, the wife of your grandfather, who went missing not long after the alleged theft of $150,000."

I run up the sidewalk to the front door. Anna's standing on the top step, arms crossed, glaring at a young woman I recognize instantly as Elisia Drakes.

"What's going on here?" I ask firmly. "Anna, are you all right?"

"I'm fine, Father Tom," Anna says. "Ms. Drakes was just leaving."

"Look, Ms. Luckgold," Drakes says with a grin. "I can leave and write my story with what I have. But you may not like what I have to say."

I take a step forward, my blood beginning to boil. "Anna," I say quietly, staring at Drakes, "go inside. I'll take care of this."

I hear Anna take two steps, open the door to the Rectory, and slam it shut. "Ms. Drakes," I say coolly, "Ms. Luckgold said she has nothing to say about this. It's time for you to go."

Drakes crosses her arms and smirks at me. "You like intimidating the press, don't you Father? I mean, your attack on Katherine Shepp is kind of legendary. I guess sleeping with a parishioner who happens to be a police detective—"

"Get off this property," I snap. "As of right now, you're trespassing."

Drakes smiles. "Did I strike a nerve? See, I've never believed that whole 'we're waiting until our wedding night' thing. Your parishioners may have bought it, along with most of the town and even the Catholic Church. But I knew it was all an act."

"You seem to have gotten off track, Ms. Drakes," I smile. "I thought you were here working on a story about the dead body unearthed a few days ago. But here, you're asking me about my sex life—or lack thereof?"

"I have a wide range of interests, Father," Drakes says. "A good reporter is always working on several stories. And I have quite a few right now."

"Well, then, I suggest you get to them," I say pleasantly. "Have a nice day."

As I walk up the steps, she says, "I intend to. I'm not so sure you will."

I pause at the door, before opening it and walking inside.

"Is she gone?" Anna calls from the kitchen.

"She's leaving," I say. "Sorry about that."

"That one's got a ruthless streak," she says. "Kind of surprising for the *Myerton Gazette*."

"She's definitely one to keep an eye on. I'm not here long, just to take a shower and change clothes."

"You found it?" Anna asks hopefully.

"Sure did, with Steve's help."

"I didn't know you'd asked Steve."

"Yeah," I say quickly. "Fortunately, he was free."

I half expect Anna to pursue the question of why Steve was there further, but instead she lapses into silence. "Did you open it?" she asks quietly.

I nod my head. "Yes."

She takes a deep breath. "And?"

"I really didn't take the time to look through it, Anna."

Peering at me. "You did see something, though. Something that told you you had the right trunk."

My first impulse is to say, "well, there was only the one trunk," or something like that. But that's not fair to her. Not after all this time. Not after all the secrets she's had to endure.

"A wedding picture," I say. "A man and a woman. Writing on the back says it's your grandparents."

A tear comes to Anna's eye. "Can—can you get it for me?"

I could kick myself for not realizing she'd want to see it. "Of course."

I go back out to the car and retrieve the old framed photograph from the trunk. Once inside, I hand it to Anna. Wordlessly, she takes it from my hand.

"Oh, my," she whispers, a slight smile on her face. "That's my grandfather—other than a few wrinkles, less hair, and a bit of a pot belly, he looked the same when I knew him."

With a finger, she traces lines of her grandmother's face. "It's funny," she whispers. "I always imagined she'd look more like me. But she doesn't at all, really." She shakes her head sadly.

Putting the picture down, she adds, "I suppose you need this back. Gladys can use it as part of her magical mystery solving."

"I'm sure there are other pictures in the trunk," I say quietly. "I don't think anyone will mind if you keep this. It's your property. You're giving it to the police voluntarily."

She nods. "Helen can have it if she needs it." Looking at me, she adds, "You look and smell awful, Tom. Go take a shower."

I smile at this woman I love so much. "Yes, ma'am. Right away."

***

"Helen, I don't know why you're being unreasonable."

I stop with my hand on the doorknob. For one brief terrifying moment, I think my Mom's inside, her trademark nasally whine sending shivers down my spine.

"Lex," Helen says, "I don't know why you're not listening to me."

With a sigh of relief, I open the door to find Helen and the Deputy Mayor—what kind of parents name their kid Lex Luther?—locked in yet another standoff about something.

"Every other department in the state—in the country—has a police chaplain," Helen continues.

"I understand that," Lex says in a placating tone. "And I also understand why you're so reluctant to do this."

"Do what?" I ask. Helen looks at me as Lex turns. "Sorry to interrupt, but I believe since I'm the topic of discussion, I think I have the right to know."

Helen says, her eyes still on me, "Lex, you care to explain?"

"Of course." Clearing his throat, he says, "As police chaplain, Father Greer, you are the only source of spiritual counsel for all twenty-three members of the department. The mayor, as part of her diversity and inclusion initiatives, believes that the police chaplain should represent more than just one narrow tradition."

"And by narrow tradition, you mean the Catholic Church?"

"Precisely," Lex says. "I mean, as a Catholic priest, some of the officers are probably uncomfortable speaking with you about their concerns or any issues they may have."

"Tell me, Lex," Helen says, "has any member of my department complained about Father Greer's performance as police chaplain?"

"Well, not to my knowledge," Lex says. "But it's not a question of his performance—though I have found no record of you ever reviewing his performance—"

"Oh, I am very familiar with Father's performance," Helen says with a smile. "But since he's a volunteer, I didn't think he was under the performance review rules of the rest of the department."

"And that's the other thing. As a volunteer, Father Greer really can't be disciplined for any infraction of department policy."

"OK, that's not true," I say. "Detective Conway's threatened to kick my ass on a couple of occasions for what he called interfering in an investigation."

"Then there's that issue, Father. You seem to spend a lot more time playing detective than you do actually serving as chaplain, if the newspapers and stories I've heard are any indication."

I take a step towards the little Deputy Mayor. "Are you suggesting that I've been neglecting my responsibilities as chaplain?"

"Well, Father," Lex says sarcastically, "I don't see how you could be a proper chaplain when you're constantly trying to show up the professionals."

I take a deep breath. "Helen, Detective Conway, and Gladys Finklestein are the only members of the department who are practicing Catholics. Officer Hallstead was raised Baptist but is now a Unitarian. Her husband, Nick, is an atheist, but not vocal about it. Officer Thompson does not go to church, but his grandmother took him to her Church of God when he was a child. Officer Potter is a practicing Baptist and teaches a Sunday school class. I know the religious preferences or lack thereof of everyone in this building. I know who has had family in the hospital in the last six months. I know who's married, who has a girlfriend or boyfriend, and who's divorced. I know most of their spouses' and children's names, and I have a fair idea of their ages."

I take another step towards the Deputy Mayor, so I'm looking down on him. "Lex, I care for every man and woman in this department. You spoke of my 'playing detective.' Helen has talked to me on more than one occasion about that, as I'm sure she's told you. It's not something I've ever gone out of my way to do. Really, most of the time I get involved, I have a personal connection to either the victim or the accused. I have no interest in trying to 'show up' the professionals. I have the deepest respect for what they do. And if I thought for a minute my getting involved with the odd criminal investigation was harming anyone, or making it impossible to do my job as their chaplain, I'd never tag along on another case."

The Deputy Mayor clears his throat and tugs at his collar. "Well, Father, I certainly will admit you know the men and women in this department very well. But the fact remains that I believe a broader representation of spiritual traditions is warranted. So, I will be recommending to the Mayor that the position of police chaplain be filled on a rotating basis from interested members of the Myerton spiritual community."

Turning to Helen, he adds, "And considering that the current chaplain is soon to be your husband, Chief, I think if you examine the city ordinances concerning personnel, even volunteer positions are covered by the anti-nepotism rule. Which means, whether or not the Mayor accepts my recommendation, you'll need a new chaplain within a couple of months."

Helen and I watch Lex as he picks up his briefcase and walks to the door. "Oh, one more thing," he says. "Any progress on identifying the body?"

"We're hoping to have more later today."

"And the missing money?"

Helen shakes her head. "There's no sign that anything else is buried in the gorge."

"So you're saying the money's not there." Lex shakes his head. "The Mayor is not going to like this. And after all the high hopes she had for you in this position."

He opens the door and I ask, "Why is the Mayor so interested in money from a hundred-year-old bank embezzlement?"

Lex smiles condescendingly. "The publicity, naturally. A cold case solved, money recovered after so long and returned to the rightful owners. The press eats stuff like this up. She'll become the best known mayor in the state."

With that, he floats out the door, closing it behind him. Turning to Helen, I say, "Boy, you really had that guy's number."

"He's going to be a thorn in my backside," she says, shaking her head. "But he is right about one thing. After we're married, you won't be able to be police chaplain anymore."

"Oh, that's OK," I say, walking up to her desk, "I'd rather be married to the Chief than be her chaplain. I mean, it's going to be hard enough being her parish priest."

She smiles at this, but seems guarded. Without looking up at me, she begins to fiddle with some papers on her desk.

"Darling," I say quietly, sitting down across from her, "we need to talk about earlier."

She sighs and covers her face with her hands. "Oh, Tom, I'm so sorry. I have no idea what came over me," she whispers.

"Probably the same thing that came over me," I say, reaching across the desk for her hand.

"When I came up those steps into the attic and saw you, all hot and sweaty and shirtless—"

"—So you do find my unnaturally pale chest attractive," I say with a grin.

"Obviously," Helen says. "I've seen you without a shirt before. But today? It was like I was hypnotized. I couldn't stop myself."

"I almost didn't stop you, darling," I say. "Fortunately, I had the presence of mind to tell you to leave."

"Yeah, thanks for that," Helen says, exhaling.

We stare at each other for a moment. "So, we're good?" I ask.

"Oh, of course," she says. "We just need to be more careful."

"Avoiding temptation and all of that."

"So, just do us both a favor and keep your shirt on. Oh, and no more gray sweats until after we're married."

"Gotcha."

We sit back in our seats and Helen says, "So, you found the trunk."

"Yes, and if the wedding photo is any indication, at least some of its contents concern Theia Stewart."

"Where is it now?"

"Nina Hallstead and Mike Thompson carried it in from my car. It's in the conference room."

"Well," Helen says, standing up, "shall we go see what secrets it contains?"

The look on my face must betray what I'm thinking, because she asks, "What is it, Tom?"

"I'm worried about what we may find, frankly."

She lays her hand on my arm. "You think we might find something that points to Ashton Stewart as his wife's killer?"

"Yes, that," I say. "But there's one thing I know from experience. You uncover one secret, you find others. Secrets are rarely singular."

Sixteen

"It's not as big as I thought it would be," Helen says to me when she sees the trunk.

Gladys erupts in giggles. We turn and give her a disapproving look.

"Ahem, sorry about that," she says, looking sheepish. "Don't know what came over me. Anyway, I need a photograph to get the ball rolling on the virtual reconstruction. More than one is ideal."

"Well, let's take a look," Helen says, putting on gloves. "Edwards, I want you to film the removal of the contents of the trunk, then everything is going to be numbered and photographed."

"Right, Chief," says the young man with a video recorder. As one of the department's crime scene technicians, it's his responsibility to make sure everything is properly catalogued and photographed.

Helen looks at me, then back at the trunk. She lifts the lid and looks inside.

The trunk is about three-quarters full, an assortment of clothing, papers, photographs, and books. There is what's most likely a jewelry box. Donning a pair of gloves myself, I pick up a pistachio green dress, its straight lines typical of the 1920s, with beadwork around the neckline. On seeing it, Gladys squeals, "Oh, what a gorgeous dress! I just love the color."

"It's a little older than you like, isn't it?" Helen asks.

"I wear 1960s, but I'm wild about anything vintage," she says. "Hmm, it gives me an idea for my—" She stops herself and whispers, "Never mind." Taking a deep breath, she says, "What else you got?"

Helen takes out a black photo album, which has a black ribbon tied along the spine to hold the pages. "I think I've got something here you can use."

She begins to open it, but I put out my hand. "Wait. Don't do that. Lay it on the table, very carefully, then open it. It's at least a century old, and we don't want to do any damage."

"Looks OK to me, Dad," Gladys says.

"Looks can be deceiving," I say with a grimace.

"Tom's the expert on this stuff," Helen says. Very carefully, she places the album on the table and opens the cover.

"Hmm," Helen says with a furrowed brow. "She doesn't really look like Anna, does she?"

"No, but her grandmother was a beautiful woman," I say.

"If Anna was as beautiful at this age, I bet she broke a lot of hearts," Gladys says.

Helen and I exchange a quick glance that Gladys, hyper-observant, catches. "What?"

"Huh? Oh, nothing," I say. "Can you do something with this?"

"The photo's in good condition," Gladys says. "Are there others of her?"

Helen turns a couple of pages. "These look to be all of her," she says. "Huh. Just her. Odd."

"What's odd about that?" I ask.

"There's photo after photo of her alone, both indoors and outdoors," she says. "There is none of her husband, or anyone else."

"That is odd," I say. "I wonder who took them?"

"Her husband?"

"That would be my guess," Helen says as she turns more pages.

"Well, let me have the album so I can get to work," Gladys says, holding her hands out.

"Be careful with it," I say. "Anna will want to see this."

"I know what I'm doing, Dad," Gladys says, rolling her eyes. "I'm not a child."

She rolls out of the room and I turn my attention back to the trunk. "There is a lot of stuff in here, but there's no real order to it," I say. "And some of the stuff is just weird. There's just this one dress, no other clothes. And look here," I say, picking up a pair of long white gloves, "just this one pair."

"Maybe they're special—she kept them for sentimental reasons." Helen says.

Looking at the jumbled contents, I say, "Maybe. Or maybe she didn't load the trunk."

"What?"

"Yeah. Helen, women are traditionally more sentimental than men."

"That's a bit of a sexist stereotype, isn't it?"

"Look, let me ask you a question. When you were packing up some of John's personal belongings, the ones that really mattered to you, or things that John gave you, how did you pack them?"

She takes a deep breath. "Very carefully," she says with a pained expression. "I lingered over each item, and then put them in a box."

Touching her shoulder, I say, "I loved Joan as much as you loved John, but in my grief, I just tossed stuff into boxes. No order, no organization, no rhyme or rhythm. Even with all my training as an archivist, as a man, I just didn't have that much sentiment about anything. I just wanted it out of my sight."

"So you think that Ashton Stewart put these things in the trunk after she disappeared?"

"I do," I say. "He did it quickly, like he wanted to purge himself and his surroundings of anything he associated with her. Whether it was grief or guilt, we don't know. That dress may have been one she wore when they courted. The photo album is obvious, as was the wedding picture. The rest of it, well, we'll just have to look at it."

Helen reaches in and pulls out a stack of letters, held together by a satin ribbon. Probably once red, it's now a faded pink. "Love letters," she says with a smile. Turning to me, she says, "Just in case you ever wondered, I kept every card and letter you ever gave me."

"I'm surprised you didn't burn them," I say.

"I thought about it," she sighs, "but I just couldn't bring myself to. I liked to believe the man who wrote those words to me was the real Tom Greer, and not the man who stormed out of my apartment that day."

The shame I feel over that one foolish, stupid act is still with me. "Have you read them at all in the last twenty years?" I ask.

She purses her lips. "Yes. You remember the day you came to the police station to ask about Joan's case?"

"The first time I came? Yes, you put me off until the next day to go shopping for a new dress and to get your hair done," I say with a grin.

"OK," she says, rolling her eyes, "not my finest hour, maybe. But that night I went home and dug them out. I read them, and I kept thinking, 'I always knew he'd come back.'"

I nod, not knowing what to say. We've discussed those first months after I came back to Myerton a number of times, how long-buried feelings for each other percolated to the surface. There's no need to rehash things.

"I wonder what these say?" Helen pulls on one of the ribbons, undoing the bow easily. She removes the ribbon from around the letters and places the stack on the table.

"Be careful," I say as she takes one of the envelopes and begins to open it. "That paper may be fragile."

"I'll be careful, Tom," she replies in a sing-song tone that she uses when she thinks I'm worrying too much. The envelope's been sliced through at the fold. She looks at the front. "No stamp, no return address. Just 'Theia.'"

"He probably left it on her night table or at breakfast," I say. "He wouldn't have mailed it."

Helen nods as she gently slides the letter out of the envelope. It's one page, with only a few lines written. She skims the contents, then exclaims, "Oh, crap-on-a-cracker!"

"That's new," I comment. "What is it?"

"It's a love note, all right," Helen says, handing it to me. "But it's not from Ashton Stewart."

I read the letter, then take a deep breath. "Oh, Lord!" I mutter.

"What did you say about secrets, Tom?"

"Yeah, well, this is a doozy."

The letter, dated March 1927, has only three lines:

My darling, He'll be going to Baltimore on business tomorrow. We'll have a few hours. Can you send the servants away? K.

"K," Helen says. "For Kent Stirling."

Seventeen

"You know what this means, Tom."

I look up from yet another letter written to Theia from K. Helen and I have read a half-dozen over the last thirty minutes, each a heartfelt expression of love mixed with a desperate dissatisfaction with K's marriage to a woman he describes as "half-mad" and "prone to hysterics."

"No, Helen," I say slowly. "I don't."

"Oh, come on, Tom!" Helen exclaims. Picking up the letters, she says, "Kent Stirling was having an affair with Theia Stewart."

"No, it looks like Theia Stewart was having an affair with someone named K. There's no real indication that K is Kent Stirling."

"This one says, 'He's going to Cincinnati on business for the bank for the next three days, and Harriet is going down to Hot Springs with her mother for the week. I can get away to the cabin. Can you meet me there?' Now, who else do you think K could be?"

I take a deep breath. "OK, I admit, but the evidence is circumstantial."

Helen's about to say something, but instead takes a deep breath and smiles. "Tom," she says quietly, "I know this is hard, because of your love for Anna—"

"Helen, this has nothing to do with my love for Anna," I say, shaking my head. "I'm enough of a realist to know that it doesn't look good. That if Theia was having an affair with Kent—and I'll stipulate that as a fact, for now—it gives Ashton a clear motive for murder, assuming he found out. But all you have right now is evidence of the affair, nothing more."

"You forget what the grandson of Kent Stirling told Nate," Helen says, pulling out her phone. She taps and swipes for a moment. "Oh, here it is. According to Roland Crescent, his father told the story of Ashton Stewart, his uncle, coming to the house and telling Stirling's wife, 'you don't know what he took from us!' Nate—everyone in fact—thought he was talking about the money. But what if he was talking about something else?"

I look at the letter in my hand, then at the stack. "You're probably right, but we're missing a big piece of the puzzle."

"Well, you're right about that," Helen says, slumping back in the chair. "How does all this relate to the embezzlement?"

"There's no mention of money at all, at least not yet. There's still a lot of stuff in that trunk."

"Yeah," she says, a pensive look on her face.

I look at her. "Something wrong?"

"One thing I don't get is why he kept all of this. She had an affair. She disappeared at the same time he was betrayed by his closest friend. He never mentioned his wife for the rest of his life.

According to Anna, she was a completely forbidden topic in her home growing up. This is a man who gives every appearance of wanting to forget he was ever married. And yet, he kept it. Why?"

I shrug. "Not an easy answer. Some people—like Mom, for example—just can't bring themselves to get rid of anything. You kept the engagement ring I gave you and the notes I wrote you. You certainly kept things of John—"

"No," she whispers, shaking her head. "My wedding ring, the engagement ring he gave me. But nothing of his."

A tear runs down her cheek, which she wipes away with her hand. "After everything I found in that storage unit—all the porn, the books, the magazines, the DVDs—I went through and boxed up everything of John's, and everything that we bought together."

"What did you do with it?" I ask quietly.

She smiles. "Well, I didn't burn it, which was my first impulse. I gave it to his parents with the excuse that it just brought back too many memories. Which was the truth, but not the whole truth. I felt betrayed. I felt like—well, I've already told you that."

I'm about to give her a comforting hug when someone knocks at the door. "Excuse me, Chief Parr?" We turn and see Edwards, the crime scene technician.

"Yes, Edwards?" Helen says.

"Chief, did you want me to catalog the contents of the trunk? Or would you and Father Greer like more time to look through it?"

Helen's eyes narrow a bit. "No, Edwards," she says coolly. "You can begin. Photograph everything. I want a complete report on my desk first thing tomorrow morning."

"But Chief, it's already close to 4 p.m."

She peers at Edwards. "Do you have a date or something?"

"As a matter of fact," he says, smiling sheepishly. "I do. New girlfriend. It's our four-week anniversary tonight and I have reservations at Scapolli's."

Helen softens at this. "I see. Well, never let it be said I stood in the way of young love. Just photograph and catalog the evidence. You can write the report and give it to me by noon tomorrow."

"Yes, Chief. And thank you," the young man says with a grin.

As he busies himself with his task, Helen and I walk to her office.

"That was very nice of you," I say.

"Well, I figure everyone deserves a chance at true love," she says dramatically.

"You old softy."

"Just don't let it get around. I have a reputation to maintain as a hard-ass."

"Don't worry. Your secret's safe with me."

She opens the door to her office and walks around her desk. Dropping in her chair, she says, "Can I go home yet?"

"You're the Chief," I say. "You can leave whenever you want to. But I was hoping you'd come to the Rectory for a little while."

Helen smiles dreamily. "Tom, that's what I was talking about. My body still lives in my one-bedroom apartment. But my heart is already living at the Rectory with you."

I smile at this. "Only for a little while longer, my darling."

She sighs. "Well, anyway, I'm hungry for Mu Shi. Should we pick up from the Golden Dragon?"

"Sounds good to me." I hesitate before saying, "Anna won't be there."

"Well," she says in that deep voice of hers that drives me crazy, "there won't be a problem as long as you keep your shirt on."

***

Later that night, I'm just drifting off when my phone rings.

For one brief second, I don't recognize the ring. I have hope that it is Helen, or perhaps some poor soul desperate for spiritual succor.

After about five notes even I, tone deaf as I am, recognize the Darth Vader March.

It's my mother.

Saying a quick prayer for strength and patience, I answer, "Hi, Mom, how are you?"

"I'm fine, Tommy, but I am worried about how you are."

This causes me to sit bolt upright in bed with shock. My mother is rarely, if ever, concerned about me, and when she is, it's usually connected in some way to how whatever has happened to me might affect her. After a brief pause, I reply, "I'm fine, Mom. Why do you ask?"

"Well, Diana saw a piece of the internet about a stabbing at a haunted house in Myerton, and she said she thought it had something to do with your church, and you know, you were stabbed a few months ago and they say things like that always come in threes, so I wondered if it might be you."

"No, Mom, it was not me," I say, gratified that she actually cares. "Sadly, it was a lovely young woman in the parish, but she is going to be fine. Everyone involved is either fine or on their way to being fine."

"Except for that poor man who stabbed her, of course," my mother says in a whine. "Diana said he fell on his knife and died."

"That's true, Mom. There was nothing anyone could do."

"You know, Trevor and I were talking over breakfast this morning and he was saying how fragile life is and that you never know when someone might stab you, or even when you might fall on a big knife and die."

"That's true, Mom." Suddenly, the warm and fuzzy feeling I have pops like a soap bubble stuck with a pin when I realize what she just said. "Wait, Mom," I say quickly. "Did—did you say you and Trevor were talking over BREAKFAST?"

"Yes." She pauses and then continues, "Oh, I forgot to tell you. Trevor's living here now."

"He is?" I ask incredulously.

Yup, warm and fuzzy's definitely gone.

"Yes, he moved in after his sister got mad and left."

"What made his sister leave?" I ask before I realize that I really don't want to know.

"Oh, Tommy, I shouldn't say anything about it. Trevor was so upset. But it seems that he stopped by last Friday morning while I was out getting my hair done, and he caught her with a man in her bed. Well, he said he was not putting up with that kind of behavior, not under the roof of a nice lady like me. Then she got mad and moved out. She was gone by the time I got home."

"But why did Trevor move in?"

"Well, you see, it turns out that he didn't really have a place of his own, and was already sleeping on the floor in her room a lot of nights, so he asked if it was OK for him to just move into that room, and I said sure. I mean, it's not like you're ever going to need it again."

"I—I—"

"Besides, as he pointed out, it's just not safe for an older woman like me to live alone in this day and age."

"I see." I don't actually, mainly because I have the eyes of my mind shut tight, but what else can I say? "I guess it's good that you have someone there to look after you."

"Oh, yes. As Trevor says, 'We take care of each other.'"

"OK, well, that sounds like an, um, convenient arrangement to me."

"That's what we think."

"Sure."

"Oh, I've got to go, Tommy. Trevor's taking a shower and is calling me. I'd better go find out what he wants. Bye."

She hangs up before I can say anything else, which is good, since I really can't think of anything else to say.

Eighteen

"Sounds like Nola's got herself a boytoy."

I slam my spoon down on the table. "Helen, that's not funny," I say, even as she begins to laugh.

"Oh, come on, Tom," she says with a grin. "I was just pulling your chain a little."

"It's damn odd—sorry, Anna—if you ask me," I say as I plunge my spoon into my oatmeal—with blueberries this time. It's good, but I'm eyeing Helen's bacon like I usually eye her.

"Of course it's odd, Tom," Anna says as she drinks her coffee. "It's your Mom we're talking about."

"Seriously, though," Helen says, "aren't you concerned about this?"

"Of course I am," I say with a shrug. "But there's not a lot I can do right now. I'm not even sure what their relationship is, exactly."

"Do you think they're—"

"Please, Helen, I'm eating." I look across the table at Anna. "I've never been as thankful for Bill as I am now, Anna. If you started seeing someone half your age, I'm not sure what I'd do."

"Don't you mean half your age?" Anna says with a smile. "You sound like I couldn't attract someone like Trevor."

I stare at her, my spoon suspended in space, and realize there is no good way for me to answer that question.

So, I decide to change the subject. To Helen, I say, "What's on the Chief's agenda for today?"

"You mean, besides a meeting with the Mayor and Deputy Mayor," Helen says, rolling her eyes. "I hope we'll have a preliminary report on those remains."

"I haven't asked Tom, but what did you find when you opened the trunk?" Anna asks.

I catch Helen out of the corner of my eye. "You know it does no good not to tell her," I say.

"Anna," Helen says carefully, "we found a photo album, full of pictures of Theia Stewart. Gladys is scanning those now. We hope we can do a virtual reconstruction using the skull."

"Good," Anna says. "Go on."

"Among other things, we found letters. Now we've just begun to go through them, but they appear to be love letters to Theia Stewart."

Anna takes a deep breath. "From the look on your face," she says quietly, "I take it they're not from Ash."

"No," I say. "We think they're from Kent Stirling."

Anna nods. "After she and my grandfather married, right?"

Helen and I both nod.

Anna picks up her coffee mug and stares at it for a moment. "I guess that makes Grandpa your prime suspect."

"Now, Anna," I say before Helen can speak, "he may not even have known."

"He knew, Tom," Anna says firmly. "He knew. He knew and he killed her. Nate wrote it in his article. He confessed to knowing when he went to see his sister."

"But even if he knew, Anna," Helen says, "it doesn't mean he killed her."

"Who then?" Anna asks with surprising calm.

Helen shakes her head. "We may never know for sure."

Anna pushes back her chair and stands up. "Well," she says as she walks over to the sink to wash out her cup, "anyway, I'd like the trunk and its contents back when you're done with them. Tom, don't forget you've got that working lunch with the Ministerial Association."

"Right, thanks for reminding me," I say. To Helen, I say, "It's about the Thanksgiving lunch. Can you be there?"

"I'll try, assuming my meeting ends in time. Where is it?

"It's at Clark's church. It's his turn to host the meeting. Listen, if you can't get there, it's really no big deal."

"If I can't, I'll send Nina. Isn't Nick making dessert?"

I pull out my phone. "According to the email he sent me, a dozen pumpkin and a half-dozen pecan pies. That's not including the pie I'm getting for us, of course."

Helen grins. "I love doing dessert, but his is always better. By the way, did you ever figure out what you want for your groom's cake?"

"All taken care of," I say.

"What did you decide?"

I start to tell her, then change my mind. "You know, I think I'll surprise you."

Helen shrugs. "Fine with me. I like surprises."

***

"Tom, Reverend Huckleberry's here to see you."

I look up from my notes about the Thanksgiving dinner, preparing for the meeting with my fellow Myerton clergy. "Did I have an appointment with him?" I ask.

"No, and he apologizes for the interruption, but promises it shouldn't take long."

I stand up. "OK, send him in."

Anna opens the door and allows in a corpulent man with a red face, no hair, and an earnest look. The Reverend Dexter Huckleberry runs a small non-denominational church just outside the town limits. Before he discovered a call to the ministry, word is he participated in a number of multi-level marketing businesses, selling everything from vitamins to cleaning products to men's grooming aids. He still comes off as more of a salesman than a minister, but I've found him relatively harmless.

Even if he refuses to call me Father.

"Reverend Huckleberry," I say, extending my hand. "This is a surprise."

"Reverend Greer," he says, his grin revealing a well-capped set of teeth. "As I told your secretary, this won't take long. I just wanted to get things settled before the meeting."

"What things settled?" I ask as I offer him a chair.

He settles in and folds his hands on his sizable belly. "This thing with Steve Austin."

"Yes, it's like I said in my email to everyone. Steve's donating a soda machine and offered to help on Thanksgiving."

"So he plans on being there?"

I pause for a moment. "Since he's offered to help, I can say that's a fair chance."

"Oh, no," he says, shaking his head. "No, no, no, that's not acceptable at all."

"I don't understand."

"I was afraid of that, Reverend Greer, since your Church has shown itself far too tolerant of perversion over the years. Just to spell it out, Steve Austin is a homosexual, isn't he?"

I'm doing my best to ignore the slap at the Church when I say, "Where did you hear that?"

"One of my congregation told me," he said. "He has a cousin who frequents Mr. Austin's establishment—a very sad case, honestly, and a matter of prayer for his entire family—and apparently mentioned the fact."

"I'd be interested to know how he found out?" I say with a smile. "So, you're getting this third-hand."

"I am, I am. I don't know the man personally, of course, since I do not associate with his kind."

"Bartenders?"

"Sodomites!" he declares with a self-righteous air.

"But you're OK with bartenders?" I say.

"I am not OK with anyone who breaks God's laws. Leviticus states that a man may not lie—"

"I am well aware of the verse, sir," I say. "Look, just spit it out. Why are you here?"

"I'm here," he says, pointing a fat finger at me, "to persuade you to tell Mr. Austin he's not welcome at the Thanksgiving luncheon."

Folding my hands on my desk, I cock my head to one side. "Now, why exactly would I do that? Mr. Austin has graciously volunteered to help with a luncheon for the entire community. I have accepted, on behalf of the Association. And, since Saint Clare's is hosting this year, and I have always been clear that he is always welcome at my church, he will be there."

"I cannot understand why you'd allow someone like that to be around children. I mean, who knows what he'll do. Those people have no sense of decency."

"Are you afraid he'll try to kiss you, Dex?" I ask sarcastically. "I mean, if he does, I'll admit to being a little hurt, since I've known him longer and he's never—"

"How can you take this whole thing so lightly!" Huckleberry declares.

"It's not the situation I'm taking lightly, Dex, it's you. What you're suggesting I do is ridiculous, not to mention un-Christian."

Huckleberry's red in the face by this time. Struggling to his feet, he says, "Well, I'm sorry. But I'm going to bring this to the Association today to vote on."

I rise and say, "Be my guest. Now, if you'll excuse me, I have a lot of work to do."

I sit down and return to my reading. I don't even know Huckleberry's gone until I hear the front door slam.

"Well, that was unpleasant," Anna says when she walks in.

"Huckleberry usually is," I say leaning back in my chair. "I should have seen this coming, though. His church is pretty anti-gay, which is ironic since I think Clark told me he's on wife number four."

Anna shrugs. "Hypocracy's nothing new. So, what are you going to do?"

I look at her. "I'm going to call Clark to give him a heads up. Maybe together we can think of something."

***

"Well, now that we've finished eating," Clark says, "let's get down to business."

As we talked about, I'm sitting next to Clark, who is sitting at the head of the table as both host and chairman of the Association this year. My eye is on the door, expecting someone to come in any minute.

"I think I can speak for everyone here, Clark," Ezekiel Thompson, pastor of the Bethel AME Church, says, "when I say please pass on to the ladies of your church our thanks for a truly delicious meal."

"I will," Clark says. "Viv will be particularly pleased to hear it."

"The food was truly delicious, sir," Officer Nina Hallstead says. Helen's meeting went over, she told me, so she sent Nina in her place. She's the only woman in the room, and by far the tallest person here.

"Well, as I say, it's our privilege to host this month," Clark says. "Dex, I think it's your turn next month?"

"That all depends on what happens in the next few moments," Huckleberry booms.

"Oh, dear," Clark says, "is there a problem?"

Struggling to his feet, Huckleberry says, "There most certainly is, one that the Reverend Greer doesn't seem to be taking seriously."

Clark turns to me and asks, "Tom, why have you upset our brother in Christ?"

"I've done nothing, Clark," I say. "We just have a little disagreement."

"Excuse me, gentlemen," Rabbi Caleb Blau says. "Can you enlighten the rest of us?"

"Certainly, Caleb," Huckleberry says. "To put it bluntly, I am deeply concerned that Reverend Greer has allowed a known homosexual to infiltrate our community Thanksgiving banquet."

"Reverend Huckleberry," Hallstead says, "I want to assure you that, in spite of my physical appearance, I am completely heterosexual, as my husband can attest. Though I will admit during my MMA days, I received numerous proposals of marriage from fans, many of them women."

I try my best to keep from laughing as Huckleberry sputters, "Officer, I am not referring to you. No, I am most certainly not. I am referring to Mr. Steve Austin."

"Sorry I'm late, Clark," Steve says as he walks into the room. "I had to finish some things up."

"Oh, no problem, Steve," Clark says. "We were just getting started."

"What—what is he doing here?" Huckleberry wheezes.

"Steve? Oh, I'm sorry, Dex, I guess you didn't get the email. Steve is the Chamber of Commerce's representative for the Thanksgiving lunch this year."

Huckleberry's eyes pop and he looks at Steve, who flashes him a grin and extends his hand. "Have we met? You look a little familiar," he says.

"No! No, we have not met!" Huckleberry declares.

"Are you sure? I've got a good memory for faces."

Huckleberry's struck dumb by Steve, who sits down at the table. "Now, what did I miss?"

Huckleberry's about to speak when I say, "Nothing of any importance, Steve."

Recovering himself, Huckleberry says, "That's not true! And my objection hasn't changed!" Turning to Steve, he asks, "Are you a homosexual?"

"Why? Are you?" Steve replies.

"No! Absolutely not! I—how dare you accuse me!"

"Hey, I was just wondering if you were looking for a date or something," Steve says, holding up his hands. "But you are seriously not my type."

"So you admit you're a homosexual!" Huckleberry declares with a tone of triumph.

"Well, yeah," he shrugs. "Though that's the least interesting thing about me. I guess the most interesting thing is I'm a trained Army Ranger with three tours of Afghanistan under my belt."

"Awesome," Hallstead whispers, the tone of admiration clear in her voice.

"But you are gay?" Huckleberry asks.

"Yeah. Now, there have been times I've found women attractive, though I haven't slept with any in a very long time."

"I prefer not to know your sordid history, sir!"

"Hey, you started this," Steve says.

"What is your point, Dex?" Clark says.

"Brothers," Huckleberry says, "this Thanksgiving luncheon has been sponsored by the Ministerial Association since 1929 to give the poor, needy, and lonely of Myerton and the surrounding area a little joy and happiness at this time of year. It's always been a Christian event, supported by the Christian churches of the area."

"Excuse me, Reverend," Rabbi Blau says, "but Mount Zion has participated since 1952."

Huckleberry inclines his head. "My apologies, Rabbi. But the fact remains that people of faith have been responsible for this event. And to now allow a known sinner a place of prominence—"

"So, Dexter," I say, "your objection is to Steve as a sinner, not as a homosexual?"

"Well—well, I suppose—"

"And, you're trying to say that a sinner shouldn't have anything to do with the Thanksgiving dinner, is that correct?"

"Finally, you understand, Reverend Greer," Huckleberry says.

"Oh, well, in that case," I say, "I'm afraid Saint Clare's can't host this year."

There's a murmur around the table as I say, "If people who have sinned can't participate, then how can I? I mean, I've sinned."

"And I can no longer serve as the chair of the Association," Clark says. "Viv has a list of mine."

Around the table, our fellow ministers nod their heads. Looking at Huckleberry, I say, "I hope you can handle the dinner on your own, Reverend, you and your lovely wife, Sheila."

Steve thumps the table. "I knew I'd seen you before!" he says, pointing at Huckleberry. "You used to come in with Sheila Quales all the time. I'd heard she'd divorced Zach and married someone else. I didn't know—"

"I have no idea what you're talking about," Huckleberry roars. "I've never been in your establishment. I do not drink!"

"Well, I am glad to hear you gave it up," Steve says. "The way you used to tie one on, I tell you what, I was worried about you."

Huckleberry's mouth is open. He sputters something unintelligible, then gathers up his things and marches from the room.

We're all looking at each other when Clark says, "Well, it appears that Dex had a meeting, or something suddenly came up. Shall we go on to our first item of business?"

Nineteen

I'm driving to the hospital to do my weekly visits when my phone starts playing 'Eye of the Tiger.'

Helen's special ring. Probably after we're married, I'll change it to 'Hallelujah.' It doesn't seem appropriate until then.

"Hey," I answer. "How was your meeting?"

"About twice as long as it had to be," Helen says. "Basically, it consisted of the Mayor telling me that she wanted me to 'tighten up' on my officers and increase the department's commitment to diversity and inclusion."

"We've heard those two words a lot lately," I point out. "What did you say?"

"Not much I could say. I told her that I was going to form a task force to study the issue and make recommendations to me within 90 days on how to implement a diversity and inclusion program."

I furrow my brow. "This is the first I'm hearing about it."

"Well, I had to think of something on the fly," Helen says. "So, whether they know it or not, Hallstead, Gladys, Potter, and Cohen are the committee."

"Why Cohen?"

"Frankly? He's the only gay officer I could think of off the top of my head."

"Ah," I say, nodding my head. "Well, we had an interesting lunch."

"Yeah, Nina told me," Helen says. "In case you hear a whooshing sound, that's me rolling my eyes. What is Huckleberry's problem with Steve?"

"Best I can figure, his only issue is Steve's orientation," I say. "Though I doubt we'll be seeing much of Dexter Huckleberry around the Ministerial Association, much less the Thanksgiving luncheon. Hey, I'm headed to the hospital. Can you join me?"

"As much as I would love to, darling, I've got a desk full of paperwork and a century-old murder case to work on."

I grip my phone a little tighter. "Any more on that?"

"Just the preliminary report from the forensic anthropologist." The sound of keys clicking comes through the phone. "He says the bones are consistent with those of a white female in her early twenties, probably well-to-do from the condition of her teeth, who was pregnant. The cause of death was a fall of approximately 100 feet, given the injuries to her skull."

"So, the fall killed her," I say. "But no indication if she was pushed or not."

"No, but there is something a little odd," Helen says. "According to the anthropologist, she suffered a fractured wrist before she died. Now, he can't tell how long before she died, but it was definitely not caused by the fall.

"That is interesting," I mutter. "Any word on the money?"

"I wish people would stop asking that!" she exclaims. "No. The money is definitely not buried there. At least not anymore."

I sigh. "Oh, well. I guess you can't answer all the questions all the time."

"How profound, Father," she says with a tinge of snark. "Maybe you should include it in one of your homilies."

"Now, there's no reason to get snippy."

"Sorry. I'm hungry."

"Then eat something," I say, thinking I'm being reasonable.

"Really? Eat something? Wow, you're just a bundle of wisdom today."

"Helen," I say with exasperation. "What do you want me to say?"

She takes a deep breath and says, "Sorry, Tom. I'm just—frustrated, I guess. I hate unanswered questions, and I'm afraid I'm going to have a lot of them in this case."

"All I can say, darling, at the risk of provoking you to snark more, is if you're not getting any answers right now, maybe ask different questions."

"And how do you propose I do that?" she asks.

"Hey, you're the professional, remember?" I say with a grin.

"Ha-ha, very funny. I'll see you tonight. You're cooking, right?"

"Chicken and dumplings, Grandmother Greer's recipe."

"Oooh, I can hardly wait. Love you."

"Love you, too," I say before hanging up.

I pull into the clergy parking space not far from the hospital entrance and look out my front window for a moment.

"Ask different questions," I mutter to myself. "Ask different questions. What *do* I mean?"

I shake my head and get out of my car, reminding myself once again that Helen's the detective, I'm the priest, and I have my own work to do.

But even as I walk through the doors of the hospital, the question still nags at me.

I'm so preoccupied that I don't notice Bridget Davis and her son Terry walk off the elevator until Terry calls my name.

"Hi, Father Tom," he says, jarring me out of my thoughts.

"Terry, hi," I say with a smile. "Hi, Bridget. What are you doing here? No problems, I hope?"

Bridget is positively beaming as she says, "Oh, no, none at all. Terry had a follow-up with the plastic surgeon and the orthopedic surgeon. Both say everything's great."

"Mom, can I go wait outside for Steve?"

"Sure, honey, but don't go too far."

"I won't!" he calls as he runs out the front door.

"He seems like he's doing better," I comment.

Bridget nods, a slight smile on her face. "We all are, Father," she says. "Especially Terry. I need to call Miriam and thank her for what Catherine said to him."

"Oh," I say warily. "Terry told you about that?"

"He barely got in the car when I picked him up before he did. He'd been so worried about Rusty, about him being in hell forever, that knowing he'll see him again in heaven someday really turned things around for him. I have to admit, it's a comfort to me, too. I mean, even after everything he did to me and the kids, I just can't bring myself to wish him in hell."

"We should never wish that on anyone," I say, "though from personal experience, I can tell you it's hard."

"Did you feel that way about the woman who shot Chief Parr?"

"I've struggled with that, yes," I say. "But most of the time, I've overcome it."

Bridget nods. "I also have to say, Steve's been great to have around. Terry's had such a bad example of a man for a father, it's good he gets to be around a good one now."

Before I can say anything, Bridget looks at me and says, "Steve told me about your conversation with him."

I shake my head. "Bridget, please understand—"

"Oh, Father Tom," she says, still smiling, "there's no need to explain. I have to admit when Steve first told me I was a little put out with you. But he helped me to see that you were just concerned that I didn't get hurt by—well, by falling in love with a man who couldn't return my feelings."

"Steve told me you asked him if he was gay?"

She laughs. "I felt foolish, really. I knew it was none of my business, but it's something I had to know."

"I'm curious. Why?"

She takes a deep breath. "To protect myself from getting hurt," she says quietly. "You see, Steve's the kind of guy I could fall for very easily. Kind, sweet, generous, soft-spoken, not to mention unspeakably good-looking. Basically, he's the complete opposite of Rusty. But knowing he's gay, well, it lets me be myself around him without worrying. I don't have to guard myself around Steve. It's kind of a relief to know that romance isn't ever going to be a factor in any relationship we have."

"What is your relationship?" I ask.

"Friends. In a short time, we've become good friends, probably because we're both outcasts. Him, from his family, not to mention much of society still. Me, from my family, even my friends, even though they're much too polite to say so."

"Now, Bridget," I say softly, "you're not an outcast. The parish cares about you and your family very much."

She laughs a short, little laugh. "I know, but the fact remains, the moment Rusty died, I became an outcast. It's OK, Father. I harbor no resentment or anger about that. And I know they'll come around in a while. Or maybe I'll stop feeling that way. But for now?" She just shakes her head.

"Is that why you haven't been to Mass recently?" I ask quietly.

"Partly. Please know how grateful I am for everything you and everyone else have done for us. But I'm just not ready. Not sure when I'll be."

Through the glass doors, we see Steve pull up in his truck. He gets out, comes around, lifts Terry up, and spins him around, the boy laughing as he does.

"I can't remember the last time he laughed like that," Bridget says softly. "That's worth the whole world to me. I'll see you later, Father."

"God bless, Bridget," I say as she walks away. I see her go through the doors and stop in front of Steve. I can't hear what they're saying, but he opens the door for her, lifts Terry into the cab, and helps Bridget climb in. As he turns, he catches my eye and gives me a little wave.

I wave back, wondering again about how such a good man can be vilified for being who he is, and remembering a time when I was not nearly so good.

*****

There are only a few parishioners in the hospital who need my attention.

Unfortunately, one of them is Gloria MacMillian.

"Thanks for coming to see me on my deathbed, Father," she says, pitifully.

"Well, as soon as I heard, I rushed over," I say with my best caring, pastoral tone.

OK, I lied. I heard this two days ago. I've been steeling myself for the experience.

"It means a lot to a weak old woman to have someone care about her so much," she sighs. "I'm alone in the world, you know, Father."

"That's not true, Grandma," her long-suffering granddaughter-in-law, Serenity MacMillian, says patiently.

"I'm just a burden to everyone," she whines.

"Not everyone," Serenity mutters. "Just. Me."

"She and that no good grandson of mine—"

"—Don't talk about Bob like that—!"

"—just want to get rid of me," she says. "I've heard them talking in whispers about disposing of the old woman."

"We've never said anything like that!" Serenity exclaims. To me, she says, "Father Tom, you know how we've cared for her for years. And I'm not going to lie—it hasn't been easy. But we've done it because we felt it was our responsibility. But the kids really require more attention the older they get, and caring for her has just gotten too much."

"They want to stick me in an old folks home and forget about me!" Gloria yells.

"We want to put her in Mountain View Assisted Living," Serenity says.

"Oh, several members of the parish live there," I say. "It's a beautiful facility."

"Who wants to live with a bunch of old farts?" Gloria mumbles. "I'm not old."

"Yes, you are!" Serenity explodes. "Grandma, you're eighty-five. You can't get around as well as you used to. You complain about how loud the kids are all the time. It's just not working anymore."

"Mrs. MacMillian, it sounds like Serenity and Bob are just trying to do what's best for you," I say.

"Huh! Selfish brats! Well, if you don't want me anymore, Serenity, I'll just move in with AJ!"

Serenity's mouth falls open. "AJ? You've got to be kidding me!"

"Who's AJ?" I ask.

"One of Bob's younger brothers," Serenity says to me. "He was there at the Bazaar when she won that painting."

I remember. They were carrying the painting when then-Officer Cupcake started barking, indicating drugs somewhere. Both grandsons looked panicked, probably thinking the German shepherd had caught a whiff of something they had. Instead, of course, Cupcake found the drugs hidden in the painting.

That's how Dan and I wound up locked in the Rectory basement by a gun-wielding Martin Maycord, but that's another story.

"AJ will be glad to have me," Gloria says. "Such a good boy."

"He's told you you could move in with him?" Serenity asks, crossing her arms.

"Well, not in so many words, but I know he'll love to have me. You just call him and tell him to start moving my things out of your place and into his. I'll go there straight from here, when those quacks let me out."

She settles into her bed. "Now, you two get out of here," she says. "I need rest."

Serenity and I leave quickly, grateful for the chance to escape. "Well, that was interesting."

"Oh, Father," Serenity says, shaking her head. "This is going to end so badly."

"What do you mean?"

She takes a deep breath. "I don't know what I mean, exactly," she says. "It's just a feeling. AJ's just this side of a criminal, and not very bright, besides. No, Father, this is one of the worst ideas she's ever had."

"Maybe you can talk her out of it?" I say.

"Oh, no," Serenity says, shaking her head. "It may be a bad idea, but I'm grabbing the chance to get that old woman out of my house!"

I open my mouth to gently admonish her, then think better of it.

Twenty

"Well, that's that, then," Helen says quietly.

We're in Gladys' state-of-the-art office, looking at the large screen on her wall displaying a 3D virtual reconstruction of the face that once belonged to the skull that landed so unceremoniously at Dan's feet.

"It's definitely Theia Stewart," I say. "Helen, what do we do now?"

She shakes her head. "Well, I'm actually not sure. The Mayor is going to want to hold a press conference, so I should let her know we have a positive ID. But beyond that, I'm not sure where the investigation should go. We've gone as far as the evidence can take us. Beyond that—I'll need to think."

"We need to tell Anna," I say.

"I know," Helen nods. "Can you call her, ask her to come down here?"

I'm about to say yes, when Gladys says, "Um, yeah, about that . . . "

"What, Gladys?" Helen asks.

Gladys takes a deep breath and blurts out, "Well, as soon as I got the file and saw the reconstruction, I got so excited and I knew she'd want to know, so I kinda called and told her and she's probably here by now."

I expect Helen to give Gladys a stern lecture, but instead she just shakes her head. "I'll tell the front desk to send her on up."

"I'm right here, Helen."

We all turn and see Anna standing in Gladys' doorway, accompanied by Officer Hallstead.

"Nina was kind enough to show me where Gladys' office is," Anna explains.

"Of course," Helen says with a smile. "Thank you, Hallstead."

"My pleasure, Chief," she says with a nod before returning to her duties.

"So," Anna says as she walks in, "Gladys said you had something to show—" She stops when she sees the image on the big screen.

"It's the facial reconstruction of the skull," Gladys says. "With the measurements of the skull, and comparing with a 3D image compiled from the photographs of Theia Stewart, they were able to do this."

Anna just stares at the image of her grandmother for a while without saying anything. She walks around Gladys' desk so she gets a closer look.

"I always wondered where I got my cleft chin," she says quietly. "Obviously not from her." Over her shoulder, she says, "There's no possibility this is wrong, Gladys?"

"There's always a statistical possibility—nothing's 100 percent—but there's less than a 1/100th chance the program's wrong."

"So it's definite, then," Anna says. "Those bones—it is my grandmother."

"Yes, Anna," Helen says.

Anna nods, but says nothing. After a few moments looking at her face, she turns around. "Is there anything else you need the bones for?"

"No," Helen says. "They can be released, just like any other body."

"I see," Anna says. "Tom, I'll want to discuss the funeral with you. Grandma Theia deserves a funeral Mass, after all this time."

"Of course, Anna," I say quietly. "Find a date and make the arrangements. Do you want me to contact Myerton Cemetery?"

She shakes her head. "I'll do it. I think there's space by Grandpa's grave. That's where I want her buried."

"Sure. That makes sense."

"Helen," Anna says, "what's next?"

Helen takes a deep breath. "The Mayor is probably going to hold a press conference to announce the identification. I'll be there. Before you ask, I'll make sure to emphasize that we still have no idea who was responsible for her death."

"Oh, I appreciate that," Anna says, waving her hands. "But it won't matter. Everyone will say it was Grandpa, and they'll probably be right. I'm making too much out of all this anyway."

She walks to the door. "You'll have to make your own plans for dinner tonight, you two. Bill's taking me out."

Without another word, Anna walks out of Gladys' office, her head held high. But I can see the sag in her shoulders.

"Poor Anna," Gladys says. "Isn't there anything you can do, Mom?"

"What do you suggest?" Helen says with exasperation.

"How about we figure out who killed her?"

"Now you sound like Anna. Look, Gladys—"

"Wait, Helen," I say, holding up my hand. "You may not be able to say definitively who killed Theia Stewart, but you don't really need to, do you?"

"I'm not sure I follow."

"Look, the likeliest suspect is Ash Stewart, based on the idea that he found out about the affair between Theia and Kent Stirling, right?"

"Right," Helen says.

"But there are two problems with that. One, we don't know he knew about it before Theia was killed."

"But there's what Roland Crescent told Nate," Gladys says.

"And that's based on something Roland's father told him. But his father was only five years old when he heard it. Besides, by the time he told Roland, he was already bitter against the man because of what he did to him and his mother."

"OK, what's the second problem?" Helen asks.

"We haven't asked who else might have had motive," I say.

Helen breaks into a grin. "And so, all we have to do is provide another possible suspect who had motive and means."

"Precisely."

"Boy, Dad," Gladys says, "you are good at this."

"OK, Tom," Helen says, beginning to pace. "Other than Ash, the only one with motive for murder was Harriet Stirling."

"The only one that we know of," I say.

"We only need one," Helen says. "You said there's a diary of hers at the college, right?"

"Right," I say. "Maybe she wrote something that will give us a clue."

"You might want to interview Roland," Gladys says. "Nate can go with you. He trusts Nate."

"Have you looked at the letters anymore?" I ask.

"I have," Gladys says. "I've scanned them into the system, along with a diary Theia kept."

"Anything jump out at you?" Helen says, remembering that Gladys' eidetic memory means she's memorized the contents of each and every page.

"It's really sad," Gladys says. "Theia and Kent were not happy in their marriages. Theia complains that Ash is distant and works long hours at the bank—apparently, days would go by and she'd only see him at breakfast. She talks about how lonely she is, and how Kent's the first man to really care about her—she refers to him by name in her diary, which was kind of stupid, if you ask me.

"Kent, for his part, describes his marriage as 'hellacious' and 'a mistake from the beginning.' There's one letter where he talks about these wild mood swings Harriet would have, shopping sprees she'd go on, and how she didn't get out of bed for days at a time."

"Sounds like she had bipolar disorder," I say. Since finding out about Joan's diagnosis, I've done a fair amount of reading on the topic, trying to understand her better but also giving me the knowledge to help others who have a family member with a mental illness.

"She may have, only the understanding of mental illness was not as advanced as it was now," Gladys says. "It's strange, because Kent expresses real affection for his wife, even as he was carrying on an affair with his best friend's wife."

"Anything that indicates he told Theia of his plan to steal the money?" Helen says.

"Nothing direct, but one of the last letters says—here, I'll pull it up." Gladys taps a few keys and a handwritten letter appears on screen. "This last paragraph," she says as she blows up the referred-to portion, "Kent wrote, 'We need to seize this opportunity, my light. This chance may never come again.' This letter is dated a couple of days before the money arrived at the bank."

"Hmm, so he saw the money as his way of getting out of Myerton," Helen says, "getting away from their unhappy marriages and starting over somewhere else."

"There's your motive for the robbery," I say.

"It's actually quite romantic," Gladys says, "if you overlook the whole adultery part."

"There's nothing romantic about adultery, Gladys," I say. "I don't care what the reason is, there's no excuse for cheating on someone you're married to."

"Hey, Dad," Gladys says, "I know that. Just so we're clear, even when I was—well, you know—I drew the line at someone who was married. No, I didn't want to be that person."

"In any event," Helen says, "that doesn't help Ash Stewart's case. Between the affair and the theft, he had more than enough reason to kill his wife."

"Is there any indication she had anything to do with the robbery?" I ask Gladys.

"No, none at all," she answers.

"He may not have told her his plan," Helen says.

"OK," I say, looking at the letter. "So Theia Stewart and Kent Stirling find themselves in unhappy marriages. Who knows how it started—probably innocently enough, two people crying on each other's shoulder. But at some point, they begin an affair. Ash is so busy, he doesn't notice what's going on. And Harriet has her own struggles, so she doesn't notice. At some point, Kent sees an opportunity, and tells Theia they have a chance at a life together. He steals the railroad payroll and—and then, what?"

"What, indeed," Helen says. "Kent Stirling, the money, and Theia Stewart go missing. Almost a hundred years later, Theia Stewart's remains are unearthed, but there's no sign of the money. Or Kent Stirling."

"Which is really strange," Gladys says, "considering he wrote Harriet that note saying that what he stole was buried in the gorge."

"Maybe he was trying to throw people off his trail," Helen says.

"But until Nate found that note in Harriet Stewart's papers," I point out, "no one knew about the gorge."

We look at each other for a moment. Finally, Helen says, "Well, we're not going to get any answers standing here looking at each other. Let's go, Tom."

"Go? Go where?"

"Your old stomping grounds," she says. "Let's see if we can get a few answers."

Twenty-One

"How can you stand the quiet?" Helen whispers.

I look at her. "It's a library, Helen," I whisper. "It's supposed to be quiet."

"Maybe, but give me a shooting range any day."

I roll my eyes and shake my head as Gwen brings the one box of Harriet Stirling's papers to our table.

"Here you go Father, Chief," she says quietly.

"Thanks, Gwen," I say.

Gwen nods, then says to Helen, "Sorry, Chief Parr, that I haven't called you. It's just—I mean, with classes and working two jobs—"

"Don't worry about it. It's fine," Helen says with a smile. "It's an open invitation—though I won't be available the last week in December and the first week in January."

Gwen looks perplexed, then her face lights up. "Oh! Of course! You'll be on your honeymoon. Wow. So—just, so—"

"Gwen!" the research room supervisor hisses.

"Sorry, I've gotta go," she says, and scurries off.

Helen looks at me quizzically. "She's a fan," I explain.

"Oh, I didn't realize that when I met her," Helen sighs. "Still, seems like a nice young woman. Just out of curiosity—"

"Oh, yes, she did."

"What did you tell her?"

"What we tell everyone."

"How did she react?"

"Same way everyone does."

"This is getting old, you know?"

"I know, I know."

I open the box and pull out Harriet Stirling's diary. It's a green, cloth-bound volume about five inches by eight inches. There's nothing on the outside to indicate what it is—the only reason I know it's her diary is because that's what the collection's description says.

"Well, Harriet," I say, "let's see what you have to say."

I open the book—and stop.

"What the frankincense and myrrh, Tom?" Helen hisses.

"What indeed, Helen," I say.

The writing isn't writing at all. It's line after line of squiggles, loops, curves, circles, boxes.

I turn one page, then the next, and then the next. "That's all that's here," I whisper. "Just these strange symbols."

"Is it some kind of code, do you think?"

"Maybe, but why would she write her diary in code?"

"Paranoia?" Helen asks. At my look, she adds, "She did have a breakdown, Tom, and you said it sounded like she had bipolar disorder."

"Well, there is that," I say, continuing to flip pages. "It doesn't look like there's any kind of pattern at all, just a series of random shapes."

"Maybe Gladys can make sense of it—or at least her computers can."

"Well, if they can't," I say, "then we'll have no way of knowing if she knew about her husband's affair or not."

Closing the diary, I stand and say, "I'm going to see about getting this scanned. Then we need to figure out what to do next."

"I already have," Helen says. "We need to talk to Roland Crescent. Maybe he can shed some light onto all of this."

"We'll have to bring Nate, you know?" I say.

"I know," Helen sighs. "Maybe the drive won't be too bad."

***

Fortunately, Gladys comes with us when we go to Baltimore the next day to talk to Harriet and Kent Stirling's only known descendant.

"So far I've come up with squat," Gladys says. "The few pages I've run through my decryption program are still gibberish. I don't think there's a code there at all."

"Maybe it is a code," Nate says, "but it's so complex, only she knew how to read it. Maybe it's like the Voynich manuscript."

"No, Bae," Gladys says. "It's nothing like the Voynich manuscript. I'm telling you, there's no code."

"If there's no code, then why did she write it?"

"I don't know, Nate," she exclaims. "She did have mental problems. Maybe she was just cuckoo for cocoa puffs!"

"That's awfully insensitive, Gladys."

"I'm sorry, but you're about to drive me crazy with this coded manuscript nonsense!"

They continue in this vein until Helen says, "Guys, can you go back to arguing about Nate hiring a hooker, because I've had enough of this."

"Helen," I say, shaking my head.

"Sorry, Mom," Gladys says, glaring at Nate, "but you know how a man can be when he gets an idea in his head."

"Uh-huh, I do."

"What does that mean?" I ask, barely concealing my hurt.

"Oh, come on, Tom," Helen laughs, "do you really want me to give you the list?"

I open my mouth to say something in my defense, then change my mind. "No. When you're right, you're right."

"So, Nate," Helen says, "how did you find Roland Crescent again?"

"I was on one of those genealogy websites, trying to find any trace of Kent Stirling that I could," Nate says. "All the information I could find was up to 1928. He was born in Dahlonega, Georgia, in 1899, son of tenant farmers, served in World War I, decorated for bravery—you know the rest."

"So he just disappears after he stole the money?" I ask.

"Almost to the day, Father. So, anyway, I came across Roland asking for any information about Kent Stirling, so I contacted him, thinking maybe he had some information about what happened. He called me, really excited to talk to me. And talk he did—more rambled, I guess, most of it was a catalog of woe mixed in with a diatribe against Ashton Stewart. I spent three hours with him. Helen, I gave you the recording."

"I know, and I appreciate it," Helen says, "but as you say, most of it was him railing against Ashton Stewart and recounting all the miseries life's inflicted on him. But it wasn't helpful in trying to figure out what happened a hundred years ago."

"I really don't know how much more you're going to get from Roland."

"Maybe he has some letters, or photographs, or something that will help," I say.

Nate shakes his head. "Father, wait until you see the place. There's stuff piled everywhere. I don't think he's thrown anything out in years."

Helen shivers a little beside me. "I remember when I was still a patrol cop in D.C. We did a wellness check on a woman in her late seventies. No one had seen her leave her apartment for a couple of weeks. When my partner and I knocked and there was no answer, we forced the door. The place smelled off—I can't even describe it. Junk was piled everywhere. There was barely enough room for us to move."

After a pause, Gladys asks, "Was the woman OK?"

Helen shakes her head. "No. We found her in her bed. She'd apparently died in her sleep." She pauses, then adds, "It was August, and the air conditioning wasn't on."

I see Nate shudder. "Yeah, that's a smell you don't forget," he says quietly.

"Bae," Gladys asks, sounding uncharacteristically nervous, "is this place—where we're going—I mean, it's in a rough part of Baltimore to begin with, and you said Roland—is it safe for us to be there?"

Nate starts to speak, but I interject, "Of course it is, Gladys. After all, Helen has her weapon. She'll watch out for us."

***

If I hadn't seen the signs for Baltimore, I'd swear we'd driven through some kind of interdimensional portal into a post-apocalyptic hellscape.

With Nate giving directions, Gladys drives us deeper and deeper into the part of the city that the tourist bureau doesn't highlight—and most people like to pretend doesn't exist. The Inner Harbor's hotels and restaurants are just blocks to the east of where we're going today. Helen and I are going to spend our first night as husband and wife together in one of the glass and steel buildings that tower over the glittering downtown.

Where we are now hasn't glittered in decades. Run-down row houses that should have been torn down years ago, many boarded up with red signs screaming CONDEMNED in big black letters, streets cracked and pot-holed. Children of people who long ago gave up hope for a better life play on sidewalks littered with trash, the weeds growing up through the cracks. Feral cats climb on garbage cans, chasing the rats away.

"It's hard to believe people live like this," Gladys says softly.

"They do, or try to," I say. "In seminary, they'd bring us down to work in one of the parishes in this part of the city during the summer to show us where we might be assigned. By the end, every year, a few quit. I guess they didn't want to take a chance."

"Did you ever think of quitting?" Nate asks.

I look out the window, vaguely recognizing a couple of the streets from my time here. "No, quitting seminary never crossed my mind," I mutter. "I only thought about quitting later."

Helen's hand squeezes mine. "And we're all glad you didn't," she whispers.

I turn and look into the smiling face of my beautiful bride-to-be and say, "I'm glad, too."

After a couple of blocks, Nate says, "Up here, Bae, on the right. The one on the corner."

We peer through the front window of the Mystery Machine at the rowhouse Nate points to. It's red brick, built, from the looks of it, around the turn of the last century. A door with peeling white paint awaits us, the three steps leading up to it sporting rusty ironwork railings and cracked masonry.

Gladys parks in front. Nate hops out to help her with her wheelchair, though I'm sure she's quite adept at handling it herself. Helen startles me by opening her coat, pulling out her

Smith-and-Wesson automatic pistol, checking the clip, and chambering a round. At my look, she says, "Look around you, Tom. This isn't Myerton."

"I know, but still—"

Leaning into me, she whispers, "I checked with Baltimore PD before we headed over here. Three drive-by shootings in the last week within three blocks of here."

"Why are we even here then!" I whisper-shout.

"Because we need answers, and this guy of Nate's might have them. It's a calculated risk. Like riding in Martin's helicopter."

She climbs out of the van, and I find myself wishing I was in the air again.

Steeling myself for whatever we're about to find out—and whatever may happen in the time we're walking from Gladys' van to Roland's residence—I step out behind Helen.

Twenty-Two

I utter a quick prayer when we step inside Roland Crescent's home.

Nate wasn't kidding.

This place looks awful, and smells worse.

I'll never complain about Mom's attic again.

"Come in, come in!" Roland says, grinning to show his missing and broken teeth. He has a two or three-day growth of beard and a tuft of white hair sprouting from his otherwise bald head. He appears to be about Anna's age, but his mannerisms are that of a much older man. Even though it's warm inside, he's wearing a faded and threadbare pullover sweater over at least one long-sleeved shirt, along with jeans that have seen better days.

Nate makes the introductions, with Roland shaking our hands with enthusiasm. He's particularly taken with Gladys, saying, "Aren't you a pretty little thing, just like Nate described."

From the scowl on her face, she doesn't look particularly pleased with the comment.

"Thank you for agreeing to see us," Helen says, looking around at the piles of papers and other assorted junk scattered around the room. Nate wasn't exaggerating—there are piles everywhere, and this is just one room.

"Well, when Nate called and said you had questions about my grandfather," Roland says, "I couldn't say no. I mean, the world needs to know about what happened to him! But where are my manners? Sit! Sit! Just throw the stuff anywhere." He waves his arm around the room before settling into an old recliner that's as threadbare as his clothes.

Nate, Helen, and I carefully move stacks of paper and—well, stuff—from a sofa and an armchair. Helen and I settle on the sofa, immediately sinking into the aged piece of furniture. Gladys, fortunately, has her own seat.

There's a scuffling behind Helen and me, and I jump when a rat the size of a large squirrel runs out from under the couch and between my feet. Gladys screeches as the foul beast makes a beeline for her. Helen reaches for her gun, but Nate leaps from his chair, grabs what looks like an old golf club—an iron, not a wood—and manages to brain the rat before it can ravage the woman he loves.

"Damn rats," Roland mutters. "Gotta get more traps, I guess."

We're looking at Nate, somewhat in awe. Noticing, he shrugs. "My dad would send us into the barn to look for rats. I got really good at killing them."

"Wow," Gladys breathes, obviously impressed with Nate's show of chivalry.

"Well," Roland says, "what do you want to know? I told Nate what my Daddy told me."

Helen pulls out her notebook from her huge tote bag. "Yes, I've perused Nate's notes and heard the recording, but I have some questions."

"OK, sure, sure, anything I can do to help."

She smiles. "Good. Now, you claim that your father was the biological son of Kent and Harriett Stirling."

"It's not a claim, Ms.—I'm sorry, I seem to have forgotten your name already."

"I'm Chief Helen Parr, but you can just call me Helen."

He smiles. "Helen. Helen. Such a pretty name, Helen. I knew a Helen once. Beautiful girl. Brown hair, long, curly." He pauses. "I remember . . . yes, that's it. She was my wife. Died a while back. Huh. I'd forgotten."

Helen and I exchange glances. I'm not confident in Nate's source, and I don't think Helen is either.

"So, what were you asking me about again?" Roland asks, looking slightly confused.

"Your father, Roland," Nate says. "Remember? Your father."

"Huh! Oh, yes, yes, of course," the older man says, waving his hand. "My daddy was a pharmacist—owned his own store, here in Baltimore. Not that far from here, as a matter of fact. That was back when this street was something—you know, I grew up here, did I tell you that Nate—oh, yes, really something. You wouldn't know it to look at it now, with the element that lives here. They destroyed this place, 1968, with their burning and looting and everything after that fella was shot. But when my daddy was alive, he was a big man here. I'd go down to his store every day and have a root beer float, and—"

"Roland," Helen says gently, "you told Nate your father was adopted, is that right?"

"Adopted? Oh! Yeah. Grandma and Grandpa—they died a long time ago—they had a farm on the Eastern Shore. I'd spend summers there. Grew corn—have you ever had fresh picked corn, Helen?"

"I have," I say with a smile. "There's nothing like it. But Helen grew up on a farm."

"A ranch in Nebraska," she adds. "Lived with my grandparents."

"Grandma and Grandpa were good people," Roland says. "Couldn't have children. Adopted daddy from an orphanage. Loved him. Raised him. Sent him to college. He became a pharmacist, you know? Owned a store—"

I admire Helen for her patience, considering I'm beginning to lose mine. From the look on Nate's face, he's afraid of what she's going to say to him.

"Roland," Nate says, a tone of desperation in his voice, "your father told you a story about Ashton Stewart and his mother?"

"Ashton Stewart!" Roland screams. "That's the man. The rotten SOB who destroyed my father! Killed my grandfather! You found his bones, didn't you! That's what you're here to tell me, isn't it! I want them. Grandpa Stirling deserves a decent burial."

"Roland," Helen says. "I'm sorry, but we have figured out that the body that we found in Myerton was not Kent Stirling."

"Nonsense!" Roland growls, bringing his fist down on the arm of his chair. "You're lying! Why are you lying!"

"I am not lying to you, Roland," Helen says patiently. "I have the documentation. The body was that of Theia Stewart, Ashton Stewart's wife."

"Oh?" Roland says, looking confused. "Not Kent Stirling?"

"No," Helen answers, slowly shaking her head.

"Oh, I see." The older man lapses into silence, just staring at the floor.

After a few moments, Helen says, "Roland, you told Nate what your father told you. You told him your father was the biological son of Kent and Harriet Stirling. But you didn't show him any proof to back up this claim."

"That's not true," Roland says with indignation. "I have the album." Looking at Nate, he adds, "I know I showed it to you."

Nate looks more confused than usual as he says, "Album? Roland, you didn't show me an album when I was here the last time."

"Oh, I know I did," Roland spits, struggling to his feet. "You just forgot. Let me run get it. I think it's just in this other room over here."

He slowly shuffles out of the room, muttering to himself. As soon as he's gone, Nate says, "I swear, he wasn't this bad when I interviewed him. All right, he rambled a bit, but not like this."

"What's wrong with him, Dad?" Gladys whispers.

"If I had to guess, dementia," I say, shaking my head. "People with dementia have good days and bad days. Apparently, this is a bad day."

"The way he lives doesn't help," Helen says, looking around. "This place should have been condemned years ago."

"Probably," I say, taking in the piles of papers. "He also suffers from some form of obsessive-compulsive disorder. It doesn't look like he's thrown anything away in years."

"Helen, I'm so sorry I wasted your time," Nate says.

"Oh, Nate," Helen says with surprising cheer, "this is hardly the first time I've had a witness go south on me. Comes with the territory."

"I knew it was in here!" Roland calls from the other room. A moment later, he shuffles back, grinning from ear to ear, clutching a black binder of some kind. "I have it. I have it right here. All the proof you need—I'm sorry, your name is?"

"Helen," she says patiently. She takes the book from Roland and places it on her knees. It's an album that looks like the one found in the trunk from Anna's attic.

"Tom," she whispers, "look. It's the same style."

"I noticed that, too," I nod.

"Well, you wanted proof!" Roland says with great enthusiasm. "Open it! It's all right there, in black and white."

Helen carefully opens the album. Looking over her shoulder, I see a newspaper clipping talking about a robbery from the First National Bank of Myerton in 1928. The article appears to have been clipped from a Baltimore paper, but the dateline says it's from Myerton.

We turn one page, then another. More newspaper clippings, talking about Kent Stirling, Ashton Stewart, the missing money, speculation about Stirling's whereabouts, speculation about Stewart's role in the theft and the possible murder of Stirling. There's even an article about Theia Stewart's disappearance, with the police questioning Ashton Stewart about the matter but ultimately concluding she left her husband for another man—though for some reason, there's no mention of Kent Stirling.

"It's a scrapbook," I say, "probably made at the time by someone interested in the case."

"There's no way a five-year-old boy could do this," Helen says. "But where did he get it from?"

Helen closes the album when something catches my eye. "Hold on," I say, "let me take a look at the back."

I hold the album close so I can see better. "Just as I thought," I sigh. "Look at that. It's a price tag."

"He bought this from somewhere?" Helen says incredulously.

"Looks that way. Maybe a junk shop or an estate sale." I ask Roland, "When did you get interested in finding more information out about Kent Stirling?"

"When?" Roland says. He strokes his whiskers for a moment, then replies, "Oh, five or ten years ago. About the time my Helen passed away, I think."

I nod. "Thank you for your time, Roland," I say, standing up. "You've been a great help, hasn't he, Helen?"

"What? Oh, yes, of course. A great help. Thank you so much," Helen says, handing the album back.

Roland holds up his hands. "No, no, you keep it. If it can help bring that scoundrel Stewart to justice for what he did, you're welcome to it."

We say our good-byes and leave the older man to his fading memories.

***

We've just pulled back on I-70 headed towards home when Nate breaths a huge sigh. "I'm sorry about that, everyone. I think I'm just going to give up writing."

"Oh, Bae," Gladys says, "don't get discouraged."

"This is the second article I've written that's caused nothing but trouble. No, my dad was right about me. I don't have the sense to be a journalist. From now on, I'll just stick to cleaning crime scenes."

"Nate, I'm not trying to make you feel worse about things," Helen says, "but didn't you check out Roland's story about his father before you wrote the article?"

Nate slumps even lower in his seat by Gladys. "Actually, no. I had a deadline, and I just found out about Roland, and so I interviewed him, and the story he told was so convincing, I just ran with it. It never occurred to me that none of it was true."

"Oh, I wouldn't go that far," I say, still looking at the scrapbook.

"What do you mean, Dad?" Gladys asks.

"I think parts of it are probably true. I think his dad was adopted from an orphanage by a childless couple who had a farm on the Eastern Shore. I think he was a pharmacist who died in the mid-1960s, leaving his family in severe financial straits. And, I think it's quite likely that Roland married a woman named Helen."

"Then what was all the other?" Helen asks.

"It's only speculation, mind you," I say, "but I think after his wife died, Roland became curious about his father's background. I don't know for sure, but he may have found evidence that his father was born in or near Myerton in the 1920s and was placed in an orphanage in 1928. There, the trail must have ended. But then, somehow, he came across this scrapbook. He took what these articles say—especially that Kent Stirling was married to Harriet Stewart and they had a five-year-old son—"

I stop mid-sentence. "Wait," I whisper. "Wait just a minute."

I begin flipping pages as Helen asks, "What is it, Tom?"

"Something that should have been mentioned, but wasn't—wait, here it is," I say. I peruse the article I was looking for, then look at Helen. "It doesn't mention one," I say with amazement.

"What are you talking about, Dad?" Gladys asks.

"The article talking about Theia Stewart's disappearance," I say. "It mentions everything about her. When she was born. When she married Ashton Stewart. The different organizations she belonged to. Everything you would expect the article to mention. Except one thing."

I can't resist pausing for dramatic effect, really feeling for once like Father Brown.

"What?" Helen, Nate, and Gladys say impatiently.

I take a deep breath. "There is no mention of her son."

"Wait, Tom," Helen says, shaking her head. "We know she had a son. Anna's father."

"There is no mention of Ash and Theia having any children when she disappeared. No, they had no children."

"So, who was Anna's father?" Nate asks.

"My guess? It was Harriet and Kent Stirling's son," I say. "Ashton Stewart wasn't a monster. After Kent disappeared and Harriet had her breakdown, Ash raised his nephew as his own son."

Helen looks out the window for a few minutes, then says, "Tom, what you say makes sense. It's easy enough to check the birth records, find Anna's father's birth certificate to see if it was re-registered, changing his last name to Stewart from Stirling."

"It's the only thing that fits what we know," I point out.

"Well, great," Helen says. "We solved one mystery that we didn't even know we had. But we still don't know who killed Theia Stewart or what happened to Kent Stirling and the money."

She slumps back in her seat. "And I'm beginning to think we never will."

Twenty-Three

One of the few perks of being a parish priest is the many invitations I receive around the holidays to attend parties hosted by the various parish groups. Most are closer to Christmas, but I've attended a few Thanksgiving-themed parties. They're usually pretty standard affairs, the food some variation of the traditional meal and the decorations including a cornucopia sitting on a brown and orange tablecloth.

But since this is the Blessed Carlo Acutis Society's party—and Gladys was the decorating committee—things are far from traditional.

She repurposed some of the decorations from the Society's Fairy Tales and Frights haunted house at the Myer Mansion and transformed the church basement into something out of Ancient Greece—or at least out of Age of Artemis, the massively multiplayer online game that's a favorite of the members of the society. Faux columns, paper mache statues, greenery, even a working fountain in the center give a definite Hellenic air.

As do the young people dressed in a variety of, shall I say, interesting costumes.

"Why didn't you tell me it was a costume party?" Helen hisses. "You know how much I like costumes."

"You just answered your own question," I say with a smile.

"Huh, you're just no fun, Tom."

"Oh, I'm all for fun. This," I say, waving my arm around the basement, "is just not my idea of fun. Besides, everyone is dressed as their Age of Artemis avatar—er, character."

Helen's surveying the crowd, then her eyes fix on one spot. "Is that why Nate's dressed as a half-man, half-horse?"

I turn and see that, indeed, Nate's costumed as a centaur, wearing a Spartan helmet and brandishing a rather formidable-looking sword.

"Do you think it's real?" Helen whispers.

"I don't think Gladys would allow him here with sharp objects, do you?"

"Normally, no, but love makes women do strange things."

Behind us, I hear an alto chipmunk squeal, "What do you guys think? Great, huh?"

As I turn, I say, "It's quite imp—Gladys Louise Finklestein, what is that you're wearing!"

"What?" Gladys looks confusedly down at the costume that barely covers her. "This is my costume. I'm a wood nymph, remember?"

"But—But—I mean, where's the rest of it?" I stammer.

"Oh, Dad," she says. "It's just a costume."

I find I've run out of things to say, so I turn to Helen. "Well? Are you just going to stand there?"

She looks at Gladys with a critical eye. "Really good work, Gladys. You do have a knack with a needle."

Gladys grins. "Thanks, Mom. Coming from you, that means a lot."

I shake my head. "Gladys, don't you have a jacket or something you can put on so you're not so—exposed?"

"Dad, listen," Gladys says seriously. "I'm not wearing anything less than you'd see at the beach. In fact, I'm wearing more. I'm wearing a flesh-colored body stocking, so no one is really seeing anything they shouldn't."

"Oh?" I say. "Really? I didn't realize that. Sorry I reacted that way, Gladys."

She smiles. "That's OK."

"Hey, Gladys!" We look up and see Martin and Mae walking towards us. Mae is dressed in a beautiful greek-style white gown cinched in at the waist with a gold belt, and she sports a ring of golden leaves in her hair. Martin's wearing a rather authentic-looking Spartan warrior costume, complete with helmet and short sword.

"Hi, Mae!" Gladys squeals. "You look great! And so do you, Dr. Maycord."

"Gladys, you're one of Mae's closet friends and our wedding planner," Martin says. "I think you can just call me Martin."

Gladys laughs and looks at me. "Remember how I reacted when you said to call you Tom?" she giggles.

"That seems so long ago now," I laugh. "A lot's changed."

"Yeah, it has," Gladys says. She nods, then turns to Mae. "Listen, I have some ideas for the wedding I want to talk about with you. Martin, mind if I steal her for a bit?"

"Not at all," Martin says. "You two go have fun."

Mae and Gladys rush off to talk, and Helen says to Martin, "Nice costume. I see some men don't mind dressing up."

"Helen couldn't get you into a toga?" Martin says with a grin.

"She didn't have a chance to try, since I didn't tell her," I say. "I will say you went all out."

Martin sighs. "Well, truth be told, I only did it because Mae asked me to. I mean, fortunately I was able to use a connection I have with a theater company in Baltimore to get it—you can't just walk into a store and pick up a Spartan warrior's costume off the rack, and I don't have the skill to make my own." Spotting Nate, he adds, "Now, his is impressive. Do you know if he did it himself?"

Helen and I shrug, since neither of us have ever inquired about Nate's sewing abilities. "I'm surprised to hear you say you don't have the skills, Martin," Helen says. "I've seen you with a needle doing stitches."

"You know, a lot of people think that just because I can stitch a wound closed or suture an artery, I must be able to do needlework or sew. But sewing in human flesh is much different than fabric. I can't even sew a button back on a shirt."

I'm a little startled by Martin's admission, though having been the recent recipient of stitches at his hands, I can attest to his skill in that area.

"So, Helen," Martin continues, "I saw they identified the remains found near the college. Is it really Anna's grandmother?"

"Yes, we were able to confirm through facial reconstruction that it was Theia Stewart."

"Any idea how she wound up there?"

"No, we're still in the dark about who killed her and why. It looks like died in a fall, and most of the injuries are consistent with that."

"But not all?"

Helen shakes her head. "No. Her wrist was fractured, but the anthropologist said it was a perimortem injury."

Martin cocks an eyebrow. "So, she fractured her wrist before the fall? Hmm, that's interesting."

"Why do you say that?" I ask.

"Because when a person falls, the impulse is to put your hands out like this," he extends his arms with his palms up. "Now, from that height, you'd expect the hands to shatter. What did her hands look like?"

"I don't remember," she says, digging through her tote bag for her phone. After a few taps and a swipe, she says, "Well, there were some fractures, but—wait, Martin, does this mean anything? He writes here that the injuries are consistent with someone landing on their back."

"But that doesn't make sense," Martin says. "If she was pushed, she'd likely land face down. The only way she'd land on her back is if she was standing with her back to the grotto, facing her killer."

"Maybe she struggled with her killer, and that's how she fractured her wrist?"

Still looking at the report, Helen says, "According to this, it looks like the wrist was extended, then bent backwards with a great deal of force."

"So," Martin says, reaching for my hand, "like this?" He pulls my hand forward, then bends it back towards me.

"Ow!" I say. "Hey! Careful!"

"Oh, Tom, I'm not going to hurt you," Martin says, "and if I do, I'll set it free of charge."

He lets go of my hand and I shake it out, rubbing my now-sore wrist. "Gee, thanks, pal," I say sarcastically.

Martin shakes his head and says, "Helen, this is a puzzle. I guess she could have flipped through the air on her way down, but she couldn't have been standing."

As Martin's talking, in my mind, I'm seeing Theia Stewart standing by the edge of the gorge.

"What was she doing there?" I mutter.

"Huh?" Martin asks.

Helen looks at me. "Tom? What is it?"

I look at Helen. "It just occurred to me—you know, we've been so busy trying to figure out first who she was, then who killed her, that we never stopped to ask an obvious question. What was Theia Stewart doing at the gorge in the first place? Today, it's part of the campus, but back then, it was in the middle of the woods. It wasn't a place you'd just go for a stroll."

Helen nods. "OK, OK," she says. "She would have had to hike there. But the fragments of clothing we found—there's evidence of a hat and coat, but her shoes weren't flats."

"And, she was wearing jewelry," I point out.

"Does this normally happen when you two are together?" Martin asks, a bemused look on his face.

"More often than you'd think," I say.

"She was probably taken out there by her killer," Helen says. "It's as simple as that. He got her out there on some pretext, or maybe he forced her."

"If he dragged her and she resisted, that could explain the wrist injury," Martin says. We look at him. "Hey, I was feeling left out."

"But Helen," I say, something slowly beginning to form in my mind, "if someone took her all the way out there to kill her, why bury her the way they did? Someone took the time to dig—"

I stop in mid-sentence when my idea bursts into my head. Pointing at Helen, I say, "We've been looking at this all wrong. The answer's been right in front of us all the time."

I turn and start walking to the stairs up to the outside entrance. Helen and Martin hurry after me. "Tom, what have you figured out?" Helen asks,

"The answer," I say, reaching the bottom of the stairs. "I think."

I turn to go up and almost run into Dominic Trent and his girlfriend, Therese Shepherd. Like every other member of the Acutis Society tonight, they're costumed as their avatars from Age of Artamis.

"Father Tom, Chief Parr, Martin," Dominic says. "Leaving so soon?"

"Just for a few minutes," I say. "We need to check something in the Rectory."

He looks at us. "All three of you?"

"Well," Helen says, "I will be living there soon, you know."

"That's true," Therese says. "Dr. Maycord, why are you going?"

"Me? Oh, ah—I just need to check, um, Father Tom's blood pressure," he says. "By the way, very nice Theia costume."

Helen and I look at each other. "Your avatar's name is Theia," I ask.

"Oh, I don't play," Therese says, "but I'm studying the Greek myths this year, and I decided to come as Theia since she's in the game. She was one of the Titans and was the goddess of light."

And with that, everything falls into place.

"That's it!" I exclaim. Turning to Helen, I say, "I know how Theia Stewart died. I know what she was doing by the gorge."

"Really?" Helen asks, a skeptical look on her face. "Do you happen to know who killed her?"

I slowly shake my head. "She wasn't murdered" I say, "but I do know who was responsible for her death."

Twenty-Four

"Tom," Helen says as I walk to the Rectory, "what the frankincense and myrrh are you talking about?"

"'What the frankincense and myrrh'?" Martin asks with confusion.

"Her attempt to stop cursing," I say. "And that's not the strangest one she uses."

"Will you just stop for a second and explain?" Helen yells, the exasperation clear in her voice. "I know you just got one of those weird things you get, but can't you tell me what it is?"

I stop with my hand on the doorknob. "Helen, it's better if I show you."

I go into the Rectory and make a beeline for my office, Helen and Martin on my heels. Sitting at my desk, I open my laptop.

"The note that Kent Stirling sent his wife," I say as I boot my system. "Nate found it among her papers at the Myer College archives, right?"

"Yeah," Helen says, still puzzled. "That's the one he wrote about, the one that said the money was buried in the gorge."

"Yes, that's what he thought it said—what we all thought it said—but he wasn't talking about the money. He was talking about something a lot more precious to him."

I open the file of my notes. "Here's the transcription of the note. Now, listen to what it says. 'By now, you know everything. I am so sorry. I've hurt you and your brother in unspeakable ways. There is no excuse for what I've done. I just couldn't take it anymore. I guess I wasn't strong enough. I needed out. I wanted out. I wanted a reason to laugh again.'"

"Sounds like a man who wanted out of a bad marriage," Martin says.

Helen nods. "That's what he was. He began an affair with Theia Stewart because, he said, his marriage to Harriet was so unbearable."

"She suffered from some kind of mental illness," I comment. "Kent wrote as much in his letters to Theia that we found. He was desperate enough to get out that he stole money from the bank owned by his best friend—though he had already stolen Ashton Stewart's wife. But this letter's from a man broken by guilt over what he's done." I sit back in my chair. "Something broke him. And I know what it was."

I read, "'But now, it's all gone. The light is broken, and all is darkness. The precious thing I stole from your brother is buried in the gorge on the edge of town.'"

I look at Helen as a smile spreads across her face. "He was talking about Theia, not the money," she says.

Nodding, I say, "Exactly. I didn't realize we'd been looking at this all wrong until it occurred to me that whoever she was with at the gorge already had a shovel. That's the only way she could have been buried as deep as she was. You couldn't dig a four-foot deep grave by hand."

"So, are you saying that Kent Stirling killed her?" Martin asks.

"Not exactly," I say. "He didn't kill her, but he was the reason she died."

"OK, Tom," Helen says. "How do you figure?"

I stand up and begin to pace. "Now, let's look at what we know for certain—which is precious little, I'll admit. At some point, a year or so before everything happened, Kent and Theia began their affair. Even though Myerton was a smaller town then than it is now, anyone seeing them together wouldn't have thought much of it—they're in-laws, and both families, I imagine, were quite close. But they were discreet enough not to get caught. Since we know that the story Roland Crescent told Nate was the product of his tortured mind, let's assume Ashton Stewart didn't know about the affair until after it happened."

"He was apparently a workaholic," Helen points out. "And from the letters, they only got together when he was out of town on business."

"So they were going on like this for a while, having their affair with no one the wiser. But at some point, it wasn't enough. Either Theia or Kent wanted more—they wanted out of their marriages, to run away together, to go somewhere they could live the way they wanted to live."

"That sounds familiar," Helen says, looking at me with a bemused smile.

Returning the smile, I say, "Yes, I guess it does. Anyway, for whatever reason, they decided to run away. Only Kent didn't have money. I mean, he had his salary from the bank, but much of that probably went to paying the bills Harriet ran up from her shopping trips to D.C. and Baltimore. He came from a poor family in north Georgia, so he couldn't very well take her there. He needed money to set up their new lives in a new place. So, he decided to steal the railroad payroll. I mean, Ash had put him in charge of receiving it. He knew the process. He knew the combination to the bank vault. And he picked the ideal time, when the money would be in the closed bank for the weekend and no one would notice it missing until Monday morning.

"If I had to guess, he planned everything ahead of time. He knew about the gorge—being from north Georgia, Kent probably knew his way around the woods pretty well—and he decided he'd hide the money there right after stealing it from the bank, then get it later."

"But that doesn't make sense, Tom," Martin says. "Why not just take the money and leave town?"

"If he was going by himself, he might have," I say. "But Theia was going with him. It's possible that Kent stole the money sometime during the night, and took it out to the gorge to bury it the next morning. He told his wife he was going fishing in the mountains for the weekend, so that explained where he was going so early on a Saturday."

"But he had to wait for a time when Theia could leave home without garnering suspicion, right?" Helen says.

"Right. I'm sure if we look in the *Myerton Gazette* for the date in question, there'd be some kind of notice for a garden club or women's club meeting on Sunday afternoon. As the wife of the bank president, Theia was more than likely a member. There was probably a pre-arranged place where she met Kent. Together, they were going to leave town and put their unhappy lives behind them. But they had to make a stop first."

"The gorge," Martin says.

"The gorge," I nod, "to pick up the money."

"I still don't understand why he buried it for so short a time," Helen says. "Why not just steal it Sunday afternoon?"

I shrug. "We'll never have all the answers, darling. What I'm proposing is a possible scenario that fits what few facts we have."

"OK," Helen nods. "They go to the gorge. How does Theia wind up dead and buried there?"

"I think it may have happened like this," I say. "Kent went into the gorge with a shovel to dig up the money. Theia stood by the edge, maybe bending over to look. It could have been something as simple as she lost her balance and fell."

"Possibly," Martin says, stroking his chin. "But there's the perimortem wrist fracture. What if he was coming up the side of the gorge, which is pretty steep, with the money in a suitcase or something. He handed her the suitcase, then reached out for her to pull him up the rest of the way. She bends over, reaches for him, begins to pull, but loses her balance and goes over. That would explain the fracture."

"Either way, she hits the rocky floor of the grotto, and dies instantly—or maybe she doesn't die instantly, but lingers for a while," I say quietly. "It was a relatively remote area, so by the time he went for help and came back, she'd probably be dead."

"Even so," Helen says, "if he did that, everyone would know he stole the money. They might even charge him with murder, saying he killed her deliberately."

Slowly, I nod. "Whatever happened next, instead of admitting his crime and his sin, he decided to hide it. But, because he loved Theia, he made sure she was buried as carefully as he could. It's possible he just dug out the hole he'd buried the money in. But he couldn't just leave her there, so he wrote that note to Harriet."

"A note that apparently no one bothered to read," Helen mutters.

"'The precious thing I stole from your brother,'" I say. "He wasn't talking about the money. He was talking about Theia."

"'The light is broken, now all is darkness,'" Martin says, shaking his head. "You're right, Tom. The answer was always there."

Helen takes a deep breath. "Well, Tom, your theory fits the little bit we know for certain. I'm satisfied. But I do have one question?"

"What happened to Kent Stirling and the railway payroll?" I shrug. "He left Myerton with it. Probably the rumors of him going to South America are true. He lived out the rest of his life quite comfortably, trying to forget all the sins he committed. In any event, Helen, we may just have to be content with never knowing. I mean, some things are probably meant to remain a mystery."

***

The last Sunday before Thanksgiving this year also happens to be the last Sunday before Advent. We're commemorating the Solemnity of Christ the King, the day in the liturgical calendar when the Church recognizes that Jesus Christ our Lord is not just the savior of each man and woman individually, but is the savior and king of the entire universe.

This Sunday is also special, because it's five weeks until our wedding.

I smile at this as I pull my white and gold chasuble on in the Sacristy before 10:30 a.m. Mass. Dominic has already come and gone, hurrying around to make sure all is in readiness for the procession, complete today with incense.

"That's seen better days, you know, Tom?" Helen says. Usually, she's not with me when I put my vestments on. But for some reason, today, she asked if she could watch me, since she'd never done it before.

"All of the vestments have seen better days," I sigh. "They belonged to Father Anthony, who probably got them sometime in the 1970s."

"Didn't you receive your own vestments when you were ordained?"

I shake my head. "I was going to the Archdiocesan Archives, remember? There was no need. So, I'll have to make do with these until I can get some newer ones."

"Maybe we can take care of that next year, hmm? A new set for Lent, perhaps?"

"Maybe, though they're not cheap."

"Excuse me, Father," Dominic says, "but I'm afraid you may have lost track of the time in talking to Chief Parr. It's already 10:27 a.m., and you are usually in place by 10:25 a.m."

"Thank you, Dominic," I say with a smile. "What would I do without you?"

"Frankly, I've thought the same thing on occasion," he replies, also with a smile. He then scurries off.

"I'd better let you go," Helen says. "I'll see you out front after Mass?"

"Absolutely. Love you," I say, kissing her chastely on top of the head.

She walks out of the room, and I pause and say a brief prayer of thanksgiving for her, Saint Clare's, and for my continued vocation as a priest.

Walking to the back of the church, I notice something that startles me.

Bridget Davis is sitting in a pew with Terry and her other children. But she's not alone.

Steve is here, looking only a little uncomfortable, sitting with Terry between him and Bridget.

I glance at the tabernacle and mutter, "Still in the business of performing miracles, I see."

***

"Are you sure it was Steve?" Helen whispers as we stand greeting parishioners after Mass.

"Look, if it wasn't Steve, then it was his twin brother," I say.

Before we can talk any further, Catherine Conway runs up and squeals, "Hi, Father Tom! Hi, Miss Helen!"

"Hello, sweetie," Helen says as she bends over to give her a hug. Max and JP come up then and mumble something that might be a greeting, followed by Dan and an increasingly pregnant Miriam.

"Morning, Father Tom, Chief," Dan says.

"Morning, Dan, Miriam," I say. Seeing the expression on Miriam's face, I ask her, "Are you doing all right?"

"About as well as can be expected," she says, wearily. "She's laying right on my bladder so I have to go every five minutes—oh, oh, dear, excuse me!"

She turns around and scurries back into the church. Dan says to me, "I understand from Helen you've solved another one for us."

Thinking I detect a tone of resentment, I say, "Now look, Dan, I—"

Laughing, he says, "Don't worry about it, Father. Hey, I was never that enthusiastic about investigating this to begin with. Bunch of old bones, no witnesses to question. This was all the Chief's case, just trying to keep Anna happy."

"Time well spent, if you ask me," Helen says.

"Eh, maybe," Dan says. "But, you're the boss."

"Hey, Catherine." We look and see Daniel Wright standing a couple of steps away.

"What do you want, Daniel?" Catherine asks, haughtily.

"I just wanted to know if you wanted to play hide and seek."

"No, thank you. And if I did, you would be the last boy I'd want to play anything with!"

Catherine turns her back on the boy, and Daniel looks disappointed as he turns to walk around. Then suddenly, he spins around and yells, "Spooky Catherine!"

Max and JP make a sound reminiscent of Mel Gibson in *Braveheart* and take off after the boy, who turns and runs as fast as he can down the steps to the lawn in front of the Rectory.

"Max! JP! Stop!" Dan yells as he runs after them.

Catherine looks over her shoulder and shakes her head. "Why are boys so weird, Miss Helen?"

Glancing at me, Helen says, "Oh, just because they're boys. They don't stay weird, most of the time."

Catherine sighs. "That's what Mommy said when I asked her. She said they grow out of it by the time they're Daddy's age. But that seems like an awfully long time." Turning to me, she asks, "Have you grown out of it, Father Tom?"

Before I can answer, Helen quips, "Mostly, sweetie, but he still has his moments."

I'm about to protest when Miriam comes out, asks where everyone else is and, hearing about the incident, shakes her head and takes Catherine to the van.

"So, I still have my moments, huh?" I say, with my arms crossed.

"Oh, come on, you know you do," Helen says with a laugh.

"Yeah, but you're not supposed to mention it." I look at the entrance to the church and smile. "Look, Helen."

She turns and says, "Well, I guess you were right."

The Davis children, Bridget, and Steve all walk out of the doors of the church together.

"Good morning, Bridget," I say. "Good to see you back at Mass."

With an uncomfortable smile, she says, "Well, Terry's been wanting to come back, so . . . "

"I see you've finally taken me up on my offer," I say to Steve with a grin.

"Yeah, well, you'd been so persistent, I finally decided to give you a try," Steve says.

"Well?"

He takes a deep breath. "Interesting. Very interesting."

Not quite sure what he means by that, I say, "Well, I'm glad to see you here."

"Mom, can we go to the playground?" Terry asks.

Bridget looks like she's about to say no, when Steve says, "Why don't you take them. I need to talk to Father for a moment."

"Oh, OK," she says with a smile. "I'll see you there in a few minutes?"

Steve nods, and Bridget walks away with her children. Turning to me, Steve says, "Now, Father, before you get the wrong idea, let me explain—"

"Now Steve, you don't have to explain anything to me."

"No, after our conversation in the attic, I think I do," he says.

"What conversation in what attic?" Helen asks.

"He didn't tell you?" Steve says.

"I considered our conversation confidential," I say. "I never share anything like that with Helen unless it's a matter of life and death."

"Oh, I see," Steve nods. "Well, it's not that big a deal, Helen. Father just wanted to make sure Bridget knew I was gay so she wouldn't get the wrong idea."

Helen nods. "I see. So, does she?"

"Oh, Helen! Of course she does. As I told him, we're just friends."

"I know that, Steve," I say. "As far as why you're at church today, I'm just glad to see you. I've invited you myself on more than one occasion."

"Yes, and I've turned you down. Frankly, as I've told you, I like you, and Clark, but I'm pretty soured on religion. Don't have much use for church myself. But I was at Bridget's yesterday fixing a faulty light fixture and I heard Terry practically beg her to take him to church. Apparently, he's been missing Mass. Bridget put him off, saying she wasn't feeling well. I knew that was a lie, so when Terry went to his room, I asked her about it."

"What did she say?" Helen asks.

Taking a deep breath, Steve says, "She said she was embarrassed to come back to the church after everything. She thought people would be staring at her, you know, talking about her, that sort of thing. Now, I know how good the church has been to her since everything happened, and I tried to point that out, but she wouldn't hear it. So I told her, since it was important to Terry—I've become really fond of the kid, you know—if she went, I'd go with her. Then if anyone was looking or talking, chances are they'd be talking about the gay bartender instead of the abused widow."

"That was a wonderful thing to do, Steve," I say.

He shrugs. "As I told you, I know what it's like to be an outcast, or see yourself as one. Well, I told them I'd take them to this little place I know in the mountains for a picnic. Terry's been after me to teach him to fish, so I thought I'd do that."

"Sounds lovely," Helen says.

"I'll see you Thursday, right?" I ask.

Steve grins. "Wouldn't miss it."

He walks off to find Bridget and her kids. To Helen, I say, "Do you think it's possible there's more going on there than meets the eye?"

"Oh, Tom," she says. "Does it matter?"

"No," I chuckle. "I guess not. Bridget's happy. The kids are happy. Steve's a good friend to her. She's someone who needs a friend."

Twenty-Five

The days leading up to Thanksgiving are a whirlwind, beginning Monday morning with the arrival of fifteen pink, plump turkeys from a local turkey farm.

"That's a lot of turkeys, Bill," I say as I look at them stuffed into one of the church kitchen's large refrigerators.

"It takes that many to feed the crowd we usually have," Bill says. "You remember last year."

"Yes, I remember the turnout, but Myerton Methodist hosted last year."

"Right," Bill nods. "The host church cooks the turkeys, the other churches provide the sides."

I look at the church's oven—which is larger than the one in the Rectory, but still seems too small to cook so many. "How do you cook the turkeys?"

"The churches share a smoker," Bill says. "That takes care of the job really well."

I shake my head. "You sound like you've done this before."

"It's been a few years, but yeah, the last time we hosted, I oversaw the cooking of the turkeys. Kind of what I do, you know? I've always loved Thanksgiving."

I nod, remembering another man for whom Thanksgiving was a big holiday.

"Well," Bill says, "I'll check with Anna to make sure all of the other churches are ready with their contributions. But it's not like the first time we've done this."

"Just out of curiosity," I say, "how long has the community Thanksgiving been going on?"

Bill shrugs. "It was going on when my wife and I moved here forty years ago, so at least that long."

"Here you are," Anna says behind me. "I wondered where you ran off to."

"I was just looking at the turkeys," I say. "Bill was keeping an eye on me."

"Hmm," she responds with scepticism. "Well, sorry to draw you away from this, but you have a visitor."

"Oh, who is it?"

"He says he's the Deputy Mayor, Lex Luther?"

I roll my eyes. "Great. I wonder what he wants?"

"Is there a problem, Tom?" Bill asks.

"Probably," I sigh. "I have no idea why he'd be here otherwise."

I walk back over to the Rectory with Anna. Deputy Mayor Luther is sitting in a chair in front of my desk.

"Good morning, Deputy Mayor," I say with forced cheer. "So sorry to keep you waiting."

"Not at all, Father Greer," he says with a condescending air. "I'm sorry to stop by unannounced, but I wanted to talk to you about the Community Thanksgiving Dinner."

I sit back in my chair. "Yes, what about it?"

"I'm still new in town, you know," he says, taking some papers out of his briefcase, "so I only became aware of it a couple of days ago. I understand it's sponsored by the Ministerial Association?"

"Yes, that's my understanding," I say with my brow furrowed. "There are several other organizations that participate. The Chamber of Commerce. The police department. Those are just a couple."

"But it's primarily put on by the churches."

"We share the responsibility, yes. We take turns hosting it each year."

"I see," he says, making a note. "And how is it funded?"

I have to think for a minute. "I'm sorry, but I'm not really clear on that. I know there is money set aside for it, but I'm not sure where it comes from. I know that Saint Clare's has never been asked for a donation. But each church donates the labor."

"I see, I see," the Deputy Mayor says. "So, it's a religious function."

"Not explicitly," I say. "But if it was, why is that your concern? Does the dinner receive city funds?"

"No. Not a penny."

"Then I fail to see—"

"The point, Father Greer, is quite simple," the Deputy Mayor says. "The Mayor is very interested in making sure Myerton is a welcoming, diverse, and inclusive community. We will not tolerate discrimination against anyone for any reason."

"The Community Thanksgiving Dinner doesn't discriminate against anyone," I say firmly. "The Ministerial Association represents each religious group in Myerton, including the Islamic Center and the Mount Zion Synagogue. I'm not aware of any Hindu organizations, but their representatives would be welcome as well. The ministers represent a cross-section of the racial and ethnic makeup of the town—which considering where we are is quite remarkable for a town this size."

"Considering how problematic commemorations of the events of this country's founding have become," he goes on to say, "I'm curious how you handle such issues as the treatment of indigenous peoples?"

"It's dinner," I say. "We serve people who cannot afford to feed their families, or who are alone and desire companionship. The local businessman who is the Chamber of Commerce's liaison with the Association for the dinner told me he wanted to participate because his family rejected him due to his sexual orientation."

At this, the Deputy Mayor sits up. "Really? You have a representative of the LGBTQ+ community?" he asks with a grin.

"Yes," I say. "Steve Austin, the owner of the Hoot-n-Holler."

"Oh, well, I must say, I am gratified by that," he says. "This shows a progressive attitude that I didn't expect the churches in this town to take, especially considering the Catholic Church's history of discrimination against members of the LGBTQ+ community."

Inwardly, I sigh. I've just about had enough of explaining to people the Church's position on same sex attraction. So, I just let it pass.

"I look forward to meeting him," the Deputy Mayor says.

"Oh? Are you planning on attending?"

"Yes, as a matter of fact I am. I want to see things for myself."

"Well, you and your family are welcome," I say.

"It will just be me and Clarise, my life partner. We've decided to remain childless."

That's a blessing.

"Oh, one more thing. Are there a variety of dietary options? Clarise and I are vegan, you see."

It's all I can do to keep from saying something sarcastic. "I'm sure you'll both find something to eat," I say, a smile pasted on my face.

"Good, good," the Deputy Mayor says as he stands. "Well, thank you for your time, Father."

I stand to say, "Oh, my pleasure. Please, stop by anytime."

He nods and walks to the door of my office. "There is one more thing," he says. "At some point early next year, we need to have a discussion about the Saint Francis Education Center."

My heart drops into my stomach. "Oh? What about it?"

He grins and says, "Nothing you need to be concerned about now. Have a nice day."

The Deputy Mayor leaves, and I sit down. Leaning back and looking at the ceiling, I say, "Helen was more right than she knew. That man is going to be trouble."

Twenty-Six

My alarm goes off at 4:00 a.m. As I reach to turn it off, I am immediately aware that it is Thanksgiving morning.

To be honest, this has been a bittersweet day for me ever since my Dad died. Christmas belonged to Mom and Sonya, but Dad and I ran Thanksgiving. For as long as I could remember, he and I would look for the biggest turkey we could find at the supermarket. After thawing in the refrigerator, Dad would brine the turkey in a mixture of kosher salt, brown sugar, and a variety of herbs. We'd get up at this time every Thanksgiving morning to take the bird out of its bath, rub it with canola oil, and stuff the cavity with apple, onion, rosemary, and thyme. We'd put it in the oven, then we'd start the other food. I still remember how the house filled with the aroma of roasting turkey.

But after he died, it was years before I could even stand the smell. Mom did the best she could, but after a couple of years, she decided that making a Thanksgiving dinner for three people didn't make much sense, so we'd travel to Tallahassee for dinner. After Sonya started acting out, and her addictions took hold, well, many years we'd just forget about it.

I wipe away a tear and begin this Thanksgiving morning as I have every year since I entered Our Lady of the Mount, by saying a prayer for Dad's soul. Once I've done that, however, I put away all sad thoughts.

After all, I have more to be thankful for this year than I have for a very long time.

Also, I have more responsibilities and need to get over to the church basement to begin to execute them.

I grab a quick shower and am about to head over to the church to say Morning Prayer when it occurs to me that I probably ought to make sure Helen's up. I call, only to be surprised by a cheery, "Good morning," when she answers.

Caught off guard, I say, "I was just calling to see if you're up?"

"Why don't you open your front door and see for yourself," she replies, again with uncharacteristic cheer for so early in the morning.

I hang up and trot downstairs. Opening the door I am greeted by my bride-to-be, already wearing her designated "Give Thanks to the Lord" apron, and holding two cups of steaming coffee. I take one and give her a quick peck on the cheek, saying, "My, but aren't you chipper this morning."

"Well," she says with a sly grin, "Knowing that there was going to be a lot of activity around here first thing in the morning, I thought it behooved me to get a good night's sleep and then make a very public arrival."

I grin back. "Well, you are a very pleasant sight this early in the morning. I was going over to the church to say Morning Prayer. Care to join me?"

"Sounds delightful," she says, kissing me again.

Together, we walk over to the church. We're alone in the sanctuary, and there's enough light coming through the windows and cast by the votive candles that I don't bother turning the lights on. We kneel together in the front pew, each of us alternating reading the psalms for the day. I love the way our voices mingle together in praise and thanksgiving to the God who has been so good to us.

Afterwards, we go down to the basement where we are met by a strangely agitated Anna coming across the floor to us.

"I see you found him," she says pointedly. "I wasn't sure what had become of you."

I look at Helen for clarification, but instead she responds to Anna, saying, "If you must know, we have been upstairs in the church praying for the success of this day and the safety of anyone who gives me a hard time." She grins at this last bit and Anna, properly chastised, does the same.

"Wait," I say, "you mean to tell me you've already been here?"

"Yeah," she replies. "I've been working so late this month that it just made more sense to me to get here with the night crew and then cut out for a nap before making our dinner."

"I see," I say. I'm about to say more, but Bill walks up, hands me an apron and says, "C'mon, Father Tom. Let's get out of here. We've got fifteen turkeys in the smoker out back, and they're not going to watch themselves."

I follow him through the kitchen and out the back door. "But Bill," I say as soon as we're outside, "I always thought one of the advantages of smoking the turkeys was that they don't have to be watched so closely."

"Shhh," he says conspiratorially. "That's true, but Anna doesn't know that. If we stay inside, they'll put us to work. Out here, it's nice and quiet, if a little cold, and we can make up for that by sitting closer to the birds."

I know I should feel guilty about this but I realize that I have not made it to a Knights meeting in a couple of months, so I justify hiding out with Bill by assuring myself that I will use the time to catch up on what's going on.

Since this is the first year during my time as pastor that Saint Clare's has hosted the Community Thanksgiving Dinner, I have never seen the famed smoker that produces some of the best turkey meat in the state. I am shocked by what I see. I had expected a smallish DIY sort of set up, but instead, I find myself standing in front of a state of the art commercial-sized smoker, complete with all the bells and whistles.

"Whoooooo," I breathe, only a little bit jealous. I'm not really a grilling sort of guy, but like most men, I can appreciate a nice piece of equipment. "That must have cost a pretty penny."

"Oh, it did," Bill says, "But we had the money, and since we're not supposed to carry over too much from year to year, the Association decided to make the investment."

"I've been wondering where the money for the dinner comes from," I say, wondering if there's a wealthy benefactor out there who would like to adopt a middle-aged Catholic priest.

"No one really knows," Bill says with a shrug. "Every year the Ministerial Association receives a check from something called the Myerton Friendship Fund. They use the money for the meal that year and place the rest of it in the bank. It accumulates there until we need to buy something big, like this, or the mobile concession stand the town uses for baseball games."

"So this fund isn't just for sponsoring this dinner?"

"'Oh, no. The funds go first to the dinner, but then can also be used for any purpose or event that feeds the people of Myerton. So the Association uses it to supplement the work of various food banks, provide food during times of natural disasters, and loan out equipment for civic events."

"What a great set-up."

"It is," Bill nods. "Now, while I've got you here, I need to ask you a couple of questions about some plans the Knights hope to put into action in the coming year."

We spend the next couple of hours "monitoring" the turkeys and talking over various aspects of church business. I do check inside a few times just in case anyone does need my help, but Anna seems happy to have me spending quality time with Bill and shoos me back outside. Other help arrives during the morning, including Steve with an entire soda machine, and Martin, yawning but obviously raring to go.

We're supposed to start serving at noon, and by 11:00 a.m. Bill announces that the turkeys are done. Several men line up to take each succulent bird into the kitchen, where Bill will fulfill his final "Turkey Chief" duty by carving each into thin slices that will soon find their way to waiting plates.

I have dropped my protein offering in the kitchen and am returning for another when Nate rushes in and demands, "We need ice, now. Bill burned his hand."

I run for the freezer as Martin heads out to the smoker. Before I can get back out there, Martin has led Bill into the kitchen and has his right hand under running water. Bill is obviously in a lot of pain and Martin is looking at the hand.

"What happened?" I ask.

"Oh, I did something stupid," Bill manages to say as he winces with pain. "I wasn't paying attention and I spilled turkey grease on my hand. Damn—sorry, Father—that hurts!"

"OK, Bill," Martin says calmly, "you've earned yourself a trip to the Emergency Room. I'm going to call an ambulance since they'll get you there quicker and have something topical with them for the pain. Chances are you'll be home in time for dessert."

"What's the hold up—oh, my God!" Anna says, turning pale at the site of Bill's hand.

"He's going to be fine, Anna," Martin says. "Tom, keep it under the water. I'm getting that ambulance."

I nod, even as Anna comes up to Bill and places her hand gently on his back. "How did this happen, honey?"

Honey? I know they're dating, but I've never heard Anna call him 'honey.'"

"Oh, angel," Bill says, shaking his head, "I wasn't paying attention and spilled turkey grease on my hand."

Angel? Honey?

"OK, they're on their way," Martin says. "I've called the ER and let the attending on duty know you were coming. Fortunately, it's quiet right now, so they should see you quickly."

"I'm going with you," Anna says to Bill.

"Now, that's not necessary," he says, shaking his head. "You're needed here."

"No, she's not," Helen, who has come in with the other Ladies of Charity behind her, insists. "We can handle things here, thanks to the great job Anna's already done. Besides, going to the hospital is something no one should ever have to do alone."

Bill continues to resist, but by the time the ambulance arrives, he gives in. Anna accompanies Bill and the EMT out of the kitchen.

"He will be all right, won't he, Martin?" I ask.

"Oh, yeah," he says. "It's a nasty burn, but it will heal. No permanent damage."

"Um, excuse me," Doris Trent says, "but we have a problem. With Bill out of commission, who is going to carve the turkey?"

"That shouldn't be a problem," Helen says with a grin. "I'm no turkey, but I can personally testify to Martin's excellent knife skills."

"Of course," I say, turning to Martin, who is surprisingly embarrassed by this attention and is beginning to blush.

Alan Trent—his future father-in-law—claps him on the back and says, "Son, it seems God has a special calling for you today. Instead of saving lives, you'll be filling bellies."

With every eye in the kitchen on him, Martin stammers, "Well—well, sure. Just get me a knife and point me to those turkeys."

"Follow me, Doctor Maycord," Helen says, directing him toward the butcher block in the back where the hot turkeys are resting.

I go back to milling about with everyone else. Since priests are considered by most to be the very most unskilled of unskilled labor, I end up mainly toting and fetching between the kitchen and the dining area. Members of the other churches arrive with their food. Clark and Vivian join us, their boys unable to make it home for Thanksgiving.

"Everything looks great, Tom," Clark says.

"Yes, you've done a fabulous job," Vivian agrees.

"Well, as always, I can't take the credit," I say. "The Knights cooked the turkeys, and the Ladies of Charity did the decorating and provided the paper goods. Oh, and the sweet tea."

"Oh, I am dying for some of that," Vivian says as she makes a beeline for the drink table. Steve's finishing setting up the soda machine and greets Viv with a hug.

At 11:30 a.m., the doors open and the first guests begin to file in. Clark and I stand at the door and greet everyone, me on behalf of the parish, Clark in his capacity as this year's chair of the Ministerial Association. The place is already beginning to fill up and people are getting in the serving line, so at about 11:50 a.m, I go back to get the first pan of turkey.

"Martin," I call, "I'm coming back to get—what in the world?"

I'm stunned to find Martin Maycord, trauma surgeon, the man who saved Helen's life, jabbing at a defenseless roasted bird in a manner more reminiscent of Freddy Krueger than Gordon Ramsey.

"Martin—what, what is all this?" I ask, surveying the damage. Two birds, once beautiful, golden-brown and delicious-looking, are mute testimony to the carnage that's obviously taken place. There's a pan filled with chunks of turkey varying in size from my hand to the tip of my finger. The remaining turkeys are lined up, awaiting their turn at the hand of this knife-wielding maniac.

"Tom, please," Martin pleads, "grab a towel and get some of this sweat off me. I don't want to drip it on the food."

And that is how I find myself mopping the forehead of trauma surgeon Martin Maycord as he continues to hack away at the unsuspecting birds.

"Martin, I don't understand," I say. "I mean, haven't you ever sliced a turkey before?"

My good friend—OK, he did pull a gun on me and lock me in my own basement, but he was under a lot of stress that day—turns on me, brandishing the carving knife. I take a small step back, hoping he's not planning on doing to me what he's done to those poor turkeys.

In a low, menacing tone, he says, "No, I haven't, and if I survive this day, I never will again."

He pauses to sweep various bits into the tray before continuing, "And don't start all that, 'but you're a surgeon' crap with me There's practically no similarity between a live human and a dead turkey. Do you know what we practice surgery on in medical school? Dead people. Cadavers, Tom. People who have donated their bodies so idiots like me know what we're doing when we cut into a live person. We don't practice on turkeys. Occasionally, we use pigs' feet for suturing practice. Again, no turkeys." He waves his hand over the slaughter and cries, "Tom, this is a nightmare."

"OK, OK," I say calmly, "Why don't you just put down the knife and we'll talk."

It takes him a second but he complies. "Good, that's good, Martin," I say. "Now, nobody wants anyone to get hurt or embarrassed. So why don't you take this tray of turkey and walk out that door. Take it to the serving area and tell them that I said I'd like to carve for a while. Then you can make a clean getaway. How does that sound?"

"I don't know, Tom. I mean, if people find out what I did to these turkeys, they could lose faith in my abilities." His eyes get big. "Alan! Oh, Lord! Tom, Alan can't find out about this! If he knows I can't carve a turkey, he might decide I'm not good enough to marry his daughter!"

"That's why you're going to drop off the turkey and leave," I say. "Tell people you're going to check on Bill. Most people will just assume that I did it and they won't care. In fact, many folks find incompetence in a priest endearing."

Martin breathes a sigh of relief and grasps my shoulder. "Thank you for this, Tom," he says as he picks up the pan. "I owe you one."

"I'll keep that in mind if I'm ever stabbed again."

Martin walks out of the kitchen, drops off the food at the serving table, and disappears from the basement. I can neither confirm nor deny that he squealed his Porsche's tires as he left.

As it turns out, I don't have to carve the turkey after all, for no sooner has Martin left than Steve arrives. "Father," he says pleasantly, "you'd better let me take over here. They want you out there to welcome everyone and say Grace. Anyway, thanks to the Army, I'm pretty good with a knife."

As I surrender my apron to him, I consider for a moment how, apparently, the skills needed to kill someone can transfer to carving a turkey, but those used for surgery cannot.

Ah, life is full of mysteries.

I don't have time to consider them any further, however, for I am soon out the door and saying, "The Lord be with you."

The Catholics present reflexively reply, "And with Thy Spirit," which quiets everyone.

"I want to welcome everyone here to the annual Community Thanksgiving Dinner. I am Father Tom Greer, Rector of Saint Clare's Catholic Church, and we have the honor of hosting this Myerton tradition this year. I want to thank the Myerton Ministerial Association for serving as the primary sponsor of this dinner every year. I also want to thank the men and women of the churches in our town who provide the help every year to make this possible. Now, I think you've heard me speak enough." There's a smattering of applause and laughs at this, and I say, "so let us first have a moment of silent prayer in thanksgiving for the many blessings we've received this past year."

I bow my head along with the assembled men, women, and children, and quietly offer my heart and mind in praise and thanksgiving to God, for all he has done for me this year.

For seeing me through a crisis of faith that almost led me to leave the priesthood.

For performing a truly miraculous work in providing a way for me to remain a priest and still marry the woman I love more than anyone else on this earth.

For giving me such a loving parish family that more than makes up for my actual family.

For saving Helen's life after she was shot.

For protecting me when I was stabbed.

For some truly wonderful friends.

I finish by saying aloud, "Now, bless us, O Lord, and these thy gifts which we are about to receive through thy bounty, through Christ, our Lord, Amen."

As everyone begins getting their plates, I try to return to the kitchen but Steve and the others insist that I remain out front and play host, so I do.

I've just greeted a family of four, new to the area, when Nate walks up to me with his notebook out. "Father Tom, I'm writing an article about the dinner for the *Gazette*."

"So, you decided not to give up writing after all," I ask with a smile.

He sighs. "Actually, Father, I have. I've told the editor there'll be no more articles from me. But he asked me to do this last one, since he knew I'd be here. I've talked to Reverend Applegate for the background on the dinner, and I've interviewed a few of the workers and a couple of the people who're here to eat. But as the host, I was wondering if you have any comments."

"Believe it or not," I say, "I do. This meal teaches us all a very important lesson, that we are all needy on some level or another. This is important because the term that is traditionally translated 'charity' in older Bible translations, is more correctly termed 'love,' and it is the need for this that binds us all together. Jesus, as God the Son, came to earth and made himself one of us. In doing so, He demonstrated that true Biblical charity is given to 'us,' not them. One of the major problems of the world today is that we want to separate ourselves from those we help. We no longer go to a neighbor's home with a bag of groceries, remembering when they did the same for us. We refer them to the Food Stamp Office. We don't offer to take an older person to the doctor, knowing that we, too, will be old someday. We refer them to Elder Services. In doing so, we wallow in the sin of pride, of saying, 'I did this for them,' when we should be thinking, 'We did this for us.'

"The true beauty of this meal is, while there are some here who do indeed need the food, others need the fellowship, or to have something to do, or to just be a part of the human community. So, when you write your article, please, remind your readers that this meal is something that we do for each other as equals in our need for love, not something that one group of people that is not needy does for another that is."

Nate looks at me and wipes a tear from his eye. "That's—that's beautiful, Father," he whispers. "I'm glad I was recording that. I'll probably have them print the whole thing verbatim."

I smile. "Happy Thanksgiving, son," I say.

"It is, isn't it," he says. "I know I have a lot to be thankful for. For Gladys. For not being in prison. For you, Helen, Dan, and Miriam. And, most of all, for my faith. Yeah, this is the happiest Thanksgiving I've had in a long, long time."

He nods and goes to join Gladys at a table, where a few members of the Acutis Society I know are students at Myer are seated, enjoying both the food and fellowship.

I begin to make my way around the room, practicing what I just preached by reaching out to the people here as guests in my home, friends as opposed to projects. Every so often, I look at the serving line, where people are still being served ample portions of turkey with all the trimmings—stuffing, mashed potatoes, green beans casserole, candied yams, fresh baked rolls from The Muffin Man. I don't see Helen, and realize she's probably gone to take a nap before our own dinner tonight. I notice Steve's still in the kitchen, but he looks out the door every few minutes like he's expecting someone.

"Good afternoon, Father," a nasally voice behind me says. I turn around and see Lex Luther with a thin, rather pale woman with dirty blond hair.

"Mr. Deputy Mayor," I say with a smile. "Thank you for joining us."

"It is our pleasure," he says. "May I introduce my partner, Clarise Dryer."

"Very nice to meet you, Clarice," I say.

"So," she says with what I think is a smile, "you're the priest who's marrying the Police Chief?"

"Ah, yes, that's me," I say, trying to keep a light tone in my voice. "I hope you won't hold that against me." I laugh, but am disconcerted when neither of them laugh.

"I find the entire concept of organized religion outdated," she says. "A relic of the dark ages, you know."

I have no idea how to respond, so I say to Luther, "Well, what do you think?"

"Well," he says, "it looks fine. Just fine. Nice diversity of people here."

"Uh-huh," I reply. "Well, I'm glad you approve."

"I'd like to talk to Mr. Austin," he says, "to get his view on things as a representative of a marginalized community."

I almost make a joke about bartenders hardly being marginalized in Catholic circles, but think better of it. "Steve's back in the kitchen, but I'll be glad to introduce you."

Just then, I see Bridget Davis arrive with her children. "Excuse me," I say to Luther and his partner, and I walk over to greet them. But before I can, Steve rushes past me. He greets Bridget with a hug, high fives Terry and the other kids, and shows them to a table. Once the kids are seated, he escorts Bridget through the serving line, helping her with the children's plates.

"I thought you told me that Mr. Austin is gay?" Lex Luther says behind me.

I turn to him. "He is," I say firmly.

"Then what is he doing with that woman?"

"Bridget Davis is a recent widow," I explain, "her children left fatherless. Steve has been doing some much-needed repairs at her house. They've become friends. And frankly, I can't think of a better example of what this dinner is supposed to represent than that. Now, I'm sure the people serving the food can help you avoid whatever it is you believe is wrong to eat."

As they walk off, I mutter, "Maybe some fava beans and a nice Chianti."

I turn on my heels and walk to another table, greeting another family. After a few tables, I make it to Clark and Vivian's table.

"Have a seat, Tom," Clark says. "You look like you could use it."

"Thanks, it's been a long day already."

"Have you eaten?" Vivian asks.

"No," I say. "Helen and I are having dinner later with Anna and Bill, assuming they get back from the hospital before morning. I think Nate and Gladys are coming. You two should stop by, at least for dessert."

"We might drop in," Clark says, "if I haven't fallen asleep by then."

"I haven't seen Helen in a while," Vivian says.

"She's probably taking a nap at the Rectory. Apparently, she was here really early this morning. Actually, I think I'll go check on her."

I stand up to leave, but Clark says, "Wait, Tom, you need to sign the book."

"What book?" I ask.

"The record book for the event. Apparently, each year we write down how many people were served and how much food we prepared. Then the pastor of the host church signs it."

He pulls a surprisingly worn, leather-bound volume out of his briefcase. Opening it to a page that's partially filled out, Clark says, "See? It's all recorded here. You just sign and date at the bottom."

Intrigued as always by any old document, I ask, "How far back does this record go?"

"All the way to the beginning, apparently," he says.

Clark takes the book and flips back to the first page, dated November 28, 1929. As I study the page, he comments, "You know, that was right at the beginning of the Great Depression. Many people would have had mighty slim pickings if it hadn't been for this meal.

Something strikes me about this date. "I know this is paid for by something called the Myerton Friendship Fund. Do you know anything about it?"

"No," Clark says. "When I took over as chairperson of the Association, the previous chair told me about the book and about the yearly check, and the rules for its use."

"Where does the check come from each year?"

"I can't say where it's come from in the past, but this year, it came from a bank in a town in Georgia. Place called Dahlonega. I'd never heard of it, so I looked it up. It's in the North Georgia mountains. Not much there. I believe it's one claim to fame is that it was the site of the first Gold Rush in the United States, years before the one in 1849."

This information sends a chill up my spine and I say, standing, "Clark, I've got to run to my office for a few minutes. I won't be long."

"Is anything wrong, Tom?" he asks, his forehead wrinkled in concern.

"Wrong? No," I say with a smile. "But if I'm right, you've just solved a hundred-year-old mystery."

Twenty-Seven

I never make it back to the community dinner. I become so consumed with figuring out if my gut feeling is right that I don't notice how much time has passed. Since no one comes to hunt me down, I assume everyone left there took care of anyone else who showed up, along with the necessary clean up.

By the time Helen wakes up from her nap in the guest room, I'm positive I'm right. Now, all I have to do is tell her.

"Is the lunch over already?" Helen yawns as she stands in the doorway to my office.

"Huh? Oh, probably. What time is it?" I ask, looking up from the papers scattered on my desk.

"About 3 p.m. What are you doing?" she asks, a quizzical look on her face.

I lean back in my chair and toss my pen on my desk. "You're not going to believe this," I say, "but I think I've figured out what happened to Kent Stirling and the stolen money."

Her eyes pop open at this. "You're not serious," she says with a skeptical look on her face.

"Helen, I've spent the last hour and a half or so looking through parish records, Father O'Connor's papers, and doing some internet research. I've come up with an answer that, while bizarre, fits what we know. Of course, most of it is speculation, but at least it's an answer."

Helen sits down and leans on my desk. "OK, well, I'm all ears."

I open my mouth to begin to tell her, but I break into a grin instead. "You know, I think I'll wait until dinner tonight. Anna deserves to hear this."

"Tom, now, that's not fair," she says firmly. "I'm the Chief of Police. This is my investigation. So if anyone's going to hear the story first, it's going to be me."

I hold my hands up in surrender. "OK, you've got me. I'll tell you now, but I get to tell the story later over dinner. Deal?"

"Deal? Now, what have you got?"

I sit back in my chair, a self-satisfied expression on my face. "It all starts after Kent Stirling flees Myerton with the money."

***

After telling Helen my theory about Kent Stirling and the missing money—a theory she agrees is plausible—she and I go back over to the dinner to check on everything. By the time we get there, everything is almost cleaned up. Clark and Vivian are still there, along with a few Ladies of Charity and a handful of Knights, Steve, Bridget, and her children. The Davis kids are running around playing some kind of game, while Bridget is helping the Ladies clear away the serving table. Steve's in the kitchen, scrubbing away at the remaining pots and pans.

"I thought you said you'd be back in a few minutes, Tom?" Clark asks when Helen and I come in.

"Sorry, things took longer than I thought," I smile sheepishly.

"And what was this about solving a hundred-year-old mystery," Vivian says.

"Helen, would you care to comment on that?" I ask.

"Well," Helen says, shaking her head, "I'll admit, I think Tom's got the only solution that fits all the evidence."

"Does this have something to do with that bank theft Nate wrote about in the paper, the one Anna tried to kill him over?" Vivian asks.

"You could say that," I say nonchalantly.

"Aren't you going to tell us, buddy?" Clark asks.

"Well, I thought I'd wait until tonight over dinner. Stop by for dessert and I'll reveal all."

"Oh, good grief," Helen says under her breath. "You're being insufferable, you know that, Tom?"

"Am I?" I say with false modesty. "I'm so sorry. I don't mean to be."

"Yeah, yeah—well, anyway, if you two want to find out what Father Brown here's figured out, you'll just have to stop by the Rectory around 8 p.m."

Clark and Vivian look at each other, then turn back to us. "We'll be there," they say in unison.

Turning to me, Helen says, "Well, if there's going to be any dinner tonight, I'd better get along with it. Is there any turkey left?"

"Yeah, quite a bit," Clark says. "I think Steve set some aside for you."

"Great. Oh, Tom," she says, "how did Martin carving the turkeys go?"

"Oh, fine," I say. "He only carved a couple, then Steve took over. Martin had to leave suddenly."

"Was there an emergency at the hospital?"

"I'm sure an emergency had something to do with it."

No, I did not just lie to Helen. I told the exact truth. But I also told Martin I would not reveal his shameful secret.

"Well, I'm glad it worked out," Helen says. "Any word on Bill?"

"Anna called me about thirty minutes ago," Vivian says. "Bill's fine. His hand is wrapped up and he's still in some pain, but she was going to take him home to get some rest."

"I'll check to make sure they're still coming," I say, pulling out my phone to send her a text.

Helen walks to the kitchen with Vivan, apparently talking about something to do with our wedding. Clark says to me, "Tom, I'd say this was a success. People ate a lot of food, and they seemed to have a good time. Well, everyone except the Deputy Mayor and his partner."

"Sorry I left you with them," I say, shaking my head.

"Oh, it's all right. I've dealt with people like him before. He means well, I think, but he's just so—so—"

"Yes, he is," I nod. "He's giving Helen a hard time about the police department, specifically the office of Chaplain."

"Yeah, I was meaning to ask you about that," Clark says. "I got a call the other day from Helen, saying you were going to step down as Police Chaplain after the first of the year?"

"It can't be helped," I say with a shrug. "The nepotism rules cover me as a volunteer, so since I'm going to be married to the Police Chief—my boss—I can't serve as Chaplain. I assume she called you to gauge your interest?"

"That, she did," Clark nods. "I told her I'd pray over it, and I'd want to talk to you first."

"My advice? Take it. She needs someone in there she knows and trusts."

"Is it a hard job?"

"Not most of the time. It's like having a small church, in a way, only it's made up of people who don't necessarily share the same faith. They'll leave you alone for the most part—they're not likely to call with minor complaints. I've learned that police officers are pretty self-reliant, up-by-your-own-bootstraps people. They try to handle things on their own—or avoid handling things at all. So when there is a serious crisis, you may have to work at reaching them. But if one of them ever comes to you for help, stop what you're doing and see them right away."

Clark nods. "I'll definitely give it some thought." Then, he grins. "Just out of curiosity, do I get a badge?"

I laugh as I pull mine out of my coat pocket and hand it to him. "It's just like the ones the real police officers carry. It's mainly to show other cops you belong."

"How do they treat you, the officers?"

At this, I begin to tear up. "Like one of their own," I whisper. "They're as much my family as the parish is."

He claps me on the shoulder. "I'll see you later, Tom. Have a Happy Thanksgiving."

"I already have, my friend. I already have."

***

"Helen, the dinner was delicious," Anna says as we sit in the living room for dessert.

"Yeah, Mom," Gladys says. "Best food I've had in a while."

"I'm stuffed," Nate says.

"I'm not surprised, Bae," Gladys says to him, "considering how much you ate at the community dinner."

"I have a high metabolism," he says, "you know that about me."

"So," Anna says, looking at me with her arms crossed, "are you going to tell us this big secret you've been keeping?"

Helen and I look at each other as Bill says, "What secret?"

"I don't know, but both of them have been dying to tell us something all through dinner. I've gotten very good at reading you two, you know?"

"We need to practice our poker faces, Tom," Helen says.

"You have a secret?" Nate asks.

"Oooh, what is it? Have you two eloped? Is that it? You're already married?" Gladys squeals.

"Oh, Gladys," Helen sighs, rolling her eyes. "Of course not."

"Well, what is it? Out with it?" Bill asks, wincing with the pain from his now-bandaged hand.

I'm about to speak when the doorbell rings. "Ah, that would be Clark and Vivian," I say, standing up.

"I'll get it, Father Tom," Nate says, getting up and walking to the door. In a minute, Nate comes back, followed by Clark and Vivian.

"Hi, everyone," Vivian says, "sorry we're late. Have we missed it?"

"They know?" Anna says.

"No, Anna, Tom wouldn't tell us anything. That's why we're here for dessert."

"Let me go get you some coffee and pie," Helen says. She stands and walks into the kitchen, returning moments later with a tray containing two plates, each with a slice of pumpkin pie, and two cups of coffee. Clark and Vivian take them and settle back on the couch.

"OK, Tom," Anna says patiently. "Clark and Vivian are here. Everyone has their desserts. Now, please, what do you need to tell us?"

I look at Helen, who says, "Go ahead. It's your story."

Nodding, I begin, "So, ever since Nate wrote that article about the theft of the railroad payroll from the First National Bank of Myerton in November 1928—"

"Oh, don't remind me about that," Nate says mournfully.

"Anyway," I continue, "everyone has wondered what happened to the money. Nate's theory, based on his interview with Roland Crescent—"

"—which turned out to be a complete bust, remember—" he mutters.

"—was that Ashton Stewart killed Kent Stirling and either made off with the money himself, or Stirling buried the money in the gorge and then was killed, taking the secret of the burial place with him."

"But we know Grandpa Ash didn't kill anybody," Anna says.

"Yes, now we do. We also know that the money isn't in the gorge now—not that it never was, but it isn't there now—and the body found there was not Kent Stirling, but Theia Stewart."

"Now if I remember your more recent article, Nate," Vivian says, "Theia was pregnant with Kent's baby?"

"Yeah, at least that's what I assume," Nate says. "After Father Tom figured out that Ashton and Theia Stewart had no children, I did a little more research. According to some records I found concerning his injuries in World War I, well, let's just say he'd never be able to father children."

"If that's the case," Gladys says, "then why did he marry in the first place?"

"It was the expected thing to do, Gladys," Anna says. "A young, handsome man like my Grandpa back then couldn't remain single without starting rumors."

"So when Theia became pregnant," I say, "she knew it was Kent's baby."

"And that's what probably prompted him to go forward with his plan to rob the bank, so he and Theia could run off together," Helen says.

"But it didn't work out that way," Clark says. "She died in an accidental fall, and Kent Stirling buried her in the gorge."

"That's right—or at least that's our theory based on the evidence," Helen says.

"It certainly answers all the questions, except for one," I say.

"What happened to Kent Stirling and the money?" Bill says.

"Right," I nod. "Now, the assumption was that after Theia died, Kent ran off someplace and spent the rest of his life living it up in some tropical country. That assumes that he was a selfish and self-centered sociopath, or something like that."

"Well, Tom," Anna says. "May I point out he committed adultery with his best friend's wife, stole from his employer—who was his best friend—was responsible for a woman's death, covered it up, and ran away? Sounds pretty much like a sociopath to me."

"I agree, except you're forgetting one thing," I say. "A sociopath doesn't feel guilt for his actions. And I'd say that Kent Stirling did."

"Oh really! How do you know that, Tom?"

"The note he sent his wife, Harriet, after the robbery," I say. "In it, he expressed remorse for hurting Harriet and Ashton. He told her where Theia is buried—which makes me think he wasn't trying to hide Theia's body, but to protect her from scavengers. No, the Kent Stirling who wrote that note was grief-stricken, burdened by what he'd done."

"If he felt so bad, Dad," Gladys asks, "why did he take the money? He could have left it for someone to find?"

I shrug. "I don't have a good answer for that, Gladys. People don't always act consistently, even when they feel guilty. But I will tell you, he didn't follow his original plan. Wondering what to do, having lost the woman he loved, his best friend, his position, and with his freedom threatened because of his crime, he decided to go to the one place he knew he'd be protected."

There's silence for a minute, then Nate says, "Home."

I smile and nod. "Exactly. Kent Stirling decided to go home, to the mountains of north Georgia."

"Dahlonega," Clark whispers. "Tom, you're not serious?"

"I am. The answer's in the timing," I say.

"What's Dahlonega?" Bill asks.

Before I can answer, Nate says, "It's a town in the mountains of north Georgia, a couple of hours or so north of Atlanta. Kent Stirling was born there. But Father, I already thought about that. I looked in the 1930 and 1940 Census for Lumpkin County, Georgia, and while there are several Stirling families, I couldn't find a Kent."

"Census records are rarely complete, or accurate," I say, "especially those of a poor, rural, and mountainous county in the 1930s and 1940s. He could be there under an assumed name, or maybe he's not recorded at all. Kent could very well have lived the rest of his life in an isolated holler in the mountains there."

"But assuming this is true," Anna says, "he had $150,000 dollars. Why didn't he use it?"

I lean back in my chair and look at the ceiling. "This is pure speculation, of course, but I think the money weighed more and more heavily on his conscience. He might have seen it as the reason Theia died—no money, no gorge, no fatal fall, you see? So, wherever he was, I believe he didn't touch a cent of it. I have no proof, but I think I'm right."

"So what are you saying?" Vivian says. "The money is buried somewhere in the North Georgia mountains?"

"Oh, that's not what he's saying at all," Clark says with a grin. "Is it, Tom?"

"You've got it figured out, don't you?" I say, returning his grin.

"Well can you explain it to the rest of us!" Anna exclaims.

"I'm getting to that right now," I say. "Meanwhile, the stock market crashed in October 1929. The country was plunged into depression, and in a short time, people were thrown out of work as businesses went bankrupt." I take a deep breath for dramatic effect—sorry, I can't help myself—and say, "One of those businesses was the Western Maryland and Ohio Railroad. I checked on the internet and found a history page for the Railroad. According to it, the Railroad was on shaky footing for a year. Within a couple of weeks of the crash, it ceased operations. Hundreds in this part of the country were thrown out of work, left penniless in many cases."

"Did the payroll theft have anything to do with the company going bankrupt?" Nate asks.

"Not directly, at least not that's mentioned in what I read. Apparently, it suffered from mismanagement."

"I don't see what this has to do with Kent Stirling?" Anna says with exasperation.

"I think that somehow he found out what happened to the railroad," I say. "Probably saw a newspaper article about it, or something. Even down in Atlanta, it would have been news. Regardless, Kent's guilt became unbearable. Being from a poor family himself, he empathized with what they're going through. Knowing Thanksgiving was coming up, he probably realized that many of those families didn't have money to put food on the table, much less have a traditional dinner with all the trimmings. So, as a way of making up for what he did and the damage he caused, he decided to do something about it with the money he stole."

"The Myerton Friendship Fund," Clark says. "The checks come from a bank account in Dahlonega."

"Uh-huh," I nod. Picking up Father O'Connor's journal, I open it to a page I've marked with a strip of paper. "This is what the Rector here at Saint Clare's wrote in November 1929, 'I received in the mail something so curious and miraculous, I can only ascribe its appearance to the hand of God. Having just returned from a meeting of local clergy, including almost all the Protestant churches in the area, where we discussed the desperate straits our town was in due to the shuttering of the railroad, I found a letter waiting for me. It was from a bank in a town in Georgia I've never heard of, and contained a check for $500. The enclosed letter, signed by the president of the bank, explained that this was from an anonymous donor who had deposited funds in his bank under the name of the Myerton Friendship Fund. This donor requests that the money be spent to feed the families affected by the closure of the Western Maryland and Ohio Railroad, as well as any other families who find themselves in similar straits. He specifically desires that the money be used to host a dinner for the community on Thanksgiving Day. I have already called the Methodist and the Presbyterian ministers, and we're meeting tomorrow to come up with a plan of action. To God be the Glory!'"

"That was the first Community Thanksgiving Dinner," Clark says, "it's recorded in the book."

"That's right, the first one. Every year since then, a check arrives around November 1 from the Myerton Friendship Fund, made out to the Myerton Ministerial Association. I plan on calling the bank tomorrow to try to get more information, but I'll bet the fund started with a deposit of $150,000 dollars."

"Wouldn't the president of the bank at the time have been suspicious of someone depositing such a large amount?" Gladys says.

"Considering there were already banks closing across the country, he probably considered it a blessing," Helen says. "I'm not sure, if I'd been him, if I'd have asked any questions."

The room falls silent for a few minutes. Finally, Nate asks, "So, you've explained what may have happened to the money, Father Tom. What about Kent Stirling?"

I shake my head. "He probably lived quietly among his family and friends, who might never have known about his transgressions."

"Well, Tom," Clark says, his forehead wrinkled with concern, "if what you say is true, the Ministerial Association has been receiving the fruit of ill-gotten gain for the last hundred years or so. What do you think we ought to do?"

I look at Anna. "It was your Grandpa's bank Kent Stirling stole from. What do you think?"

Anna takes a deep breath. "That whole thing caused my family so much pain and suffering through the years, I'm actually comforted that the money's been used to help people here in my hometown. I'm not sure what Grandpa would think, but I think Kent Stirling's made up for his sins hundreds of times over."

I smile and say, "Amen, Anna. Amen."

***

I am dead tired by 10:30 p.m. Everyone leaves, and Anna goes upstairs to bed. Helen and I finally collapse on the couch to watch *Plymouth Adventure,* Hollywood's version of the Mayflower story starring Spencer Tracy as the captain of the rickety vessel. I have to admit that, as good as the movie is, I drift in and out of consciousness most of the time.

Finally, I hear Helen saying my name, softly, and drift back into consciousness with my head on her shoulder.

"Tom," she says softly, "it's after midnight."

"I know," I mumble, taking her word for it. "You need to go home."

"Yes," she says softly, "but it's also the 26th."

This gets my foggy attention and I smile contentedly.

Only one month to go.

The Father's Family

The Father Tom Mysteries, Book 12

By

J. R. Mathis and Susan Mathis

Mercy and Justice Mysteries, 2021

First Printing, December, 2021

Contact: mercyandjusticemysteries@gmail.com

Cover Photo: Depositphotos

Cover: Millie Godwin

Editor: Anna Palmer Darkes

One

It's a beautiful late November morning. Helen and I are on our way out of Myerton for one last trip to Hagerstown before the wedding. We've made this trip monthly, at least, ever since the announcement of our engagement. Helen would spend a few hours shopping for our honeymoon, then we'd have a nice, long lunch together.

But today, we're not going shopping. As Helen pointed out, "It's the Saturday after Thanksgiving, there are only twenty-seven shopping days until Christmas, and everyone will be acting crazy."

"Well," I had said, "what do you want to do?"

"Let's just drive up into the mountains to that state park, have a picnic, then take a nice, quiet walk in the woods. One last day together before the craziness starts."

Our day trip is such a relaxing ritual for us, I am thinking about putting it on our calendar
With just a little something added.

After we're married, we can spend the night. Maybe in some little out-of-the-way cabin?

I am pondering this happy thought when Helen knocks on my window, jarring me out of my reverie.

"Hey!" she says through the glass. "Are you going to let me in? It's a bit nippy out here."

I unlock the door and she slides into her seat, leaning across the center console to kiss me. "You were lost in thought," she comments as she buckles her seatbelt.

"Oh," I grin, "I was just thinking about what these trips will be like after the wedding."

She leans back against her seat and smiles. "Oh, yes," she whispers. "I've thought about that myself. Care to share with the rest of the class?"

"Probably not a good idea right now," I say, certain that she can see me blushing.

Helen nods and I shift my car into gear. I press the accelerator gently to move away from the curb—when my engine cuts off.

"Darn it!" I curse as I turn the key and the car comes back to life. "I just got you out of the shop a couple of weeks ago!"

"Did they say what was wrong with it?" Helen asks as I turn onto a main street.

"Jake said this time it was . . . something, I didn't really understand," I say sheepishly. "But he also said—or rather implied—that the main reason my car's been in the shop three times in the last two months is simply a matter of its age."

"Well, Tom," Helen says, "the car is over fifteen years old. How many miles does it have on it?"

"It's pushing 175K," I say. "But most of those I've racked up since coming to Saint Clare's. I do a lot more driving than I used to. When I worked at the Archdiocese, it just sat most of the time."

"That's not good for cars. As much as you love them, I'm surprised you don't know that."

"I love cars, true. I love how they look. I love the speed, even if I don't drive like you do—"

"—have I ever had an accident?—"

"—but I don't know a whole lot about them otherwise."

Helen opens her mouth to say something else, but she's cut off by a staticky squawk from her police radio.

"How can you understand anything?" I say, shaking my head. "Most of the time it sounds like a frog croaking in a downpour."

"Sshh," she says, straining to listen. After a minute, she says, "There was a robbery earlier today. That was Nina Hallstead leaving the scene."

"A robbery? What'd they get?"

"I don't know, Tom, and I don't care. I'll find out Monday. Right now, I'm looking forward to just spending the day with you."

As always, we stop by The Muffin Man for coffee and muffins. Since opening earlier this year, Nick Hallstead's bakery has become so popular that the line this morning is to the door. There's a steady murmur as people talk and wait patiently to purchase some of Nick's spectacular baked goods. Since we're not in a hurry, I take my place at the back of the line just as my phone starts playing 'Ave Maria.' The talking stops as every head turns. Seeing it's me—even though I'm in a sweater and jeans, they all know I'm a priest—they return to their conversations or own phones.

Inwardly, I groan, hoping it's yet another offer for an extended warranty on my car. But when I see the number, my groan becomes audible. I answer in what I hope is a pleasant tone, "Good morning, Father Tom Greer."

"Father Tom, it's Serenity MacMillan," says the tired voice on the other end of the call. "I am so sorry to bother you on a Saturday morning, but I was wondering if you could stop by sometime today."

"Of course, Serenity," I say. "Is Mrs. MacMillan not well?"

"No, Father," she says, "It's much worse than that. She's mad."

I shudder *and* groan. Gloria MacMillan is an eighty-something-year-old widow in my parish and a constant thorn in my side. Worse than that, she is a continuing source of angst for her long-suffering granddaughter-in-law, Serenity.

"Oh? Has something happened to upset her?" I ask, knowing all too well it doesn't take much. In the time I've known her, she's subjected me to tirades on everything from rigged bingo games to the portion sizes at Knights of Columbus fish fries.

"Well, yes," she sighs. "This time, it is kind of a big thing, I'll admit. We've been robbed."

"Robbed?" I say, upset myself now. "Serenity, I assume you've called the police?"

"Oh yes, Father, as soon as we found out. The officer just left. She was very nice, but I'm afraid Grandma was pretty hard on her."

I manage to keep from saying, "I'm sure." Instead, in what I hope is my best comforting pastor voice I say, "I'm sure the officer thought nothing of it." I look at the time and say, "I'm on my way out of town right now but I can stop by for a few minutes."

"Oh, Father, I don't want to put you to any trouble."

"None at all. I'll be out there as soon as I can."

"Thank you so much. I'll let Grandma know you're coming."

I hang up just as the customer in front of me leaves. Nick Hallstead, the tall, beefy owner of the shop, looks harried—and with good reason. In the past few months, he's lost a partner and gained a devoted clientele. I know Nick both personally, since I love his baked goods, and professionally, since his wife, Nina, nearly as tall and muscular as he is, is one of Helen's best officers.

"How's it going, Nick?" I ask.

"I'd love to tell you, Father, but I just don't have time. What'll it be?"

"One Bavarian cream, one blueberry, two coffees," I say as concisely as I can. "You really need to get some help, Nick."

"Oh, don't I know it," he says as he takes a delicious-looking blueberry muffin out of the case. "I've managed OK the last couple of months since they arrested my former partner, but with the holidays, it's only going to get worse. Fortunately, I've hired a girl from the college to take over the counter through New Years. She starts Monday."

"I know that's a relief."

"Yeah, maybe I'll actually get more than three hours of sleep a night." As he's bagging my order he says, "At least I'm having a better day than Nina. I just got a text from her. She's already been called out to a robbery at some crazy woman's house a few miles out of town."

I nod, a bad feeling forming in the pit of my stomach.

I get back to the car and tell Helen about the call and what Nick said.

"Oh, boy," she says, "That's not good."

"Why?" I ask.

"Let's just say that Nina is not someone with an excessive amount of patience. Knowing Gloria, I should probably go ahead and begin work on the citizen's complaint report."

"Against Nina Hallstead? You're kidding. She's delightful and one of the nicest people I know."

"She is, and very professional. But she does not take well to being told by civilians how she ought to be doing her job. I'm not saying that she actually told Gloria to shut up, but it's likely Nina pretty firmly suggested that she should stop talking."

I pull out onto Main Street. "Robbery isn't all that common around here, is it?"

"It's more common than murder," Helen says. "Even though this year we've had four of those, we've had about thirty robberies. Mostly petty stuff, a couple of grand thefts. We always see a bit of an uptick in the weeks leading up to Christmas."

"So it's not that big of a deal?"

"Not really. But since it's my first holiday season as Chief, I'd like to try to get out ahead of this if I can. So, my darling, I am going to make the incredible sacrifice of riding out there with you instead of insisting you drop me off at my apartment."

"Do you think we'll still have time to get up into the mountains?"

"Well, we can always drive that way when we're done and if we don't have time for a hike, I'll spring for lunch at that nice Greek place you like."

"Hey, big spender," I say playfully, "if I'd known you had that kind of money, I'd have married you a long time ago."

I immediately regret my words as a shadow passes over Helen's face onto my own. I could have married her twenty years ago, had I not walked out in a jealous rage and then been too proud to come back and make up. We might have had children, an entire life together.

"Or we might have killed each other," Helen says, saying what she always says when we lapse into "what might have beens."

She's right, of course. And we've had good lives without each other, loved and lost other spouses and, in my case, even a child.

Now we have each other, and that is plenty. "Good point," I reply as we head out of town. I am about to add that I have never contemplated killing anyone.

Then I remember where we're headed, and decide not to jinx it with such a bold statement.

Two

As soon as we pull up to the MacMillan homestead, a hundred-year-old or so farmhouse about twenty minutes from town, I groan.

"There she is," I say. Rather than propped up in her bed as she usually is when not out visiting friends or playing bingo, Gloria MacMillan sits on the porch in an ancient rocking chair that looks worse than she does.

"I don't see the kids," Helen observes. "I guess they're not home."

"They're probably hiding," I snort. "That's what I'd be doing."

"Now, Tom," Helen chides. "She's a harmless old woman."

"Helen, you've met her," I say. "What about her is harmless?"

"Just remember, she's been through a shock. Being robbed is very traumatic for people."

I'm about to say that visiting her is very traumatic for me, but that would sound like whining, so I don't.

Characteristically, Gloria starts in on us before I can close the car door. "'Bout time you got here," she bellows. "I called more than two hours ago."

"Mrs. MacMillan," I say gently, "I came as soon as Serenity—"

"I'm not talking to you," she says with a dismissive wave of her hand. "I'm talking to your little girlfriend."

Now, most women in her position—one of the few female police chiefs in the state—would be infuriated by such a statement. But Helen takes it in stride. "Fiancée, Mrs. MacMillan," she says with a smile, "but I do appreciate being called little."

"Ha, ha, ha," Gloria says, fuming. "You like making fun of a frail old lady who has been viciously wronged, do you? Well, go ahead. Have your fun."

"Now, Mrs. MacMillan, you're about as frail as I am small," my voluptuous bride-to-be says with a laugh. "I believe an officer has been out here, hasn't she?"

"Bah, that smart aleck chit of a girl. Acted like she knew everything, like it's no big deal that a poor old lady like myself was robbed of precious family possessions."

I'm beginning to wonder if dementia has a firm grip on Gloria, because no one who knows Officer Nina Hallstead, over six feet tall and a former Mixed Martial Arts champion to boot, would ever describe her as a 'chit of a girl.'

Trying to mollify the old parishioner, Helen says gently, "I am sorry to hear that, Mrs. MacMillan. I haven't seen the report yet, so why don't you tell me what they got."

"My big screen TV with the surround-sound speakers and built-in DVD player," she whimpers. "Went into MY bedroom. I've never felt so violated."

Hardly family heirlooms, I think, as Helen continues, "Anything else?"

"Isn't that enough? How am I supposed to watch my stories? I just bought that TV a few months ago after I sold that gosh-awful painting."

"Wait a minute," I say, forgetting myself. "You sold the Our Lady, Queen of Peace? But you were so thrilled when you won it."

"I was, because it was the first time in my life I actually won anything, but I didn't like the painting that much. Too big and modern looking. Mary looked like some kind of Arab or something."

Before I can jump in to point out Mary was born in the Middle East, she continues, "As soon as I got it home, I got my grandson, Jack, to list it on that Internet store thing and I sold it for more than I'd have ever thought it was worth, probably because I had Jack write down all about how this was one of that artist woman's last works and how she was murdered in such a grisly way. Stuff like that sells, you know?"

"Yes, ma'am, I know," I say, too stunned by what I'm hearing to process my friend's murder being used to line this old lady's pockets.

Oh, wait. She's talking again.

"But what I want to know, missy, is what you're going to do to get my TV back. I need to have it in time to watch my stories this afternoon."

"First, Mrs. MacMillan," Helen says patiently, "we're going to do everything we can to find the person who stole your TV. Second, you're not going to be getting it back today or tomorrow or the next day, no matter what. Things don't work that fast."

"That's what you told me when you kept my prize from me all those weeks, but as soon as I threatened to sue, you got busy pretty fast!"

"That's because you threatened to sue us just a few days before the culprit took a deal and the case was closed."

"You know what I think I'll do?" Gloria says with a distinct gleam of malice in her eye. "I think I'll call Dan Conway. Now there's a man who knows how to get things done. You know, back in my day, Dan would be the Chief of Police and you'd be home baking brownies. And," she continues, staring pointedly at me, "not for no priest, either. He'd be too busy caring for the sick to have any thoughts about getting married."

"If it makes you feel any better, Mrs. MacMillan, the first time Father Greer comes out to see you after we're married, I'll send a nice plate of brownies with him."

"Can't eat 'em if they have nuts in 'em," she says in the tone of a woman placing an order with a bakery that is about to go out of business.

"I'll keep that in mind," Helen says.

Serenity joins us on the porch, arms crossed and glaring at her grandmother-in-law. "Thank you for coming, Father Tom, Chief Parr," she says. "I'm sorry we interrupted your plans."

"Oh, not at all, Serenity," I say.

"I was just explaining to Mrs. MacMillan that, while we'll do everything we can, we can't guarantee we'll get her television back anytime soon," Helen says.

"We understand," Serenity says.

"Huh!" Gloria snorts. "That's only because you didn't have your precious possessions stolen!"

Helen glances at me, then back at Serenity. "I haven't read the report yet, but nothing else was stolen?"

Serenity's about to answer when Gloria snarls, "Of course not! She don't have anything worth stealing. Besides, it's her fault my TV was stolen anyway!"

"How is it my fault?" Serenity asks.

"You left the door unlocked."

"That door was locked, Gloria! Bob was the last person out and he locked it himself."

"Bob's an idiot and you know it!"

"I am sick to death of you running down Bob every chance you get!"

Helen holds up her hand and says, "Excuse me." The two women stop arguing and turn their attention to her. "Serenity, I know you told Officer Hallstead what happened, but why don't you tell me?"

I look at Helen, wondering why we're still here and not on our way out of town. "Helen, can't this—"

A quick side glance from her cuts me off. Serenity says, "Yesterday morning, at the crack of dawn—at Grandma's insistence, I might add—we all loaded up and left to drive to the annual MacMillan family reunion."

"The day after Thanksgiving?" I say.

"It's always held the weekend after Thanksgiving, for reasons no one can figure out."

"Always been that way," Gloria says. "Forty years, always been the weekend after Thanksgiving."

"Anyway," Serenity says, shooting Gloria daggers with her eyes, "we drove all the way to Quarryville, which you know, Father, is a three-hour drive from here. Of course, it took five hours because someone insisted on stopping for breakfast, then at an outlet mall."

"I had Christmas shopping to do," Gloria spits.

"So we finally got there about noon. We checked into our hotel, then went over to see family. Well, everything was going fine until the talent show—"

"—The family reunion has a talent show?" I ask, incredulous.

"Yes, every year," Serenity says. "It's usually painful—especially when cousin Emma reads her gosh-awful poetry."

"It is pretty bad," Gloria nods her head in agreement.

"Well, everything was going as it usually does. Uncle Greg had just finished his harmonica medley of songs from *Hamilton* when Bob's third cousin Virgil came on stage. Now, Virgil's in college, a theater major, so usually, he does some kind of dramatic reading from a play." Serenity takes a deep breath. "This year, he decided to come out."

"Oh, I see," I say.

"Yes, and he introduced his friend Colin as his fiancé to boot."

"I wouldn't have it," Gloria says with a sharp shake of her head. "No, no queers in my family. It ain't natural. Couldn't stay after that."

"Mrs. MacMillan," Helen says with her brow furrowed, "do you mean to tell me that you left the reunion because of that?"

"Oh, yes," Serenity sighs. "We had to pack everything up and leave because she demanded it. I mean, it's not like we could stay after the scene she made."

"I didn't do anything wrong!" Gloria insists. "I wasn't the one bringing disgrace to the family."

Serenity rolls her eyes. "So, we left about 11 p.m. and finally pulled in about 2 a.m. We were all exhausted, and all we wanted to do was sleep. But as soon as Grandma walked into her room, all hell broke loose."

Helen nods. "The door was locked when you came back?"

"Both front and back," Serenity nods.

"Bah!" Gloria says dismissively.

"Did it look like the locks had been tampered with?"

"Officer Hallstead looked at them and didn't say anything like that."

"Chit of a girl," Gloria mutters.

"Ok, Serenity. Thank you. Detective Conway may be around with more questions. In the meantime, Mrs. MacMillan," Helen says to Gloria, "is there anything else Father Greer or I can do for you before we leave?"

"Yes, you can go in there and tell Serenity how to clean off that gosh-awful fingerprinting stuff your girl officer spread all over the house. She's having the devil of a time with it," Gloria replies.

"I'll do that," Helen says, "while Father Greer here has a word of prayer with you."

I want to insist that I know all about removing fingerprint powder, but instead I say, as Helen and Serenity go inside, "Shall we bow our heads?"

"No," Gloria says sharply, causing me to jump. "I want to tell you something while we're alone."

I reach for my stole, saying, "If you want me to hear your confession, perhaps we should go somewhere more private."

"No, I don't want to talk about me, Father. I want to talk about you." Shaking her bony finger at me, she hisses, "Now, when you get to that hotel, don't you just jump on that poor woman. Young girls may like that these days, but grown women don't. You take your time, I don't care how long you've been without a woman. You understand me?"

I manage to choke out, "Yes, ma'am," even as I hear the weird buzzing in my ears that signals that I may be about to have a panic attack.

But that's always over something simple, like the fear of death.

This is so much worse.

Fortunately, having said her piece, Gloria MacMillan stands up suddenly and goes into the house, slamming the door behind her.

Alone now, I manage to breathe again and grope my way to the car, where I take a seat and rummage through Helen's giant tote bag for the bottle of water I know she always keeps in there. She comes out a few minutes later and says pleasantly, "Well, did you manage to straighten Gloria out?"

I nearly choke as I croak out, "Not nearly as much as she straightened me."

Three

Much to my delight, instead of going on a hike, we have an early lunch about an hour outside of Myerton. The foliage is far past its prime by now, but that just means that more light can get through the branches. We are seated by a window overlooking the increasingly bare mountains, but I only have eyes for the sunlight playing on Helen's raven hair.

The main reason that we come to out-of-the way places like this is so that we can indulge ourselves by acting like two people in love, instead of two pillars of a small-town community that is always on the watch for anything that someone somewhere might consider inappropriate. So, we indulge ourselves in ways we wouldn't at home.

Holding hands.

Whispering.

Discussing topics of a very secret nature.

"So," I whisper, "who do you think stole the TV?"

"No idea," Helen admits, rubbing her thumb over my hand and looking deeply into my eyes, "but I'm going to guess it was an amateur. I mean, there were a number of lighter, more valuable things they could have taken. When I went inside with Serenity, I peeked into Mrs. MacMillan's room. Her jewelry box was open and I noticed that there were a couple of what were obviously wedding and engagement rings. With the price of gold right now, those would have been much easier to take and to sell."

"And it happened when they were on their trip," I mutter. "Hmm, so whoever it was knew they were out of town?"

"Hold it right there, Father Brown," Helen says with a playful smile. "This is not a case for you. In fact, it's not even a case for me. Hallstead is a good officer and Dan is a great detective. Besides, someone at this table is always after me to delegate more, so I plan to do just that so I can concentrate on other things."

"Like what?" I ask with what I hope is a sly grin but probably looks more like nausea.

She leans forward and says seductively, "Like getting ready for our wedding and our new life as man and wife."

"Ooooh," I say, "I like the sound of that. Care to share any details with me?"

"Only if you'll lean in close so I can whisper it in your ear. You see, it involves matters of the bedroom."

I think my heart is going to stop and I am thankful that we are in a very public place as I lean forward and she whispers, "I have about 15 years worth of—"

Pent up passion, I think.

Lust and desire, I hope.

"—junk cluttering up my closet that I have to go through and pack up, not to mention all the stuff under my bed and in my storage room."

I deflate in a very obvious way and sit back in my chair, scowling at her. For her part, she feigns innocence and says, "Why, Father Greer, what ever did you think I was going to say?"

***

With nothing else to do after lunch, Helen and I drive back to Saint Clare's, where preparations for the first Sunday in Advent are in high gear. Marion Glass is putting the final touches on the Advent wreath and I must admit, she's outdone herself this time. Made as always from trimmings from the church's own box hedges, it measures nearly two feet across and, with the candles, more than 18 inches high. Satin ribbons, three purple and one pink, hang down below their respective candles, each taper standing ready to be lit, a new one each week as we, Christ's people, countdown the days to the anniversary of his incarnation.

I admit that Advent is my favorite season of the Church year, this year more than ever, as I have not one but two countdowns to celebrate. Helen and I are admiring the arrangement when someone calls Helen over to discuss some details concerning the decorations. The altar has no flowers on it, and will not until we welcome Christmas with banks of poinsettias.

I notice that the Book of Remembrances from All Souls month—November—is still lying on the altar, so I take this opportunity to gently close it and carry it reverently back to the sacristy. There, I lock it away, but not before I kneel for one last time to offer prayers for all the names of departed saints and sinners that it contains. "God, grant me the grace to escape being the latter and to become the former," I conclude before making the Sign of the Cross and rejoining the men and women working out front. I look at my watch and realize it is after 3 p.m., so I leave Helen there and return to the Rectory to relax a little before the 5 p.m. Vigil Mass.

During Advent, in order to take advantage of the shorter days to lower the lights in the church and thus draw more attention to the candles, I have moved the Mass time back to 5 p.m. This seems to be a popular idea, since it is better attended than usual. This doesn't surprise me, since the First Sunday in Advent is also the first day of the new church year and, just like those wanting to get in better physical shape often start going to the gym on January 1, so those who want to get in better spiritual shape will start coming to church during Advent.

Deacon Roderick does his usual excellent job with the Gospel, proclaiming with a firm but loving voice, "And then they will see the Son of Man coming in a cloud with power and great glory. But when these signs begin to happen, stand erect and raise your heads because your redemption is at hand."

Since I know that most of the folks present are parents with children, I tailor the length of my homily accordingly and, with the Deacon Roderick helping to distribute Communion, we are out of church in record time.

This works for me, since I have a surprise for Helen.

***

"OK, Tom," Helen says later that evening at the Rectory. "You've been acting mysterious long enough. What do you have up your sleeve?"

"Trust me, it's something you'll like. Just make yourself comfortable, honey," I say, disappearing into the kitchen.

Now, Helen is a mature, serious woman with a job that regularly puts her in contact with the worst side of our community. Because of her position as Chief of Police, she likes to present herself as the consummate professional. Perhaps because of that, when she lets herself go, she does so with complete abandon. That's why she's sitting on the couch now, clapping her hands and saying, "You know how much I love surprises, Tom."

"Well, I hope so, because I have been planning this one for a while." It is then that I come back to the living room and set a covered tray down in front of her.

"But first," I say dramatically, "you have to guess what it is."

"Ooooh. Even better. You know how much I love solving mysteries."

I remove the first napkin to reveal a bowl of popcorn.

"We are going to see a movie," she says with excitement.

"Correct," I say, removing the second napkin to reveal a plate of Christmas cookies.

"It's a Christmas movie."

"Very good," I nod. I pull back another napkin to uncover a bowl of teriyaki shrimp.

She looks confused and says, "A Japanese Christmas movie?"

"Sorta," I say, before removing the final napkin to uncover a box of powdered donuts.

She just stares at this for a moment, muttering, "A Japanese Christmas movie with powdered donuts . . . " Her eyes get big and she grins, "Oh, Tom, really?"

"Yes. I thought it would be a great way to get our first Advent together off to the right start." And with that, I hit 'play' on the remote and 'Jingle Bell Rock' begins to play as an unsuspecting John McClane lands in L.A.

John and Holly are walking off into the sunset, more or less, and the credits are beginning to play with a reprise of 'Jingle Bell Rock' in the background when Anna gets home. Even though it's nearly 9 p.m., she comes into the living room and asks us, without preamble, "Did you two finish the seating chart?"

Helen looks at me and I admit, "Anna, I am sorry. I completely forgot."

"That's OK, Tom," Anna says testily, turning a glare on Helen. "It's usually the bride's job."

"Now, wait a minute, Anna," I say, beginning to get aggravated.

Helen stops me by saying, "Anna, I am going to be gone for two weeks. I need to get as much done at the station as I can between now and then. Not to mention I need to pack up my apartment and get things moved over here. I don't have a lot of extra time. So please, tell me again why people can't just sit anywhere they want to?"

"Because there will be a lot of young families there, and they'll need to sit near the dance floor so they can dance and keep an eye on the kids," Anna says with precision. "There are also going to be a lot of old people, so they need to sit in the back, away from the band and near the restrooms. The gamers are going to be there, and they need to sit together because no one else can understand what they're talking about. Your officers will be there, and cops make people nervous, so we need to keep them together, and—"

Helen raises her hand. "You're right, Anna. I was a fool to ask. I'll tell you what, just give me the names of everyone who's RSVP'd and the diagram of the table set-up, and I'll take care of it at work on Monday."

"Thank you, dear," Anna says with a smile.

"No, Anna, thank you for keeping us on track."

Anna leaves and I ask Helen, "So who're you going to get to do it?"

"Well, I obviously can't assign it to anyone in the department, but Miriam has been insisting that she wants to do something, so I thought I'd ask her."

"Perfect," I say, popping the last donut in my mouth.

Helen turns and looks at the screen as the last credit rolls past. She snuggles closer to me, resting her head on my chest. "Tom," she says quietly. "Does it bother you?"

"Does what bother me?" I say, kissing the top of her head and inhaling deeply of the vanilla scent of her hair.

"That I haven't done more of the planning for the wedding," she sighs. "I mean, other than my dress and the cake, I've let Anna and Gladys do the heavy lifting."

"Don't forget the Archbishop providing the caterer."

"Oh, I won't forget that, Tom. Especially not after all he's done for us."

"Why are you asking this now? I mean, do you regret not doing it?"

"See, that's the thing," she says. "I really don't. I planned one wedding in my life down to the smallest detail. I thought I'd never have another one, and I wanted it to be the perfect start to our lives together. And my wedding to John was perfect. My dress, the flowers, the setting, the reception, the food—everything was exactly like I wanted."

She falls silent as a cloud crosses her face. I pull her closer and whisper, "But?"

"But," she says softly, "I now know something was missing. I was so intent on being the center of attention that I forgot completely about God. I guess that's why I'm so hands off. I don't want to make that mistake again, not after all He's done for us."

Kissing the top of her head again, I say, "I understand that, and I don't think anyone minds—certainly not Gladys, you know how much she loves this stuff."

"Ultimately, I just want to marry the man I love, in front of our family and friends, with God at the center. I don't care about flowers, or seating charts, or anything like that."

"Well, in that case," I say, holding her tight, "let others handle those things. Whether you do the seating chart or Miriam does it, we're still going to be married in twenty-eight days."

Four

I get into my office about 8:00 a.m. on Monday, figuring I might as well get some extra work done since Helen is working. As I've often mentioned, Monday is a parish priest's traditional day off to rest and recharge after a weekend of celebrating three Masses plus hearing confessions. But since I'm going away for two weeks for my honeymoon—a very non-traditional thing for a Catholic priest—I think I need to be in my office as much as possible in the little time remaining before the wedding.

I am going over the report of the previous day's offerings when the Rectory doorbell rings. Since Anna hasn't arrived yet, I answer the door myself. On the front porch is Dr. Martin Maycord, bundled up against the early December chill.

"Hey, Tom," he says, steam coming from his mouth and nose, "do you have a minute?"

"Sure, Martin, come on in out of the cold," I say. He comes in and I take his hat and coat. He removes his gloves and scarf, stuffing the former in his coat pockets and hanging the latter with the coat on the hall tree.

"I was just on my way to the hospital, and thought I'd stop by," he says. "I don't want to interrupt you, but since I know Monday's your usual day off—"

"You, my friend, are never an interruption," I say, clapping him on the shoulder. "Coffee?"

"Sounds great."

I go into the kitchen, pour two mugs of steaming morning brightener, and carry them into the living room where Martin is warming himself by the fire. He takes one of the mugs gratefully and sits in a wing chair. I take my place in the old burgundy recliner, which is my favorite place to sit in the room.

"Here to check on your patient?" I ask with a smile. "This is only my second cup, so after this, I'm done."

He laughs. "No, you seem to be doing fine. Unless you've been lying about the numbers you've been sending me, somehow your blood pressure's been stable through the holidays."

"Speaking of the holidays, I didn't have the chance to ask you after Mass yesterday about the rest of your Thanksgiving."

Martin sinks in his chair. "Insane and exhausting. If I wasn't on call Friday, I wouldn't have been able to get out of bed."

"What in the world happened, Martin?" I ask, incredulous. "You seemed fine when you left Saint Clare's."

"I was," he nods. "I was just thankful to get out of there after you rescued me from the turkey debacle. I went by the hospital to check on Bill's hand, you know, after he burned it getting the turkeys out of that smoker. I never realized how dangerous turkeys could be. They should come with some kind of warning label."

I try to suppress a laugh at the good doctor's expense. Certainly, his recent experience with turkeys hasn't been a good one.

"After I was done at the hospital, I went over to the Trents to help out. The next thing you know, I'm rearranging furniture and eyeing tablecloths with Mae to see if they were even and stuff like that. I tried to slip into the family room for a few minutes of peace and quiet, only to find that my Aunt Louise had taken that over and had the younger Trents and my nieces cutting fall leaves out of construction paper and writing what they were thankful for on them. She caught sight of me and told me to go out and find 'a nice limb that we can use for our thankful tree.'

"I liked this idea, especially after Mae said she'd go with me. I figured we'd go for a nice walk in the woods, maybe sit in the gazebo and, you know, talk."

"Oh," I say with a smile. "Talk."

Martin blushes a little. "Well, maybe not *just* talk. But it didn't matter anyway."

"What happened? Did Dominic come looking for you?"

He glares at me. "You know, sarcasm is unbecoming to a priest. We never got anywhere near the gazebo. The next thing I know, I'm struggling through fallen leaves, branches, and brush, while Mae stands on the path trying to direct me to the perfect branch." Martin snorts. "Branch? Hah! Log is more like it. I managed to drag it to the path, which wasn't easy, I'll tell you. Once I had it, I tried to interest her in the gazebo, but she insisted we had to get the limb back to the house so Aunt Louise and the girls could finish their project.

"After Dominic helped me carry it through the house and to the living room, I thought I could relax." He takes a deep breath. "Then, the worst happened."

Somehow, just from the look of horror on his face, I know what he's about to say. "Oh, no! Did Alan—?"

Martin nods. "Alan finds me and says, 'Martin, if you're not too tired of the job, could I get you to carve the turkey? I mean, you have had a lot of practice today.'"

"What did you say to him?"

"Tom, what could I say? I asked if I could have a quiet word with him. From the look on my face, he probably thought I was about to tell him I was dying of a terminal illness. We went into his den and, after he closed the door, I spilled everything. I told him that I'd never carved a turkey before in my life, that I'd probably committed some kind of crime in the way I hacked that poor bird at the Community Thanksgiving Dinner, that I could explain that being an excellent surgeon doesn't mean you know anything about slicing holiday poultry, and begged him not to tell anyone because I didn't want people to lose faith in my abilities."

"Martin," I say with a smile. "I have to say, I applaud your courage. It couldn't have been easy."

"I figured it was either that or being responsible for ruining Doris' beautiful turkey. I'd take Alan's disappointment in me as a future son-in-law and hope he could see past it. But I never in a million years imagined that he'd react the way he did."

I'm feeling a little queasy as I ask, "He didn't do something rash, did he? I mean, he's still OK with you marrying Mae, right?"

Martin laughs. "Not only that, I think he likes me better than ever."

"I don't understand," I reply.

"When he finished laughing, he told me a story. Apparently, the first time he went to Thanksgiving dinner at Doris' parents, they were all seated at the table around a turkey that would have put Norman Rockwell to shame. Well, Doris' dad stood up and announced that, as the newest member of the family, Alan was going to do the honors of carving the turkey that year. Alan said he'd never been so shocked in his life, but everyone was applauding and Doris was looking at him the way women look at the men they love, you know, so he took the offered carving knife and fork and, well, carved the turkey."

"I take it it went well?"

"Oh, no, it was a complete disaster. Alan says he started to carve, but he was shaking so hard, the knife slipped and he cut his wrist. He showed me the scar, and I can tell you it was a bad one. Doris wound up taking him to the ER for stitches. Alan said it was years before he could even look at a Thanksgiving turkey. He said to this day, he wishes he'd just had the courage to pass. At the very least, it would have saved him the embarrassment of bleeding over Doris' grandmother's Battenburg lace tablecloth."

"So, it all worked out, huh?"

"Yeah, after that, everything was just a blur of turkey and prayers and speeches and howling children fighting over the wishbone. By the time everything was over, I was actually looking forward to going home and sleeping alone, something I do not enjoy nearly as much as I used to."

I sigh. "Well, I can certainly relate to that. At least everyone had a good time."

"I did too, just so we're clear. It's just so exhausting. That's the thing. You know, my parents only had me and my sister, so holidays were pretty quiet, to say the least. And Sundays—well, you know about that. That's why I love being with Mae's family on Sundays and holidays. A part of me really enjoys the beautiful chaos of the Trent household. But another part of me is having a hard time getting used to the idea of this being my life, in our home, all the time, without being able to leave it and go somewhere quiet."

"Martin, you know we've talked about—"

Martin holds up his hand to stop me. "But I didn't come over here this morning to talk about that. I came to ask you a question."

"Oh, OK," I say, a little perplexed. "What do you want to ask me, Martin?"

He leans forward slightly in his chair and asks in a lowered voice, "What do you and Helen have planned for your wedding night?"

This obviously catches me off guard and I turn beet red as I stammer, "Uh—uh—well—you know—I mean, this is kind of personal, don't you think, even if you are my doctor?"

He laughs and says, "Sorry Tom, I worded that badly. What I should have asked was, do you have a place to stay yet?"

I laugh at my own embarrassment. "Oh, yes. We're driving up to Baltimore and staying at a hotel near the Inner Harbor. It's not exactly the honeymoon suite, but it's a very nice room. Why do you ask?"

He hesitates before answering, "Well, I happen to have a credit with the Beaumont for a luxury suite with a balcony overlooking the Inner Harbor. I have to use it by the end of the year, and since I'm not going to, I'd like you and Helen to have it. I've already checked and it is available that night. It comes with unlimited room service and a direct line to the concierge. Everything's already paid for, so all you have to do is check in."

I'm unable to hide my surprise. "Wow, Martin. That's amazingly generous of you. But why haven't you used it yourself?"

Now it's his turn to blush. "Look, Father, truth be told, it's the room I booked for Mae and myself a few months ago. You remember that big mistake, right?"

I nod. Martin, having spent most of his adulthood outside the Church, had previous relationships with women that, by his own account, consisted primarily of dinner together at night and breakfast the next morning. He'd taken Mae to dinner at the same hotel where he had a room already booked, believing that that particular date would end the same way. When she gently and lovingly set him straight on a few things—first, that she was a virgin, and second, that she was going to remain that way until she was married—Martin had cancelled the room and, as he told me, ordered dessert. It was only a few weeks later that he proposed to her.

"Well, I hope to stay there sometime in the future," Martin continues, "but not until Mae can go with me, if you see what I mean."

I grin at him and nod. "I do see. But it's so generous, I don't know—"

"Look, Tom," he says with a twinkle in his eye, "There is one thing you may not know about me. I hate waste. If you don't take this luxurious suite off my hands, there's no guarantee that I won't find a way to persuade Mae to go with me before the end of the year."

"I find that highly unlikely, knowing Mae."

"You don't know. I can be very charming and persuasive when I have to be. But think of the consequences. If we did that, then we'd have to elope and break her parents' hearts, or live in sin, or something like that. I mean, do you really want that on your conscience?"

I laugh as I hold up my hands in surrender, "OK. As long as it's OK with Helen, it's OK with me."

Myerton General's chief trauma surgeon breathes a huge sigh of relief. "Great. Thank you, Tom. This really is a load off my mind. I was wondering how long I could last thinking of that lovely room going to waste."

We stand and I shake his hand. "I'm glad I was able to remove temptation from your path, Martin," I say with a grin.

***

After the Noon Mass, I decide to walk to the Police Station for my daily lunch with Helen. Having gotten over my initial resistance to Martin's recommendation that more exercise is the key to controlling my blood pressure, I've begun walking more as the weather turns colder. Riding my bike is a bit uncomfortable in the chill.

I'm walking past The Old School, a charming building that was the Myerton Community School at one time. Tim Cooper, the young architect responsible for the redesign of the Myer Mansion into the Saint Francis Education Center, turned the building into a comfortable apartment complex with about 10 units.

A pickup truck is backed up to the front door. Always curious, I slow down and see two young men wrestling a large chest of drawers down a makeshift ramp. I rush up to help but by the time I get there, they have it on the ground.

"Can you guys use any help?" I ask, knowing that it's my obligation as a servant of God to offer but, as always, hoping they'll turn me down. Before either of the two young men can say anything, Gloria MacMillan pops her head out the door and says, "No need for that, Father. You're too old for this kind of lifting, You'd probably herniate yourself and sue me."

Before I can reply, she screeches at the younger of the two men, "AJ, be careful with that. My grandma brought that with her all the way from South Carolina more than 50 years ago."

AJ, who's red-faced and sweating in forty-degree weather, gasps, "Yes, Grandma. You've told me that a dozen times since we put it on the truck at Bob's house."

"If you weren't so thick-headed, I wouldn't have to repeat myself," she snarls. Looking at the other young man, who I now recognize as another of her long-suffering grandchildren, she snaps, "Jack, get around here and help him. You know he's not very strong."

They wrestle the dresser up the steps to the main door of the complex. I am about to try to slip away when Gloria says, "I'm moving in with AJ. I should have done it right after I got out of the hospital this last time. But Bob said it wasn't a good idea, what with AJ only having the one bedroom. But after being violated the way I was, I decided that place out of town's not safe for a frail old woman like me. Next thing you know, I'll be murdered in my sleep. I mean, I'm not saying AJ's worth much but at least he's sorta like a man."

"Of course," I say, trying to think of something encouraging to say. I look at the young man, who is leaning against the dresser just inside the door and trying to catch his breath. "AJ," I say with my best pastoral smile, "you're doing a good and noble thing, taking in your aged grandmother. I'm sure you'll be rewarded in heaven."

Under his breath, he replies, "Well, Father, that's good, 'cause I sure as hell ain't gettin' anything here on earth."

***

I'm walking back to the Rectory from lunch—a hearty vegetable beef soup, one of Helen's favorite recipes—when I get a call. A small shiver goes up my spine when I see the number.

I answer with a wary, "Good afternoon, Your Eminence."

"Father Tom," a boisterous Archbishop Walter Knowland replies, "I am glad to catch you. I know Monday is traditionally your day off."

"That's true, sir, but since I'm going to be gone for a couple of weeks at the end of the month I decided to be in the office as much as I can for Advent. Though right now, you've caught me walking back from lunch with Helen."

"And how is your lovely bride?"

"Very well, thank you. Hoping for a relatively quiet December crime-wise," I say.

"No murders, I hope?" he asks warily.

"None, your Eminence. In fact, the last murder in town was in October. Helen's not counting the body found near Myer College before Thanksgiving."

"No, considering that happened, what, a hundred years ago?"

"Yes, though interestingly enough, it turned out to be Anna's paternal grandmother."

It's actually more complex than that, but I doubt the Archbishop cares about the details.

He's quiet for a moment. "I read that in the paper," he says. "How is Anna dealing with everything?"

I take a deep breath. "About as well as can be expected. She's just going forward. You know how she is."

"Yes," he says quietly. "Yes, I do." He pauses, then clears his throat and continues, "I trust all of the wedding preparations are going well?"

"They certainly seem to be," I say. "Anna's handling the logistical details of the day. Our cake is in good hands. And Gladys Finklestein is coordinating the decoration for the reception."

"Aren't you confirming Ms. Finklestein soon?"

"Yes, Your Eminence. I'll receive her into the Church during the Midnight Mass of Christmas."

"Sounds like you have a busy month, the wedding aside."

"Well, you know how busy Advent is," I laugh.

"Yes, yes, I do," the Archbishop says. "Well, Tom, I do have a reason for calling today. When I was a parish priest, it was my practice to meet with the couple getting married for a private lunch a week or two before the big day. It gave us a chance to go over any details that might have come up about the Mass and to celebrate their imminent transition to marriage. I know this is short notice, but I am hoping that you and Helen can join me on Saturday, say around noon, for lunch. Father Wayne will be around and you can use that time to bring him up to speed on anything he will need to know while filling your pulpit during your honeymoon."

"That is fine with me, Sir. Let me check with Helen and get back with you."

"Excellent," he says. "Oh, and you can also carry the Gypsinian Christ Child back to Myerton with you."

The Gypsinian Christ Child is a life-sized model of the Infant Jesus, carved in walnut by the little-known Renaissance sculptor Geraldo Gaspar Gypsinian. I've seen and held the statue; it's lighter than it looks, with each detail of the infant carved in exquisite detail, and painted so it looks almost lifelike. Pope Leo XIII gave it to the Cardinal Archbishop of Baltimore in 1880, and it was the center of the Nativity scene at the Cathedral until 1965. The then-Archbishop, returning from a session of the Second Vatican Council, decided it should be passed from church to church in the Archdiocese, adorning a different local creche each year. This is our year.

"We'll be glad to do that," I say.

"Good, good," he says jovially. "I guess I will see you both on Saturday. Please, give my love to Helen and A—ahem, I mean, give my regards to Anna."

I smile, wondering again about his relationship with my mother-in-law, and say, "I will, Your Eminence. God bless you."

We both hang up. I text Helen about the lunch, and she says she'll put it on her calendar.

Five

The remainder of the week is surprisingly quiet. I'm actually able to finish my homilies for the second and third Sundays of Advent and make notes for my Christmas homily. We're having two Masses on Christmas Eve—one at 4 p.m., primarily for those with little children, and the traditional Mass at Midnight, which was well attended last year. There is a 10 a.m. Mass on Christmas Day, but fortunately, I have a priest from Frostburg coming to celebrate that one.

It is, after all, the day before my wedding, and Helen and I have something special planned in the morning.

On Friday, I'm walking past some store windows on Main Street. Now, like most small towns, Myerton's Main Street primarily contains quaint specialty stores—a candle shop, a bath shop, a yarn and quilting shop, and a couple of small dress shops, to name a few. In shopping for our honeymoon, Helen decided to go to the Hagerstown outlet malls because, as she said, "None of the shops here would have anything in my size."

One of the front windows of Patricia's Dress Shop catches my attention. It's a beautiful Dickensian Christmas village, complete with lights and small figures on the fake-snow-covered streets. I have to admit, I'm kind of a sucker for displays like this. *A Christmas Carol* is one of my all-time favorite Christmas stories, and I try to re-read the book and see one of the movie versions every year.

The fact that Dickens was a favorite of my Dad, I'm sure, has nothing to do with it.

After looking with childlike wonder at the display for several minutes, I begin to turn away and continue to my destination—Primrose Florists, to check on Helen's bouquet—when something—or I should say, someone, catches my eye.

"What are you doing in a dress shop, Steve?" I mutter.

Inside the store, Steve Austin is standing around, hands behind his back, looking here and there at the dress racks and mannequins. Not exactly where I'd expect the bartender of the Hoot-n-Holler to be a few weeks before Christmas.

I know I should just walk away. After all, it's his own business why he's here. It's nothing for me to be concerned about.

But my curiosity gets the best of me, so I walk into the shop.

"Oh, Father Greer," a young woman says. "Can I help you with something?"

Steve looks in my direction and appears startled. I say to the store clerk, "Um, ah, well yes. I wanted—oh, a scarf for my fiancée."

She smiles and says, "Let me get you a few things." She goes off and Steve walks up to me.

"Oh, Steve," I say, feigning surprise, "I didn't see you there."

"That's strange, Father," he says with a grin, "since you only came in when you saw I was here."

"Well, I hadn't seen you since Thanksgiving, so I thought—"

"Well, Steve, what do you think of this one?" a woman says behind us. We both turn to see Bridget Davis modeling a forest green wool dress with matching heels. Her mouth falls open when she sees me and she stammers,"Oh! He—Hello, Father Tom!"

"Hi, Bridget," I say. "Buying a new dress?"

"Yes," she says. "Yes. Um, for your wedding."

"Oh, I am so glad you're going to be there," I say. "You'll be at the reception, too, won't you?"

"Yes," she says. Glancing at the man standing next to me, she adds, "Steve invited me to go with him."

I look at Steve, who's trying to hide his embarrassment. "Really? That was very nice of you, Steve."

Steve opens his mouth to say something, but Bridget says, "I wasn't going to go—I mean, the reception. Still not really in the mood to celebrate love and happiness, you know. But Steve said he was going, even though he really didn't know many people, and he knew he'd stick out like a sore thumb, so he asked me to go with him. He convinced me that a night of dancing and good food is just what I need."

"I think that's very good advice."

"And when I told him I really didn't have anything appropriate to wear, he insisted on taking me shopping. So," she says, spreading her arms, "here we are!"

"To answer your question, Bridge," Steve says, "I think that one's perfect for you."

"Really?" she says, swishing back and forth slightly. "You think so?"

"Oh, yes. It really sets off your eyes and goes great with your red hair. Don't you think so, Father?"

I nod and say, "Yes, I agree with Steve. Very nice."

Bridget turns and practically skips back to the dressing room. "I think you've made her very happy, Steve," I say.

Steve turns to me and sighs. "Now look, Tom," he says quietly, "I don't want you getting the wrong idea."

"Hey," I say, holding up my hands, "I don't. I know you're just friends. I just think it's a very nice thing you're doing."

"Well, she's a great person," he says. "We've . . . we've really become pretty close in a short period of time. As friends, nothing more."

"Here you go, Father Greer," the store clerk says, returning from the back with some boxes. "I'm sure you can find something for her."

"Hmm," I say, stroking my chin, "do you have anything in a sapphire blue?"

"As a matter of fact," she says, shuffling the boxes like a deck of cards, "here you go."

I take the box from her hand and open it. "Yes, very nice," I say. "It'll go with her eyes."

"Excellent choice," she says. "Is there anything else?"

"I have another stop to make," I say. "Can you hold it for me? I promise I'll be back."

"Of course, Father Greer," she laughs. "Mr. Austin, are you ready to check out?"

"Oh, yes," Steve says. "Bridget—here she is. That's the dress, right?"

"Yes. It's the one you like, isn't it?" she asks with a smile.

"It looks great on you. Yes, I think we're ready. Father, good to see you."

"Good to see you too, Steve, Bridget," I say. I walk out of the store and turn towards the florist.

But when I glance back through the window, I see Steve looking at me.

Six

There are many things Helen and I see eye to eye on.

Time is not one of those things.

"We don't have to get there until noon," Helen says after picking me up from the Rectory at 9 a.m. We're heading to Baltimore on a rather dreary Saturday morning for our final lunch with the Archbishop.

"I know," I say. "But this way, you can give your lead foot a rest."

"After me about my driving again? You know I've never had an accident." she retorts.

"Oh, I know," I say with a grin. "But we're getting married in just three weeks and I don't want to take any chances. Besides, we'll have time to stop by The Muffin Man."

Helen pauses a moment, then says, "OK, I'll concede you made the right decision. This time. But your obsession with time's something you're going to have to work on."

I'm about to point out that maybe—just maybe—she should work on getting to places on time, but before I can, she pulls up to The Muffin Man.

The store's as crowded as it was last Saturday, but I don't see Nick behind the counter.

In fact, I don't see anyone behind the counter. I know someone's there, because the line's moving quickly and I hear a young woman cheerfully saying "Happy Holidays!" as each customer takes their order and the line moves up one.

I get to the counter and the young woman says, "Good morning, what—Oh! Father Greer!"

"Gwen?" I ask, startled to see the Myer College student behind the counter. "Have you started working here, too?"

Gwen Tolson brushes a stray blond hair out of her eyes and says, "Only on Saturdays. The Archives and Manuscript Reading Room is closed, of course, and I work at The Bistro Sundays through Thursday."

"Three jobs and going to school full time?" I shake my head. "When do you sleep?"

She sighs, and I see the weariness on her face. "Sleep? I remember sleep. But I have bills to pay, you know?"

"I know," I say, "And Myer's not cheap."

Her smile fades. "No, it's not," she says flatly. "Some people ask why I didn't go to a cheaper school closer to home, but that wasn't an option for me. What can I get you, Father?"

I look at her for a moment, wondering at what caused this bright and cheerful young woman to suddenly go dark, then say, "Two blueberry muffins, two coffees. One coffee with one sugar, the other cream and two sugars."

Gwen nods in acknowledgment and efficiently gets my order. I pay, and as she's handing me my receipt I say, "You know, Gwen, I don't know if you're Catholic or not, but if you ever need to talk—"

"Thank you, Father," she says quickly. "I'm not much of anything, truth be told. I'm fine. You have a Happy Holiday—oh, sorry, I guess I should say, Merry Christmas."

I smile and shake my head. "Either's fine," I say. "Take care of yourself, you hear?"

She nods and turns her attention to the next customer in line. I walk out, wondering what dark secret this young woman is trying to hide from the world.

***

We haven't even cleared the town limits when Helen's police radio goes off.

Once again, what sounds to me like someone trying to say the Gettysburg Address with a mouthful of marbles is instantly understandable to Helen. "Tom," she says without preamble, "there's been a robbery out this way. Do you mind if I stop in and check out what's going on? We have to drive right by the location."

"Helen," I say, "we need to be at the Archbishop's Residence by noon, remember?"

"Of course I remember," she says. "and you made us leave 30 minutes earlier than we needed to, as usual, thanks to your time fetish. So, we are already going to get there early."

"But if you stop—"

"Don't worry, Tom. I can always put on lights and sirens if I need to."

This thought terrifies me. But I know that interruptions like this are sure to be part of our lives together, so I put on a brave face and ask, "You're not going to have to work it, though, right?"

"Oh, no. They've already dispatched Potter to the scene. It's just that I'm right here and can do a little hand holding and hopefully keep anyone from messing with the crime scene."

We drive another mile or two before turning left onto a dirt road that meanders for what seems like forever. We eventually arrive at an early 1970s style concrete block house with several old cars on the lawn and numerous pieces of what appear to have once been types of mechanical equipment, now more rust than metal.

The victim of the crime, a man in his mid-fifties wearing denim overalls, sits on the porch swing, holding a shotgun across his lap.

Helen reaches into the glove compartment and pulls out her badge. She slips it over her head and looks at me. "Tom, stay in the car," she says firmly, reaching under her skirt for her backup. She gets out of the car and stands by it, not pointing her gun at the old man but making sure he can see it.

"Sir," she says firmly while holding up her badge, "I am Chief of Police Helen Parr, and I need you to put down that shotgun."

"Yes, ma'am," he says cooperatively, bending over and lowering the gun to the ground. "But you ain't got nothin' to worry about. It ain't worked in over 10 years."

"I understand that, sir, but I need you to walk down those steps and over to me, now." He complies and Helen pockets her own weapon. "Now, sir, why don't you tell me what was stolen?"

"My brand new welder," he says with disgust. "It just got here all the way from the Amazon last week. I hadn't even had time to use it." He pauses and then adds, "And my wheelbarrow, but it was pretty beat up, so I don't care about that."

I know what he means about Amazon, but I still can't keep visions of anacondas swimming in and out of a new welder while exotic birds call to each other from the tops of trees.

"Where was the welder?"

"Right up there on the porch," he says, pointing behind him.

Potter arrives now and Helen motions him over, saying, "There's a shotgun up there you need to secure and then I'll leave you with this. We've talked for a few minutes but I haven't taken a formal statement."

"Right, Chief," Potter says. "I'll get a description of the item and take a report. Anything else you want me to do?"

She looks around. "See if you can find anything that looks like wheelbarrow tracks. Mr.—"

"Spencer," the old man says, "Roscoe Spencer."

"Mr. Spencer," Helen says, "how big was the welder?"

"How big? Oh, I dunno. Maybe three feet tall, not including the tank of acetylene—they took that too."

"Could someone have carried it away?"

"I suppose, if they were like Andre the Giant—you ever see him wrestle, ma'am? Now, that was a wrestler, not like the prettified showboats they have now. I remember one time he was wrestling—"

"Thank you, Mr. Spencer," Helen says, holding her hand up. To Potter, she says, "They stole the wheelbarrow to carry the welder. Just see what you can find. Mr. Spencer, this officer will take your report so you can turn it into your insurance company."

"Don't got no insurance," he snaps. "I want my welder back."

With a patient smile, Helen says, "I understand, and we will look for it, but it's unlikely we'll be able to find it to return it to you."

"But without my welder," he says pitifully, "I cain't do my work. I've got all this to do," he adds, waving his arm over his yard of wrecked and rusting machinery.

"I am very sorry," Helen says. "We'll do our best. Potter, I'll leave you to this."

When she gets back in the car, I quip, "You know, Helen, I'm trying to decide if I should feel my manhood insulted that you told me to stay in the car."

"Look, Tom," Helen says with a hint of exasperation, "unless you're Superman—in which case I have to wonder when you're going to tell me—the strongest, most manly man in the world is no match for a bullet. My weapon, along with the training to use it, is."

"As always, you make a good point," I admit as we turn back up the road. We're driving along pretty slowly, since this is what my grandmother called a 'washboard road.' I admit to getting a little impatient as I see the time approaching 9:30 a.m., knowing that Archbishop Knowland is punctual to a fault, and expects punctuality in others.

But, with the way Helen drives, there's little reason to worry.

Suddenly, she slams on the brakes. We skid to a stop as she exclaims, "What the frankincense and myrrh!"

"What in the world?" I ask, looking around to find why she stopped so suddenly.

"Look at that," she says, pointing at the road and getting out. I get out, too, and follow her to where she's pointing. There, in the damp clay, is a rather deep impression of a wheel.

"Bicycle?" I ask, unimpressed.

"Maybe, but that's a mighty wide tire for a bicycle. Also, there are a couple of footprints behind it." She squats down and studies these for a minute before adding, "Look at the footprints. They're not nearly as deep as the tire track. Whoever was walking along here was pushing something pretty heavy."

"You mean like a welder in a wheelbarrow?" I ask.

"Yep. I'm going to walk a little ways and see where this goes. Can you just follow me in the car, please?"

"Sure," I say, always enjoying watching her work. Helen walks about 100 yards up the road while I creep along behind her. Then, she turns sharply and stops at the edge of the road, peering into the ditch running alongside. "Hey, Tom," she yells. "Come look at this."

I get out again and walk to where the wheel suddenly turns off the road, with the footprints behind it. There, well buried in the brush, is an overturned wheelbarrow and what appears to be a new welder and tank of acetylene gas.

"Come on," she says, "and watch your step." We walk back to the car and she grabs her radio mic. "Potter, tell the gentleman we found his welder. It's about a mile from his place, in a ditch along the dirt road leading to County Road 15. Radio for a couple of officers and the crime scene techs. I'll wait here."

She replaces her radio mic and I say, "Helen, do we really need to wait here? I mean, it's almost 10 a.m."

"I know what time it is, Tom," she says matter-of-factly. "You've been around enough crime scenes to know we can't leave it unsecured. There's always a chance the thief will come back."

"But we're supposed to be at the Archbishop's Residence by noon.," I point out. "You know what a stickler His Eminence is for promptness."

"What are you afraid of Tom? That if we're a few minutes late he'll say you can't get married? I think he's put a little too much effort into everything to pull the plug because we're not knocking on his door right at noon."

I open my mouth to say something, but Helen puts up her hand and says, "Listen, I've driven from here to Baltimore in under two hours. I'll put the lights and sirens on and put the pedal to the floor. It will be fine."

I turn away from her and look out the window. "Only if we get there in one piece," I mutter.

"I heard that!" Helen snaps.

"Sorry."

We lapse into a tense silence. Helen knows how I am about time, and I know how she is about speed limits. Every couple has their "thing," the one thing about the other person that drives them crazy. It's just something we're going to have to get used to.

Besides, I'm mature enough to admit that nothing bad will happen if we're a few minutes late. I also know that Helen's an excellent driver, and has never had a single accident even when driving at top speed. Of course, other cars get out of her way when she runs lights and sirens.

And if I'm being completely honest, I get kind of a thrill when Helen drives fast.

I'm just never telling her that.

After about 15 minutes or so of waiting, a couple of her officers get there along with the department's crime scene van. Helen shows them what we found, gives a few instructions, and then we're on our way again.

"So what do you think happened back there?" I ask, trying to distract myself both from the clock and the speedometer once we're on Interstate 70.

Helen's eyes are glued to the road in front of her as she replies, "My best guess is that whoever did this parked his car or, more likely, truck somewhere near the main road, maybe not wanting to wake Mr. Spencer, or maybe not wanting to leave tire tracks on the road. He walked to the house, snuck onto the porch, then tried to carry the welder. When he realized how heavy it was, he managed to get it into the wheelbarrow along with a tank of acetylene—probably not his best plan. Then, he got tired of pushing it, or maybe someone unexpected came down the road, so he dumped the evidence and planned on coming back later to get it."

"Mr. Spencer's place is off the beaten path," I say. "He has no neighbors, and it's not like that dirt road is a major thoroughfare. Who would have known he had a new welder in the first place? That can't be a long list."

"I'm sure Potter will ask him if he can think of anyone who'd try to steal his welder."

"Do you think it could be the same person who broke into the MacMillans' place?"

She shakes her head. "No. For one thing, two completely different items were stolen. I doubt the person who'd steal a TV would know anything about welders or what they were worth. Besides, Tom, it's not my case. Dan'll look into it. But it's not like there's much to investigate. Mr. Spencer will get his welder back and that's enough. Chances are, whoever did it was just trying to score some money for Christmas and will probably think better of it now."

Unfortunately, Mr. Spencer's welder is probably safer than we are as Helen puts her foot to the gas, determined to make up the time to Baltimore. My stomach drops when I see traffic slow in front of us but, as promised, she puts on her lights and siren and soon gets through, weaving in and out of the slowed cars and often driving in the break-down lane.

Helen and most of my body arrives at the residence at 12 p.m. sharp.

My stomach catches up with the rest of me a few minutes later.

Remember what I said earlier about the thrill I get when Helen drives fast?

Forget it.

***

"Tom, Helen, I'm so glad you could make it."

Archbishop Walter Knowland, the seventeenth Archbishop of Baltimore, clasps my hand in both his big, beefy ones and embraces Helen in a bear hug. The Archbishop is an imposing figure, both in terms of height and width. He's over six feet tall and sports a tuft of white hair on his otherwise bald head. I'm not sure of his age, but I think he's in his early sixties.

Probably his most striking feature is his expansive belly. Usually a very jovial man, he looks like Santa Clause without the beard.

"Thank you for inviting us, Your Eminence," Helen says with a smile.

"Well, as I told him—are you feeling OK, Tom? You look a little pale," he says with concern.

"No, no," I say quickly. "Fine. Just fine."

"I had to make up some time driving here," Helen says.

"Ah, I see," the Archbishop nods. "Now where—oh, here's Father Wayne."

Out of nowhere, Knowland's right-hand-man and personal assistant appears. He warmly hugs Helen—the ex-Marine chaplain is her spiritual director and frequent shooting partner—and shakes my hand firmly, his trademark scowl in place.

"Good to see you both," he rumbles. "Helen, how's that arm?"

"Better every day, Father," she grins. "My aim's almost back to where it was before I was shot. Dan's coaching really helped."

Father Wayne snorts. "Good to know Conway's good for something other than—er, well, never mind. Your Eminence, everything is ready."

"Will you be joining us?" I ask.

"Oh, no, no," he says with a quick shake of his head. "His Eminence wanted to meet with you privately."

He tells us good-bye and leaves, while the Archbishop shows us to the dining room where a delicious feast awaits us. According to the printed menu placed on each of our plates, we are having Watercress and Cauliflower Soup, followed by Pork Tenderloin with Braised Fennel and White Beans. Then for dessert, Pears with Maple Walnuts and Gorgonzola Cheese. The Archbishop is his usual jovial self and I finally relax by the time the pears are served.

"So, Helen," Knowland says with a smile, "how have your first few months as Chief of Police been?"

"Well," she says, "it's been an experience. The people who work under me are great—they're almost like family, frankly. The people I answer to?" She shrugs. "I'm still not used to the bureaucracy and the politics. I'd expect it in a city like Baltimore or D.C., but I'm kind of surprised that there's so much of it in Myerton."

"My dear," the Archbishop laughs, "you'll find that everywhere, in any organization, no matter what the size. Frankly, I feel the same way about my position. Love the priests, religious, and laity under me. But the internal politics of the Church above me?" He rolls his eyes.

"If we're any indication, Your Eminence," I say, "you seem pretty adept at navigating those waters."

He grows serious for a moment. "On this one issue, yes. But I had the support of the Holy Father. On other issues? Tom, I'm just another bishop."

We finish our pears in silence and the Archbishop escorts us to the sitting room where I take advantage of the fact that Helen is driving to enjoy a snifter of brandy while she makes do with a cup of coffee.

"Tom, how are things in the parish?" the Archbishop asks after taking a sip of his own brandy.

"Very good, Your Eminence," I say. "I'm baptizing at least two babies a month. Our religious education program is doing well, even in the absence of a Director of Religious Education. And thanks to the generosity of an anonymous donor, we're on track to open the Saint Francis Education Center by next fall."

"Good, good," he says with a smile. "Um, I don't want to get your hopes up, but I heard from Nashville the other day."

I sit up in my chair. "Yes?" I ask with excitement.

"According to the Mother Superior, they have several sisters completing training for their teaching certificates in the next couple of months. She may—may, Tom—may be able to assign one to Saint Clare's."

"Really? Oh, Your Eminence, that's just wonderful!" I say. After the disaster that was Leslie Williams—it doesn't get much worse than a Director of Religious Education who turns out to be the psychotic daughter of a serial killer who tries to kill Helen—I've resisted advertising for a layperson. I requested a sister from the Nashville Dominicans, an order known for their young and enthusiastic women dedicated to religious education. They're in such demand, I've had little hope of ever getting one.

"Oh, Tom," Helen says, grinning and grasping my hand, "I'm so happy for you."

"Now, now," the Archbishop says, "nothing is certain."

"Still, it's a ray of hope," I say.

We chat about other things for a few minutes, then Knowland says, "Now, with regards to the wedding. Tom, I will be staying at the Rectory and will make myself available to hear your confession that morning. It is a rare day when one can receive three sacraments within a few hours and the opportunity should not be missed." Turning to Helen, he adds, "Father Wayne will be available to meet with you, too, if you wish."

"Of course," Helen says, nodding.

"The Archdiocese official photographer and videographer will be there to document the ceremony. We'll provide any photos or video to the media outlets upon request. The Papal Nuncio will be in attendance at the ceremony, but not the reception—apparently, he has an engagement in the afternoon. After the ceremony is over and everyone's cleared out, you'll appear at the front of Saint Clare's for a photo op. There will probably be questions, and you can choose if you want to say anything or not."

"The press office let the media know they won't be allowed at the reception, right?" I ask. "We don't want our friends and family harassed."

"They've been told in no uncertain terms," the Archbishop nods. "And if any paparazzi show up, I'm sure there will be enough of Helen's officers in attendance to deal with them."

"It would be their pleasure," Helen says with a smile.

"Father Wayne's been coordinating the caterer, and everything's set with that. So," he says, clasping his hands together, "if you two can avoid a knock-down drag-out fight, we're going to have a wedding in a couple of weeks."

"Your Eminence," Helen laughs, "even if we do have a huge argument, we're still getting married. I'm not letting this man get away from me again."

We all laugh at this, then the Archbishop stands. "Tom, you have Mass at 5 p.m., so you two better get going. Father Wayne will walk out with you and give you the Gypsinian Christ Child. Take good care of it. It's priceless, you know?"

"We will," I assure him, "and don't worry about me being late for Mass. I'm sure Helen can make up any time we need. She certainly did on the way here."

She shoots me a look but says nothing. The Archbishop gives us a final blessing, we thank him for his hospitality, and take our leave.

Seven

I get back to the Rectory about 4 p.m. and find Anna in the kitchen. I pour myself a cup of coffee as she asks, "How was lunch? And where is Helen? I thought she was coming back here. Nothing's wrong between you two, is there?"

Less than a month to go now, and I swear that Anna is more nervous about this wedding than Helen and I are. "Everything's fine, Anna. Helen just dropped me off and went to the station to check on a robbery that happened this morning. We stopped by on our way to Baltimore, and she wanted to follow up with the officers."

"Wait," Anna says, a voice tinged with panic, "did you say there was a robbery? Wasn't the MacMillans' place robbed last week?"

"Yes, when they went to Pennsylvania for a family reunion. But Helen's not concerned. She says this always happens this time of year."

"But Tom, what about the Gypsinian Christ Child?"

"What about it?"

"Tom," Anna says, with more than a little exasperation, "have you forgotten that it is Saint Clare's turn to have it this year?"

"No, Anna, I haven't forgotten. How could I, since you've mentioned it to me at least once a day for the last two months. Helen and I brought it back with us from the Archbishop's."

"You did? Well, where is it? Someplace safe?"

"I brought it in with me when Helen dropped me off. It's on the coffee table in the living room."

"You left it in the living room!" Anna yells. "You can't leave it there! We're responsible for its care through Christmastide!"

"I know that, Anna"

"Well, what if it's stolen?" she blurts as she hurries out of the kitchen.

I follow her into the living room. "Why would anyone want to steal it, Anna?" I ask, beginning to be exasperated.

"Because it is priceless."

"To us, yes. But to most of the world, not so much. And anyway, no one even knows it's coming but you and me—oh, and of course Helen, who I certainly hope we can trust."

"And what does she suggest we do?" Anna says, glaring at me and crossing her arms.

"What do you mean?" I ask, my exasperation giving way to confusion.

"I mean, we are going to need some extra security around here, you know?"

"Again, Anna," I sigh, "I'm sure that Helen will agree that the best security is the fact that no one knows it's coming and won't find out it's here until the Christmas Eve Vigil Mass."

Anna doesn't respond to this. Instead, she looks away and bites her lower lip.

"Anna?" I say slowly. "No one else knows, right?"

"Well," Anna says reluctantly, "I might have told a few people." I stare at her now and she declares, "No one ever told me it was a secret. Not you, not Wal—the Archbishop, not anyone."

"So," I ask, crossing my arms, "who exactly did you tell?"

"Just Bill," she says, referring to Bill Brandt, the head of the Knights of Columbus and Anna's 'gentleman friend.'

"OK. Anyone else?"

"No, but Bill may have told the Knights, since I asked him to task them with building a new creche to house the statue."

I shake my head, but she continues, "And once I got to thinking about it, I thought that the Ladies of Charity would probably like to be involved, so I suggested at the last meeting that we make new robes for the figures in the existing scene, so they know."

"So Helen knew already?" I ask, wondering why she hadn't mentioned it to me.

"Oh, no, she didn't. I brought it up at the sewing meeting."

"What sewing meeting?"

She looks flustered and stammers, "Why, the—the one to make the robes for the figures, of course."

"But how could you already be meeting to make them if you hadn't proposed it until then?"

She's now red in the face and says forcefully, "Listen, Tom, I am not a suspect that you're trying to grill. I am a parishioner telling you that we have a problem, and I expect you to get on top of it."

"All right, All right," I cry, raising my hands in surrender. "I'll talk to Helen and see what can be done."

"Good," she says, stomping out to her own office and then, pausing, saying, "I'm going to make some tea. Would you like some?"

"No, no, I'm fine. I need to get over to the Church for 5 p.m. Mass."

"Of course," she says. "What are you going to do with the Gypsinian Christ Child?"

I take a deep breath. "Since I presume you're going to be here until I get back," I say, "how about I lock it in my office? Helen's coming over for pizza and Risk, so I'll talk about it tonight."

Anna nods and walks out, leaving me wondering once again what's going on in my own parish.

***

"Ah, Father Tom, here you are."

I smile at the older man in the Sacristy. "Hello, Deacon Derek," I say, extending my hand.

"How was your lunch with the Archbishop? No problems related to the wedding, I hope?"

"Oh no, no," I say, shaking my head. "He has a tradition of having lunch with a couple he's marrying a couple of weeks before the ceremony. It was a formality, really."

"Of course," I say. "Did he happen to say what my responsibilities would be that day?"

"No, but I can't imagine they'd be any different than a normal Sunday Mass. I believe Father Wayne's concelebrating. He said the Papal Nuncio is attending, but nothing about participating in the Mass. I think if you're at the rehearsal on Christmas evening, you'll have more clarity."

"I'll be sure to be there."

"Are you sure Linda won't mind?" I ask, referring to his wife.

"Huh?—Oh, no. I'll spend Christmas Day with my wife, but be back in Myerton in plenty of time for the rehearsal."

"Good, good," I nod. "By the way, I don't remember seeing your RSVP for the reception. You are going to be there, aren't you?"

"I'd been meaning to mention that to you," Derek says slowly. "I will be there, but Linda won't be able to be at the reception or the wedding, for that matter. She needs to take her mother to Delaware to see some relatives to celebrate their Christmas that day."

"Oh, well, Helen and I will miss her. But Derek, don't you need to go with her?"

"I have my responsibilities here at Saint Clare's," he answers matter-of-factly.

"I appreciate your commitment," I say, "but if you have family obligations—"

"I don't," he blurts. Then, more softly, he adds, "I mean, they're her family. I don't really get along with them, you see?"

At this point, I could take the opportunity to remind Derek of his obligations as a husband to be supportive of his wife, even in difficult family situations.

But, instead, I say, "Well, again, I appreciate your loyalty. But if something comes up and you need to go with Linda, I'll understand."

"I appreciate it, Father," Derek says. Looking at the clock on the Rectory wall, he says, "It's almost time for us to begin. Dominic's probably beginning to panic because we're not where we're supposed to be."

I laugh and say, "Well, we'd better get out there then."

**

"Tom," Helen says as she moves her pieces around the board, "this is not D.C."

"I know that," I say as I study the board. "But Anna's half-convinced herself that organized gangs of thieves are just waiting for the chance to steal the Gypsinian Christ Child."

"I mean, if we were in D.C., her concerns might be justified. Theoretically, some high-end thief might want to steal a valuable art piece to sell on the black market. But this is Myerton, where some low-life thief wants to steal something he can sell at the flea market or pawn for some quick cash."

"Look," I say, moving some of my pieces, "I'm on your side on this. I think she's being ridiculous. But Anna's not someone we can just ignore. Don't you have any professional advice on how we can keep the figure safe?"

Helen sighs and shakes her head. "The best thing you can do is just keep quiet about it and keep it locked up in the church."

"Well," I say reluctantly, "we can certainly keep it locked up in the sacristy, but I'm afraid it's too late now to keep it a secret."

"What do you mean?"

"I mean, darling, that Anna's already told Bill, who told the Knights of Columbus so they can start building a new creche, as well as the Ladies of Charity so they can make some new costumes for the other figures in the Nativity scene. And considering how gossipy both Knights and Ladies can be, it's probably common knowledge in the parish by now. So given all that, what do you recommend?"

"What does Anna want?" Helen exclaims. "Does she want me to assign an officer to guard the statue 24/7? I can't do that, Tom. I don't have the manpower, not to mention the fact that I'm pretty sure that Balaam's donkey of a Deputy Mayor will say I'm using city resources in the unconstitutional support of religion. The Christ Child's still going to be safe enough locked in the church. There's nothing about any of these break-ins that indicate the thief is any kind of professional. In fact, the evidence we have points to a rank amateur."

"OK, I see your point about that."

"Besides, most people are still reluctant to steal from a church, whether because of superstition or just a sense of honor. So yeah, it should be perfectly safe in the sacristy."

I grab my phone, prompting Helen to say, "We agreed, no devices during date night."

"Except for an emergency," I point out, "which is why you have your radio. I'm just texting Anna to tell her what you said. She's over at Bill's house."

I do that then watch Helen study the board. "Do I have you confused?" I say with a wry grin.

She fixes me with a stare. "Confused, Father Greer? You underestimate me. How many games have I won?"

"Thirteen."

"And, let's see," she says, tapping her chin, "how many have you won since we started playing Risk?"

I sigh and slump a little. "None," I mumble. It was my idea that we play something besides Monopoly all the time—which, ironically, I finally won a couple of months ago.

Of course, that's the last game I won.

"Tom," Helen says with a wicked smile, "I never knew you were this much of a masochist. And I know how much you dislike board games in the first place."

"Oh, I really can't stand them," I nod.

"Then why?"

I chuckle. "Come on, Helen. You're a great detective. You know the answer."

She leans on her elbows and says, "Oh, I do know, Tom. I just want to hear you say it."

"I subject myself to this torture," I say in a low voice, "because—"

Just then, my text message alert dings. Then dings again. Then again.

"What the heck?" I say, looking at the phone.

"You'd better check it, in case it's important," Helen says as she picks up the dice and shakes them.

I do just that. I furrow my brow when I see who the messages are from.

"Oh, boy," I sigh. "They're all from Anna. 'Is that the best she can do?' says the first one. She follows that up with, 'I'm leaving Bill's right now.' Finally, she says, 'Don't move the GCC without me!'"

"Dang it," Helen says, tossing the dice wildly. "And I was hoping not to make her mad before the wedding."

"She's not mad. She's just concerned about the statue."

True to her word, Anna flies into the Rectory about fifteen minutes later. We've abandoned the game and are snuggling on the couch nursing a couple of beers.

"Should you really be drinking, Helen?" Anna asks without preamble.

"I am off duty, Anna," Helen replies. "Besides, I've just started this one, and it's the only one I've had so far."

"I just—I mean, can you be alert with alcohol in your system?"

Helen stiffens in my arms. "Anna," she says carefully, "what exactly do I need to be alert for?"

"We're taking the Gypsinian Christ Child from the Rectory to the sacristy," she says. "We'll be outside in the dark. What if someone jumps out of the shadows and tries to take it?"

"If that happens, I'll throw Tom at them to distract them while I run into the church with the box."

Anna glares at Helen while I try not to laugh. "I'm hurt, Helen," she says, "that you would take this so lightly."

Helen sighs. "I'm sorry, Anna. You're right. I should take this more seriously." She stands up and says, "Let's do it right now."

Standing, I say, "I'll go get the box."

I walk to my office, get the Christ Child, and return to the living room.

"Have you seen it?" Helen asks me.

"I saw it years ago," I say. "Anna?"

"It's been a long time," she says quietly. "I remember thinking it was the most exquisite Christ Child I'd ever seen."

"Well," I say, sitting the box on the coffee table, "let's take a look at our precious charge."

I lift the lid and we peer inside. Nestled in straw is the Gypsinian Christ Child. The statue itself is smaller than I remember it, but then people, and babies, were smaller 500 years ago. It is indeed beautiful, with the child appearing almost lifelike, with smooth skin and small, delicate features. Our Lord's depicted with brownish hair and brown eyes, befitting a child born in the Middle East. He has a slight smile, and his hands reach upward. Looking closely, I notice the fingers of his right hand are formed to give a blessing.

"It's beautiful," Helen whispers. "So lifelike."

Anna's transfixed by the statue, and I see tears come to her eyes. She reaches out and gently strokes the fingers of the baby, just as she probably once did Joan.

"I won't lose you this time," she says in a barely audible whisper. "I won't do that to him."

Not certain I heard her right, I ask Anna, "What was that?"

"Huh?" she starts. "What?—Oh, nothing. We need to get this under lock and key as soon as possible." Glaring at Helen, she asks bluntly, "Where's your gun?"

"Locked up in the safe at the police station where it always is when I don't need it."

"But what if someone tries to mug us as we're walking over?"

We both look at Anna incredulously as Helen says, "Anna, I have my backup in the gun safe here, but I can tell you I am not going to shoot someone, or even threaten to, over a statue, I don't care how irreplaceable it is."

Anna squares her shoulders and looks like she's about to say something, but I pick up the box and head to the door, saying, "Well, we'd better get this over to the sacristy before it gets any later."

We walk to the side door of the church, Helen making exaggerated movements to indicate she is on alert while Anna just glares at her. Unlocking the door, I let Helen go in first to assure Anna that no one is crouching in a pew waiting to steal a 500-year-old statue of the baby Jesus to sell it to the Chinese—or whoever would want one. The door to the sacristy is unlocked, but there is a cabinet where all the altarware is kept.

"Anna," I say, "I'm putting it in this cabinet. It's kept locked, and I'll even lock the door to the sacristy."

I unlock the cabinet and place the box carefully inside. After locking the cabinet, we walk out of the sacristy together and, with a flourish, I lock the door and place the keys firmly in my pocket. "There, Anna. The statue is locked up and anyone wanting it will have to kill me to get the key."

"Fine. Now, if you two are finished making fun of me for taking proper precautions to protect the Church's property, I will go to bed now."

"Anna," I say, "we weren't—."

Turning to me, she points her finger at me. "Yes, you were, Tom," she says. "You think I'm being a foolish old woman. Well, the Archbishop has given us a great responsibility. And I for one am going to make sure that we don't let him down."

She turns on her heels and marches out of the church, the bang of the closing door echoing through the empty space.

"What is it with her?" Helen whispers.

"I don't know," I say. "But something tells me there's more to it than just the statue."

Eight

I'm at my desk on Monday morning, reviewing some papers for the Parish Council meeting on Tuesday, when my phone rings. Since Helen hasn't called yet this morning, I pick it up and say, "Hey, honey, I've missed you today."

Instead of Helen, I hear the giggling of an alto chipmunk. "I've missed you too, Dad," Gladys Finklestein laughs.

"Oh, Gladys," I say to my surrogate daughter, "I thought you were Helen."

"Obviously." Then, turning uncharacteristically serious, she says, "Dad, you need to come to the Mansion right away."

Something in her voice causes my stomach to sink. "What's wrong, Gladys?"

She takes a deep breath and says, "Well, you see, it's like this. We're over here beginning to decorate for the reception—"

"You're decorating for the reception? But, that's not for over two weeks yet. And don't you have to work today?"

"To answer your first question, yes, Dad. These things can't be left until the last minute. Besides, Mom's entrusted me with this. As for the second, I've taken the entire month off. Turns out if I don't use the leave I've accumulated, I'm going to lose it. It's that jackass Deputy Mayor's idea, frankly. For some reason, he doesn't like the idea of a member of city government never having taken a vacation. So, here I am."

"Can Helen get along without you for a whole month?"

"I guess we'll find out. If there's a murder or a crime spree or something that requires my unique set of skills, I'll just come in off the clock. It's not like I really need the money."

After losing her parents in a hit-and-run accident when she was 8 years old, Gladys' grandparents raised her. When she turned 21, she came into possession of a trust fund left her by her parents and prudently invested by her grandparents. In fact, she's worth several million dollars.

"Anyway, that's not important," she says frantically. "You've gotta get down here."

"Just tell me what happened."

"OK, well, now, you know how Nate isn't very adept mechanically?"

I don't, but having known Nate Rodriguez for quite a while, I'm not surprised.

"Well, I rented one of those mechanical scaffolds—you know, the ceilings in the ballroom here are really high—and Nate was moving it and he kind of lost control and he bumped into a wall."

"Is Nate OK?" I ask, proud of myself for asking after his welfare instead of the condition of parish property.

"He's fine—upset, convinced you're going to kill him, you know, the usual. The wall—well, OK, he sorta went through it."

"Gladys!"

"Before you start yelling, you need to come down here and see. It's—it's just incredible."

"What is?" I ask.

"What we found behind the wall."

***

By the time I get to the Mansion, Tim Cooper is standing with Nate and Gladys in the Myer Mansion's ballroom. The piece of equipment Nate rammed into the wall has been moved, and the damage is apparent.

Seeing me, Nate and Gladys rush over to me. "Father Tom," Nate says frantically, "I am so, so sorry about the wall. I'll—I'll pay for the repairs."

"Bae, Father Tom's not angry—or at least won't be when he sees it."

"Gladys," I say, surprisingly calm in the face of the carnage, "You keep saying that. Well, I'm here. Show me. And by the way, what's Tim doing here?"

"He was the second call I made. Come on!" she says with excitement. She spins her teal wheelchair around and rolls back to where the young architect's staring at some blueprints and shaking his head.

"Tim," I say. "Good to see you."

Looking at me, he points to a spot on the blueprints, which I now see are of the ballroom. "See," he says, almost as excited as Gladys. "It's not here! It's not shown on the plans for the addition from 1925. And these are the oldest blueprints I've been able to find."

"Whoa, whoa, Tim," I say. "I still don't know what you're talking about! What is going on here!"

"Come on, Father," Tim says. He starts walking toward the large hole in the wall. I know enough about houses to see that the wall's not modern drywall. Instead, it's plaster over a metal mesh. Plaster bits and dust cover the floor right under where Nate made impact, the mesh bent inward and broken.

"Is there a room behind there?" I ask Tim as I peer inside. "There's not a lot of light."

"Not just a room, Father," Tim says with a grin. Taking a flashlight out of his pocket, he shines the beam inside.

When I see what the light hits, I cross myself and whisper, "Jesus, Mary, and Joseph!"

Tim's flashlight reveals a beautiful wood altar with an exquisitely carved crucifix. There are two rows of pews in the same style as the altar. On the altar, on either side of the crucifix, are statues of Our Lady and Saint Joseph.

"What's that in the corner? Is—is that a little shrine?" I whisper.

"The votive candles, I can't identify the saint statue, but that's what it looks like to me," Tim says in a hushed tone.

"What is it, Dad?" Gladys asks quietly.

"It's a small chapel," I say. "Wealthy Catholic families would often have them in their homes. The Myer family would have used it for family prayers, maybe the occasional private Mass."

"If I'm right," Tim says, continuing to look around the room, "this was part of the original house. It was probably walled over when the ballroom was expanded in 1925."

"Why would anyone do that?" Nate says. "I mean, the Myers were a pretty devout family, weren't they?"

"Well, the original family was. They helped finance Saint Clare's reconstruction after the original church burned in the 1850s. But by the 1920s, I think the family was far from devout."

"The fact they just walled this up confirms that," Gladys mutters.

"Tim," I say, "can you get some workmen out here to finish what Nate started? Then, I don't know, frame it out and maybe put some doors?"

"Sure," he says. "I'll get a couple of guys from a project in the historic district. I'll need to make some measurements, but it will be done in a few days."

"Good," I nod.

"What are you going to do with it, Father?" Nate asks.

"Do with it? Why, Nate, you found the chapel for the education center."

***

"So the workmen came," I say to Helen over dinner that night. Once again, we've opted for the couch instead of the dining table as simply more comfortable. "Once they cleared what was left of the wall, Tim said it was safe to go inside. The wood altar and pews are just gorgeous! I mean, they need some restoration work, and we'll have to expand it, but it's going to make a great chapel for the center. Imagine! I can say Mass right there for the children. Isn't that fantastic?"

I look at Helen, expecting an enthusiastic answer. Instead, she's looking at her plate and pushing the Brussels sprouts around her barely-touched chicken.

"Helen?" I prompt, but she doesn't answer me. "Hey, Helen?"

"Huh?" she finally says. "What? Oh, sorry, darling. You were saying?"

It's unusual for Helen to just zone out like this, so I place my hand on her shoulder. "Darling, have you heard anything I've said in the last fifteen minutes?"

"Don't be silly," she says, dismissing the statement with a wave of your hand. "You were talking about—about—the birthday party for Jesus?"

I shake my head. "No. Not even close. What's wrong, honey?"

"I don't know," she sighs, "and I'm probably making a mountain out of a molehill, but I think the Ladies of Charity are mad at me."

I look at her with astonishment. "What—what in the world makes you think that?"

"A couple of things, actually," she says, placing her plate on the coffee table and turning to me. "For one thing, there's this sewing meeting Anna mentioned. No one told me about that."

"They don't know that you sew. In fact, you've gone out of your way to keep them from finding out."

"But they could have at least invited me. I mean, no one's even asked me if I could sew or not."

"Well, they know how busy you are, being Chief and getting ready for the wedding."

"I could understand that, and what you say makes sense. But the last couple of meetings, when I get there, it's like everyone else has been there for a while, and they're finishing up something that I don't know about."

"Have you asked Anna about this?"

"Yes, and she insists that I'm imagining things. She says the other women get there early because they have nothing better to do. But it still feels weird."

"Honey," I say, taking Helen's hands. "Anna loves you and I'm sure the other women do, too. I think you're just stressed out and looking for problems where there aren't any."

She snuggles down next to me, and I put my arm around her shoulders. "I guess I'll just be glad when it's over."

"The wedding?"

"Yes, and all the hoopla around it. I mean, Gladys is about to drive me crazy with everything she wants to do for the reception. Thank goodness Miriam had time to do the seating chart, or Anna would still be giving me grief about that. Tom, the fact of the matter is, I'm too old for this. Unlike the first time I got married, I know that the joy of sharing a life together far outweighs the wedding day, no matter how splendid. My heart already lives here," she says, waving her hand around the room, "and here," she adds, touching my chest over my heart. "Until the rest of my body can join it, I feel separated, torn apart."

"I know, darling," I say, kissing the top of her head. "I feel the same way. Honestly, if we weren't Catholic, I'd propose we elope, just slip down to the courthouse and be done with it. But, as I've told you again and again, you are the most precious person in the world to me, and you, and all that we will have together so soon now, is worth planning and waiting for. Besides, it's just a few more weeks."

"But Tom," she says with a naughty gleam in her eye, "if we elope, you wouldn't have to deal with your mother and her boytoy."

Suddenly, what Helen says makes sense to me. I actually ponder checking with the Archdiocesan canon lawyer to see what my options are. But after a few minutes, I admit, "OK, that is tempting, but she'd probably come here anyway, insisting that she'd already bought the plane tickets and Trevor—I have asked you not to refer to him as her 'boytoy'—wanted to see snow for Christmas or something gross like that, so no, I still think we should just tough it out."

She fakes a pout at this, but a smile soon gets the best of her and we move on to watching one of my favorite Christmas movies, *The Bells of Saint Mary's*. Later, as we're saying our goodnights, I remind her, "Don't forget, we have the Knights' Christmas Party tomorrow night."

"I won't forget," she assures me. "I'm looking forward to it."

Nine

I get over to the church basement early on Tuesday evening so I can help the other members of the Knights of Columbus get the food ready. I'll admit that I've never been one to join clubs or organizations—I'm kind of like Groucho Marx, you know? He once said, "I refuse to join any club that would have me as a member." But since becoming Saint Clare's Rector and being committed to being the best priest I can, I've become a fairly active member of the Knights. I don't make every meeting, but I attend those I can and help out at events like this.

The main ministry of the Knights is making wooden toys for children by hand, which they pass out every Christmas to the poor and needy. Since I have no carpentry skill—my one attempt at shop class in high school resulted in five stitches and an immediate transfer to home economics—I figure I can at least help in the kitchen.

When I arrive, I notice the men are all in a good mood. With the food in the oven and the tables set up, they're gathered around telling stories and drinking adult beverages of various kinds. Since the wives—and in my case, fiancée—will not arrive until time for the party to actually start, the men take this opportunity to give me advice.

About, shall we say, the wedding night.

Not necessarily good advice or sought-after advice or even needed advice, but mainly alcohol-fueled advice.

Bill gets the ball rolling. "You know, Tom," he says, clapping me on the shoulder with one hand and holding a beer with the other, "I envy you, getting a fresh start at your age. I mean, I've been a widower now for almost a decade and it sure does get lonesome." He lowers his voice and says, "Especially at night. You know what I mean?"

Not knowing what to say, I manage, "Well, I—"

"I know you do," he says with a wink. "Now, you'd think that having Anna would make things better, and in some ways it does, but in others, well, let's just say that going home to a cold house after being out with a warm woman can be pretty miserable."

I am desperately trying to get away from him while trying to erase the idea of Anna being warm from my mind when he claps me on the shoulder again and says rather loudly, "Of course, those days are almost over for you, Father, aren't they?"

"Ahem, yes," I say, managing a weak smile. "I guess they are."

"Darn right they are, thank the Lord," Bill says before walking off to join the conversation a group is having in the corner.

I breathe a sigh of relief just as Dan comes over and says, "Hey, Father, can you help me get the paper goods out of my car?"

"I'd be happy to," I say, thankful to get away before another man decides to counsel me.

We head out into the cold and Dan says, "I don't really need help. It's just that I wanted to talk to you, you know, alone, before Helen gets here."

"Is anything wrong?" I ask, nervous now.

"No, not really, at least nothing that's not to be expected." He pauses and studies his shoes, rocking from one foot to the other as I stand there getting colder. Finally he says, "Umm, I went into Helen's office the other day without knocking and, ah, I mean the door was open and everything. But, umm, she was, uh, looking at a magazine."

"What kind of magazine?"

"Well, see, that's the thing. It was, ah," and here he lowers his voice, "Cosmopolitan."

"Oh, I see," I say, even though I have no clue what he's trying to say.

"Well, I just hope you do," he says. "I mean, she's obviously nervous about something, because otherwise, why would she be looking at something like that?"

"What could she be nervous about, Dan?"

"She's a very special woman," Dan says, not answering my question. "Very, very special. There's not another woman in a million like her."

I look around just to make sure Miriam isn't nearby.

"She's had a lot of sadness in her life—some of it caused by you, remember. But you've got another chance with her." He stabs me repeatedly in the chest with his finger as he continues, "It's your responsibility to see to it that she's happy, you got that? Otherwise, well, you'll have to answer to me. And I think we both know what that means."

"Of course, Dan," I nod, completely flustered by now. "I appreciate your concern and how much you care about Helen but, you know, I have been married before."

"Yes, and I'm sure Joan was a fine person, but Helen is special and I don't want you to ever forget it. OK?"

"Sure, Dan. Sure."

We shake hands like two little boys told to make up after a fight and then turn to go back inside. I pause and say, "Go ahead. I just need to check something on my phone. You knew there's not much of a signal down there."

"Sure, Father," he says. "I'm glad we had this little talk."

As he walks away I text Helen:

Can you go ahead and come over now? I am being inundated with unwanted advice. Save me, please!

Thankfully she quickly replies:

Heading over in five minutes. Hang in there.

I initially plan to stay outside until she arrives but the cold soon drives me back inside. I haven't been back inside the basement for two minutes when Herbert Geoffs walks up to me—actually, I should say, staggers up to me.

"Well, Father," he slurs, "I guess your life as a free man is about to end."

"Ah," I say with a strained smile, "I guess that's one way of looking at it?"

"I feel so, so sorry for you," he says with a mournful expression. "To tie yourself down like that, to one woman. Hell, I've had two wives myself—not at the same time, you know, one right after another."

I nod, remembering that on the rare occasions when Herbert attends Mass, he slips out right before communion.

"My first wife, now, she was a beauty. But a she-devil. A real she-devil. You know, I actually caught her in the act—you know, *the act*. And who do you think it was, Father? Huh?"

"I, ah, I have no idea," I say, looking furtively at the entrance to the basement.

"Guess," he says.

"Beg pardon?"

"Guess? Guess who I caught my first wife in the act with?"

"Oh, I don't think—"

"My brother. Can you believe it? My own damn brother. My older brother, not my younger one."

"Oh, I am so sorry. I bet that was a shock."

"Not as much as you'd think," Herbert says sadly. "Always wanted everything I had. Took my bicycle when we were younger. I guess if you steal your brother's bicycle, it's no big deal to steal his wife, huh?"

At this point, I have no idea what to say, so I just shrug like an idiot.

"So I dragged him out of the bed and beat the crap out of him—made for an awkward family Thanksgiving that year. Divorced her first chance I got. But did I learn my lesson? Noooo, not me. I got married again. Now, my second wife, she was something else. She didn't cheat on me."

"Well, that's good," I say, because what else can I say?

"No, she didn't cheat on me. Just made every day a living hell. I tell you, Father, that woman had only one way of communicating, and that was full volume. Sometimes, I can still hear that shrill voice of hers." He takes a deep breath, then screeches, "Herrrrrrberrrrt!"

A hush falls over the entire basement as every eye turns to Herbert and me. After a second, people resume their conversations, I guess satisfied that nothing too terrible is happening.

Herbert just stands in front of me, shaking his head. "No matter what you think, nothing will ever be as good as you think it will."

He wanders off, and I am now staring at the door, willing it to open. But when it finally does, I face the disappointment of seeing, not Helen, but various and sundry other women. One right after another, they arrive, joining their husbands, leaving me standing like a wallflower at the junior high dance.

On the one hand, I'm thankful that this will at least stop the unwanted marital advice. On the other hand, I am wondering where Helen can be. Her text a half an hour ago said she was on her way, but since then, I've heard nothing. Knowing service in the basement is spotty at best, I keep trying to get back outside to check my phone. But every time I do, someone buttonholes me with a question about the wedding or Advent or something equally mundane. I'm almost to the door when Anna comes up to me.

"Tom," she whispers. "Where's Helen?"

"I don't know," I say. "She texted me a while ago that she was on her way."

"She knows she's supposed to be here, right?"

"Yes, Anna," I say with thinly veiled irritation, "she knows that. I'm sure she'll be here in a few minutes."

"That's all well and good, but it's time to eat. You need to say grace."

I nod and manage to get everyone's attention. After blessing the food, Bill comes up and says, "Father, you should go through first."

Not wanting to draw attention to the fact that Helen is not here by trying to wait for her, I say, "Thanks," grab a plate, and start serving myself portions of ham, macaroni and cheese, broccoli casserole, green beans with bacon, and fresh made rolls. There's a designated table for the officers and their wives. As their chaplain, they made a place for me—and Helen.

Time ticks by. I check my phone every five minutes, both for the time and to see if there are any messages from my tardy bride-to-be. The more time passes, the more concerned I get. Has something happened to her? Has she been in an accident? I look over to where Dan is sitting with Miriam. He seems unconcerned. I'm pretty sure someone would have told me if she was hurt.

Suddenly, I'm seized with a sense of panic. I look around the basement, crowded with people, with only two ways in and out.

Are the walls closing in? What's that I smell? Is—is it blood? No, it's just damp—the damp I remember from another basement just a few months ago. Helen lay dying on the floor as I tried to save her. No, not tried, I did save her. She survived that. But what if something really bad has happened? I haven't heard from anyone because she's—she's—and they're trying to figure out how to tell me.

My blood pressure's up. My ears feel like they're on fire. My heart is pounding in my ears. My breathing is heavy.

There are various speeches happening, reports from the different committees on what the Knights have accomplished during the year. The last speaker has sat down when I decide I've had enough. I need to get out of here. I need to get somewhere I can call someone to find out what's happened to Helen.

I'm not very steady when I get to my feet. I've just about tamped down the worst of the panic using the techniques my counselor taught me. I manage to walk from my table to the basement door without drawing attention. I am almost out the door when I hear Bill say, "Now, if Father Tom and his lovely bride-to-be will join me up on the stage."

I freeze, not quite sure what to do. As applause begins behind me, I pull myself together, turn, and head towards the front of the assembly. I take my place up on stage with Bill, plastering what I hope is a sincere-looking smile on my face as Greg Jamerson comes forward with a large, beautifully wrapped box.

I hope no one notices I'm up here alone.

Bill continues, "Father, this Christmas, which shall see God reward your faithfulness with a blessing 800 years in the making, we want to present you and—." He pauses here and looks around. "Oh, I don't see Helen."

"No," Dan pipes up, "She got called out to a robbery. She sends her apologies."

I manage to conceal my surprise.

Well, at least she's alive. But what the hell?

It is all I can do to keep a smile on my face as Bill continues in a slightly disappointed tone, "Well, anyway, we have this gift for the two of you, for your new life together. But you may not open it until after you receive your gift from the Ladies of Charity. You see," he says jovially with a wink, "like you and Helen, they go together and are well worth the wait."

This brings the house down. I shake Bill's hand and thank him, then I take my place behind the microphone. "Thank you all for this," I say. "Helen and I are so blessed to have such loving and supportive friends behind us. God bless you all."

More applause, and I stand there nodding with that stupid smile on my face, wondering how Dan knows more about where my soon-to-be-wife is than I do.

***

As soon as I get back to the Rectory, I open my phone and see that Helen did try to contact me. This mollifies me a little, but I'm still not happy, especially since the text says:

> *Sorry. Got called out on a robbery. Will call if I finish up in time.*

I text back:

> *I just got this. Why don't you stop by?*

It takes her a few minutes to reply. When she does, it's not what I want to hear:

Sorry, Darling, I have an early meeting with the Deputy Mayor tomorrow so I can't. Lunch?

I text back:

Sure. See you around 1.

I don't sleep well that night, but instead spend much of the time caught between fuming over being stood up and reminding myself that this is something we knew would happen.

Ten

By the time I get to the police department the next day, I am no longer angry at Helen. After a sleepless night, I decided to just let what happened drop. After all, we've talked about things like this. Because of our vocations, we can be called away anytime because of an emergency. I shouldn't have been as upset as I was.

There is one thing, though, that I need to know.

"Helen?" I ask as we tuck into the vegetable soup Anna sent with me. "Why did Dan know what was going on with you when I did not?"

"What are you talking about, Tom?" she asks, reaching for a roll.

"He knew about the robbery, and that you sent your apologies."

"Honey," she says, looking genuinely apologetic now, "I tried to call you. I sent you the text you saw later that night. I was only able to reach Dan because he had his radio with him. I told him to tell you what happened, that I was sorry, and would try to get there if I could. I guess he either didn't hear me or forgot."

"I see," I say, a little embarrassed about how I reacted. "Well, Dan had a bit to drink by that time. Probably he just forgot. Since you went through all that trouble, I guess it's OK, then."

She arches her eyebrows. "You guess it's OK? What does—?"

There's a knock on her door. "Yes!" Helen says sharply, still glaring at me.

Officer Mike Thompson comes in with a cheerful, "Hi, Father Tom," before turning to Helen and saying, "Here's the report on the robbery, or whatever it was."

My curiosity drives away any residual anger as I ask, "Whatever it was?"

Helen looks like she's about to dismiss him, but Thompson is a talker. "Yeah, Father. Darnedest thing I've ever seen. Looks like someone got in through the bedroom window and raided the jewelry box. Took a string of pearls and a couple of pairs of expensive earrings but left behind a wedding band and a couple of diamond rings."

Helen's looking at the report. "According to this, there were a lot of expensive electronics and other items left behind."

"Just like at the MacMillans," I mutter.

"Yeah, but in the end they didn't get away with anything," Thompson says. "We found it all in a zip-top bag right below the window where they gained entry."

"What, so the culprit dropped it?" I ask, looking at Helen.

"That's what it looks like," she replies before adding, "That'll be all, Thompson."

Thompson leaves and I ask, "Do you think it's the same person who broke into the MacMillans' and stole that welder we found?"

"Either that, or there are several incredibly incompetent crooks around," Helen says. "But I don't want to talk about that right now. I think you were saying something when Thompson interrupted?"

She's leaning back in her chair, arms crossed, the glare she had earlier returned. I sigh and say, "Listen, I shouldn't have said that. I guess I'm still a little hurt that you weren't there."

"Now, Tom—."

I hold up my hand. "I know, I know. You had a good reason for missing the party. We've had this discussion before."

"And I guess I should have tried harder to contact you," Helen sighs. "Did you worry?"

I look at my hands. "Oh, Tom, I am sorry," she says softly.

"It's OK," I say with a strained smile. "I got through it. I guess now I have another trigger for my panic attacks."

"Do you want to go back to the counselor?" she asks.

"I may if it happens again," I say. "It caught me off guard. If there's a next time, I'll know what it is."

Helen reaches across the table and takes my hand. "I promise, Tom, there won't be a next time. I'll send an officer to find you if I have to."

I laugh. "You don't have to do that, Helen."

She shakes her head. "No, I'll do it if necessary. But enough of this for now. What did I miss?"

I recount the attempts of Bill, Dan, and Herbert to advise me about married life, being sure to emphasize Dan's promise to deal with me if I didn't 'make her happy.'

"What did he mean by that?" Helen laughs.

"Somehow, it's connected to a magazine he found you reading?"

"Oh, no!" she laughs harder. "You mean this one?"

She reaches into one of her desk drawers and pulls out a copy of *Cosmopolitan*, complete with a well-known actress partially clothed on the cover.

"Ahem," I say, averting my eyes. "I—yes, that's the one."

"Oh, good grief!" she says, rolling her eyes. "Tom, I was going to show this to you. It has an article—."

"No, no, that's OK," I say quickly, holding up my hand, "you don't have to tell me."

"—About women in law enforcement," she says with a chuckle. "I did a phone interview with the author of the article about a month ago. Didn't I tell you?"

I search my memory. "Yeah, that does ring a bell, actually. Are you telling me the article is about you? That's great!"

"Well, not just me," Helen says. "She profiles about half a dozen women. But yes, I am in it."

"I'm so proud of you," I say with a grin. "But why didn't you tell Dan that? It gave him the idea that you were—ah, worried about things."

She takes a deep breath. "I shared my concerns with you months ago. And while I am still nervous about our first night together, I'm certainly not going to go to a woman's magazine for advice. As for why I didn't tell Dan, I tried. But he got so flustered that he left before I could."

"You know, for having as many kids as he has, he seems a little squeamish about sex."

"I don't think it's that so much as he's squeamish about *us*," she says. "By the way, he said something to me today about a gift?"

"That's right," I nod. "We have a big box at the Rectory from the Knights, waiting for us to open, but we can't until we get the gift from the Ladies of Charity. You will be at that party, won't you?"

She smiles and says, "Yes, Tom. I will be at the Ladies of Charity party, come Hallelujahs or high water."

"What?"

"I'm still trying words out."

***

Later that night after Helen leaves, having handed me another loss at Monopoly, I am about to go upstairs for the evening when I realize I left my phone in the Sacristy earlier. We'd been in the church to say Evening Prayer together. I'd gone in there to turn the lights on the altar off, and in the process, I'd laid my phone down.

I suppose it must be the stress I'm under because of the wedding, but I'm beginning to think I'm losing my mind. I have to lock up the church anyway—I keep it open for prayer until 11 p.m. or so, much to Helen's chagrin because I refuse to install security cameras inside—so I just grab my keys and head over.

The interior of the church is lit only by the votive candles and the presence candle, signalling that the body of Christ is present in the tabernacle. I flick on one of the light switches so I don't trip going up the steps, walk to the altar, make a bow, and go to the right side of the altar area where the sacristy is.

I am about to unlock the door when I hear glass break inside.

I freeze, straining to hear if there's movement in the room. My first impulse is to call Helen, but that's impossible, considering my phone is locked inside. I could go back to the Rectory and call from there, but I don't want anyone getting away, either.

I'm really left with one option—to confront whoever is in there myself.

Now, the last time I did something like this, I wound up trying to take on two huge thugs by myself. The result? A twenty-four hour coma, a concussion, and a severely injured groin that my mother still insists turned me into a eunuch.

But, in spite of that experience, I decide to take my chances. I tip-toe back to the altar, suddenly aware that Saint Clare's really has an echo. I grab one of the candlesticks, looking to the tabernacle and whispering, "forgive me." Creeping as softly as I can back to the sacristy, I unlock the door as quietly as I can and then throw it open, brandishing the candlestick like a club.

All I find is an empty room and a broken votive cup by an open window.

I rush to the window, hoping to catch a glimpse of the potential thief, but see no one. Knowing the rules, I step out of the room after grabbing my cell phone—whoever broke in left it behind—and dial Helen.

"Missing me already," she purrs when she answers.

"Helen, I need you right now," I say.

"Whoa, Tom," she says, "we still have a few weeks—"

"That's not what I mean, and you know it," I say firmly. "Someone broke into the sacristy."

She says nothing for a moment, then replies, "I'll be there in ten minutes. An officer may get there before I arrive. Where are you?"

"In the church."

"OK. You know the rules, Tom."

"Don't touch anything," I say. "I remember."

She arrives a short time later, walking into the church along with Officer George Bailey, who is carrying a large crime scene kit.

"What happened, Tom?" she asks.

I give Helen a quick rundown of everything as Bailey begins processing the room, beginning with photographs. I've just finished recounting my attempt to catch the thief in the act when Anna rushes into the church, pale and out of breath.

I realize that I should have called and warned her so she wouldn't see a police car out front and panic. Bill is on her heels as I hurry to assure her, "Everyone's fine, Anna. No one's hurt."

She seems not to hear me but pushes past, running to the sacristy and crying, "The Christ Child! Helen, is the Christ Child safe?"

Bailey appears confused by this but Helen assures Anna, "Yes, the cabinet is still locked. It has not been tampered with."

"But did you check?" Anna asks, lunging for Bailey, who raises his hands to restrain her.

Helen takes her by the arm and says calmly, "Tom, please give Officer Bailey the key to the cabinet."

I do so, and Bailey opens the door to reveal the wood box we placed in there earlier in the week. Pointing to it, Helen asks, "Satisfied?"

"No," Anna says firmly, "not until you open the box and show me it's there."

Helen nods at Bailey, who opens the box, revealing the small statue safely nestled in its straw bed.

"Good," Anna says. "Now give it to me."

We all stare at her like she's lost her mind. "Chief?" Bailey asks.

Helen pauses for a minute, obviously evaluating the situation.

"OK," she says finally. "It's pretty obvious that whoever broke in here did not get into the cabinet, so yes, Anna, you can take the statue with you. But I am curious. What are you going to do with it?"

"I am taking it to my bedroom and locking it in with me for the night. That will give you, Helen Parr, until morning to figure out a safer place to keep it." With this, she storms out of the room, carrying the wood crate with her. Bill looks back apologetically before following her.

"Is she for real?" Bailey whispers.

"Oh, yes," Helen mutters, "and she's also the least crazy of my future mothers-in-law."

I spend about an hour watching Bailey process the sacristy, all the time searching for something missing, but everything appears to be in its appropriate place. After the officer leaves, I lock up, and Helen and I walk back over to the rectory for some late-night hot cocoa.

"Tom," she says as we settle in on the couch with our mugs, "I'm beginning to worry about Anna. I mean, this obsession she has with the Christ Child is beginning to border on the insane."

"I know," I sigh. "I've been trying to figure her out since the Gypsinian Christ Child arrived. But isn't there something you can do? You know, to secure it? Just to satisfy her?"

She considers this for a moment and then says, "I guess I could lock it up in our evidence vault until Christmas. That's about the safest place in town."

"Oh, would you, darling? I mean, if you think she's driving you crazy, imagine what it's like to live with her."

"OK," Helen laughs. "Just to preserve your sanity before our marriage. I'll stop by for it tomorrow after lunch. I'd take it in the morning, but I have a meeting with the deputy mayor first thing."

"You had one this morning," I say with exasperation. "What does Lex Luther want now?"

Yes, that's right. The Deputy Mayor's name is Lexington Luther.

You can't make this stuff up.

"Oh, Lex just wants to make sure that the department's giving equal protection to all parties celebrating the holidays and not, as he put it in his email, 'favoring those of my own faith tradition.'"

"And are you giving equal protection?"

"I will as soon as anyone asks for it," she says. "Hey, wait. I just realized something. I guess I've really opened the floodgates now with harboring this Christ Child. Next thing you know, I could have an evidence locker full of plastic reindeer, Menorahs, and Druid staffs."

Perplexed, I ask, "Are there many Druids in Myerton?"

"I'm sure they'll come out of the woodwork—or woods, I guess is more accurate—once they hear about this."

"I'll try to keep this little favor quiet," I say.

Eleven

"So Helen said she'd keep the Gypsinian Christ Child in the evidence locker at the police station until Christmas Eve."

I look at Anna over my oatmeal, coffee, and orange juice, waiting for her reaction. She finally nods. "Yes. That will work. I'll let Walt—the Archbishop know."

As she stands, I say, "I don't think you need to tell His Eminence. I mean, he doesn't really care where the statue is as long as it's secure."

"No, I want him to know," Anna says. "I want him to know we're keeping his statue safe."

His statue? "Anna, you know it's not his personal property, right? It belongs to the Archdiocese."

"Tom, Archbishop Knowland is the head of the Archdiocese, isn't he?"

"Of course."

"And Saint Clare's is one of his parishes, right?"

"Yes."

"And you're one of his priests, correct?"

"Uh-huh, but I don't—"

"Then the Gypsinian Christ Child is his for as long as he's Archbishop."

And with that, she walks out of the kitchen. A minute later, I hear her office door close.

I pick up my coffee mug and nod. "That's it, isn't it, Anna," I whisper. "Can't disappoint Walter, can we?"

Once I finish my breakfast, I wash out my dishes and head to my office. When I'm passing the front door, someone rings the bell.

I open the door and am surprised to see Officer Nina Hallstead standing on the porch.

"Good morning, Father Tom," she says. Hallstead's a good two inches taller than I am, and her usual bulk is enhanced by her uniform coat.

I'm suddenly seized by a flash of panic. "Nina? Is—is Helen—?"

"Oh, I am sorry! I bet you think I'm here to tell you something happened to Chief Parr. No, she's fine. In fact, she said I could come talk to you. As police chaplain? I mean, you are still police chaplain, right?"

I breathe a sigh of relief and step back so she can come in from the cold. "Yes, until the first of the year," I say. "Come into my office."

She takes off her coat and knitted cap, hanging them on the hall tree, before following me. I close the door so we can have some privacy, Hallstead taking a seat at my desk.

"I think this is the first time we've talked like this, isn't it?" I say with the best pastoral smile I can muster.

"Yes," she says. The normally calm and collected former MMA fighter seems uncharacteristically nervous.

"So, Nina, tell me. What's on your mind?"

She takes a deep breath. "I'm not Catholic, you know, Father."

"I know. You're Unitarian, correct? Raised a Baptist by your single Mom in Tennessee."

She smiles sheepishly. "You have a good memory. I forgot I'd even mentioned that. Yes, I'm technically a Unitarian, but I don't really know what I believe. I believe in God, but beyond that, I really don't know, you know?"

I smile. "Actually, I do know. There was a time, not too long ago actually, when I wasn't sure what I believed anymore."

"Anyway, the Chief's really good at reading her people, you know? I—I haven't been myself for about a week. She called me into her office to find out what was up."

"You're not in any trouble, are you, Nina?"

"No, no. Nothing like that. At least, not a lot of trouble. That MacMillan woman got under my skin, but I understand she does that to everyone."

"Yes, she does. Myself included."

"I, ah, heard that too."

"So, you didn't get in trouble for that. But you did get in trouble about something else?"

She takes a deep breath and looks at her hands. "I—I kind of lost it with a suspect. I didn't lay a hand on her—well, I did, but I didn't hurt her. I know how strong I am, and between that and my training, I could really hurt someone, so I'm always careful to keep my anger in check. And you know, Father, you see a lot to get mad at in this job."

I nod, but say nothing.

"Potter and I were dispatched to a home for a wellness check," Hallstead says. "A grandmother had called the station, saying she hadn't been able to get in touch with her daughter in a couple of days. The address was right outside the city limits down a dirt road. I don't know if you know the area, but we've nicknamed it Shantytown. It's mostly old mobile homes that look like they're about to fall down. Lots of single parents there, some drug activity." She sniffles and wipes a tear away. "And kids. Lots of kids."

She pauses for a second. "The place we went to was like the other places—a single-wide mobile home, plywood over one window that was apparently broken, a rickety set of steps. There was a kid's bike in the front yard, looked brand new. Somehow these parents live like this, but always manage to scrape money together for toys. I figured someone just had a birthday.

"Potter knocked, we identified ourselves, and asked that someone open the door. Because we never know what we're walking into, we had our hands on our weapons—not unholstered, but so we would get them quickly. We waited a few minutes, then Potter knocked again. This time, someone answered."

She swallows and whispers. "She looked to be about ten years old. Didn't look like she'd had a bath in days. The place smelled to high heaven—we noticed it even before we went in. The little girl looked at us and asked, very politely, 'Yes, can I help you?' Just like police officers came to her door every day.

"Sometimes kids seem more comfortable around me, I guess because I'm a woman—sometimes, sexist stereotypes have a little bit of truth to back them up, you know? I asked if we could speak to her mommy or daddy. 'We don't have a daddy. Our mommy's asleep,' Father, it was four o'clock in the afternoon.

"'Is she taking a nap?' Potter asked. The little girl said, 'No, sir. She's been asleep all day. I've been taking care of my brother and sister, like she told me to. I made breakfast and lunch for them, and I've even changed Nina's diaper. She had a couple of really stinky ones.'"

I look at the officer, who has tears flowing down both cheeks, and say, "There was a baby named Nina?"

Hallstead nods. "She looked less than a year old. The place was as filthy as you can imagine. The baby—she looked healthy enough, but she was dirty, too. She wasn't even in a proper crib or anything, just a box on the floor. When I saw that, I just lost it. I kicked the bedroom door open and dragged the mom out of bed. I screamed in her face for I don't know how long, until Potter pulled me off of her and told me to take a break. I went out to my patrol car and just started sobbing. Potter called Child Services and they came out. I don't know what happened after that."

She's crying softly now. I just look at her, processing what she told me. Nina Hallstead is a consummate professional. What she saw involved children. That triggered her reaction.

Something involving a child. A baby.

Oh, of course.

"So, Chief Parr urged me to come talk to you. So, I'm here," Hallstead says.

I lean forward and look at her across my desk. "Nina, when did you lose the baby?"

Hallstead's shocked by my question. "Who told you?" she whispers. "Has Nick been here?"

"Nina, you just told me," I say quietly. "I suspected that was it, though, from your story. The baby's name was Nina. That had to get you."

Hallstead nods. She swallows, then says, "I—it happened the day before. I was at home when I started feeling wrong. I went to the ER, and there they told me I was losing the baby. I was about eight weeks along."

I push a box of tissues across the desk to her. "How many before this?"

"How did you know this wasn't the first?"

"Oh, personal experience," I say with a bitter smile. "My first wife suffered several miscarriages. She was pregnant when she was killed."

"I'm so sorry, Father," Hallstead whispers. "To answer your question, this is number four. We've tried—we've been trying for about four years to have a baby. One thing after another happened, one failed pregnancy test after another. I've been tested, Nick's been tested, and no one can tell us why we have such a hard time even conceiving. I mean, we're both in good health. We don't drink—well, not very much. We've never smoked. We've never done drugs. When I was fighting, I never used any kind of performance enhancing drugs because I knew I wanted to be a mother someday and I didn't want to take a chance wrecking my system. But even with all that . . ."

Hallstead slumps in her chair and dissolves into tears. I come around my desk, squat beside her, and give her a hug. She cries on my shoulder for several minutes. Finally, the crying subsides and she sniffles, "Sorry about that. It's such a girly thing to do, crying like that, you know?"

I stand up and pull the other armchair over so I'm sitting next to her. "Nina, you're grieving. Tears are natural when you suffer any kind of loss, especially of a child. It doesn't make sense. It seems like some kind of horrible trick of nature. If you believe in God, it may seem like he's a cruel deity to do that to someone."

"I have thought that, actually," Nina nods.

"And that's natural too, to be angry at God. But Nina, you need to understand that miscarriages just happen for reasons we don't understand. People have trouble conceiving children in the first place for reasons we don't understand. And you get angry when you see people who have children and don't take care of them. Is that what happened to you?"

She nods, and I continue, "Well, I guess since Helen told you to come talk with me, she's not going to discipline you?"

Nina shakes her head. "When I told her about my miscarriage, I think she came to the same conclusion you did. She just wanted me to talk to someone about it."

"Well? Feel any better?"

She takes a deep breath. "Actually, I do," she says. "Everyone's right. You are really good at this, Father."

I laugh, and I say, "I am glad I was able to help a little. Is there anything else I can do for you since you're here?"

Nina looks like she's about to say something, then shakes her head. "No, Father. I don't want to bother you with this."

"It's no bother, Nina. What is it?"

She clears her throat. "Nick and I've been looking at IVF. But the cost—I mean, we just can't afford it, and it will take us forever to raise the money."

"I remember," I say. "Joan and I looked into it, and it was expensive fifteen years ago. We weren't very Catholic, so we didn't care that the Church is against IVF, for reasons we don't need to get into."

"Well, that doesn't matter to me, you know," Nina says. "But the cost is the barrier. I was doing some research on the internet for alternatives, and I came across something on a Natural Family Planning site. Apparently, a couple had been trying to have a baby for several years, even had a couple of miscarriages, and finally conceived using something called Napro. Have you heard of that?"

"Yes, actually. I have a brochure about it," I say as I stand and walk to my desk. "It's called Natural Procreative Technology. It's not IVF or anything like that. They use a woman's natural rhythms to help her conceive. Many infertile couples have had success using it. There's a clinic in Baltimore that specializes in Napro. You should give them a call."

Nina takes the brochure and flips through it. "I'll talk to Nick about it. I mean, what do we have to lose, right?"

She stands up and shakes my hand. "Thank you, Father. I want to say that everyone at the station's really upset that you won't be our chaplain anymore."

"I appreciate that, but Reverend Applegate is a good man. I think everyone will like him."

Nina nods and says, "Well, I better get back out on patrol. Thanks again."

She walks to the door and stops. Turning around, she says, "I just want to say, Father, that I think the Chief is an awfully lucky woman."

I grin. "I appreciate that, Nina. Now, you and Nick will be at the wedding and the reception?"

She laughs. "Aside from the fact that Nick's not letting your cakes out of his sight, I'll go anywhere there's free food and dancing. I'll be seeing you Father."

She leaves, and I sit in my chair. Shaking my head, I say, "I think I'm going to miss being police chaplain more than I thought I would."

Twelve

Helen's at Noon Mass, which is actually a rather rare occurrence since she became chief.

Greeting her afterwards with a peck on the cheek, I say, "Just couldn't wait to see me, huh?"

"Fortunately my meeting with the Deputy Mayor was cut short," she says, "so I decided to come to Mass and get the Gypsinian Christ Child."

"Well, Anna will be glad. I think she's had it on her desk all day. She even locks the door to her office anytime she leaves for a few minutes."

"Does she think you're going to steal it?"

"I asked her that. She said she wasn't ruling anything out."

Helen rolls her eyes. "Oh, brother! We're getting that out of the Rectory just in time."

We walk over to the Rectory, finding Anna in the kitchen. "I made stew today, Tom," she says. "Helen, would you like some?"

"Don't mind if I do," Helen says, sitting at the table.

After lunch, Anna and Helen go to Anna's office, leaving me with the dishes. I've just finished up when the doorbell rings. I answer it, only to find the very pregnant Miriam Conway shifting from foot to foot.

"Come in, come in," I say as Miriam rushes past me, saying, "Excuse me, Father Tom, may I please use your—." The door to the bathroom closes before she can finish her sentence.

I look outside, where the three oldest Conway children, six-year-old Catherine and the four-year-old twins, JP and Max, are waiting outside. As always, Catherine kicks things off by running inside, saying, "Hi, Father Tom. Mommy had to pee and she can't just go behind the bushes like we can so we came here."

"I'm glad she did," I say, giving her a hug and waving the boys in. Anna and Helen have come out with the box, Helen setting it down to give her favorite child in the parish a big hug.

"Hi, sweetie," she says to Catherine. "How are you doing?"

"Fine, Miss Helen. Have you changed your mind about not having a flower girl?"

Before Helen can answer, Miriam comes out of the bathroom and says, "Now, Catherine, we've talked about that."

"I know, Mommy," the precocious child says, "I just thought I'd ask."

"You just thought you'd ask," Miriam says. Turning to Helen, she says, "Sorry about that."

"Don't worry about it," Helen laughs.

Miriam spies the wooden box. "Is that it?" she asks in a hushed tone.

As Anna nods, I ask, "How did you know?"

"Oh, I told Dan so he wouldn't freak out if he found a baby in the safe," Helen says casually.

"A baby in a safe?" Catherine asks, heading toward the box, but Miriam heads her off, saying, "Mind your own business, Catherine. Now, let's head home."

"Where's Andrew?" I ask, missing the smallest Conway tornado.

"At my Mom's house, asleep. I told the kids we'd take a walk but I think I may have pushed it a little too much. So we're heading home now."

"Why don't you let me give you a lift," Helen suggests. Then, glaring slightly at Anna, "You can ride shotgun, just like in a western when they were moving a gold shipment. I'll even let you hold my back up if Anna thinks it necessary."

"Oh, no, that's OK," Miriam says wistfully. "Catherine's pushing her carriage and the twins have their bikes and—."

"They can ride on the sidewalk all the way there while we drive slowly behind them," Helen says. "The Chief of Police will see to it that they're safe, and they can be our guards." Then turning to the kids she says, "How'd you like to be our guards, guys, and ride ahead of us to your house?"

"Yay!!!" the Conway kids all yell, jumping up and down. Catherine turns to Max and JP, saying, "I'll lead. You two stay behind me."

"Do we get guns, Miss Helen?" Max says—or JP, I can never tell them apart.

Before Helen can say anything, Miriam says, "Maximillian Kolbe Conway, you know better than that!"

"What about sticks?" JP asks. "Can we get sticks?"

"No. Sticks. John Paul," Miriam says firmly.

"But how are we supposed to guard Miss Helen's car?" Max asks in all sincerity. "We need something to scare the bad guys off!"

"You and your brother are scary enough," Miriam says. "The bad guys will take one look at you two and run in the other direction."

Max and JP look at each other, then back at their mother. "OK," they say in unison and run out to their bikes.

"Max and JP!" Catherine yells. "I'm your leader! You're supposed to wait for me!"

The little girl runs after them as Miriam and Helen just look at each other and laugh. "She takes after you, I think," Miriam says to Helen.

"Oh, she came by that naturally," Helen replies. She picks up the box, looks at Anna, and says, "Do you want to watch me put the box in my car? You know, just to make sure?"

"Bah!" Anna says with a dismissive wave of her hand. Turning, she stalks back to her office.

"What's wrong with Anna?" Miriam asks me.

"Oh, nothing. She just wants the Christ Child to be safe," I reply. "Come on, darling, let's get this thing out of here."

We walk out to Helen's car, where Catherine has arranged her brothers on either side. For their part, the boys are on high alert, probably wishing that bad guys do attack the car so they can heroically fight them off.

Helen places the box on the backseat as Miriam asks with only a little sarcasm, "You gonna buckle that baby in, Helen?"

Helen laughs and says, "Not a chance."

***

I have just poured myself a glass of lemonade when 'Eye of the Tiger' comes from my phone.

"Hey," I answer. "Did you get the Christ Child locked up?"

"Tom," Helen says, without preamble, "You need to come to the Conways right now."

She hangs up before I can ask any questions, so I dash to the foyer and grab my coat. Anna comes out of her office and I say, "I just got a call from Helen. Something's wrong at the Conways."

She puts her hand to her mouth. "It's not the Gypsinian Christ Child."

"No."

"Did she say it wasn't?"

"She didn't say anything, just that I needed to go over there right now."

I'm wrapping my scarf—knitted by Elizabeth Bentley and consisting of alternating stripes of black and white—around my neck when Anna says, "Well, then, you don't really know, do you, Tom?"

I pull on my knitted ski cap—black with a white pom-pom—and say, "Anna, I know it's not anything to do with the Gypsinian Christ Child, because if it had anything to do with the Gypsinian Christ Child, Helen's first words would have been, 'Tom, something's happened to the Gypsinian Christ Child'!"

Before Anna can say anything else about the Gypsinian Christ Child, I dash out the door to my car. Because of the cold, it takes a few turns of the key, a couple of Hail Marys, and a choice word or two questioning the car's heritage before it will start.

"I really need a new car," I mutter as I pull out of the driveway and head down the street towards the Conways' neighborhood.

Ten minutes later, I pull up in front of their house. I notice the Conway children in Helen's car along with Miriam. There's a police cruiser parked across the street, but Helen is nowhere to be seen.

I walk up to the car, where Miriam has the passenger side window down. "What's going on?" I ask. "Are you OK?"

"Yes, Father, I'm fine," she says, looking a little flustered, "but it looks like someone broke into our house. Helen's in there now with Mike Thompson, looking around. She told me to wait here until she came out."

As if magically summoned, Helen emerges with Thompson. The officer goes to his car and Helen comes over.

"Miriam," she says gently, "I am so sorry, but it looks like whoever it was really trashed the place. There's definitely no one inside anymore. I'd like for you to let Tom watch the kids while you come inside and take a look around and tell us what you notice missing. Do you feel up to that?"

"Sure," Miriam says, "And I called my Mom, so she's going to come over with Andrew as soon as she gets him changed and dressed. Father, why don't you take everyone in the backyard to play."

The kids are already piling out of the car and running for the backyard utopia that Dan has built for them through the years. Bikes and carriages are forgotten as they rush to the maze of wooden tunnels and slides that gush forth from a massive treehouse built in the middle of the lot. I marvel at this as the children play, but am thankful when Mrs. Rumstead arrives with Andrew and I can join the adults inside the house.

In order not to touch anything, I go around to the front door, which is still standing open. I'm shocked by what I see.

Chairs are turned over near the dining table, along with bowls of cereal and a couple empty glasses that look like they once contained milk. The couch cushions are on the floor where someone obviously threw them while looking for—what, loose change? The TV is gone, but strangely enough, the DVD player and their streaming box were left behind.

"That's odd," I mutter. "Why not take everything?"

What I find even more odd, though, is that the rugs have been pulled up and are piled in the corner. The lower doors to the china cabinet are open and the cabinet itself emptied.

I walk back outside and see Catherine at her pram, covering her baby with the blanket she'd apparently gone inside to get. I join Mrs. Rumstead in watching the spectacle of the Conway children at play.

"I remember having that much energy," she says as the twins chase each other with sticks. "Max! JP! Don't hit!" she hollers.

"I'm not sure I ever had that much energy," I say. "Was Miriam like this when she was young?"

"Oh, Mir? No, not so much. She was the quiet one in the family, actually. Didn't like roughhousing or sports. But, oh, did she love to dance," Mrs. Rumstead says with a smile.

"I remember she was a dance major at Myer?"

"That's right," she nods. "She wanted to go on and get her MFA in dance, maybe open up her own studio to teach dance here in town. But, she met Dan and fell in love. So, she became a mom instead."

I sense a hint of disappointment in her voice. "It's a great and noble thing, you know? I mean, you have ten children, right?"

"Oh, yes, I know that, Father," she sighs. "But I wanted something more for my girls. All of them have careers and families. But Miriam, well, she wanted this."

I don't know what to say, so I just stand with her watching her grandchildren play. Catherine's now on the porch swing, rocking and singing to her baby tightly swaddled against the chill.

Helen finally emerges from the house and, after kissing Catherine on the head, walks over to me. She says hello to Mrs. Rumstead before we walk to her car.

"It looks like someone was in there," she says softly. "But there is nothing missing except Dan's laptop. Miriam tells me it hasn't worked since one of the twins spilled grape juice on it. A new one's coming in today, but fortunately, it hasn't arrived yet."

"Any other clues?"

Helen shakes her head. "Not yet. There's no sign of forced entry but Miriam's not sure she locked the door. She's taking the kids to her Mom's house while Thompson processes the place."

"And what about you?" I ask as we walk back to her car and she pulls out her keyfob to unlock it.

"I'm going on to the police station and get this precious—."

She glances into the back seat and screams, "Oh, God! NO!"

I look through the window to see what she's looking at. "No," I whisper in horror. "No! No!"

In the seat is the open and now empty box that once held the Gypsinian Christ Child.

Thirteen

"No, no, no, no no," Helen keeps saying as she snatches the door open and begins to search the car. She looks under the front seats, in the floorboards, and even the trunk. But finds nothing.

"Oh, my Lord, Tom," she whispers, clutching my coat. "Someone stole it. Out of my car. A plain car, yes, but one with lights and a siren. That's pretty brazen."

She lets go and begins to pace back and forth. "Oh, my God, Tom! This is awful. I've let the Gypsinian Christ Child be stolen. By a real pro, it seems, someone who was not afraid to break into a police car."

She stops and grabs my arm. Frantically, she says, "Don't touch anything, Tom. We've got to get the crime scene techs out here to process this."

Helen pulls out her cell phone and is about to dial when she stops. "No, wait. I can't tell anyone. Word will get out. Then everyone will know what I did. Or didn't do. I don't know."

She starts to cry and lays her head on my chest. "Oh, Tom! What a disaster! I—I can't believe this has happened. We were so close!"

I put my arms around her, saying, "Honey, calm down. It's not the end of the world."

She jumps away from me like I'm on fire. "Not for you maybe," she hisses, "but for me, it is. I mean, no one in the church or the Archdiocese or even the whole world will ever trust me again if this gets out. They probably won't let me marry you! Oh, God! The Archbishop will find another wife for you. I can't let that happen. I love you! I can't stand the idea of him cancelling our wedding!"

"He won't do that, Helen," I say. "He'll understand. You just need to explain what happened."

"No. No. We can't tell anybody." She paces back and forth again for a minute, then gets right in my face. "The only thing to do is find the statue before anyone finds out it's missing. Yeah, yeah, that's good, that's good. All I have to do is find it, then the problem's solved."

"But Helen, don't you think—"

"My prints are already in the car," she continues, "so I'm going to drive it to the station and process it myself. If anyone asks, I claim that I'm just cleaning it out for Dan to use while I'm gone. He's always complaining about me having a messy car anyway, so it will make sense. I'll find the prints, match them to the scumbag who left them, then hunt him down like the rabid dog he is and rescue the statue from his clutches."

"You're going to do this all by yourself?" I ask, folding my arms.

"Yes. Hopefully. If I have to involve Gladys—well, she'd die for me, so she'll keep this secret. If I have to involve Dan, I will, I'd trust him with my life. But no one else can know." She whirls on me and says, "And you, Father Greer, will tell no one—I mean NO ONE—about this. Understand?"

I want to tell her the truth—that I don't understand any of this, that we really need to let the Archbishop know, that I have no idea how we're going to keep something like this a secret for very long, especially from Anna.

Instead, I realize Helen's beyond reasoning right now, and say, "Yes, absolutely. So, what do you want me to do?"

"Nothing right now," she says as we walk around to the driver's side. "Just go back to the Rectory and act like everything's fine. I'm going to put the lid back on the box. When I get to the station, I'm going to walk this box into the station, slap an evidence seal on it, and lock it in the vault. If Anna asks any questions, you can tell her that's exactly what I did."

She's about to get in her car when she says, "Oh, and get online and find me the best photo you can of the statue. I might need something to show around the area."

"Will do," I say, leaning in for a kiss as she turns away and jumps into her car.

As she speeds off, I shake my head and whisper, "This is never going to work, Helen."

***

After checking with Miriam to see if she needs anything, I leave Catherine pushing her pram and the boys wrestling on the ground for reasons known only to them, and drive back to the Rectory. When I walk in, Anna pops out of the kitchen and asks anxiously, "Well, what was all that about?"

I hesitate, then decide to tell her because she's going to hear anyway. "Someone broke into the Conways' house," I say. "Helen was going through the house with Miriam, and she needed some help with the kids until her mother arrived."

"What!" she exclaims. "What did they get?"

"Believe it or not, only a broken laptop," I say. "Once again, whoever broke in left a bunch of other more valuable things behind."

Anna breathes a huge sigh of relief. "Oh, my goodness! Thank the Lord that's all they took." She pauses and then gets back to her real concern. "What about the Christ Child?"

"Helen wanted me to assure you that she has sealed the box with an evidence tag and placed it in the safe, where it will remain until she herself unseals it and brings it to the church on Christmas Eve."

"Speaking of which, have you nailed down that schedule yet?"

"Yes, I have. I will celebrate the 4 p.m. Christmas Eve Vigil Mass for Families, at the end of which we will place the Christ Child in the Creche. Then you, Helen, and I, along with

Bill, will have our Christmas celebration here. I will then return to the church and celebrate the Midnight Mass, after which I will come back here, collapse into bed, and not emerge until sometime mid-morning on Christmas Day. I have Father Small coming from Frostburg to do a Christmas Day Mass at 10 a.m." I pause. "You remember we're going to be gone for a few hours."

Anna smiles. "I remember. I think it's a lovely idea." She pauses and adds, "What time is the rehearsal?"

"Everyone is supposed to meet at the church at about 5 p.m., but I don't see it taking very long. There's no need for a full blown rehearsal. It's really just a normal Mass except for the marriage part."

"Yes, Tom, except for that," Anna says with only very thinly veiled sarcasm. I ignore this and she continues, "Then why don't you invite everyone back to the Rectory for dinner?"

"Oh, Anna," I protest, "there's no reason for you to go to that much trouble."

"Tom," she says, placing her hand on my arm, "it will be the last meal I cook in this house for you. I want it to be special, for you and Helen to be surrounded by people you love and who love you."

I look in wonder at this woman who has given so much to me. I wrap her in a hug and choke up as I say, "That would be lovely, Anna. Thank you so much."

I release Anna from the hug, only to see tears on her cheeks. She wipes them from her face, pats me on the cheek, and whispers "Well, I should let you get back to work."

Going into my office, I very much want to call Helen and see if she's calmed down. Instead, I go online and locate a photo of the Gypsinian Christ Child, which I forward to her by email. A few minutes later, she responds with a terse, "Thanks," and I decide that my best strategy is just to leave her alone for a while.

I turn my attention from the missing Gypsinian Christ Child and my rather frantic fiancée to preparing for my next meeting with Martin Maycord and his lovely bride-to-be, Mae Trent. I'm sure no one who knows them has any idea about the difficult time I've had preparing them for the sacrament of marriage. True, they are people who are twelve years apart, who fell in love at first sight, and became engaged after only a few months—all things which would be challenging with any couple.

But even though they are in love—of that, I have no doubt—they are very different people. Mae comes from a very large, very devout Catholic family, and is one of the most grounded young women I've ever met. Martin came from a small family that, from his own testimony, wasn't very devout. Until just a few months ago—in fact, right before he met Mae—he hadn't exactly lived according to the teachings of the Church. This difference, more than anything, has proven to be the challenge, particularly when it comes to how many children they're going to have.

Which is what we're talking about again at our next meeting. After much discussion and no small amount of struggle, both Mae and Martin agree that they want a large family. But while Martin accepts the idea, he still finds the idea very intimidating. Since this has evolved from an issue of Church teaching to one of faith and trust in God's providence, I am focusing on those topics and have sent them several readings that we will review together.

The afternoon passes and I hear nothing from Helen. Finally, I can wait no longer.

"How's it going?" I ask when I call

"Not good. No prints that pop in the system," she replies. "Just mine, yours, and Miriam's. Some smaller prints I presume are the kids, since I've never had a team of midgets in the car."

"Any on the crate?"

"No. The surface is too rough and porous," she replies.

"Are you coming for dinner?" I ask hopefully.

"No. I don't want to see Anna until I fix this."

"She's not even going to be here tonight," I say. "She's got some Ladies of Charity meeting at someone's house."

She's quiet. "Oh. Another mysterious meeting I'm not invited to. It's just as well. If I don't find that statue, I'm going to be a pariah in the church, anyway. Do you think it will affect your priesthood very much, having a wife who is a parish pariah?"

I ignore her question and instead ask, "So, since she's not going to be here, how about coming over for dinner?"

She hesitates. "OK. Text me when she leaves. I'll come over and leave right after we eat. That way, I should miss her."

"Helen," I say, exasperated, "don't you think you're carrying this a little too far?"

"No."

I roll my eyes. "OK," I sigh. "What are you going to do next?"

"I'm going to visit all pawn shops within an hour's drive of Myerton, giving them the photo and assuring them of a sizable reward if they turn it in. Double if they turn in the thief, also. I'm offering the same deal to anyone in the fence database."

"Where's the sizable reward coming from?" I ask.

"Our savings account. You got a problem with that?"

"Not at all," I assure her, only too aware that all the money in our now joint savings account was, until recently, in her personal savings account. Priests don't make a lot of money and I have terrible spending habits, as Helen knows all too well.

"Good," she says. "Are you cooking or do you want me to bring something?"

"How about pizza tonight? I'll call the order in when Anna leaves."

"Sounds good. You know what I like."

"Sausage, Canadian bacon, and onions with alfredo sauce on your half." I chuckle and add, "I'm not sure I can marry a woman who insists on onions on her pizza."

She doesn't laugh. Instead, she says seriously, "If I can't find this statue, darling, you may not be."

***

I'm relaxing for a few minutes looking at our honeymoon cruise—seven nights out of the port of Baltimore, down the coast to the Bahamas, with stops in Nassau and the cruise line's private island. Just being able to get out of the cold for a few days is going to be fantastic.

Of course, most of my plans for the cruise include spending a lot of time alone with Helen. After having to be careful about our every move, I'm really looking forward to not having to be careful anymore, so to speak.

I allow my mind to transport me to the ship, standing on the deck under the warm tropical sun as the ship cuts through the waters, holding Helen as we look to the horizon. I can feel her in my arms. I see myself leaning in for a kiss—.

My thoughts are interrupted by my phone playing the Darth Vader Theme.

"Perfect timing, Mom," I grumble. Clearing my throat and putting a smile on my face, I pick up the phone and say, "Hi, Mom. How are you?"

"I'm fine, Tommy," she says.

I'm shocked.

My mother is never fine.

What is all this about?

"That's good, Mom. I'm glad to hear it. So what's up?"

"Well, Tommy, I've been thinking about this business of flying to your wedding and I'm a little nervous about coming alone. I mean, I haven't flown in years and you know, you hear such horror stories about strip searches at airports and women being taken into other rooms to be questioned by strange men. Tommy, I just don't know what I'd do if that happened to me."

I am holding my breath now, hoping against all hope that she's decided not to come to the wedding. I am forming the words, "Oh, Mom. I understand. Helen and I can just come see you" in a decade or two.

She continues, "So I was wondering if I could bring Trevor with me."

"What," I ask, snapped out of my reverie. "Trevor?"

"Yes. I was talking to him and he said that he'd really like to meet you. I've told him all about you and Helen, and he said he'd be glad to escort me to the wedding."

I pause to think about this. I mean, it might be nice to have someone to take care of Mom while she's here—someone who is not me.

"Sure, Mom, that will be fine," I say. "We've got a block of rooms set aside at the Myerton Inn so I can get him one there."

"Don't worry about that, Tommy. I'll have him book it himself and that way, we can make sure to get what we want."

I'm not sure I heard her right. "Wait, what did you say?" I ask.

"I said," Mom says quickly, "that way he can get what he wants."

I breathe a sigh of relief. For a second, I thought—but no, I just heard wrong. Must be the stress.

"Great," I say, "because you're staying at the Rectory, right?"

"Well, Tommy, about that," she says. "You know, my back isn't what it used to be. And you know I have a hard time sleeping in a bed that's too soft or too hard. It needs to be just right. So I'd rather give you an answer after I get there and try out the bed. You understand, don't you, Tommy?"

No, Goldilocks, I don't understand AT ALL is what I want to say to her. Instead, I say slowly, "Yes, Mom. That's fine. But I'm not sure I'll be able to book anything for you later, especially since you're coming in the day before Christmas Eve."

"Tommy, don't worry about that," she says cheerfully. "You just focus on getting ready for your wonderful day, and Trevor and I will take care of ourselves."

At this point, I want to ask, "Who are you and what have you done with my mother," but I think better of it. "Thanks for that, Mom," I say. "Helen and I will get with you closer to the day you're flying in and will be at Dulles International Airport to pick y'all up."

"That sounds just wonderful, Tommy. I love you. Give Helen my love, too."

"I will, Mom," I say, dazed at what she just said. I can't remember the last time she said "I love you" to me, much less gave Helen her love. "I love you, too," I manage to add before ending the call.

I lean back in my chair, struck by an odd feeling of happiness after talking to my mother.

But in the back of my mind, a little alarm rings.

Fourteen

As she requested, I text Helen as soon as Anna leaves for the Ladies of Charity meeting.

"Uh, how late are you going to be?" I had asked Anna.

"Why?" Anna had said. "Is Helen coming over?"

"Why do you think Helen is coming over?"

"Because she usually comes over in the evening for dinner."

"Oh. Well, yes, she's coming over."

Anna must have sensed my nervousness because she peered at me and said, "Are you two up to something?"

"No. Why do you ask?"

"Because you're acting jumpy. Like a teenager who's trying to figure out how much time he has to—well, you know—with his girlfriend."

"Oh, Anna! No, it's nothing like that. Nothing like that at all."

She didn't look entirely convinced by my protest, but she said, "OK. Well, we're trying to finish up a special project, so I don't know when I'll be back. You don't have to wait up for me."

I was never so glad to see Anna leave. Helen arrives about ten minutes after I text her.

"You didn't say anything to her, did you?" Helen says as soon as she walks in the door.

"I haven't said a word, Helen," I say. "I told you I wouldn't."

"Good. Good."

She takes her coat off and plops on the couch. I offer her a beer, but she shakes her head. "No, I need my mind clear," she says. "Just in case I get a call. I've got feelers out all over this part of the state. Every pawn shop's been alerted. They're to call me as soon as someone comes in with the Gypsinian Christ Child."

"Do you really think someone will try to pawn it? I mean, we're talking about a 500-year-old one-of-a-kind sculpture."

"I. KNOW. That. Tom," she growls. "I can't think of anything but that. I'm just hoping that the same idiot burglar who's been behind the break-ins stole the Christ Child and thinks it's just some purty piece of art."

Purty? "Have you asked the Conways' neighbors if they saw anyone around your car?"

She glares at me. "Wow, I hadn't thought of that. Gee, you are some kind of genius detective, aren't you?"

"Oh, good grief, Helen—"

"To answer your question, of course I have. Thompson canvassed the neighborhood to see if anyone saw anybody strange around today. No one did. I even asked Dan to ask his kids if they saw anyone hanging around my car. They hadn't." She sits back. "Maybe this is some kind of professional. A master criminal. Maybe they've had their eye on the Gypsinian Christ Child for a while. Maybe they followed us here from Baltimore."

"You don't really think—"

"I bet they had the Rectory under surveillance," Helen goes on. "Maybe it was a team of master crooks. They were waiting for just the right time." She suddenly sits up. "The break-in at the sacristy! That was their first attempt. But you scared them off."

She's getting more fevered as she spins a story that sounds like a low-budget heist film. "Helen," I say calmly, "the pizza will be here any minute. Why don't you—"

"Shush, Tom," she says with a dismissive wave. "I think I'm on to something. They saw me walk out of the Rectory with the box. They followed me to the Conways—wait! I bet they staged the break-in to distract me! Tom, that has to be it!"

"Helen!" I snap. "Get a grip on yourself! You're driving yourself crazy!"

"Well, fine, Father Brown!" she spits. "What's wrong with my theory?"

"Besides everything, you mean? Helen, you're trying to piece together a theory out of things that may have no connection at all. You've taught me a lot about investigating a crime. But the main thing I've learned from you is that you have to follow the evidence, right?"

"Right," she nods. "That's just basic police work."

"Well, you have no evidence at all that the break-in to the sacristy is connected with the theft of the Christ Child from the car."

She opens her mouth to say something, then closes it.

"Did you find any fingerprints in the sacristy?"

"Plenty."

"Whose were they?"

She takes a deep breath. "Most of them were yours. The others were Deacon Derek's, Dominic Trent's, and Anna's, along with other altar servers."

"Just out of curiosity, how do you have their fingerprints?"

She shrugs. "Anyone employed by or who volunteers in a parish in the Archdiocese has to have a background check done. We have their fingerprints on file."

I actually remember that I was fingerprinted when I entered seminary. Of course, my prints and DNA are in the system for other reasons.

"But there were no prints you couldn't identify?"

"A professional would have worn gloves," she protests weakly.

"Would a professional have come in and out of the window? Wouldn't a professional know how to pick the lock? I mean, the sacristy has an outside entrance, and I know for a fact there's nothing special about the lock."

Helen's sitting back now, her hands folded in her lap. "Darling," I say, putting my arm around her. "There's no grand conspiracy here. I'm sorry the Christ Child was stolen, and I have every confidence that you'll find it. But you're not going to find it by chasing fantasies."

The doorbell rings. "That's the pizza," I say as I stand up. "I found the Christmas episode of *Magnum PI* on one of the streaming channels. It's all queued up. Let's just eat our pizza, relax, watch that guy you had an adolescent crush on, and forget about the Gypsinian Christ Child for a couple of hours."

Helen sighs. "That sounds wonderful, darling."

I nod and am about to walk out of the living room when she says, "Tom?"

"Yes?"

"Thanks."

Smiling, I say, "I'm always here to talk you down out of a tree."

The rest of the evening consists of pizza, sodas, and a good number of explosions—pretty much ideal. Helen doesn't mention the Christ Child anymore. I'm actually proud of myself for what I did. It seems like all of Helen's anxiety over the theft has dissipated.

About 9 p.m., Helen's cell phone dings. She digs it out of her gargantuan tote bag—I should say her gargantuan *Christmas* tote bag—takes one look, and stands up.

"I've gotta go, darling," she says, leaning over and kissing me.

"Is there an emergency?"

"Yes. Anna's on her way home."

"How—?"

"I had Nate follow her from here to where the meeting was. He's been staking the place out. That was him telling me she just left."

"Helen, I just don't—"

"Sorry, can't stay, gotta go!" she says cheerfully as she flies out of the living room. A moment later, I hear the front door close, leaving me dazed, confused, and worried for my bride.

***

What happens Sunday doesn't lessen my concerns about Helen.

We're standing outside of the church, greeting the 8 a.m. Mass-goers as they leave. Helen's perusing the bulletin when something catches her attention.

"Tom," Helen says, grasping my arm, "what is this about Bambinelli Sunday?"

"You've never heard of that? I'm surprised, considering how devout you were when you were younger."

"I'm still devout, Tom. Now what is it?"

"It's something that's relatively new. On the Third Sunday of Advent, which this is, people bring the Christ Child from their home creches to be blessed by the priest. We'll do it at the end of the 10:30 a.m. Mass."

"I see," Helen says with surprising interest. "And this is open to everyone, even people who are not Catholic?"

"Yes, but I doubt anyone who isn't Catholic would care about anything like this."

"You're probably right, but then again, you never know," she mutters. Just then, Agnes McGillicudy walks by. "Oh, Mrs. McGillicuddy," Helen says with a smile, "good to see you today. That's such a pretty scarf. Be sure to keep warm."

"Mrs. McGillicuddy," I say to the elderly parishioner. "Good to see you." As she walks away, I ask Helen, "I never know what?"

"Who might show up, and why," she says as she watches for other departing parishioners. "I mean, someone could stop by because they have a guilty conscience."

"Helen, you have got to be kidding me!" I say, incredulous she'd even suggest such a possibility. "Why would someone steal the Gypsinian Christ Child and then bring it to the church to be blessed? Wouldn't they be afraid of getting caught?"

"Well, it doesn't have to be the person who stole it," Helen says. "Someone could have bought it innocently enough from a pawn shop, or even just off the street. You really never know."

I certainly don't now, I think. To Helen, I say, "So let me get this straight. You're saying that somewhere in the seedier part of Myerton, some guy is standing on a street corner in an overcoat talking out of the side of his mouth and asking people walking by, 'Hey, you want I should hook you up with a primo Christ Child for Christmas?'"

"Listen, Father," she says, beginning to turn red with anger, "you work your side of the street and I'll work mine."

"OK, OK," I say, holding up my hands in surrender. "What would you like to do?"

"Nothing you need to worry about. You won't even notice anything. I promise."

Like a fool, I believe her.

At the end of the 10:30 a.m. Mass, I announce, "Before the final blessing, we shall now have the Blessing of the Bambinelli."

Because the practice is still relatively new—anything thirty years old or so in the Church is considered 'relatively new'—I have some leeway in how to do the blessing. "Let us pray," I say. Dominic comes forward with a leather portfolio where I've placed the words I'm going to use. I've chosen some of a previous Holy Father for the occasion.

"God, our Father, you so loved humankind that you sent us your only Son Jesus, born of the Virgin Mary, to save us and lead us back to you. We pray that with your Blessing, these images of Jesus, who is about to come among us, may be a sign of your presence and love in our homes.

"We ask you this in the name of Jesus, your beloved Son who comes to give the world peace. He lives and reigns forever and ever. Amen."

"Amen," comes the response. "Now," I say, "you may bring your Christ Child forward."

Helen stands as the families begin to straggle forward, Dan and Catherine Conway leading the way with their Christ Child. For some reason, little Catherine looks displeased about something. Probably her nemesis, Daniel Wright, irritated her before or during Mass.

Dan's allowed Catherine to hold the Christ Child statue, probably because it's made of a non-breakable material. She resolutely presents her charge to me. I take the water sprinkler from the holy water bucket and lightly sprinkle the figure while saying, "I bless this image of Jesus in the name of the Father, and of the Son, and of the Holy Spirit, Amen."

I glance at Helen, wondering why she's standing in the first place, especially considering everyone else not coming forward with a Christ Child is still sitting. It's not until Catherine returns to her seat alone, while Dan remains in the pew opposite Helen, that I realize what's going on.

As I sprinkle each figure, Helen and Dan study it briefly. They exchange glances, usually a slight shake of the head, while I try desperately not to roll my eyes at both of them.

There's not really a problem until old Mrs. Riley comes forward with a rather large bundle wrapped in newspaper and bubble wrap. As I am raising my hand to sprinkle the package, Helen steps forward and pulls back the wrapping. She reveals a cheap plaster figure with bright yellow hair, cobalt blue eyes, and lips that appear to have been painted on with bright red lipstick.

When Mrs. Riley turns to look at her, Helen whispers, "The head has to be uncovered for the blessing to count."

She then steps back and gives Dan a quick OK sign while Mrs. Riley and I both stare at her like she's crazy—which I'm beginning to think she is.

Mass ends, and Helen joins me at the door to shake hands. As Dan walks past Helen, he says under his breath, "Sorry we didn't catch anyone, Chief. I did a double take on the Harbingers' until I saw the Valumart tag still on it."

"It's OK, Dan," Helen mutters as she smiles at the people passing by. "We've still got some time left."

"So, are you satisfied that a member of our parish isn't in possession of a hot Christ Child?" I whisper.

Before Helen can answer, Catherine tugs on my vestments and says loudly, "Father Tom, Daddy would not let me bring my Baby Jesus to be blessed. I had him all wrapped up, too, but he told me to take it back to my room."

"Catherine," Dan sighs. "We have talked about this already. You can't just pick a doll and call it the Baby Jesus. The baby in the manger at home is special. Now come on, your mom's already in the van."

"But Daddy," I hear her whine as Dan drags her off. Helen and I finish shaking hands and walk back to the sacristy. I remove my vestments and say, "Well, are you satisfied?"

"All this proved, Tom, is that no one brought the Gypsinian Christ Child to be blessed," she says. "It doesn't prove that it's not in the possession of someone in the parish. We just need to keep looking and remain alert."

"Alert for what, Helen?" I ask, really getting exasperated by now. "What are you going to do next? Are you going to have Sergeant Cupcake stand with us next Sunday sniffing every parishioner that comes by for the scent of 500-year-old wood and paint?"

She snaps her fingers. "Tom!" Helen exclaims. "That's a great idea. I'm sorry I didn't think of that."

She rushes out of the room. "Helen? Where are you going?" I call as I follow her.

"To the station to talk to Cupcake's partner about next Sunday!" she says over her shoulder.

"No, Helen, you can't—."

"It's outside the church, Tom!" she exclaims as she walks out. "My turf. We agreed."

Before I can say anything else, she's gone, and I'm left wondering if my beautiful bride-to-be has lost her ever-loving mind.

Fifteen

I don't see Helen for the next couple of days. We do text, however, so I know she's continuing her frantic search for the Christ Child. I'm very glad she decided to tell Dan what was going on, after swearing him to secrecy. This actually makes me feel better, because I know that Dan's the only other person she'll listen to when she's like this.

I finally decide that I need to take matters into my own hands. Without letting her know, I go to the police station at our usual lunch hour.

But instead of heading right to her office, I go to Dan's.

The door is closed, and I think the light is off. Still, I knock. When there's no answer, I knock again. "Dan?" I say. "Are you in there?"

I hear a chair move, then quiet footsteps approach the door. "Tom?" Dan whispers. "Is that you?"

"Yes, it's me, Dan. Are you OK?"

"Are you alone?"

"Yes, it's just me."

Suddenly, the door opens, a large hand grabs me, and I'm yanked inside the dimly lit office. Dan quickly shuts and locks the door.

"Phew," he says, shaking his head. "I'm glad it's you."

"Dan, what's going on? Why are you hiding in your office?"

"Why? Why? Tom, that fiancée of yours is driving me crazy!"

"Oh," I say, nodding. "The Gypsinian Christ Child."

"Please!" he says, holding his hand up. "Don't mention that name. If I hear about the Gypsinian Christ Child one more time today, I may shoot someone."

"I haven't really talked to her in a couple of days," I say. "Is she any closer to finding it?"

"No, and she's getting weirder and weirder about it. I mean, you and I both know how she can be with a case. But I've worked with her for a while now, and I've never seen her like this. I tell you, Tom, I'm getting worried about her."

"I'm just glad she told you about it," I say. "She was going to try to do this all by herself."

"Well, now that she's Chief, she has too many responsibilities to do that. Besides, I knew something was wrong—I've gotten pretty good at reading her, actually better than I can read Miriam sometimes—so I confronted her. It took a while, but I finally convinced her to come clean." He paused. "Do you know why she's acting so nutty about this?"

"Sort of," I say. "She doesn't want anyone to find out, because she's afraid she'll lose the respect of the parish. She's worried Anna will be mad at her. And I think she's worried the Archbishop will tell her she can't marry me because she allowed the statue to be stolen."

"That's all crazy," Dan says.

"I've tried to tell her that, but she won't listen to me. I came over today, hoping to drag her away from the office for a while."

"Well, good luck," Dan sighs. "Except for traveling around checking pawn shops, she hasn't left the building in a couple of days. She's living on delivery and sleeping in her office. I tell you, Tom, if she doesn't let this go, I'm not sure what's going to be left of her for you to marry."

***

I am barely able to persuade Helen to ride with me to Sprockets for a quick lunch. We pull into our usual stall and I place our order, only to find when I turn back that she's on her phone texting someone.

"What are you doing?" I ask. "Besides breaking our 'no phones when we're alone together unless there is an emergency' agreement, that you talked me into, by the way."

"I was just texting Dan. It occurred to me that since more than a day has passed since the statue disappeared we should probably expand our search radius. I'm going to have him contact local LEOs in Pennsylvania and West Virginia, to get them to check their pawn shops."

She must notice my disappointment, because she adds with a fairly good attempt at a smile, "But now I am all yours. What have you been up to?"

"Thank you for asking. I spent most of the morning with Deacon Derek, going over what he'll be responsible for while we're gone. He's done most of it, but he's going to be on call for hospital emergencies, so I was giving him some pointers about that.

"Deacon Derek, huh?" she says, a curious expression crossing her face. "You know, I haven't really spent a lot of time with him, except for that dinner we had for him and Linda back in October. How long has he been here now?"

"I don't know. He got here the day I was stabbed. I don't think I'll ever forget that."

"I don't think he will, either," she says. "You were pretty out of it on morphine. So, a little over three months then, huh? And his wife's still not here, so he's still renting that apartment, and possibly making a house payment. I wonder how he affords that?"

"I don't know. I assume he has military retirement and that whatever he earns with us is just a supplement."

"But he could be worse off than we think," she says. "Maybe he's deeply in debt. Maybe he has a gambling problem no one knows about. Has he ever mentioned being strapped for cash?"

"Not that I can remember," I reply, becoming more confused by the second. "Why are you saying all of this?"

"Well, you know, Tom, a man who needed money and knew the value of a religious statue, not to mention a good place to sell it—"

"Helen!" I cry. "You really can't be serious. Deacon Derek is a delightful man in his 60s who has given over his retirement years to the service of God. For heaven's sake, the sacrifice he's making by living apart from his wife is a testimony to his commitment to his ministry. How can you possibly think he would steal *anything*, much less something that belongs to the Church?"

"I'm not saying I believe he did it," she says, sounding defensive. "I am just saying that I would like to know where he was around the time the Christ Child was stolen."

"I admit that I don't know, and I am not at all inclined to ask him. If you want to, go ahead, but leave me out of it!"

Our order finally arrives, providing a needed break in the argument while we sort out our food and begin to eat. I, for one, am starving.

Oatmeal may be good for my blood pressure, but it doesn't fill me up the way Anna's full breakfasts did. Eggs, bacon, toast, usually pancakes on the weekends—

"You're certainly singing a different tune than you usually do," Helen says. Her voice has an edge that could cut glass.

"That's because I think the composer has lost her mind," I reply firmly.

"Well, that's not very nice."

"I don't enjoy saying it, Honey. But really, don't you think you're getting a little obsessive about this?"

"Look, Tom. Consider it from my perspective. That priceless statue was stolen from my car. My police car. The statue belongs to the Church. The car belongs to the department. No matter how you slice it, letting this happen has tainted my reputation in both areas of my life."

"Again, Helen, I think you're exaggerating. I mean, no one even cares right now."

"That's because they don't know. When word gets out, it'll be a different story."

Helen lapses into silence, her full attention on her hamburger and cheese-covered tater tots. The sag in her shoulders is mute testament to the despair she feels over the statue. Her raven black hair is unbrushed and, considering how dull it looks, unwashed. Her rumpled clothes are the same ones she wore the last time I saw her.

"Helen," I say quietly. She turns to look at me, and for the first time I notice her normally bright, azure-blue eyes are dull from lack of sleep.

"Darling," I say. "OK, finding the statue is important to you. But you need to go home. Sleep in your own bed. Take a shower."

A weary grin spreads across her face, and a dim sparkle flashes in her eyes. "Do I smell that bad?" she asks.

With a smile, I lean towards her and take an exaggerated sniff. I wrinkle my nose and say, "Phew. Actually, you're close to making my eyes water."

Helen hits me on the shoulder, and we both burst out laughing. The tension broken, she says, "OK, OK. I see your point. I'll sleep in my own bed tonight. Anyway, that couch in my office is doing a number on my back." She sips her drink, then adds with a mischievous smile, "And I can't have a bad back before our honeymoon, can I?"

I choke on my drink as it goes down. "No," I cough. "No, definitely not."

She reaches over and strokes my cheek. "Thank you for trying to take care of me. It's been a long time since anyone did that."

I take her hand in mine and kiss it, saying, "I've told you before, it's my pleasure."

We eat in companionable silence for a while. When our food is finished, I ask, "So? The station, or your apartment?"

Helen starts to say something, then shakes her head. "My apartment. I'll let Dan know I'm taking the rest of the day off. He can carry the water on this for a while."

"Very wise decision, Chief."

I pull out of Sprockets and drive back to town. Along the way, I say, "Remember the Ladies of Charity Christmas Party is tomorrow night."

"I promise I'll be there, Tom." She looks out the window and mutters, "I've let enough people down this week."

Sixteen

The Ladies of Charity Christmas Party is one of those annual church events that I feel largely neutral about. I neither look forward to it nor dread it. It consists of a potluck dinner, followed by a couple of Christmas-themed games and ends with a Secret Santa gift exchange. It starts at 6 p.m. and I'm usually back in Rectory, watching television by no later than 9 p.m.

I am looking forward to it a little more this year because Helen will be with me, but still, I'm not what I'd call excited.

It doesn't help that Helen is running late, and Anna has noticed.

"Tom," Anna says to me as I stare at the door to the basement, "Helen did know she was supposed to be here tonight, didn't she?"

"I reminded her several times," I reply. "She promised she'd be here."

"Well, we can't wait much longer," she says before turning and walking off.

I check my phone one more time. Nothing from Helen. No replies to my texts.

"Ladies," Anna says, amplified by the speakers, "welcome to our annual Christmas Party. We've got a lot of good food and some really fun things planned. But before we begin, I'd like to ask Father Tom to come up to the stage to bless the food."

I check my phone one more time before shoving it back in my pocket, plaster a fake smile on my face—I've gotten very good at hiding my disappointment in being stood up by the woman I love—and walk to the stage.

Looking out over the gathering, I say, "Thank you, Anna. Well, I've seen the food table, and everything looks delicious. So let's get this party started, shall we?"

There's polite applause at that comment. Once it dies down, I say the blessing, then Anna takes back the microphone. "Father Tom, I know you were raised as a southern gentleman. But since you and Helen—" she pauses a second and glances at the door "—are the guests of honor, you get to go through first."

Covering the microphone with her hand, she whispers in my ear, "You really have no idea where she is?"

"No. I haven't heard from her since lunch. I suppose maybe something came up."

"I just hope it's nothing trivial," she whispers back, her tone dripping with irritation.

Before I can say anything else, Anna walks off the stage, leaving me alone with about twenty pairs of eyes looking at me expectantly.

"Thank you for that honor, Anna," I say. "You—you may have noticed that Helen is not here yet. She assured me that she was very much looking forward to this, and I'm sure whatever's delayed her is important police business. She'll be here shortly."

"She'd better be trying to find my TV," Gloria MacMillan yells from the back of the crowd. She's sitting in a chair at a table, her grandson AJ standing by her. "Doesn't need to be at a party when a poor old woman's TV was stolen right out from under her."

I smile weakly, then walk off the stage and take my place at the head of the buffet line. The Ladies are almost universally good cooks, and there are only a couple of dishes I discreetly avoid. The deviled eggs, of course, I pass up, along with Mrs. Cole's potato salad. By the time I get through the line, there's so much food on my plate I'm afraid I might drop it on the way to my table.

I've just sat down when Helen finally rushes in, out of breath and obviously flustered. It's obvious she did not take time to change, because while most of the other guests are clad in festive sweaters and scarves, she has on a gray tweed suit with a button missing.

I expect her to go through the serving line before joining me, but instead she comes right to our table and plops in the chair next to me.

"Sorry I'm late," she says breathlessly. "I'm not that hungry. Can I just nibble off your plate?"

"Sure," I say, because, what else am I going to say? I mean, I could point out to her that she never nibbles, especially not when she's under stress. But I still want to marry her, and I'd like to avoid a trip to the emergency room tonight.

The next thing I know, she is wolfing down my green bean casserole while glancing at the program. She gets to the bottom and then says under her breath, "Oh, dern. No. Oh, man, how could I have forgotten!"

Helen looks around the room furtively. "Oh, no," she whispers. "She's here."

Before I can ask her what's going on, she hisses, "Tom, give me the keys to the Rectory."

"What?" I ask.

"Hurry. I need to run to get something."

I dig my keys out of my pocket and hand them to her. "Helen, what the—."

"Thanks," she whispers quickly before scurrying across the basement and dashing up the stairs.

"Tom—oh, I thought Helen was here. Finally."

I look up at Anna, who has her arms crossed and a look of displeasure on her face.

"She was," I say. "She had to run to the Rectory for a minute."

Anna sighs. "Well, anyway, can you help judge the Christmas sweaters again this year?"

"If not me, then who?" I say dramatically.

"Oh, good grief," she mutters and walks off.

After fifteen minutes, Helen still hasn't returned. I'd go look for her, but instead, I'm sitting at a table with this year's chairwoman and an elderly member who once worked in the local dress shop and is therefore considered an expert on fashion. It's a pretty easy job, actually. They discuss the choices, and I agree with both of them. My main purpose for being there in the first place is to announce the winner.

It's not until I stand to hand over the prize—a $5 gift certificate to The Perfect Cup—that I see Helen return. I go back to our table where she slips me a white card.

"Sign this," she hisses under her breath.

"What is with you tonight, Helen?" I whisper, even as I do as she asks.

She plucks the card from my hand and slides it in a white envelope. "I forgot completely about the Secret Santa," she says as she licks and seals the envelope. "Let me use your pen."

"What do you mean you forgot?" I whisper.

"Well, you know, I've had a lot on my mind lately," she mutters. With my pen, she writes *Misty* in her tortured handwriting. "Look, I have to go. There's been another robbery and I need to check it out."

"What?" I whisper. "When did this happen?"

"The call came in about thirty minutes ago. Dan called me when I was at the Rectory."

"Why can't Dan handle it?"

Helen hands me the envelope. "Can you please just slide this under the Christmas Tree in the corner as soon as you can. I love you."

With that, she's gone, without so much as a chaste peck on the cheek.

Flummoxed, and more than a little put out, I casually saunter over to the Christmas Tree and place the envelope among the other presents. It's only later, when the Ladies start passing out their gifts, that I realize that something very, very bad is about to happen.

"Oh, no!" I mutter to myself. I try to get back to the tree to retrieve the envelope, but I don't get there in time.

All I can do is watch the disaster unfold.

Misty Newton, who, at 40, is one of the younger women in the group, is also one of the few that has never been married. She opens the envelope in front of everyone to find inside the Mass card I just signed. She starts to hold it up for everyone to see, but then pauses, turning it around and around. Then, she says aloud, "It's a Mass card, signed by Father Greer, but given by my Secret Santa, in honor of the birth of my new baby."

There are a couple of gasps, not to mention a fair share of murmurs. Watching the confusion spread, I am suddenly inspired to tell a small lie to prevent a big problem.

"Oh, this is my fault," I say with an embarrassed smile. "A woman who I know is a member of this organization came to me recently for a Mass card. I must have given her the wrong one."

There are more murmurs, with some of the ladies saying things like, "well, he is under a lot of stress, you know," and "he already has his mind on the wedding night."

"Misty," I continue, "I assure you the Mass will be valid and given for your real intentions, no matter what the card says."

Fortunately, this elicits a laugh, and everyone returns to oohing, ahhing, and otherwise commenting over their presents. Anna walks up to me, even more irritated than before, and says, "That was a good save, Tom. I hope Helen appreciates it. I see she's gone off again."

"Yes," I say. "Another robbery, apparently."

"Another one!" she exclaims. "It's a regular crime wave! I am so glad the Gypsinian Christ Child is safe and sound."

It is all I can do to maintain a neutral look as Anna walks off. A couple of ladies walk up and begin telling me about this news special they saw about the dangers American tourists face in the Caribbean—something about pirates, drug wars, and rabid monkeys—when the chairwoman of the Ladies of Charity announces, "OK, everyone, let's gather around. Can Father Tom and Helen come up on stage please?"

The ladies begin to applaud as I make my way up to the front in a replay of the Knights of Columbus party. Once up on stage, two of the ladies come forward with a large, beautifully wrapped gift.

"Father Tom," the chairwoman says, "the Ladies have worked on this gift for the last few months in cooperation with the Knights of Columbus. You received their part of the gift at their party. We are so pleased to present you, and Helen, of course, with our part."

Everyone applauds as I take the large package and turn to face the gathering. "Normally, we would ask you to unwrap it here, so we could see your expressions," the chairwoman continues. "However, since Helen had to leave, why don't you two just open it the next time you're together."

There's more applause. I say, gratefully, "Thank you so much for this. I know Helen will be terribly disappointed that she was not here to receive it."

As the ladies applaud one more time, I walk off the stage with the package. I have only one thought in mind.

This is the last straw.

***

By the time I get back to the Rectory a little after 9 p.m., I know what I need to do.

At least I hope I do.

I text Helen:

Please stop by the Rectory on your way home.

It takes her a few minutes to reply:

I really don't know when I'll be finished. It'll probably be pretty late.

I answer immediately:

That's fine. Anna's here. I'll wait up.

This time, it takes her even longer to reply:

OK. I'll be there as soon as I can.

"You've said that a lot lately," I grumble.

I turn on the TV and flip through the channels to find something to take my mind off of things. Almost two weeks before Christmas, there's nothing but sickly-sweet holiday movies.

Where's a good explosion when you need one?

I finally settle on a holiday movie on a channel named after a famous greeting-card company. Why I start watching it, I don't know. I've already missed the first thirty minutes or so, but I have little trouble figuring out what passes for a plot. Apparently, a top CIA agent inherits her great-aunt's all-natural, hand-dyed wool yarn business in a small town somewhere. She's on suspension after assassinating the wrong drug lord or something, so she takes the time to travel to this small town she's never been to—I'm still unclear about why the great-aunt left the business to her in the first place—intent on selling the business as quickly as possible. She's cynical and lonely, as I guess most spies in the movies are, and quick with a knife. Her first day, she runs some handsome guy in an old pickup truck off the road. She's eventually arrested for a hit and run, only to have the handsome guy not press charges because—surprise, surprise—he's in love with her. Lots of other things happened involving the yarn shop, sheep, and an anthrax outbreak, all culminating in the town's holiday dance which for some reason is held outdoors in the cold.

By the time the now ex-spy and the handsome guy—turns out he's the town vet—finally kiss, it's a little before 11 p.m. I've just turned the TV off when I hear the door open.

"Hi, darling," Helen says from the hallway. "Sorry I took so long."

I'm determined not to lose my temper. I say, "Oh, no problem. So, what was taken?"

"Ultimately, nothing," she says. "Hey, you want a beer?"

"Sure, thanks," I say. "What do you mean, nothing?"

She returns from the kitchen with two beers and hands me one. "Whoever it was had some pretty valuable jewelry when they left, but dropped it on the sidewalk in front of the house."

"You're kidding?" I ask.

"Nope. But there is good news. We might be able to raise some prints but I won't know until tomorrow. Maybe we can finally catch this guy and find the Christ Child before anyone else discovers it's missing."

She drops on the couch beside me and asks, "So, what's up with you? This is way past our curfew. I hope Matron doesn't get upset."

"Helen, I'm not in the mood to be flippant," I say firmly.

She sits up and puts her beer on the coffee table. "OK," she says slowly. "What is it?"

Looking at her steadily I say, "We need to have a talk."

Her eyes meet mine just as steadily as she asks, "About what?"

"About why you were late to the Ladies of Charity Christmas Party, ran into my office, and then disappeared again."

"I was late, Tom, because I had a call from a pawn shop in Oaksborough about the Gypsinian Christ Child. That turned out to be a wild goose chase—apparently the owner can't tell the difference between a 16th Century Renaissance statue and a twenty-first century baby Jesus from Valuemart. I ran into your office to get a Mass card for Misty, since I'm her Secret Santa and I forgot to get her a gift. I left again because, as I've already told you, there was another break in."

"And Dan couldn't handle it? Or one of your officers?" I ask, trying to keep my tone even.

"Probably," she replies, "but I thought it might have something to do with the statue."

"And you couldn't have waited until after the party was over to find out?"

"I could have, but I was anxious to know. Now, Tom, why don't you tell me what this is really about?"

I take a deep breath and, trying to weigh my words carefully, say, "This is about you not taking the feelings of the members of this parish seriously. This is about you promising you're going to be at a parish function, then either being very late or not showing up at all. This is about you running off to every case, whether it needs your attention or not. This is about you disappointing your fellow Ladies of Charity and leaving me to clean up your mess."

"What are you talking about?" she asks with indignation. "There were several dozen women there. They probably didn't even notice I was gone."

"Oh, they noticed, all right. Misty certainly knew something was wrong when she received a Mass card from her Secret Santa in honor of the birth of her child."

Helen goes white at this and says, "No. You're kidding me. Please tell me you're kidding me."

"Unfortunately, I'm not. But don't worry. I covered for you—I've had a lot of practice lately, becoming quite good at it actually. I told them that I had picked up the wrong card by mistake. Fortunately, most people consider priestly incompetence charming. I also didn't tell them who sent it."

"But Misty and everyone else will know at the end of the year," Helen says mournfully, "and then I'm sunk."

"I doubt that, because they'll remember what I said and you can tell them, 'You know Father Tom, typical man,' or something else like that. But I do know that everyone—especially Anna—was disappointed when they presented us with a gift and you weren't there to receive it with me."

"Tom, we've talked about this," Helen says firmly. "There will be times when I will have to miss things because of a case."

"Yes, I know that. But tonight was not one of those times. You could have waited. Someone else could have handled it."

Her face reddens and her eyes flash with anger. "You don't get to make that call," she says through clenched teeth.

"No," I reply, "but I get to point out when you have made it incorrectly." She's about to flare up again when I add, my voice rising, "Which you as good as admitted yourself. You didn't need to be there."

"Yes, I did, Tom!"

"No!" I snap, shaking my finger at her. "The only reason you left the party was because of that damn statue!"

We both pause for a reprimand, but Anna is obviously asleep.

"You can't curse a statue of the Baby Jesus," Helen says, the edge of a smile appearing on her lips.

"Good point. Allow me to rephrase. The only reason you left the party was because of your damn obsession with that statue!"

"I am not obsessed," she blurts. "I am reasonably concerned."

"Oh, really? In what universe is anything you've done in the last couple of weeks reasonable?"

"In a universe where the Holy Roman Catholic Church has granted me special permission to marry the man I love without dooming both of us to Hell," she says, her voice cracking. "In a universe where thousands of people are watching, hoping, and praying that we blow it, that I let you down and mess your work in the parish up so that they can say, 'See, I told you so.' In a universe where I have willingly given up so much of myself and what I want to be with you. In a universe where, if I fail, if I fall, I take you down with me, the one thing I could never bear to do. That's the universe we're living in, Tom—both of us, not just me—and I'm not about to let some darn statue be the reason all all hopes and dreams turn to ashes!"

She's sobbing now and pacing around the room. "Tom, I love you so much it scares the hell out of me. I love you too much to let you down. That's been what I've been most afraid of ever since we received permission to marry. That I'd do something to ruin your priesthood. You know, sometimes I wish I'd said yes to you back in that cabin in Bellamy and ran away from our lives here. You wouldn't be a priest, sure, but I wouldn't be going through this!"

Helen collapses on the couch and leans her head on my shoulder. "All I want to do is to be the best wife I can be, and I've already messed that up!"

She dissolves into sobs, burying her head in my chest, her tears wetting my shirt. Wrapping my arms around, I say gently, "Helen, my darling. I don't know what universe you're in, but you need to get out of there and come back to mine—to ours—where people love us and want us to succeed, where neither the Church nor I want you to give up anything that is good for you, where

where if you fall, you won't pull me down with you because I'm strong enough to grab your hand and hold both of us up."

"But Tom," she rasps. "You trusted me, and I let you down."

"You didn't let me down," I whisper. "It's not your fault someone stole the Christ Child."

"I left the car unlocked."

"You made a mistake. You're human."

"I'm Chief of Police, Tom," she whispers. "When I make a mistake, people might die."

"Well, no one's died over this. And no one is going to."

She sits up, sniffling. I grab the box of tissues off the coffee table and hand it to her. She blows her nose and wipes away her tears. I brush hair that's fallen in her face back behind her ears.

Taking a deep breath, Helen says, "So, what should I do? Just forget about finding the statue?"

"Of course not," I say. "I'm not asking you to. I'm just asking you to get some balance back in your life. I'm asking you to remember that if you don't find the statue, nothing catastrophic is going to happen. You and I are still getting married the day after Christmas, and nothing in Heaven or on Earth is going to keep that from happening."

Helen grins, then leans in and kisses me deeply and passionately. So deeply and passionately, in fact, that I'm very glad Anna's upstairs.

Fortunately, my strong and stoic bride-to-be is an absolute child when it comes to presents and she quickly loses interest in me when she sees the two wrapped gifts on the coffee table. "Oh Tom," she nearly squeals with delight, "is that the gift from the L of C? I do feel bad about disappointing them and I will apologize to everyone at the next meeting, but does this mean we can open it and the gift from the Knights now? I'd like to be able to write them thank-you notes before we leave town."

"And you'd like to see what's in the boxes, too, I bet."

"You know me too well," she says, pulling the box from the Ladies toward her.

"Not yet, but I intend to keep trying," I say as she suddenly shocks me by reaching down the front over her blouse and pulling out a small pocket knife. She sees me staring and laughs, saying, "Oh, c'mon Tom. You've known I carried a knife on me for months. Surely you must have figured out where I carried it."

"I did, but just didn't expect to see you suddenly whip it out like that."

"Calm down, Father," she says playfully. "I can assure you that this knife is all I'll be whipping out for another 12 days, 6 hours, and an odd number of minutes."

I'm still blushing over this when she opens the box to reveal multiple bubble-wrapped items. She unwraps the first to reveal a delicate, obviously carefully and lovingly hand-painted statue of a woman in Biblical garb. "Mary?" Helen asks with wonder.

"No," I say, "Look at her gray hair. It must be St. Elizabeth." I set the statue on the table as she unwraps a man whose priestly robes and gray beard identify him as St. Zechariah. Next comes an angel, then the Blessed Virgin herself, then St. Joseph, his face lined but his body obviously muscular from years of hard work. There are shepherds and wise men, sheep, camels and a very patient-looking donkey, Then, in the very bottom, carefully wrapped and stored in his own separate box, the Christ Child. As Helen and I marvel at his perfect features, a note falls out. "I painted Him myself, to remind you of the Gypsinian Christ Child, so that you'll never forget it. Love, Anna," I read aloud, holding my breath to see how Helen will react. I am thankful when she laughs out loud and declares, "Small chance of that."

We soon move on to open the Knight's gift, which proves to be several beautifully hand-carved buildings to house our new treasures. There's a comfortable looking home for Zechariah and Elizabeth, a delicate tree under which Mary can be praying when the angel appears, a backdrop of a starry night for the shepherds and even a Oriental tent for the wise men. But the centerpiece is the creche itself, with stalls for the animals, soft hay for Mary to rest on, and a warm, welcoming manger in which she can lay her newborn son.

We spend the next half-hour arranging our gifts perfectly on the entryway table, leaving the infant Jesus in his box until Christmas Eve and placing the Wise Men far away. For this, Helen insists on pulling out her compass for, as she says, "They must come from the east."

By this time, it is after midnight and we have badly broken our curfew, so I give her a quick kiss and send her out into the night, watching once again as her bundled-up back disappears into the cold.

"12 days, 6 hours, and an odd number of minutes, my love," I say quietly to myself, "and I'll never have to drive you out into the cold again."

Seventeen

The Birthday Party for Jesus is a well-loved tradition at Saint Clare's, normally held on the last Saturday before Christmas. In order to help the children better understand my role as *in persona Christi,* standing in the person of Christ as a priest, they present Jesus' birthday cake to me, then sing Happy Birthday, and watch me blow out the candles. I also get the first piece of cake. Miriam asked me weeks ago what kind of cake I wanted, so I selected my favorite—chocolate—and she got it from The Muffin Man.

Hey, it's a tough job, but someone has to do it.

I get to the church basement early so I can welcome the children and their parents. The food table is all set up, complete with a scrumptious-looking cake and hot apple cider. Anna is putting the last minute touches on everything but pauses to ask, "Where's Helen?"

"She's on her way," I say, hoping I sound casual. "She's following up on a lead on these robberies."

"But she is going to be here, isn't she? I mean, this isn't going to be a repeat of the Ladies of Charity Christmas Party is it?"

"Of course not," I say. "We had a long talk the other night, and she promises that she's going to be here before it starts."

Anna looks dubious, and shakes her head. "Honestly, Tom, I don't think she worked that murder case involving you with as much determination. Of course, I'm not surprised, given everything."

"What do you mean, everything?" I ask, fearing the worst.

"She is obviously nervous about getting married and she's working hard to distract herself."

"Oh yeah," I say, breathing an inward sigh of relief, "That's probably it."

"I was so nervous before marrying Drew that I actually picked a fight with him over something trivial. I can't even remember what it was about. After yelling at each other for about half-an-hour, I felt much better."

"Fascinating, Anna," I say.

"Anna! Do you know where the pin-the-tale on Joseph's donkey game is?" Misty, who seems to have recovered from the faux pas committed by her Secret Santa, calls from across the room.

"For heaven's sake, Misty," Anna says, marching across the basement, "it's in the container marked 'donkey.'"

Soon after, Martin and Mae arrive with an entourage that includes his three nieces and Mae's four youngest siblings. "My," I say as the kids run squealing toward the games being run by the Ladies of Charity, "you two certainly know how to make an entrance."

Mae just laughs, but Martin says, "That's what I've been talking about in our meetings. I don't know if I can get used to moving through life like I'm leading a parade."

Mae turns to her fiancé. "Marty, you know we won't start out with this many."

"That's where you're wrong," Martin says. "We'll already have three, which means we're almost halfway to being able to field our own softball team."

"You know," I say, "why don't we put a pin in this discussion—"

"You're exaggerating again, Marty," Mae says, rolling her eyes.

"I don't think now's the time to get into this again," I interject.

"You only think I'm exaggerating because you're downplaying how difficult it's going to be," Martin says.

"Difficult for *you,* not for me," Mae says, her voice rising just a little. "Don't forget, I grew up like this."

"And I didn't, Mae," Martin replies. "I just—"

"Stop," I say firmly. "Both of you, stop right now."

"Father Tom?" Mae says with surprise.

"Really, Tom," Martin says, shaking his head.

"This is not the time or the place for this discussion," I point out. "Let's revisit this at our next meeting. In the meantime, just go and enjoy yourselves, OK?"

Mae and Martin look at each other, then break into giggles. "Of course, Tom," Martin says. "Sorry."

"Yeah," Mae says. "Sorry."

"Now, go get some hot cider and don't talk about this anymore today. That's an order from your priest."

"Yes, Father," they say in unison before going arm-in-arm to the table to partake of the hot apple cider.

I look at the clock on the wall. The party doesn't officially start for another ten minutes, so Helen isn't technically late. But parents and children are beginning to come, and I really hope—

"Let me help, Miriam," I hear Helen say.

I smile, thankful that she's arrived. I turn to see her holding the door open for Miriam, who is coming in carrying Andrew and trying not to trip over the twins hanging onto her legs. Catherine's carrying the diaper bag for her mother while admonishing her brothers, "You're going to make Mommy fall and hurt herself!" Fortunately, as soon as they see the other kids, they squeal and run off to join them.

"Whew, thanks," Miriam says as she rubs her back.

"Are you OK?" Helen asks.

"Oh, fine," she laughs. "She's just putting a strain on my back, and carrying Andrew didn't help. I swear, that boy gets heavier every day. But then I guess I do, too."

"Not at all, Miriam," I say with a smile.

"I thought priests aren't supposed to lie, Father?"

"Self-preservation is permitted," Helen says before I can defend myself. "Besides, he has a lot of practice not commenting on my weight."

Miriam pats me on the arm and winks. "Good man."

I shrug. "I try. But let's find you a chair."

We walk over to where Martin and Mae are sitting, observing the growing gaggle of children playing pin the tail on Joseph's donkey. Miriam hugs Mae and asks, "How are you, Dr. Maycord? Are you and Mae busy making plans?"

His Georgian drawl suddenly more evident than usual, Martin replies, "My friends call me Martin, ma'am. And I hope we can be friends, even if I did once lock your husband in a basement at gunpoint."

"Oh, that," she says nonchalantly. "Don't worry about it, I've done worse to him. We both understand the desperate circumstances that led you to do that, and hold no grudge." She looks over at the group of children gathered around the "Find the Pearl of Great Price" sandbox. "If you don't mind me asking, how are the girls?"

Martin looks at Mae, and she says quietly, "They're still working through some things, but they seem to be growing stronger every day."

As if to confirm her evaluation, Therese squeals and runs across the room, with Max and JP in hot pursuit.

"Boys stop chasing Therese. She doesn't like it," Miriam scolds, heading their way.

Mae catches her by the arm and says, "Let's watch a minute. If she's like most five-year-girls, she actually does." Sure enough, as soon as the boys back off, little Therese turns around and starts chasing them.

Reassured, Miriam turns to Mae and asks, "Did you learn that in college?"

"Oh. no," Mae laughs. "Most of what I know about the average kid, I learned from my mom."

They both laugh and Miriam says, "Well, I come from a big family but I'm the baby, so I certainly don't know much, but I know a lot more than I used to." She then says to Martin, "We'd love to have the girls over for a play date sometime after the baby gets here. Well, more precisely, a few weeks after," she adds with a smile.

"I've got a better idea," Mae says brightly. "Why don't the girls have Catherine over sometime soon? They seem to do better getting to know new people on their own turf."

"Well, Catherine can certainly be intimidating so that's probably a good idea. Just let me know."

There's some sort of commotion over by the games. We turn and find Catherine has Daniel Wright down on the ground in a headlock.

"What have I told you about calling me spooky!" Catherine yells.

"I'm sorry! I'm sorry!" the struggling boy shouts "Just let me go!"

"Do you promise!"

"I promise! I promise!"

"Catherine Elizabeth Conway!" Miriam shouts, "You let him go!"

Helen says, "Little son of Satan probably deserved it. Dan teach her that?"

"Yes!" Miriam says with exasperation as she waddles over to her oldest daughter, who's let her tormentor go. Daniel, for his part, at least has enough sense not to hang around.

"Why does that boy call Catherine spooky?" Martin asks, surveying the scene and looking a little pale.

Mae, Helen, and I look at each other. "You haven't heard the stories?" I ask.

"No, but then I don't know a lot of people in the parish."

"Well, it's kind of complicated, but here's the gist of it. About eight months ago, Catherine fell out of a tree in her front yard. She hit her head and was unconscious for several hours."

"Just a few hours?" the trauma surgeon asks. "That's curious. A fall like that should have put her into a coma for several days. Or . . . " he trails off and shakes his head.

"Anyway, when she woke up, she told Helen and me that a woman wearing a white dress with a blue ribbon had told her that we were getting married."

Martin shrugs. "She dreamed it, based on what she'd heard. The human brain is a tricky thing."

"Well, that's true," Helen says. "But this was before we received official permission. It was a closely guarded secret, and when she had her accident, Anna was the only person in town who knew."

"Still, there were probably rumors about you two. She also seems to be a very observant girl."

"Again, both those things are true," I say. "But there were details that have no rational explanation. For example, remember I said the woman she saw wore a white dress with a blue ribbon?"

"Yes," Martin says slowly. "What about it?"

"What she described was my late wife Joan's wedding dress."

Martin considers this, then shakes his head. "It's just a coincidence. She may have seen a picture of a dress she liked."

"Oh, Marty," Mae says with a smile. "You're such an old skeptic."

"I am not! Old, that is. The skeptic part, well, yeah. It was a dream, brought on by the concussion and probably the medication they had her on."

"I'm surprised you didn't treat her," Helen says. "It wasn't that long ago."

"It was probably when I was in Ottawa for a conference. I presented a paper on applying battlefield surgical techniques in the ER."

"Anyway, Martin," I say, "I might agree with you if that were the only thing. But there have been other things."

One of Martin's nieces comes up and wants to show them something, so she leads him and Mae to the craft table, leaving Helen and I alone.

"I was afraid you weren't going to make it," I say quietly.

"What, and miss seeing my 46-year-old fiancé wearing a Birthday Boy crown and blowing out the candles for God the Son's birthday," Helen says with a grin. "Oh, no, I'm not just here, I plan to take and post video."

"You wouldn't!"

"I might. Gladys does keep saying that Saint Clare's website needs more pizazz."

"Yeah," I sigh. "It looks pretty dismal. But that's what you get when your webmaster is a 70-year-old retiree who took a class on web design at the senior center."

"Have you thought about getting Gladys and Nate to take it over?"

"Yes. On the one hand, it makes perfect sense. On the other hand, the thought makes me nauseous."

Helen's laughter is cut off by her phone playing the Marine Corps Hymn. My heart sinks as I say, "Dan's calling you."

She nods and digs through her tote bag for the phone. "Maybe we got a hit on the fingerprints," she says.

I'm about to ask her if she can just call him back after the party, but before I can, she answers.

"Yeah, Dan?" she says. I see her eyes widen before she looks at me and then replies, "Great. Hold him but do not talk to him until I get there. . . Hold on a second." She asks me, "How much longer will this last?"

I shrug. "About another hour, I'd guess."

She nods and says, "Dan, I'll be there in about an hour." She hangs up and says to me, "They've got a match off the fingerprints on the bag of jewelry. They're on their way to pick the guy up."

"Helen, that's great news. Who is it?"

"You are not going to believe this. The fingerprints came back to AJ MacMillan."

"Gloria MacMillan's grandson?" I say, startled by this turn of events.

"The very same," she nods. "It will be interesting to hear what he has to say for himself when they bring him in."

"And you don't need to be there?" I ask.

She flashes what I call her brave smile and declares, "Not as much as I need to be here."

I am once again bowled over by this woman I love, whom God has given me. And that is why I am wearing such a goofy grin in all the pictures taken of me cutting Baby Jesus' cake.

Eighteen

As soon as the last child leaves, Helen reverts to Chief of Police mode.

I realize this as we speed through town.

"Helen," I say, wincing as she sails through a red light with full lights and sirens, "Dan's not going to do anything before you get there, you know. Can't you just slow down?"

"Tom," she says, keeping her eyes fixed on the street ahead of her, "the quicker I get there, the quicker we can get the Gypsinian Christ Child back."

"You don't even know if this guy knows anything about the Christ Child."

"I know, but you don't know he doesn't. Now shut up, darling, so I can concentrate. Traffic's heavier than I thought it would be."

I shut up, take my Rosary from my pocket, and begin to pray a decade for both our safety and the safe return of the Gypsinian Christ Child.

When we find it, I'm going to strongly suggest to His Eminence that he keep it safe at his Cathedral next Christmas. I'd hate for another priest to suffer the way I have.

Of course, no other priest is engaged to a half-crazed Chief of Police.

She squeals her tires as she pulls to a stop in her designated parking space outside the department. I'm certain that the car hasn't finished moving before she's out and striding across the lot to the back door of the station. I hop out and hurry to catch up with her.

"Where is he!" Helen cries as we come through the door. "Where is the reprobate scumbucket!"

She heads toward the interview room, only to run into Dan as he emerges from his office.

"Is he in interrogation?" she asks her chief detective.

"No, Helen, he is not," he says calmly. "He's in a cell, cooling his heels."

She starts to walk toward interrogation again. "Well, pull him out of the cell and drag his butt in there. Time's a'wastin', Dan!"

Time's a'wastin'? Apparently, just as I fall back into the colloquial terms of my youth when I'm under stress, so does Helen.

"Helen, stop," Dan says calmly. "We need to talk first."

She stops and turns to her detective, a scowl on her face. "No, *I* need to talk to *him*."

"Let's just go in here for a minute," he says, pointing back to his office. Helen glares at him, then says, "OK. One minute." She follows Dan inside, and I follow her, closing the door behind me.

"What is this about, Detective?" she asks as Dan sits behind his desk.

468

"Helen, please," he says, holding his hands up. "Let's just sit together for a few minutes and figure this thing out before you do something that will blow this case and possibly wreck your career."

He utters the last with the stern tone that he typically uses for his kids. This gets her attention. She sits down and waits for Dan to speak. I sit in the chair opposite her.

"First, Helen, you need to let me take the lead in this," Dan says. "The investigation was one thing. But you are too emotionally involved in this to actually interview this or any other suspect."

"Dan," Helen starts, "we don't have a lot of time—."

"No, Chief," Dan interrupts her. "You don't have a lot of time. This department, which represents all the citizens of this town, has plenty of time. The suspect in these robberies is in custody. This is not a murder case, so no one is likely to get hurt if we've got the wrong person. We can afford to take our time and do this right, by the book."

"Dan, I don't think you understand. If I don't get that Christ Child back . . . "

Demonstrating the interrogation skills that he has mastered under Helen's tutelage, Dan says nothing, waiting for her to finish. When she just looks at him, he asks quietly, "What, Helen? What is the very worst thing that will happen?"

This catches her off guard, and she says nothing as I reach over and take her hand. "He asks a good question, Honey," I say. "What will happen? The Archdiocese is well-insured. There is not another Gypsinian Christ Child out there, but there are other statues. No one will die, no one will even get hurt. The Archdiocese will just have to get a new one."

"While everyone knows that Helen Parr, the Chief of Police of Myerton, Maryland, allowed it to be stolen out of her own car because she didn't bother locking it," Helen says sharply. "That the future Mrs. Father Tom Greer lost one of the most valuable art objects in the Archdiocese before she was even married. No, gentlemen, I will not back down from this."

She pauses and then says quietly, "Now, Dan, I admit that you make a good point. But I am still head of this department. You can interview the suspect but I will be watching and I want you to pull out all the stops. I'll even turn off the cameras if necessary. There will be no record, just his word against yours."

"Helen!" I say, incredulous. "You can't expect Dan—"

"Father, I've got this," Dan says firmly. "Chief, if you expect me to rough someone up over a property theft, then you can have my resignation right now, because I will not do it."

"Now don't you get all high and mighty with me, Dan Conway," she shouts. "You and I both know that we've pushed the limits a few times."

"In a life and death situation, yes, but not for something like this," Dan growls. "Human dignity and safety is much more important than the most valuable possession in the world. Or at least that's what one detective told me at a stake out a few years ago, when I wanted to rush a gambling den."

This gets her attention, and she seems to calm down some. "OK. The cameras stay on. But Dan, please, please, find out what he did with that statue," she pleads quietly.

"I will do my best," Dan replies solemnly.

***

Less than an hour later, Helen and I are once again in Gladys' office, looking at the interior of the Myerton Police Department's interrogation room on the big flatscreen wall monitor. Dan is sitting across from AJ with his back to the camera, just looking at the suspect, not saying anything at all. AJ, for his part, looks like he's about to throw up or wet himself or both.

"Your sensors are all functional, Gladys?" Helen asks as she stands with her arms folded behind the quirky genius' wheelchair.

"Yes, Chief," she replies. She taps some keys on the keyboard. "Man, he's as nervous as I used to be in church."

"He's hiding something," Helen comments.

"Or, he's scared of Dan," I suggest. "Or, he's nervous about being in that room."

Helen cuts her eyes to me, a clear sign that she wants me to be quiet.

"Dan," Gladys says into her microphone. "Scratch your ear if you can hear me."

We see Dan do just that, indicating to Gladys that he's reading her loud and clear though his earpiece.

Helen leans across Gladys and says into the mic, "OK, Dan. This is your show."

Dan leans back, throwing his arm over the back of his chair, and says casually, "You know, I've had some pretty sorry characters in this room, but I've never had someone so rotten that they'd steal from their own grandmother."

"Whoa!" Gladys says.

"What?" Helen asks.

"Dan's mention of his grandmother got a sharp reaction."

"That's hardly surprising," I mutter.

AJ slumps further in his chair and shakes his head. "You don't understand," he moans.

"You're right," Dan says, leaning forward. "I don't. So why don't you help me out."

AJ buries his head in his hands. "I stole the TV and all the other stuff. But it was all because of her. She drove me to it!"

"Because of Mrs. MacMillan?"

"Yes!" he cries.

"So she what, got you hooked on drugs? Forced you to gamble? Maybe introduced you to a pretty girl with high end tastes? Exactly how is that sweet little old lady responsible for you becoming a thief?"

Helen and I look at each other when Dan calls Gloria MacMillan "sweet," but we say nothing.

"No, it's not like that," he whines. "I don't do drugs or gamble or have a girlfriend. Grandma would never let me do anything like that. Hell, she won't let me do anything at all."

"Except steal?"

"No, not that either." He takes a deep breath and says, "I had to steal the TV. I was desperate. I have got to get out of this town, away from her."

"From who?"

"Grandma! I just had to get away!"

Dan says nothing for a moment. "AJ, what you say makes no sense. She wasn't living with you when you stole her TV. She was living with your brother, right?"

"But ever since she got out of the hospital, she kept calling me, saying I needed to get her stuff moved out of Bob's and into my apartment. I kept putting her off with one excuse or another—my apartment was being painted, it had to be fumigated for termites, it was being cleaned for mold—but I knew I couldn't put her off forever. That's when I decided I had to get away."

Dan nods. "OK. Go on."

"I knew they were going to be out of town for the weekend," AJ continues. "Bob gave me a key a while back, so getting in was no problem. No. That was the easy part. Then what happens? She insists on moving in with me. Says Bob's place isn't safe." The young man sighs. "She's made my life a living hell ever since she moved in with me. She spends all day in bed, only getting out to go to the bathroom or take a shower. She just lays there and yells at me. First, she says I need to get a job, but then, when I try to go out to look, she insists that she can't be left alone. Then she wants to know if I'm gay, because she says it's weird that I don't have a girlfriend. The fact is, I did, but she broke up with me the day Grandma moved in. Then she wants me to take her somewhere in my truck, but as soon as we get out to it, she insists that she can't climb up into it and that I need to trade it for a car. I'm telling you, sir, I just can't take it anymore."

"Ask him about the Christ Child," Helen says into the mic but Dan ignores her.

"OK, so you needed money to get out of town. You should have been able to pawn that TV for enough for a bus ticket and then some. So, why were you still here for her to move in with?"

"Because I broke the TV!"

"What?" Helen and Dan say at the same time.

"Yeah. I was trying to get it in my truck when I dropped it and the screen shattered. At first, I thought this was like a sign, you know, from God, warning me to stop. So I did. I prayed and asked God to give me the strength to stand her. But then she actually moved in and Grandma mentioned that she might have to have me help her in and out of the bathtub. I decided that was the actual sign, that I should steal something else and get the hell out of Dodge."

I can't help but smile a little at this but Dan says, "Did you try to steal a welder and a tank of acetylene?"

AJ nods. "Yeah. I've worked some for Roscoe, so I knew he had just gotten it. I grabbed it when I knew he'd still be asleep. I just didn't know it would be that heavy, even with the wheelbarrow. I couldn't get it back to my truck, so I just ditched it."

"So after that you took the laptop?"

"Yeah, but that didn't work. Honestly, given what a mess that house was, I'm not surprised. I mean, you just can't believe how some people live."

Dan ignores this and says, "The laptop didn't work, you said?"

"No. When I took it in to pawn, the guy said it looked like someone had poured soda in it or something."

"Grape juice," Dan says, obviously without thinking. When AJ looks up, he clears his throat and continues, "Then you dropped the necklace."

"Uh-huh. And I thought about giving up again but I figured with Christmas coming, I'd try one last time. But I dropped the bag when a dog started chasing me. That's how you caught me, right? I forgot my gloves, but didn't realize it until I was inside the house."

"OK," Dan nods. "So you admit to the five break-ins. Now, tell me about the statue."

AJ looks at Dan, clearly confused. "What statue?"

"Gladys?" Helen asks.

"I need a minute, Chief," Gladys replies.

"The one of the Baby Jesus. What did you do with that?" Dan asks.

AJ shakes his head. "Sir, I don't know what you're talking about."

"Well?" Helen asks.

"Nothing yet." Gladys replies.

"Someone stole a statue of the Baby Jesus out of the back of someone's car, and obviously, you are our prime suspect," Dan says.

"Look, sir," AJ says, "I've told you about everything I took. I don't know anything about no Baby Jesus. I mean, wouldn't stealing something like that, I don't know, send me to hell?"

"That's not my department. But just to recap, you stole a big screen TV, a welder, a laptop computer, a string of expensive pearls, and a bag of other jewelry, but you did not steal a statue of the Baby Jesus."

"That's right."

"Chief," Gladys says quietly, "there's nothing to indicate he's lying. His breathing, heart rate, perspiration—everything shows he's nervous, but there's no evidence he's trying to hide something."

Dan rubs his hand through his hair and turns to the camera, a look of defeat on his face. Then he says, "OK, son, write that down for me and we'll figure out what should happen next."

As Dan leaves the room, Helen dashes out of Gladys' office and catches him in the hallway. "Why are you letting him off the hook like that! You have got to drill down on him and find that statue!"

She's about to say more when I say, "Helen, this is no conversation for the hallway."

The three of us step into a vacant office. As soon as the door closes, Dan says, "Helen, it is obvious to anyone in their right mind that that guy knows nothing about that damned statue. I'll let you figure out what the fact that you don't recognize that means."

"You're skating on thin ice, Detective," Helen growls,

"And you're—"

"OK, stop it!" I demand. "You both need to take a deep breath and let me talk for a minute. Helen, I love you and I hope that I always want what's best for you, which is why I have to agree with Dan. I am so sorry, Honey, but that kid wouldn't know a valuable statue from a box of rocks."

Helen stares at me for a moment, opening and then closing her mouth. She then takes a deep breath, lets it out slowly, and says much more calmly, "You're both right. I can see that. I just hate it, because it means that all this work has been for nothing."

"No, Helen," Dan says gently, "Not for nothing. We caught a thief and, if all goes well, may have stopped an otherwise good kid from getting into worse trouble down the road. That's not nothing, not by a long shot."

Helen sighs. "Good point, Dan. The problem is, I just don't know where to go from here. I mean, we really are running out of time."

***

I would love to hang around the police station and comfort Helen, but I have to be back at the church by 3 p.m. to hear confessions. When I arrive a few minutes before the scheduled time, there's already a good crowd gathered of about a dozen or so people. Unlike Lent, Catholics are not required to go to confession during Advent. But since it's a minor penitential season, I've noticed an uptick in people choosing to partake of the sacrament. Everyone is praying or using a popular Catholic phone app to examine their consciences.

At least, that's what I choose to believe.

We're about 20 minutes in when the door opens and I hear a familiar voice that I recognize as Dominic's say, following the preliminary exchange, "Father, I broke into the sacristy last week and accidentally broke a votive candle holder. I will be glad to pay to replace it. For these and all my other sins, I am truly sorry."

This catches me completely off guard, and I'm uncertain how to proceed. I mean, this really is something Helen needs to know. But he's telling me in confession, so I can't say anything.

After wrestling for a moment, I finally say, "I have reason to believe that what you did may have had unforeseen consequences, ones that I would like to discuss with the police. In order to do that, I am requesting that you speak with me about this matter outside the confessional. This is not your penance and you may decide not to do it, in which case, as always, everything you have said here remains under the seal. Now, for your penance, say three Hail Marys."

Before he says the Act of Contrition, Dominic says weakly, "May I stop by your office after Mass this evening?"

"Yes, of course."

***

As soon as I've changed out of my vestments, I hurry back to the office. Dominic is waiting there, looking forlorn. As soon as we're seated he begins, "You need me to tell you everything that I told you in the confessional again, right?"

"We can only discuss what you tell me now. And as always, I will keep what you say as confidential as I can."

Fortunately, Dominic repeats the entire story to me. When he finishes, I say, "I don't understand why you didn't just come ask for the key? I would have let you in."

For some reason, the question makes Dominic uncomfortable. He squirms in his chair and says, "Well, you see, Father. I thought that the window was unlocked because I always open it to air out the room after I extinguish the incense and I couldn't remember locking it back. I figured I'd climb in, lock it and then go out the door and lock it behind me."

"But Dominic, if it was just that you forgot to lock the window, you could have texted me. I would've taken care of it."

He turns a bit red at this and studies his well-worn sneakers as he says, "Well, Father, it was more than the window being unlocked."

I say nothing and he continues, "You see, it's like this. Someone, ah, had given me a note before Mass the previous Sunday. I'd remembered putting it in my pocket, but when I checked the next day it wasn't there. I thought I'd dropped it in the sacristy. I didn't contact you about it because—well, it wasn't exactly the kind of note that I'd want your help in finding. If you understand what I mean."

"I see," I say with a smile. "So I'm guessing it was from Therese?" He nods and I continue, "Dominic, you and Therese are both old enough and have been brought up well enough to know right from wrong. If there was something in that note that concerned your involvement in something you're ashamed of, having me or Deacon Derek or anyone else find the note is the least of your worries. God already knows about it."

"Oh, no, Father Tom," Dominic says quickly. "It's nothing like that. I'm not ashamed. Just a bit embarrassed." He studies his shoes again. "See, we've been spending more and more time alone lately. Don't misunderstand me, we haven't been doing anything—well, not much. Just kissing. We thought we could handle it but things got a little out of hand Saturday night—don't misunderstand me, nothing bad happened, it was just—oh, this is so embarrassing!"

"It's OK, Dominic."

"Well, Therese was just sort of reminding me that after what happened we should probably invite another couple to go with us when we went anywhere, if you see what I mean."

I smile at him, reassured that all is right with the world, before adding, "Dominic, it sounds like you two have things well under control, but please, remember, you can still talk to me if you have any questions."

"Oh, I will. I've also talked to my Dad. He's given me some good advice."

"Glad to hear it. Now, Dominic, I have a favor to ask. At this moment, Chief Parr thinks that someone broke into the sacristy to try to rob it. I would like to let her know that I have learned differently. I don't need to tell her anything beyond that, just that someone from the church was in there and didn't want me to know, so they climbed in and out of the window. Is that OK with you?"

"Sure, Father. You can tell her it was me if you need to, just, um, maybe not about the note."

"Absolutely. That will stay between us."

Nineteen

I am in my office Monday morning going over my notes for the Christmas homily—I'm giving the same one at the Vigil and Midnight Masses—when Anna pokes her head around my door.

"Tom, Steve's here," she says. "Do you have a few minutes to see him?"

"Sure, but why didn't I hear the doorbell?"

"I was walking from the church and he was coming up the sidewalk, He said he just needs a minute of your time."

"Sure, sure, show him in," I say. A moment later, Steve comes in, carrying a wrapped box.

"Hi, Father," he says, "Merry Christmas."

He hands me the box. "Well, this is a pleasant surprise, Steve. What is it?"

"Just open it and find out," he laughs.

I unwrap the box and open it. "Steve!" I say, pulling out the bottle. "My favorite brandy. How did you know?"

"Oh, a bartender can't reveal all his sources of information. Consider this a wedding present as well."

"As much as I appreciate this," I say, "Helen and I did say on the invitation that we wanted donations to the education center in lieu of presents. I mean, we have everything we need."

"And I'll be making a donation," he nods. "Bridget—" He stops, his face reddening slightly. "That is, her kids are really looking forward to the center opening, and I want to do my part. This is, well, for those times when married life may not be too easy and you can't make it out to my place."

I laugh and offer him a chair. "This will also come in handy after parish council meetings," I say.

Steve nods. "Yeah, I can imagine."

We both lapse into silence, Steve leaning forward looking at his hands and shoes. "Something on your mind, Steve?" I ask.

"No," he says quickly, looking at me. "No, I just wanted to make sure I got this to you before Christmas."

"I see."

"Yeah," he says. Clapping his hands together, "So, I guess I'll let you get back to work. I have some last-minute Christmas shopping to do, so I'm heading to Hagerstown."

"It'll be packed," I say.

"Well, most of the things I ordered online," he says. "But some things wouldn't get here in time."

"That happens," I say, nodding my head. Cocking my head to one side, I ask, "Are you sure there's nothing else?"

He opens his mouth to say something, then closes it and shakes his head. "No, no, nothing. I'll see you at the Christmas Eve Mass. Bridget and I—that is, Bridget's bringing the kids and I said I'd come along."

"See you then, Steve."

I watch him leave my office, a moment later hearing the door close.

***

I come back to the Rectory from saying Noon Mass to find Martin and Mae sitting in the living room.

Noticing my surprise, Mae says, "Don't we have a pre-marital counseling appointment this afternoon?"

"No, Mae," I say, "It's tomorrow. At least that's what I have down."

"That's what I had, too, Honey," Martin says gently.

"Why didn't you say something?" she asks.

"Because I thought I might be wrong."

"Oh, Marty," she says, "if you had said something, we wouldn't be wasting Father Tom's time."

I hold up my hand and say placatingly, "Look, this is no big deal. In fact, I can go ahead and see you now. I just need to let Helen know that she's on her own for lunch."

"No, Tom, don't do that." Martin says, "I've got a better idea. Why don't the four of us go out for lunch to Spacolli's. I'll treat."

"Wonderful idea, Marty," Mae says with a grin. "How about it, Tom?"

I'm about to say no, but it occurs to me that this is the perfect opportunity to distract Helen from the case of the Gypsinian Christ Child.

"Let me call Helen and see if she can spare the time," I say. "I'll be right back."

I go into my office and shut the door. Normally, I'd text her, but I think I need to talk to her about this.

"Hi," she says cheerfully. "You are bringing lunch today, aren't you?"

"That's why I'm calling, actually," I say. "Martin and Mae have invited us to go out with them to Spacolli's for lunch, his treat."

She's quiet for a moment, then says, "Oh, darling, that sounds great, but I—"

"Helen, darling," I say, "I know you're still anxious about the Christ Child."

"Yes, Tom, because I only have five days to find it."

"I'm aware of that, mainly because you've been counting down the days ever since someone stole it. But you need to eat, and I think you could also use the distraction."

She sighs. "Tom, I don't think—"

"Helen, a couple of hours won't make a difference. Let someone know you're going to lunch, and if any leads come in to follow up on them."

I can hear her thinking through the phone, turning the possibilities over in her mind. "Tell them yes," she says. "You're right. I could use a break, and besides, I've been craving their veal scallopini for a while now."

"We'll pick you up in ten minutes?"

"I'll be waiting." She pauses, then says, "Thank you, darling."

"For what?"

"Oh, for watching out for me, keeping me sane, you know, the basics."

"It's my pleasure."

We hang up and I rejoin Martin and Mae in the living room.

"Well, she's game," I say with a grin. "I said we'd pick her up at the station in about ten minutes."

"Good," Martin says, "good. We'll take my car."

As soon as he says 'my car,' a thrill runs through me. His Porsche. We're going to ride in his Porsche. I have been wanting a ride in that car ever since I saw it.

To say I'm excited as we walk to the Rectory driveway is an understatement.

To say I'm disappointed when we get to the driveway is an even bigger understatement.

"Oh," I say. "I thought you said we were taking your Porsche?"

Martin's about to climb behind the wheel of the minivan he bought just after becoming his nieces' guardian. "No, it's getting serviced for the winter," he says.

"Besides," Mae says, "the back seat is a little cramped."

Martin begins coughing at that, I cock one eyebrow, and Mae turns fifty shades of red. "Er, that is," she says nervously, "ah, you're tall, and Helen is—well, what I mean to say is—"

"Shall I sit in the back?" I ask as I climb in, putting her out of her misery.

Soon, we have Helen and we're driving out of town. We're talking about our upcoming wedding, what Martin's nieces want for Christmas, and the Trent family's plans for the holiday.

"So your dad always cuts your Christmas tree in the woods near your house?" Helen asks. "How fun. I used to go with my dad to pick out just the perfect tree for our house. He even let me use the chain saw once." She takes a deep breath. "That was the last Christmas before I went away to college."

"I've never gone," Mae says. "That's for the men of the family. Dad, Vince, Domi, and this year, Marty, right honey?"

"Mae, about that," Martin says. "You know, I grew up in a suburb of Atlanta."

"I know," she says. "I've seen the house."

"We always got our tree from a tree lot the Kiwanis Club ran."

"OK."

"So, well—do you know how many injuries there are every year from inexperienced people trying to cut down their own Christmas trees? I mean, have you ever seen a chainsaw injury? They're not pretty, Mae. I remember one year when I was in Baltimore, some poor guy came in with his hand dangling by a flap of skin because he tried to cut down his own tree."

"In Baltimore?" I ask.

"Yes, exactly."

I think for a minute. "Where can you cut your own Christmas tree in Baltimore?"

"I didn't say he cut it in the city, he just came to the Emergency Room in the city. But that's besides the point."

"Marty," Mae says, patting him on the shoulder. "Dad and the boys know what they're doing. They don't expect you to cut the tree down, I promise."

Considering the mess he made of the turkeys for the Community Thanksgiving Dinner, that's a blessing. I'd hate to see what he'd do to a defenseless evergreen with a chainsaw.

"I didn't notice a tree in the Rectory, Tom," Martin says.

"No, we decided not to put up one this year," I say. "Helen and I will be on our honeymoon, of course, so we won't be able to enjoy it anyway."

"Besides, we'll go all out next year for our first Christmas together as husband and wife," Helen says.

"By the way," Mae says to Helen, "I heard you arrested AJ MacMillan for those break-ins?"

"Yes," Helen says. "He was trying to get the money to leave town and get away from his grandmother."

"I heard some of the nurses talking about her," Martin says. "Can't say I blame him."

Just then, Helen's phone rings, "Excuse me," she says, "This is Dan. He had to go over to Hagerstown today." She answers the phone with a cheerful, "Hi, Dan."

I hear Dan speaking pretty forcefully but I can't understand what he's saying. Instead, I just hear Helen say quickly, "Will do. We'll meet you there."

She hangs up and says to Martin, "Sorry about this, but it looks like we're going to have to take a raincheck. Miriam's in labor and needs a ride to the hospital. Tom, I need you to either drive her or watch the kids."

"Oh, I'll watch the kids," I say firmly as Martin begins to look for an exit.

"Marty and I can watch the children," Mae says and Martin nods, though I can see he's not thrilled about the change of plans.

Twenty

We pull up in front of the Conways and everyone heads for the door as Helen says, "I'll just take her in their van." We knock, and Catherine opens the door.

"Hi, sweetie, where's your Mommy?" Helen asks with a big smile. "We've come to take her to the hospital so she can have your baby sister."

Wide-eyed, Catherine points down the hallway. "Mommy went to get her suitcase," she says, "but she hasn't come back."

Helen goes down the hall as Mae begins calmly gathering the children together. Before she can find Andrew, I hear Helen yell, "We need some help in here!"

Something in the sound of her voice tells me this is not a spiritual crisis, so I stay put as Martin goes, taps on Miriam's door and disappears inside. A moment later, Helen comes out and says to Mae, "he wants you."

"Me?" Mae says with surprise.

"Yes," Helen says. "He needs you to assist him."

Mae's confusion quickly changes to understanding, and she trots from the living room to Dan and Miriam's bedroom.

Helen looks down at the children and says with a big smile, "It looks like your mommy is not going to have to go all the way to the hospital to have your little sister after all. Now, Father Tom is going to take the boys outside. Catherine, you show me where your mommy keeps the clean towels."

Thankful to have instructions, I spend the next several minutes trying to round up coats, hats, and gloves for everyone, taking care to keep them as far from their parent's bedroom as possible. I have just gotten everyone dressed when Helen and Catherine come back. "They have everything they need," Helen says with exaggerated calm, "So Catherine and I are going to go outside with you."

We get out the back door and the boys make a break for the large tree fort/jungle gym Dan adds to every Christmas and kid's birthday. Catherine, on the other hand, stands close to Helen and me. "Don't you want to go play, sweetie?" Helen asks.

"Yes," Catherine says, "but I want to play Bethlehem."

I smile at this and ask, "How do you play Bethlehem?"

She looks at me as if she's wondering what exactly they're teaching priests in seminary these days. "I'm Mary," she explains with all seriousness. "JP and Max take turns being Joseph. We walk all around the yard and ask people for a place to stay but everyone says no. So we go and stay in that pile of straw over there. Then I have Baby Jesus and I wrap him in a blue blanket and put him in the straw, and somebody is an angel and somebody else is a shepherd and everyone brings him presents, but I keep them for him because he just got born and I'm his mom."

"I see," I say, nodding with approval. "That sounds like a fun game. Why don't you go get your brothers and see if they want to play?"

"I can't. I don't have my baby Jesus doll. Can I go get him?" she asks, heading for the house.

Helen stops her, saying firmly, "Not right now, Catherine. Everyone inside is busy. You can go later."

This seems to placate her and she runs off as I hear an ambulance arrive. Helen goes inside to let them in. When she comes out, she says softly, "The baby's out but Martin is not thrilled with how she looks. The paramedics are giving her oxygen and getting her ready to transport, but Miriam wants you to go along, just in case."

We both share a look and I give her a quick hug as I head through the house toward the waiting ambulance. I know only too well what she means. Miriam wants to be sure that in case something goes terribly wrong, someone will be there to baptize her daughter.

Fortunately, that proves not to be necessary. I pray and Martin barks orders, taking the baby in his arms and removing the oxygen mask. He studies her for a few minutes and then says to the mother, again showing his Georgia roots, "Miriam, she's as pink as an Atlanta belle and twice as feisty. Just listen to her howl."

Minutes later, we get to the hospital and the crew rushes off with Miriam. One of the nurses reaches for the baby, but Miriam balks. Martin, using a tone that allows for no reproach, orders, "Everyone stop." He then says to Miriam, "Your little girl seems fine, Miriam, but we need to have someone check you out and her out, so if you'll let me take her for a few minutes, Tom or I will be with her the whole time until we bring her back to you. Is that OK?"

She stares at him for a brief moment, but then nods her head. The orderlies take off with Miriam. Martin then heads inside with his wailing bundle.

"Is Miriam all right?" I ask as we walk inside

"Yes, almost certainly, though we shouldn't stop praying yet," Martin says. "She seems to me to have lost more blood than she should have, but I am no expert."

He looks down now at the bundle in his arms and says, "Would you believe I've never held a baby before? When I've had to do an emergency C-section, or deliver one in the ER, I've always passed them off to nurses as soon as they're out. She's rather interesting, isn't she?" He's staring into her eyes and commenting, "It's funny how they'll look toward voices. Of course, she can't see anything."

He's smiling as he says this and again surprises me by bypassing the Emergency Room and getting on an elevator. "Press 4 if you don't mind, Tom."

I press the button, and moments later the door opens onto a hall labelled prominently, "Neonatal Unit," Walking up to a nurse, Martin says professionally, "38 week female, emergency birth at home, received about 15 minutes of oxygen, is now breathing on her own. Please check her out and get her cleaned up. Her parents are going to want to see her before long." He pauses and then, "Oh, and a whole houseful of siblings." He then hands her over, almost reluctantly, to the nurse, and turns back to me, saying, "You go get washed up, I'll stay here."

By the time I get back, Martin has washed up as well. "I'm going to check on Miriam," he says. "You stay here and keep an eye on that precious bundle."

He's back in about 15 minutes. "She's stable, alert, and demanding to see the baby," he announces with a smile. "Let's take this little girl to her."

I watch him, dumbfounded, as he walks back to where "Baby Girl Conway" is being carefully examined by a young doctor in a white coat. "Any problems, Jessie?" he asks.

"None that I can find, Martin," she replies. "You say she took a minute to pink up immediately after birth?"

"Yes, that's right. I put her on oxygen in the ambulance."

The doctor looks at Martin and says, with a grin, "Well, I don't see anything that concerns me. I wonder if she may have been the victim of an over-anxious trauma surgeon who was in a bit over his head?"

Martin laughs at this. "You're probably right," he nods. "I guess babies are resilient and can survive even the most incompetent doctors."

"Well, you did a good job, Martin. Baby and mom were lucky you were nearby. Is she a friend of yours?"

"Yes," he says. "I owe her husband a favor."

"Well, I think you're probably even now," she laughs.

The doctor scoops up the baby and takes her back to the nurse. After speaking to her for a few minutes, the doctor starts to leave, then says to Martin, "By the way, I haven't had the chance to congratulate you on your engagement. She's a lucky lady."

"Frankly, I think I'm the lucky one," he replies. "Mae—she's special."

"Hmm, I guess she'd have to be to hook you," she says with an almost wistful smile, then walks out of the room.

I tap Martin on the shoulder. "Ah, do you know her?"

He takes a deep breath. "Yes," he admits. "We—we went out a couple of times."

"Oh, I see."

He looks sharply at me. "I never claimed I was a saint, you know," he whispers. "That was long before I got back into church. Long before I met Mae."

"I believe you, Martin," I say.

"Well, anyway," he says, "let's get this little girl to Miriam before she tears my E.R. apart."

We approach the nurse and Martin says, "I'll take Baby Girl Conway to see her mother."

The nurse looks Martin up and down critically and says, "I need to see your I.D."

Martin seems taken aback by this. He turns, walks to a nearby wall, smiles broadly and strikes a pose next to a large poster introducing, "Dr. Martin Maycord, Myerton General's New Chief of Trauma Surgery."

The nurse, who seems not the slightest bit amused, says, "I know who you are, Dr. Maycord. But no newborn leaves my nursery without either a hospital I.D. or patient bracelet getting scanned."

She walks over to what I assume is the scanner and stands by it with her arms crossed. Martin sheepishly joins her and scans his I.D.

"There, that wasn't so difficult, now was it?" she says with a smile before retrieving the littlest Conway, scanning her tiny hospital bracelet, and handing the baby over to the doctor.

"I'm sure when your fiancée has a baby," she says, "you'll appreciate our security measures."

Martin nods. "Of course, nurse. I understand."

We walk out of the nursery, the door closing behind us. "Well, she's charming," he mutters.

"She does have a point, Martin, in this day and age," I say, trying to placate him.

"I suppose," he nods. On our way back to Miriam's room, Martin says softly to his little bundle, "You are something else, you know that? Your mommy and daddy, not to mention your siblings, are so looking forward to meeting you. You're going to fit in just fine. And wait until you meet your godmother! She's pretty special too."

"Ahem!" I clear my throat loudly.

"Your godfather, who's a priest, is not bad himself," he says with a twinkle in his eye.

For my part, I am all smiles as I congratulate myself on guiding a young couple through the bumps of marital preparation, with help from this little lady.

When we get to the room, Martin pushes past the nurses adjusting Miriam's IV and hands the baby to mommy, then steps back.

"Watch this," he says to me, pointing at the monitors. Before our very eyes, Miriam's still low blood pressure rises, her racing pulse falls, and her respiration and heartbeat steady.

"I've never seen it fail," he says, softly. "I instruct every nurse caring for a patient I've had to do a c-section on to get the baby into the mom's arms as soon as possible."

"Did you learn this in medical school?"

He laughs. "No. A young and arrogant resident trauma surgeon learned this from an old nurse-midwife with a patient whose stats kept crashing."

We don't bask in this calm moment long before Dan bursts through the door.

"Miriam," he says, gasping for air. "Martin—Father—is—?"

Martin grabs him by the shoulders and says forcefully, "Dan, they're both fine. Now calm down and go meet your daughter." Dan kind of staggers over to Miriam, who's sitting up and smiling at her panicked bear of a husband.

Martin looks at me and says, "That's our cue to leave, Father. Let them have some peace to get to know each other."

We leave mom and dad with their latest addition. "Martin," I say, as we walk down the hall, "I have to say this is a side of you that I've not seen before."

He shrugs his shoulders as he says, "Blame Mae. One of the things she's taught me is that, while detachment is good in the operating room, in the end, my patients are people who just want to be cared for and cared about. And after what happened with her, I now know first hand what it's like to be on the wrong side of the charts."

I clap him on the shoulder as I say, "That's something I understand." Then, with an air of mischief, I add, "Does this mean you're going to be nicer to me if I ever get stabbed again?"

Without missing a beat, he replies with a grin, "If it's for doing something stupid like you did last time, no. If that happens, I'll give you a bullet to bite on and sew you up with a rusty needle and sewing thread."

"Fair enough," I admit, laughing.

Twenty-One

Helen and I return to the hospital the following morning to check on our new goddaughter. When we arrive, it appears that Miriam's just finished nursing the little girl.

"Is this a bad time?" Helen whispers as we come into the room.

"Of course not. Come meet your goddaughter," she says with a tired smile.

Helen peers down at the little pink bundle with an expression I've not seen before. She's obviously thrilled to be a godmother, but there's just a touch of sadness in her eyes from never having her own newborn to cradle.

"You want to hold her?" Miriam asks.

Helen shakes her head. "Oh, no, I haven't—"

"Look, Helen," Dan says, "if I can hold something that small without breaking it, you can, too. Now come on and hold your goddaughter."

Helen swallows nervously and nods. She reaches out as Miriam hands her the precious bundle. Cradling the infant and supporting the head like she's done it a hundred times before, Helen grins and starts whispering to—

Who? Dan and Miriam haven't mentioned her name yet.

I ask them, "So, when do you want to baptize this precious gift?"

"We've been talking about that, Father," Miriam says. "We'd very much like you to baptize her before you leave town."

"That's fine," I say. "Will you be out of the hospital by then?"

"Yes, if all goes well, they'll let me go home Thursday afternoon."

I think for a minute and then suggest, "If you think you'll feel up to it, we could baptize her at the Christmas Eve Vigil Mass at 4 p.m. I love the idea of having a baptism at Christmas time."

"Since I'm planning on being at your wedding on Sunday, that should be fine."

"Great," I say, pulling out my notebook. "The parish has all the records from your past baptisms so all I really need is her name." I pause with the pen in my hand as they look at each other briefly.

Then Miriam says with a smile, "Helen Joan Conway."

I freeze at this. Helen has a look of rare shock plastered over her previously serene face. She then looks at me and we both break out in smiles, even as tears well up in our eyes.

"Oh, Miriam, Dan," I say, choking up, "I don't know what to say."

"I don't either," Helen adds, wiping away a tear.

"Well then," Dan says jovially, "that makes it all worthwhile, to have both of you stop talking at the same time."

We all laugh at this, causing little Helen Joan to let out a wail and Helen to hand her back over to her mother.

"Dan and I decided this months ago when we found out we were having a girl," Miriam says as she manages to calm the infant. "You both mean so much to us and our family. We wanted to honor both of you in this way."

Before Helen or I can reply, Miriam's mother arrives with the other kids and pandemonium breaks out. We are about to beat a hasty retreat when Helen stops and bends down to Catherine, saying softly, "Catherine, do you have a baby doll at home that could be the Baby Jesus this year?

"Of course, Miss Helen," Catherine says confidently. "My Baby Jesus."

"Can you bring her to the Baptism?"

"Yes, but Miss Helen," Catherine says seriously, "Jesus was a boy so I will bring HIM to the baptism."

Helen chuckles. "Of course. Thank you, Catherine. You can just bring him up when your family comes up for the baptism. Is that OK, Father Tom?"

"I think that's a splendid idea." I say with a smile.

We leave a few minutes later and, slipping my hand in hers, I ask Helen, "Does this mean you've given up on your search for the Gypsinian Christ Child?"

"Not exactly," she says, thoughtfully. "It's just that yesterday afternoon, when Miriam was in labor and we couldn't get her here in time, I thought nothing at all about that statue. In fact, I forgot all about it until we got ready to leave today. And I want to be the kind of person, Tom, who does forget about statues and shoes dyed to match and candle heights when people are in danger, either physically or spiritually. In just a few days, I am taking on a new vocation as your wife, and I just realized that I need to start working harder to become the person I want to be rather than just falling back again and again into the person I am."

We're at the car by now, and after she climbs in, I pause before closing the door and bend over to kiss her. "First," I say, "I'm proud of you. But I also want you to know that the person you are is pretty wonderful as she is."

This makes her smile and as we drive home, I am relieved that Helen has finally seen sense—this time, with several days to spare.

***

The next day's a Wednesday, and Helen's promised to accompany me on my last scheduled visits to the hospital as well as the assisted living center. But when I arrive at the police station, I see she's heading to her car.

"Hey," I say. "What's up?"

"I was just about to text you," she says cheerily, "but now you can ride with me."

"To the hospital for visits, right?" I say slowly.

She places her hand on my chest. "Yes, of course. I promised I'd go with you—"

"But—?"

Helen takes a deep breath. "I got a call from a pawn shop."

"Oh, Helen," I say, shaking my head. "I thought you were over your obsession with the Gypsinain Christ Child?"

"I am over my obsession. But the fact remains that the statue was stolen. It's still an open case. And since I was going out anyway, I told Dan I'd check it out. If it turns out to be something, I promise I'll call in a uniformed officer to take him into custody."

I look down at her and sigh. "OK, Chief. Where to?"

She smiles and starts walking again to her car. "Braley's, here in town. The owner says there's someone there with a valuable-looking statue of the Baby Jesus. He's going to try to get them to hang around until we get there. I know it's a long shot, but stranger things have happened."

Braley's is in Myerton proper, so we arrive there in just a few minutes. She parks, gets out of the car, and rushes in as I try to keep up with her. I throw the door open in time to hear someone say, "You better not try to swindle me on this!"

I recognize the voice. Helen's stopped just inside the door, her eyes huge. We glance at each other, then attempt to beat a discreet retreat back to the car.

"Father Tom! This is your little chippie's fault!" Gloria MacMillian says. We both turn around, trying to look as pleasant as possible. Pasting on my best pastoral smile, I say, "Why Mrs. MacMillian, what brings you here today?"

She glares at Helen as she replies, "Trying to raise money for poor AJ's defense, that's what. Lawyers cost money, and that public defender is an idiot. So I've decided to sell off some of my precious family heirlooms to hire someone who can save my grandson from the slammer."

"Mrs. MacMillian," Helen says calmly, "I told AJ and I am telling you—."

"Don't talk to me, Heler Parr. I don't have time to listen." Then, turning to the owner she demands, "Well, how much will you give me for this?"

The owner shows the Christ Child to Helen, who just looks at it and shakes her head. "No, that's not it."

"Don't look at her," Gloria screeches, "She doesn't know anything about this. I bought this more than 50 years ago down in Mexico. It is an original, and I want a good price for it."

"Thanks for the call," Helen says to the owner. "If anything else like it comes in—."

"Would you leave him alone!" Gloria yells. "He'll never give me any money at this rate!"

The owner just nods and turns his attention back to Gloria. Helen and I leave the shop before she learns how much her Christ Child is worth.

"Sorry, Honey," I say as we slip back in the car.

"Oh, that's OK," she sighs, "I pretty much knew we were sunk as soon as I saw who was there. I mean, it's not like Gloria MacMillan would be able to tail my car and then get in and out without being seen."

"No, I guess not."

She lays her head back and closes her eyes. "I really thought I could find it, Tom," she whispers. "I really thought I did. But it's long gone by now."

"Don't give up hope, Helen," I say.

"Tom, at this point, it will take a miracle for the Gypsinian Christ Child to be placed in the creche at the end of Saint Clare's Christmas Eve Vigil Mass."

I shrug. "Well, this is a season for miracles, you know?"

She turns to look at me. "You're being optimistic this afternoon, especially considering what's happening tomorrow."

I slump in my seat. "I know. And if I can get through picking up my Mom and Trevor from the airport tomorrow without losing my mind, it really *will* be a miracle."

Twenty-Two

The only way Helen got me in the car to start the two-hour drive to Dulles International Airport was the promise of a donut from The Muffin Man.

"I'll be right back," Helen says as she pulls up outside Nick Hallstead's bakery.

"No, that's OK," I say. "I'd like to say hi to Nick."

I walk into the shop, which isn't busy at all considering it's two days before Christmas. In fact, Nick isn't even out front.

"I'll be right there!" he calls from the back.

"It's just me, Nick."

A moment later, the smiling baker comes out wiping his hands off. "Well, this is a coincidence," he says. "I was doing some work on your groom's cake."

"I hope my request hasn't caused too much trouble for you," I say apologetically.

"Nah!" he says, waving his hand. "I like doing something unique. People will definitely talk about it. I'm pretty happy with your wedding cake as well."

"Can't wait to see it," I say. "But for today, I'll have a chocolate donut and a blueberry muffin, with two coffees."

"Your and Chief Parr's regular?"

I nod and he bends down to retrieve the donut and muffin from the display case. "By the way," he says as he bags them and walks over to the coffee pots, "thanks for talking to Nina."

"I hope it helped a little," I say.

"It helped a lot," Nick says. "Her miscarriages, our having such a hard time having a baby, I knew that upset her. It upset me too—I mean, I'd like to be a father someday. But I never knew how guilty she felt about them. Nina's a strong woman. Tough, you know? Sometimes I tell her she's less emotional about things than I am. Each miscarriage, I knew she was upset even if she didn't cry. But when she told me about her meeting with you, she broke down and cried. Father, believe it or not, that's the first time I'd seen my wife cry in—well, I can't remember the last time. She told me about how empty she feels inside, about how she blames herself for her infertility problems."

"She told me the same thing," I say. "I told her there was no way of knowing."

"Yeah, she told me that, too," he nods. "She showed me the brochure from the clinic. We talked about it, and she's going to make an appointment sometime after New Year's. I mean, what do we have to lose?"

Nick pauses, then says, "You know I don't believe in God, Father. I'm not anti-God, I've just never had much use for him myself, if he exists or not. But I'm glad there are men like you who do."

"Thank you, Nick," I say. "And if you ever want to talk to me, just stop by the Rectory. Or, I can stop by here."

He looks serious and nods. "I may just do that sometime."

I pay for the coffee and pastries and leave. When I get back in the car, Helen says, "That took you long enough."

"Just another satisfied customer, Helen," I say, buckling my seat belt.

"Nina talked to you," she says.

"Yes."

Helen nods. "Good."

***

I'd like to say that Helen and I spent the time driving to the airport singing hymns and praying the Rosary.

I could say that, but I'd be lying.

Instead, I spend my time dreading meeting my mother and the mysterious Trevor.

I guess I grouse about this a little too much, because Helen finally says, "Look, Tom. I have some bad news. I hadn't laid eyes on your mother in over twenty years when I met her again in January. She hadn't changed one iota. If Nola Greer was going to be any different, she would have changed by now. So, my darling, I need to tell you that you are not going to change your mother. You are not going to fix her. There is absolutely nothing at all that you can say or do that will make any difference."

"I know that—"

"No, you don't," Helen says, shaking her head. "Oh, you might know it in your mind, but you don't believe it in your heart. That's because you have given your life to trying to make people better. You've gone as far as any human being can in that department, actually taking vows before God to represent him on earth in trying to help people become kinder, gentler, and more loving. The good news is that there are people like me out there who truly want to be better, and you provide a wonderful service to us. But the bad news is that there are also people out there who do not want to be better. Richard Davenport was one of those people. And, my darling, so is your mother. Now don't get me wrong, I'm not saying Nola Greer and Richard Davenport are cut from the same cloth. But just like Richard was satisfied with the way he was, your mother's content with who she is. That is never going to change."

I stare out the window at the passing scenery, the trees denuded of their leaves and the bare branches looking black and gray against the sky. With each passing mile, I try to process what Helen said.

I know she's right. I really do. But it's so hard to accept.

Finally, I ask, "So what do I do?"

She takes my hand in hers and says softly, "Stop trying to rationalize the irrational. When you and your Mom have a good moment or two, enjoy it, thank God for it, but never think it's going to last. And never, ever think that you can make one come again, or even get her to stop doing things that hurt you because for her, you're an easy target. She knows that you'll always come back, so she is perfectly comfortable lashing out at you whenever the mood strikes her."

This does not exactly make me feel better, but it also doesn't make me feel any worse.

For now, that's the best I can hope for.

***

We get to the airport. Helen pulls into the Arrivals area and stops, moving her "Police Business" placard to a prominent place on the dash. "I'll stay here with the car," she says. "You go help your Mom."

"And Trevor," I say with a phony smile on my face. "Don't forget Trevor."

I begin to open my door when Helen puts a hand on my shoulder. "Tom?" I look at her, and she says, "It's going to be OK."

I nod and get out of the car. Walking away, I mutter, "No, it's probably not."

I go inside and check the arrival and departures board. The flight from Tallahassee, Florida should be landing right about now, so I take a deep breath and prepare to put a smile on my face. The airport is bustling with activity two days before Christmas, as people rush through to get wherever they're going.

Fifteen minutes after her flight landed, I'm getting concerned that Mom's lost somewhere in the vast expanse of the terminal. Dulles is much larger than the airport in Tallahassee, and she doesn't have the world's best sense of direction.

Not to mention, I hold out little hope that this Trevor guy has much sense at all.

I mean, for someone half my age to get involved with my mother—

"Tommy!" I hear a high-pitched nasally voice call across the loud, bustling room.

I turn, the smile firmly plastered on my face—and immediately notice a problem.

There she is, Nola Greer, my mother.

But she's wearing someone else's clothes.

Now, I probably should explain something about my mother. Until today, I have never seen her in anything that was not at least partially polyester, usually in the form of a pantsuit. She was never what one would call stylish or trendy in her choice of clothes—or anything for that matter. Beyond the regular forays to the beauty salon to have her hair done by an old high school friend—for some reason, she couldn't stand Wendy Lyles but still let the woman be around her with sharp objects—Mom didn't really care too much about her personal appearance. I never remember her wearing a lot of makeup, nor anything I would consider immodest.

Today, however, is a much different story.

As soon as she spots me, my nearly 70-year-old mother rushes towards me in a denim skirt that barely brushes her knees, and a low-cut red sweater that is at least one size too tight. She's wearing more makeup than I've ever seen her wear before. In spite of the fact that she is teetering on spiked red heels, Mom manages to get to me and wrap me in a big hug before I can process what I'm seeing.

Fortunately, kids in the South are trained from the cradle to always show good manners to their elders, so I say reflexively, "Mom, it's so good to see you. How was your flight?"

"Fine, Tommy, just fine," she says, her voice already grating on my nerves. "It was like being on vacation, the way Trevor fussed over me and ordered drinks. I can hardly wait for you to meet him."

"Well, I can't wait to meet this mysterious man in your life," I say, still trying to smile.

"Oh, don't be jealous," Mom says. "You'll always be my little Tommy, no matter that you so cruelly abandoned me and Sonya so many years ago. Trevor will never replace you."

I take a deep breath. "Thanks, Mom," I manage to say.

"Besides, you're my son, and Trevor is—well, you'll see."

She begins giggling, and I'm beginning to feel my blood pressure rise.

"You stay here, Mom. I'll go get your bags," I say, and walk toward the luggage ramp. It has already begun to send luggage from Mom's flight on its way to its rightful owners. Mom has had the same luggage for the last forty years, so I won't have any trouble picking it out.

I guess I've been hanging around Helen too much, because I begin eyeing this suspicious-looking guy waiting for his bags. He's in his late 20s, I think, with wavy black hair and a three- or four-day growth of beard. He's wearing jeans that look a couple of sizes too tight for him, a white t-shirt, and a leather jacket. He already has two rather large suitcases next to him, and is apparently waiting on more.

I know you're not supposed to judge people by their appearance, but this guy has "drug mule" written all over him. He's nervous, like maybe he's afraid of being recognized or detained. I'm trying to decide if I should snap a discreet photo of him that Helen can have Gladys run though facial recognition, when I see Mom's gray and pink plaid suitcase come sliding down the ramp.

I start walking toward it when the guy I've been watching reaches out to grab it. I am trying to decide if I should call security or try to stop him myself when he swings around and almost tosses the bag to me.

"You must be Tommy," he says in a much too familiar tone. "Take this one and I'll grab my luggage and meet you two at the car."

"Oh, Trevor, honey," I hear Mom say. She's walked up to join us. "Thank you so much. Tommy, let's do as he says."

She turns toward the exit, leaving me the choice of following her or hanging around to see if Trevor makes it out without being arrested. I decide on the former, mainly because if something bad does go down, I want to be with Helen.

I'm hoping she's at least carrying her backup.

As we come out of the double doors, Helen gets out of the car and waves at us. Mom says, "There she is." She adds under her breath, "Well, I guess being shot didn't damage her appetite any."

I want to say something to Mom, but Trevor catches up with us about that time. I'm astonished by the number of bags he's carrying.

"You packed quite a bit for a five-day trip, Trevor," I say pleasantly.

"Well, you know what they say," Trevor replies with a sly smile. "Be prepared."

"Were you a Boy Scout?" I ask before I can think.

He winks and says, "That, Tommy, is something I've never been accused of being."

Helen's standing on the sidewalk, grinning as we approach. "Nola," she says as she hugs Mom, "so good to see you."

"You, too, Helen," Mom says. "I'm so glad to see you up and around."

"Why, yes, I'm fully recovered from being shot."

"That's good to hear," Mom sighs. "You just never know, being in such a dangerous profession. I'm just thankful you weren't killed. I'm not sure Tommy would have survived another woman he loved dying so violently."

Helen's jaw tightens and her eyes narrow. "Well, you never had to find out," she mutters, her smile looking more like an upside-down frown."

"Tommy," Trevor oozes, "aren't you going to introduce me to your beguiling fiancée?"

"Of course," I say, my facial muscles straining to keep my smile in place. "Helen, this is Mom's friend, Trevor—I'm sorry, I don't know your last name?"

"Deveraux," he says, taking Helen's hand in both of his. "Trevor LaSalle Fontaine Deveraux. So nice to meet you."

Helen's eyes narrow. "Likewise, I'm sure."

Having stood there as long as I can stand it, I pick up Mom's suitcase and say, "Well, let's get this show on the road. We've got dinner reservations at 6 p.m., and I'm sure you'll want to freshen up a bit, right, Mom? Helen, pop your trunk please?"

Helen opens the trunk with her keyfob, and soon Trevor and I are loading the luggage.

"How was your flight, Nola?" I hear Helen ask.

"Oh, just lovely," Mom says. "I had a window seat. It was so comfortable and roomy."

My ears perk up. *Please, dear God, don't let Helen say anything.*

"I've been on flights quite a few times," Helen says in spite of my prayer, "and I've always found the seats to be a little snug."

Please, dear God, don't let Mom say anything.

"You know," Mom says, "I saw a report on the news saying that because of the obesity epidemic in our country, airlines are letting large people buy two seats for their comfort for just a little bit more than one seat. Maybe you should do that the next time you fly."

"OK," I yell. "All loaded. Let's get going! Mom, you can ride in the back with Trevor. I'll sit up front."

I'm about to get in, keeping an eye on Helen to make sure she doesn't accidentally push Mom into oncoming traffic, when Trevor says, "Why don't you ride in the back with your Mom so you can catch up and Helen and I will get to know each other better. That'll be fun, won't it Helen?"

"Sure," she says through only slightly gritted teeth. With Trevor sliding into the front seat, I have no choice, so I join Mom in the back. As soon as I close the door, Helen takes off, obviously as anxious as I am to get this drive from hell over with.

As we veer onto the highway Trevor turns to Helen and says, "You're a fast one, aren't you? No wonder Tommy is smitten."

"Oh," she says casually as the needle nears 80, "I get a lot of practice chasing down fleeing felons."

"From what I hear, you weren't always so successful. I mean, Tommy got away the first time, didn't he?"

I open my mouth to say something, but before I can Helen says pointedly, "I don't know anyone named Tommy. Who are you talking about?"

"Your fiancé back there," he says, looking my way.

"You mean Tom?" Helen says cooly. "Well, that's what threw me off. You see, no one calls him Tommy, except his mother, of course. His friends call him Tom, but you are certainly welcome to call him Father until you get to know him better."

"Sorry, no can do," Trevor says, shaking his head emphatically. "You see, I don't believe in all this religious stuff. I don't call anyone by titles because I believe in complete equality, especially between the sexes," he adds, patting Helen's knee.

"Really? So when in court, you call the judge what? Bob?"

"Well, no, since last time it was—"

He stops cold here and cuts his eyes toward Helen. She gives him a knowing look and says, "If you like, why don't you call me what some of my closest friends do? Chief."

He pauses a minute before saying slyly under his breath, "Oh, so that's the way you like it, then?"

I'm about to say something that I'll definitely need to go to confession for when Mom affectionately slaps Trevor on the back of the shoulder. "Oh, Trevor," she says playfully, "you are such a naughty boy." Turning to me, she says, "You and Helen will just have to get used to his sense of humor. He is such a cut-up; you never know what he'll say next."

"I'm learning that," I say through gritted teeth.

***

We stop by the Rectory to freshen up and change clothes. Helen had dropped off a dress before we left for the airport, so she goes into Anna's office to change while I run upstairs. Mom and Trevor each grab something out of their bags and take turns—at least, I hope they take turns—in the guest room.

Fifteen minutes later, I come downstairs in a freshly-pressed set of clericals to find Helen standing at the staircase, looking absolutely lovely in a ruby-red dress with a black belt.

She also has a concerned look on her face.

"Tom," she says, "stop and take a breath."

"What?" I ask.

"Just do as I say, please."

"OK," I say slowly, but do as she says. "Now, can you tell me what this is all about?"

She takes a deep breath. "Darling, you're going to see something shocking. But you need to remember, she's your mother. Please, don't lose your mind."

I'm now wondering what the hell's going on in my Rectory.

"Well, we're ready, Tommy," Mom says as she and Trevor emerge from the living room.

It's a good thing Helen warned me, because what I see leaves me speechless.

Mom's wearing the gaudiest dress I've ever seen, all shiny greens and reds with white fur. The skirt—what there is of it—ends just above her knees and shows off far too much of her legs.

Her legs. Those are the worst part. My almost 70-year-old mother is wearing red fishnet stockings with the same red spiked heels she hobbled through the airport on.

"Isn't your Mom a picture," Trevor says with a grin. He's actually dressed nicely in a dark blue suit and a white dress shirt open at the collar. I admit, he does wear clothes well. What I don't like is his arm around my mom's waist.

Still unable to speak, I simply nod. Helen slips her arm through mine and says brightly, "Well, shall we?"

Mom and Trevor go out first. As Helen and I follow them, she whispers, "I'm very proud of you."

"Don't be," I whisper back. "The night is still young."

***

Needless to say, I am thankful when we get to the restaurant.

Looking back, I don't know why.

First, the hostess seats us at a table not terribly far from one occupied by Martin and Mae. The last person anyone wants to run into when they're out on a date is their priest and his crazy family, so I just give them a quick wave and take my seat. Mom's on one side, Helen on the other. Trevor is right across from me. Thankfully, he has his back to Martin and Mae.

Our waiter comes up and says, "Good evening, Father Greer. Can I start everyone off with a drink?"

Since Helen's driving, she sticks to iced tea. Thankfully, I'm not driving, so I order a Cuba Libre.

"And for you, ma'am?" he asks my mother.

"I'll have a Drunken Sailor," Mom says, a little too loudly. I look at her, then Helen, who just shrugs, but I say nothing.

"I'll just have a beer, thanks," Trevor says. Looking at me, he adds, "I really don't care for mixed drinks. It's either beer or straight bourbon for me."

I nod. "Good for you," I say with a weak smile.

We sit just looking at each other for a few minutes. I ask about the weather in Bellamy, which prompts Mom to complain about the Courthouse Square Diner raising their prices. What the connection is, she never adequately explains, so I just smile and nod.

Thankfully, our waiter brings our drinks and takes our orders. When he leaves, I say as pleasantly as I can, "Trevor, " I say, again trying really, really hard to stay pleasant, "I understand from Mom that you're an Uber driver?"

"Yes, that's how I met Nola," he grins, looking at her and taking her hand. "It was fate that brought us together. I wasn't even supposed to be driving that day. I had a party cancel at the last minute. Some kind of stomach bug went through an entire bridal party."

For some reason, Helen's eyes get big. She glances at me and shakes her head, just as I ask, "Oh? Are you a caterer?"

He laughs and shakes his head. "No, no, nothing like that."

"He's an entertainer, Tommy," Nola says.

Helen says quickly, "Nola, has Tom told you about the education center the parish is starting?"

"No, Tommy never tells me anything. Even when I call, he doesn't tell me anything. I didn't even know he almost died a few months ago. Found that out from Diana looking on the internet."

"So, you're an entertainer," I say to Trevor. Now Helen for some reason is gently kicking me in the shin. I try to ignore her as I continue, "Are you a singer, or do you play an instrument?"

He stretches in the chair. "No, I'm completely tone deaf," he says. "I like to call myself an erotic dancer."

I start so quickly I knock my drink over. The flow narrowly misses Helen as I wheeze, "E—e—erotic dancer! You—you're a stripper?"

"He's very good, too, Tommy," Mom says admiringly. "He does this thing with his—"

"Mom!" I say a little too loudly. Martin and Mae look over at our table, obviously wondering why their priest is yelling in a restaurant.

It's a good thing my doctor is at the next table, because I'm sure my blood pressure's through the roof.

Before I can regain my powers of speech, Mom asks, "Tommy, who is that older man with the young girl who's staring at us?"

"Mom," I say in a low voice, "please keep your voice down. That's Dr. Martin Maycord and his fiancée, Mae Trent."

"Oh, is he the one who treated your injury?" she says even louder.

I start coughing when Trevor chimes in. "Yeah, Tom, Nola told me all about that. Tough break, my man." He turns to Helen and with a leer says, "I bet it's a really tough break for you, too, huh, Helen?"

"Speaking of tough breaks," Helen says very softly so that Mom can't hear, "You're going to suffer one if you ever—and I do mean even one time—touch my knee again."

Suddenly, Trevor has both his hands on his table, while Helen smiles like the cat who ate the canary.

The rest of the meal pretty much follows this pattern. Both Mom and Trevor down one drink after another—Mom switching to martinis and Trevor ordering straight bourbon—as Helen and I look on in horror. The more they drink, the louder they get, the more I pray I just survive the inevitable stroke I'm sure to have as a result of this dinner from hell. All through the appetizer, main course, and dessert, I keep smiling and remain surprisingly calm.

"Will there be anything else?" the waiter asks.

Before Mom or Trevor can order another drink, I say, "No. Everything was lovely. We're ready for the check."

"Sir, your check's already been taken care of by Dr. Maycord."

I look up to see Martin and Mae walking towards us. I stand and say, "Martin, you really shouldn't have."

"Consider it your Christmas present," Martin says.

"Tommy," Mom slurs, "are you going to introduce me to your friends?"

"Oh, where are my manners," I say nervously. "Mom, Trevor, this is Dr. Martin Maycord and his fiancée, Mae Trent. Martin, Mae, this is my mother Nola Greer and her—her friend—Trevor Deveraux."

Martin takes Trevor's hand, then bows to Mom. "Mrs. Greer," he says, pulling out his Georgia accent to full effect, "it is a pleasure to finally meet you. Your son has mentioned you frequently. I'm proud to number him among my closest friends."

"Oh, Dr. Maycord," Mom gushes, "I just want to thank you for patching up my boy after his injury."

He must think she is referring to my stabbing, because Martin insists, "Oh, Mrs. Greer, it was my pleasure."

"Really?" Trevor says, trying to get to his feet. "You don't seem like the type." He leers at Mae. "Well, hello there," he slurs. "Aren't you a pretty little thing—ow! Dammit!"

Trevor collapses back in his chair, a look of sheer agony on his face. Helen glances at me and winks. I can't help but smile.

"Honey, are you OK?" Mom yells.

"Fine, love, just fine," he says, still grimacing. "Old football injury."

Martin says politely, "We'll leave you to your dinner. But Father, could I possibly speak to you for a moment alone?"

"Of course," I say, excusing myself and following him and Mae into the foyer. Mae discreetly slips into the Ladies' Room as Martin shoves a sheet of paper into my hand.

"What's this?" I ask, trying to read his terrible handwriting in the dim light.

"It's a script for a few sedatives," Martin whispers with a smile. "Not many, just enough to get you through the wedding. After what I've seen and heard tonight, I figure you might need them."

"Bless you," I say, resisting the urge to hug him.

"I guess that makes us even," Martin says. "You'll be in my prayers."

"Thanks. I'll need them."

***

Of course, when I said that, I had no idea just how soon and how badly I'd need both the prayers and the sedatives.

We arrive at the Myerton Inn and Trevor gets out and goes to the trunk to get his luggage. Anxious to leave him, I go back to help him unload his several bags. When he reaches for Mom's suitcase, I say casually, "No, that one goes with us."

"'Fraid not, Tommy," Trevor says with a grin. "Nola and I talked about it, and she's staying with me."

"What?" I nearly scream as Mom and then Helen come around the car.

"Now, Tommy," Mom says, "Trevor and I don't share your outdated sense of morality. We just want to be who and what we are, today and always."

I open my mouth to say something but Helen steps between me and Mom. Her arms are crossed, and her stance—well, let's just say I've seen it before.

"Oh, I see," Helen says in a voice overflowing with venom. "So now caring about the feelings of others is outdated morality? Well, I must have missed that one. But let me tell you one thing, Nola Greer. I don't care who you sleep with. In fact, if you get tired of Trevor here, I know of at least a half a dozen guys just like him that I've sent to prison. Let me know and I'll give you their release dates and you can take your pick. But you need to know one thing. The only thing that has kept me from already running a background check on this sorry Son of Beelzebub is my own outdated sense of morality that tells me not to hurt the families of those I love. Now, if we're throwing that out the window tonight, in the next ten minutes I'll know everything he's ever been in trouble for since the day he turned 18, which I know is not that long ago."

She takes a breath here and allows what she's just said to sink in. "But if we are going to care for each other," she says slowly, "I suggest you shut that trunk, get back in this car, and leave Romeo here to his own devices. I'll give you two sixty seconds to discuss it."

With that, she gets back in the car and I join her. She looks at her watch and about 45 seconds later, opens her window a crack and keys her mic. "Chief Parr here. Stand by to run a check on—."

Before she can finish her sentence, the trunk slams and Mom gets in the car. Trevor stands by the car with his hands in his pockets, glaring at me through the window. I roll it down and say with a grin, "Have a good night, Trevor."

As we pull away from the entrance, Mom whines, "I can't believe you let her talk to your mother that way, Tommy. I'm so disappointed in you."

Over my shoulder, I say, "Mom, it wasn't the first time, and it probably won't be the last time."

"Are you going to do anything about what she said?"

"Actually, yes."

I lean over and kiss Helen on the cheek. "Thank you, darling."

With a smile, she says, "It was my pleasure."

As soon as we get to the Rectory, Mom storms right past Anna, who has waited up to welcome her. She marches into the guest bedroom and slams the door. I follow her, but instead of going in, I leave her luggage outside her door.

Returning to the foyer, Anna asks with confusion, "What in the world was that about?"

Helen puts her arm around Anna. "Come on. Tom needs some hot cocoa. We'll tell you the whole story."

Twenty-Three

The next couple of days are a whirlwind of Christmas and wedding preparations. Fortunately, the decorating of the interior of the church is in the capable hands of the Ladies of Charity. I talk to Clark a couple of times, and he assures me that everything is OK and if I need to talk to him, he's available. Helen, for her part, is busy at the office—not continuing to search the countryside for the Gypsinian Christ Child, but briefing Dan and preparing everything he needs to serve as Acting Chief while we're gone on our honeymoon.

Mom's still decidedly cool to me, barely speaking to me at breakfast the day after she arrived. By the evening, however, she's almost back to normal.

Well, normal for Mom.

"I hope you don't mind, Tommy," she says, "but Trevor and I are going out tonight."

"Oh," I say, surprised. "OK. I mean, I'd planned on cooking for the four of us—"

"You're sweet, Tommy. But Trevor wants to take me dancing. He found a place just outside town."

I'm not familiar with a place that has dancing outside town, but I don't know every place a gigolo might take the older woman he's dating.

"Mom, one question," I say. "How are you going to get there?"

"Oh, I rented us a car," she says. "Trevor's going to drive. We want to have our own way to get around, especially since you're going to be leaving on Sunday."

"Well, I guess that makes sense. What time will you be back?"

"Oh, Tommy," she says with a smile. "I'm a grown woman. Don't wait for me."

I do. But Mom doesn't arrive back until 3 a.m., and she looks disheveled. She has a smile on her face, says goodnight, and goes into the guest room.

I hear the door close and begin lightly banging my head on a pillow.

***

The Christmas Eve Vigil Mass for Families is my personal favorite. While the Midnight Mass is a joyful and reverent celebration of the Nativity of our Lord, the Vigil Mass is alive with the sound of excited children anticipating what Santa Claus may leave for them under their Christmas Trees.

I come into the Mass behind Dominic Trent holding the processional crucifix aloft, two torch bearers flanking him. Deacon Derek is behind them, holding the Gospel aloft for the people to adore. I bring up the rear, as I usually do. Our choir master, Meshach Jackson, chose a personal favorite of mine, "O Come, All Ye Faithful," for us to process into the sanctuary. Because I can't carry a tune in a bucket, I usually refrain from singing during the Mass.

Today, I'm overflowing with the joy of the season. I sing this hymn of thanksgiving with all my heart, my voice mingling with everyone else's in a great song of praise to Our Lord, whose coming we're celebrating.

I pass the Conways seated on the front row, little Helen Joan wrapped in a beautiful white blanket. I understand from Dan that she's wearing Miriam's christening gown, the same one that Catherine wore when she was baptized. Catherine, for her part, is sitting between Dan and Miriam, her own baby doll carefully bundled in a blue blanket.

I say the opening greeting, then announce, "We will now have a baptism. Will the Conway family and the godmother come forward."

As they gather themselves, Dominc helps Deacon Derek move the small font into place at the front of the altar. First comes Miriam, radiant and holding my first goddaughter. Helen slips up beside me now as Dan, with his left hand on Miriam's back and his other hand holding Andrew's, completes the circle of adults. The twins come next, pushing and shoving each other as they jockey for position. Catherine is last, all dressed up for the occasion and carrying her doll wrapped in a soft blue blanket.

Then, just as she reaches the altar, she veers off and walks, not to where we are gathered around the font, but to the creche.

Miriam opens her mouth to call her when Helen says quietly, "Oh, I asked her to bring a doll for the creche. She must be going to put it in place." We all smile as Catherine bends over the straw bed carefully and gently lays down her precious bundle.

It is only when she unwraps the doll that we realize what she has.

There, in perfect, radiant condition, lies the Gypsinian Christ Child.

As the congregation oohs and ahs, I hear Helen whisper, "Well, I'll be damned."

The next few moments are a blur. Catherine walks serenely over to join us, and Dan and Helen stare at each other and then at her. I know that we all have questions but quickly realize that this is not the time to ask them. Pulling myself together, I go through the rites and readings leading to the all important question, "What name have you chosen for this child?"

Smiling, Miriam says in a firm voice, "Helen Joan Conway."

She then slips the baby into Helen's waiting arms and, with a huge lump in my throat, I pick up the silver shell, dip it in the water, and pour over her head as I say, "Helen Joan Conway, I baptize you in the name of the Father, and of the Son, and of the Holy Spirit. Amen."

For my efforts, I am rewarded not with the screams so many infants are inclined to, but with what I will always insist is a real smile, no matteer what anyone else may say. Then, against all protocol but with overwhelming joy, I bend over and give my new goddaughter a kiss on the forehead from me and her other namesake. I detect something salty and I realize it's Helen's tears.

Little Helen Joan, who has put up with a lot by now, decides that she has had enough of these adult carryings-on and begins to howl, causing Helen to quickly pass her back to her waiting mother.

***

The rest of the Mass is a beautiful, sacred blur, for as much as I love the Christmas liturgy, I cannot help but have dozens of questions lurkiYbi

Yng in the back of my mind. Miriam and the younger children leave right after the final min)

s. Dan and Catherine remain, hanging back until Helen and I have shaken hands with and wished Merry Christmas to all who were present.

We find them when we head back to the sacristy to hang up my vestments. Dan still looks incredulous and Catherine forlorn as we sit down.

"Catherine Elizabeth," Dan says quietly, "What do you have to say to Father Tom and Miss Helen?"

Bursting into tears, the little girl cries, "I'm sorry! I didn't know it was wrong! I was only trying to be a good helper!"

Helen immediately wraps her arms around the sad little figure, saying comfortingly, "I'm sure you were, Honey. You are a good, sweet little girl."

She holds her like this for a few minutes until Catherine calms down. Then Helen asks, "Can you tell me what happened?"

Sniffling, Catherine begins, "The day that you took us to our house but we couldn't go in, I went to play because you told us to. But then I remembered that I'd left my pram on the sidewalk by the car. I went back to get it, and Baby Jesus was there all by Himself. And Miss Helen, you're not supposed to leave babies in the car alone, not even for a minute."

She says this with such seriousness that it's all I can do not to smile. "So I put him in my pram and I pushed him out to the backyard," she continues. "Then you left without him, so I figured I should babysit him until you came back for him."

"So he's been in your room this whole time?" Dan asks, his incredulity appearing to grow.

"Uh-huh. I think he liked sleeping in my pram. I'd always wrap him up real tight and make sure he laid on his back so he wouldn't suffocate. Then, in the morning I sang him songs and told him stories." Then the budding theologian adds, "But not Bible stories because I'm sure he already knows all those."

Dan opens his mouth to say something that I am afraid might be a scold so I cut him off, saying, "Catherine, I wish everyone in the world would care as much about Baby Jesus as you have. I'm glad He was able to spend the weeks leading up to his birthday with you."

***

After the Vigil Mass, Helen and I enjoy a traditional Christmas dinner with all the trimmings at the Rectory. We're joined by Anna and Bill, who's admiring the Nativity scene he and his Knights worked on as the backdrop for the Ladies of Charity's hand-painted figurines.

"Now, each of these pieces," he says to me, "was worked on by a different Knight. Each has a slightly different style, you might notice."

"Oh, certainly," I say, even though I can't tell the difference between them.

"Now, I handled the creche personally," he says. "I think it's just the right proportion to the figures—not too big, not too small."

"You did a fine job," Helen says.

"Speaking of creches," Anna says. We turn to look at her. She's eyeing us with that penetrating look of hers.

Helen looks her squarely in the face. "Yes, Anna?"

"How did Catherine Conway come to carry the Gypsinian Christ Child to the Nativity Scene?"

"It was her turn to bring the Christ Child to the creche," Helen replies.

"How did she get it? I saw her bring a baby wrapped in a blue blanket with her. That was the Christ Child. So, I ask again, how did she get it?"

Very calmly, Helen says, "I asked her to bring the Christ Child from her house."

"And how did it get there?"

"Really, Anna, how do you think it got there?"

Anna studies Helen for a moment, then smiles. "Well," she says, "the important thing is the Gypsinian Christ Child is safe and sound where it belongs this Christmas."

I breathe an inward sigh of relief.

No, Helen didn't lie to Anna. Everything she said was the absolute truth.

Besides, I'm pretty sure Anna knows there's more to the story. But she'll never mention it to Helen.

***

The Midnight Mass actually begins at 11 p.m. There is a stillness as people arrive early to sing carols and hymns welcoming the Newborn King, and it's followed by singing that seems to become more and more filled with joy as the Mass progresses, that moves me to the very core of my being. Tonight's Mass is even more intensely joyful for me personally, since I will be confirming my surrogate daughter in her Catholic faith.

When the time for this arrives, Helen, Gladys' sponsor and surrogate mother, rolls her forward. For her part, Gladys has pulled out all the stops for this occasion and is dressed in a traditional winter white wool suit with a boxy, buttoned-up jacket. On her head, she wears a white mantilla that I know belonged to her grandmother, whose rosary she holds in her white-gloved hands. Helen remains behind Gladys as I anoint her and confirm her in our faith. She even smiles when I lightly slap Gladys with the traditional reminder that the life of a Christian is never meant to be an easy one. I'm sure that this must seem as redundant to her as it does to me, for Gladys already knows more about life being hard than most people her age do.

Helen wheels Gladys back to their seat on the front row and I continue celebrating the Mass, reminded once again of how much all of us truly have to celebrate.

Twenty-Four

I pick Helen up on Christmas morning. She's carrying two small potted poinsettias as she walks from her apartment to my car. I get out to open the door for her and suddenly feel awkward. I mean, while what we're about to do makes perfect sense to us, I know it would seem strange to many.

"Those look nice," I say, trying to hide my embarrassment.

"Thanks," she says, "I thought we ought to take something, and this is the only thing that I thought would hold up."

"Sure," I agree. "Good thought."

We drive along in silence for a while as I pull onto the Interstate and head toward Baltimore. Finally, Helen says, "Everything ready for tomorrow?"

"As far as I know. Gladys and Vivian seem to have everything well in hand with the reception. We'll iron out any bumps in the Mass tonight during the rehearsal. So, yeah, it's all good on my end. What about you? Have you finished packing?"

"Just about. I've still got a few things that need to go into the big suitcases but the overnight bag is done."

Suddenly, we're both blushing and I find myself needing to change the subject.

"So," I ask, "have you gotten over the shock about the Christ Child?"

"Just about, though the moment Catherine unwrapped that baby is engraved permanently in my mind."

"Mine, too," I agree.

After a couple of hours driving, during which we try to make small talk, we finally pull into a cemetery just outside of Hyattsville. We get out of the car and Helen brings one of the plants as we walk hand-in-hand across the frozen ground. We're both bundled up and the sun is shining brightly, so it is not terrible.

At least not physically.

We soon reach a grave marked, "John Edward Parr." Tucking our coats under our knees for protection and cushion, we kneel on the cold grass. Holding hands, Helen says, "John, if you can hear me now, you know what has been going on and who Tom is. I trust that you also know that I love you very much and regret that we had so few years together. Tom and I pray for you every night and always will. I hope that you are happy and at peace and that we will all be together again someday."

She stops here and I add, "John, you love Helen and that makes you my brother. We will pray for you and ask your prayers for us. I promise I will take good care of her."

Then, passing Helen a handkerchief, I pull out my breviary and begin the prayers for a visit to a grave. Steam comes out of my mouth and nose as I read, "O God, the Creator and Redeemer of all the faithful, hear our supplications, and through Thy infinite love and mercy graciously grant to the soul of Thy servant departed the remission of all his sins, by which he may have deserved the severity of Thy justice and punishments in the world to come. Grant to him grace and mercy before Thy tribunal, and let him attain to everlasting rest and happiness through the infinite merits of Jesus Christ. Amen."

I continue with the Our Father, the Hail Mary, and Psalm 123. I finish by saying, "Eternal rest grant unto them, O Lord. And let the perpetual light shine upon them. May they rest in peace. And may their souls and the souls of all the faithful departed, through the mercy of God, rest in peace. Amen."

Our prayers concluded, Helen reaches out and pats the ground, saying softly, "I love you, John." She then brushes her hands together briskly and allows me to help her up. We return to the car and pour mugs of hot cocoa from the thermos she brought along. Then we begin the long drive back to Myerton.

Helen is silent for a while, but finally says, "I'm glad we're doing this, but I wonder what made you think of it?"

"It's actually a Jewish custom that I learned about in seminary. Typically, the bride and groom visit dead parents or grandparents, but I thought this would be good for us."

"It has been," Helen says softly. "It helps both bring forward and put away the past."

I take her hand, saying as I do, "I'm glad."

We drive on for a while, talking some but not a lot, until we get back to the Myerton Cemetery, where Joan is buried. I carry the plant this time, and place it on her grave. Stepping back, I say, "Joan, you know why we're here. You were right. The reason I was here in Myerton was right in front of me the whole time. Thank you for praying for me—for us. We pray for you and our daughter every night and will for the rest of our lives."

Then it's Helen's turn. "I'm so sorry that your life ended the way it did," she says softly. "I'll take good care of Tom for both of us." I read the office for visiting a grave and then, after helping Helen to her feet, lean over and gently kiss the headstone, saying yet again, "I love you, darling. I always will."

***

We drive straight to the Rectory to exchange our wedding gifts.

"Open yours first," I say, handing a small box tied with a red ribbon. I'm anxious to see the expression on her face.

"Hmm, I wonder what it could be," she says before quickly tearing the ribbon off and opening the box. Inside is a blue velvet box, reminiscent of the one I gave to her last Christmas. This time, instead of a St. Michael medal, it is a pair of sapphire earrings that match her engagement ring and, more importantly, her eyes.

"Oh, Tom!" she cries. "They're gorgeous! Thank you so much!" She punctuates her words with a big hug and delighted kisses.

"I'm so glad you like them," I say with a smile.

"I'll wear them tomorrow," she says. "They're both new and blue." She takes a deep breath. "Ready for your present?"

I nod, though I'd be content to bask in the glow of her pleasure instead of receiving a present of my own.

"I'll be right back," she says, and disappears. I'm trying to figure out what it might be when she returns and places a large and rather heavy box in my lap.

"What in the world?" I ask, looking at the package.

"Why don't you open it and find out, Father," she says with a grin.

I untie the forest green ribbon and lift the top off the box.

As soon as I see what it is, I'm left speechless.

Inside, nestled in white tissue paper, is a green chasuble. However, unlike the threadbare polyester one from the 1970s that I've been using since coming to Saint Clare's, this one is made of pure silk and decorated with the most intricate embroidery I've seen since entering the priesthood.

I look up at Helen and say, "Darling, next to you, this is the most beautiful thing I have ever seen. Where did you get it?"

With shining eyes, she proclaims softly, "I made it, Tom. For you. For us. For God. I contacted some sisters who offer online classes in vestment making. They helped me with the pattern and design, but I did all the needlework myself."

I trace the intricate stitching with my finger. "This must have taken you months. When did you start it?"

"Ash Wednesday, the day the Archbishop gave us permission to create a relationship based on mutual love and respect for both our callings."

I look at her. "So you knew I'd stay a priest the whole time," I whisper.

She strokes my cheek. "I knew that's what I wanted for you, more than I wanted anything for myself."

Overwhelmed by her incredible faith, I draw her close to me, hoping that by hugging her, I'll keep her from seeing the tears in my eyes. I kiss the top of her head and whisper, "This is the most wonderful gift anyone has ever given me."

***

There's not much left to do that afternoon, and I confess that time weighs heavy on our hands. I saw Mom briefly before we left, but she's nowhere to be found—I assume she's with Trevor. We grab a bite to eat, then try to play a game of Monopoly neither of us really can concentrate on. Nate stops by to pick up the luggage, which Gladys has assured us 20 times he will deliver safely to the ship Monday morning.

"He has a meeting at his company's headquarters in Baltimore," she told us. "He's leaving early enough to get to the harbor before the meeting. He won't let you down."

We try to make small talk but fail miserably. After Helen beats me again, I suggest a walk.

"Can we go to the station?" she asks. "I'm still on duty, technically, until four. I just want to take a last look around."

"I think that's just fine, considering that's the place we reunited," I laugh.

Bundling up against the cold but bright day, we set out for the police station. The stores are closed, so the sidewalks are basically empty except for children trying out their brand new bicycles, scooters, and skateboards.

The station's quiet, most of the officers either off or coming in later. Thompson's at the front desk when we arrive.

"All quiet, Thompson?" Helen asks.

"Quiet as usual, Chief," he answers with a smile. "Christmas Day has been quiet, except for a few reports of drunk and/or loud neighbors."

"Potter's relieving you at 4 p.m, right?"

"That's right," he says. "Then I'm off for Christmas with my family."

We leave and make the walk back to Saint Clare's, arriving at the Rectory just as the Archbishop and Father Wayne arrive.

"Your Eminence," I say, shaking his hand.

"Father Greer." he says with equal formality. He then breaks into a smile and adds, "Tom, how are you? And as always, more importantly Helen, how are you?"

She smiles broadly as she gives him a hug and says, "We're both fine, sir, and delighted to see you."

"I'm certainly delighted to be here, but it's a little chilly out here. Can we go in?"

"Oh, of course," I say.

Once we're settled in by the fire, the Archbishop says, "If I understand correctly, everyone is meeting us here about 5 p.m. for the rehearsal. That should not take long. Then, you mentioned that Anna is preparing dinner here at the Rectory. As we discussed earlier, Father Wayne will be staying in the Myerton Inn while I take advantage of the second bedroom upstairs. He will remain in Myerton for the next two weeks until you return from your wedding trip, celebrating Mass with the help of Deacon Roderick. Where is the deacon, by the way?"

"He left town after the Midnight Mass so that he and his wife could spend Christmas with her mother. He should be back soon, but I told him I didn't think he'd have any special duties that I know of."

"No. Father Wayne will be assisting me so there's really very little for him to do."

The Rectory door opens, and Gladys and Nate walk in. "Hi, Mom! Hi, Dad! Merry Christmas," she says cheerfully.

"Merry Christmas, you two," Helen says, giving Gladys and a very confused Nate a hug.

Gladys rolls into the living room and looks up at the very imposing figure of the Archbishop. Uncharacteristically for her, she looks nervous.

"Your Eminence," I say, "may I introduce Gladys Finklestein, one of Helen's employees at the police department and, most importantly, her maid of honor."

"Ms. Finklestein," Archbishop Knowland says, extending his hand. "Very nice to meet you. I've heard many things about you."

"Ah-ha," she says nervously. "All good, I hope."

"Oh, yes," His Eminence says. "I understand you were confirmed at Midnight Mass?"

Relaxing, Gladys smiles. "Yes, Your Eminence. Helen was my sponsor. I—I owe so much to them."

"And this is her boyfriend, Nate Rodriguez," I say. Nate steps forward, and I notice beads of perspiration on his forehead.

"I'm familiar with you, Mr. Rodriguez," the Archbishop says slowly, "from your newspaper work."

Nate swallows and blurts, "Your Eminence, I am so very sorry about that article I wrote about the Myer Mansion. What I did—well, as has been pointed out to me on numerous occasions since, it was wrong. A huge mistake. Frankly idiotic. I'm sorry."

The Archbishop chuckles and extends his hand. "Young man, if I had a dollar for every mistake I've made in my life, I'd be a wealthy man."

"But you'd still be where you are today, Your Eminence."

I look up and see Anna's standing in the doorway to the living room, Clark and Vivian standing right behind her. "Tom," she says, "Clark and Vivian are here, and Deacon Derek's in the church."

"Hello, Anna," Archbishop Knowland says with a hint of a smile. "It's good to see you."

"Well," she says with a smile, "if you visited Saint Clare's more often—"

"I know, I know," he says.

"Tommy!" Mom screeches before making her appearance, with Trevor in tow.

"Mom," I say. "Where have you been?"

"Oh, Trevor and I've been having a little fun," she says. "You must be the man responsible for all of this."

The Archbishop bows slightly. "Walter Knowland, at your service, ma'am."

"This is my mother, Nola Greer, Your Eminence," I say.

"I suspected from her calling you 'Tommy'. My mother insisted on calling me Wally until the day she died."

"I remember you hated it," Anna says, blushing when she realizes what she said.

"Well, er, you have a good memory," His Eminence says.

"This is my boyfriend, Trevor," Mom says, pushing him forward.

"Hey, man," he says, "good to meet you."

"Likewise," His Eminence mutters.

"Clark, Vivian, come here," I say quickly. "Your Eminence, you've heard me speak of Reverend Clark Applegate and his wife, Vivian."

"I've been wanting to meet you, Reverend Applegate," the Archbishop says with a smile. "I want to thank you."

"Thank me, Your Eminence?" Clark says, a look of confusion on his face. "What for?"

"Well, two things really. First, for not stealing a good man for your church."

Clark and I both laugh. "There was never a chance of that, Your Eminence," I say. "Clark and I often discussed the dangers of thinking the grass was greener on the other side of the Reformation."

"The other thing, Reverend," the Archbishop continues, "is for being such a good friend and supporter for Tom during his trials early this year. He told me how much he grew to value your counsel. In a way, you're as responsible for all of this as I am."

"I am honored you say that, sir," Clark says. "All I did was help a good man through some problems. Along the way, we became good friends. You know that friends are few and far between in our business."

His Eminence takes a deep breath. "Yes, they are," he says quietly. Looking at Vivian, he adds, "And you are his lovely wife, Vivian, right?"

"An honor to meet you, Your Eminence," she says with a smile.

"You're the one in charge of everything tomorrow, hmm?"

"Well, it's just my job to make sure these two get to where they're supposed to be when they're supposed to be there," Vivian laughs. "With these two, that can be a tough job."

"I take it, Helen," Father Wayne pipes up, "you've ordered all the criminals in Myerton to refrain from killing and pillaging tomorrow?"

"Yes, sir," Helen laughs. "They've all promised to wait until after the wedding to start their crime spree."

Everyone laughs at this, and I say, "Well, seeing it's almost 5 p.m., shall we go over to the church?"

Everybody leaves, with Helen and I hanging back. I take her hand and say, "You know, you can still back out if you want to."

She cups my face in her hands. "Tom, there is nothing in Heaven or on Earth which is going to stop me from marrying you. Now, let's join everyone before Anna runs back here to make sure we're not doing something we shouldn't."

***

The rehearsal over, we all begin to walk back to the Rectory for the dinner Anna has prepared. When I tell Mom this is where we're going, she sort of pouts and says, "Oh, Tommy. I thought we'd be going out to dinner, since this is such a special occasion. To tell the truth, Trevor isn't really much into traditional home cooking. He says it's just full of fat and salt and stuff like that."

"You mean unlike those nachos he was wolfing down the other night?" I ask.

"Well, that's different. Anyway, I think it would just be best if he and I went somewhere on our own, maybe some place we can unwind a little. This whole wedding thing has really been stressful, especially for Trevor. He's just not used to being around so many new people."

I want to say, "Unless they're slipping fives into his g-string," but I bite my tongue, saying instead, "That's fine, Mom. You have a key to the Rectory. Feel free to let yourself in if I've gone to bed."

It sounds cold and uncaring, because that's how I feel at that moment. For years, Mom put my drug addict sister Sonya ahead of me. Now, I suppose, it's this—I hate this word, but it fits so well—boytoy of hers.

Of course, on the other hand, I'm actually delighted that they won't be here having dinner with the Archbishop and the rest of us, but still, it's the principle of the thing.

Right?

I get to the Rectory and find everyone else already inside with champagne glasses in their hands.

"Sorry everyone," I say, shucking off my coat and hanging it up. "I was talking to Mom."

"Is she joining us?" Helen asks.

"No," I say slowly. "She and Trevor are on their own tonight."

Helen looks at me with a mixture of "I'm sorry," and "That's a relief."

"Well, that's unfortunate," the Archbishop says, "but now we can get started with the festivities. Clark, you're up."

Because of the attitude many in his congregation would have toward Clark making a toast with alcohol at a Catholic wedding, we agreed to hold those sorts of festivities during the rehearsal dinner. I walk over to the fireplace and put my arm around Helen's waist as Clark says solemnly, "If you had told me the day I met Tom Greer that this Catholic priest would one day be one of my dearest friends, I would have been surprised. If you had told me that I would one day be the best man at his wedding, I would have been stunned. But if you had told me that the woman he was marrying would be as beautiful and as brave and as accomplished as Helen, I would have punched you in the face for lying."

Everyone bursts out laughing at this as Clark raises his glass and says, "To Tom and Helen, may God give you love and joy beyond anything your earthly minds can hope for."

As everyone toasts, I look into Helen's sparkling eyes and kiss her chastely on the forehead.

Now it's Gladys' turn. Rolling into the center of the room, she begins, "When I lost my parents, I never thought I would ever again know what it was like to love and be loved so sincerely. These two have told me the truth when I wanted to hear lies, told me they loved me when I was being completely unlovable, and have taught me that, no matter what, God is in the business of turning our mistakes into masterpieces. To Tom and Helen, who I have the privilege of calling Mom and Dad."

She raises her glass and begins to sing with surprising strength and feeling:

"The Lord bless thee and keep thee:

The Lord make His face to shine upon thee,

And be gracious unto thee,

The Lord lift up the His countenance upon thee,

And give thee peace."

As the entire room says together, "Amen," Gladys shouts, "And love, but then, you've already got plenty of that."

I look at Helen again as the Archbishop says, "Tom, if you can't kiss her better this time than you did last time, I'm going to have to haul you in for some remedial pre-Cana."

Everyone laughs as I go out of my way to demonstrate to one and all that will not be necessary.

Twenty-Five

With the rehearsal dinner over, everyone says their goodnights and leaves the Rectory for their respective homes. Father Wayne leaves for the Myerton Inn, but not before telling Helen that he'll hear her confession tomorrow morning before the wedding.

Helen and I are left with the Archbishop, who asks, "Tom, do you have any cigars?"

I say, "Certainly, Your Eminence. Your preferred brand. I also have a very nice brandy I'm sure you'll like."

He smiles. "Ah, that sounds like a fine way to end Christmas." He approaches Helen and gives her a hug. "Good night, my dear. The next time I see you will be at Mass tomorrow."

"Good night, sir," she says with a smile.

He looks at her and nods. "Tom," he says, "I'll meet you on the patio."

The Archbishop leaves, and suddenly, Helen and I are alone together for the last time before the wedding. She slips her arms under my suit coat and lays her head on my chest. I wrap my arms around her and say, "This time tomorrow, we'll be married."

"But until then," she replies.

Burying my face in her hair for one last sustaining memory of vanilla, I whisper, "Until then."

She pulls away but takes my hand. I walk her to her car and give her one final kiss and she drives away. After all this time, I am shocked at how hard it is to let her go. I stand there for a moment or two before I turn and go into the Rectory.

Anna, ever generous, has left a tray of brandy and snifters, along with the box of cigars, on the kitchen table. I take these outside, where the Archbishop has a surprisingly good fire going in the fire pit.

"Don't be surprised, Tom," he says jovially. "I'll have you know I was once an Eagle Scout."

"Indeed, sir," I reply, pouring us each a brandy and taking a comfortable chair.

"Oh, yes. But that was a long time ago." He sits in the chair next to me and I pass him his brandy. He savors the aroma, then takes a sip. "Very nice, Tom," he comments. "Are we paying you too much?"

I laugh. "Hardly sir. This was a gift from a friend of mine. He owns a bar outside of town."

"Well, he sure does know his spirits." He pauses and then says carefully, "Tom, you and Helen have been faithful to everything I've asked of you since well before your engagement. Now I'm going to ask you something. Do you need or even just want anything from me?"

I ponder this extraordinary offer before saying, "Just the answer to one question, sir."

"What is that, my son?" he says, reaching for a cigar.

"How did we get here?" I ask. "I mean, it was not that long ago that I would never have considered serving in a parish church, much less being married. What is it that you haven't told me?"

He says nothing at first, just takes another sip of his brandy. "To answer that question, Tom," he says quietly, "I must share something with you that I ask you to keep as sacrosanct as you would a confession. Meaning, you can't tell anyone, not even Helen."

I nod my head. "I will never tell another person what you tell me tonight, sir."

"Very well, then," he says, taking another rather large swallow of brandy, emptying his glass and passing it to me for a refill. "It all started with a call and a debt I did not know I owed, and that I can never repay."

He takes a deep breath. "Tom, you may remember that not long before I assigned you here, we were talking about you moving to Rome and joining the Archival staff at the Vatican."

That seems like a lifetime ago now, but I do remember and nod my head.

"You'd probably be there now had I not gotten a call from Anna." He pauses again and takes another sip of his brandy before continuing. "You had mentioned the Rome assignment to her in one of your phone calls, and she wanted to know if I thought it would be permanent. I said probably, and she replied, 'You can't do that to me, Walter. I want you to send him here. We both know Father Anthony is losing it, and I want Tom to take his place.'

"Needless to say, I was stunned by this and replied, as you might assume, by reminding her that the needs of the Church must come first, that you had never expressed an interest in parish work, that the Vatican Archives would be an ideal assignment for someone with your training. Then she said, 'But Walter, he needs to be here. His soul is fading into dust, shut up away from people, from life.'

"I'll admit that statement gave me pause. More than one of your colleagues had described you as 'cold,' 'aloof,' even 'secretive.' But I didn't feel that I could give in to her demands, not until she said, 'You owe me, Walter. I will not lose another child.'

"This got my attention, and I reminded her that I knew all too well what she'd gone through with Joan—the loss, the sorrow, the loneliness. And that's when I learned that she did not mean Joan."

He falls silent here. I feel as though I need to breathe, but I am afraid to take a breath, fearing that any sound I make might break the spell. So I let myself breathe as softly as I can and wait as he takes one, and then another, sip of the amber liquid in his glass.

"Tom, neither you nor I nor any other man is born a priest—I think you know that more than most," he says. "We're born little boys and we go to school with little girls. We live in homes with families and assume that one day, we'll have ones of our own. Of course, most little Catholic boys go through a phase of thinking they have a vocation to the priesthood, but most do not.

But some men know, even from childhood, that they have the calling. That's how it was for me, and Anna Stewart was the first person I ever confided that to. We were in the 10th grade and I had just asked her to the sophomore dance. 'We'll have fun, but just as friends,' I insisted, stating boldly, 'I'm going to be a priest.'

"She seemed OK with this, and so we went to the dance, and other dances in the years that followed. We'd sit together and talk for hours after Mass on Sundays, and she'd always cheer me on at baseball games. I guess I should have known she was falling in love with me, but I was young and stupid. Toward the end of our senior year, however, it finally dawned on me that not only was she in love with me, but I was in love with her.

"I went to my priest for advice. Actually sat in what's now your office. He knew I was discerning a vocation but advised me to, as he put it, 'explore my feelings' toward Anna. So I did."

I have stopped breathing, waiting for what he's going to say next—and almost certain I know what it's going to be. He takes another swig of his brandy and says, "Well, one thing led to another and, after our senior prom, we went for a long drive on a deserted road. And I asked her if she wanted me to stop the car. She said she did, so I did. And we did."

He stares sadly into his empty glass. "Afterwards, I felt such a sense of guilt, not because of what we had done in those moments of weakness but because I realized I had led her on."

He looks at me, and I see the first tear I've ever seen Archbishop Walter Knowland shed. "I loved her, Tom. Oh, how I loved her. But she was never going to be enough. I think she sensed this because, when I drove her home, and went around to open her door, I said, looking at the ground, 'Look, I love you and I'll marry you if you want me to.' But there, in the moonlight, she turned me down. Instead, she squared her shoulders, raised her chin, and said firmly, 'You can't do that, Walter. You're going to be a priest.' I was searching for something to say. I had the radio on and I heard what was then a new song, 'Bridge Over Troubled Waters,' come on and I took her in my arms and I held her as it played, promising, 'Anna Stewart, no matter what happens, no matter where we both go in life, I promise to always be this to you.'

"She didn't say anything—you know how she is when she has her mind made up—but she gave me a sweet kiss on the cheek, turned her back, and ran up the steps into the house."

Again the long pause, and then, "We never saw each other alone again, but we did stay in touch. I married her to Drew and was Joan's godfather. I attended the funeral when he died and then, when Joan started having problems, I was able to help pay for some of her treatment. I would have given her away when you two married, but I got appendicitis."

I speak now for the first time in what seems to be hours, exclaiming, "Uncle Walter! I remember now. Joan had to get someone at the last minute to give her away because 'Uncle Walter' was in the hospital."

"That's right," he says, nodding. "And Tom, I was at her funeral, though I know you don't remember me. I didn't speak to you. Well, I was a stranger to you, wasn't I? I just sat with Anna and did what I could for her.

"So, the years passed. Anna and I stayed in touch. She gave me a heads up when you entered seminary. I was an auxiliary bishop at the time, so I could and did keep an eye on you for her. But at no point did I interfere with your discernment process or with your training. When Archbishop Gray needed a new archivist for the Archdiocese, I admit I did use my influence to get you the position. But that's because of you, not Anna. I knew that a man with your experience would be especially useful in the Archdiocesan Office, considering the state of some of our more recent records."

"And Anna?" I ask, dreading what I am about to hear.

"She and I spoke often by phone, especially when she wanted something for the parish or the Ladies of Charity. But for herself, she asked for nothing. She told me nothing, not until the day she called in the debt."

He sighs, "I'm pretty sure you've figured this out by now. At the end of the summer, when she told everyone she was going away to college, Anna actually went to St. Monica's Home for Unwed Mothers in Philadelphia. She had a baby and she surrendered it to be adopted by a devout Catholic family. She never told me, Tom, or as God as my witness, I would have come home. I would have married her. I would have been good to her. I swear!"

He's nearly shouting now and I assure him, "I know that, sir, I know."

He calms down and says, "Apparently, after Joan died, Anna put her name and information on some sort of registry that allows adopted children to get in touch with their birth parents. The girl—the baby was a girl—got in touch with her a few years ago. They began corresponding and things were going pretty well, as I understand it, until the girl started asking about her father. Anna wanted to protect me, protect my position in the Church. It had just been announced that I was to be made Archbishop, and she thought the publicity would prove damaging. So, she insisted she would not tell her, and that created a rift between them. I think there was also some talk of money, and when she found out Anna was not particularly wealthy and that she would not reveal my name, she cut off contact. Obviously, this nearly killed Anna. Then, when she found out you might be going to Rome—well, I just told you the rest."

We say nothing for several minutes as the Archbishop finishes his drink. I have other questions but I cannot bring myself to ask them now. Instead, I say nothing until His Eminence finally stands up and says unceremoniously, "Well, Tom, it's late and we both have a busy day tomorrow. We should turn in. Good night, son."

"Good night, sir," I say, also standing.

And so, with the earth-shattering news still reverberating in my ears, we turn in.

Twenty-Six

I sleep surprisingly well, probably as a result of being emotionally spent and well-lubricated with brandy. My alarm wakes me at 7 a.m. When I turn off the alarm, I notice a text message from Mom that she sent about 3 a.m.:

Trevor needs me, so I'm staying with him. I'll see you at the wedding.

I toss my phone on the bed. "Mom, I just don't care anymore," I mutter.

I shower before throwing on some casual clothes and going downstairs. As promised, Anna has returned to make a fine breakfast that I find I am way too nervous to appreciate. The Archbishop, on the other hand, digs in with relish and seems to enjoy himself immensely until 8:30 a.m., when Anna says firmly, "OK, you two. Clear out. Vivian and Helen will be here soon. Tom, do you have everything?"

"Yes, ma'am, I do," I say, falling back on my Southern upbringing, as I always do in times of high emotion.

The Archbishop stands and says, "Anna, thank you for this delicious breakfast. Tom, I'll wait for you in the living room."

He leaves Anna and me alone in the fragrant kitchen. "Anna," I say, wrapping my arms around her in a bear hug, "There is nothing I can ever say to tell you how much you mean to me, how important you have always been and will always be to both Helen and me. I love you so much and will always—and I mean always—be here for you."

In a voice choked with emotion, Anna croaks, "You two just be happy. That's all I need." Then, reverting to form, she pushes me out the door of the kitchen.

I join the Archbishop in the living room. He asks, "Do you still want me to hear your confession?"

"Yes, please," I say. "Shall we just go to my office? I'm not sure I'm up to running into anyone in the church right now."

"Of course," he agrees. We go from the living room to my office, and I close the door behind us.

One of the cool things about the sacrament of reconciliation is that, no matter who is hearing your confession, the form is the same. The man and his rank mean nothing. It is God, our heavenly Father, who is hearing us and forgiving us our sins. So I begin with the same "Bless me, Father," that I have used and have heard used so many times. I then tell him of my struggles concerning my mother, of when I was so angry at Helen, recent issues I'd experienced concerning the wedding, lying to the woman at the dress shop, that kind of thing. Then I conclude, meaning it sincerely, "For these and all my sins, I am truly sorry."

"Tom," His Eminence begins gently, "I don't need to tell you that issues with family members are among the most trying in our lives. God gave you Nola Greer to be your mother in order to shape you in a particular way. Pray for her, try to love her, try to see Christ working in her and through her, pray for her—um—ah—pray for Trevor, that God will give you grace to influence him for good. But today, for your penance, say a decade of the Rosary, meditating on Christ's first miracle at the Wedding at Cana, and reminding yourself that He will be a guest here today, turning the water of your life and Helen's life into the wine of your life together." His voice chokes as he grants me absolution and then slips out, leaving me alone with my happy penance.

***

I decide to walk to Clark's to get a little fresh air, relax, and clear my mind. Unfortunately, the Darth Vader ringtone disrupts my plans.

I want to cuss and throw the phone in the bushes, but Helen and I are committed to making this a day of love and rejoicing in the Lord, so I answer pleasantly, "Good morning, Mom!"

"Oh, Tommy, I'm afraid it's not," she says in a dismal tone. "Trevor is sick and I really don't think he's going to be able to make it to the wedding."

So it's actually a great morning, I think. To Mom, I say, "I'm sorry to hear that. What's wrong?"

"Well, Tommy, I wasn't going to tell you this but I kinda got my feelings hurt at the rehearsal last night. I mean, I just couldn't believe that you had not thought of having someone escort me to my seat. You are my son, after all, and after everything I've done for you and Helen—welcoming her with open arms even though I'm not even sure you should be allowed to marry—I would have thought that you would have created at least some special place for me in the wedding party. That's why we didn't stay for dinner, that and the fact that Trevor felt that everyone was judging him for not being Catholic."

I want to say, "No, everyone was judging Trevor for being a twenty-something gigolo taking advantage of an elderly woman who is well on her way around the bend." But the sacrament of confession is still fresh on my soul, so God gives me the grace to say, "I am sorry you and he felt that way, Mom. As I told you, we're not—."

"It doesn't matter now, Tommy. Remember, I called about poor Trevor, not you."

I do remember this and so shut my mouth as she continues, "After the rehearsal, he and I went out to that bar on the edge of town, the Hoot-n-Holler. He wanted to get a drink and so did I, but I guess he may have had a few too many because he got kinda loud and that bartender—oh Tommy, he's a nasty one—threw him out. Well, Trevor was still thirsty so, and I told him not to, but he was just so upset, he came back to our room and finished off a bottle of rum we had brought with us."

"So he's not really sick," I say as I knock on Clark's door. "He's hung over."

"Well, yes, I guess you could say that."

"OK, but can you still drive yourself to the wedding?"

"Yes, but it just won't be the same without Trevor."

Clark opens the door as I say, "No, Mom, it certainly will not. But I need to go now. I'll see you in a couple of hours."

I hang up and Clark asks, "What was that all about?"

"Oh, nothing really. Mom's boytoy got drunk at the Hoot-n-Holler last night and started some problems, so Steve threw him out and now he can't come to the wedding."

"The Lord does indeed work in mysterious ways, my friend," he says, clapping me on the back. "Now, Vivian has the guest room all ready for you. Just make yourself at home. If you need anything, including company, come on out. Otherwise, I'll leave you alone."

It only takes me about ten minutes to get dressed. After all, it's the same clothes I wear everyday, though Helen did insist I buy a new black suit. I look at my watch and am shocked to see that it's just now 9:30 a.m. Desperate for something to kill time, I decide to call Steve and find out what happened last night.

He picks up on the first ring and greets me with, "Hi, Father. I'm surprised to hear from you this morning. Need a dose of Dutch courage?"

"Maybe, but not yet. I'm calling to find out what happened last night with my mother and her, um, you know."

"Oh, yes, Father, I know. And after what happened, I suspect every drinker in Myerton does, too. But that's a mark in your favor, not his."

"I don't understand."

"Well, Father," Steve says, "the last thing I would ever want to do is cause you any trouble or embarrassment, but I had to kick that Trevor guy out or he'd be dead and my place would be in shambles."

"What happened?" I ask, certain Mom didn't tell me the whole truth.

"So, here's the story. He and your mom came in. They wasted no time telling me who they were and how they were related to the celebrity couple. They ordered a couple of drinks, and then your Mom switched to soda. But that guy just kept drinking."

"Doesn't surprise me one bit," I say.

"Yeah, well, after five, he began to get real loud, which a lot of guys do. But he started spouting off some less than stellar comments about you and Helen and what he suspected you two got up to when you were alone. I was heading over to the table to try to settle him down, but I forgot that there was another couple sitting at the next table. By the time I got there, Nick Hallstead had him by the throat and Nina was in his face, giving him a detailed description of the beat-down she was about to give him. I broke it up pretty quickly, and then escorted him and your Mom to their car."

"You're kidding?" I say, incredulously.

"Nope."

I cannot help but laugh out loud at this and say, "I'd offer to buy you a drink but I guess that's not very appropriate. I will look forward to shaking your hand at the reception this afternoon."

"I was glad to do it. You know, he's a real piece of work. For what it's worth, I got a certain vibe that tells me he may be a switch hitter."

"Oh, man, that's all I need." Then I add, "Look, I guess I'd better go. But I'll see you in an hour or so."

"We'll be there," he says, then hangs up.

"We, Steve?" I say with a smile.

I settle into the comfortable wing chair by the window to spend a few minutes in prayer and praise for all God has done. Time seems to both speed forward and stand still until I hear Clark knocking at the door.

"Tom," he says, "you about ready? It's 10 a.m."

"Yeah," I say, taking one last look in the mirror. I check my pocket for the fiftieth time for the rings and then come out. For reasons that escape my rattled mind, Clark is perfectly calm and looks well put together in a black suit and gold tie. He offers to drive us to the church but I really prefer to walk. The day is cool but clear and we both have coats.

As we walk, he says, "Look, Tom, you're a grown man and have been married before. I know you don't need any advice from me, but I'm going to give you some anyway. If you've got any sense at all, and I think you do, you're more nervous about this evening than you are this morning."

I am thankful for the cool wind that is now blowing on my hot face.

"I know," Clark continues, "you're all wound up about the mechanics of everything and how it will be and how you'll do and heaven only knows what else. So, I'm going to share something with you that I wish someone had told me way back when I married Vivian. She's not just any woman, she's Helen. The woman you take to bed tonight is the same woman that you bickered with last week and the same one you danced with last month. She kept you out of prison and lay in your arms on that basement floor. Tonight is just the next glorious chapter in the book that you have been writing together since the first day you met. So forget about everything else and just focus on how much you love her, personally, and everything will be fine."

"God, I hope so," I admit and we both laugh.

Fortunately, we're at the Rectory by now and, as arranged, Clark goes in and runs everyone out but Helen. Meanwhile, I pace back and forth like the nervous bridegroom I am.

As they come out, Gladys gives me a big hug while Vivian stops and whispers in my ear some of the most beautiful words in the English language.

"She's waiting for you, Tom."

They disappear into the church and I take a deep breath before opening the door.

Twenty-Seven

I have spent the last several days trying to come up with something suave and meaningful to say at this moment.

Unfortunately, my excitement and nerves have driven every thought from my head.

So, I simply step to the base of the stairs and say in a voice choked with emotion, "I'm here, Helen."

The first thing I see as I look up the stairs is the hem of a long, sapphire blue skirt, or maybe dress. I really don't know and don't care. Then I see ribbons, the white satin ones I chose to match the Christmas season. Next, her curvy hips, with the bouquet of red roses sprigged with vanilla pods and set off by green leaves, her creamy hands hidden, her white arms mostly covered by some sleeves of the same fabric as the skirt. Then, finally, what I've been waiting for over the past interminable hours, her face, her smiling, radiant face. Her hair is pinned up and she's wearing a small hat with a delicate veil that brushes over her forehead and draws attention to her eyes, which sparkle this morning like they never have before.

Has someone ever come up with a word for this much happiness? I don't think so.

I want to say something sophisticated, something to forever mark this moment. But I've got nothing. Instead, I say simply, "My darling," and offer my arm. We walk together, whispering, to the church and join the rest of the party.

The Archbishop is there, beaming almost as much as we are. As always, he takes charge of the situation and gets everyone in place. He nods to Vivian, who opens the door. Dominic rings the bell, people stand, the organ begins the strains of "Oh God, Beyond All Praising," and we progress forward.

"O God beyond all praising,
We worship you today
And sing the love amazing
That songs cannot repay."

I cannot join in the singing. I'm too choked up, and anyway, my voice is nothing to write home about, even on a good day. But Helen sings in the deep throaty alto that won her a spot in our college glee club. So I listen, and contemplate the "love amazing" that we especially "cannot repay."

Then, of course, there is what comes next:

"For we can only wonder
At every gift you send,
At blessings without number

And mercies without end."

Wonder, gifts, blessings, mercies. All these things have been ours, poured out on us by our gracious Lord, and there is so much joy now in my chest that it's a wonder I can even breathe. But onward we go, as "We lift our hearts before you."

We reach the altar and make our bows as the second verse begins. I thought Meschach might wonder why we included this one, but when we were going over the music, he nodded approvingly and said, "This is what you two understand that young people don't. I've been married 22 years this May and I can tell you, the first verse is for the wedding, the second is for the marriage."

"Then hear, O gracious Savior,
Accept the love we bring,
That we who know your favor
May serve you as our king."

We are both vowing ourselves to serve God as our king, me to a dual vocation as priest and husband, Helen to being married to a man who can never put her first. But we both know this, and together we kneel at the rail, promising that,

"Whether our tomorrows
Be filled with good or ill,
We'll triumph through our sorrows
And rise to bless you still."

Of course, we both know that there will be both good and ill. I've tried to tell Martin and Mae that, and I'm sure they believe me. But Helen and I know on a different level. We know what it will be like to be hurt, angry, betrayed, and, of course, widowed, which one of us almost certainly will be—please, God, make it Helen, not me—and we also know the necessity of carrying on. This is why I am finally able to join Helen in promising Our Lord,

"To marvel at your beauty
And glory in your ways,
And make a joyful duty
Our sacrifice of praise."

I soon become eternally grateful for my familiarity with the Mass; the responses come automatically and there are only a few times when I chime in with the Archbishop in places where today, I'm supposed to be silent.

Then, things take a different turn. Following the Gospel reading, the

the Archbishop begins his homily. He has promised us that he will keep it brief, and we are grateful.

"My friends," he intones in his deep bass voice, "it is good and right that we are here today on the feast of the Holy Family. Please take a moment to admire the Gypsinian Christ Child lying in the manger. It is five hundred years old and was created by human hands to remind us that God did indeed become human and was born into a family made up of a man and woman who would love and protect Him. Today, Tom and Helen come together to promise to love and protect you and each other, just as they, and hundreds of others, have cared for this statue."

I feel Helen grip my hand and I know that if I look at her, I'll either burst out laughing or pass out or both, so I keep my eyes straight ahead and wait patiently for her to start breathing again. Just as I am thinking I may have to slap her, she takes a deep breath and lets it out very, very slowly.

Fortunately, the Archbishop does not seem to notice this, for he continues, "Tom and Helen, you are here to vow to each other that you will live and love as husband and wife for the remainder of your lives together. We have talked extensively about what all this means and I know that you both understand this as well as two people beginning their lives together can. Every couple is unique, but you two more obviously than others.

"Helen, you are not just marrying Tom, but in a very real sense, you are entering into a covenant with the Church itself. You are agreeing to accept the unique challenges that will come along with being the first woman in over eight centuries to marry a Catholic priest. Among these challenges is moving wherever the Church chooses to send him, accepting his sacrifices of missed dinners and middle-of-the-night emergencies as your own, and being under constant scrutiny, not just in Myerton, but around the world.

"Tom, in addition to the challenges I just mentioned, in marrying Helen, you are also taking on the responsibility of loving and caring for her as a wife deserves without letting your priestly ministry suffer. This is a difficult challenge, in fact, an impossible one.

"It goes without saying that at times you will fail each other, you will fail the Church, and you will fail God. The tragedy is that when you do so, others will look at you and say, 'See, I knew a priest could not be married and still serve God well.' They will not know, as I and all the others in my office do, that priests fail all the time, as do Archbishops. We fail God, but He never fails us.

"What few will consider is the number of times you *might* have failed but did not because you have in Helen a 'helper,' as Eve was to be to Adam. But unlike the first Eve, who failed so miserably, Helen is a daughter of the 'Second Eve,' our Blessed Mother, and I have absolute faith that she will be more of the helper God originally envisioned.

"This brings me to a few words I have to say to those here today, and who will hear or read these words in the future. Tom and Helen have come here today, not just because they love each other, but because they love God. Indeed, it is their love for God that led them to sacrifice their love for each other so that Tom might remain a priest. Then, as he did for Abraham after he willingly offered up his son, Isaac, God provided another way—a legitimate dispensation to marry granted by the Holy Father with the support of the Holy See. So, please remember that when you feel the need to criticize, lay the blame where it belongs, on me and my colleagues who brought this about, not on the two brave pioneers who opened themselves up to have their life together placed daily under a magnifying glass. And when you see one of them live out their vocations less than perfectly, be sure to ask yourself how well you're doing in yours before you comment.

"Tom, Helen, this is a glorious day for you and it is with a heart full of joy that I commend your future to God and each other."

Suddenly, Helen and I are standing, and this moment has my full attention. Reading from the The Celebration of Matrimony, the Archbishop intones solemnly, "Dearly beloved . . ."

After this, everything is a blur.

The Consents—yes, we are here by our own free wills and we will love and honor each other as long as we live. There is no question of children so we join our right hands and, looking into her eyes, I say, "I, Thomas, take you, Helen, for my lawful wife, to have and to hold, from this day forward, for better, for worse, for richer, for poorer, in sickness and in health, until death do us part." She responds the same way, grinning as we have had more than one teasing argument about her promising to obey me, or anyone else for that matter.

Suddenly, we're kneeling and Archbishop Knowland is blessing us, saying, "May the Lord in his kindness strengthen the consent you have declared before the Church and graciously bring to fulfillment his blessings within you. What God has joined, let no one put asunder. May the God of Abraham, the God of Isaac, the God of Jacob, the God who joined together our first parents in paradise, strength and bless in Christ the consent you have declared before the Church, so that what God joins together, no one may put asunder. Let us bless the Lord."

At this, the church resounds with adult and child-like voices together, "Thanks be to God." Clark hands His Eminence the rings, which he blesses, and we place them on each other's fingers, asking that each "receive this ring as a sign of my love and fidelity. In the name of the Father, and of the Son, and of the Holy Spirit."

And then, finally, the kiss. I take Helen in my arms and kiss her in front of God and everybody, as my ever-so-large family applauds.

Then, everyone settles down and the Mass continues, with Christ Himself coming in the form of the Eucharist to share our happiness. The Conways come forward with the gifts, led by Catherine wearing her emerald green Christmas dress with a red satin sash and carrying the hosts that will become the body of our Lord. Behind her are Max and JP, each dressed in their Sunday best, with one carefully carrying a carafe of wine and the other one of water. Dan is behind them, carrying a suddenly shy Andrew as Miriam walks beside him with the tiny white bundle that is our new goddaughter. As they had practiced, each bows before Father Wayne, who receives each gift, passes it off to Dominic, and gives each child a blessing.

It's only when they are supposed to return to their seats that things go a little off the rails. Instead of joining her family, Catherine veers off to the side altar where she carefully tucks her own blue baby blanket around the Baby Jesus. Dan turns and heads to get her, but Father Wayne stops him, taking his arm gently and saying quietly, "Let her alone. She knows what she's doing."

Sure enough, satisfied now that the baby will not catch a cold, she joins the rest of her siblings, with her father following cheerfully behind.

I look at Helen, who whispers quietly in my ear, "She's taken care of him this long, you know?"

From this point on, the Mass seems to fly by, with us kneeling together to receive our Lord, one of the few times we'll ever get to do so. Then comes the recessional, after which Helen and I take a moment to kiss again in the narthex before taking our places by the Archbishop to welcome those coming out.

Of course, there are some things that can't be prevented. I am, let's just say, shaken up when my mother rushes forward to hug us.

For one thing, I am nearly blinded by the sequins that cover every square inch of the bright red cocktail dress she is wearing. I know that I should be grateful that there's not more of the dress than there is, but I'm not. It stops a few inches above her knee and starts only a few inches above that. All I can think of while we are in the receiving line is that the press will have a field day with this.

Of course, I keep smiling and introducing Helen to various churchmen she has not yet met, just as I'm supposed to. But then I have to introduce them to my mother and watch as each and everyone studiously ignores her high—and, if my recollection of my childhood is correct—obviously augmented bust.

Thus, it is with tremendous relief when Vivian sidles up to me and whispers, "Don't worry about your mom. I've taken care of it." She says nothing else but I still relax, thankful that I can trust her with this.

Dan does his usual superb job keeping everyone moving and after what seems to be an eternity, Helen and I are at the front of the church with the rest of the wedding party, posing for pictures with the photographers sent from various newspaper outlets. We have agreed to give them anything they want at the church but nothing at the reception. There is too much of a chance that something could happen that might be caught in such a way as to make it embarrassing for someone.

We almost renege on our promise of any photo they want in the church when they ask us to pose by the creche. I very much want to bail, but Helen walks over keeping a mostly straight face. We pose briefly as the reporter assigned comes forward to ask us a few questions about the Gypsinian Christ Child.

"Yes," we say, "it really is 500 years old."

"No, it does not belong to Saint Clare's, but to the entire diocese."

"No, it was not loaned to us because of the wedding. It was just our turn."

"Yes, it has been an honor to care for it."

And finally, "Yes, the church and the police department did cooperate in protecting it."

Twenty-Eight

The photographers and reporters leave. Helen and I walk down the front steps of the church and get into the limo that we rented to take us to the reception.

"Take the long way around," I whisper to the driver as we get in. I slip him a $20 as I add, "and put your privacy screen up."

For the next 30 minutes or so, while various scenes of the outskirts of Myerton slip by, Helen and I enjoy champagne and snacks and each other, whispering and cuddling and kissing like the bride and groom we are. This is paradise, a little time just to ourselves before we have to face the crowd again.

At one point, I startle Helen by reaching down and picking up her feet. Removing the heels she's wearing, I reach under the seat and pull out a small box that I had Nate place there earlier today.

"What is this?" she asks with a giggle, as I indulge myself by rubbing and massaging her feet with more passion and pleasure than I have allowed myself before. She opens the box and pulls out a pair of soft, pale blue slippers that I slip on her waiting feet.

"There," I say, lifting each briefly to my lips before lowering it back to the floor, "now you can dance the afternoon away, Cinderella."

"Thank you my dear, dear Prince," she replies, before rewarding me with a kiss that would make both Cinderella and her prince blush.

Finally, we arrive at the Mansion, looking beautiful in the crisp cold of the winter midday. Vivian holds us outside until Bill, who is acting as our Master of Ceremonies, calls for everyone to quiet down as he announces our arrival.

As planned, Meshach begins to sing the chorus from "Hallelujah," as we walk in, hand in hand. Vivian escorts us straight to the multitiered masterpiece that is our wedding cake. It is based on photos Helen had of her own parent's cake and is completed by their topper, hand painted by Helen so that the bride's dress is blue and the groom is wearing a Roman collar. I laugh at this and then whisper in her ear, "Please tell me that you're going to use the knife that Nick provided and not whip out your own."

"Certainly not for another few hours," she declares with an innocent smile on her face, and the cameras capture her pushing cake into my very red face.

Now it's my turn to surprise her. At the other end of the table is my groom's cake, which Nick himself designed for us. It is a large chocolate sheet cake cut in the shape of a magnifying glass. The top is frosted white with a pair of thumbprints crossed to make a red heart. On the edge of the cake and running down the side that is frosted in black is a white tab, making the circular frame of the magnifying glass itself a Roman collar.

She laughs joyfully at this as I carefully cut a small slice and gently pop it in her mouth. The crowd groans in disappointment, I guess because I did not shove a large piece into her face. But I can't stand to see good cake go to waste.

Vivian now helps us navigate the crowd to our own private table, where we are soon served piles of delicious food. We revel in being able to sit and eat, my appetite coming back and hers probably having never left. People stop by to say congratulations, but Vivian proves to be quite the bodyguard, gently assuring everyone that we need a few minutes to catch our breaths before we feel up to visiting. That doesn't stop people, especially Gladys, from tapping their glasses insistently so we will have to stop and kiss. Not that this is a major hardship, but I haven't eaten all day, and—

Our reverie is soon broken as Vivian comes to our table and says, "Time to get the dancing started." We make our way toward the dance floor as everyone begins to applaud and Meschach begins to play the opening strains of "Hallelujah."

Now, I have great intentions for our first dance. It will be dignified, with Helen and I dancing gracefully while looking into each other's eyes. We both agreed that we are uncomfortable being on public display, and so have asked that the wedding party join us on the second verse of Meschach's carefully edited version of "Hallelujah."

But something goes terribly wrong when he begins to sing.

Suddenly, I am in Bellamy, and facing losing her. Then I'm in the basement, holding her as life drains from her body. I am in the Archbishop's living room, hearing we can marry. I'm on my knees, washing her feet. I'm cleaning and rebandaging the gunshot wound in her shoulder.

I am drifting away to somewhere amazing, and I bury my face in her hair, giddy with the smell of vanilla. Somewhere, far away, a voice is saying that I should not be holding her so tight, that people are staring at us, but I can't stop myself.

I know Helen. She'll stop me any moment now, just as she did in the cabin.

But this time, she doesn't, for while our momentary lapse could be considered tacky, it is in no way sinful.

Not now.

Not ever again.

I feel tears well up in my eyes as I think of this. Then, I feel moisture on my shirt front. Helen is weeping also—tears of joy, I trust—as she buries her face into my chest, and her breath warms me on this cold December evening.

We are one now, and are not just allowed, but charged—ordered—to keep each other warm, and whole, and comforted. I never want to leave this place—no, not even for the promised joys to come. But there are others dancing now. The song has carried forward, even as I have tried to drag it out, to keep the music going.

As the last Hallelujah escapes from Meshach's throat, I know I have to let her go, after being able to hold her with love instead of desperation for longer than I ever have before. Thank God she proves herself to already be a help to me, as she slowly lowers her hands from around my neck, allowing me to gently reenter the world in which we belong to others.

It is not a pleasant landing, but at least it is a soft, and for today at least, temporary one.

***

Moments later I find myself transferring from the sublime to the ridiculous as Vivian reminds me that I have to dance with my mother.

In a fit of utter insanity, I had allowed Mom to pick our song. I shudder at the possibilities, until I hear the first strains.

Wait, I think, *this sounds soft. Gaelic. Maybe it will be OK.*

I begin to relax as Mom and I walk to the middle of the dance floor. It's only when I recognize the lyrics that I realize that I am dancing with my mother to the theme song of *Titanic*.

That's when it all comes back to me. I've brought Helen home to meet Mom, and she insists that the three of us should go see *Titanic*. Then she proceeds to sit between Helen and I in the theatre. Afterward, she sobs all the way home that she understands how Rose felt now, being left all alone in the world. I try to comfort her while Helen sits wide-eyed in the back seat. We leave the next day, telling Mom that my apartment flooded and that I have to get home to save my books.

And yes, I did deliberately decide on a water-related disaster to get me out of there.

"Mom," I say softly, "this is an interesting choice of song. What made you think of it?"

"Oh, Tommy," she says in that nasally tone of hers, "how like a man. This is from *Titanic*. You know, that disaster movie that you and Helen and I went to see when you brought her home to meet me years ago. I never hear this song that I don't think of you two."

"Oh, I see," I say.

Then, thankfully, I feel a tap on my shoulder. I turn to see who's cutting in, and for the first and probably only time in my life, I am thankful to relinquish my mother to Trevor.

It's only when I see the look on Helen's face as I walk back to our table that I know I relaxed too soon.

We make eye contact and she mouths, "Don't turn around." Of course, I have to as soon as I sit down. That's when I see Trevor running his hand up and down my mother's—

Nope, I can't say it. I can't even think about it.

Fortunately, the song soon ends. I am about to ask Helen to dance, knowing that she must be missing her Father-Daughter dance, when Dan approaches Helen, puts out his hand and says, "Shall we?"

She smiles and takes Dan's hand as he glances at the DJ, who gives him a big thumbs up. She looks at Dan, who is grinning ear to ear as a familiar refrain comes through the sound system.

Helen gasps and gets a surprised grin on her face. "Dan, you didn't?"

"Oh, yes, I did," he says with a laugh.

"It's been a long time," she says.

"Not that long. Miriam and I talked about it, and she thinks we've still got it."

"OK," Helen says. "I've had just enough champagne to be willing to try. But don't let me look too foolish, please. I am the bride, not to mention your boss, after all."

"You know you can always trust me," he replies.

Dan escorts her to the dance floor. I watch in shock as Helen rolls up the waistband of her skirt, revealing more of her shapely calves than she normally would at a church function.

I am trying to figure out what's going on as the familiar rhythm continues coming from the speakers, getting louder along the way. I'm trying to place it as Helen and Dan pause on the edge of the floor, then rush, hand-in-hand, to the center. They both freeze, bent over at the waist, until the first words, words I can't believe I'm hearing at my wedding reception, start playing.

"Rising up, back on the street, did my time, took my chances . . . "

The next thing I know, they are dancing and spinning. At one point, Dan grabs Helen around the waist and actually raises her off the ground. By this time, Miriam has come to sit beside me. I'm looking at her incredulously before finally getting my mind together enough to say, "What the—what in the world is this?"

"Oh this?" she says casually, a smile that matches Dan's on her face. "You remember, don't you, that I was a dance major in college? Well, this is something I choreographed for them a few years ago when they entered the police fund benefit contest. They got second place. When Dan found out that you two were getting married, he insisted that he was going to ask Helen to dance to this again at the reception."

I can't help but smile at this, exalting with Helen as Dan spins her and then dips her with a final, dramatic pause that brings the house down. I stand and lead the cheers and applause, as Ginger Rogers and Fred Astaire walk lightly back to the table, out of breath and collapse into their chairs.

I lean over and kiss Helen, whispering in her ear, "You're just full of surprises, aren't you?"

Taking another sip of her champagne—really more of a gulp—she replies with a grin, "You have no idea."

I hear the strains of "What a Wonderful World" begin. I look at the sweet, beautiful young mother next to me and say, "Miriam, if your expectations are low enough to dance with a humble priest, I would love to take you out for a spin."

She smiles, hands a sleeping Helen Joan to Helen, and joins me on the floor.

As we dance, I tell Miriam, "You don't know this, but you were one of the first people that I met when I came to Saint Clare's."

"Really?" she asks, deftly avoiding my two left feet.

"Yes. You came to the church office to ask about having a Christmas Pageant, and I said yes."

"But it didn't happen that year," she replies with just a hint of sadness. "And then when it did—"

"Listen, all that's in the past now, including the incident with the alpaca. I am looking forward to many pageants to come. In fact, I have one in particular I'd like you to consider. It's based on a book written back in the early 1970s, and there's this kid named Gladys that Catherine would be perfect to play."

"Oh, no," she says with surprising force. "I was in a production of that when I was a kid and promised myself that if I survived it, I'd never have anything to do with that play ever again."

I'm about to ask why when the music ends, so instead, I escort Miriam back to their table and sit down for a minute to catch my breath and chat with Dan. "So, you and Helen looked pretty good out there."

"Thanks," Dan says. "She's a good dancer but not nearly as good as Miriam."

"Well, obviously she's your favorite partner."

"More or less," he says with a grin, catching Miriam's eye as a new song comes on.

"Oh?" I ask.

"Wait for it," he says quietly, obviously listening for something in the cacophony around us.

Then I hear it.

Running feet in soft slippers and a squeal, "Daddy, shut up and dance with me!"

I jump at these words as Catherine makes a dash for Dan's arms. I am waiting for him to scold her when he instead swings her into his arms and carries her to the dance floor, where they begin to dance and spin to a song I don't recognize, both with the happiest, most joyful looks that I have ever seen on their faces.

I glance at Miriam and she explains, "'Shut Up and Dance With Me' is their song. When I was pregnant with the twins, I was on bed rest for a couple of months. Dan was working like crazy, often pulling double shifts, so Catherine spent most of her time either with my mom or piled up in bed with me, reading and drawing. But no matter how many hours he'd worked, as soon as he'd open the door, he'd turn the CD player on to this song and they would dance together until it was over. They still do it sometimes, but now she's older and is often too busy playing, so this means the whole world to him."

I watch father and daughter spinning and laughing. "Did you plan this?" I ask.

Miriam shrugs. "You're not the only one who can keep a secret, Father."

Twenty-Nine

Everything is going so splendidly and I feel almost giddy, especially after watching Helen and Dan's dance. It's my wedding day, and this time, I'm old enough and wise enough to know that it is a sacred day, not just because the spiritual dimensions, but also because I will need these memories of these people, of this time, of Helen looking more beautiful than I've ever seen her, on the dark days to come.

And I'm now wise enough, I think, to know they will come.

I am basking in the joy of everything when "Bridge Over Troubled Waters" comes through the sound system.

I lean over to Helen and ask, "How'd this end up here?"

With a soft smile in her eyes, she says, "It was one of my parents' favorites and I love it, too. Is there a problem?"

"I hope not," I reply as the Archbishop cuts me a look, not one of disapproval but more of bittersweet memory. I'm about to go over and apologize, explain everything, when he stands up and goes over to Anna. He says nothing, but instead puts his hand out. She takes it, they walk together to the dance floor, and they begin to dance.

"When you're weary, feeling small,
when tears are in your eyes
I'll take your side
when times are rough
and friends just can't be found
like a bridge over troubled waters
I will lay me down."

He's staring straight ahead over her shoulder, but she's looking at him, not obviously but nonetheless with barely hidden emotion. Thankfully, the dance floor has become crowded with others who love this beautiful song of love and friendship, of a passion that goes beyond any that could ever be expressed physically.

In addition to the Archbishop and Anna, I see Steve dancing with Bridget. At first, he's holding her at arm's length, in a very friendly, almost brotherly way. It is only when the second verse begins and I catch the sight of tears in her eyes that I see him reach up and pull her head gently to his shoulder.

"When evening falls so hard, I will comfort you."

Walter's hand is on Anna's back now and I see it making small circles, tiny indications of the pain in both their hearts. But then she stumbles and I realize it's too much for her, to be so close to him and yet never able to be close enough. I stand up and start over to cut in when out of the corner of my eye, I catch Bill approaching them. With a big smile, he taps Walter on the shoulder and takes her away, placing his hand on her head so that it's buried in his shoulder. If anybody does choose to watch them, they will only think it's romantic that a couple their age is dancing so close.

The Archbishop does not return to his table but instead goes outside, only to return a few minutes later perfectly composed and in a jovial mood, making his way over to the Maycord table to offer Martin his congratulations in person. Bill and Anna go back to their table, and all is well again, currents set in motion so long ago once more flowing within their designated banks.

***

Part of me wants this afternoon to last forever, while another part is desperate to finally be alone with my wife. So for once in my life I decide to view this as a Win-Win, instead of a Lose-Lose. So when Vivian comes to us and says softly, "It's time for your last dance," I'm ready.

Taking Helen in my arms again, we dance to "The Way You Look Tonight," the song we danced to on one of our earliest dates when we were awaiting word from the Vatican. I feel her trembling slightly in my arms and I hold her closer, whispering into her ear, "I've got you."

I am startled when she shudders slightly, but then I feel her relax. "I feel ridiculous," she whispers with a soft giggle.

"Don't," I say. "Whatever has happened to or between us in the past is different. This is something brand new. Wonderful, but a bit scary, too."

The music ends and I see that she's blushing, her face aglow with happiness and nerves combined. Vivian meets us at the edge of the dance floor and announces, "Everyone, please make your way out the front doors and gather around the porch. Tom and Helen have a few special goodbyes to make, and then they'll be out to throw the bouquet."

As everyone begins to leave, I grab my mother and give her a quick hug and kiss. Helen does the same and for once in her life, she seems to take the hint. She leaves with the rest of the crowd, running a little to catch up with Trevor, who seems to be hurrying to put as much distance as possible between himself and the Hallsteads.

As I had requested, Anna hangs back, as does the Archbishop. Helen goes first to Anna, enveloping her in a hug. Anna kisses her cheek gently and says, "God bless you, my dear, and may you always be as happy together as you are today."

Helen then goes to the Archbishop and gives him a big hug, standing on tiptoe to kiss his cheek. "I'll take good care of your boy, sir," she says with a smile.

His Eminence nods. "I'm sure you will, and he of you."

I hug Anna, longing to tell her how much she means to me, how grateful I feel for all she has done for Helen and me, but my voice cracks and I can only manage, "I love you so much. Thank you for everything."

She pats my back and says, "Be happy, be holy, be in love together, now and forever."

She then beats a hasty retreat outside as I turn and put my hand out to the Archbishop. "Thank you, sir, so much, for making all this possible."

Pulling me into a bear hug, this model of piety almost growls, "Tom, it has all been my privilege and my joy." Then, collecting himself, he says, "Now let me get out of the way so you too can make your well-deserved exit."

He goes out the door, now being guarded by Vivian, who pauses a minute before waving us forward. She throws the double doors open and Helen and I exit under the crossed swords of Saint Clare's Knights of Columbus, with Bill giving me a wink as we rush by. Then, at the end of the gauntlet, Helen turns and quickly tosses the bouquet.

It's at this moment that I remember her telling me she used to pitch for her high school softball team. The bouquet sails in a beautiful arc over the heads of most of the crowd, only to land at Bridget's feet, who was standing way in the back.

There is only the briefest of pauses before Steve steps forward, picks up the delicate flowers from the ground, and hands them to Bridget in a manner so gallant that Sir Walter Raleigh would have been impressed. She turns bright red as the crowd erupts in applause and then turns its attention again back to Helen and me.

This is the moment when we're supposed to run through a shower of birdseed to the car. The problem is, I don't see the car.

I turn to Vivian. "Where's the car?" I ask.

She smiles. "There's been a slight change in plan. Follow me."

She then walks into the house, Helen and I following obediently behind her. We go down a long hall and through the back doors. As the door opens, I hear a familiar whirring sound.

There's a helicopter on the back lawn.

Martin is waiting at the door and says with delight, "Tom, Helen, I'd like for you to meet Danny Bradford. He's a friend of mine and a certified search and rescue pilot. Tonight, he's your ride to Baltimore."

"Wait," I say. "I don't understand."

"I do," Helen says gleefully, "We're flying to our hotel. But where will he land?"

"Well, that's part of the surprise. I happen to know, for reasons Tom has my permission to share with you, that the place you're staying tonight has a helipad on the roof of its parking garage. So he'll set you down there and a limo will pick you up tomorrow to take you to the ship."

I don't know what to say but apparently Helen does, for she gives Martin a big hug and grateful kiss on the cheek before taking Danny's hand and getting in. Realizing that I have to act quickly or Helen is liable to leave on our honeymoon without me, I shake Martin's hand firmly and jump in behind her.

We quickly lift off, and before I know it we are hovering over the Myer Mansion, waving joyfully to the crowd below as they wave back. Nate and Gladys are throwing confetti in the air, as are many from the Acutis Society, while Miriam places her hand over Helen Joan's tiny head and Dan picks Andrew up to wave. Anna blows us a kiss and the Archbishop makes the sign of the cross in one final blessing.

Then, the helicopter turns, and we're off to Baltimore.

As the family we have known falls behind us, we fly into the winter's twilight to our new life together as a family ourselves.

Epilogue

I wake up the next morning to the sun streaming through the window of the amazing suite Martin reserved for us. The light is casting cascades of glitter over Helen's raven hair and creamy skin.

I shift slightly, my forty-something body struggling to adjust to once again sleeping with someone in my arms. My movement wakes her and my bride sighs gently, "Good morning, Darling."

"It is a good morning, indeed," I see, kissing her. "Did you sleep well?"

She looks at me through slitted eyes as she says, "I slept better than I ever have in my adult life."

I take this as a compliment, but also know how much she hates mornings. I suggest, "How about I order some coffee and maybe some breakfast. I bet you're hungry."

"I am. Pick something good."

By the time the server arrives with our breakfast, we are dressed enough to let him in. Just like in the movies, he has our food on a rolling cart which he parks in front of the large window overlooking Baltimore Harbor. He opens the curtains wider and places chairs in front of each place, removes the domed covers from our meals, and takes his leave with my thanks and what I hope is a generous tip.

Wanting to make a good impression on my first day as a husband, I seat Helen before sitting down myself. We begin eating when something on the front page of the Baltimore paper catches my eye.

"Helen," I say, "I think there's something about us in here."

I find the "Local" section and nearly choke as I turn the page for Helen to see. Her reaction is even more violent. Together, we gaze at a large photo of ourselves yesterday around the Saint Clare creche.

The headline reads, "Priest weds with Blessing of 500 Year Old Gypsinian Christ Child."

***

The story of Father Tom Greer and Chief of Police Helen Parr Greer—as well as the rest of their family and friends in Myerton—continues in **The Mercy and Justice Mysteries**.
Turn the page for a sneak preview of Book 1, *The Honeymoon Homicide*

A MERCY AND JUSTICE MYSTERY

THE
HONEYMOON

Preview of The Honeymoon Homicide

"Tom, wake up!"

Helen's voice cuts through my foggy brain like a searchlight—a very loud searchlight.

"Stop yelling," I demand, pulling my pillow over my head, "and stop banging on the walls."

"I am not yelling, I am whispering, and I am not banging on the walls, someone is banging on our door."

Our door. We have a mutual door now. If my head didn't hurt so badly, this would make me smile, but it does not.

"Tell them to go away," I groan from under the pillow.

"I can't do that," she hisses. "I'm not dressed."

"Neither am I."

"Yes, but you're the man and you're supposed to protect me."

I poke my head out from under the pillow. "By checking a door?"

"Yes."

"Of a stateroom on a cruise ship?"

"Yes—Oh, shit!" she exclaims.

"You really have given up trying to give up cursing," I say, rubbing my head.

"Tom," she says, "we're not supposed to be here!"

Helen rolls over to look at the clock as I grab my robe and rush toward the door. "What time?" I call back over my shoulder.

"9:30 a.m."

"Oh, no! We were supposed to be off the ship a half hour ago!" I whisper back in the false hope that my head will not explode.

I reach the door and open it slightly to see a very determined-looking steward standing outside.

"Mr. Greer," he says without preamble, "you and your wife have exactly 30 minutes to disembark or I will have to report you to the authorities."

"No, no," I insist. "That won't be necessary. We just overslept."

"Yes," he says. "I'm not surprised." He then leaves before I can say anything else.

By the time I turn around, Helen has her robe on and is flinging clothing into an overnight bag. I grab a shirt from her hands and put it on while I begin walking around looking for my pants. I don't see them right away but finally find them under a chair.

"Helen," I ask, "what did we do last night?"

"Hell if I know," she says, grabbing a sweater, sniffing it and then slipping it on. She's now on her hands and knees looking under the bed, from where she pulls a number of garments, including a pair of black slacks. "I think we ordered some champagne."

"Yes, I do remember finishing a bottle." I'm in the bathroom now sweeping our toiletries across the counter into Helen's substantial make-up case. "But really, that shouldn't have been such a big deal."

"It wouldn't have been," she says, brushing her raven hair quickly, "if we hadn't ordered a second bottle."

"Are you sure?"

"Yes."

"Then what happened?" I ask, picking up our bags and heading for the door while she grabs our coats from the closet.

She joins me, stopping to pick up the bill placed under our door. Glancing at it she says, "Apparently, we ordered a *third* bottle of champagne and various snacks, including escargot and cheese puffs."

"That would be you," I say.

"As well as chocolate mousse, chocolate cake, and a tray of chocolate petit fours."

I suppose that explains why my stomach feels nearly as bad as my head.

"Well," I say, yanking the door open, "all that matters is that we get off this ship before we are arrested and tomorrow's headline reads, 'Newly married priest and wife arrested after a night of drunken debauchery.'"

"You know what the real shame is?" she says, slipping on her sunglasses against the winter are and giving me a kiss.

"What's that?"

"I don't remember the debauchery."

***

e good thing about running late is that the nice people from the cruise line are more than ppy to expedite our way off the ship.

They are even nicer when Helen and I both tip them generously.

Once we are in the port, though, we are on our own. I realize for the first time how much ıggage Helen actually brought on our honeymoon. The thing is, everything that stands out in my mind was pretty flimsy so I don't really know . . .

We get to the port lounge and I learn that the shuttle for our hotel just left so we have about an hour to wait. This suits us fine, since we are both anxious to catch our breaths.

As soon as I sit down, I reflexively pull my phone from my pocket. Before I can turn it on, though, Helen says with a smile that grows dearer to me each day, "Oh, no, you don't, Tom. We agreed, no phones on our honeymoon."

I grin back as I put it away. Since my hands are now free, I slip my arm around her and we turn our eyes to the local station playing on the muted TV. There's nothing much to see and we begin talking, whispering quietly about our first week of married life, when something on the screen catches my eye.

The chyron reads, "Man found dead near St. Clare's Catholic Church in Myerton."

"Helen," I say, pointing to the set just in time to see none other than Gladys Finkelstein come on screen. I look around quickly and find the remote just in time to hear her say "withheld pending family notification."

"What the hell?" Helen whispers. Digging through her tote bag, she says, "Where's Dan? Why was Gladys on there? What's going on?"

"I'm sure everything is fine, Helen," I say, not really believing it myself.

"No," she says as she pulls out her phone. "Something's wrong."

She's calling Dan Conway, her Chief Detective and the man she left in charge while we were gone. There's no one else in the room so she puts her phone on speaker as I hear, "Daniel Boone Conway's phone. Catherine Elizabeth Conway speaking. Who may I say is calling?"

Apparently, Miriam has been working with 7-year-old Catherine on her phone manners. "Hi, Catherine," Helen says calmly, "it's Miss Helen. Why are you answering Daddy's phone?"

"Because he fell and broke his leg and he won't rest, and so Mommy had to take it away from him so she could have a few moment's peace. Then Helen Joan threw up on her so she had to change shirts."

"I see. Well, can I speak to your Daddy, please?"

"Sure," she says before we hear her running down the hall yelling, "Daadddy! Miss Helen's the phone." I hear grumbling before Dan says brightly, "Helen, I didn't expect to hear from y Is everything OK?"

"With us, yes. With you and the rest of the department, not so much. What the hell is go on?"

"Now calm down, Helen, I can explain. I'm just running a little late. That's the only reas I'm still at home."

"Oh, so it doesn't have anything to do with your broken leg?"

There's a pause on the other end. "Who told you about that?" Dan finally says quickly. "W all agreed that y'all didn't need to know anything until you got home."

"Your little secretary told me, and I learned about the murder from Gladys."

As always, I am impressed with Helen's ability to get the truth without quite telling a lie.

"Gladys? Why did she call you? I mean, I have everything under control. I've got calls out all over the state to get a temporary chief in. It's just that a lot of guys are out of town still for the holidays."

"And until then, Gladys is in charge?" Helen asks incredulously.

"She and Hallstead. They're going to work together and run everything past me before they do anything."

"Like talk to the press?"

"Well, Helen, someone had to do it, and Gladys is the ranking person in the office after us."

"No, Dan. Gladys is a civilian with no police training."

"You're kidding? You mean she lied to me? She said that she took a crash course in police procedure online last year and made a perfect score."

"She did, because she's a genius. But she is not suited to leadership." Helen then pauses to think. Dan, being as familiar with this tactic as I am, volunteers nothing. Finally, she says "I'll text you in a few minutes."

She hangs up and calls Gladys. "Mom," she says in a voice faster and higher-pitched than usual, "before you say anything, there is no need for you to come home. We have everything under control."

"I just got off the phone with Dan," Helen says calmly. "What I want to know from you is why you still haven't notified the family?"

"I've tried, Mom. I got his file from Anna, but the only next of kin listed is his wife, and she's not answering her phone."

"I see," Helen says. "Well, just keep trying. I'll get back with you."

I'm already dialing my phone when Helen finishes. Anna answers tersely, "Tom, you're supposed to be on your honeymoon. Why in the world are you calling me?"

"Helen and I just learned what happened and I wanted to know if there is anything I can do."

Anna sighs at this and complains, "We all agreed to keep this from you two. As Dan pointed, he was probably mugged because he had the offering bag with him, though why he did, I'll never know. I always take care of that."

I feel panic well up in my throat as I ask, "Who had the offering bag with him?"

"Deacon Roderick. That's what we think they killed him for."

"Wait, Deacon Roderick's been murdered?"

"Yes, who did you think I was talking about?"

Helen takes the phone as I slump down. Speaking to Anna firmly, she says, "Anna, Tom and I will be home in a few hours. I would really appreciate it if you'd turn on the heat in the Rectory."

"Where?" Anna asks, seeming startled.

"The Rectory. Tom's home, and mine now, too. Could you please have someone stop by and turn on the heat?"

"Umm. I can't."

"Why not?"

"Because the heat is out," Anna says quickly. "There was a problem with the flue last night and the fire department had to seal it off. No one is allowed in there until the carbon monoxide dissipates, and then they'll have to send someone in to repair it, and then the inspector will have to come out and certify that it is habitable. I told them to not rush, since you two weren't supposed to be back until a week from today."

There's something funny about the way she says this. It's almost like she's trying to figure it out herself, but I'm too upset to give it much thought.

Deacon Dereck Roderick, well loved servant of God and one of the kindest, gentlest men I have ever met, is dead. As soon as Helen is off the phone, we both cross ourselves and pray for the happy repose of his soul.

Then we pick up our phones again, and start making plans to find the one who killed his body.

Lightning Source UK Ltd.
Milton Keynes UK
UKHW031501090223
416681UK00013B/3079

9 798215 62